Courting Kay

Courting Kay

A single mom, love at first sight, small town, happily ever after romance.

Heart's Destiny Book 1

Leah Mae Wright

Copyright

Contents

Dedication

To my Mom and Daddy. If you happen to have access to books in heaven, I hope you'll enjoy the first story in my literary world. And send me any inspiration you can for the next book in the series. Love and miss you both!

Introduction

After tragic losses in his past, and recovering from injuries that led to his medical discharge from the Navy, Anthony Burleson used his job as a pilot for the Galactic Wrestling Association to search for the woman he'd been dreaming about for over a year. Anthony knew the instant he saw her for the first time that she was his dream woman—his soulmate. Now he just had to figure out how to win her heart when he had to fly out of town the next morning.

Kay Lee was a single mom healing after divorcing her abusive ex-husband. While she'd always been a romantic at heart and secretly longed for the whirlwind, passionate romance she'd only read about, she didn't think it could happen for her. Until she met her knight in shining armor at the castle-themed hotel where she worked.

After an incident with her ex-husband derailed their first date, Anthony's plan for courting Kay on his days off was quickly replaced with a new plan to protect the woman and children he saw as his future family. Their adventures as they fall in love while dealing with the issues of Kay's past run the gamut from wholesome family fun with her precocious daughters to hot sexy desire behind their locked bedroom door. They blend their families publicly for a small town happily ever after, while sneaking off for alone time to stoke the fires of their off-the-charts heat.

DISCLAIMER: This single mom, love at first sight, small town, happily ever after romance contains profanity, graphic sex scenes, and references to past abuse, as well as current atrocious behavior by

Kay's ex-husband. It is intended for adult readers (18+) who are not easily offended.

Chapter One

Friday, September 28, 2018

"Where are you going this week?" Hazel Burleson smiled at her youngest son, Anthony, as she handed him the basket of rolls across the table. The Burleson family normally met weekly for a family dinner on Sundays at the family ranch just outside the little town of Heart's Destiny, Texas. Unfortunately, Anthony's unusual work schedule meant she had to insist on a Friday family dinner this week, too. Hazel wished all six of her children were there, but since her two middle sons, the twins, Josh and Jake, were on base in the Navy, she was glad to have her two oldest children, Bobby and Charlotte, and her two youngest children, Becky and Anthony there. Especially Anthony after how hard the last few years had been on him.

While Hazel worried about all her kids, and probably babied them all a bit too much since they were all in their mid to late twenties now, she worried about her youngest the most. At twenty-five, Anthony had already gone through more loss than anyone should in life. He'd lost his high school girlfriend and unborn son when he was only eighteen years old. Then after burying his feelings and running away from the memories by staying in the Navy and deploying as much as possible, he was injured when there was an explosion on the aircraft carrier he was on, and he was exposed to radiation that sterilized him.

Hazel knew that his accident brought back all the pain of losing his first love and their child. He'd tried to shut his family out after their deaths by being away in the Navy, but at least he seemed closer to the family when he was home on leave for the first few years. After his accident, he seemed to shut down even more. After only a few months of recovering from a collapsed lung and broken arm and ribs, he took a job traveling all the time, so he wasn't on the family ranch, trying to avoid the memories. Hazel hated that he didn't feel comfortable at home anymore and really wished she could figure out how to find a way to make him want to come home to the family again.

Of all her children, Hazel believed that Anthony would be the first to settle down and get married. He'd always been the one who embraced his softer side and was the most affectionate as a child. Since he was the youngest of her six children, all born within five years, she figured it was because sitting on her lap as a small child was how he got more of her attention than his older siblings. Besides that, though, he was also the only one of her children who seemed to want to be a parent. It was heartbreaking to Hazel that Anthony was injured in a way that would prevent him from being a father in the traditional way.

She decided that getting Anthony to open up to the family again, and maybe feel more like moving home to them, would probably require him to meet a woman who already had children, so he could not only fall in love with her, but also with the children he could be a loving stepfather to, as well. If only she knew some women with children to introduce him to, who lived there in Heart's Destiny.

For the past few years, her matchmaking had been focused on her oldest son, Bobby. Since he was obviously not ready to settle down, Hazel decided that she needed to change her focus. She would have to talk to her friends to see if any of them had any suggestions about whom she could set up with her youngest son.

Anthony didn't answer and seemed to be lost in thought, so Hazel raised her voice a little higher than she normally would speak to anyone to get his attention. "Anthony Ray Burleson! Are you even listening to me, or are you already on the plane in your head?"

~~~

"Sorry, Ma." Anthony took a moment, trying to remember what his mother asked him. *Oh yeah, where I'm going.* "Tomorrow I'm flying to Tulsa, Oklahoma to meet up with my crew. Then Sunday, I start my five days of flying to different cities in California."
~~~

As a pilot working for the Galactic Wrestling Association, Anthony flew to the city where the wrestlers were performing the day before his scheduled days of flying the corporate jet. His best friends, James and Dean Hunter, helped him get the job a little over a year before when he was medically discharged from the Navy.

Anthony had been on an aircraft carrier in the middle of the Mediterranean Sea for six months when there was an explosion on one of the lower decks. While he wasn't close enough to the actual explosion to suffer any burns from the fire, the jolt to the ship caused him to fall down the stairs he was descending at the time. He suffered from a broken arm, three broken ribs, a punctured lung, and a concussion from how he landed. He thought at the time that the breathing difficulty he was suffering through from the punctured lung was his worst injury. Little did he know that he was actually close enough to the ship's nuclear core to be exposed to enough radiation to sterilize him. Waking up in the hospital to have the doctor tell him that he would never be a father was way worse on him mentally than any of his other injuries were on him physically.

As soon as he was cleared to leave the hospital he came home to the family ranch in Heart's Destiny, Texas. He lived in his old bedroom in his parents' house for a few more months, not even moving to one of the ranch houses like his siblings all had when they turned eighteen or came home from college. He needed to be home with his family until he built his lung capacity back up to normal, but being on the ranch was difficult emotionally. Everywhere he looked, he saw memories of his childhood, especially his teenage years with his high school girlfriend, Nancy Parker.

While his family saw that it was bringing up bad memories for him to be home, they weren't much help in making them recede or at least be more bearable. Anthony was grateful that the Hunters came home from traveling for Independence Day and were able to see through the façade he put up for everyone else. They knew him well enough to see that he needed to get away from the ranch and Heart's Destiny for a while to heal mentally.

James and his twin brother, Dean, grew up on the next ranch over and had been Anthony's best friends since they were all in diapers. When the twins graduated high school six years ago, they started going through training to become professional wrestlers while they were also in college. They worked with a few different smaller organizations before they made it to the GWA, which was the most widely known wrestling company in the world. They'd been working in the GWA for about a year and really pushed Anthony to meet their boss when they were home and saw his need to mentally heal.

Anthony didn't graduate with them. Their senior year hadn't started yet the summer he turned eighteen and joined the Navy. Two weeks before his eighteenth birthday, Nancy told him she was pregnant. Although their parents didn't agree, Anthony and Nancy wanted to get married and raise the baby together. Anthony dropped out of high school, got his GED, and joined the Navy on his eighteenth birthday. Since Anthony hadn't inherited his share of the family business yet, he wanted to have a good-paying job to be able to provide for Nancy and their baby. Because Nancy's parents wouldn't sign off for them to get married while she was still seventeen and living at home with them, Anthony and Nancy planned to save up Anthony's pay until she turned eighteen. Then he planned to come home on leave to get married and move her to the base where he was stationed. His leave was scheduled for the week after her eighteenth birthday. The baby was due three months later, so they figured it would give them plenty of time to get her changed to a base doctor and everything set up for their child's birth.

Unfortunately, fate intervened, and their plans never came to fruition. Nancy's parents took her out to dinner for her birthday and they never made it home. Nancy and her parents fought about their plans to get married and move away. Anthony was told conflicting stories about what happened that night, so he still didn't know if her dad was drunk and caused the accident, if they were hit by a drunk driver, or if they were still fighting in the car on the way home and that distraction caused the wreck. Nancy and the baby died before the paramedics even made it to the site of the crash. Her mom died the next day in the hospital. Her dad was in a coma for over a month. When he finally came out of it, Anthony's oldest brother, Bobby, had to arrest him because he showed up at the Burleson Ranch with a gun, looking for Anthony.

"Anthony, Son, you alright?" Bob Burleson's question shook his son Anthony out of his mental trip down memory lane.

"Yeah, Pop, I'm fine," Anthony replied. "Just thinking." He wasn't really sure why he'd been thinking back to that time seven years before. It was the hardest time in his life, and he thought he'd gotten to the point where he wouldn't have random flashbacks to that pain anymore. His accident eighteen months ago brought it all back when the Navy doctor told him that the radiation he was exposed to would make it impossible for him to become a father. *It was like I lost my son all over again.*

"Whatcha thinkin' 'bout?" Anthony's brother, Bobby, queried with his strong Texas drawl as he finished sopping up his gravy with a roll. Bobby only did one stint in the Navy before he came home to South Texas to start working at the Heart's Destiny Police Department. He said he was afraid he'd lose his Texas drawl if he stayed around all the funny accents of his fellow sailors any longer. Anthony wondered if they actually kicked him out because they didn't have a Texan-to-English translator on board his ship. "Looked like you're dread-un this trip."

"Naw," Anthony replied, reverting to his own drawl, so Bobby could understand him. "Just a trip down memory lane to how I got this job."

"I thought James and Dean got you this job?" Anthony's sister, Becky, interjected. She practically glowed when she said their names. She was ten months older than Anthony but only about five months older than the Hunter twins. Back when they were in school, Anthony had to make sure they both knew his sister was off-limits. Seeing that dreamy look on her face when she brought them up, made him think it might be time to let them know that the ban on them dating his sister was lifted now that they were all in their mid-twenties.

"Yeah, they did," Anthony replied, wondering what she was trying to say without really coming out and saying it. "I was thinking about how they introduced me to Rick, and how my interview went that led to me being hired," Anthony lied. He didn't want to explain to his family how thinking about the accident that led to him leaving the Navy brought back all the pain of losing his only chance at being a father.

"Then why are you making the same face you make every time you think about Nancy and the baby?" Becky whispered while looking at Anthony with sympathy in her eyes.

Anthony didn't know how to respond to her. It had been seven years since their deaths. Up until his accident, he hadn't thought about them in two or three years. It was easy to block them out when he was on an aircraft carrier because they were never in that part of his life, so he didn't see reminders of Nancy everywhere he looked, unlike being home in Heart's Destiny and especially on the Burleson Ranch.

He ended up getting an apartment in San Antonio right after he started his job with the GWA, so he'd be close to the family and could come to Sunday suppers regularly, but he wasn't in Heart's Destiny all the time to constantly see all the places they used to hang out as teenagers.

One of the perks of being a pilot was the freedom of being able to live anywhere in the country, even if having to fly commercial to and from the crew on his days off was annoying. He was just too big at six-foot-six and two-hundred-and-twenty pounds to fit comfortably in a commercial plane seat.

Looking around at his family, Anthony realized that during the time he was living at home and dealing with the pain of losing the ability to father a child, he hadn't hidden his emotions from the family as well as he thought. *I wonder if Becky is the only one who recognizes this look I get when I think about never being able to play catch with my son, or teach him how to drive, or help him navigate his way through the perils of being a teenager.* He gazed around the table, closely examining his family. They all looked back at him with sad, stoic faces. *Shit, they're all worried about me!*

"I, uh," he started to stutter out but didn't know what to say. He took a deep breath and decided to bite the bullet and just tell them how he was really feeling. "I guess thinking about getting this job made me think about why I needed it." He could feel himself shaking as he tried to get the words out. "Every time I think about the accident that led to me leaving the Navy, I hear that doctor in my head."

"Oh, Anthony," his mom, Hazel, sobbed as she reached over and put her hand on Anthony's to give it a squeeze. "That makes you think of the baby, huh?" She had tears in her eyes when he looked at her, and it was clear she was fighting to hold them back.

"Yeah," he replied, turning his hand in hers so he could squeeze her back. "But it's not always a flashback to losing them both. Most of the time it's more thinking about the things I'm gonna miss out on by not being able to be a father."

Anthony glanced around the table again, making sure to make eye contact with each of them so they knew what he was about to say was the truth. "I know I'll always miss Nancy and AJ, but I am actually doing okay and have moved on from their loss. Ya'll don't have to worry about me spending the rest of my life grieving for them. I just have a few moments once in a while, which is totally normal and not enough to worry about."

"Ya know, Son," his dad, Bob, started as he pointed at Anthony with his fork. "You shouldn't resign yourself to never being a dad. There are a lot of kids in this world who need to be adopted. I'm sure you can find 'em when you're ready to do all those things you're thinking about missing out on now."

"He has to find a wife first, Dad," his oldest sister, Charlotte, smirked. "He's not going to do that while he's traipsing all over the country with a bunch of rowdy wrestlers."

"Oh, you never know, Char," their mom grinned, making Anthony uncomfortable. "Some women are more adventurous than you, and wouldn't mind traveling the world with him."

Anthony shuddered at the thought of his mother playing matchmaker with the limited prospects in their small hometown. Heart's Destiny, Texas was a super small town about an hour outside of San Antonio. Anthony used to joke that his dad had more cows on the ranch than there were people in Heart's Destiny. None of the girls he knew from there were what he was looking for as a possibility to date, much less a potential future wife.

It wasn't that he was opposed to dating, or even settling down and getting married. He actually liked the idea of finding someone he could truly connect with and adopt a few children with. He just didn't think his mother should be the one to pick out a wife for him.

He actually had an idea of the perfect woman for him, he just hadn't met her yet. She haunted his dreams every night, though, so he thought he'd know her when he finally met her. None of the girls he knew from Heart's Destiny were anything like his dream woman. He wasn't sure how to stop his mother from trying to fix him up with one of them, though.

Leah Mae Wright

He knew his mom had good intentions when trying to find the right woman for each of her sons. Unfortunately, the dates he'd heard about that she'd set up for his brothers over the years had all been disasters that he had no intention of repeating. She just didn't understand her sons' taste in women and kept trying to set them up with the daughters of her friends from church, or their cousins who were visiting from out of town. While they'd all seemed to be nice girls when his brothers met them for dates, the Burleson boys all preferred girls that would be on Santa's naughty list instead of in the church choir.

"I wouldn't mind traveling the world with the right man," Becky added. The wistful look on her face told him that he should definitely let the Hunters know they could ask her out if either one of them was interested.

"How many ring rats have you spent time with since you got this job?" Bobby's lips turned up in a devilish grin. *Yeah, he may know too much about the nightlife of professional wrestlers to have this conversation in front of our mother*, Anthony thought.

"What's a ring rat?" Charlotte narrowed her eyes and looked back and forth between Bobby and Anthony.

"Rasslin' groupies," Bobby chuckled. "From what I hear, they're about the same as what we call buckle bunnies at the rodeo. So how many, little brother? I can tell by how red you're turnin' that it's more than one."

Anthony felt himself turning red all right, but not because he'd been with a bunch of ring rats. He was embarrassed because Bobby was talking about this in front of their mother. He thought of his mother as a saint and didn't feel comfortable talking about anything sexual in her presence. He didn't think she needed to hear about the sexual escapades of some of his coworkers.

Most of the people that worked for the GWA were family oriented and actually traveled with their wives and children. There were several, though, that were single and liked to hang out in the hotel bar after a show on a regular basis. Just because they met women at those hotel bars, didn't mean they took them back to their hotel rooms every night. Had it happened on occasion? Sure, but it wasn't as regular an occurrence as Bobby was trying to make it sound. *He wouldn't believe me if I tried to tell him that, though.*

Anthony hadn't actually hooked up with anyone since before he started the job with the GWA. His last time with a woman was a one-night stand about six months before his accident when he went to a club right before the deployment that led to his injuries. *Damn! That was over two years ago!* There were no opportunities on deployment or while he was home healing after being discharged. Then his first night on the road with the GWA, he started having nightly dreams about the woman he believed he'd one day find and marry. He looked for her everywhere he went since then, and had no interest in hooking up with anyone else.

"Robert Adam Burleson!" Hazel reprimanded her oldest son using the scary mom voice that got the attention of all of her kids, even when Anthony would rather keep daydreaming about his fantasy woman. "We do not speak of the debauchery you and your friends get up to after a rodeo in this house, so don't try to use it to embarrass your baby brother by implying that he and his friends do the same." The look she gave Bobby was the one that all mothers have that told every kid on the planet to hush because they were already in deep trouble and didn't need to dig any deeper. It was scary enough to make Anthony not care that she still pointed out that he was the baby of the family.

"Sorry, Ma," Bobby half-heartedly apologized as he ducked his head. "I didn't mean that he was doing anything wrong. I just wondered if he'd met any girls that he might like to date or marry eventually."

"No, you implied that the girls he might meet while traveling with his job aren't nice girls that he might want to marry one day. You would've asked if he'd met any nice girls if that's what you wanted to know."

Fuck, I need to figure out how to change the subject!

"So, Son, have you met anyone special recently?" Bob pointedly looked at Anthony.

Thanks, Dad! Way to help me change the subject.

"No, not yet, but you know I'm always looking for her," he replied. His dad was the only person Anthony had told about the dreams he'd had about the woman he thought of as his soulmate. He'd told his dad because he was worried that the only time he got an erection was when he was dreaming about her, or fantasizing about her to take matters into his own hands. His dad had reassured him that after his accident, it was normal to have arousal issues until he was fully healed.

When it persisted for a few months and Anthony felt like he was healed, he went back to his dad because he still didn't get aroused any other time than when he was dreaming or thinking about his mystery woman. That's when his dad told him that she was probably someone he'd seen and felt a connection with but didn't realize it at the time because of all the other things going on in his life. His dad thought it was because she was his soulmate, and his dreams were how the universe told him whom to look for in the future once he was fully healed and ready to meet her.

Anthony wondered if maybe he should tell his mom about the dreams. If she knew he was looking for his soulmate, maybe she wouldn't feel the need to fix him up with anyone else. "I'm still dreaming about her every night, so I know I'll know her when I meet her."

"You have sex dreams about the same woman every night?" Bobby shouted at the same time Becky cooed softly, "Aww, how romantic, you dream about your soulmate."

Shit! I should not have said anything in front of my siblings! Anthony looked over at Charlotte, expecting her to have some kind of reaction like his other two siblings, but she just shook her head like she thought their conversation was ridiculous.

"I, uh, yeah, I've been dreaming about my future wife and family for a little over a year." Anthony scratched the back of his head, trying to figure out how much of the dreams he could tell them about. He definitely couldn't tell them all the kinky sex dreams, but they were only about half of them, so he figured he could skip admitting to them. "Most of the time it's family game night or taking them to the beach."

"Yeah, right," Bobby smirked. "I'm sure they're all about family time and not how you plan to make that family with the hot wife."

"Shut up, Bobby!" Becky glared at Bobby from across the table. Then she turned to Anthony and smiled before asking, "So what do your future wife and kids look like?"

"I don't really know all the details. Their faces aren't really in focus in my dreams." Anthony tried to figure out how to describe the family he saw in his dreams. "I can say that she's a petite brunette with long, straight hair and we're gonna have two blonde daughters and two brunette sons."

"So, you're definitely adopting two blonde daughters since you and your future wife are both brunettes," Bobby said. "Do you at least dream about making the two sons?"

They all looked incredulously at Bobby, who held his hands up in surrender.

Damn it, Bobby! Do you have to keep bringing up sex? It's not like you don't know I can't make a baby that way!

"You really believe your dreams are prophetic?" Charlotte looked at Anthony like she thought he was nuts.

Anthony was grateful for the change of subject from Bobby's desire to hear about Anthony's sex dreams, but he wasn't sure how to respond to his sister with the incredulous look on her face. *Yeah, Sis, I probably am a little crazy believing I'm dreaming about my future family.*

Anthony wasn't sure if his dreams were prophetic or not, but he sure as hell hoped so. If not, then he hated the thought of continuing to be tortured by them nightly, when he couldn't look forward to actually living them.

"I, uh, don't know," Anthony shrugged. "I hope they are, though."

"Of course, they're prophetic!" Becky squealed. "That's so awesome! I'd love to have a dream about my future husband and kids!"

Anthony looked over at his parents to see his mom shaking her head at his dad. His dad then tilted his head at his mom and gave her a look like he was trying to get her to say something. They went back and forth for a few minutes and the whole room got quiet as the siblings all caught on to what Anthony was watching between them. They all stared back and forth between their parents.

"Fine!" Hazel finally huffed out. "I dreamt about all of you before you were born. I guess Anthony gets it from me."

"Seriously, Mom?" Charlotte gave Hazel a look that clearly said she still thought the whole family was crazy for believing their dreams.

"You dreamt about all of us before we were born? Like while you were pregnant with each of us? Or before you even met Dad?" Becky asked imploringly.

Hazel took a deep breath before speaking. "It was a couple years after your dad and I got married. I was having a rough time because we were having trouble conceiving. Then I started having dreams about our six children. I had them nightly for about a year before we finally found out Bobby was on the way."

"So, I came along and scared away your nightmares about having six kids?" Bobby gave their mom a big grin.

Luckily, Hazel's glare at Bobby caused enough of a pause to the conversation that when someone finally got brave enough to speak, the subject changed to how Charlotte liked the change she'd made that year to teach a different grade in the middle school and what play Becky was going to put on next at the local theater. After another hour or so of chit-chat, Anthony was able to head out to his apartment to be able to pack for his next week of work.

When he went to bed, he tossed and turned. He had a hard time falling asleep because he was thinking about everything his family discussed that night, especially what his dad said about kids who need to be adopted. While most of Anthony's long deep conversations had been with his dad, they were always when they were alone. Anthony knew his dad was a man of few words when even one other family member was around, so he knew there was a lot more meaning behind those couple of sentences. His dad knew that Anthony had always wanted to be a dad like him. When he spoke that night, Anthony could see in his eyes that his dad wanted him to realize that being a dad wasn't about the biology of the relationship, but about how Anthony would interact with any kids he may get to play a part in raising. It was more important to show them that they were loved than to have participated in their creation.

It reminded Anthony of a conversation they had when he was in middle school and one of his friends found out he was adopted. Nick Martin didn't deal well with finding out his dad wasn't his biological father. He threw a fit at one of their baseball games and screamed "You're not my father!" at his dad.

Anthony's dad was the baseball coach and stepped in to defuse the situation. Afterwards, Anthony asked his dad how Nick's dad couldn't be his father because it didn't make sense to him at twelve years old.

Bob explained that any man could become a father because that was just biology. He explained that a father isn't anything special because a man just has to have sex to make a baby. He said that being a dad is what is important because being a dad is about the time spent with the kids. Dads show their kids how much they love them, respect them, and want to make their lives happy and fulfilling, regardless of whether or not they are the biological father of their children.

Anthony was glad his dad reminded him of that. *He's right. I don't need to be upset that I can't be a father because I'll be a good dad one day.* Just before he fell asleep, Anthony sent his dad a quick text to thank him for the lesson.

~~~

Saturday, September 29, 2018

Kay Lee woke up Saturday morning way earlier than normal. It was the one day of the week she could sleep in as late as she wanted, so she wasn't thrilled to be awake before five in the morning. She tossed and turned for about thirty minutes before giving up on going back to sleep. She turned on the bedside lamp and dug a book out of her bedside table. If she was going to be awake anyway, she may as well take advantage of the unexpected free time to enjoy her favorite hobby. Back when she was in college, she actually studied English because she wanted to write her own romance novels eventually. Not that she had the experience to be able to write the steamy scenes she was most fond of reading.

Being a single mom, she didn't have the free time or extra funds to indulge her love of reading romance novels often. Usually, it was only what she could check out at the library, and her reading time was limited to the nights her daughters were on their every other weekend visit with their father. Unless she took advantage of their time with him to pick up an extra shift at work.

The book she was currently reading was actually a splurge she'd bought on the clearance rack the previous Christmas, but she needed to take the girls to the library soon. Hopefully, when she did, she'd find something new for herself. *Not that I'll find anything as steamy as this one at our local library,* she thought to herself.
~~~

Kay lived in Tulsa, Oklahoma. Right in the middle of the Bible Belt. More specifically, she lived in West Tulsa, which was more like a small town in and of itself, instead of a part of the second-largest city in the state. In West Tulsa, everybody knew everything about a majority of their neighbors. If Mrs. Redman, the head librarian at the library for the last twenty years, knew what the main plot of the book series Kay had been reading for the past ten months was, she'd probably pull them all from the library shelves.

While the rest of the world seemed to have embraced the erotic romance genre by making movies about some of the more popular ones, those books weren't available at the local library and the movies weren't shown at the Admiral Twin Drive-In. Kay was lucky to find a few books by lesser-known authors on the clearance rack at Barnes & Noble and was even luckier to find a few more by those authors at the library.

She hoped Mrs. Redman wouldn't flip through one while she was checking it out or returning it one day to see that they were laced with profanity and graphic descriptions of kinky sex. If her favorite books were removed from the shelves at the library, it would be devastating to Kay because it would mean she could no longer escape her boring life for a few hours every month in a whirlwind book romance.

After a few hours of reading, Kay was wide awake and slightly aroused. It was rather disconcerting to be aroused by reading books that she knew were all fiction. Granted, her experience was limited, but she wasn't sure there was a man alive who could make her feel the way the heroines in those books described.

Sex in real life wasn't as great as the authors depicted it on the pages of their books. It was uncomfortable and embarrassing. Kay preferred cuddling and kissing and only put up with the rest of it to get to cuddle afterwards. *Thank goodness, I'm divorced, so I don't have to put up with it anymore,* she thought. *Cuddling with Mark wasn't worth it at all.*

Kay was also completely confused about why she couldn't shake the feeling that there was something special about the day that caused her to wake up so early. She felt like she was excited about something important happening that day and couldn't sleep in anticipation, but for the life of her, she couldn't figure out what. It was her weekend with her daughters, so she knew it wasn't anxiety about having to see her ex-husband, Mark Fox. Her birthday was still a few weeks away, so she wasn't anticipating celebrating with her family over the weekend.

Maybe it's because it's the first Saturday in over two years that it's just me and the girls?

A little over two years prior, she and her daughters moved in with her parents in the house she'd grown up in. The previous weekend, while Kay's daughters were with Mark, her mom and dad moved into a new house a couple blocks away, leaving her alone to rearrange her childhood home and start moving her daughters' things so they no longer had to share a room.

The house was only a three-bedroom, so when they moved in, Kay took her brother's old room, and the girls took the room Kay used to share with her sister. Now that her mom and dad had moved out, Kay moved into the master bedroom and had tried to start separating her daughters into their own spaces.

Kay decided that her excitement and feeling like the day was special for some reason had to be because of her plan to help her daughters personalize their individual spaces while they were all home for the afternoon. *I really hope that improves Tia's mood from last weekend's disaster of a visit with Mark.*

Her oldest daughter, Tia, was twelve and had struggled all week to understand her emotions after Mark yelled at her the previous weekend. Her younger daughter, Maria, was eight and had also questioned why her dad was telling them lies about the divorce and child support and acting so different from what they remembered from a few years ago. But Maria seemed to be handling her emotions better than Tia. Kay really wished she could get them to give her more details, but she didn't want to push and upset either of them more than they already were, so she backed off for the time being.

When she got to a stopping point, she put her book away and grabbed her phone off the charger to text her best friend, Deanna Wolfe. They'd been best friends since Deanna and her parents moved in right next door to Kay's family before Kay and Deanna started sixth grade. They were polar opposites these days, having grown apart since Kay didn't go back to college for her junior year when she realized she was pregnant with Tia. Kay got married and was happy being a stay-at-home mom while Mark was in the Army. Dee went on with school and graduated with a bachelor's degree in business administration and worked downtown at an oil company for the past ten years.

Kay only got her job as the hostess at the restaurant inside the Camelot Hotel four years ago because Mark was having trouble finding a job after getting out of the Army. It was definitely not her dream job, but it was enough to keep the lights on and food on the table. Plus, her normal, seven in the morning to three in the afternoon, Monday through Friday shift coincided perfectly with the girls' school schedule.

Dee made what Kay would think of as a boring secretarial job sound glamorous and exciting with the title of executive assistant and stories about trips all over the world with her sexy-as-sin boss. While Kay would love to be able to travel the world, she would never want to complicate her life by working so closely with someone she was attracted to, but who was completely off-limits.

Who am I kidding? Books are the only fuel for my fantasies, and I'll only have book boyfriends for at least the next ten years, until both my girls go off to college. Maybe then I can meet a man who makes me feel a little of the flutters and excitement my books describe.

Kay sighed and shook off those thoughts as she sent the text to her childhood BFF.

Kay: Whatcha doin' tonight? I'm thinking a Girls Night In w/ mani/pedis after rearranging the girls' rooms today.

After no response for several minutes, Kay finally got up about nine o'clock. She made breakfast and started her weekly house cleaning. She'd always tried to keep the house picked up all week by having her daughters pick up after themselves and cleaning the kitchen every night after dinner, but she usually spent her Saturday mornings helping her mother with the chores that they hadn't had time for during the week. Now that it was just her and the girls, she had to get back into the routine she had before moving back to her parents' house.

Tia and Maria always tried to help with the Saturday chores before they moved in with Kay's parents. When Tia was only three years old, Kay let her start helping by sorting laundry. When Maria got old enough to want to help too, Kay had to let Tia graduate to more challenging tasks like dusting furniture and using the vacuum cleaner, so her younger daughter could take over sorting the clothes. For the past two years, since they'd moved in with Kay's parents, while Kay was going through the separation and divorce from their father, Kay's mom insisted the only chore the girls were to perform was cleaning their room. Since it was just the three of them in the house now, both girls were insisting on helping Kay with the house cleaning once again.

Since Tia was now twelve and Maria was now eight, Kay figured they were old enough to do a little more than dusting, vacuuming, and sorting laundry, so she had to figure out what else she was going to let them do that wouldn't actually cause her to have to spend more time cleaning up after they were done cleaning. *Maybe I can come up with chore charts next weekend when they're at Mark's?* For this weekend, she decided to just let them do what they'd previously helped with so she could focus on cleaning the bathroom and kitchen and then start moving furniture and Tia's things to the room that she'd been using until the previous weekend.

About Noon, when they were done with the chores and about to start moving the girls into separate bedrooms, Kay's phone rang with a call from her boss.

"Hello, Mr. Brooks," Kay answered the phone with more of a smile in her voice than she felt.

"Kay, I'm sorry it's such short notice, but are you available to work the three to eleven shift this evening?" Mr. Brooks didn't sound nearly as happy over the phone as Kay had.

"I have my daughters this weekend," Kay answered.

"Is there anyone you can get to watch them for the evening? Valarie called in with a family emergency, so I don't have a hostess for our busiest shift of the weekend."

"Yeah, I'll call my parents." Kay realized this shift was going to derail her plans with the girls for the rest of the day, but she couldn't pass up the extra money. "I'm sure it won't be a problem."

"Thank you!" he said a little louder than she expected, causing her to jump slightly. "See you in a few hours."

Kay shook off the startled feeling as she hung up with the boss and called her parents' house.

"Hello," her mom, Mary Lee, answered.

"Hey, Mom." Kay flopped down on the couch to talk to her mother. "Can you watch the girls tonight so I can cover a shift at work? The other hostess had a family emergency and Mr. Brooks just called to see if I can be there by three."

"Of course!" she shouted. "You know I love having time with the girls."

"I won't get off until eleven tonight, but with closing, that means closer to midnight. You're good with a sleepover?"

"Perfect!" Her mom squealed with glee. "Just meet us at church in the morning to pick them up. Your sister is working tonight, too. At least that's what she told me when I talked to her this morning. See if you can get her to talk to you, either while you're working or maybe go for a late dinner after work. I'm not sure what's going on with her, but she seemed aggravated when I talked to her and she wouldn't tell me what's wrong, so I'm worried about her."

Kay's sister, Randi, was seven years younger than her and also worked at the restaurant in the Camelot Hotel. To look at the two of them, nobody would believe they were sisters because they were so different. Randi was tall and blonde with green eyes and Kay was super short with dark brown hair and blue eyes. Randi was outgoing whereas Kay was more introverted. But even with their differences and large age gap, they were super close and shared everything like best friends. Hearing that Randi was aggravated made Kay wonder if she was having problems with a guy or just didn't want to work on a Saturday night.

As soon as she hung up with her mom, Kay called Randi.

"Hey, Sis," Randi answered, sounding much too cheerful to be as aggravated as their mother said. "What's up?"

"Not much. Just got called into work the three to eleven tonight. When I called Mom to have her watch the girls, she said you're also working tonight, so I figured I'd see if you want a ride to work and would be interested in having a mini girls' night out after."

"Are you suggesting giving me a ride to work, so I can actually drink on this mini girls' night out?" Randi sounded hopeful.

"Yeah, I figured I'd be the designated driver tonight," Kay replied, smiling at her sister's enthusiasm. "Mom said you sounded aggravated when she talked to you earlier, so I thought you might need some girl talk and might want a drink or two to chill."

"Yeah, I'm sure I sounded aggravated when I talked to Mom," Randi chuckled. "I wanted to talk to Dad, but Mom said he was working and then wouldn't let me off the phone."

Kay chuckled, thinking about how their mother probably kept talking about inane things that were of no interest to Randi, like she usually did to Kay. They chatted for a few minutes to decide on what they were going to do after work and then hung up, so they could each get ready for work.

Kay broke the news to her daughters that they wouldn't be working on their bedrooms that day after all, but they were both excited to get to spend the night at their grandparents' new house.

After a shower, changing clothes, and packing bags for the girls and one for herself, so she didn't go out after work in her uniform, they finally left the house, so Kay could pick up Randi and drop Tia and Maria at her parents' house before going to work.

Anthony Burleson woke up Saturday morning massively aroused from the dream he just had. It started off relatively tame with him dreaming of his future wife and children. Then it morphed from playing on the beach with their two boys and two girls to him playing with their mother alone in a hotel room. He couldn't describe most of her facial features because he had her blindfolded and tied to the bed. *But she has pretty pink lips that looked amazing wrapped around my cock just before I woke up.*

He was frustrated that he didn't get to finish the dream but hoped it would come true soon. He really wanted to one day find a real-life version of his dream woman. He knew it was always the same woman in his dreams, even though he couldn't ever see her face clearly. He'd certainly seen every other part of her, since he spent most of his dream time touching and tasting every inch of her petite, curvy body.

As he showered, he closed his eyes and fantasized about fucking her perfect double D's to lessen the pressure in his cock, so he could get on with his day. With his final cry of release, she disappeared from his mind's eye, and he prayed he would meet the real woman he was meant to be with soon.

His trip to the San Antonio airport was short since his apartment wasn't too far from there. *Maybe I'll meet my dream woman on this trip*, he thought as he boarded the plane.

Thinking back, he realized that this trip to Tulsa was somewhat nostalgic as it was the first place he went to meet with Rick Robertson when the GWA had a pay-per-view weekend there at the end of July a year before. His interview had actually been in the restaurant of the hotel where the staff and talent stayed while in Tulsa. Anthony did the interview with Rick on a Friday morning, then stayed in the hotel for the next three nights and filled out all his paperwork, so he could be the pilot for the company jet on Monday morning when they flew out of Tulsa.

I wonder if Dad was right when he said my dream woman was someone I saw but didn't realize I had a connection with on that first trip to Tulsa? Maybe I'll get lucky and see her again on this trip!

Neither of the women he was seated between on the plane came close to being that woman. The one on his right in the window seat was a tall blonde who looked like a model. Beautiful face, way too thin body, and total diva attitude. She demanded the window seat, so she could keep it closed. *Definitely not my type if she can't handle seeing the clouds while flying.*

The woman on his left was a tall, thin redhead who had to have the aisle seat because she needed to go to the lavatory a half-dozen times in the first hour they'd been waiting to pull back from the gate since boarding the plane. At first, Anthony worried that she was sick, but after seeing all the changes to her hair and makeup, he realized she was also a model or wanted to be a model.

"Sorry for the delay," the male flight attendant said over the intercom. "Our captain just informed us that he's talking to Air Traffic Control and looking at the weather between here and Tulsa to determine how much longer we'll be delayed. Please feel free to stand up and stretch your legs for the next fifteen minutes. Hopefully, it won't be much longer than that before we can take off."

Fuck! I have to start insisting on first class for these flights to and from work. Anthony was so cramped in the middle seat in coach that his toes were already going numb. Since he couldn't fully stand up, he was grateful the redhead went to apply another coat of makeup to her face so he could stretch his legs a little into the floor space in front of her seat.

The only thing he hated about flying was how cramped he was when he was stuck in coach, but weather delays were quickly making him rethink that short list of dislikes. He was supposed to check in at the arena by five o'clock in the evening, so the boss knew he could let the lead pilot on the other crew go home. Anthony scheduled his flights no later than noon, so he had time to go check in at the hotel before going to the arena to be able to get a king suite. He had to have the king-sized bed, so he could sleep at an angle and not have his lower legs hanging off the bed. This weather delay was seriously affecting his ability to stay on schedule, and Anthony hoped it didn't cause problems with his ability to sleep tonight. *Yep, I also hate weather delays when I'm flying.*

The flight attendant informed the passengers that the fifteen-minute stretch break was up, so Anthony pulled his legs back into the space in front of only his seat to allow the redhead to sit back down without his legs in the way. The flight attendant then walked down the aisle to check that the passengers were all buckled in properly with the tray tables in the upright position and all electronics were put away. Anthony wasn't sure why since it was another hour before the plane taxied to the runway to wait in line to take off.

Anthony's noon flight finally took off at two-thirty-six in the afternoon. The plane landed just after four o'clock, so he hustled through baggage claim, only stopping long enough to call the hotel to find out he'd already lost his king suite for the night. Then he got a rental car with just enough time to go straight to the arena. *So much for the hotel and food first.*

<div align="center">~~~</div>

The sound of trumpets signaled the entrance of a couple arriving at the restaurant of the Camelot Hotel as if they were the king and queen entering a royal ball. Kay Lee really wished she wouldn't get in trouble for wearing earplugs, so she could muffle the sound of those freaking trumpets. Since her boss would probably frown on that, she resigned herself to having a headache by the end of her shift. Most of the time at the beginning of a Saturday afternoon shift was spent filling condiments and rolling silverware, but the restaurant also had a few seniors who came in for the early bird special.

"Welcome to Camelot," Kay smiled at the elderly couple. That was the standard line she was required to greet every customer with when they walked through the door. "A table for two?"

Both of them nodded their heads, so Kay grabbed two menus and escorted them to a table that allowed for easy access and a shorter distance for them to have to push their walkers. Before they were even seated, the trumpets blared again, so Kay had to quickly put their menus down and rush back to the hostess stand.

The hostess stand was really a cabinet with an open back where the hostess stood. It had shelves to hold menus and the silverware she spent half her shift rolling. The front was made up to look like a medieval cupboard. The dark wood went well with the red and gold carpets, drapes, and table linens, but the suit of armor beside the door really set the stage for the castle feel the hotel owners were going for when they built the hotel a few decades before. The hotel actually looked like a castle from the outside.

Luckily for Kay, the medieval castle theme included her uniform. She had to wear a long gown appropriate for a fair maiden in King Arthur's time. At barely five feet tall *(Fine, I'm only four-foot-eleven-and-three-quarters, but I round up.)*, Kay wouldn't be able to see over the hostess stand if it weren't for the high-heeled boots she wore under her long, poufy skirt. The boots didn't exactly match the dress, but she needed the four extra inches of height they provided, and they were a lot more comfortable than the dress shoes she had to wear all summer. Thankfully, Tulsa finally realized on the last weekend in September that it was time to cool off for Fall, so her boots were no longer too hot to wear.

"Welcome to Camelot," Kay said automatically as she got back to the hostess stand.

When she looked up to count the number of people in the group to be able to seat them at the right size table, she realized that they were definitely not the normal early bird customers. She had to look way up because all six of the guys that were standing at the hostess stand were well over six feet tall. They looked to be about her age, early thirties, at most. Most women would probably say they were ruggedly handsome, her sister Randi included.

Kay decided to seat them in Randi's section because she knew Randi would appreciate the eye candy. They were all overly muscular in Kay's opinion. At her size and with her history with men, Kay found men who were that large very intimidating. Adding in the long hair, beards, and the tattoos that showed on the one guy's wrists where his sleeves were rolled up made their appearance scream "bad boys".

If Kay were meeting them anywhere but at work, she would probably be too scared of them to say anything to them. At work, though, she had to make sure they weren't waiting for more people in their party to be able to seat them, so she had to swallow her fear and speak. "How many in your group?"

"Six," the clean-shaven, long-haired, blond man at the front of the group replied with a smile. "Unless you want to join us? We might need a couple suits of armor, so we could joust for you, Princess." He winked at her and elbowed the tattooed, bearded, brunette beside him in the ribs.

Kay fought to not roll her eyes as she grabbed the menus. She hated dealing with flirtatious customers, especially when she already felt uneasy because of the massive size difference. She tried to think of one of the sarcastic lines her younger sister would use in these situations.

Randi was only twenty-five, but she was much more confident and outgoing than Kay. Randi was only five-foot-six, so not overly tall for a woman, but tall enough that she wasn't as intimidated as Kay was by big men. Randi probably got some of her confidence from being cheer captain in high school, too.

Finally thinking of one of Randi's go-to lines for unruly customers, Kay spoke as she turned to show them to their table. "Sorry, my manager doesn't like me to hang out with the Court Jester, so you'll just have to stay a group of six. This way."

Yep, Randi is going to love cutting their egos down to size all evening, Kay thought as she seated them in Randi's section of the restaurant. "Your waitress will be right with you." Kay flipped her ponytail over her shoulder like Randi had been known to do with her long, blonde locks. "She's a true princess, though, so she'll only be won over by the boldest and bravest of knights."

The guys were all smiles as they took their seats, especially when they saw Kay walk over to her beautiful sister and point out their table. "Just a heads up, Sis, that table is in need of jousting supplies and a beautiful princess to fight over," Kay smirked.

Randi looked where Kay pointed at the table of men and put on a fake, sweet smile. "Awesome. I needed some entertainment for tonight. It's not been a great week."

"Mine either," Kay replied, thinking back to the conversations she had with her daughters earlier in the week.

It had actually been over two years since she'd left their father, but the divorce had only been final for about a year. When Kay and her girls first moved in with her parents, her ex-husband, Mark Fox, was so livid he refused to work with her to put together a visitation schedule. Then when the judge finally put together a visitation schedule as part of the final divorce decree, he claimed he didn't have room to have them on weekends in the tiny apartment he moved into after having to sell their house as part of the divorce settlement.

It was like pulling teeth to get him to finally start spending time with their daughters. Finally, about six months after the divorce was final, Mark started acting more like the man Kay married and had been following the visitation schedule, until the last few visits. Now, he seemed to be reverting to the behaviors that led to Kay leaving him. He'd been late picking them up multiple times. At their visit the previous weekend, Mark yelled at the girls and told them all kinds of lies about Kay and the divorce. Kay spent all week trying to get Tia and Maria to open up to her about everything that happened during their last visit.

"I'm so glad the girls are staying with Mom and Dad tonight, so you and I can have some sister time after work."

"Yeah." Randi grabbed silverware and water glasses to take to the table of guys. "I hate that it's just the bar here at work, but I don't really feel like going to a meat market. I just want to sit and relax and talk to you."

"Yeah, I don't want to deal with men either, but I am looking forward to hearing all the jabs you get on this round of court jesters tonight," Kay chuckled as Randi walked away.

The rest of her shift was pretty much business as usual in the restaurant. She went through the motions of rolling silverware and seating patrons in the restaurant while thinking back over her life. She hoped to remember something from her marriage to Mark that would help her figure out why he was being such a jerk.

Kay thought back to when she first met Mark. She'd just broken up with her high school boyfriend, Doug Jacobs, during Spring Break because it was too hard to maintain a long-distance relationship while he was in college out of state, and she was going to the University of Tulsa. It was the end of her sophomore year when she saw Mark in the dining hall for the first time.

It was actually the end of his senior year, so she didn't know why she hadn't ever noticed him before she got back to campus after that Spring Break trip. *I guess I'm just so much of a one-man woman that I didn't notice any other guys until after I was single again.*

Mark was in the ROTC program, so after he graduated, he went into active duty in the Army. They basically only dated for a month before he graduated and left town. A couple weeks after he went to live on an Army base overseas, Kay found out Tia was on the way. Even though they hadn't planned on trying to make a long-distance relationship work, she felt like he would want to know he was going to be a father. She wrote him a letter to let him know, but she also made plans to be a single parent.

Mark surprised her, though, by calling her as soon as he finished reading her letter. He was excited about being a dad and said it was fate telling them they could make long-distance work until he finished his time in the Army. They got married when he was home on leave in December. Tia Lee Fox was born on January first, nine months to the day from the day Kay met Mark. *Maybe meeting him on April Fool's Day should have been my first clue not to marry him.*

The first couple of years they were married, Kay and Tia lived with Kay's parents while Mark was overseas. They took that time to save up enough money for the down payment on a house. They basically only saw him when he came home on leave, even after Kay and Tia moved into the house they bought. Maria was conceived on one of those leaves. It wasn't until after he'd served eight years in the Army that Mark actually came home full-time. By then, Tia was seven and Maria was three.

Whenever he would come home on leave, he was a great dad. He was attentive to the kids and loving with Kay. She thought she had a great life with the perfect husband. He changed after he came home full-time, though.

Mark had a rough time transitioning to being a civilian again. He got irritated by the schedule Kay and the girls lived by. He had a hard time finding a job. He was so stressed that he became short-tempered. Back then, he would only raise his voice to Kay, never the girls. *I wonder if his yelling at the girls last weekend is because he's stressed out again and I'm not there to buffer his temper?*

When eleven o'clock finally rolled around, Kay flipped the sign on the door to closed. That didn't mean she got to leave yet. She still had to stay until all the customers finished their meals and left. Then Kay had to help Randi and the other two waitresses clean and reset the restaurant for the morning shift to be able to open on time. It was after midnight before they finished the closing tasks at the restaurant.

Kay and Randi both changed out of their uniforms and into jeans, t-shirts, and comfortable tennis shoes. While they were looking forward to a girl's night and unwinding after a long week at work, they didn't want to dress provocatively, and risk being hit on by the usual crowd of guys who enjoyed the medieval times décor and came to the bar to role-play as if it were a renaissance fair.

Since her divorce, Kay was on what she called a Man Fast, where she wasn't dating. She didn't want her daughters to see her going out with anyone unless she thought it could be a serious enough relationship to get married one day. Since she didn't think there was any way to know that when she first met someone, she decided not to date, so she didn't introduce her daughters to a string of first dates that wouldn't lead to anything more.

Randi had recently told Kay that she wanted to take a break from the dating scene as well after breaking up with her last boyfriend. Kay still didn't understand why Randi had even dated Billy. He was always rude whenever she saw them out together, which was luckily infrequent since he seemed to prefer spending his time hunting instead of actually with Randi.

Kay might have understood Randi putting up with being ignored if Billy were more attractive. She honestly couldn't name one redeeming quality about the man. But Kay hated that Randi was so heartbroken over him. She was glad, however, that her younger sister didn't want to use their night out to look for her next boyfriend, so

Kay could have a night out without having to be a parent once in a while.

~~~

By the time Anthony made his way through the backstage area of the Tulsa Fairgrounds to find his boss, Rick Robertson, it was five-fifteen that evening. Rick was looking at his watch as Anthony walked up, and Anthony knew he was going to give him shit for being late. Rick was a really cool guy. He was only about ten years older than Anthony, but the silver strands mixed into his dark hair at his temples made him look older. He was a wrestler before he took over the promoter's role from his father a few years back, so he was still muscular and outweighed Anthony by twenty or thirty pounds, even though he was four inches shorter. Luckily, Anthony knew Rick would just hit him with a little trash talk and not challenge him to get in the ring with him as punishment for being late.

"I never thought I'd see the day that the always punctual Anthony Burleson would be late, but I guess I was wrong," Rick smirked. "You know that's a fireable offense."

"Being fifteen minutes late to check in when I don't actually get to work for almost fifteen hours?" Anthony wondered where Rick was going with that statement since it wasn't his normal trash-talking.

"No, making me be wrong about something." Rick grinned as he slapped Anthony on the back and chuckled.

"Sorry, Boss," Anthony replied with a chuckle of his own. "Blame Delta or Mother Nature. Storms delayed my flight over two-and-a-half hours, so I figured I was doing good only being fifteen minutes late."

"Damn, you made up over two hours? Guess that means I have to cut you loose early so you can get checked in at the hotel, huh?"

"Naw, I called them while I was in baggage claim. I've already lost my king suite and am in no hurry to sit on a tiny standard bed for the evening."

"I won't fire you, then," Rick chuckled as they walked toward the catering area. "Having to sleep in a standard bed is punishment enough for making me be wrong."
~~~

They each grabbed a plate and sat down to discuss flight times for an international tour the next year while the rest of the company made their way through catering for their normal six o'clock dinner break. When they finished eating, Rick went back to his temporary office space to triple-check that everything was set up for that night's show, and Anthony made his way to the dressing room to find his best friends.

"There you are," Dean Hunter shouted as Anthony walked into the locker room. "Thought you were gonna meet us at the hotel."

"Flight delay," Anthony explained in place of a greeting.

"You should've kicked the pilot out of the cockpit, so you could have flown here faster." Dean finished lacing his wrestling boots before looking back up at Anthony.

"I doubt the air marshal would have allowed that." Anthony took a seat on the bench across from him, so he wasn't in the way where he or his brother, James, were getting ready.

"Probably not," James chuckled as he shut his locker. "Have a good visit with your family?"

"Yeah," Anthony replied, thinking back to the family dinner the night before. "Speaking of family, Becky was real interested in how ya'll are doin'. Last night at dinner, she got this dreamy look on her face when she said your names, so I figure it's time I lift the ban on dating my sister."

James looked like he was going to be sick. It was a rare look on him. He was six-foot-four and two-hundred-and-fifty pounds of ripped muscles, who looked like he would never be afraid of anything with his long hair, beard, and tattoos. But the way he just turned green was a good indication that he might be afraid of Anthony's five-foot-four, one-hundred-and-twenty-pound sister.

"Nope," was all James said before bending over to hide his reaction with his pre-match stretching routine.

"Oh, hell yeah," Dean shouted. "I've been waiting years for you to lift that ban."

"Seriously?" James stood back up and looked at Dean like he was confused. "She's like our sister, too."

"Dude, I have never thought of Becky like a sister." Dean went into his own stretching routine. "I may have fantasized about her in that nun's habit she wore in that play in high school, but that's the type of sister I want to corrupt, not my sister."

"Don't say another word, Dean." Anthony pointed at his friend, feeling like he might puke. "I don't need to know what you wanna do with my sister."

"Sorry." Dean apologized, but he didn't look like he meant it.

"Seriously, though, if you want to date her, I don't have a problem with it. But don't do it unless you think she's the one woman for you because I don't want to see her get hurt." Anthony hoped Dean knew Becky was not the type of girl who would have a fling and be happy when it was over. Becky was a forever girl. She was the type who went all in and thought every relationship could last forever.

"Dude, you know I would never intentionally hurt Becky." Dean looked at Anthony imploringly. "I've always been attracted to her, but I've held it all back because I didn't want to risk our friendship, so I've never allowed myself to even think about how I could really feel about her. Now I'm going to think about her and the possibilities, but I won't act on anything until I know exactly what I want with her."

He moved to another stretch before continuing. "Is she still looking for love at first sight like your parents? If so, she may not really be interested in me since I can't even remember the first time I saw her."

"How do you know about my parents? And when was Becky looking for love at first sight?" Anthony felt slightly blindsided by what Dean just said.

"Becky told me how your folks met when we were in high school. She asked me to morp, and I had to tell her about your ban on dating her. She tried to convince me that it wouldn't really be a date because she was holding out for love at first sight like your folks."

Morp was the backwards prom for seniors at Heart's Destiny High School. Anthony missed it since he got his GED and joined the Navy instead of going to his senior year. Since the Hunters, Becky, and Anthony were all in the same grade all through school, they all three got to do the fun stuff Anthony missed by skipping his senior year. They all ended up in the same grade because of how their birthdays fell and the requirement to be six years old before the September first cut-off date for starting Kindergarten at Heart's Destiny Elementary. Becky's birthday was in October, so she didn't turn six until after the cut-off the year she actually turned six. Since Anthony's birthday was in August ten months later, they were both six on September first the year Anthony turned six, so they started kindergarten at the same time. For a while, they had to explain to the other kids that they weren't twins. *Twins. Fuck. What was I saying to the Hunter twins?*

"Oh, I, uh," Anthony stuttered. "I never knew she thought she would find *The One* like Mom and Dad. I just know that she always thinks whoever she's dating is *The One*. I don't want her to start planning your wedding if you don't intend to walk down the aisle."

"So, I gotta be ready to propose before I ask her out to dinner?" Dean laughed.

"Something like that." Anthony laughed with him.

"You really think love at first sight is real?" James asked. Anthony glanced over at him and saw James looking deep in thought. Anthony wondered if James was thinking about someone specific or if he was just ready to settle down and start looking for his future wife.

"Mom and Dad sure claim it is," Anthony answered. "I think there's definitely someone out there who is perfect for each of us, and I hope I'll know it when I meet her."

"But how are you supposed to know it when you meet *The One*?" James still looked thoughtful.

"I imagine my cock will tell me by getting hard as soon as I see her." Dean grinned.

Anthony laughed at Dean's obvious locker room talk. "I'm sure instant lust is part of it, but I don't think that's the main sign that it's real love." Anthony thought back to what his dad said he felt the first time he saw his mom and tried to figure out how to explain it to James and Dean. "Dad said Mom glowed, like a beacon calling him from across the room. He felt drawn to her like a magnet. He said that when he looked at Mom the first time, it was the first time he thought about getting married and was excited about it instead of sick."

"That how you felt about Nancy back in school?" James looked over at Anthony with a curious expression.

"No, not really," Anthony replied with a sigh. "Don't get me wrong, I loved Nancy back in school, but I don't remember the first time we met. She was just always around and grew on me from being Becky's annoying friend to Freshman year when I finally saw her as an attractive girl and asked her to Homecoming."

Nancy was Anthony's first at everything his freshman year and his only long-term girlfriend. She was a grade behind him in school, but with such a small school they all mingled between grades when they hung out after school. She was also his only sexual partner until almost a year after she died. The guys in his squadron decided he'd grieved long enough and started dragging him out whenever they were on leave, so he had a few one-night stands over the years until his accident. *Damn! I still can't believe it's been two years since I've had sex!*

Since Anthony started having nightly dreams about his soulmate, he hadn't wanted to be with anyone but her. She was like a needle in a haystack to find, so he was a little worried it was going to be a long while before he finally found her and ended his dry spell. He wondered if he should tell the guys about the woman he was looking for, to have them help him search.

"Actually, I think I'll know my soulmate when I finally meet her because I've been dreaming about her for a little over a year," Anthony finally managed to tell them.

"Seriously?" James inquired as he and Dean both looked up at Anthony from their stretched positions.

"Yeah," Anthony practically whispered. "She's a petite brunette, with long, straight hair almost down to her ass. Curves in all the right places, perfect double D's, and pouty pink lips."

"Damn!" Dean came completely up out of his stretch. "You really should have been with us at the hotel earlier. I saw more than one petite brunette there."

"How often do you dream about the same woman?" James asked as he, too, finished his stretching.

"Pretty much every night," Anthony answered.

"That's why you think she's your soulmate?" James queried. "Because it's always the same woman and nightly for a year?"

"Yeah," Anthony replied. "Always the same woman, doing different, um, things." Anthony struggled to decide how much detail he wanted to give them about his dreams. "Sometimes we're hanging out with our kids at the beach or having a family game night, and other times it's just her and I, um. I guess you could say she's my fantasy woman, but I also see her as the mother of my children, so I think that makes her my soulmate, my one and only." Anthony shrugged, not sure what else to say.

"That's awesome." James gave him a sincere smile.

"Hope you find her soon. Not that your dreams really help us out, other than to know that when we go out, we can have all the blondes and redheads." Dean grinned as he mentioned the blondes and redheads.

Anthony shook his head and chuckled at him.

"You're on deck," one of the production assistants pointed back and forth between the Hunters before bouncing back out the locker room door. Anthony hadn't even seen him come into the room because he was too focused on his own thoughts about his dreams and his fantasy woman.

Not wanting to be rude, he tried to stay out of his own head and focused on watching his friends perform the rest of the night. The Hunters wrestled as a heel tag team, which meant they played the role of the bad guys. Since most Saturday shows weren't televised, they were working with two babyfaces (guys playing the good guy role) from the local promotion instead of their normal GWA rivals. This let the local crowd cheer for their hometown favorites and gave the local wrestlers a chance to show Rick and his team of writers what they could do to possibly earn a place on the GWA roster. The Hunter brothers got their jobs the same way a couple years back.

After the Hunters finished their match, they all hung out backstage watching the rest of the show on monitors. Rick recorded every show even if they weren't televised, so he could review the performances to help everyone improve. Anthony appreciated that he did, so he could watch every show without leaving the backstage area.

When the show was over, James and Dean went for a late meal with a few of the other people on the crew, but Anthony had to go check in at the hotel for the night. *UGH! I have to unwind a little or I'll never get any sleep in that tiny bed.*

After checking in at the Camelot Hotel, Anthony made his way to the hotel bar. He was going to order a beer, thinking that would be just enough to help him sleep, but would wear off quickly, so he would be safe to fly the GWA plane the next morning. His plan for a beer changed the instant the most beautiful woman he'd ever seen climbed up on the barstool next to him. *It's HER!*

She's gorgeous. So short that she had to step on the bottom support bar on the barstool to use it like a ladder to sit on the stool. If it weren't for the womanly curves in all the right places, he would have thought she was still a child because she was so small. *DAMN, I want to pick her up and carry her with me everywhere.*

When she first walked up, he was drawn to her full chest that couldn't be concealed by her light blue t-shirt. She didn't notice Anthony at all and immediately turned to talk to the blonde who came in with her. Even with her mostly turned away from him, Anthony hadn't been able to look at anything in the room but her.

All his life, he'd heard the story of how his dad fell in love with his mom the first time he saw her across the room at a church potluck. His mom was five years younger than his dad, so he couldn't ask her out then because she was only fifteen at the time. Bob Burleson did point Hazel out to his brother, Jon, that day, though, and said she would be his wife one day. *I wonder if this is what Dad felt that day?*

Anthony pulled out his phone and started texting his dad. Anthony described his future wife while watching her while she talked. Her hair was dark brown, long, and straight. The shiny, dark locks hung down to the middle of her back. Anthony imagined how it would look up in a ponytail, so her neck would be exposed for him to kiss. That led him to thinking about kissing her further down. *Those have to be double D's.* He had to stop that train of thought because his pants were starting to feel too tight, and he didn't want to scare her off with a visible erection before he even knew her name. His phone vibrated in his hand, so he looked down at his dad's reply.

Anthony: Hey Dad! Just thought I'd let you know that I'm sitting in a bar in Tulsa, OK next to my future bride. She's exactly who I've been dreaming about. Petite, brunette, and the most beautiful woman I've ever seen. ;)

Dad: ;) Glad to hear it, what's her name? What's she like?

Anthony: Haven't heard her name yet, but she has a heart-shaped face & a button nose & pouty lips I can't

wait to kiss. I'm trying to find a way into the convo
she's having w/ the other woman who walked in w/
her, so I can find out her name.

Dad: Good luck, Son! Maybe by this time next year, you'll
be adopting that first baby.

Anthony: Fingers crossed!

Chapter Two

Sunday, September 30, 2018, 12 a.m.

Kay and Randi weaved their way through the crowded tables to the bar and found two stools side by side so they could chat.

"Alright, Sis, tell me about your bad week," Kay urged as soon as they were both seated.

"Ugh!" Randi groaned and laid her head on her hands on the bar. "Billy is driving me nuts!" She sat back up and turned to look at Kay with irritation written all over her face.

"I thought you broke up with him." Kay leaned her head to the side to look at her sister questioningly.

"I did!" Randi exclaimed and threw her hands up in the air. "A month ago! But he was apparently too focused on the hunting trip he was leaving on and didn't hear me when I told him it was over and to never call me again." She waved her hands around agitatedly. "He called me Monday to let me know that he was back in town and wanted to bring a deer to my house so he could hang it in my carport to dress it out. Like Amy and I want a dead deer hanging in the carport forcing us to park on the street. Then when I reminded him that we broke up, he got pissed and claimed that it hadn't happened."

Kay sat there dumbfounded by the nerve of Randi's ex-boyfriend. *Seriously, this guy sounds like he's gone completely off his rocker!*

"I finally got sick of trying to get through to him and just hung up on him. He's called me daily since, so now I'm screening all my calls and quit answering when it's him. I'm going to ask Daddy to talk to him for me tomorrow after church."

"You know you can block him on your phone, so he can't call you anymore, right?" Kay felt more than a little fear for her sister.

"Yeah, I didn't want to do that until after Daddy talks to him, so he doesn't just start coming by the house or work. But as soon as I tell Daddy what's going on, I'm definitely blocking him." Randi sighed and her shoulders slumped. "So, how was your week?"

"It was a week," Kay replied and thought back to her conversations with her daughters. "The girls were irritable all week after having to spend the weekend with Mark. I wish I could get his visitation revoked, so the girls don't have to suffer through the visits."

Randi looked dumbfounded as she gaped at Kay. "But you don't want to be the bad guy who takes their father away from them."

Kay took a deep breath and thought for a minute to figure out how to explain to her sister that she was worried that Mark would escalate from yelling at the girls to physical abuse, like he had with her right before she left him. *But I can't tell her that because I never told her about him hitting me!*

"I don't think taking Mark away from them would make me the bad guy anymore." Kay finally admitted with a sigh. "All he does, on every visit for the last couple of months, is complain about how he has to cancel his plans to have them there. And he seems to take great pleasure in telling them that they can't do anything but sit at his apartment, or go to his dad's farm, because he doesn't have the money to do anything."

Kay felt her cheeks heating and knew they were turning beet red from how hot her anger made her feel just thinking about the lies Mark told the girls. *He's telling them all this BS to make me look bad in my daughters' eyes. I don't know what he thinks he'll gain by turning the girls against me, other than making all three of us miserable. I do know I'm sick of seeing my daughters hurting from the emotional turmoil he's causing them every other weekend.*

"Get this!" Kay shouted at Randi. "He told Tia that he has to send all his money to me to pay to see them!"

Randi looked back at Kay with wide eyes, obviously shocked by what Mark told Tia.

"He had Tia convinced that he had to pay me, so I would let him see her and Maria every other weekend. She was in tears, asking why I charged him so much to see her!" Kay had to pause while she took a deep breath and tried to calm down, so she could quit shouting.

"I had to explain that I didn't charge him to see her or Maria. I didn't really want to explain to my twelve-year-old how divorce works and that a judge ordered the child support he pays to help cover the expenses of our household. Thankfully, she's gifted, because I had to show her the court orders to convince her that he only pays three-hundred dollars a month in child support, and not his full paycheck like he told her."

"I bet she loved reading that," Randi laughed. "After reading that dry, confusing language, does she still want to be a lawyer when she grows up?"

Kay's oldest daughter, Tia, decided she wanted to be a lawyer back when they were going through the divorce. She wanted to go with Kay every time Kay had to go to court. When Kay told Tia she was too young, she said that kids need their own lawyer to represent them when their parents get divorced, so she wanted to grow up to be the lawyer for all the kids like her.

"Yes! Crazy kid asked me for not only the divorce decree, but also the entire court transcript because she was so fascinated by it." Kay practically shouted. "I told her that she's too young to read the transcript, but I'm going to let her frame the divorce decree to hang over her bed."

Randi laughed and shook her head. "Why does she want to frame it and hang it up?"

"I'm not entirely sure," Kay answered. "She just wanted to know if she could after she read it. Seemed strange to me, but it finally put a smile on her face after the week of irritability from spending the weekend with Mark, so I was glad to let her hang it up. Plus, I'll get to see it every morning when I wake her up and thank God that I don't have to spend another day of my life with Mark."

"Amen to that!" Randi shouted, raising her hand for a high five.

Kay slapped her sister's hand before asking, "So, how much fun did you have this afternoon waiting on that rowdy group of guys?"

"Oh, girl, they were hilarious and so over the top!" Randi gave her a wide smile. "I was asked to dance, asked on a date, challenged to a wrestling match, and proposed to, all in the time it took for their dinner."

"Seriously?" Kay giggled. "What did you tell them?"

"I basically roasted them," she replied. "I insulted their looks, their intelligence, their attitudes, anything I could think of to insult, and the more I insulted them, the more they threw out cheesy lines. But I kind of felt bad for the one guy, who was so shy he could barely speak to order his dinner. I think his friends embarrassed him."

Randi shifted in her seat and looked down at her hands in her lap. "I actually thought he was the only one I would have liked to have flirt with me. I thought about giving him my number and telling him that, but I was afraid I would just embarrass him more, so I didn't."

"Isn't that how it always goes? The ones who are actually attractive and act like gentlemen are either already taken or are too shy to ever politely flirt," Kay replied.

"Are you talking about a guy who's staying at the hotel?" a guy to Kay's right asked. Kay turned to look at him and about fell off her barstool. He gently clasped her elbow to steady her, but she was so enchanted by his dark brown eyes and the tingles running up her arm from where he was touching her that she couldn't speak to answer his question. When she didn't say anything, he continued by saying, "Because if he's staying in the hotel, maybe you can find him when he's not with all his friends and talk to him without embarrassing him."

Randi looked past Kay at the stranger and then back at Kay. Randi widened her eyes and twisted her mouth in a look that told Kay she noticed the obvious chemistry Kay shared with the man. Kay realized that she didn't hide her feelings well enough that her sister couldn't read them in her eyes. They had a silent conversation with just their eyes where Randi asked, *"What's going on?"* And Kay told her, *"That is the most attractive man I've ever seen and just looking at him is riling up a bunch of butterflies in my stomach!"*

Randi straightened her face and looked back at the guy beside Kay. "I don't know if they're staying here or not. We get some people who just come in for the theme restaurant that aren't hotel guests, so I may never see him again. But if I do happen to see him in the lobby alone, I'll definitely go talk to him."

"Good. Hopefully, you'll see him soon. I see you ladies haven't gotten a drink yet. Can I buy you a round and see if I can help you figure out if he's in the hotel or not? I'm Anthony, by the way." Anthony raised a hand to flag down the bartender.

"I'm Randi, and this is my sister, Kay," Randi replied, nudging Kay in the side. She leaned in to whisper in Kay's ear, "Say something, Sis, before the hot guy runs away thinking you're rejecting him."

"Um, uh, hi," Kay stammered out, hating that she was presenting herself in such an unflattering way because she was so tongue-tied at the mere sight of this gorgeous man. She squared her shoulders and sat up as straight as possible before trying again. "Kay Lee." She extended her hand toward Anthony.

He took it in his much larger hand, but instead of shaking it as Kay expected, he lifted her hand to his mouth to kiss her knuckles. When his lips touched her hand, she felt tingles up her arm and a resurgence of that swarm of butterflies in her core. *Holy moly, the fluttery feelings described in those books are real!* Kay didn't know what to think about the way her body was reacting to Anthony. She'd never had such a strong attraction to anyone before, not even her ex-husband.

Anthony touched her elbow or her hand, and she felt tingles running all the way from the innocent places he touched her straight to the not-so-innocent womanly body parts she wished he was touching instead. *What kind of woman starts thinking about having sex with a man within seconds of meeting him? This is so not me!*

"What can I get for you?" The bartender came over to the section of the bar beside them.

Anthony looked to Kay, indicating to the bartender that she should order first. The way he looked at Kay, as if he could see through to her very soul, had her flustered to the point of stuttering as she answered, "Jus-just ah, a, Pep-Pepsi."

"She's my designated driver tonight." Randi smiled at the bartender. "You can add some rum to my Pepsi, though, Tom."

Tom acknowledged her order with a wink before looking back at Anthony.

"I guess I'll have a Pepsi, too." Anthony shook his head with a small lift of his lips. "I'm not sure I'll ever get used to these places that have Pepsi instead of Coke."

As he shook his head, his dark brown hair fell down over one eye and caught Kay's attention. She finally stopped looking into his eyes long enough to notice the rest of him. Since she had to look up at him, even though they were both seated on barstools, she figured he was way taller than she. He had straight, dark brown hair that just touched the collar of his navy-blue dress shirt. It was parted on one side and the side without the part was just long enough to cover the one eye when it wasn't brushed back. He had high cheekbones and a nose that looked like it might have been broken at some point in his past. His rugged jaw had a slight five o'clock shadow that indicated he hadn't shaved since the morning or maybe the night before. Kay couldn't take her eyes off his lips because she noticed they were what she considered perfect. Not too thin, or too full, just perfect.

Thoughts of how much she wanted to kiss him made her force her eyes down to look at the rest of him. Broad shoulders, narrow waist, and long legs in navy, pinstriped dress pants that ended with large dress shoes. *I wonder how true the old saying about big feet meaning a man is big in other places actually is?*

Kay wasn't sure if she was really hoping that it was true or not. Part of her worried that it would just hurt more if he was too big. And another part of her was wondering if the book descriptions of steamy sex with big men were actually correct and she'd just never been with a big enough man.

Maybe I need to think about testing that theory before just believing that all sex will be as bad as what I've had in the past. It has been a few years. So, maybe I just don't remember the good parts because of who it was with?

Anthony's really big feet were flat on the floor with his knees bent, even on the tall barstool. That made Kay realize that he was definitely much taller than Kay, probably at least six-foot-four, if not taller. That made her feel even more petite.

Oddly enough, she didn't have the normal feelings of discomfort at being so much smaller than him that she normally had around large men. Normally, she was scared of men his size, but she didn't feel afraid of Anthony at all. Instead, she felt like she wanted to cuddle up on his lap and let him protect her from the rest of the world. When she looked back into his eyes, they seemed to tell her that he would like that, too.

The bartender setting their drinks down finally brought Kay's attention back to where they were, and she realized what he'd just said. "I'm sorry?" Kay tilted her head and looked at him quizzically. "What's wrong with Pepsi?"

~~~

Anthony didn't really mean to eavesdrop on their conversation, but the melodic tone of her voice was like a siren song to his sailor's ears. *She has daughters, Tia and Maria.* Anthony liked the sound of their names. *I wonder if they have blonde hair? She also has an ex-husband, Mark, who sounds like a jackass. Mark the Jackass. Yep, that's definitely what I'll call him from now on.*

Anthony hoped he could maintain his focus, so he didn't say that out loud when he met her ex-husband. He knew he would definitely be meeting her ex at some point. He knew he would because he knew he would have to deal with her ex-husband when he became her new husband.

Anthony had been skeptical of his parents' claims of love at first sight when they told all six of their kids about how they met. His mom claimed to have known that first day at church when she was fifteen, too. But since she hadn't mentioned his dad to any of her friends before he actually asked her out a few years later, Anthony believed she might actually have had to be convinced to fall in love with his dad.

One look at the beautiful woman sitting beside him convinced him that love at first sight was real. He just hoped that he wouldn't have to convince Kay to love him back or wait a few years to date her like his dad had to do with his mom. *She said her daughter is twelve, though, so she is probably a year or two older than me instead of underage like Mom was back then, no matter how young she looks.*

When Anthony interrupted their conversation about the wrestlers (or at least he thought the guys they were talking about were wrestlers), and she looked him in the eye for the first time, he fell instantly. Anthony fell into those pools of ocean blue and couldn't look away. He knew right then that he would love her for the rest of his life. He was so lost in her eyes during their introductions that he ordered a Pepsi instead of a beer.

"What's wrong with Pepsi?" Kay asked after looking Anthony over from top to bottom.
~~~

Damn, I hope my erection isn't too obvious, Anthony thought, then smiled when he realized that Dean was right when he said his cock would tell him that she was *The One*.

"It's too sweet," Anthony replied as he put his wallet back in his pocket after paying the bartender and picked up his glass to take a drink. "Coke has a sharper taste. Plus, it's what I grew up with, so I'm probably just more used to it. It seems like it's more popular in most places, but for some reason, Pepsi is more popular in Oklahoma. I was just wondering why."

"That's because the bottling plant for Pepsi is just across the river from here." Kay took a drink of her Pepsi.

Seeing those perfect pink lips wrapped around her straw caused Anthony to have a flashback to his dream the night before, only now he saw all of Kay's heart-shaped face as she sucked his cock. *Fuck, I can't wait for that to be real life.*

"We buy it straight from the plant for the house because it's cheaper than buying any other sodas from the store."

"That makes sense. If the plant is local, then I'm sure it's much cheaper to get than Coke for the businesses, too." Anthony didn't want to think about how tight her budget must have been as a single Mom, but he knew he would be changing it as soon as she would let him. It was going to take a lot of self-control to keep from coming on too strong and scaring her away.

To change from that train of thought, Anthony looked at Randi and asked, "So, you're a waitress at the restaurant here? Is that where you met the guy you wish would have flirted?"

"Yeah, Kay is the hostess, and she sat a group of guys in my section this afternoon that were over-the-top flirts. They were all attractive, but the outrageousness of most of them was a real turn-off." Randi moved her hands around like she couldn't keep them still. "The one guy, though, I wish he'd come in by himself because I would have definitely enjoyed getting to know him, without the clowns he was with being so embarrassing. Do you really think you can figure out if he's staying here or not?"

"Maybe," Anthony shrugged. He realized then that if Kay had been the hostess at the restaurant in this hotel a little over a year before, he may have seen her there when he went for his first interview with the

GWA. That would explain why he started having his dreams that weekend and felt drawn to her still, now that they'd actually met.

He tried to appear to be looking at Randi while he was speaking to her, but he was actually watching Kay through his peripheral vision because he couldn't stop himself from looking at her. "Did I hear you mention that they challenged you to a wrestling match?"

Randi nodded her head, so he continued. "I work with the Galactic Wrestling Association as a pilot. They had a show at the Tulsa Fairgrounds tonight. If you describe them, I might be able to tell you who they are and if they're staying at the hotel. That is, if they're actually GWA wrestlers. They could also be local wrestlers who just came to the hotel because they found out our crew was here, and they were looking to get a tryout. But mentioning wrestling is kind of strange for someone who isn't in the business, so there's a good chance I know them."

Kay took her foot off the top rung of the barstool and used it to push against the bar to move her stool back, so Anthony didn't have to lean around her to talk to Randi. While he appreciated her trying to move to include him in their conversation more comfortably, he worried that she would topple the stool and fall. So, he grabbed the bottom of her stool seat and pulled her back at the same time to prevent her from possibly getting hurt. His protective instincts were extremely high with Kay, which in his opinion was just more proof that she was his soulmate.

"Well, the guy I liked was tall. I don't think he was as tall as you, but close. He had long hair, a little lighter than Kay's but not much." Randi started her description while also talking with her hands to show how tall the guy was. "He had a neatly trimmed beard." She punctuated her statement by rubbing her own jaw. "He had tattoos on his arms, but I couldn't tell what because they were mostly covered up where he'd only rolled the cuffs of his shirt sleeves up." She demonstrated by slicing her right hand over her left wrist. "He had brown eyes." She pointed to her own eyes. "I think he was Caucasian with a really great tan, but he could be Native American or mixed race to get that golden-brown skin." She let out a long sigh as she settled her hands in her lap.

"How many guys were with him?" Anthony asked while noticing that Kay's eyes were focused on him. He hoped thinking about the wrestlers he knew would keep him from tenting his pants while she was looking him over. There were a couple of guys who worked with the GWA who matched Randi's description.

"It was a table of six, so him and five others," Randi replied, holding up a hand and marking each of the others off on a finger as she described them. "The one right beside him at the table was a blond-haired, blue-eyed, clean-shaven surfer."

Anthony fought to maintain eye contact with Randi as she went through her descriptions. He was so drawn to Kay that his focus was still on her, and he was fighting himself to keep it to just through his peripheral vision. Kay seemed lost in thought as she sat there, as if she couldn't even hear her sister talking.

"The one on the other side of the surfer kind of looked like a lumberjack in a plaid shirt with long, sandy brown hair, and a bushy beard." Randi continued with her description as she pointed at her next finger.

Anthony smiled when a brief flicker of his eyes at Kay showed him that she was no longer lost. Well, maybe she was still lost in thought, but at least now he was hopeful that the way her eyes were wandering back down his body meant she was thinking about him.

"Neither of them had their shirt sleeves pushed up, so I can't tell you if they had tattoos. The lumberjack was the most flirtatious." Randi paused to take a drink before continuing.

Anthony took advantage of that pause to look directly at Kay, but he couldn't make eye contact because her gaze was focused on his waist, or slightly below. His cock responded to her focus by immediately standing at attention. He knew he would have to teach his cock to stand down or he wouldn't stand a chance of earning Kay's heart. So, he turned his eyes back to Randi where she was continuing her descriptions, and tried to think of anything that would reverse the growth in Mr. Happy. *Sweaty wrestlers. Smelly locker rooms. Dirty socks.*

"The one directly across the table from my guy looked like he could be his brother, like not quite identical twin, but he didn't have tattoos on his wrists and was almost as boisterous as the lumberjack."

As soon as she mentioned twins, Anthony knew who she was talking about, so he pulled out his phone to text his friend.

Anthony: Hey James, are you at the hotel?

James Hunter was the quiet one of the Hunter twins. His brother Dean was the outgoing one. So, Anthony knew that when she was describing the quiet twin, she meant James. He smiled when he thought about his lifelong buddy James and how he might react to hearing Randi was interested in him. Anthony hoped James didn't freak out so bad that he couldn't even talk to her. Anthony had seen him have that problem a few times in the past. It wasn't that he was so shy he couldn't talk to women like a lot of people thought. He was just hyperaware when a woman felt intimidated by his size, so he didn't talk to keep from scaring them more. Sometimes, Anthony thought James read a woman's anxiety due to interest as fear of him instead and shut down when he shouldn't. *Hopefully, Randi won't give him any minute signals that she's intimidated or afraid of him.*

"Beside him was a bald, African American who never stopped smiling. He was the most laid back of the group and mostly just laughed at the other's antics."

Anthony looked down at his phone when he felt it vibrate.

James: Yeah. Why?

        Anthony: Did you eat dinner at the hotel restaurant? Have a hot blonde waitress?

James: Yeah. How'd you find out? Which asshole told you about her?

        Anthony: Nobody told me about her. I'm at the hotel bar & she's here.

        Anthony: She's telling her sister about you.

James: No way. I didn't even really talk to her.

        Anthony: That's why she was telling her sister about you.

Anthony: Wished you'd have come into the restaurant alone so she could have gotten to know you.

James: Seriously? She was too busy turning down Dean, Josh, Red, & Crockett to notice me.

Anthony: Dude, she's so into you that she just described you to me with so much detail she was trying to figure out your racial breakdown to get that golden-brown skin.

James: You sure she didn't mean Dean?

Anthony: No, she said he was too flirty.

Anthony: She likes the shy, quiet type apparently. Probably because she wants to be the outgoing one in a relationship.

James: You think I have a chance with her?

Anthony: Yeah, definitely. If you get your ass down here to the bar before she & her sister finish their drinks.

James: On my way.

"And the last one was a redhead with an accent. Irish, I think. I wouldn't say he had a beard, but it looked like he might have skipped shaving for a day or two." Upon seeing Anthony's huge smile, Randi stopped talking and started making a squeaking sound as she pointed at his phone.

"I think you're talking about James Hunter. So, I texted James and asked if he had dinner at the hotel restaurant and had a blonde waitress." Anthony told Randi as he put his phone back in his pocket. "He confirmed by asking which asshole he was with had told me about you. So, I told him you were here and were telling us how you wished you could have gotten to know him. He's on his way down."

Randi squealed and put her hand up, so Anthony put his hand up for her to slap.

~~~

Kay zoned out as Randi described the guys to Anthony. While she probably should have been paying attention to what Randi was saying, she couldn't focus on anything but staring at Anthony. While he maintained eye contact with Randi to listen to her descriptions, Kay figured he wouldn't notice her close examination of every inch of his body.

Kay thought about how strong and fit he looked. But he wasn't overly bulky like the wrestlers Randi was describing. Kay imagined how it would feel to be wrapped in his arms, how he could probably pick her up and carry her off to his bed with ease.

Her ex-husband had only picked her up to carry her once, on their wedding night. He picked her up right outside the door of the hotel room, took two steps through the door, and put her down. All while complaining about how she was too heavy to have to carry over the threshold. At the time, Kay thought it was because she was eight-and-a-half months pregnant with Tia, but when she wasn't pregnant, then he would be able to carry her to bed every night. Unfortunately, Mark never understood her fantasy of wanting to be carried to bed and made her feel like she was stupid for wanting to live out some fantasies instead of sticking to the harsh reality of life. She learned over time that the harshest reality of life was that she was married to Mark Fox, whom she now realized she never really loved.

Kay wondered if the instant connection she felt with Anthony was closer to love than what she felt with Mark. She speculated that the tingles and the swarm of butterflies in her stomach she felt when Anthony touched her were signs that she'd fallen in love at first sight like a fairy tale. She pondered whether Anthony would be more open-minded, or if he too would hate her flights of fancy. She wasn't sure how she would be able to figure out if he was more open to indulging her fantasies, and also believed in fairy tales.

Kay also wasn't sure how she was going to deal with her intense feelings for Anthony or if she should even try to act on them. Falling
~~~

for Anthony certainly didn't fit into her Man Fast so maybe she would have to figure out how to go off of the fast. Seeing the size of the bulge in Anthony's slacks was certainly giving her ideas of how she would like to switch over to an Anthony Feast instead. *What if the books are right about bigger being better?*

Kay was startled back from her thoughts by Randi leaning across her to give Anthony a high five and jumped slightly in her seat. Anthony slid his arm behind her back to keep her from falling and she felt goosebumps from the contact with him. *Is that another sign that this instant connection I feel is more than lust?*

"Kay, did you hear any of that?" Randi looked at Kay quizzically.

"No, I guess I zoned out," Kay replied, turning to actually look at Randi instead of Anthony.

"He knows the guy!" Randi exclaimed, practically bouncing on her stool with excitement. "Anthony's already texted James and he's on his way down here to meet me!" The look of glee on Randi's face told Kay that she was a lot more interested in this guy than just wanting to ease his embarrassment.

"So, Kay, now that I've helped your sister, how about you tell me more about you?" Anthony still had his arm around Kay and used it to pull her closer to him, so he could whisper in her ear. "I didn't mean to eavesdrop on your conversation when you first sat down, but I was glad to hear that the most beautiful woman I've ever seen is divorced. I hope that means you're still unattached and available so I can ask you out to dinner."

Kay felt herself flush at his words and had to take a moment to compose herself before speaking. "I, uh, am available to go to dinner with you, but I wouldn't say I'm unattached. I have two daughters that I'm very much attached to, and I don't usually date because I spend all my free time with them."

"I understand." Anthony traced small circles on her shoulder. "I would never want to take you away from them because I know how much children need their mother. Perhaps we can schedule our dates for the weekends they're with their father, until you get to know me well enough to let me meet them?"

"Maybe," Kay replied, feeling a bit overwhelmed by the strong desire he stirred in her. "But I think I need to get to know you better now before I decide on possibly going to dinner with you next weekend."

"Alright, well, you already know I'm a pilot." Anthony was still running his fingers over her shoulder and looking into her eyes. "I travel constantly flying the crew around the country. I actually grew up in South Texas. I'm the youngest of six kids. I love classic rock music and played bass in a rock band when I was in high school."

"We rocked back then," Kay heard a strange deep voice say from behind her.

"'Bout time you got here, James," Anthony grinned as he and Kay turned around to see his friend. Kay recognized him from the restaurant earlier. "Since you didn't get a proper introduction earlier, this is Kay and her sister, Randi. Ladies, this is one of my best friends, James."

"Nice to meet you." Kay tentatively extended her hand. She was correct in her earlier appraisal of James and the other guys he'd eaten dinner with this afternoon. He was very intimidating outside of her work environment. He gently shook her hand, but quickly released it to turn to Randi.

"Hi," Randi squeaked out the word in a more reserved manner than she normally had when meeting new people. Instead of extending her hand to shake his, she gave him a little wave.

"Hi," James returned her greeting as he gave her a slow small smile. James and Randi didn't break eye contact as Anthony told Kay that James and his twin, Dean, had been his neighbors since birth and his best friends since they were all toddlers.

As they continued chatting, Anthony and Kay turned to each other while Randi and James had their own conversation. Sitting there looking into Anthony's eyes and talking, Kay got a form of tunnel vision where it was like they were the only two people in the room. She couldn't even hear Randi's conversation and she knew she was sitting right beside her.

Kay's connection with Anthony was so strong, it was like they were the only two people in the world at that moment. Kay had never felt this connected to anyone in her entire life. *Yep, I'm definitely having a Cinderella night. Since it was after Midnight when I met him, does that mean I can skip straight to the happily ever after?*

"Did you grow up here in Tulsa?" Anthony rubbed his thumbs on the backs of Kay's hands. They were sitting face-to-face with Kay's stool pulled between Anthony's knees and he was holding her hands while resting the backs of his hands on her knees.

"Yes," Kay replied with a shy smile. "Mostly, anyway. My parents also have a cabin in River's End. It's a small town about an hour and a half from here. We go there for vacations and during the holidays."

River's End, Oklahoma was so small there weren't any stoplights. It was really just one road that ran along the Illinois River in a spot that was only about two feet deep. They named the town River's End because the people who settled there said the river was too shallow to be considered a river anymore. The business district along the west side of the river's edge was called the Creek Walk because the people who lived there thought the river should be downgraded to a creek. There was also a resort on the other side of the river and the houses on dirt roads within a ten-mile radius of the Creek Walk were all considered to be in the town of River's End. It was an interesting little community to visit, and Kay had always wished she could move there permanently. Anthony didn't want to know about River's End, though, he wanted to know about Kay, so she shook away the thoughts about the town that had sidetracked her thinking.

"I actually live in the same house I grew up in," Kay continued telling Anthony about herself. "It's in West Tulsa, on the other side of the Arkansas River from here. When I left Mark, my daughters and I moved in with my parents. They just bought a new house a couple of blocks away, so now it's just the girls and me in my childhood home." Kay didn't tell him that the only reason she still lived there was because she couldn't afford the rent on anything even a quarter of the size with her only income being a minimum wage job and three-hundred dollars a month in child support. Kay's parents let her, and her daughters, live there rent-free, only moving out because she convinced them that she could cover the utilities by herself. She planned to cover the property taxes every year from then on and put any extra money she earned over the household expenses into savings to be able to cover them when the time came. Kay thought her parents were planning on signing it over to her when her dad retired in a few years as kind of an inheritance while they were still alive to see her use it. She also thought they were going to do the same thing with Randi and their new house and move to their cabin in River's End full-time.

"You must have a lot of happy memories there." Anthony's smile didn't quite reach his eyes.

"Yeah, I do. I actually lived there while going to college since I went to school locally. I only did two years before I found out Tia was on the way. I stayed there the first couple of years I was married to Mark, too, because he was in the Army and spent most of his time deployed." Kay didn't mention that the reason she was there was so they could save up the down payment on their own house, or that Mark was still stationed overseas for several years after Kay moved out of her parents' house. Kay really didn't want to get into her history with Mark during her first conversation with Anthony, so she tried to change the subject back to him. "So, how did you become a pilot?"

"As a little boy, when my older brothers were all into the rodeo and ranch life, I only wanted to learn about planes and flying." Anthony squeezed her hands. "I went in the Navy as soon as I turned eighteen because I wanted to learn to fly."

"If you wanted to learn to fly, why the Navy and not the Air Force?" Kay was confused by his answer and gave him a quizzical look. She could understand the Navy if he'd been interested in boats but not planes.

"Because Air Force pilots don't get to take off and land on aircraft carriers." Anthony's smile was as big as Texas. "Anyone can take off and land with a long runway, but Navy pilots have to be the best to be able to take off and land on a ship."

"So, you're a cocky guy who thinks he's the best, huh?" Kay smirked at him.

"No, not cocky at all," he smirked back. "But I believe if I'm going to do something, I'm gonna do the best job I possibly can, and in order to do that, I had to learn from the best. I chose the Navy so that I had the best pilots teaching me to be a pilot. Now, I use runways like everyone else."

Kay tried to stifle a laugh but couldn't stop the smile at his attempt at humility. "Okay, I'll try to overlook your ego."

Anthony threw his head back in laughter at her statement. His joyous roar sent tingles throughout Kay's body. When he looked back into her eyes, she saw more than just joy in his dark chocolate orbs.

While there was definitely amusement and excitement in his eyes, Kay also saw affection, desire, and lust. *Oh my! I really like that look.*

"When you meet the rest of my friends and family, be sure to tell them how big my ego is." Anthony grinned as he reached for his drink. "They will never believe that I've come across as cocky. I'm normally not nearly as outgoing as you're seeing me tonight."

"Really?" Kay looked at him with her head tilted to the right to show that she was asking a question. He seemed so at ease that she found it hard to believe that he wasn't being his normal self.

"Really," Anthony replied, moving his left hand up and down her right arm and causing goosebumps to follow in his wake. "I normally have a hard time talking to new people, especially attractive women. And I only have a few friends that I'm close enough to that they've heard me say more than a half-dozen words in a social setting. But for some reason, when you sat down, I felt drawn to you more than I've ever felt drawn to anyone in my life. I had to talk to you, to get to know you, to find out what this strange feeling is, and see where it leads us."

Kay stared down at their joined hands, feeling small when she noticed that her hands looked like a child's being cradled in his large ones. Keeping her eyes down and feeling slightly embarrassed, she whispered, "I feel it, too. Not when I first sat down, but when you first spoke and I turned to look at you, I felt drawn to you, too."

Kay was so nervous about admitting that to him. She knew there was something strong between them, but she was afraid to act on it. She worried that if she allowed that feeling to lead her into a relationship with Anthony, not only would she get hurt when it ended, so would her daughters. He'd already said that he wasn't acting like he normally did when he met someone. What if he couldn't keep up his charming behavior and was normally more like Mark had been acting lately? Kay couldn't take that chance with her daughters' fragile hearts. *I really should end this now before either of us develop real feelings.*

"I've never felt anything like this, either. But I don't think I can act on it. I really should go." Kay tried to pull her hands from his to be able to stand up, but Anthony wouldn't let go of her.

"Please don't go," Anthony pleaded as he leaned down so they were eye to eye. "Talk to me a little more. Tell me why you don't think we should explore this when we both feel this connection."

Kay looked down at their hands for a moment before she looked back up into his eyes and tried again, unsuccessfully, to pull her hands away. "I'm not in a place in my life where I'm looking for a relationship. I don't think it would be good for my girls." Kay shook her head thinking about how her daughters would perceive her dating.

Anthony's eyes never left Kay's, imploring her to continue explaining because he didn't seem to understand her reasoning. "They need to see me as a strong, independent woman, so they can grow up to be strong, independent women. I've been divorced for just over a year, but when we first separated over two years ago, I had to move in with my parents because I couldn't afford a place of our own. My parents just moved into a new house and basically gave me their old house, so I have a place on my own with my daughters, but I'm only able to afford it because I don't have to pay rent. I basically went from being dependent on my ex to being dependent on my parents. I don't want them to see me dating and think I'm just moving on to the next person I'm going to be dependent on. It may be fake independence, but it's better than them thinking I have to have a man in my life to survive."

"Kay, sweetheart," Anthony cooed as he moved one hand up to stroke her cheek. "I'm not asking you to marry me, or even to move in with me. Like I said, we can go out on the weekends when they're with their father, and they don't even have to know we're dating." He smiled at her before continuing. "Then in a few months, or a year, or whenever you finally feel like you've shown them how strong and independent you are, you can introduce me to them, and we can start planning our wedding." He punctuated that statement with a wink, so Kay knew he was trying to lighten the mood with a joke.

"We can plan our wedding in a few months or a year?" Kay sputtered incredulously, regardless that it was a joke.

"Well, I'd fly you out to Vegas and marry you tonight if you wanted, but since you need me to spend some time convincing you, I'll wait a few months or a year to marry you." Anthony smirked and Kay hoped it was because he was still joking.

"Last call," the bartender said as he walked by them behind the bar.

Leah Mae Wright

"How about we continue this conversation over breakfast? I think I saw a twenty-four-hour diner a couple of blocks from here."

"I have to drive Randi home," Kay replied, looking around for her sister. "Where's Randi?"

"She left with James about twenty minutes ago." Anthony stood up and offered a hand to assist Kay off the bar stool. "Come on, let's go get some breakfast."

"Fine, but I'm driving myself and will meet you there." Kay took his hand to let him help her hop down from the stool. "I need to call Randi to make sure she's safe first."

Kay pulled her phone from her purse and called Randi as she walked to her car.

"Hello," Randi greeted her when she answered the phone.

"Hey, Sis. I didn't see you leave, so I wanted to make sure you were actually safe at home before I leave the Camelot."

"You didn't see me leave?" Randi chuckled. "I don't think you saw me at all once you locked eyes with Anthony." More laughter from Randi. "Yeah, it was too loud to talk in there, so we left. We've just been driving around talking for the last half hour or so."

"So, you're not home yet?" Kay worried her bottom lip with her teeth. "Do I need to wait here for him to bring you back or is he taking you home?"

"He's taking me home," Randi giggled into the phone. "Eventually!" More giggles. "Don't worry, I'll be home in time for church in the morning."

The line went dead, and Kay let out a frustrated sigh.

"Everything okay?" Anthony asked from behind her, causing Kay to jump at his unexpected presence.

"No, everything is not okay!" Kay shouted. "My sister is off God knows where with your friend and you just scared the crap out of me by following me to my car like a stalker. I thought we were meeting at the diner?"

"Well, babe, since I don't even know the name of the diner, I didn't know where to meet you, so I figured I'd have to follow you to know where we're going," Anthony smirked. "Unless you'd be okay with me riding with you?"

Kay looked up at him and realized just how much taller he was than she originally thought. *Geez, he has to be at least six-and-a-half feet tall!* She grinned at him, thinking about how he wouldn't fit comfortably in her compact car, and smiled. "Sure, you can ride with me." *If you're a contortionist.*

~~~

Anthony's eyes widened when he saw her car. He had to think fast to figure out how he was going to fit in a Volkswagen Beetle. While he had to admit it was the perfect size car for Kay, it was going to be a tight fit for him, if he could even get in it at all.

Originally, he thought riding with her would be the best way to make her feel comfortable with continuing their evening. After seeing her smirk when she said he could ride with her, he wondered if her discomfort was actually a ploy to cover her sadistic side that was clearly taking pleasure in seeing him struggle to fold his body small enough to get in her car. She certainly hadn't stopped laughing the entire time it took him to get settled in the passenger seat.

She has a great laugh. It was like music to his ears. Music that made his heart beat faster in his chest. Her laugh made his numb legs worth it. *If I have to get in her clown car every day for the rest of my life to hear her laugh, I'll gladly volunteer to do it.*

She continued laughing as they put on their seatbelts and as she pulled out of the parking lot and drove to the diner. Her constant laughter made Anthony laugh, too. More than he ever remembered laughing in his life. So much that it reminded him of when he was a kid and his sisters had friends over for slumber parties and the girls all got the giggles and couldn't stop laughing. Anthony pondered if Kay and Randi had those kind of childhood memories, or if Tia and Maria have slumber parties like that now. That was the kind of fun he would want for his own children if he'd have been lucky enough to have them.

Remembering that he would never be able to be a father stifled his laughter. *Maybe I can be Tia and Maria's stepfather?*

To see if he could get Kay back to laughing, Anthony decided to make a big show of his struggle to get out of the car. Once he was out, he slapped both hands on the top of the car, pretending to need it to hold him up until he could feel his feet again.
~~~

"I hope sardines are your favorite food." Anthony pointed to Kay over her car.

"Sardines?" Kay grimaced. "No, definitely not."

"Then why did you just try to turn me into one?" Anthony smiled and winked to show her he was joking. Sort of. *Damn, I want to be her favorite thing to put in her mouth.* He adjusted himself to hide his body's reaction to that thought while he had the cover of her car between them.

Kay groaned and shook her head as she walked around the front of the car toward the diner. "We definitely need to work on your jokes," she chuckled as she started to pass him.

Anthony reached out and put a hand on her shoulder before she could get too far ahead of him. "Hold up." He moved to put his arm around her shoulders and pulled her into his side. "I need you to help me walk until my legs quit with the pins and needles feelings from going numb in your car."

Kay laughed again, but she put her arm around his waist as if she were going to hold him up if his legs actually went out from under him. With the top of her head barely reaching the bottom of his chest, her shoulders were literally at his waist.

Anthony assumed their huge size difference must be why all eyes in the diner turned to them when they walked in. The staff and customers all must have thought an old-fashioned sideshow was in town when they saw such a mismatched pair. *Or that I have a little girl fetish.* Their rude glares kind of made him want to pick her up and carry her like a child on his hip to really give them a show and a reason to stare, but he didn't. He didn't want to embarrass Kay by doing something so unexpected.

She didn't seem to notice that they were the center of attention as she led him to a booth and sat down. Probably because she was used to being the most beautiful woman in any room and having all eyes on her was nothing new.

She grabbed the menus from the back of the table and handed him one. He took it, but just held it while he looked over it at her. The lighting at the diner was much brighter than it had been at the bar or in the parking lots, so now he could see her features much better. Her hair was such a dark brown that it was only a shade lighter than ebony. With her looking down at her menu, he couldn't see her blue eyes behind her long, dark eyelashes. Her face was almost heart-shaped. She had a cute little button nose and perfect pink lips.

Oh, how I wish I could see those lips wrapped around my cock like in my dream last night, he thought and instantly realized his mistake in thinking that when his cock stood at attention. *Stand down, she's not ready for anything even remotely close to that yet*, he mentally told his cock.

If she were wearing makeup, Anthony couldn't tell. Surely that meant she wasn't because he didn't think it was possible for makeup to look that natural. He wished he could see more of her creamy, tan skin to know if she had tan lines from the summer or if she had that olive tone everywhere.

It was a good thing he was sitting on the opposite side of the booth from her, so the table blocked her view of his bulging pants. Anthony wasn't sure how he was going to survive months of dating and going slow to keep from scaring her off, when just seeing her made him hard. *Think about cold showers, flying missions in the Navy, my ugly brothers, anything to decrease the pressure behind my zipper*, he told himself mentally.

"I think I'll have the French toast." Kay laid her menu down on the table and looked up into Anthony's eyes. "What are you thinking?"

Anthony knew he couldn't tell her what he was really thinking. He couldn't even tell her what he was thinking about eating because he was thinking about eating her pussy. And now he was thinking that his attempt to deflate his over-eager cock definitely didn't work. He smiled, hoping she couldn't read his dirty mind, and tried to cover his true thoughts. "I was thinking French toast, too."

She smiled at him, and it made him feel like his heart skipped a beat. *Mine*, he thought. *Now I just have to convince her of that.*

Anthony wasn't sure why he felt so possessive of Kay. He knew a woman wasn't a piece of property. For some reason, though, Kay brought out a primal need in him to take control of her. He wasn't sure he liked that deeply buried part of himself that wanted to step in and take charge of her life. It wasn't how he was raised to treat women.

All his life, his parents had taught him that couples were equal partners. His parents worked together to take care of the ranch. Bob Burleson focused on the animals and managing the work of the ranch hands and Hazel Burleson made sure they were all well equipped for their tasks by feeding the whole lot daily. While they may have taken on traditional roles, his parents made sure their children all realized that each role was equal in their importance to the running of the ranch.

With his parents as his role models, he was uncomfortable with the thoughts he was having about Kay. He didn't want her to be his partner. He didn't want her to have to work as hard as his mother did. He wanted to do all the hard work for her. He wanted to take care of her, cherish her like she deserved. He wanted to hide her away from the rest of the world, so he could protect her from anyone or anything that might hurt her. He wanted to keep her all to himself, spending all of his time worshiping her like she was his queen because she was precious to him.

"I guess great minds think alike." She smiled and started to look around the room. Her change of focus brought Anthony back to the moment. "Do you think they even noticed we came in? It seems like someone should have at least brought over water by now."

That statement made Anthony realize that his earlier thoughts about her being accustomed to all eyes being on her beauty were wrong. *What was she so focused on to not look around the room and see that everyone saw us arrive?*

"I'm sure they'll be here soon." Anthony put his menu down and reached across the table to slip his fingers under her hand. They both smiled when she grasped them with her own. "Tell me more about you."

"Um, okay," Kay fidgeted. "What do you want to know?"

"Everything," Anthony implored just as a waitress finally showed up at their table.

"What can I get you?" The waitress put down two water glasses and silverware and looked at Anthony.

"Ladies first." Anthony nodded at Kay.

"I'll have the French toast and a chocolate milk," Kay ordered with a wide smile.

"And I'll have the same." Anthony never took his eyes off of Kay as he placed his order.

The waitress wrote their order on her notepad and left their table without another word.

"Chocolate milk?" Anthony thought it was adorable that she still drank it as an adult. "Why no juice or coffee?"

"Orange juice and maple syrup do not taste good together." Kay adorably scrunched her nose in distaste. "And if I were to drink coffee this late, I'd never get to sleep tonight. I have to meet my parents at church in the morning and can't do that if I don't fall asleep until right before I'm supposed to be there."

"What church?" Anthony hoped to find out how religious Kay was, so he would know just how slow he would have to take things with her. *Please don't be super religious. I don't know if I can wait until we're married to be inside you.*

"Southern Baptist." Kay's cheeks turned slightly pink as if she were embarrassed to admit to her religion. "My parents go every time the doors open. I only go on the weekends I have the girls and usually work on the Sundays they are with Mark. Mom and Dad have the girls tonight, so I have to go to church in the morning to pick them up. It's their way of making sure I go to church."

"I get it." Anthony gave her a reassuring smile, as he stroked his thumb over the back of her hand that was still holding his. He was grateful that she didn't sound like she was as religious as her parents. "My folks are the same with us. One of these days I may get brave enough to tell my mom that my relationship with God is between Him and I and has nothing to do with where I am on a Sunday morning. But since I haven't been that brave in my first twenty-five years of life, I'll probably be on the pew beside her every time I'm within fifty miles of Heart's Destiny on a Sunday morning for at least the next twenty-five years of my life."

Kay jerked her hand back from his and shouted. "You're only twenty-five?" She made a face of shock before covering it with both of her hands. She mumbled something into her palms that he couldn't understand.

"What did you say?" Anthony tried to pull her hands down so he could see her face. Kay kept facing down even after he had both of her hands in his on the table. "I couldn't understand what you said into your hands, please say it again."

Kay still wouldn't look up at Anthony, but he could see that her whole face was blushing, and he couldn't figure out the reason.

"I said everybody is going to think I'm robbing the cradle if I date you," Kay practically whispered while shaking her head down toward the table.

Anthony laughed at her words and reached out to lift her chin, so she had to look in his eyes before he spoke. "I don't even think that will cross anyone's mind. Since the only reason I know you aren't still a teenager is because I heard you mention that one of your daughters is twelve, anyone who sees us together is probably going to think I'm older than you." Anthony tried to make his smile look like a comical version of a dirty leer. "In fact, when we walked in here, I thought everyone looking at us had to think that I'm a dirty old man out with a little girl. I briefly thought about shocking them by picking you up like a child to give them a reason to stare, because I'm sure I look more like your Daddy than your date."

"You'll have to do that next time, Daddy." Kay smiled then and it actually reached her eyes. She was still blushing, though, and he thought he saw something else in her eyes besides her smile.

Is that arousal? Does she like the idea of calling me Daddy? Anthony hadn't ever thought of himself as the type of guy who would want to be called Daddy by a woman he was involved with, but the thought of Kay calling him that certainly seemed appealing.

He didn't continue that train of thought, though, because the waitress brought their food, so he shifted to focus on it instead.

After they each poured on the syrup and took a few bites, Anthony broke the silence. "Okay, I know you're a beautiful woman, slightly older than me, even if we won't tell anyone that," he whispered conspiratorially. "And you work as a hostess at the Camelot Hotel restaurant. You have a sister. And religious parents. And your daughters are Tia and Maria. Now, tell me everything else about you."

Kay giggled and squeezed Anthony's hand. That was when he realized that he was still holding her left hand in his right hand. *How perfect that I'm left-handed and she's right-handed, so we can keep holding hands while we eat.*

"Slightly older?" Kay whispered. "Yeah, we'll go with that. I'll actually be thirty-three in about three weeks."

"No way!" Anthony whisper-shouted and leaned down closer to her eye level. "I seriously thought you must have gotten pregnant at fifteen because I wouldn't have thought you were a day over twenty-seven, and that was pushing it."

Kay's eyes widened as she leaned across the table to whisper. "You thought I was having sex at fifteen? What kind of girl do you think I am? That's a horrible thing to think about someone."

Fuck, what is she going to think of me if I tell her I started having sex at fifteen? Anthony sat there looking into Kay's beautiful blue eyes and tried to figure out how to dig himself out of the hole he'd stumbled into with her. He had to let her know that he wasn't thinking she'd ever done anything wrong, regardless of when or how she started having sex. *Ugh! I hate thinking of her having sex with anyone but me! She's mine and I have to make her want me and only me from now on.*

Anthony lifted his left hand and waved his napkin in surrender. "Hey, I don't judge people like that. I honestly hadn't thought about it that much. I certainly didn't think anything bad about you if you had chosen to be sexually active at a young age. To be blunt, I've completely blocked the thought of you having sex with anyone but me out of my mind. And when you finally agree to have sex with me, I plan on making it so good that you forget you've ever been with anyone but me, too." *Shit, I didn't mean to say that last part out loud!*

Before he could backtrack, Kay burst out laughing. She was laughing so hard her eyes were watering. *I hope this means I didn't just scare her off.*

When she finally got it under control, she pointed at Anthony with her fork and giggled out, "And you claim you aren't cocky!" before taking her next bite.

Anthony smiled in what he thought looked like a cocky way to smile. *I'll own the cocky title if it keeps her laughing. Although, I really hope to own her with my cock soon!*

Again, he was back to thinking of possessing her, even if it was just in the bedroom this time. He thought about the dream he had of her tied to his bed, blindfolded and at his mercy. He wanted to live out that dream, spending hours touching and tasting every inch of her delectable body, making her come repeatedly before finally giving in to his primal urges and fucking her so deep that they couldn't tell where one of them began and the other ended. He definitely had to stop thinking like that if he wanted his cock to deflate before he had to leave the booth.

"Alright, enough laughing at me." Anthony grinned, hoping to move on to safer topics. "Seriously, tell me more about you."

"Okay," Kay sighed between bites. "I'm actually the oldest, even though I'm the smallest of my siblings. I have a brother, David, but he moved to Kansas when he got married a couple years ago, so I never get to see him. Randi is the baby of the family. Well, she was until I started having babies. I was actually nineteen when I got pregnant, not fifteen, and twenty before Tia was born."

She paused to roll her eyes and took another bite. He sat there absentmindedly eating while focusing on her every movement and word.

"Tia is twelve but is the smartest person you'll ever meet. She scores off the charts on all the standardized tests they give her in school. They keep trying to convince me to let her skip grades because she's smarter than all her teachers, but I can't bear the thought of them wanting her to go off to college and not getting to just be a kid. Maria is eight and while I think she's just as smart as Tia, she has no desire to let anyone else know it."

"Really?" Anthony interrupted her, so she had a chance to take a few more bites. He loved watching her eat. Every time she closed her mouth around her fork, he imagined replacing it with his cock. *Stop! Deflate!* He had to make himself focus on what she was saying. He wasn't comfortable getting hard from the visual of her eating while talking about her daughters. "Why do you think she doesn't want anyone to know she's smart?"

"Because she's seen how people treat Tia different than other kids and she doesn't want to give up being a kid. I think she sandbags her tests, so they don't know how smart she is and treat her the same way they treat Tia. To be honest, I wish I could go back and change Tia's test scores, but I don't know that it would even help. She learned to read at three and was bored with storybooks at four. My dad bought her a dictionary and encyclopedias to give her something harder to read. She had such a large vocabulary when she started kindergarten that the teachers started talking to her like she was fifty instead of almost five. It's just gotten worse every year."

"And you haven't let her skip grades?" Anthony wondered how bored Tia must be in school with lessons that were so far beneath her abilities.

"No, she's twelve. She should be with other twelve-year-olds, not off at a school I can't afford, with grown men who might not recognize that she's still a kid." Kay huffed in frustration. "I know I can only keep her safe at home until she's eighteen, but I'm hoping that in the next six years I'll learn how to not worry so much about her living in a dorm at college."

Anthony gently stroked the back of Kay's hand with his thumb. He hoped she didn't notice the sudden rush of anger he felt at the thought of Tia being off at college with no one to defend her from the advances of a bunch of frat boys. He hadn't even seen a picture of Kay's daughter, but he envisioned her as a smaller version of Kay. He felt such a strong connection to Kay that the possessive and protective feelings he had for Kay extended to her daughters. Anthony knew they already had a father, but he couldn't stop himself from feeling like being their dad was supposed to be his role in their lives. *How am I going to be able to make myself hold back and just be their stepdad?*

"Wow!" Anthony thought about how strong Kay had to be to handle the challenges of being a parent. He wanted to take some of those worries off her shoulders, so she could have some time to relax and enjoy life. "I hadn't even thought of the logistics of her having to live in a dorm." *Can I handle how scary that will be?* "I was just thinking about how bored she must be in school with material that isn't on her intellectual level."

"She's in special classes for gifted students, but yeah, she's still bored a lot of the time." Kay shrugged one shoulder before finishing her last bite of French toast. "The school recommended a private tutor and homeschooling her to give her tougher material, but even if I could afford it, I don't want her to miss out on having time each day with friends her own age. Socialization is just as important for children as education. What good is it to be the smartest person in the world if you don't know how to interact with people to be able to implement all of your brilliant ideas?" She paused to finish her milk. "She also found a website to do college classes that are free as long as they don't count as actual college credits. So, instead of watching TV or playing like most kids do when they get home from school, she gets online and studies things that are way over my head."

Anthony quickly swallowed his last bite so he could smile at Kay. "You are an amazing mother. When you talk about your daughters, all the love you have for them shines in your eyes. I think that's the most beautiful thing about you."

"Thank you." Kay lightly blushed. "What about you? Do you have any children or ever thought about having children?"

Anthony took a deep breath before slowly letting it out. He wasn't sure he was ready to tell her everything about his past but knew that if he didn't open up to her then, she might be hurt by him not being completely honest when he eventually did tell her in the future. He knew he wanted to have a future with Kay, so he knew he had to tell her everything. *Fuck, I don't want to tell her everything now!* He took another deep breath and squeezed her hand before speaking. *I'll just give her the basics, no details now, so I don't frighten her away from getting involved with me.*

"I've always wanted to be a dad. I almost got the chance when I was a teenager." *God, how do I tell her about losing my son?* "I joined the Navy on my eighteenth birthday and planned on marrying my pregnant girlfriend as soon as she turned eighteen. I had leave scheduled for the week after her birthday." Anthony's voice faltered and he had to take a few deep breaths before continuing. "Unfortunately, she and the baby both died in a car accident on her birthday."

"Oh, Anthony," Kay sobbed as a tear ran down her cheek. Anthony reached up and wiped it off her jaw with his thumb.

"So, instead of getting married on my leave, I used the money I had saved for having a baby to bury my son and his mother." Anthony had also paid for Nancy's mother's funeral, but he didn't tell Kay that because he didn't want to have to explain how Nancy's father went nuts blaming Anthony for all of their deaths. Nancy's father ended up having to be committed and Anthony hadn't heard any more from him in the last seven years. He was always worried that eventually Mr. Parker would get out of the mental health facility he'd been in and would come looking for Anthony with a gun again. Anthony didn't want Kay to be afraid that she or her daughters would be around when that happened and could possibly get hurt.

"I'm so sorry for your loss." Kay squeezed Anthony's right hand with her left and stroked his right forearm with her right hand.

"Thanks, but you haven't heard everything yet." Anthony stopped her right hand with his left, so he could hold both of her hands in each of his. "I knew back then that I wanted to be a dad, and I was going to be a good one because I learned how to be a dad from the best dad I could ever ask for. Unfortunately, getting to be a dad isn't going to happen the normal way for me. I was medically discharged from the Navy last year after an accident that left me unable to father a child."

"Oh, Anthony, are you okay?" Kay exclaimed and looked down as if she could see his dick through the table. "Can you even, uh, you know?" Kay looked back up with wide eyes and a panicked expression on her face.

Anthony chuckled at her obvious thoughts. "Don't worry, Baby, I'm not deformed or suffering from E.D. I was just exposed to some radioactive materials so now I'm shooting blanks."

"Oh, thank God!" Kay exclaimed as her shoulders visibly relaxed. "You had me worried there for a minute."

"Um, did you forget me saying it's going to be so good you'll forget everyone but me?" Anthony had a huge smile on his face from realizing that she was having some of the same sexual thoughts he'd been having all night.

"No, I just figured it would be so traumatic from your horrible scars and weird shape that I would block out all memories of sex forever," Kay joked with a little grin.

"You're a little smartass," Anthony playfully chided with a grin of his own before turning serious. "I know your daughters already have a father and I don't plan on trying to take his place in their lives. But if," *when*, "I do become their stepdad, I promise I will love them as if they were my own. And if you want more children in the future, I'll adopt and love as many as you want."

"Okay, your joke about getting married in a year was a little funny, but this isn't. Please don't joke about my daughters." Kay frowned. She looked so dejected that Anthony was concerned that he may have said too much too soon. *Damn it, I have to remember not to rush her. I don't want to step too far backwards either, though.*

"Baby, I'm not joking." Anthony reached over to tuck a lock of hair behind her ear. He thought for a moment to figure out how to word what he wanted to say. He wanted to let her know that he was serious about her but didn't want to freak her out or cause her to want to run from him. "I wasn't joking about marrying you either. I knew when I first looked into your eyes that everything my parents ever told me about love at first sight is true, and you're it for me. I know that even though you felt it too, you don't believe it yet. So, I'm not going to pressure you to go faster than you're ready for in this relationship. I'll let you set the pace for how fast we progress, but know that I'm already one-hundred percent committed to you and fully intend to be your husband as soon as you'll let me."

Anthony couldn't read more than confusion in her baby blues, but he prayed she could see all the love and sincerity he felt in his eyes.

"Okay," Kay sighed. "I guess that means we should plan our next date."

"Let's plan it in your clown car. You need to get home and get some sleep, so you can be on time for church in the morning." Anthony stood and grasped both of Kay's hands, so he could pull her up from the booth. He paid their check, and they walked hand in hand out to the car.

After five minutes of laughter as Anthony squeezed back into her passenger seat, they decided to go to dinner at the end of the week. Anthony was scheduled to pick Kay up at seven Friday evening, so she would have a couple of hours to get ready after her ex picked up her daughters. Anthony programmed Kay's address and phone number into his phone while she drove back to drop him off at the hotel. He immediately called her phone, even though she couldn't get it out of her purse to answer it while driving.

"Why'd you call me when you're sitting right next to me?" Kay raised an eyebrow quizzically as she glanced at him. "Did you think I gave you a fake number?"

"No, silly," Anthony chuckled. "Now you have a missed call from my number so you can save it in your phone when you get home and don't have to try to remember it to add it when you can get it out of your purse."

"Hmm," Kay looked dumbfounded. "I guess you can tell I don't exchange phone numbers much since I didn't even think about doing it that way."

"Good," Anthony crowed as they pulled into a parking spot at the hotel. "I don't like the idea of you exchanging phone numbers with any other guys."

"Caveman," Kay retorted with a big smile. "You better not exchange phone numbers with any other girls either."

I'm more of a caveman than you think, Anthony thought. He hoped he could control the inner caveman that Kay brought out in him.

"No worries, Baby. You're the only girl I even see," Anthony replied as he got out of the car. He walked around to the driver's side and opened her door. "I know you need to go so you can get some sleep, so I won't keep you long, but I have to ask you one more question before you go."

"What's that?" Kay unbuckled her seatbelt and got out of the car. Anthony was glad when he realized it was the only way she could look up at his face instead of talking to his groin.

"Can I kiss you goodnight?" Anthony inquired hopefully.

"Yes," she answered breathlessly.

It felt like he was folding in half as Anthony bent down and brushed his fingers across Kay's jaw before tilting her chin up toward him. He slowly lowered his mouth to hers and gently brushed her lips with his. When he pressed a little harder with his lips and cupped his hand behind her neck, she let out a little moan. Her soft sounds sent a jolt of electricity down his spine and all of his blood flow straight to his cock.

Anthony took advantage of her lips parting to deepen the kiss. His tongue explored Kay's mouth as his other hand went to the small of her back to pull her closer to him. Both of her hands were on his chest, and he fretted for a moment that she would push him away.

Then Kay stroked her palms across his pecs, up over his shoulders, and settled her arms around his neck, so that she could pull him down closer to her. She returned his kiss with so much passion it made him see stars. Time stood still as he got lost in her.

Eventually, he had to pull away from her mouth, so he could take a breath. He straightened back up and hugged her to him, so her head rested just under his heart.

"Goodnight, my beautiful Kay," he drawled before kissing the top of her head and enjoying the soft scent of strawberries that he assumed was from her shampoo.

Leah Mae Wright

"Goodnight," Kay whispered as she hugged him back. They reluctantly let each other go so Kay could get in her car. Closing her car door and watching her drive away had to be the hardest things Anthony had ever done. It was going to be a long week at work waiting to see her again.

Chapter Three

Anthony struggled to wake up Sunday morning because he was enjoying the dream he was having about Kay. It was so much better than normal since he could finally see her face clearly, so he wasn't really ready for his alarm to bring him back to reality. After swiping his phone to snooze the alarm a couple of times to stay with Kay in dreamland as long as possible, Anthony ended up running late. Spending some extra time in the shower to deal with his morning wood while imagining Kay was in the shower with him, probably contributed to his late arrival at the airport, too.

"Hey Nate," Anthony greeted his co-pilot as he got to the gate at Tulsa International Airport where the GWA plane was parked. "Sorry, I'm late."

"Dude, you're not really late," Nate Rogers, the co-pilot, replied as he shook Anthony's hand. "Nobody else is here yet, so I was going to grab a cup of coffee before starting our preflight. Want me to get you one while you're storing your stuff?"

"Yeah, thanks," Anthony nodded as he stepped onto the ramp leading to the plane. "I'll meet you in the cockpit."

Anthony went out to the plane and put his stuff in the closet under the cockpit before going up the secondary stairs that allowed the pilots access without having to go through the upper deck bedroom. He started the preflight checklist to prepare for when the rest of the crew arrived to fly to California for the week.

The way the flight crews were scheduled with the GWA was as two teams alternating five days on, and five days off, so they had a travel day to get home, three days off, and a travel day to meet back up with the crew. The flight crew then spent five days covering any flights to wherever the wrestlers and upper management needed to go for shows. Most of the time, that meant flying to a different city each day, but if the company had a pay-per-view weekend and the flight crew didn't switch in the middle of the weekend, they flew in on Friday and didn't fly out until Monday. Anthony hated it when he got stuck in one place when his five days on the job were all over a pay-per-view weekend because he preferred being in the air every day instead of killing time in a hotel for two or three days between flights. When he first saw his schedule for this flight rotation, Anthony was grateful that this weekend was not a pay-per-view weekend. But now he wished he could spend one more day in Tulsa to see Kay, instead of flying the company plane on a west coast loop before swinging through the southwest.

Anthony pulled up the schedule on his phone to see his next two flight rotations. While he had his phone out, he changed his flight home on Friday, October fifth to a flight from San Diego to Tulsa, and his flight on Tuesday, October ninth to a flight from Tulsa to DFW. He hoped he could convince Kay that their date on Friday didn't have to end until she had to pick up her daughters on Sunday. Anthony wasn't sure if she would have any free time on Monday while her daughters were in school, but if so, he wanted to spend that time with her, too.

He wanted to spend as much time with her as possible, but it wasn't just physical desire. He wanted to get to know everything about her. Unfortunately, he had to turn his phone off before take-off and didn't want to start a text conversation that he couldn't finish.

~~~

Sunday, September 30, 2018, 1 p.m., Central Time

Kay looked down at the plate in her hand and realized that she didn't know where she was or what she was doing. She'd just been floating through the tasks she would have normally done without really paying attention to them. Her head had been in the clouds since the early hours of the morning when Anthony kissed her. When his lips pressed
~~~

into hers, it was so amazing, so perfect, so out of this world, that she felt like she had an out-of-body experience. She didn't float back down from the clouds after the kiss. Everything she'd done since was more like she was watching herself in a movie instead of actually living in the moment.

She was so distracted from her life because she couldn't stop thinking about Anthony. She felt so drawn to him and wasn't able to make herself turn him down, even though she knew she should avoid dating, so her daughters wouldn't think she was weak for needing someone to take care of her. The instant his lips touched hers, whatever force was making her unable to resist him transformed her inner thoughts to nothing but him. If she didn't know better, she'd have thought he was somehow brainwashing her to make her need him more than she needed air to breathe.

Kay had driven home, gone to bed, and dreamed of Anthony. It was like her dreams didn't stop when she woke up. She'd been daydreaming about Anthony all through her shower, getting dressed, going to meet her parents at church, and even driving to their favorite buffet.

My parents' favorite buffet for our weekly family meal together! Kay thought and looked down at the plate in her hand that she'd put way too many potatoes on because she'd been lost in a daydream. She looked around and was glad to see her oldest daughter, Tia, walking toward her from where she'd been at the other buffet table with her sister, Maria, and Kay's parents.

"Tia, grab two more plates." Kay motioned toward the end of the table to show her daughter where the plates were located. "I got distracted and only grabbed one when I need three for you, Maria, and me. So, since you're here, you can help me divide these potatoes into thirds and carry your own plate to the table."

Tia scrunched up her face as if she was confused, but she got the two plates and set them down beside the one Kay had already put down on the buffet table. "Are you okay, Mom?"

"Yeah, sweetie, I'm fine." Kay answered offhandedly as she scooped potatoes from her plate to the other two. "I'm just distracted."

"Mom, you haven't made our plates at the buffet for years. I think being distracted is a symptom and not the diagnosis. There is something else that you're thinking about that is causing you to be distracted. I just can't tell if it is a good thing or a bad thing that you're thinking about that's causing you to be so unfocused that you didn't pay attention to how much you were putting on your plate." Tia smiled as she picked up one of the plates of potatoes and moved down the buffet to add other foods to her plate.

Kay slightly moved her head from side to side, looking at her daughter and trying to stifle a little giggle. *Symptom and diagnosis? I have to make sure those college classes she's doing online aren't actual MD credits.*

Kay watched as her daughter walked over to the other buffet table where Kay's mother, Mary Lee, was already helping Maria make her plate. Luckily, Kay also saw her sister, Randi, leaving the restroom and walking toward the buffet tables, so she had someone she could hand her extra potatoes to, and maybe nobody else would notice how sidetracked she'd been all day.

"Randi," Kay called out louder than she intended. "Here, I started you a plate." Kay handed Randi the other plate and went back to putting roast beef and gravy on her own.

"Really?" Randi arched an eyebrow at Kay.

"Fine," Kay huffed, looking around to make sure her parents or daughters weren't standing close by. "I got distracted and put too much on my plate. Just take the potatoes, so Mom and Dad don't ask why I was preoccupied."

Randi laughed as she picked up the plate and added to it. "I'm assuming you don't want Mom and Dad to ask because you don't want to tell them about the long, tall, Texan you met last night?"

"Exactly!" Kay whisper-shouted with an ornery grin. "And you'll help me cover or I'll tell them you went home with a tattooed bad boy last night instead of running interference for me."

"No problem, Sis." Randi hit Kay with a wide, conspiratorial smile. "But you have to share the deets on what happened that you keep daydreaming about."

"How did you know I was daydreaming?" Kay looked at her sister quizzically as they made their way to the next buffet table.

"I could tell by the look on your face all through the service." Randi looked slightly up at the ceiling with doe eyes and parted lips as if she were demonstrating Kay's daydreaming face. Then she straightened and looked back down at Kay. "What were you daydreaming about? Or should that be who?"

"A Jedi," Kay replied. Randi looked at Kay quizzically. "He had to be using the Force on me last night. There's no other explanation for how I felt so drawn to him. It was like we had some kind of invisible strings connecting us, and I couldn't walk away or tell him no when he asked me out."

Kay wasn't ready to tell her sister that he believed it was love at first sight because she was afraid that Randi would think she was being flighty and hoping for a fairy tale. Kay did have to tell her more, though, or she wouldn't drop it. Kay looked around to make sure nobody was close enough to hear as she whispered, "And when he kissed me goodnight, I had an out-of-body experience."

"So, you weren't really daydreaming." Randi wiggled her eyebrows at Kay. "You were reliving the kiss."

"The kiss and the more interesting dreams I had during the four hours of sleep I got early this morning." Kay smiled as she remembered the large bulge she'd seen in Anthony's pants that starred significantly in her dreams. *Oh, I hope my romance novels are accurate in the descriptions of how much better sex is with a well-endowed man!*

Randi's mouth formed a perfect O before she changed the subject. "So, do you need me to tell you about the sermon before we get back to the table?"

"Yes, but no," Kay replied as they finished filling their plates. "There's no way we have time for you to catch me up on everything I've missed this morning."

They both laughed as they made their way over to the table where their parents and Kay's daughters were already seated.

"Sunday school was fun," Maria declared as Randi and Kay sat down beside her and across from their parents. "I wish we could do it all week instead of regular school."

"I'm glad you like Sunday school, but regular school is important, too," Kay's father, Charles Lee pontificated as he looked quizzically at Maria. "What is it that you don't like about regular school? Is there something that can be changed to make you like it better?"

Leah Mae Wright

"Can we make it only an hour a day like Sunday school?" Maria looked hopeful as she smiled up at her grandfather. Kay recognized that smile as the one she thought of as her daughters' ornery smile.

Maria and Tia both did this thing where they smiled only slightly, like they thought they were being sweet. The glint in their eyes they got when they did their little half smile told Kay that they really thought they could get away with doing or saying something mischievous.

Charles leaned his head back and roared his deep, baritone laugh that caused several people at the tables around them to turn and look their way. "No, sweet pea. I don't think I can convince your school to only teach for an hour a day."

"Sure, you can, Grandpa!" Maria bounced in her chair. "You can arrest them if they don't change to only an hour."

Everyone in the vicinity of their table laughed, not just Kay's family, but also several people at the surrounding tables.

"Sorry, Maria," Charles chuckled. "I can only arrest them if they break the law. Technically, since the law says how many hours you have to go to school, I'd be super busy picking up all the kids who left after only being there for an hour a day."

"Wouldn't it be the truant officer who had to pick them up, Grandpa?" Tia scooped a bite onto her fork.

Kay wasn't surprised that her oldest child was the one who questioned whether or not her grandfather would be personally responsible. Tia had always been so inquisitive about how things worked and who was responsible for each task at their job. She'd known who did what at the Sheriff's Department since before she even started school. She knew so much about police work that she corrected her kindergarten teacher, Mrs. Comstock, when she didn't know the difference between a sheriff's deputy and a patrol officer on their kindergarten field trip to the Tulsa County Sheriff's Department.

"Yes, Tia, it is the truant officer's job to pick up the kids who miss too much school. But if all the schools in Tulsa County went to only an hour a day, the truant officers wouldn't be able to pick them all up, so I'd have to reassign everyone in the department to help them. Which means, even me as the sheriff, would have to act as a truant officer. It would cripple the whole department and we wouldn't be able to solve any other crimes." Charles turned to Maria, narrowed his eyes in an overacted glare, and pointed at her. "My granddaughter better not be a criminal mastermind trying to undermine my department to get away with committing a crime."

Again, they all chuckled at his joke. Then Tia turned serious and looked at her grandfather. "Grandpa, I know lying is a sin. That's why they teach us not to lie in Sunday school. But is it against the law to lie? Can you arrest someone for lying?"

"Well," Charles pondered, putting his fork down to focus on his oldest grandchild. "It depends on the lie and to whom it is told. There are specific laws about specific lies. Most of them are civil laws, which lead to monetary penalties between individuals or businesses and are dealt with in civil courts and with lawyers, but people aren't arrested for them. There are some criminal laws for lies told to specific people, like lying under oath to a judge, that are grounds for an arrest, though."

"Is there a law that says you can arrest my dad for lying to me about what a judge said?"

Kay couldn't tell if the worry she saw on Tia's face was because she was afraid Mark Fox would or wouldn't be arrested.

"No, baby girl." Charles placed his hand on Tia's shoulder. "I'm not going to arrest your dad. While it is still a sin, there's no law against lying to your family like that."

"If there was a law against lying to your family…" Mary pointed her fork at Charles. "…I'd have had your grandpa arrested every week for the last thirty years for lying to me about getting into the cookie jar before dinner, or claiming he'd picked up his socks and shoes in the living room when he hadn't."

"Those aren't lies, Grandma," Maria shouted while pointing at her grandpa. "Grandpa taught us that those are times we're supposed to tell you what you want to hear so we make you happy, like how your pants don't make you look fat."

Randi spit out the tea she'd just drank as she busted out laughing. Kay giggled, too, and enjoyed watching her father blush.

"Charles Allen Lee," Mary scolded. "I can't believe you've taught our granddaughters to lie to me!"

"Mary Mae Lee," Charles replied as he put his arm around Mary and pulled her into his side. "You know I would never do that. I always admit it if I've gotten into the cookie jar within five minutes of you asking if I had." He paused to kiss her forehead. "And when I say *yes* when you ask if I've picked up my shoes and socks, it's not a lie because your question reminded me to do it, so I have picked them up right before I answer you. I just have them in my hand and haven't made it to the closet or hamper with them yet." He paused again to kiss the tip of her nose. When he pulled back from pecking her on the nose, he smiled at her with love shining through his eyes. "And there isn't a garment made that would make you look fat because you aren't fat. You are perfect. I love every inch of you and don't want you to get some harebrained idea that you aren't the perfect size and try to lose some of the womanly curves I like to cuddle with every night." With that, he planted a chaste kiss on her lips before returning to his meal.

"Aren't you a sweet talker." Mary smiled at Charles before kissing his cheek and changing the subject. "Kay, Randi, what did you girls end up doing last night?"

Kay choked on the bite she'd just swallowed. Thankfully, Randi had her back and spoke up to cover Kay's cough.

"We just had a Pepsi and some girl talk after work. Nothing too exciting."

"At the lounge at the hotel?" Mary looked back and forth between Kay and Randi like she saw through Randi's lie.

"Yep," Kay squeaked out before drinking half her glass of tea to finish clearing her throat.

"Hmm," Charles looked at Kay quizzically. "I guess Don saw someone else's red Beetle at Allie's Diner, then. I'll have to let him know that he needs to get his eyes checked since he thought it was you out with some fella too tall to fit in it."

Crap! What was Dad's friend Don doing out at two in the morning? I hope he wasn't in the diner and close enough to hear any of our conversation. Kay felt her cheeks flush and struggled to think of what to say. It wasn't that she was embarrassed about having gone to eat breakfast with Anthony. They didn't do anything wrong or even anything too scandalous to tell her parents about. *Well, I can't tell them specifics about our conversations, but they won't think just talking in a diner is as scandalous as they would think our discussion was if they knew the details.*

It was just that Kay was so confused about the instant connection she felt with Anthony and didn't know how to explain it to herself yet, much less anyone else. Plus, she didn't want to confuse her daughters by talking about someone she just met, at least, not with them at the table. She knew by the questioning looks on the faces of both her parents that she had to tell them something, though. Kay just hoped they wouldn't make a big deal out of her confession in front of the girls.

"No, Dad," Kay finally admitted, squaring her shoulders, and lifting her chin to look him in the eye. "It was my car he saw at the diner. After Randi left, I went to breakfast with someone I met at the lounge."

"Oh, really?" Mary practically cooed. "What's his name? Are you going to be seeing him again?"

"His name is Anthony." Kay sipped her drink to buy a moment to think of what all she wanted to tell them about him. "We exchanged phone numbers and may go out the next time he's in town. But he lives in Texas, so it may not ever happen."

Kay really hoped her mother would believe that and drop the subject because she really didn't want to hear a lecture about dating like she was back in high school in front of Tia and Maria.

"Oh, it'll happen." Randi winked and smiled impishly. "The way he was looking at you all night, he will definitely make it happen."

"How was he looking at Mommy?" Maria swallowed her last bite.

"Like he hadn't eaten for days, and she was a nice, juicy steak," Randi replied with a chuckle.

I should throw her under the bus by mentioning who she left with because this is definitely not having my back and helping me cover.

"Oh, please, he did not!" Kay exclaimed. "He was a perfect gentleman and looked at me respectfully, like he genuinely wanted to get to know me." *I hope I'm not blushing, or they'll never believe that.*

"He'd better not have been leering at my daughter." Charles gave both Kay and Randi each a pointed look.

"I was kidding, Dad," Randi smirked. "Kay was actually the one drooling when she looked at him."

"I did not drool," Kay rebuked her sister. *At least not until I was at home and dreaming about him.*

"Still kidding!" Randi held her hands up to show that she was stopping with her joking around. She then turned to look at Maria and angled her head to point at her mom and dad. "Seriously, they looked at each other like Grandma and Grandpa look at each other. You know, like they are so in love that they don't see anyone else in the room because they have hearts in their eyes."

"Like love at first sight?" Tia looked at Kay with an optimistic expression on her face. "That's so romantic, Mom. Did you feel a kaleidoscope of butterflies in your stomach when you met him? Is that how you knew it was love at first sight? When will you get married and make him our new dad? When do we get to meet our new dad? And since we have a new dad, does that mean we can get the judge to change his orders, so we don't have to see our old, lying dad anymore?"

"When you marry our new dad, do we get to change our last names too?" Maria looked enthusiastically at Kay. "I want us all to have the same last name, like before you and Daddy got divorced, but with our new daddy's last name."

"Whoa!" Kay exclaimed. She was feeling extremely overwhelmed by how both of her daughters jumped straight to marriage and replacing their father after hearing she'd met someone the previous night. *I guess my dreams of fairy-tale love are hereditary.* "I just met Anthony last night. I only spent a couple of hours talking to him. I don't know him well enough yet to know if I even want to go on more than one date with him. And I definitely don't know him well enough to think about marrying him."

At least not enough to let anyone know I was dreaming about that possibility anyway, Kay thought while finishing her food.

"And even if I do eventually get married again, whomever I marry would be your stepdad, not your new dad. Your dad will always be your dad, even though he's not my husband." Kay looked back and forth between her daughters. "Just like if your dad ever gets married again, his new wife would be your stepmom, but I will always be your momma. You don't replace your parents with new ones. You would just have more people to love you like a parent."

Tia's shoulders slumped and Kay longed to be able to read her daughter's mind, so she could understand why the preteen looked so bummed.

"What's wrong, Tia?" Charles reached over to tilt her chin up, so she had to look up at him instead of down at her empty plate. Kay yearned for Tia to open up to her grandfather more than she had to her all week. It had been worse than pulling teeth to get her oldest child to tell her about Mark's lies from the previous weekend. And Kay wasn't sure Tia had actually told her the whole story or all of her feelings.

"Nothing, Grandpa." Tia's bottom lip quivered as she spoke. She looked like she was on the verge of tears. Kay's heart was breaking from seeing her daughter trying to hide her emotional pain.

"Baby girl." Charles's voice seemed even deeper than normal as he spoke to his granddaughter. "Remember what we were saying about lying being a sin? I can tell you're upset, so saying nothing is wrong is a lie. Want to try again with that answer?"

"Sorry, Grandpa." Tia sat up straight and looked up at him confidently. "I didn't mean to lie. I just thought it was one of those times that if you can't say something nice, it's better to say nothing. So, I said nothing because saying what's wrong would not be saying something nice."

"I can understand that," he replied, poking her on the nose with his fingertip. "It can be hard to keep all the rules of etiquette clear when you're talking about some things, huh?"

"Definitely," Tia agreed.

"If something is bothering you, I'd much rather you tell me the whole truth even if it is downright mean than to say nothing." Charles smiled at Tia. "You know I will do everything in my power to fix any problem you have, but you have to tell me what's wrong so I can figure out how to fix it."

"I know, Grandpa." Tia looked up at her grandfather with a cynical smile. "But I don't think even you can fix this. You already said you can't arrest my dad, and Mom just said that we can't replace him with a new dad, so I'm just going to have to go to his house again next weekend, even though I don't want to ever see him again."

"Oh, sweetie," Mary sighed as she reached across Charles to place her hand on Tia's. "I know you think that now because he hasn't been doing a great job of being a dad recently, but trust me when I say that you don't really mean it. I know you love your dad and don't really want to cut him out of your life." Mary patted Tia's hand.

Leah Mae Wright

Kay knew her mother meant it lovingly, but Kay could see by her expression that Tia felt her grandmother was being condescending. Mary's tone didn't improve when she continued speaking. "He loves you too, so please give him some time to deal with whatever he's got going on. He'll be back to being a good dad soon, I'm sure."

Kay didn't agree with her mother's assessment of the situation. Based on the look on Tia's face, Kay didn't think her daughter really bought into it either. Tia just nodded at her grandmother, probably saying nothing because what she wanted to say wasn't nice.

Thankfully, they were all finished eating, so after exchanging meaningful nods with her father, Kay was able to take her daughters home, so Tia didn't feel like she had to justify her feelings or argue with her grandmother.

As they walked into the house, Kay's phone beeped with a new text notification. Since the girls ran off to their room to change and play, leaving her in the living room with a little privacy, she pulled out her phone to check the message.

Dad: I just talked to Matt Monroe. Told him what's going on with Mark. Asked about options.

Kay: What did he say? Any way to get Mark to stop lying & bad-mouthing me to the girls?

Dad: He said you can petition the court to change his visitation to supervised, but it may take a while.

Dad: Said to try talking to Mark 1st & see if he's willing to skip a couple of visits so Tia can get over his bad attitude last weekend.

Kay: I don't know if that will work, but I'll call him & try.

Dad: If he doesn't agree, call Matt in the morning so he can get started with the petition to change visitation.

Kay: Okay. Thanks Dad.

Dad: If Mark gets belligerent or you think he might get violent, call me immediately.

Kay: Hopefully, it won't be necessary, but I will. Love you, Dad!

Dad: Love you, too, baby girl!

When she finished her text conversation with her dad, she scrolled through her phone contacts and called her ex-husband. After only two rings, it rolled to voice mail.

"Ugh!" Kay was frustrated by how obvious it was that Mark intentionally refused her call. "Hey Mark, it's Kay. We need to talk about canceling a couple of weekends. Tia is really upset about some things you said last weekend and I think she might need some time to understand her feelings before she'll be willing to go for your visits. Can you please call me back so you can talk to her, and we can work together to explain what was said, so our daughter can get over the emotional pain she's currently in?"

After hanging up, Kay pulled up the main text message screen as she walked to her room to change clothes so she could spend the afternoon rearranging her daughters' rooms. She had a new text from her best friend, Deanna Wolfe.

Dee: Hey Girly! Sorry, I couldn't make girls' night last night, but I had a great date I can't wait to tell you about!

Kay: You were missed, but I can't wait to hear about your new guy. I might have one of my own.

Dee: Seriously? What happened to the Man Fast?

Kay: Currently still on it, but I met someone who might make me want to end the Man Fast. Who did you go out with? Tell me about your date first!

**Dee: His name is Kenton. We went to PRHYME for dinner
and then to a symphony at the Performing Arts Center.
It was the classiest date I've ever been on!**

Kay rolled her eyes and shook her head. What Dee thought of as
classy, Kay believed sounded pretentious and boring. But they'd been
best friends since middle school, so Kay would never hurt Dee's
feelings by telling her how horrible that date sounded.

**Kay: Sounds like you had a great night. You think Kenton
is the one?**

**Dee: Maybe. I had a great time at the steakhouse and
the symphony, but I'm not sure there's much
chemistry. He only kissed me on the cheek at the end
of the date. :(**

**Kay: I'm sorry. Maybe he just didn't want to mess you up
since you were probably dressed to the 9s. How about
doing something more playful on your next date so he
doesn't have to worry about messing up your hair &
makeup?**

**Dee: God NO! I don't do playful dates where I don't have
my hair & makeup on point.**

*Yeah, well, I'd rather have kisses like Anthony gave me last night
when I was barely wearing any makeup and had just taken my hair
down and brushed it out from the ponytail I wore it in to work.*

**Dee: So, tell me about your new man who is ending your
Man Fast.**

**Kay: His name is Anthony. He's a pilot for a wrestling
company. He was sitting by us at the bar & figured out
that the guy Randi was interested in yesterday is one of**

the wrestlers he works with & has known since they
were kids. He introduced them & then he & I went to
breakfast at Allie's.

Dee: So, you've already gone out with him & broken the
Man Fast?

Kay: Not really, we just ate breakfast & talked, not really
a date. We're going to try a real date on Friday.

Dee: Did you kiss him? Was there chemistry?

Kay: Yeah, definitely lots of chemistry. It was surreal. I
tingled wherever he touched me & had a swarm of
butterflies in my stomach just from looking at him. I
was drawn to him like a magnet & couldn't say no
when he asked me out. I told Randi I think he's a Jedi
& using the Force to make me dream about him
constantly since.

Dee: Awesome! Girl you needed some good ol' Lust in
your life!

Kay: You think it's just lust?

Dee: Yeah, that's all chemistry is.

Kay: You don't think it could be love at first sight?

Dee: Please! Love at first sight doesn't exist. It's just lust.
But enjoy it! So, tell me about those dreams.

Kay: Oh, Girl, they are wild! Sexiest dreams I've ever had.

Dee: DETAILS!!! Tell me all about them!

**Kay: While in church, I was thinking about him coming in
& saying he can't fly out without me, so he throws me
over his shoulder & takes me with him. Like my knight
in shining armor taking me & the girls along on his
flights so I don't have to worry about dealing with
Mark & visitation anymore. Then while we're in the air
& the girls are napping, he sneaks me into the cockpit,
holds me up against the instrument panel, & rocks my
world!**

**Dee: OMG! That's never going to happen! Mark is their
dad & no new guy is going to want to step in between
the girls & their dad. You have to quit with the
schoolgirl fantasies of a knight in shining armor coming
in to fix your life. Enjoy the lust but don't break your
own heart by thinking it's true love.**

UGH! I should have just skipped telling Dee! Kay really wished her best friend wasn't always so negative about love. Kay realized that Dee didn't believe in true love or the possibility that there was a perfect person for everyone, but Kay hated how Dee kept preaching her views to the detriment of anyone else's beliefs. Kay didn't try to change Dee's opinions. She also didn't push her to quit having random one-night stands and try to find her Prince Charming, so she didn't understand why Dee couldn't respect Kay's life choices and views the same way. Kay really didn't want to get into an argument with her best friend, so she sent her a quick text telling her she had to go so she could move the girls' furniture.

I'd rather go back to my daydreams about Anthony. Kay didn't normally have those types of daydreams, so she presumed she should enjoy them while they lasted. She was normally a pretty asexual person. Kay had honestly thought that there might be something wrong with her because she wasn't as sexual as her friends, or even her sister, until she met Anthony. Sure, she had the occasional fantasy after reading a steamy romance novel, but never about anyone she actually knew, until she met Anthony the night before.

She'd only ever had sex with two people, her high school boyfriend, and her ex-husband. Neither had been mind-blowing. It wasn't bad, per se, but it wasn't the multi-orgasmic, out-of-this-world experience the heroines in her favorite books described. Kay felt like having sex was just what a woman had to do to keep a man in a relationship, but it wasn't really what she needed in a romantic partnership.

Orgasms just hadn't been that important to Kay. She needed more affection and comfort and feeling like she had a partner that she had a lot in common with to do things together, but she hadn't felt like she needed sex. *Until I met Anthony!*

Since starting to read more erotic romance novels, Kay had started to wonder what it would be like to find a partner that made her feel the overwhelming desire that book heroines felt, but she still couldn't imagine it actually happening. Since meeting Anthony, she was actually having those kinds of fantasies. More than just her normal dreams of being rescued by a handsome prince and living happily ever after like a G-rated movie.

Now her visions were much more sexual, and they weren't necessarily the sweet, loving kind of sex scenes you'd expect from being with Prince Charming. Even if Kay were to compare them to a fairy tale, like ***Beauty and the Beast***, she would say that the sexual fantasies she'd been having were more like the Beast and not the Prince he turns into at the end of the movie. Kay's fantasies became animalistic and primal and intense beyond anything she'd ever experienced before.

As she went through her day, alternating between moving furniture and texting with Anthony and Randi, Kay was concerned that if she broke down and told Anthony what she was daydreaming about, she would give him a false impression of who she really was. *What will happen if I tell him these graphic sexual fantasies and he thinks I'm some wild sexual woman? Will he be turned off by thinking I've done any of the things I've only imagined in the last twelve hours or so? Or will he be excited by thinking I'm the wild sexual woman of his dreams and then disappointed by my lack of sexual prowess when we eventually do have sex?* Either way, Kay feared it would be the end of them as a couple.

~~~

Sunday, September 30, 2018, 1 p.m., Pacific Time

When Anthony finally landed in San Francisco, he couldn't wait to get off the plane to turn his phone on and start texting Kay.

Anthony: Good afternoon, Beautiful. How was church this morning?

Kay: Good afternoon. Church was …

Anthony: "…"?

Kay: IDK Had my mind on other things so I kinda daydreamed through it.

Anthony: What kind of other things? Good things? Bad things?

Kay: ;)

Anthony: {devil emoji}

Kay: Yeah, I'm probably going to hell for what I was thinking while in church.

Anthony: Naughty thoughts? Please tell me in detail all your naughty thoughts.

Kay: Oh no! I don't know you well enough to share those.

Anthony: Lucky for us, we can call & text all week while I'm in CA to get to know each other better before our date Friday.
~~~

He put his phone in his pocket so he could carry his bags off the plane. When he got to the rental car counter, he ended up in line behind several of the GWA wrestlers.

"Dean, you've gotta drive today," James Hunter pointed to his brother who was beside him in line. "That couple hours of sleep I got on the plane wasn't enough for me to be safe behind the wheel."

"Oh no," Dean replied. "I'm not driving you anywhere until you tell me where you went last night. You were supposed to explain on our flight why I had to grab your gear from the hotel and bring it to the airport this morning. Since you slept on the plane instead of telling me then, you need to start talking now."

James looked tired and was still wearing the same clothes he had on when he came down to the hotel bar the night before. *I guess he had a really good time with Randi last night,* Anthony thought and smiled knowingly at him.

About that same time, he felt his phone vibrate in his pocket. He knew it was Kay texting him back, but he wanted to find out about James's night with Randi before he pulled his phone out.

"I, uh, was just," James started, but then saw Anthony in line behind him and changed his train of thought. "Hey Anthony, help me out here."

"Help you out?" Anthony chuckled. "How? I only saw you for a few minutes last night before you took off with Randi. I have no idea where you two went or what you did after that, so I don't know how I can possibly help you explain it to Dean."

"Randy?" Dean looked at his brother like he was confused. "You were out with a dude all night?"

"No, Randi with an I," James started explaining as he held his hands up in front of him. "She was our waitress at dinner, remember?"

"Whoa!" Dean shouted. "You hooked up with Blondie last night? What the fuck?"

"No way!" Brent Crockett threw his arms up in frustration. He must have been who Randi described as a lumberjack since that was his wrestling gimmick. "We all tried to get her number and she had no interest in sharing it!"

"Yeah, because she has no interest in any of ya'll," James smiled. "Lucky for me," he paused to slap a big hand on Anthony's shoulder, "Anthony is a much better friend than any of you. When he met Randi and her sister, he helped Randi figure out who the hot guy she's actually interested in was, and texted me to come meet them at the hotel bar."

Several of the guys groaned and shook their heads as if they didn't quite believe that Randi was interested in James.

"I owe you one," James told Anthony as they moved closer to the rental car counter. "Best night of my life." His phone beeped in his pocket and when he pulled it out to read his text, James had the biggest smile Anthony had ever seen on his friend's face.

"That her?" Anthony arched an eyebrow at James.

"Dude, are you sexting her?" Josh Parker, the blond wrestler with a surfer gimmick looked at James with a shocked expression.

"No," James replied as he sent a quick text and pocketed his phone. "Not that I would tell you even if I was."

"Dean, James, Anthony," Liam Connery, the Irishman with the ring name Red, called out as he stepped away from the counter with keys in his hand. "Ye boyos are ridin' wit me. Den I want ta 'ear all about Randi and her sister."

Anthony followed the other guys out to the silver SUV and was glad that at least they were all almost as tall as him, so he wouldn't be cramped in a compact car while they interrogated him about Kay. As soon as he was buckled into the back seat, he pulled his phone out of his pocket to read Kay's message.

Kay: You really think I'll tell you about my naughty thoughts after only a few days of texting?

Anthony: That's the goal, but I'll be happy to just find out if your naughty thoughts are about me.

"So, Anthony." Liam got his attention as he pulled out of the parking lot, reverting back to his normal New Yorker accent now that they weren't out in public where he had to maintain his wrestling character. "What's Randi's sister's name?"

"Kay," Anthony answered, knowing that was going to be the only question they would ask that he would be comfortable answering with one-hundred percent honesty. It wasn't that he didn't want to be truthful with his friends, but he hadn't fully processed all of his feelings about the instant connection he felt with Kay. It was so new and so strong that he felt overwhelmed by all the ways he knew his life was going to change now that they'd met. He wasn't sure he would be able to find the right words to adequately explain the depth of his feelings for Kay to his friends.

"Is she as hot as her sister?" Dean turned in his seat to look back at Anthony. "Maybe a couple of brothers need to date a pair of sisters."

Anthony's fists clenched involuntarily as he processed the fierce wave of possessiveness over Kay that hit him with Dean's words.

James noticed Anthony's reaction and smiled as he wobbled his head. "Stand down, Sailor," he instructed Anthony before turning to face his brother in the front seat. "She was the hostess at the restaurant yesterday afternoon, so you already know she has no interest in dating you. Besides, she was so focused on Anthony when I got to the bar that I don't think she even knew anyone else was in the room but him." James's phone beeped and he pulled it out and typed another reply.

Anthony inhaled a deep breath to calm down and smiled at the reminder of how Kay had looked at him the previous night. He loved knowing that she was as affected by him as he was by her. "Yeah, she kind of freaked out at last call when she realized ya'll had left a half hour earlier."

"I figured as much based on the phone call to Randi," James chuckled before looking back down to his phone when it beeped again.

"So, where did you go?" Anthony asked James. "I half expected to see you at the diner where Kay and I went to breakfast." His phone vibrated, so he plucked it back out of his pocket.

Kay: I plead the 5th {Winking Face with Tongue emoji}

Kay: Where are you in CA? What are you doing?

> **Anthony: San Francisco, sitting in the backseat of an SUV with James while his brother and Red glare at us from the front.**

> **Kay: Why are they glaring at you?**

> **Anthony: Because we're both focused on our phones instead of telling them all about you & Randi.**

> **Kay: He's texting Randi?**

> **Anthony: Don't know. He hasn't said who he's texting. Based on his :) I think it's her.**

"Alright, enough sexting." Dean pointed back and forth between Anthony and James. "Start talking. I need all the dirty details from both of you."

"Sorry, Bro," James half-assed an apology, while still focusing on his phone. "No dirty details to tell you. We just drove around for a little while talking and then ended up at a park where we climbed through these huge boulders their grandfather moved when the park was designed years ago. Sat up there talking and watched the sunrise. Then we went to breakfast, and I dropped her off at her house on my way to the airport."

"Did she make it to church this morning?" Anthony questioned James as his phone buzzed again. "Or was she too sleepy after you kept her out all night?"

"Yeah, she made it to church," James chuckled. "Did Kay?"

"Yeah, but she couldn't tell me about it because she was *'daydreaming'* instead of paying attention." Anthony used air quotes around the word daydreaming.

"Daydreaming, huh?" James grinned at Anthony. "About what? Or should I say who?"

"She won't tell me," Anthony replied, shaking his head. "But I hope they were similar to what I was thinking about in the shower this morning." His phone vibrated again. "Ask Randi if Kay told her what she was daydreaming." Anthony looked down at James's phone. James started frantically texting, so Anthony looked at his own phone.

> **Kay: Yeah, he's texting Randi. She's also texting me about her night with him.**

> **Anthony: I wonder if their stories match up? He's not making eye contact as he's saying what they did so I'm not sure he's telling us everything.**

> **Kay: OOOOOOOHHHHHHH!!!!!!! What's he saying?**

> **Anthony: Just that they drove around talking, then rock climbing at a park your grandpa designed & more talking until sunrise & breakfast.**

> **Kay: He's definitely not telling you everything. Thanks for fixing my sister up with a guy who doesn't kiss & tell. I hope you're a good guy like that, too.**

Anthony turned his phone to show James Kay's last message and gave him an I-Know-What-You-Did look before replying to Kay.

> **Anthony: I would never tell them anything that you should be embarrassed about.**

And you shouldn't be embarrassed about our kiss.

"Damn!" James shouted before punching Anthony in the shoulder. "Did your shower fantasy include storming into the church and throwing Kay over your shoulder like a caveman claiming his woman because you couldn't leave town without her, and then fucking her against the instrument panel in the cockpit during our morning flight?"

Anthony's jaw dropped as he turned to look at James in disbelief. "Um, no, I just pictured her in the shower with me. Is that what she told Randi she was thinking while in church this morning?"

"Yep!" James turned his phone so Anthony could read his screen. He slowly scrolled through the last few messages.

Randi: Yeah, she was daydreaming about Anthony. Not just in church. She was so lost in her fantasy that she overflowed her plate with mashed potatoes at lunch.

James: Did she tell you what she was fantasizing about? He wants to know so he can make it come true.

Randi: I think he'd crash the plane if he made it come true. Unless he got arrested for the 1st part.

James: So, her fantasies are wilder than yours?

Randi: No, just not set in practical locations. Very similar in sexual content. ;)

Randi: While I love the idea of the possibility of being seen while being forked against a wall or boulder in a public park, I wouldn't imagine that same rough forking against the instrument panel of an airplane @ 30000 feet.

James: Yeah, that sounds like a good way to die. But how would he get arrested?

Randi: By Caveman Kidnapping Kay from the church in front of our Sheriff Dad.

"Holy Shit," Anthony said under his breath. He wasn't sure if it was because of the content of her fantasies or because James had just inadvertently told her fantasies to Dean and Liam.

"Sounds like your lass is some freak." Liam looked at Anthony in the rearview mirror. "So, what did you do last night to give her those dirty ideas?"

"Obviously, I told her about my job," Anthony admitted defensively. Then he chuckled, thinking back over their time together. "I guess she figured that if I could contort to fit in her Beetle to go to the diner, then I could make having sex in a cramped cockpit possible."

"You rode in her Beetle?" Dean exclaimed. "How? I can't fit in a Beetle and you're what, two or three inches taller than James and I."

"I'm six-foot-six, but I don't have as much muscle mass as either of you so I can bend easier than ya'll," Anthony replied. "But seriously, we talked at the bar and more over breakfast, but it was mostly getting to know each other, a little personal history stuff, and how we both felt this instant connection. I tried to avoid scaring her off, so I toned down or didn't say what I was really thinking about what I wanted to do to her sexually. I only kissed her once. A goodnight kiss right before she left, so she could get some sleep before she picked up her daughters and went to church with her parents this morning. It was a great kiss, but…" His words trailed off as he contemplated how Kay came up with such rough and wild ideas about him from one passionate kiss. Not that he would object to a little role-play if she wanted to pretend her bedroom wall was the instrument panel in an airplane.

Anthony's phone vibrated in his hand, and he had to laugh at the irony in Kay's text.

**Kay: Good because I would be horribly embarrassed if I
    ever met them & they knew details about our kissing.**

Before he could think of a way to break the news that they knew more details about her fantasies than their relatively tame kiss, she changed the subject. *Yeah, I just won't tell her everything they know.*

**Kay: Have you ever played "Would You Rather"? It's a
    game I play with the girls on long drives. Basically, one
    person asks a Would you rather do this or that
    question & then everyone answering has to explain
    why they chose their answer.**

**Anthony: I haven't played before, but I think I understand
                the concept. What's your 1st question?**

Kay: Would you rather live at the beach or in the
mountains?

Anthony: That's a tough one. Part of me wants to say the
beach because I loved going to the beach all the time
growing up in South Texas.

Anthony: But I think I'll say mountains because I've
always wanted to learn to snowboard but haven't ever
lived where it snows enough to be able to. I can
always fly to the beach for vacation.

Kay: The Ozark Mountains are only a couple hours
outside of Tulsa & we definitely get snow in OK, but I
don't know if they are really big enough to be called
mountains or if there's enough snow for
snowboarding.

Kay: We've enjoyed sledding at my parent's cabin in the
Ozarks the past couple of years. Maybe next year you
can come with us.

Anthony: That sounds awesome. So, now do you answer
the same ? or do I ask you a different ?

Kay: Ask me a new one.

Anthony: WYR...ride a trolley in San Francisco or ride the
subway in New York?

Kay: Easy. Trolley because you're in San Francisco.

Anthony: But I'm not on a trolley & will only be in San
Francisco for about 20 hours. Which would you rather
ride if I weren't with you or in either city?

Kay: I'd still say trolley in SF because I think it's safer than the subway in New York, but I would never go to either by myself.

Anthony: Would you ride them if I were with you?

Or would you just ride me? Anthony stifled a groan knowing he had to stop that train of thought, or he would have to try to hide an erection while checking into the hotel. Luckily, looking up at his travel companions was an instant boner killer.

"What did she say about James telling you her kinky fantasies?" Dean prodded when Anthony looked in his direction.

"I didn't tell her that Randi told him or that he told us," Anthony confessed, thinking there was no way he would risk losing Kay by telling her that the guys knew something about her that would make her embarrassed to meet them if she knew they knew. "She just told me that she would be embarrassed to meet any of you if I told you details about us kissing. If I told her that we all know her fantasies, she'd probably break up with me, so she'd never have to meet any of you. Hell, since she's too embarrassed to tell me herself, she may break up with me if she finds out I know before she's comfortable telling me."

"Then what were all those long texts?" James pointed at Anthony's phone.

"We're playing a game to get to know each other, answering questions with detailed explanations of why we chose that answer," Anthony explained as he unbuckled his seatbelt since they'd arrived at the hotel.

"Would you rather?" James got out of the SUV. "Randi and I were playing that all night."

Anthony nodded as he also got out and walked to the back of the SUV. "Yeah, that's it."

"Which version?" James queried as they grabbed their bags and started walking to the hotel entrance.

"I didn't know there are different versions." Anthony opened the door to the hotel lobby.

James laughed as he walked through the door. "You're still on the basic version then. Randi and I only stayed on that one for about ten minutes. Then we moved on to what she called the naughty version. I should have known that if she wouldn't tell you her fantasies yet, she wouldn't have told you about the naughty version either. Sorry man."

Anthony hung his head as they made their way to the counter. He wasn't sure if he would be able to keep his questions for Kay in the right version of the game all week if she didn't bring up the naughty version. After James mentioned it, now all he could think of were sexual questions. He was anxious about being the one to bring up the more risqué questions, afraid that she would figure out that James had told him about the naughty version of the game and also the other things Randi had told James.

As soon as he got checked in at the hotel and dropped his stuff off in his room, Anthony pulled his phone back out of his pocket to see Kay's reply.

Kay: Yes, I'd ride them with you.

Kay: WYR watch a romantic comedy movie or perform in a comedy club?

Anthony: Watch a romantic comedy movie. I'm not a performer.

Kay: Not a performer? I thought you were in a band in high school.

Anthony: Okay, I'm not a comedian. The only way I was able to perform in the band is because I just played the guitar & didn't actually sing.

Kay: Still more of a performer than me.

Anthony: You've never been on stage for anything?

Kay: I twirled a baton at high school football games, but that takes way less talent than playing a guitar.

Chapter Four

Monday, October 1, 2018

Kay woke up Monday morning dreading her day at work. She would much rather stay in bed dreaming of Anthony. She was more than a little worried that she would get lost in her daydreams about him again and mess up something at work bad enough to get fired. She was definitely way too distracted the previous day by thoughts of Anthony. Very inappropriate thoughts considering her surroundings.

Kay was only slightly embarrassed about sharing the same daydream with Randi that she'd shared with Dee. While Randi called Kay out on the practicality of sex while flying, she wouldn't ever be truly negative about the fantasy or make Kay feel bad for having any off-the-wall ideas for creative sexual activities. Kay was actually relieved that she was able to share her secret thoughts with her sister, especially since Randi confessed to having similar fantasies. It was good to know that the crazy, wild things she'd been daydreaming about were normal. *Maybe now that I've started having them, I won't go back to being the asexual person I used to be.*

Kay had to push all of that from her mind, so she could get herself and her daughters up, fed, and ready for the day. As soon as she clocked in at work, she checked the schedule to see if they needed her to cover an extra shift over the weekend like she did Saturday.

While she could definitely use the extra money from the overtime, Kay was not as eager as she would normally be to work extra hours while the girls were at Mark's. During their text conversation the previous night, Anthony told her that he would be in Tulsa all weekend, and wanted to see her on Saturday and Sunday, too, not just for their dinner date Friday night. He wanted her to think about her favorite activities and places and show them to him when he got back in town.

After reading Randi's texts about everything she did with James Saturday night, Kay knew she had to take Anthony to Chandler Park. She didn't intend to repeat Randi and James's performance with Anthony while they were there, though. Kay had to admit to herself that Randi's detailed description of their sexcapades was arousing. Kay just didn't think she could ever be as wild and free as her baby sister.

Besides, they went to Chandler Park in the middle of the night when it was too dark for anyone to see their naked bits even if they'd been caught in the act. Kay was planning to take Anthony there on Saturday morning in broad daylight when the park was full of people. There was no way Kay was going to get naked at the park no matter how much she really wanted to have sex with Anthony.

And I really want to do a lot more than just getting naked with Anthony this weekend!

Kay really wished she could understand what was going on between her and Anthony. When she tried to explain it to Dee, she seemed to think it was just lust and said that Kay was being naïve by thinking it was anything more. Since the majority of Kay's daydreams had been her wildest fantasies of all the ways she wanted Anthony to make love to her, she wondered if Dee was right. *Maybe I am naïve and want to believe I've met my Prince Charming, who will swoop me off my feet and carry me off to live a fairy-tale life, where I won't have to worry all the time about work, having enough money to pay the bills and provide for my daughters, or if I'm doing everything right to raise them in a safe, happy, and loving home.*

Kay was afraid that meeting Anthony in the castle where she worked might have influenced her perception of him as her knight in shining armor, coming to rescue her from her dragon of an ex-husband. Combine the atmosphere where they first met, Anthony's belief in love at first sight, Tia and Maria wanting a new dad, and Kay's fear of what Mark might do next, and you had the perfect recipe to make her confuse intense lust for true love and want to jump straight to happily ever after.

"Earth to Kay." Randi waved a hand in Kay's face. "You need to come back from wherever Anthony has you tied up and look like you're actually working before Brooks comes in for breakfast."

"Geez, Randi, don't say that so loud," Kay whisper-shouted and batted her hand away. "I get that you aren't ashamed to talk about, um, stuff in public, but please don't embarrass me by mentioning my private fan, uh, thoughts where anyone can overhear them." Kay looked around to make sure nobody was close enough to hear their whispered conversation and started rolling silverware to look like she was busy working.

"Nobody heard me," Randi claimed as she wobbled her head and started helping Kay with the silverware. "And you shouldn't be embarrassed even if someone did. You're a beautiful, vibrant woman who should never be ashamed of anything. You should be proud of every part of you." She leaned in close to speak in a really low whisper. "Especially the kinky parts."

Kay felt herself blush as Randi put the silverware she just rolled in the bin and walked away to go check on her customers. Kay somehow managed to appear focused on work for the rest of the morning.

During her lunch break, Kay called and left a message for her lawyer, Matt Monroe. He was not only a close friend of her father's, but he was also an attorney who specialized in family law and had been representing Kay since the day she left Mark. As far as Kay knew, he was the only person her dad told about the scene he walked in on when Mark thought he could physically stop her from leaving. *Thankfully, Mom had already left with the girls and their suitcases in her car.*

Kay had been loading boxes in her car while waiting on her dad to get the big stuff in his truck when he got off work, and Mark came home earlier than she expected that night. Mark was so mad that he spent twenty minutes yelling insults and obscenities at Kay before realizing she was ignoring him and continuing to pack. Kay made the mistake of turning her back on him. He then grabbed her from behind and shoved her into the wall. When she tried to fight him off, he grabbed her wrists and pinned them both behind her back with one hand, so he could punch her with the other. Luckily, he only got in a couple of hits before her dad walked in and pulled him off of Kay.

Kay should've let her dad arrest Mark right then, like Charles had wanted. But it was the only time Mark ever hit her when anyone else was around to witness it, so she didn't think it was enough for any charges to stick. If Kay had ever mentioned any of the other abuse to anyone else, she might have had a solid case against him, but nobody knew about the things Mark did when he came home drunk during the last couple of years of their marriage.

Kay hoped that keeping the divorce as amicable as possible would lessen the chances of Mark retaliating in court. She also knew pressing charges would make that unfeasible. Now that Mark was lying to and yelling at their daughters and not returning Kay's phone calls, she was concerned he was going to escalate to physical violence again. Kay was terrified that it may not be limited to just her this time. She didn't know what else she could do to protect her daughters, so her message for Matt was that she needed to talk to him about requesting a change to supervised visitation.

As she went through the rest of her day at work, she couldn't stop herself from imagining what life would be like if this intense connection she felt with Anthony was actually love and not just lust. She wanted desperately to give Tia and Maria the new dad they wanted. She longed to live peacefully with Anthony and her daughters, not having to worry about their safety every other weekend. She pictured the four of them going to the beach Anthony had mentioned in his texts the day before. They were all happy playing in the water and burying each other in the sand. She also imagined Anthony as her husband, spending Christmas at her parents' cabin in River's End. She envisioned him putting new sleds under the tree for the girls and bending his long legs enough to be able to sit on one to ride down the hills with them.

Kay thought back to the conversation at Allie's Diner and tried to gauge how real and honest Anthony had been in all the things he said he felt. *Does he really want to be a good stepdad to my daughters? Will he really love them like they're his? Does he really think he loves me when we've only just met? He said it was love at first sight, but he never actually said the words "I love you."*

Kay was unsure if she believed in love at first sight or not. She knew she instantly felt a powerful connection, but she didn't know that it was more than a strong physical attraction. Kay hadn't ever felt anything like it before to know how to tell the difference.

She thought about it for a while and fantasized some more about Anthony being her husband, taking care of her, showering with her so he could spend the time touching every part of her, carrying her to bed every night, dressing and undressing her, holding her in his lap to cuddle and stroking her hair while they watched TV, and doing kinky things to her after they closed the bedroom door each night.

Anthony as her husband would be a dream come true. The perfect happily ever after for their fairy-tale romance. Kay just wasn't sure she could believe it was really real, though. *Did he really fall in love with me at first sight? Is that what I feel for him? UGH! I'm so confused!*

When her shift was finally over, Kay rushed to pick up her daughters and went home. As they were walking in the door, her phone rang. Kay recognized her attorney's name on the caller ID, so she went to her bedroom to answer, where the girls wouldn't overhear the conversation.

"Hi, Matt." Kay sat down on her bed. "You have perfect timing in returning calls. I just got home where I can talk without distractions."

"Well, you did say this is the best time to reach you on your message," Matt Monroe chuckled over the phone. "Have you had any luck talking to Mark?"

"No," Kay huffed. "I've left two messages so far. He hasn't called back. I think he's declining my calls because it rings twice and then goes to voicemail."

"Okay, when is he supposed to see the girls next?"

"Friday," Kay told him while fighting the urge to get up and pace around her bedroom. "He's supposed to have them from five o'clock Friday evening to five o'clock Sunday evening, but I'm worried about what might happen if they go with him."

"I know, but I don't know that the one bad weekend will be enough to convince a judge to change the visitation. I still think the best course of action is talking to Mark."

"Yeah, well, how am I supposed to do that when he won't return my calls?" Kay was so upset that she couldn't sit still. To stop her legs from shaking, she bolted off the bed and started walking laps around her room. From one bedside table, down the length of the full-size bed, past the bookcase, dresser, and oval standing mirror, back up the length of the bed to the other bedside table. Kay turned around and went back the way she came and just kept repeating laps for the rest of the conversation.

"I think you might have to wait until you see him Friday." At least Matt sounded as irritated as Kay felt by that statement. "I'll go ahead and draw up the petition to change visitation, but there's no way I can get it in front of a judge before Friday. Let me know if you actually get to talk to him, and how he reacts to you, and whatever he does with trying to explain himself to the girls, so I can put it all in front of the judge when we get a court date set."

"Okay," Kay sighed. "What do I do if he won't give Tia the break from visitation she needs? Do I have to make her go with him Friday?"

Matt let out a long, heavy breath over the phone before speaking. "Unfortunately, you can't stop his visits without his cooperation, or you'll be in violation of the court order, and we don't want to deal with the consequences of that."

"Even if I'm in fear for their safety in going with him?" Kay hoped she'd found a loophole to help keep her daughters safe at home with her. She would rather cancel her weekend with Anthony, and keep them at home where she knew they were safe, than have their time together ruined by her constant worry about the safety of her daughters.

"That's a gray area. If you think he's just going to yell or lie to them again, no because it's not a physical danger even though his actions are causing emotional trauma. If he had a history of hitting them, and I don't mean a spanking, then yes because it's a physical danger. But the only time he's even been a physical danger to you was when the girls were not present, so it doesn't provide enough evidence of a history of violence to show the courts a fear for the girls' safety." Matt groaned and Kay could tell he hated having to tell her all this. "I'm sorry, Kay, but unless Mark agrees to skip a couple of visits or does something to physically harm the girls, you have to make them go until we can get in front of a judge."

Kay couldn't stop the tears from falling as they said goodbye and she promised to call him immediately after she had any communication from Mark. Kay threw herself face down across her bed and screamed into a pillow to let out as much of her anger and frustration as possible without making enough noise to alert her daughters. She knew she had to get it together before she went back out to the den where the girls were playing and working on the computer. She had to be strong for them. She couldn't let them see how weak and vulnerable she felt, or they would just be scared that she wasn't able to protect them from Mark, much less anything else they were afraid of.

Suck it up, Buttercup! Kay told herself as she pushed up from the bed. She made a quick pitstop in the bathroom to wash her face and put some drops in her eyes to lessen the redness from crying.

When she felt like she looked presentable, she went into the den to play Barbies with Maria while Tia tried to explain a complex math problem that she was working on for the online calculus class she was enrolled in that semester. Most of what she was saying was going way over Kay's head, but Tia seemed to enjoy explaining how she was working through it and Kay always wanted to encourage her daughters to talk to her about anything, so she tried to listen and really pay attention, even if she only understood part of it.

While they were hanging out, Kay wondered what Anthony would be doing if he were there with them. That's when she realized she left her phone in her bedroom and hadn't checked her texts all day.

She never checked them at work because her phone was in her locker since they weren't allowed to have them on the floor. Kay usually checked her texts when she first got home, but her call with Matt sidetracked her that day. She told the girls she was going to fix dinner and made a beeline to her room to grab her phone, so she could read her messages while she made spaghetti.

Kay swiped to her text inbox to see multiple missed messages. New message notifications from her dad, Randi, Dee, and Anthony. She knew she struggled to juggle multiple conversations, so she decided Randi and Dee could wait. She checked her dad's message first to make sure it wasn't urgent.

Dad: Have you talked to Matt yet?

Yeah, I should probably answer him, so he doesn't get worried and send multiple messages.

>>> Kay: Yeah, he's going to file the petition to change visitation, but said to stick to the current schedule until we see the judge.

Dad: I'm sure he'll get it to a judge as soon as possible. Hang in there, kiddo!

>>> Kay: Will do! :)

Kay had made it to the kitchen by the time she was through texting her father, so she washed her hands, started some water boiling, and crumbled ground beef into a frying pan before washing her hands again and opening Anthony's messages.

Anthony: Good morning, Beautiful.

Anthony: I know you're at work and can't reply, but I just had to let you know I'm thinking about you before I shut my phone off for my flight to Fresno.

Anthony: I'll text again when we land. Don't want you to get worried if you try to text on your break & I don't reply because I'm in the air.

Anthony: Good afternoon, Gorgeous. This is your pilot speaking. I've just landed in Fresno, CA where it's sunny & 88 degrees. Wish you were here with me.

Anthony: I'm checked in at my hotel and have nothing to do until the show tonight & I don't even have to go to it. I really hope you get off work soon.

Anthony: Did I scare you off with too many texts today? I didn't text @ 4 when you said you normally get home

because I figured you'd reply to one of the ones I'd
already sent.

Anthony: But it's after 5 there now so I'm wondering if I
freaked you out with too many messages. I hope not.

Anthony: I'm sorry if I've texted too much, but it's 6 there
now & I'm really worried that I haven't heard from
you. Even if you're mad or overwhelmed by me, please
just text & tell me you're okay.

Kay looked at the time and realized the last message came in while
she was reading the others, but her phone didn't beep since she already
had the text screen open. So, she quickly typed a reply, so he could
quit worrying.

Kay: I'm fine & I'm not mad or overwhelmed. Got
sidetracked on the phone when I 1st got home & then
left it in the bedroom while I was in the den & didn't
hear any notifications.

Kay: Not too many texts. I wish I could have my phone at
work so we could text all day.

Anthony: Good. Me too on the wishing we could text all
day. Maybe we should have scheduled times to text,
so you don't leave your phone in another room again &
cause me to have a heart attack from worrying about
you.

Kay: Sorry, I know I'm bad about not keeping my phone
on me or answering it promptly. The only reason I
realized it was in the bedroom is because I was
thinking about you & it wasn't in my pocket when I
went to ask you a question.

Anthony: Yeah? Now I feel better. What's your ?

Kay: WYR play Barbies or try to understand calculus?

Kay pondered telling him that those were the things she was doing with the girls and the reason she was asking was because she wanted to know how he would fit in her family. She wanted to know how he would interact with the girls to see if he really would be a good stepdad, or if she should stick to her current plan of not introducing him to the girls for a few months.

After seasoning and stirring the ground beef and putting the pasta in the boiling water, Kay looked back at her phone.

**Anthony: Interesting question. Can I answer with neither
     or both? Neither would be my first choice of things to
     do, but I would happily do both with your daughters. I
     just hope I don't disappoint them with my lack of
     experience to know how to do either correctly.**

Kay: Perfect answer.

Can you swoon via text? If so, I think I just did.

Anthony: I guess that means I can't ask you the same ?

**Kay: I was actually doing both when I came up with the ?
     so you know my answer is both, but I do have a lot
     more experience with Barbies. I'm so confused by
     calculus that I honestly have no idea if Tia has the right
     answer to the problem she was telling me about.**

**Anthony: Yeah, I'd have to read her textbook to know
     how to try & solve it to check her work. Just listening,
     it would all go over my head.**

**Kay: Yeah, I gave up trying to read & comprehend her
     textbooks when she got past basic algebra. I used to**

think I was good at math. Tia has proven me wrong
about that for several years now.

Anthony: Just because you aren't interested enough to
want to learn complex math doesn't mean you aren't
good at math.

Kay: No, but the fact that I can't comprehend anything
I've tried to read in her books does. I suck at complex
math.

Anthony: Do you need me to look up calculus to figure
out if her answer is correct?

Kay: No, we've already moved on to other things.

Anthony: Oh, what are you doing now?

Kay: Making dinner.

Anthony: What's for dinner?

Kay: Spaghetti.

Anthony: Yum! Can you text & cook, or do I need to let
you go for now?

Kay: I can text & cook.

Anthony: WYR...Be on top or on bottom when you sleep...

What? Is he asking me about sexual positions? Kay was flustered
by her mental image of sex with Anthony and wasn't sure how to
answer his Would-You-Rather question. Kay had never done anything
but basic missionary position, so she guessed bottom. But then when
she thought about how much bigger Anthony was than her, she was a

little perplexed by how their bodies would line up for basic missionary position. Trying to imagine how their disproportionate sizes would impact their ability to engage in intercourse, Kay rationalized that she may have to be on top for it to even work. Before Kay could figure out how she could answer the question and not be totally embarrassed by having to explain how she reasoned out the answer, Anthony sent her the rest of the question in another text.

> **Anthony: In bunk beds?**

Oh, thank goodness! Kay shook her head to clear it of the images of sexual positions with Anthony and typed a quick reply before finishing up fixing dinner.

> **Kay: Top bunk. I ended up with a really bad haircut after trying to sleep on the bottom bunk as a child & my hair got caught in the springs under the top bunk.**

Kay sat the phone down, dished up plates, and set the table. When she called the girls to dinner and sat down to eat, she glanced at her phone that she'd put beside her place setting.

> **Anthony: Ouch! Yeah, I'd avoid bottom bunks after that, too.**

She picked up her phone to text him another Would-You-Rather question when her daughter interrupted her.

"Who are you texting, Mom?" Tia placed her napkin on her lap.

Crap! Kay didn't want to lie to her daughters, but she also didn't want to tell them about how much she was communicating with Anthony, either. She'd assumed that if she didn't mention him again for a few weeks, then they would forget his name and wouldn't realize she was dating while they were on their visits with Mark.

"Just a friend," Kay finally answered.

"Aunt Dee?" Maria asked between bites.

"No, I have other friends besides Aunt Dee." Kay stuffed a forkful of spaghetti in her mouth, so she couldn't keep talking. She made sure her phone was face down, so the girls couldn't see the screen to see his name.

Of course, her darling daughters wouldn't drop it there, though.

"What's your friend's name?" Tia inquired between bites.

"It's nobody you know." Kay was feeling put on the spot and uncomfortable talking about Anthony with her daughters. "Now hurry up and eat so you can get a bath before bed."

"Is it Anthony?"

Kay choked on the bite she'd just tried to swallow. She was sure her blush gave Tia the answer to her question. Kay wasn't sure if she should be proud of how smart Tia was to figure that out or worried about what the ornery smile she was currently giving her meant.

"Mommy and Anthony, sitting in a tree, K.I.S.S.I.N.G." Maria sang.

"Alright, no picking on your mom!" Kay interrupted her song. "Yes, I'm texting Anthony, but we're not doing any of the things in that song. Now eat!"

The girls both giggled but they finished their food without teasing Kay anymore. After the table was cleared, Kay did the dishes while the girls bathed and got ready for bed. When Kay was almost done cleaning the kitchen, Tia came back and handed Kay her phone. Kay hadn't realized that when Tia was helping clear the table, she picked it up, too.

"You should really ask him more of his favorite things instead of just playing Would You Rather over text." Tia hugged Kay, saying "Goodnight, Mom," and went off to her room.

Oh Crap! I hope she just looked at my texts with Anthony and not the ones with Dee or Randi!

~~~

Thursday, October 4, 2018

Anthony's week in California felt like the GWA writers were remaking the movie **Groundhog Day**. While he woke up in a different hotel each morning, his routine was pretty much the same day after day no matter what city he was currently inhabiting. He woke up
~~~

every morning after dreaming about Kay, fantasized about Kay in the shower, got dressed, ate a quick continental breakfast as he checked out of the hotel, and headed to the airport. He flew the plane to the next city, alternated with his friends to rent a car to get from the airport to the hotel, got in a workout in the hotel gym, ate lunch in the midafternoon, went to the arena to watch the show while texting Kay, ate dinner in catering at the arena, went back to the hotel to call or Skype with Kay, and dreamt about Kay overnight, just to wake up and do it all again in the next city the next day. By Thursday, while he was at the arena waiting to make sure the pilot on the other crew arrived to relieve him, he was extremely ready for his flight back to Tulsa on Friday.

Besides his communication with Kay, the only real change to his routine from any other week over the last year was that now he knew Kay, so he was seeing her clearly in his dreams. That was a change he really liked this week, but it was also making him start to wish he had a job in Tulsa, so he could see her every day instead of just texting and calling her.

Anthony was thoroughly enjoying all of their texts and calls. After Kay told him Monday night that Tia read their text conversation, he'd taken extra care not to accidentally send her a text that would be inappropriate for her kids to see. They'd mostly stuck to texting while the girls were awake and then he would call or Skype with her after they'd gone to bed, so his conversations with Kay could be a little more flirtatious. He struggled to keep from telling her all the things he wanted to do to her sexy little body, but he knew he had to take things slow, or their relationship would end before it really began.

Since Kay took Tia's advice and started asking Anthony about his favorite things instead of just playing the Would-You-Rather game, he'd been surprised to learn that they had a lot of things in common. They had the same favorite color (royal blue), the same favorite food (steak), and the same inability to name a favorite song because they both loved listening to a wide variety of music. While they didn't agree on a favorite book, because Kay said she loved going to the library and reading a large variety and couldn't choose a favorite, Anthony still felt like his favorite book, **Where the Red Fern Grows**, was something they had in common because she told him that her family's vacation cabin was in the Ozark Mountains, which was the setting for the book. They'd already made plans to drive out that way for a day on one of his weekend visits to see her.

Hearing that Kay's love of reading was only fed by library visits, Anthony immediately ordered her an e-reader for her upcoming birthday. He sent it with a very large gift card for her to be able to load it up with all the books she wanted but hadn't had the chance to read yet because of her lack of access. When it arrived at her house on Wednesday, she immediately called to tell him it was too much, and she couldn't accept the gift.

Thinking back to that conversation, Anthony closed his eyes and sighed. He hated that it was a fight to get her to accept even a little birthday present. He was afraid he was going to scare her off by pushing too fast to get her to let him take care of all her wants and needs.

He still wasn't completely comfortable with his feelings of ownership over Kay. He knew that a man couldn't own a woman. No one person could own any other person. *But she's mine! Mine to protect, mine to provide for, mine to cherish.* He just had to figure out how to do all those things without overwhelming her or making her feel like he wasn't respecting her boundaries.

Anthony also worried that Kay was still holding back from him when they talked. She was open and excited when she talked about her favorite things and mostly open when she talked about her daughters. But Anthony still felt like Kay was putting up walls to keep him out when it came to anything really important about the things she was dealing with in life. As soon as the conversation about her daughters came close to mentioning their father, Kay shut it down and changed the subject.

Anthony wasn't sure he really wanted to hear all the details about Kay's relationship with her ex-husband. He cringed at the thought of Kay telling him about sex with her ex. But Anthony also knew that the little bit he overheard the previous Saturday, when Kay was talking to Randi about Mark's behavior on his previous weekend visit with their daughters, was only the tip of the iceberg of the issues he was causing in Kay's life.

Anthony feared that if he knew everything that had transpired between Kay, Mark, and their daughters, he would have a hard time controlling the rage inside him that he wanted to unleash on Mark. *If that bastard ever physically hurt them, I'll kill him!*

Not that he would get the chance anytime soon. Anthony hated that he was only going to be able to see Kay on the weekends about every six weeks due to his strange work schedule. His days off only fell over a weekend every other time he had days off. And since she was not ready for him to meet her daughters, Anthony wouldn't be able to see her on his days off when they fell in the middle of the week.

With Tia and Maria going to their father's every other weekend and Anthony's weekends off being every third weekend, the weekends both he and Kay were free only lined up to be the same weekend every six weeks, so that was the only time she was willing to go out with him. It was frustrating, but Anthony was willing to suffer through it just so he could see her when she would let him.

Anthony didn't plan on it being that way for long, though. His lease was up on his apartment in San Antonio at the end of October. Since he wouldn't be going to San Antonio every time he was off work anymore, he decided not to renew it. He called the management company and let them know earlier in the week. He also called his parents and set them up to be there to help him pack his stuff when he had time off in the middle of the week and on the weekend he couldn't see Kay in October. His parents were pushing him to move into one of the ranch houses to move back to Heart's Destiny, but he just wanted them to store his stuff at the ranch until he could find a place in Tulsa.

He didn't plan on having Kay help him look for a place this first weekend, but in six weeks when he got to see her again, he wanted her to help him find a house in Tulsa. He hoped being in town every time he was off would tempt her to want to see him so much that she would let him meet her daughters sooner. If she helped him find a house in her neighborhood, all the better. Anthony was willing to take things slow, but he wasn't above accidentally (on purpose) bumping into her at the grocery store or church to push things along a little faster.

"What's that smirk for?" Rick, his boss, arched an eyebrow at Anthony as he walked up to where he was sitting backstage.

"Smirk? What smirk?" Anthony looked around to make sure Rick was talking to him and not someone else.

Rick just shook his head and smiled as he sat down across the table from Anthony in catering. "You were smirking when I walked up. It looked like you were plotting something, and I just want to make sure I'm not the one you're going to be pulling a prank on."

"No," Anthony laughed in response. "I'm not pranking anyone. Just thinking…" Anthony's voice trailed off because he wasn't sure how to finish the sentence. *Damn, he's right! I was plotting. Plotting to get Kay to move our relationship along faster.*

"Thinking about the new girlfriend?" Rick looked at Anthony with a knowing smile.

Anthony couldn't help the grin he got when he thought of Kay as his girlfriend. "Yeah," he finally admitted. "Who told you about her?" Anthony had to ask because he didn't think he'd mentioned Kay to Rick this week.

Rick shook his head again. "Dude, nobody had to tell me about her. I recognize the signs. You're distracted and off by yourself, texting constantly every evening when you would normally be hanging with the Hunters and watching the show. The only reason a man changes his habits that drastically is because of a woman. So, you gonna tell me about her, or do I have to wait to meet her when you get to your breaking point and start bringing her with you because you can't stand to be away from her while working?"

Wow! I guess I'm not as private a person as I thought I was.

"Her name is Kay." Anthony shifted in his seat. "I met her in Tulsa, last Saturday. And we're going on our first date tomorrow night."

"You just met her?" Rick looked at Anthony like he must be crazy.

"Yeah, I've only known her five days, but…" Again, his voice trailed off while he decided how much he wanted to open up to his boss. He'd become more of a friend over the last year. Rick hadn't ever talked about his past relationships, but his daughter traveled with him all the time. Anthony wondered if maybe Rick's experience as a single parent could give him insight into Kay's situation that Anthony didn't already have, so maybe he could give some advice on how not to screw this up. "She's different than any other woman I've ever met."

"Different how?" Rick leaned back in his chair.

"I don't know, just different," Anthony shrugged, not knowing how to describe how she made him feel. "Just looking at her, I feel different."

"So, she's hot," Rick laughed.

"No, I mean, yeah, she's hot, but that's not what I'm talking about." Anthony stumbled over the words, not sure how to explain it. "Obviously, I feel attraction, but I also feel like I just want to know everything about her and do anything I can just to make her smile."

Anthony paused to take a drink of bottled water, using the time to figure out how to word his next statement. "She's a little older than me and divorced with two daughters. We had an instant connection, like so instant that I knew she's *The One* as soon as I saw her. She felt the connection too, as soon as we looked into each other's eyes, but she's fighting it and I'm afraid of doing something to scare her off."

"What do you mean, she's fighting it?" Rick looked concerned. "Like she's trying to ignore you and you're harassing her via text every day?"

"No, she's not ignoring me, but she's keeping walls up and doesn't really get too deep when we're talking. And she's only willing to see me when her daughters are with their father for the weekend. She doesn't want me to meet them, at least not yet, and it's driving me crazy because I want to not only meet them, but I also want to adopt them and learn how to help Tia with calculus and build Maria the ultimate Barbie dreamhouse. She's having issues with her ex, but she won't talk to me about them, and it's killing me because I want to protect them all from whatever he's doing that's causing her so much grief, but she won't even tell me what's going on so I can."

Anthony realized he'd just blurted out way too much information to his boss and snapped his mouth shut. Rick looked at Anthony with a knowing smile and then nodded slowly.

"I think that's the most words I've ever heard you speak in one conversation," Rick finally chuckled. "She's obviously got you tied up in knots with no idea how to untie yourself."

Anthony chuckled with him before asking, "Do you have any advice? Being a parent, how would you want someone you were dating to approach meeting Britney?"

"I don't know that I'll ever date anyone that will get to meet Britney." Rick's posture stiffened obviously in his seat. "But I've also never met anyone that I've felt an instant connection with, so that's more of a doubt that I'll ever meet someone that I'll feel like I need to introduce to her. If she's divorced and having problems with her ex, then I'm betting her reluctance is more to do with him than you."

"Yeah, I figured as much." Anthony let out a sigh and slumped in his seat. "I overheard some of her conversation with her sister on Saturday and what she was saying about him…" Anthony trailed off, trying to keep himself from getting angry again. Just the thought of Kay's ex-husband yelling at the girls made him see red and clench his fists.

Anthony was raised to never resort to violence except in self-defense and even then, only if it was a life-or-death situation, so his desire to punch Kay's ex-husband was completely out of character for him. He took a few deep breaths to clear those thoughts from his head before continuing. "At the very least, he's emotionally abusive to Kay and her daughters. I worry that it's worse than just the little bit I overheard. It's making me want to do things I wouldn't normally want to do, and I'm struggling with that. But most of all, I want to protect them, and I'm frustrated because I don't know how I can. How crazy is that? I haven't even seen a picture of Kay's daughters, and I already love them so much that I want to beat the hell out of their abusive father and then fly them all to Vegas, so I can marry Kay and adopt her daughters and never let the asshole near them again."

"Remind me never to make you mad." Rick shook his head with a chuckle. "I wish I'd have had a camera on you just now because I have a few people on the roster that need to be able to make that angry face during promos."

Anthony laughed and felt his anger dissipate.

"Seriously, though," Rick finally finished laughing. "Don't push for a quickie Vegas wedding or even for meeting her daughters for at least a month or two. It sounds like she's got some valid reasons for not trusting you immediately, so give her time to get to know you and realize you aren't an asshole like her ex. And instead of sitting in catering texting, go spend some time in the ring while everyone else is sparring, so you can release some of that anger. Maybe you'll learn a few things to be prepared if you ever do get a chance to kick her ex's ass."

"Thanks, Boss," Anthony chuckled as he shook his head at Rick. "I'll get right on that." He started to stand up to head to the ring, thinking Rick may be right about his need to take out some frustration through sparring with his best friends. Before he could even take a step, though, Rick started speaking again.

"You do know that I encourage all my married talent to bring their family on the road, right? That goes for you, too, if you think being on the road with you would be safer for Kay and her daughters than being in the same city as her abusive ex, even before you get married." Rick rubbed his chin.

"Thanks, Rick." Anthony thought about what a great guy his boss was for the offer.

"In fact, I've been thinking about adding a second flight attendant to the crews since we have so many families traveling with us. Let me know if you know of anyone with childcare experience who might be interested in a job." Rick punctuated his statement with a smirk.

Anthony smiled and shook his head at his boss. He liked the way Rick was thinking and would love for Kay to come to work on the flight crew, but he was unsure how receptive she would be to a job offer so out of the blue.

Before they went their separate ways backstage, Rick to his office and Anthony to the ring to see if he could spar some, Anthony spoke again. "As much as I would love to have them all with me, I doubt Kay would go for it. But I'll keep that in mind just in case."

Anthony hated that her need to appear independent to her daughters meant that she was insisting on continuing working and struggling instead of letting him take care of her. *Maybe a job traveling with me will help her still feel like she's showing her independence but will at least be with me even if she won't let me take care of her the way I want.*

Since his Pappaw Jerry died a couple years ago, Anthony had been collecting the dividends on five percent of Burleson Incorporated, and a salary as a board member on top of his salary for his job with the GWA, so he had plenty of money to take care of her, even though he wouldn't get the trust fund his grandfather left each of his grandkids until he turned thirty and was married.

The way Burleson Incorporated was set up, the stock in the corporation was divided up to fifty percent going to the oldest generation in the family and the other fifty percent going to the second oldest generation. For as long as Anthony could remember that meant his Pappaw Jerry owned half and his dad and Uncle Jon each owned a quarter. When Pappaw Jerry died, his fifty percent was divided evenly between Anthony, his siblings, and their four cousins. So, now they had twelve board members that had to meet every quarter, even if some of them just Skyped into the meetings.

All of his cousins had actually started working for the company, expanding it out to other things besides the cows and oil. While Anthony appreciated the fact that they'd increased his bank account by diversifying the company, he didn't really keep up with everything going on there like he probably should.

Having taken as many CLEP tests as possible to quickly earn a general education degree in order to become a naval aviator, he didn't feel like he knew enough about business to do much more than talk to his dad to figure out how to vote when he had to at board meetings. Now that he was thinking about the family business, Anthony wondered if Kay had taken any business classes in college.

Maybe I should take a few business classes myself, so I can be more knowledgeable in what I need to do in my family business. I wonder if Kay's ever thought about going back and finishing her degree? Maybe we can take a few classes together and have some fun with some college co-ed role-play, Anthony thought.

Anthony managed to get through a few rounds of sparring with his friends and headed back to the hotel just as soon as he got the "all clear" that the pilot for the other flight crew was there to take over.

He wanted the privacy of his room to call Kay. He couldn't stay up too late talking to her, though, because he had to get up early for his morning flight to Tulsa. *I can't wait to see her again!*

As soon as he got to his room, he settled on the bed and pulled up his computer to Skype with her. He knew she was just expecting a phone call, but he couldn't go another minute without seeing her. Not being able to see her but a few minutes when they Skyped the first time over the past five days was killing him. He didn't know how he was going to get through six weeks without seeing her every day.

As much as he loved his job, especially all the time he got to spend in the air, Anthony was beginning to think that he might be ready to settle down to a normal job so he could be in Tulsa to see Kay daily.

"Hello, Beautiful," Anthony grinned when Kay finally appeared on his computer screen. "I know I'm early for our normal call time, but I couldn't wait a minute longer to see you."

"Hi," Kay laughed, and Anthony loved the twinkle in her eyes when she smiled at him. "It's okay, I'm already in my room. The girls are finishing up their baths and will probably come in here in a few minutes to tell me goodnight, so I may have to go pretty quick, but I can call you back right after."

"Or just lay your phone on your bed while you go tuck them in and I'll wait." Anthony hoped he wasn't being too pushy, but he needed to stay connected with Kay, even if it was just looking at her ceiling while she wasn't in the room.

He was afraid that his brothers would tell him he was behaving like the stage-five clingers they avoided when dating. As much as he didn't want to overwhelm Kay with his possessive need for her, he couldn't control his obsession with her. *I'm addicted to her, and I've only spent a few hours actually with her!*

"Yeah, I can do that," Kay uttered slowly, looking perplexed by the request.

Anthony heard a knock through the computer and realized that it was probably one of Kay's daughters knocking on her bedroom door. He felt terrible for jumping the gun and Skyping before their bedtime. *I have to quit being so damn pushy and demanding her undivided attention when she has so many other responsibilities that are more important than me.*

"I'll be right back." Kay placed the phone face down on the bed, so her image on Anthony's screen went black.

Not even a ceiling view, he thought to himself with a chuckle.

He heard muffled voices but couldn't make out any of the words being said by Kay or her daughters.

A few minutes later, Kay picked up her phone again and he got a panoramic view of her bedroom as she rolled onto the bed to sit and chat with him. He was shocked by the old-fashioned quilt on her bed because he expected her to have something more modern.

From his quick glimpse of the whole room, he realized that her bed was only a full-size, definitely not big enough for him. He stifled his groan at the mental image of them trying to fuck in the tiny bed. *Maybe I'll just fuck her against the wall and pretend to live out her fantasy of fucking in a cockpit. If I can get her to tell me about it soon!*

Once she was settled, Kay had her phone propped up, so his view was of her beautiful heart-shaped face and down to her shoulders, where he could see that she was wearing an oversized t-shirt. He wondered if that was her normal sleepwear and if she had anything on under it. *Fuck! I wish I could see down further to find out what her panties look like, if she's even wearing any.*

Kay bit her lip as she muttered, "Sorry about that."

"Nothing to be sorry for, Baby," Anthony replied, wishing he could soothe the light marks her teeth left on her bottom lip with his tongue. "I'm the one who should've been more patient and waited to call until our normal time. I'm sorry. I just couldn't stop myself. As soon as I got to my room, I had to see you. If I'm this desperate to see you after only five days, I'm not sure I'm going to survive not seeing you for six weeks before our next date."

"Do you really miss me that much?" Kay looked at him skeptically. "Or are you just trying to sweet-talk your way into my panties?"

"Oh, I want in your panties." Anthony gave her a lustful smile. "But needing to see you every day isn't about that. I just need to see your smile to make my day complete."

Kay's lips turned up slowly, ending in the secret smile that Anthony loved seeing. The one she only gave him when her thoughts turned naughty, like when she was trying to see his cock through the table at the diner the night they met, or when she was reacting to him calling her Baby.

"Seriously, Baby." Anthony leaned into the computer to feel closer to Kay. "Sex isn't nearly as important to me as seeing you happy. If you're not ready for us to be physical, I can wait. I'm much more interested in building a strong foundation for our relationship because I want it to last forever."

"It's not that I'm not ready," Kay sighed. "I'm just..." Her voice trailed off as her face contorted in confusion.

"Just what?" Anthony cajoled in a soothing tone, hoping that Kay would open up to him.

"I don't know." Kay still looked confused but also a little anxious, or maybe worried.

Fuck, I don't want her to be scared of me!

"Well, we don't have to do anything but talk until you're ready, Baby." Anthony gave her what he hoped was a comforting smile. He wanted her to feel safe with him. He wanted to protect her from anything and everything that could possibly hurt her, even himself. "Would it help to talk through how you're feeling?"

"Maybe," Kay whispered sheepishly. "But maybe not." She shrugged her shoulders.

"You know you can talk to me about anything, right?"

"I know you keep telling me that," Kay replied with a wry smile. "But I have a hard time talking about some things." She closed her eyes and took in a deep breath. She held it for a moment before blowing it out and opening her eyes again. "I want to trust you, but I'm afraid that you're too good to be true."

"I'm definitely not too good to be true," Anthony chuckled. "And I most certainly have my flaws, but I don't think my clown feet make me untrustworthy."

"Clown feet?" Kay chortled.

Anthony loved making her laugh. "Yeah, they're so big I have to buy clown-sized shoes." Anthony waggled his eyebrows at her, hoping to keep her laughing.

Kay giggled and her wide smile showed through in her eyes. When she started to blush, Anthony wondered if she was thinking about what other supersized body parts he had. His smile grew as he thought, *Yeah, Baby, my cock is supersized too!*

When her giggle subsided, Kay stated, "It's not that I think you're perfect and don't have any flaws. I know nobody's perfect." She sat up straighter and took on a serious expression on her face. She looked down away from her phone and whispered to herself, "Don't be embarrassed. Just tell him. You'll be okay, no matter how he reacts."

Anthony felt his heart skip a beat and choked on a lump in his throat when he realized that she was having to give herself a pep talk to be able to tell him whatever she was about to say. He feared that it was because she was about to end things with him before they'd really even begun.

"I'm scared," Kay finally choked out, still not looking up into the phone so he could see her eyes.

"Of me?" Anthony hated the thought that Kay would be afraid of him. "Baby, I would never hurt you." His voice broke as he choked out the last word.

"No, not of you," Kay replied, looking up at him imploringly. "I'm scared that I'm going to disappoint you."

"Baby, you could never disappoint me." Anthony finally felt like his heart restarted, and he could breathe again since Kay wasn't physically afraid of him.

"Don't be so sure of that," she replied.

Her face went blank, and Anthony disliked the fact that she was putting up walls between them. He much preferred being able to see her thoughts and feelings in her ocean blue eyes.

"I'm not any good at sex," Kay stated flatly. "I've only been with two people in my life. The first was my high school boyfriend. I thought it was just bad because we were both inexperienced. The second was my ex-husband." She shuddered as she stopped speaking to take a few more deep breaths to compose herself.

Anthony bit his tongue to keep from interrupting her. He wanted to tell her that her prior experiences didn't matter because she'd been with guys who weren't right for her. He wanted to tell her that the sexual chemistry between the two of them was so palpable he could taste it, so he knew that when they were finally together it would be explosive, the most intense passion he could imagine. But he didn't say either of those things because he wanted her to feel safe to tell him everything about her past.

"When Mark and I were first together, it wasn't as bad as it'd been with Doug, but it wasn't the mind-blowing experience my friends talked about, either. I didn't figure it was a big deal because it wasn't often since he was deployed most of the time. When he got out of the Army, it got really bad."

A single tear rolled down Kay's cheek and Anthony wished he was there in person, so he could wipe it away. He longed to hold her in his arms and comfort her as she relived her painful past.

She closed her eyes and looked down again before continuing. "He made it clear that the issues were mine. The last two years before we separated, we never had sex. He told me he preferred his hand because it was more responsive than me." She sobbed out the last few words.

Anthony clenched his fists, trying to hold back his fury at her ex-husband for how he'd emotionally abused Kay. "He's a moron," he said in a low growl.

"I think I'm just asexual," Kay stated emotionlessly. "I don't get aroused like most women."

Leah Mae Wright

"Bullshit," Anthony bellowed. "You were aroused when we kissed Saturday night."

Kay jerked her head back up to look at Anthony through the screen of her phone. "How do you know that?" Her voice took on a high-pitched tone that told him she was surprised by his recognition of her arousal.

"Baby, you were very responsive when we kissed. And your nipples were hard enough to cut glass. I could see them through your shirt." Anthony smirked at the memory of how passionate their kiss had been.

Kay blushed. *Damn, she's adorable!*

"Oh, okay," Kay stuttered. "But that's not normal for me. What if it was a fluke? What if I don't have that same reaction when we see each other again?"

"Sweetheart, lean back against your headboard and push your phone far enough away that I can see your entire upper body," Anthony commanded with a deeper bass tone than his normal voice. He planned to prove to Kay that he could arouse her without even having to touch her because he knew that their connection was stronger than either one of them had ever experienced before.

She did as he ordered, making Anthony's already hard cock more engorged than he'd ever felt. Her light pink nightshirt was fairly thin, giving him a glimpse of the darker peaks of her breasts. *I'll definitely be able to see how hard her nipples get in that shirt.*

"I want you to stay focused on looking at me, because I want you to know exactly who is arousing you while we chat," Anthony ordered with a gravelly tone. "I know you feel too embarrassed to tell me your fantasies, but I want to tell you some of mine to show you how responsive you are to me."

Kay's eyes widened and her mouth opened as if she were about to object. Anthony shook his head at her, hoping she understood his unspoken message to just relax and listen to him. She closed her mouth but still sat stiffly. He didn't want to leave her with too much time to think and disconnect from him, but he wished she would at least loosen up a little before he spoke.

"Every night, I dream about you, and every morning I relive those fantasies while showering," he confided in a low, sensual tone. "I stand there under the spray of the shower with my eyes closed, stroking my cock while picturing you there with me. I imagine running my hands over every inch of your delectable body as I soap you up. You're the perfect height for me to wash between your beautiful breasts with my dick. Sometimes I imagine doing that until I come all over them."

Kay's breathing quickened and her nipples hardened to stiff peaks that looked to Anthony like they were about to cut through her thin nightshirt. *Wow, one of my tamest fantasies, and she's already aroused.*

"Sometimes I imagine rinsing the soap off, so you can take me in your mouth," he crooned. "But most of the time, I imagine picking you up, so you can wrap your legs around my waist, and I can kiss you while fucking you against the tile wall of the shower."

Kay moaned and Anthony felt his cock twitch in response to the sultry, sexy sound. Based on her glassy-eyed look and how much harder her nipples appeared, Anthony knew she was more aroused than she'd probably ever been before.

He ached to tell her to touch herself and aim the camera so he could see how soaking wet her pussy was, but he didn't want the first time he saw her that way to be over Skype. He stifled his desire for Skype sex and told her, "Baby, I can see how aroused you are, just from hearing my tamest fantasies, so I know you are definitely not asexual."

Kay opened her mouth as if to speak but closed it again before saying anything. Anthony smiled at her floundering as she did it a few more times, reveling in the feeling of leaving her speechless. The flush of her cheeks became deeper, and he longed to stroke his hands across them just before kissing her.

"Don't be embarrassed, Baby," Anthony crooned in a soothing tone.

"Bu-but, I don't," Kay stuttered with a quiver of her lower lip. "I don't normally…" Her voice trailed off as she struggled to deal with the emotions she was obviously grappling with.

While Anthony loved seeing her innocent vulnerability, he hated that she felt uncomfortable with the strange sensations their connection evoked in each of them. He hoped that he could put her at ease by admitting to his own overwhelming feelings.

"Baby, it's okay," Anthony consoled, speaking softly. "This is different for me, too." He ran a hand through his hair, trying to think of how to comfort her from long distance while also showing her his own vulnerability. "I think the ease with which we're each aroused by one another is just one of the signs that we're supposed to be together."

"You aren't easily aroused normally either?" Kay appeared shocked at the thought.

Anthony chuckled at her adorable expression. "Don't get me wrong, Baby," he grinned. "I was a typical hormonal teenager and had the normal struggle to hide the fact that I was hard eighty percent of the time."

Fuck, how do I explain the last two years and not sound like a lunatic? She's going to think I'm crazy if I tell her about my dreams.

"After Nancy died, it took a while before I was interested in anything again," Anthony finally choked out. "It was a year later before I actually had a one-night stand after a night out with the guys in my squadron. I had a few more over the years when I was on leave, but none of them were ever anything more than a way to let off steam between deployments. The last one was a couple of years ago. I've never felt a connection with anyone, the way I feel with you."

Anthony took a deep breath and struggled with whether or not to try to explain his lack of interest in anyone since his dreams started. Looking into her eyes, he saw that she was truly listening to him and seemed open and understanding, not judging him for his sexual history. He decided to take a chance and trust her with his truth.

"I was on deployment for six months before there was an explosion on the ship." Anthony's voice was full of emotion as he flashed back to the accident briefly. "I had just taken the first step down a metal stairway and the explosion violently rocked the ship, causing me to fall to the bottom. I broke my arm and a couple of ribs, one of which punctured a lung." He paused to take a deep breath, grateful that his injuries had healed, so he could without pain.

"The worst of it was that the nuclear core was damaged and leaked enough radiation to sterilize anyone on that level of the ship." Anthony heard how his voice was filled with sorrow, but he couldn't hold it back from her. "I couldn't get aroused for a while after that. I was worried it was because of the radiation, that I'd be impotent forever. But the doctors said it was more of a mental thing while I dealt with my feelings about not being able to procreate."

Kay sat silently, allowing Anthony to take his time in gathering his thoughts and explaining his feelings.

"While I was home with my folks recovering, I talked to my dad about it." Anthony was surprised by his desire to share things with Kay that he'd only spoken to his dad about before. "We've had a lot of long talks on the back of a horse over the last eighteen months. He got me through the worst of it, making me realize that DNA doesn't matter and I'm still able to be a great dad to whoever I'm able to play a part in raising. He also reassured me that my impotence was a temporary thing."

Anthony chuckled, remembering his dad explaining that only a boy who hadn't grown up and met the love of his life could be aroused easily by any woman he saw. Becoming a man meant only being aroused by his one true love. Kay gave him a quizzical expression at his chuckle, so he explained that horseback ride with his dad to her. She giggled when he got to the part where his dad told him that he was just showing signs of being a man and would only be aroused again when he found *The One*.

"And you've only been, um, aroused, again since meeting me?" Kay questioned with a twinkle in her eye.

"Yes, and no," Anthony answered sheepishly, hoping admitting to his dreams wouldn't scare her off. "Last year, I started getting aroused again, but only after very specific dreams. I think I was dreaming about you, even though we hadn't met yet. Saturday night was the first time I've gotten aroused while looking at a woman, *you*. Now I get hard just thinking about you. Hell, I got hard in catering from smelling strawberries and thinking of how you smelled on Saturday."

Anthony cringed inwardly at his bold admission. The slight upturn of Kay's lips made him hopeful that she wasn't offended, though.

"You really think you've been dreaming about me?" Kay smirked. "How long have you had these dreams?"

"Since the day I interviewed with Rick for this job," Anthony replied, relaxing as he saw the twinkle in Kay's eyes as he went on. "My interview was actually in the restaurant at the Camelot Hotel in Tulsa. I think I saw you that day but was too focused on the interview to recognize our connection, so I've subconsciously maintained our bond via my dreams for the last year."

Kay's hand went up to cover her mouth as her jaw dropped in surprise. She dropped her hand and looked at Anthony in awe before speaking. "Or maybe the timing just wasn't right because I was in the middle of my divorce proceedings then, so you subconsciously realized I wasn't ready to meet you yet?"

"Maybe?" Anthony replied with a wide smile. *Thank fuck, she doesn't think I'm crazy!*

"How do you know our time is right now?" Kay had a hopeful expression on her face.

"I don't think we would have met until it was the right time for us," Anthony replied. "I don't think God, or fate, or whatever you believe in, would be so cruel as to show me the woman of my dreams without intending us to be together. Knowing you and not being able to be with you would be the worst form of torture I can imagine. I've certainly felt tortured this week."

"Yeah, the fact that we can't see each other but every six weeks is part of why I think it's not really the right time for us." Kay worried her lip with her teeth again.

"Naw." Anthony tried to ease her fear with a smile. "I think that's just a way of making us take things slow, so we build a strong foundation. It's certainly making me think about what I want to do, so we don't have to be apart so much."

"Maybe," Kay whispered as she closed her eyes and took in a deep breath. "Maybe it's because I need more time to deal with things, too."

"Anything I can help you deal with?" Anthony hoped Kay would finally open up about the major stressors of her life.

"No," Kay sighed. "Nothing I can really do until my lawyer gets us a new court date."

"Your ex?" Anthony hoped she'd finally open up to him. *Please talk to me, Baby!*

"Yeah," she replied, her shoulders sagging as if she felt defeated. "The girls told me about some issues after their last visit with him that are concerning. He's not answering my calls, so I have no way of resolving the issues before he picks them up tomorrow. Hopefully, we'll fix it tomorrow when he comes to pick them up. But if not, then I'll have to take him back to court to request supervised visits."

Fuck! I hate the thought of her being alone with him tomorrow! But if I tell her that, she'll realize it's jealousy and not all fear for her safety. Fuck! Fuck! Fuck! What can I say to be the supportive boyfriend and not sound like the angry, jealous caveman I actually feel like?

"I wish there was something I could do to fix it for you," Anthony finally offered, trying to speak in a soothing tone of voice.

"Like I said, nothing you can help me with." Kay gave him a wry smile. "But definitely something I need time to take care of before we get too serious."

"I may not be able to help, but I can definitely be there to offer moral support when you have to go to court. In fact, if I don't have any delays on my flight tomorrow, I can come over early…"

Anthony's offer to be there to have Kay's back when she met with her ex was cut off by Kay's exclamation of, "No! Don't do that." Her eyes were wide with fear, making Anthony think he'd screwed up by pushing her boundaries.

"Sorry, Baby." Anthony held his hands up in surrender. "I wasn't thinking about the fact that I'd meet your daughters if I showed up too early. I, uh, I just thought you might need someone to lean on, to support you while you discuss things with your ex. I want to be your person, the one you can lean on, and know I'll always have your back."

Kay's expression softened as she tilted her head and tried to smile at him. "I know." She still sounded dejected. "But I have to do this on my own. My girls need to see me being strong enough on my own to stand up for them."

"That strong, independent woman thing you were talking about last weekend?" Anthony smiled at her.

"Yeah, that strong, independent woman thing," Kay chuckled. "Thank you for wanting to be there for me. You don't know how much that means to me." She let out a long sigh. "Unfortunately, right now I think seeing you would just make Mark act out more, so I can't let you be there for me to lean on. But I'll probably be pretending that you're standing at my back, even when you aren't in the room, so I can project that needed strength."

Anthony smiled at the thought of Kay imagining him there at her side to provide the strength she would need. "So, tomorrow at five, I should close my eyes and imagine I'm holding you in my arms to give you all my strength?" he suggested in a slow seductive drawl.

Kay blushed, making Anthony think her thoughts were a lot more salacious than just him holding her fully clothed.

"Baby," he crooned, drawing the word out to three syllables. "Please tell me what you're thinking right now."

"I, um," Kay stammered, her eyes looking downward, coyly. "Was wondering if that's all you'd be imagining or if you'd be having another fantasy like you told me earlier."

"Really?" Anthony grinned. "It looked more like you were having a fantasy of your own. I've shared mine, surely you can share one of yours now."

"I suppose it's only fair, huh?" Kay took a deep breath to bolster her courage to tell him. "You said you'd be imagining holding me and I kind of branched off from that, picturing you holding me where I could wrap my arms around your neck and my legs around your waist."

Anthony wouldn't have believed her cheeks could turn a deeper shade of pink until he saw them do just that.

"But it wasn't because I needed to channel your strength to confront my ex. It was because we were alone and naked."

Thank fuck! Anthony thought.

"Where were we?" He hoped she would finally tell him about her cockpit fantasy.

"I have no idea," Kay answered, breaking out in a burst of laughter. "I couldn't see anything but you and me in my mental picture."

"Well, then, let's imagine it together and come up with some possibilities of when we can make your fantasy come true. I've already imagined that in the shower. Is your shower big enough for both of us?"

"Nope, just a standard tub and shower," she replied, giggling. "You'd probably have to bend over to put your head under the showerhead to get your hair wet."

Anthony chuckled with her, knowing that the mental image of him bending in half to get his head wet in her shower was what caused her to giggle. "Okay, your shower is out."

"I, um, have thought of something similar earlier this week," Kay confessed shyly.

Anthony loved how adorably innocent she looked even as she was trying to push past her comfort zone to tell him her dirty fantasies. *Oh, Baby, I'm going to make you so dirty!*

"When Randi told me about what she did with James at Chandler Park, I told her about the daydream I had in church Sunday morning." Kay shifted on her bed like she was physically uncomfortable and not just emotionally discomfited by what she was about to say. "I wasn't sure I should tell you about it because Randi pointed out that while it was hot, it wasn't physically possible to do and stay safe."

"Not safe?" Anthony grinned, feeling relieved that he was about to hear the fantasy he already knew about. "Was it the danger that was the turn on or what we were doing?"

"Oh, no, I didn't think about the possible danger." Kay shook her head earnestly. "I liked the idea of, um, having sex in the cockpit of your plane. But I figured people could see in the windows if we did it on the ground, so I imagined it while flying on autopilot. Randi pointed out that we'd probably knock the autopilot off when you pushed me up against the instrument panel and we'd crash the plane, so obviously, that's out."

"You want me to not just pick you up but to push you against the wall while I fuck you?" Anthony's voice took on a deep gravelly tone as his arousal increased with the thought. "Oh, Baby, I can definitely do that in any room we can be alone in, and I'll gladly pretend it's the cockpit."

"You would do that?" Kay looked surprised that he was willing to role-play with her to live out some of their fantasies.

"Baby, I'll do you any way you want it." Anthony lowered his tone to his deepest, most seductive voice. "All you have to do is tell me what you want, and I'll make it happen."

Kay looked as if she practically melted at his words. "I wish you were already here to actually do that." Her voice was also low and sultry.

"I can't make it happen immediately, but I will be there tomorrow. Don't be surprised if I pin you against your front door as soon as I get there tomorrow night." Anthony wagged his eyebrows at Kay. She gave him that special, secret smile before losing it by yawning.

"Get some sleep, Baby." Anthony hated that he had to end their conversation, but she obviously needed her rest. And he now considered it his number one priority to give her everything she needed. "Dream about what you want me to do to you as soon as I get to your door tomorrow. And when I get there, you can tell me exactly what you want me to do, and I'll fulfill your fantasies."

"Goodnight, Anthony," Kay smiled through another yawn. "I would wish you sweet dreams, but I don't think your normal dreams are all that sweet."

"Some of them are sweet." He winked at her. "At least you taste sweet in them."

She giggled at his flirtation.

"Goodnight, Baby," he said just before she clicked to end their Skype session.

He closed his laptop and put it in its case before stripping down for a shower before bed. The wait to see Kay made it feel like the longest night of his life.

Chapter Five

Friday, October 5, 2018

On Friday evening, Kay paced nervously while waiting for Mark to come pick up the girls for the weekend. When she called him as her attorney suggested to see if they could talk about the visitation schedule, he hadn't answered any of her calls. He also hadn't responded to any of the voice messages she'd left him every day that week. Kay made the girls pack for the weekend because she knew he was going to refuse to cut back on his time with them, even though it would be in their best interest to not be around his negativity every other weekend. The girls weren't happy about having to go with him, so Kay worried that there would be tears or a fight to get them to actually go for the weekend.

Mark was supposed to arrive at five o'clock to get them and was late as usual. That also made Kay worry that she should have planned her date with Anthony for a different day because she didn't know if she would have time to get ready before Anthony arrived to pick her up at seven with Mark being an hour late already. At least she'd done her hair and makeup earlier in the day and would just need to do a little touch-up to those and change out of the jeans and t-shirt she had on and into the dress she was planning on wearing on the date.

All week Kay had been talking, texting, and Skyping with Anthony. Not just the Would-You-Rather game, but also so many other conversations about all their favorite things. In those conversations, Kay really felt like she'd gotten to know Anthony and he'd gotten to know her. Kay was looking forward to their date with hopes of moving their physical relationship to more than just a goodnight kiss.

Leah Mae Wright

It had been a long time since she'd actually wanted to be touched by a man. Even before her divorce, it had been years since her relationship with Mark was sexual. Even early in their marriage, sex with Mark was more of a chore than pleasurable. Kay thought she'd actually come closer to orgasm from the talk the night before with Anthony than she ever had from sex with her ex.

Kay fanned herself at the memory of talking with Anthony the night before. Just the memory of his dirty talk got her hot. She still wasn't sure why she ended up telling him about some of her fantasies when she'd intended to hold them back for a few more weeks while they got to know each other.

"Baby, I'll do you any way you want it," Anthony had said when they were discussing acting out some of their fantasies. "All you have to do is tell me what you want, and I'll make it happen."

Remembering his words sent a flutter of desire straight to her core. She couldn't believe how lucky she was in meeting Anthony. He not only wouldn't berate her like her ex for having whimsical fantasies, but he actually wanted to make them all come true for her. His statements like that were making it hard for her to remember why she had to take things slow with him.

Their conversation the night before had definitely not been on the slow track to a relationship like the rest of their discussions had been. While their calls were much more flirty than their texts, the ones earlier in the week were nowhere near as explicit as their Skype session Thursday night. They were more innuendo and double entendre than actually talking about progressing the sexual side of their relationship. Well, with the exception of their conversation on Wednesday when he tried justifying his outrageous birthday present to her.

"I want to take care of you, more than just in the bedroom," Anthony had said, and Kay could picture his sexy smile and the way he wiggled his eyebrows suggestively.

"But you don't even really know me yet," Kay had replied. *"What if you get to know me better and regret spending so much money on something like this for me."*

"Baby, that's never gonna happen. I told you, I'm in this with you for the long haul. You're my forever and I'm yours. And while I don't mind waiting for the sexual benefits of our relationship, I want to go ahead and start enjoying the other benefits, like pampering you with gifts just because I think they'll make you smile."

"Mom, can we unpack now since Dad isn't coming?" Tia walked into the living room and brought Kay back to the present.

As much as Kay wished she could live in fantasyland with Anthony, she had to come back to the reality that was her real life. *Too bad real life is more of a nightmare because of Mark*, Kay thought as she turned to face her daughter.

Kay's oldest daughter was already as tall as Kay, so they looked eye to eye as Kay told her, "No, honey, he's just late, but he's still coming to get you for the weekend. I never got to talk to him this week to change the schedule, so I'm sure he won't cancel."

Tia's shoulders slumped as she let out a huge sigh. She obviously struggled with her feelings about her weekend visits with Mark. Kay wished she knew how to help her but was at a total loss because she still struggled with her own issues with Mark. Kay wondered if the therapist she'd seen during her divorce could give her a recommendation to a therapist that specialized in working with children.

At six-thirty, just as Kay picked up her phone to call Anthony to cancel their date, Mark finally knocked at the door. Kay put her phone in the back pocket of her jeans and went to greet her ex. As soon as the door was open, she could smell the beer on Mark. There was no way she was going to allow him to take her daughters with him after he'd apparently been imbibing, so she tried to hold the door only partially open while they talked. "Mark, it's obvious you've been drinking. You can't drive our daughters…"

Kay's words were cut off as Mark pushed his way into the house yelling, "Like hell I can't!"

Kay stumbled backwards but, thankfully, she didn't fall to the floor as he pushed past her. She reached out and clasped his forearm and tried to stop him from getting too far into the house. As she grabbed him, she shouted, "Tia! Maria! Lock yourselves in your bedroom and call Grandpa Lee, NOW!"

"Let go of me!" Mark yelled as he yanked his arm out of Kay's loose grasp and flung her a few feet away from him.

"No!" Kay moved toward him to try to get by Mark, and between him and the hallway, where the girls were. "The girls aren't going with you after you've been drinking. You need to leave before my dad gets here. We'll let our lawyers renegotiate the visitation schedule since you wouldn't talk to me about it all week."

Kay didn't make it around him, but she got to just a couple of feet behind him when he turned back toward her. The look on his face terrified Kay. While Mark wasn't an exceptionally large man at only five-foot-nine, he was still nine inches taller than Kay and outweighed her by at least seventy-five pounds. She knew she couldn't actually drag him outside to protect her daughters, but she hoped she was tough enough to keep him in the living room until her dad got there to make sure they were all safe.

"I'm not gonna change the visitation schedule," Mark slurred as he advanced toward Kay. He grabbed her by the shoulders and pushed her back toward the front door. "I gotta send all my money to you, so I'm gonna get what I'm paying for by taking the girls every time the judge said I'm suppose ta have 'em." He turned again toward the hallway and started yelling again, "Girls, get out here now with your suitcases, so we can leave!"

"No, Mark, they aren't going with you. Come outside and let's talk this through, so we can do what's best for Tia and Maria."

He turned again and raised his fist as if he was going to hit Kay. "No," Kay screamed as she jumped back toward the door to get away, only she ran into a wall that shouldn't have been right inside her open front door. Kay didn't realize what was happening until she found herself behind Anthony, who apparently came in the open door when he got there and heard the shouting.

"I believe you were asked to leave." Anthony looked down at Mark as he held Kay safely behind him. "I'd advise you to lower your fist and leave now."

"Who the fuck are you?" Mark shouted, but he lowered his fist since it was obvious that he didn't stand a chance in a fight with Anthony, who was as much taller than Mark, as Mark was taller than Kay. Seeing them both in the same room, Kay also thought Anthony had forty or fifty pounds on Mark since Anthony was all muscle and Mark was on the softer side.

"Your worst nightmare if you even think about coming near Kay again." Anthony's voice seemed deeper than Kay remembered as he growled out the words. "I'm assuming you're her ex-husband. Again, my advice is to leave now."

Is it wrong that I'm really turned on by Anthony right now? Kay wondered, feeling not only aroused but also safe and protected by Anthony's unexpected rescue. *He's definitely my knight in shining armor.*

"I'm not leaving until the girls get out here to go with me," Mark snarled as he puffed out his chest and tried to stand as tall as he possibly could. If it weren't for the fact that Kay was so worried about her daughters seeing this fight, she would've laughed at how ridiculous Mark looked trying to be a badass in front of Anthony.

"I already told you, Mark…" Kay slid under Anthony's right arm to be able to stand beside him. She may have only known Anthony for six days, but having him by her side made her feel not only strong enough to stand up for herself and her daughters, but also safe in doing so because she knew Anthony would protect her from Mark. "The girls aren't going with you when you've been drinking."

"And I told you, they are, 'cause the judge said I gotta take 'em every other weekend!" Mark spit out. "If you don't let me take 'em, then I'll call my attorney and tell him I want full custody because you won't honor the judge's orders."

"No judge would order kids to be put in a car with an inebriated driver," Anthony stated matter-of-factly. "And if you think I'm going to let you take Kay's daughters tonight, you're obviously too inebriated to drive. Now, this is the last time I'm going to tell you, leave or I will physically remove you from the premises."

"Please try," Mark spat at Anthony. "Then I can tell the judge that this slut had her john of the week rough me up and it'll make my getting custody even easier."

Anthony growled and started moving toward Mark. He was stopped by a large hand on his left shoulder as Kay's dad, Charles Lee, stepped into the room. "That won't be necessary. I've got this." He walked past Anthony and Kay and pulled the handcuffs off his belt. "Mark, you're under arrest for trespassing."

"Trespassing?" Mark sputtered as he tried to back away from Charles. "I'm here to get Tia and Maria for my weekend visit. I'm not trespassing. If you're going to arrest someone, arrest Kay for disobeying the judge's order for visitation by keeping the kids from me and this jackass for threatening me."

"Threats? I didn't hear any threats." Charles looked around the room as if he were looking for witnesses to the supposed threats. "But I did hear you being asked to leave and refusing, so therefore, you are technically trespassing. And I won't be arresting my daughter tonight unless she actually agrees to let my grandbabies go with you. If that were the case, I'd be arresting both of you for child endangerment, and you for driving while impaired." He turned and looked at his daughter. "You alright, baby girl?"

"Yes, Dad, I'm fine. But I want to go check on the girls to make sure they aren't freaking out. Do you think you can get Mark to leave without arresting him? I really don't want them to see their father being arrested by their grandfather."

Her father nodded at her to show he understood her wishes. "Alright, Mark, let's call you a cab and wait for it outside." Charles pointed toward the door. Mark's eyes darted between Charles, Anthony, and Kay before he reluctantly started to walk out the door. Charles followed him.

Kay turned to look up at Anthony. "Give me a few minutes to check on my daughters, and then we can figure out when we can reschedule our date."

"Take all the time you need, Sweetheart." Anthony rubbed a hand down her arm and gave her a tender smile.

As she walked down the hall to her daughters' rooms, she realized that she would be introducing Anthony to her girls a lot sooner than she'd planned. She wasn't sure how to feel about that. Her brain still thought it was too soon, but after spending the last few days falling more for him with each new thing she'd learned about him, her pulse quickened with excitement about taking this major step in their relationship. And if she were really being honest with herself, she hoped her daughters would feel the same sense of safety and strength from Anthony that she did. They certainly needed it to be able to deal with their feelings about Mark's recent behavior.

Kay knocked on the door to Maria's room since it was closed and the door to Tia's was standing open. "Tia! Maria! You can come out now."

The door opened slowly; Tia stood behind it with her baseball bat in her hands. "Is Dad gone? I was gonna come back to help you, but Maria got scared and hid under the bed, so I was trying to calm her down first in case she needed to call nine-one-one."

"You were going to help me with a baseball bat?" Kay shook her head and took the bat from Tia. "Tia, what were you thinking? You were supposed to stay in here, where it was safe, and call Grandpa, not go putting yourself in danger by coming back out there and letting him get ahold of a weapon." Kay trembled with fear as she hugged her daughter tight after setting the baseball bat down beside the door.

"He pushed you, Mom!" Tia shouted, pulling back from Kay's embrace. "The only way he was going to get my baseball bat was upside his head, so he couldn't hurt you anymore!"

"Tia!" Kay shrieked. "He could have easily grabbed the bat from you and then who knows what he would've done." Kay sat down on the bed, gently pulling Tia down by her hand to sit beside her. "Maria, come out here and talk to me, too." Maria poked her head out from under the bed between Kay's feet. "All the way out from under the bed. I need you both right beside me, so I can hug you."

Maria crawled out and jumped on the bed to sit, so Kay was between both her daughters. She put an arm around each of them and squeezed them close. "I know you're both upset about how your dad has been acting lately. I'm still working on fixing it, so you don't have to go visit him so much."

Kay thought about how much detail she wanted to tell her daughters about the phone calls she'd made that week to her father's friend and her attorney, Matt Monroe. Kay had spoken to him several times, so he had all the details of every message she'd left Mark and the new things Tia finally opened up and told her about what Mark had said on their last visit with him to be able to put them in the petition to change to supervised visitation. Kay didn't really think now was the time to bring any of that up again because she didn't want Tia to get more upset and shut her out once more. Kay decided to just focus on letting them know the goal she was working toward for the moment.

"I'm trying to make it where he can only see you with someone else around, so he can't yell at you or tell you lies anymore." Kay looked back and forth between her daughters. "But until I can get the court to change the orders, we have to do what we can to keep you both safe. If you have to be around him and he's acting mean like tonight, I don't want you to try to fight him to protect me. I want you to get away from him and lock yourselves in a room where he can't get in and call Grandpa Lee or nine-one-one."

Kay paused to take a deep breath. "You two staying in here where he couldn't hurt you was exactly what needed to happen tonight. I'm an adult and can defend myself if he does try to hurt me again, but I can't do what I need to do to protect all of us if I'm worried about one of you getting hurt because you're too close to the fight."

Kay tried to think of a way to get her point across to her daughters and remembered a similar scenario on the local wrestling show they'd watched a few weeks back. Kay didn't have cable to be able to see the wrestling company Anthony worked for, but Mid-American Wrestling was based in Tulsa and the girls loved watching Mid-American Wrestling shows every Saturday on the local station they could watch with just an antenna.

"Remember last month when we were watching wrestling and the valet, Victoria, got hurt because she was too close to the fight between Bobby Brooks and Steve Starr?" Both girls nodded their heads. "If you had come back in there when your dad was pushing me, you could have gotten too close and might have gotten hurt just like Victoria. We never want to take a chance on that happening." Kay looked directly into Tia's eyes. "Calling Grandpa was perfect. He got here in time to make your dad leave before anyone could get hurt. You did exactly what you needed to do by staying in here."

"Okay, Mom." Tia looked down at her sneakers. "I understand. I won't try to help you with my baseball bat if he does it again. But if he gets in the bedroom with us, I still want Louie to hit him with, so he doesn't hit me."

Kay wondered if Tia still hadn't told her everything about that last visit with Mark. She feared that he may have done more than just yell and lie if Tia felt like she needed a baseball bat to defend herself from her father. Kay inhaled another deep breath and held back from flat out asking because she didn't want to risk her daughter feeling embarrassed or defensive and shutting down again.

"How about we go talk to Grandpa Lee and see if he knows about some self-defense classes?" Kay hoped learning some self-defense might help Tia feel safe and empowered, so she could finally talk about everything that happened at Mark's. "He's probably still out front waiting on the cab he called for your dad."

"Yes!" Both girls shouted as they jumped up and ran out of the bedroom.

~~~

While Kay was down the hall talking to her daughters and her father and ex-husband were outside, Anthony took a few moments to look around her home. It was a quaint nineteen-fifties style white house with black trim and a one-car garage on the left side when looking at it from the road. The front porch was just to the right of the garage. The wrought iron railing around the porch was also black to match the shutters and doors. Just inside the front door was an organ and Anthony wondered if Kay or her daughters played it, or if it was something left over from her parents living there. There was a soft, blue sofa to the right of the door in front of a picture window to the front yard. While he was tempted to move to sit there immediately to watch what transpired between her father and ex-husband, Anthony also felt the need to pace a little to expend some of his excess angry energy, so he could calm down before Kay came back and was alarmed by his furious scowl.

Anthony walked across the room to the archway that led into a formal dining room. He peered into the kitchen that was off to the left of the dining room. There was a door that Anthony assumed went to the garage to the immediate left, and when he continued around to the right past the refrigerator, he saw that there was another living room that extended a lot farther back than he expected from the looks of the other houses on the block. It had a built-in table extending into the room from the kitchen counter and Anthony finally saw the television at the other end of the room, along with another sofa. *I guess that's a family room?*
~~~

He quickly walked back to the formal living room where he'd walked in. Anthony wanted to walk down the hall off the right side of the room but with a glance down it, he saw the doors were all too close together for him to be able to find a restroom or explore Kay's bedroom without being caught. *Dude, get it together! I can't be thinking about Kay's bedroom because it's obvious I'm not going to get to spend any time in it this weekend!*

Anthony needed to keep himself in check, so he didn't push for too much too soon from Kay. Even the brief thought of her bedroom being just a few feet down that hall was sending all the blood from his brain to his cock at the thought of what he could do to her in there if they were only alone. Anthony had to find a way to stop himself from thinking about sex with Kay quickly, or he was going to be really embarrassed when her dad walked back in the house, or if he got to meet her daughters.

To make himself focus on something less sexual, he made his way over to the wall of family portraits on the wall between the hallway and the sofa. There were a bunch of larger photographs of little girls that looked like school pictures. Anthony didn't know if they were all of Kay's daughters or if they were possibly her nieces, too. There were some of Kay and Randi and a guy Anthony assumed must be the brother Kay told him about as well. There was a picture of Kay's parents right in the middle, but it looked like it was from a portrait studio.

Not a single picture that was on the wall looked to be a spontaneous moment. They were all extremely formal and it reminded Anthony that Kay lived by a strict schedule and set boundaries that he was going to have to respect, or he wouldn't have any chance at getting farther in their relationship the way he wanted. *Damn, I hope we can find a happy medium between her strict schedule and my traveling chaos!*

Anthony moved over and sat on the couch and glanced out the window at Kay's ex-husband getting in a taxi. That sight brought back some of his anger from earlier. He struggled to maintain his composure while turning away from the window, hoping to find something else to focus on to help him calm down.

When he'd stepped on Kay's porch and heard the commotion with her ex, he didn't stop to think before he ran through the door. Seeing

Mark, the jackass, with his fist raised about to hit his precious Kay brought out a primal, animalistic part of Anthony that he hadn't even known he possessed. He saw red, and it took every ounce of self-control he had to keep calm. Anthony really wanted to grab the jackass by the throat and choke him out.

Never before had he ever had a violent thought like that, but his need to protect Kay was so strong it caused him to have vicious thoughts about anyone who would hurt her. He normally tended to follow his mother's motto to "kill them with kindness" whenever he had a disagreement with anyone.

Thinking about the possibility of either of his sisters dating someone like Kay's ex-husband made him decide to teach them some self-defense moves the next time he went home to the small town of Heart's Destiny, Texas. He wondered if he should teach Kay and her daughters some self-defense techniques as well before he had to leave for work on Tuesday. His whole body shuddered at the thought of having to leave them defenseless, so he could report to work.

"You're not Grandpa Lee!" squealed the younger, platinum blonde little girl who just ran into the living room. *Maria,* he thought with a smile.

"Maria, run back to the bedroom!" shouted the older, darker blonde little girl who had also run in. *Tia.* Anthony felt his heart growing in his chest to accommodate the love he already felt for Kay's daughters. "Mom, bring Louie, someone broke in the house!" Tia grabbed the biggest dictionary Anthony had ever seen from the coffee table and held it over her head like she was going to hit him with it.

Anthony raised his hands in surrender to her just as Kay and Maria came back out of the hallway and Kay's dad came back in the front door.

Kay's dad started laughing and walked over to Tia to take the book from her hands. "Alright, Tia the Terminator, remember what I taught you about when it's okay to hit someone and when it's not?"

She looked up at her grandfather and bobbed her head in the affirmative.

"Just because we haven't been introduced to this man, doesn't mean he actually broke into the house. You've got to step back and get all the facts before you decide if it's better to fight back or run away." Kay's dad set the dictionary down on the coffee table and turned toward Anthony. "Since I came in and saw you protecting my daughter, I'm assuming you didn't break in, but I would like to know who you are and what you're doing at my daughter's home."

Anthony stood and extended his hand to the man in a police uniform. While Kay's father was a good four or five inches shorter than Anthony, the gun on his hip and badge on his chest garnered a lot of respect. "I'm Anthony Burleson, sir. I met Kay and Randi last weekend and I'm here because Kay and I were going to dinner tonight." They shook hands while Anthony continued speaking. "While I don't think I was breaking in, I did walk in without being invited in because the door was open, and I saw…" His voice trailed off as he tried to choose the right words. He cleared his throat and started over. "I saw a situation that I wasn't going to let happen."

"Nice to meet you, Anthony." Kay's dad released Anthony's hand from his strong grip. "I'm Charles Lee, Kay's Dad, and the Sheriff for Tulsa County. I appreciate you stepping in to stop that, um, situation."

"You stopped Dad from hurting Mom?" Tia gave him a questioning look as she stepped up to Anthony. "I was going to come back and help her, but I had to calm Maria down and grab Louie, my Louisville Slugger baseball bat, first."

"Tia, we already talked about this," Kay started, but didn't get to finish her thought as Maria tore out of her arms and ran to hug Anthony's waist.

"Thank you for saving us!" Maria screamed into his belly button. "We saw him push Mom and I was so scared he was going to start hitting her and then come hit us since Tia wasn't going to stay in the bedroom with the door locked. You're my hero!!!"

Anthony reached down and put his hand on the back of Maria's head and rubbed his thumb over her baby soft hair. Anthony's heart broke at the thought of Kay or her daughters ever being afraid. He knew at that moment that he would do anything to protect all three of them, so they never had to be fearful of anything ever again.

"Oh, Sweetie, you don't have to worry about that anymore. I won't let anyone hurt you or your mom or your sister ever again." Anthony meant that as a solemn promise. He gently pulled her arms from around his waist and squatted down to get closer to her eye level. "You must be Maria. Your Mom told me you like to play games. Do you like to play mini-golf?"

"I don't know," Maria whispered, shyly looking up at Anthony. "I've never played mini-golf."

"How about you, Tia? Do you like to play mini-golf?" Anthony turned his head to the older child, who he realized then was the same height as Kay.

"It's okay. But the only time I went to the fun park was for a friend's birthday party and I enjoyed the batting cages more than mini-golf."

Anthony chuckled and smiled at Tia. "I should have known that since you named your baseball bat, huh?"

Tia looked back at him with an expression that appeared to say *"Duh,"* and he couldn't help but chuckle again.

Anthony looked over to Kay and asked hopefully, "Well, Kay, since I messed up and only made restaurant reservations for two, how about we scrap our dinner plans and take the girls to the fun park for some pizza, mini-golf, and batting practice instead? Maybe some arcade games, too?"

"Oh," Kay replied, looking a little unsure of what she should say. "I assumed we'd just reschedule for another time when I could get a sitter."

"We can do that if you want." Anthony smiled at her before standing back up from his crouched position and turning to look at Charles. "Mr. Lee, do you think they will be safe here alone?"

Anthony hoped he wasn't the only one who was worried that Mark would come back as soon as Kay was alone with her daughters. He wanted to honor Kay's wishes if she wasn't ready for him to spend time with her girls, but he could only leave to do that if he knew her father would be able to keep them safe.

"I honestly don't know what to expect Mark to do anymore." Charles ran his hand through his salt and pepper hair in frustration. "I can have a patrol come by a few times overnight, but I need a formal order of protection to assign a protective detail full time."

Anthony didn't think that sounded like enough to protect them. He couldn't, in good conscience, leave them alone without a full protective detail. If he left them now, he would spend the entire time he was away from them worried sick.

"Kay, I know you wanted to get to know me better before you decided to let me meet your daughters, so I understand if you want me to leave and reschedule." Anthony turned to look at Kay. He took a step toward her and reached out to take her hands in both of his. "I also already told you how I feel and where I see our relationship going, so I really hope you'll let me skip some of the going slow and getting to know each other dates, and let me take ya'll out for a fun evening, so I can make sure you're all safe. I haven't checked in at my hotel yet, so I can crash on your couch and protect you until your dad can get a protective detail set up."

"I, I, I don't know," Kay stuttered, looking up at him with uncertainty in her eyes.

"Anthony, I appreciate you wanting to help my daughter and granddaughters, but I don't know how comfortable I feel with you wanting to stay overnight with them." Charles moved to try and get between him and Kay. "We know nothing about you."

Anthony pulled his wallet out of his back pocket and removed his driver's license and social security card. He handed them to Charles. "Here, sir, I know you can do a background check through your job, so check me out. I'm not perfect, but I'm a decent guy. If you need the word of a fellow law enforcement officer, you can call the police department in Heart's Destiny, Texas, where I grew up. My oldest brother, Bobby Burleson, is the Chief there, but everyone in the whole department knows me. They can tell you anything you'd ever want to know about me."

Charles looked up at Anthony skeptically, so Anthony figured he needed to put all his cards on the table to earn Charles's trust. "I fell in love with your daughter the instant I looked into her eyes last weekend. I plan to come ask you for permission to marry her one day. It may take me a while to win her over, but I promise you, my intentions are honorable." There was no way Anthony was going to mention any of the dirty things he intended to do with Kay to her father, though. "I will do whatever I have to do to keep them safe and make your daughter happy."

"Love at first sight, huh?" Charles looked questioningly at Anthony as he took the cards. He inhaled deeply and Anthony saw the slightest upturn of the corners of his mouth as he blew out the breath. "I remember the first time I saw Kay and her momma and felt something similar myself," Charles confided, his voice barely above a whisper. "Alright, I'll check you out and see what I find. Give me a few minutes." He then walked outside to his patrol car to get as much information on Anthony as he could.

"Can we have spinach and pineapple on our pizza?" Tia tugged on Anthony's shirt sleeve.

"Spinach and pineapple?" Anthony made a face down at the precocious little girl. "Is that your favorite or are you just trying to gross me out?"

"See, Tia, it is gross!" Maria shouted.

"It's not gross!" Tia rolled her eyes at her sister. "It's good!"

"She's always trying to eat weird stuff to gross me out." Maria grabbed Anthony's hand. Her hand was so small that she could only wrap her digits around his first two fingers. The sight of her little hand clinging to his gave Anthony a sense of awe at how quickly she seemed to trust him. "She dips her fries or chips in ice cream, too, and it's really gross."

"That's not gross. That's just me trying to decide if I want something salty or something sweet," Tia shrugged. "I quit trying to gross you out when Mom made me eat the pizza with anchovies and I puked."

"EEWWW!" Anthony exclaimed while making a sick face at Tia. "I'll try your spinach and pineapple as long as you promise to make sure Mom doesn't make me eat anchovies."

Both girls burst out laughing.

"I guess I've been outvoted." Kay smiled at her daughters before looking up at Anthony. "But there's no pizza at the fun park, so we might want to stop at a pizza place before going there."

Charles came back in and handed Anthony's identification back. "Alright, you came back clean, so I guess I won't make you leave my daughter and granddaughters alone. But if you even think about sleeping anywhere but the couch before you put a ring on her finger, I'll rescind my permission to stay and protect them."

"Dad!" Kay shouted. "I'm almost thirty-three years old…"

Her words were cut off by Charles saying, "And you'll always be my baby girl, so I'll always want to protect you." Charles hugged Kay and smiled down at her. "Just be glad I didn't pull my gun like I did on some of those boys who thought they wanted to date you in high school."

Kay started to laugh, but Anthony wasn't sure Charles was joking. Anthony was just grateful that Charles didn't feel the need to pull that gun off his hip.

"Kay, I'm going to have a patrol take a few extra trips by here to keep an eye out in case Mark decides to come back here tonight. If you end up getting a sitter to be able to go on your date, I need to know where the girls will be, so I can have some extra patrols there, too, to make sure Mark can't get to them. I'm having his car towed to the impound lot, so he won't have a legitimate reason to come back here. But I don't trust him not to try to pick up the girls for his weekend before Matt can get something drawn up and to a judge to change the visitation."

"Thanks, Dad." Kay hugged her father. "Matt was already working on the petition but won't be able to file it until Monday. I have to call and tell him about this evening, so he can add an order of protection to the paperwork." She looked up at her father with a hopeful expression. "But if he shows up tomorrow and he's sober, can your guys keep him from taking the girls?"

"Until you get a judge to sign off on something saying he no longer has visitation rights, you know they can't keep him from taking them unless there are extenuating circumstances, like him drinking or verbally threatening them. But you also know that when my guys find out he pushed you, they won't let him make it to your door to even knock, much less find out if the girls are here and take them." Charles flushed lightly as he spoke. Anthony wondered if it was in anger or embarrassment that he couldn't guarantee Mark wouldn't get near them.

What happens if the Jackass comes by between the extra patrols when the deputies are on the other side of the county? Anthony could protect them all weekend but wanted to know they would still be safe when he had to leave on Tuesday. If they weren't going to be safe when he had to go back to work, then he desperately felt he needed to convince Kay to come with him so he could keep them all safe.

"Would it help if they weren't here where he could find them for a few days?" Anthony straightened up to his full height and was now being flanked by Kay's daughters. "I just flew in today for our date but am scheduled to fly out Tuesday to meet up with my crew in

Dallas. They can come with me and stay out of town for as long as it takes for your attorney to get the legal stuff done."

"What crew? What do you do in Dallas?" Charles glared at Anthony.

Before Anthony could answer, Kay interjected. "That won't be necessary. Matt can file everything Monday morning."

"He can file it Monday morning, but that doesn't mean the judge will sign off on it then." Anthony took Kay's hands in his again. "It's more likely that he'll set a date for a hearing to allow Mark to respond before making a decision. That can take a while. And I don't feel comfortable leaving you and your daughters without twenty-four-seven protection."

Kay closed her eyes and it looked like she was fighting to keep from crying. Anthony couldn't handle seeing her struggle with using such a great effort to be strong. He didn't care that her father or daughters were watching. He had to pull Kay into his arms to show her that she could lean on him to take care of her, so she didn't have to struggle anymore.

Kay's arms went around his waist, and he reveled in how tight she clung to him. As he held her close, he looked over her head at Charles. He hoped the older man could see just how much he cared for Kay.

"I'm a pilot for the Galactic Wrestling Association," Anthony explained to Charles. "My flight Tuesday will be commercial, just to meet up with the crew in Dallas. They have a show in Dallas Tuesday night. Wednesday through Sunday, I'll be flying the company plane to a different city in Texas each day. Then I'm off Monday through Friday. Well, I just have to fly to whatever city they are in on Friday to start my five-day rotation flying the company plane again on Saturday."

Kay loosened her grip on Anthony and lifted her head off his chest. He noticed that while her eyes were now dry, there were some wet spots on his shirt. He gave her a small smile before continuing.

"I have family all over South Texas, so we can hang out down there on my days off if we need to be gone that long. The company plane is actually a converted airliner that now only holds a hundred-and-twenty passengers because they pulled out all the cramped commercial seats and replaced them with the largest first-class pods they could find.

Since there are only about fifty people who work for the company and travel to every show on the plane, a lot of the guys bring their families along. I can change my Tuesday flight to tomorrow and get tickets for all four of us if you want to get out of town until you have to come back for the hearing."

"You don't seriously think I'm going to let my daughter and granddaughters fly off with a bunch of wrestlers indefinitely?" Charles barked.

Kay inhaled a sharp breath and pulled out of Anthony's arms to turn to her father. Anthony prayed that was so she could tell her dad that she didn't need his permission.

~ ~ ~

Anthony, Kay thought with a sigh, drawing strength from him as he held her close. Anthony had shown her that the butterflies and goosebumps were real. She felt them every time they were in the same room. She also felt them when he called, or her phone beeped that she had a text from him. The butterflies were like her internal Anthony Alert.

His arms around her now made her feel safe and protected. She knew that if she let him, he would be by her side every minute of every day. Anthony would never let anyone hurt her if he had any way of preventing it. Kay knew from their Skype sessions, phone calls, and text conversations that he was a man of honor and outstanding character. Kay really wished she could continue to just lean on him and let him protect her and the girls from Mark's escalating temper.

That's not going to teach the girls to be strong and independent, though, Kay's inner voice that sounded a lot like her dad told her.

But I want to run away with him, she mentally told her inner Dad voice.

"You don't seriously think I'm going to let my daughter and granddaughters fly off with a bunch of wrestlers indefinitely?" Charles growled in his deepest, gravelly, indignant voice.

Crap, now I have to try to keep Dad from trying to protect me from the wrong man, Kay thought as she reluctantly pulled out of Anthony's embrace. She turned to her father, but she wasn't sure what to say to him. Then she realized that as much as she would love to run away with Anthony, she couldn't even if her dad weren't objecting.

"We can't do that." Kay turned back to Anthony. She looked up into his dark chocolate-colored eyes and spoke with regret. "The girls can't miss that much school and I can't miss that much work."

"Whoa!" Anthony held his hands up like a stop sign for Charles and Kay's arguments. "I'm not talking indefinitely or as a permanent solution. I just hoped a week or two of vacation would keep ya'll safe until the hearing."

Anthony reached out and took Kay's hands in his. It was in no way a sexual touch, but the instant their fingers entwined, Kay felt a jolt of electricity shoot through her from her hands, up her arms, through her heart, all the way to her most womanly body parts. In his eyes, Kay saw longing, a look of need and love.

"Do you not get any vacation time, Kay? Or can you maybe call in sick for a few days?" Anthony questioned beseechingly. "From what you've told me about your daughters, I'm sure they are both smart enough to make up any work they might miss if they're out of school for a week. Plus, there are a couple of tutors who travel with us for the guys with families, so if they already have any assignments, we can make sure they complete them while we're traveling."

Kay released the breath she hadn't realized she'd been holding. Anthony wasn't just suggesting that they go away with him spontaneously as a way to take over her life and make her dependent on him. Kay could see in his expression that he'd truly thought through the options. He not only saw what he thought was the best one, but he also saw her thoughts and concerns to make sure he could address them before he suggested the best option. As he stood there looking into her eyes, it was like he was really seeing her, like he could see deep inside her soul.

Anthony turned his head to look at Charles while still holding Kay's hands. "Charles, just as I'm sure your deputies would step up to protect them if Mark showed up drunk or trying to hurt them, I'm positive that anyone I work with would do the same. The only difference in how Kay, Tia, and Maria would be treated and respected, would be that my crew wouldn't be legally bound to enforce the current visitation order."

Kay felt her face drain of all color and she looked up at her dad in fear. "If Mark showed up sober with the current court order, would your guys have to enforce it?" Kay hated the tremble she heard in her voice. "Would they legally have to make the girls go with him?"

As Charles looked down at his granddaughters, who were so distraught they were shaking, Kay could see from his expression that he hated having to answer honestly. "Technically, yes, they are legally obligated to enforce the current court order," Charles bit out. "But," he stammered as he squared his shoulders, "knowing that Mark is so short-tempered, none of the deputies I'd assign to watch the house would do it."

"But Grandpa, what if Dad brings a city cop who doesn't work for you with him? Will we have to go with him?" Tia reached out and grabbed Anthony's wrist to pull his hand from Kay's. Once it was free, Tia placed her palm on Anthony's and laced her fingers with his. Kay could see that Tia was scared, but she knew she could trust Anthony to keep her safe. Tia was so afraid, she squeezed his hand so tight that her knuckles turned white, and her nailbeds turned bright pink.

Charles paled as he looked at Tia and nodded his head.

Tia grabbed Kay's free hand with her other hand and squeezed with a death grip. Her little voice trembled as she spoke, "If so, then I'd rather go with Anthony. He didn't let Dad hit Mom, so I know he won't let him hit Maria or I either. And maybe his wrestler friends can teach us some self-defense stuff, too."

Kay took a deep breath and looked up at Anthony. "I guess I should listen to the smartest person in the room, huh? Will it really be okay with your job for us to travel with you for a few days?"

"Yeah, they won't have a problem with it." Anthony smiled reassuringly. "And since I'm going to have to rearrange my flight to add three more seats, how about I change it to tomorrow instead of Tuesday, so there's no chance of him coming by before we're able to leave?"

"Um, maybe," Kay started to agree, but then realized that she needed to make sure this wouldn't be a problem with the court before she could take off with Anthony. "Dad, can you give me Matt's home number, so I can call him to make sure this won't complicate things with the court? He said something the other day about if I don't follow the current court order, it can cause some complications we don't want, so I need to make sure he is at least prepared for the fallout."

Charles pulled out his cell phone and placed the call. "Hey Matt," he barked into the phone. "We have a situation."

Instead of handing Kay the phone, he walked outside with it, so she couldn't hear his conversation with her attorney. Kay was sure it was because the girls were in the room and he didn't want them to hear him if he lost his temper while explaining what had happened to Matt, but Kay really needed to be a part of that conversation.

"Okay, girls, go get your jackets and anything you need to go to dinner and the fun park while I go out and talk to Matt." Kay directed the girls before turning to Anthony. "I'll be right back and then we can go eat and figure everything else out."

As the girls rushed back down the hall to their rooms, Kay hurried out the front door to find her dad leaning on the porch rail with a white-knuckled grip on it. He was red-faced and obviously fuming from what he'd already told Matt. His frustration was amped up by whatever Matt was saying while Charles was standing there listening.

"Can you at least put him on speaker, so I can hear what he has to say?" Kay walked up beside her father and put a hand on his forearm.

Charles didn't look like he wanted to, but he pulled the phone from his ear and pushed the speaker button.

"I'm not sure going to River's End will work," Matt's voice boomed through the phone. "It's too close. Mark will probably try to find them tomorrow and if he can't find them at home or your house, then the next place he'll look will be the cabin in River's End."

Dad was suggesting I go to River's End instead of going with Anthony?

"But I have connections in River's End. It's an old-fashioned community that protects women and children. I know the sheriff there will keep Mark out of the county if he goes after them." Charles sounded adamant as he spoke to Matt.

"You may think the sheriff will do what you want, but it's still in the state of Oklahoma, and it'll put him in a bad position with his job if Mark takes the right paperwork to the sheriff's department there. He'll have to enforce the current court order," Matt sighed. "Besides, if we try to use her moving to River's End as a reason to sever his parental rights and stop visitation, I don't think we'll be able to get a judge to agree. Since it's only a couple hours away, the judge will probably make it where Kay has to meet Mark halfway to lessen the burden of the drive for each parent while dropping off and picking up for the visits."

Crap, Dad's really worried about what Mark is going to do if he's thinking of having us move to his vacation cabin long-term!

"So, what can I do to protect my daughter and granddaughters?" Charles's normally rumbling voice sounded deflated.

"I think the idea to go out of state is a good one. That way they're far enough away that Mark can't follow them. But she has to have a reason to take them out of state or it will just look like she's running away with them. If the judge thinks she's running with them, it could cause her to lose custody altogether because he may see it as her kidnapping them."

CRAP! I can't lose custody of my babies!

"Does a job interview qualify as a good enough reason?" Kay was surprised to hear Anthony's voice coming from behind her.

Charles and Kay both turned to look at him where he was standing just outside the door. Kay didn't realize he'd followed her out. She hadn't expected him to when she told him she would be right back in, but if he had a valid reason for her to take the girls out of state and away from Mark, she didn't care that he was overstepping the boundaries she'd set.

"Who's that? And what job interview?" Matt asked through the phone.

"I'm Anthony and I have a couple of options for companies that Kay can interview with down in Texas this week. Would interviewing for a better paying job be a valid reason for Kay to leave the state and take her daughters with her?" Anthony walked across the porch and took Kay's free hand in his.

What on earth could he possibly think I'm qualified to interview for in Texas?

"I suppose, depending on how much better the pay is." Matt sounded contemplative. "And if she actually gets a job that she has to move out of state for, it would be another reason for the judge to sever Mark's visitation rights, even if he isn't willing to go as far as to issue an order of protection."

"Well, the one job I know about pays about fifty thousand a year, but I'm not sure of the salary for the other job."

"Fifty thousand a year," Kay whispered in awe, worried she would never be qualified to get a job that paid that well. "That's more than twice what I make now."

Kay looked up at her dad but couldn't read the expression on his face. It looked like he was only partially relieved that they may have found a way she could get the girls safely away from Mark, but the rest of him was a mixture of mad at the whole situation, and sad or disappointed for some reason. His expression didn't make sense to Kay, but she didn't have time to figure it out right then.

She had a decision to make, and she needed to make it immediately. She didn't have time to second guess her qualifications for the jobs Anthony mentioned or to feel guilty for not being strong enough to stand her ground at home and be the independent woman her parents kept pushing her to be. Keeping her daughters safe from Mark's excessive temper was her number one priority. Their safety was more important than Kay appearing to be strong and independent. Maybe she wouldn't feel too guilty for leaning on Anthony and letting him be her shining knight if she could show that she was still somewhat independent by getting one of the jobs he mentioned.

"Okay, Matt, file the papers on Monday to sever Mark's visitation and request an order of protection." Kay squeezed both Anthony's hand and her dad's forearm. "I'll have my cell phone, so you can call me as soon as you have a court date set to let me know when I need to be there."

"So *we* can be there," Tia demanded as she and Maria ran out the door. "I have a lot to tell the judge."

"Tia," Kay started to tell her daughter that she didn't think she should go to court but was interrupted by Matt.

"Excellent! I think having the girls and anyone else who witnessed Mark's behavior tonight testify on your behalf will be exactly what you need to win this. I'll get a list from you, Charles, of full names, addresses, etc. to put on the witness stand. Bring it to church Sunday. Now, go, get on the first plane out of Tulsa and I'll call you soon."

"I'm not sure I'm really comfortable with this, but since Matt thinks he can spin it to the judge to make your case stronger, I'll go along with it for now." Charles hung up his phone and put it back in his pocket. He turned and pointed at Anthony before saying, "You'd better keep my girls safe."

"I will, sir," Anthony replied, reaching out to take Charles's hand to shake it. "I promise." It appeared that Anthony wanted to say something more but when he didn't, Kay wondered what it was and why he didn't say it.

"We're ready to go to the fun park." Maria grabbed the first two fingers on Anthony's free hand.

"After we go to Mazzio's first," Tia added as she ducked under Anthony and Kay's clasped hands, putting an arm around each of them with their joined hands behind her back like she was getting a double hug. "We have to eat first to fuel the exercise at the fun park."

Chapter Six

Anthony took a few minutes on his phone to book their flight to Dallas the next morning while Kay called her boss to tell him that she was going to need to take some time off for a family emergency. The way she cringed while talking to her boss made him wonder if she was going to have a job when she got back to Tulsa from their impromptu vacation.

Anthony was ninety-nine percent sure Rick would hire her for the flight-attendant position he mentioned the day before as soon as he met her on Tuesday, so he wasn't too worried about the possibility of Kay losing her job. If Kay decided not to take the flight-attendant job, he could still get her a position at Burleson Incorporated, and move them all to the family ranch to keep them safely out of her ex's reach.

Anthony hoped he wasn't coming on too strong and overwhelming her by having a plan in place to have her with him twenty-four-seven, but when he heard the attorney say that she had to have a reason to leave town with her daughters or it would appear as if she were running away with them like a kidnapper, he couldn't stop the words coming out of his mouth.

He didn't consciously plan it to make her have to be with him. It just seemed like the hands of fate had put all the pieces into place for them to be together all the time to protect her and the girls and for her to still feel independent with a good-paying job. It was a win-win he just couldn't stop himself from suggesting. *I really hope she doesn't think I'm trying to take over her life.*

As soon as Kay got off the phone, she went to her bedroom to get a jacket, so they could leave. Anthony finished booking four first-class tickets for the first morning flight and pocketed his phone. As soon

Kay came back out, he walked them all out to the SUV he rented when he landed in Tulsa. He opened the doors for Kay and her daughters and was tempted to pick them all up and help them in the tall vehicle.

Tia jumped in before he could help her, but Kay did at least take his hand to allow him to help her step up into the front passenger seat. As soon as he shut her door, he stopped Maria from trying to jump like Tia by putting a hand on her shoulder.

"Let me give you a boost," Anthony suggested when she looked up at him. He moved behind her and placed his hands on her tiny waist. "Jump on three. One. Two. Three!"

Anthony had to laugh as she jumped, and he felt her full weight in his hands before she got a couple of inches off the ground. He was happy to put her all the way up in the vehicle, where she landed on the floorboard with both feet planted. She had the biggest smile on her face when she turned to sit in the seat.

After closing the back-passenger door, Anthony walked around behind the vehicle to get in the driver's seat. "Now, you'll have to give me directions to Mazzio's." Anthony looked in the rearview mirror at Tia. "Since you picked the restaurant, I'm sure you know how to get there."

Anthony wasn't surprised that Tia was able to give him turn-by-turn directions to the restaurant, even though she wasn't nearly old enough to drive. He could tell by looking at her that she was observant of her surroundings and her intelligence carried over from traditional learning environments to learning everything she could about anywhere she went or the people she met.

During the drive, Tia gave them a detailed explanation of how pizza was the perfect food to eat because it had something from all the food groups, and even how the various components of pizza would be utilized as fuel for the activities they would be doing at the fun park. Anthony was completely lost when she started talking about glycolysis and the Krebs' cycle, but he was thrilled when she said they needed to make sure they got a thick crust, so they had plenty of carbohydrates to fuel their fast-twitch muscle fibers. Anthony didn't have to understand it to know he liked being told to eat more carbs.

Anthony noticed Kay was awfully quiet as they drove, and she was fidgeting with her hands in her lap. He was sure it was because she was stressed about what all had happened that night. Anthony wanted to help her calm down and take her mind off the scene with her ex, but he wasn't sure what he could do to get her to let him carry part of that burden for her.

So, he did the only thing he could think of to do and reached over and grasped one of her hands in his, leaving them both resting on her thigh. Even if he couldn't completely fix the situation immediately, he could offer her comfort and reassure her that he was there for her.

When Tia finally came to the end of her nutrition and physiology lesson to take a breath, Anthony inquired, "Are you planning on being a nutritionist when you grow up, Tia?"

She certainly knew a lot about nutrition and how food fueled the body, so he presumed it would be an ideal career for her to use that knowledge. She apparently didn't agree with him, though, based on the face she made in the rearview mirror.

"No," she replied and leaned up so she could see him in the mirror too. "I'm going to be a lawyer and represent kids in divorce cases."

Well, that's not the answer I expected. Anthony smiled at her. *I'm going to enjoy you keeping me on my toes as you get older, Tia.*

"I didn't know kids could have their own lawyer to represent them in a divorce." Anthony wondered how she was planning on getting that to happen.

It was fascinating how her eyes lit up as she got started on her next monologue. Her eyes were more of a blue-green than Kay's bright blue and Anthony swore they looked like they went greener as she started talking.

"Well, right now, kids don't get their own lawyer, but I think they need one. So, after I finish college and law school, I'm going to petition our state lawmakers to change the law to make the parents split the cost of a third attorney to be involved in the court proceedings to represent what the kids want. By having the parents split the cost evenly, neither one of them can have any extra influence on the kid's attorney, so even though I won't be the only attorney representing kids, I'll know that the other lawyers won't be biased either. I'm also going to take some extra classes in school on psychology and social work and maybe some early childhood education, so I can most effectively communicate with my clients. The children of divorced parents need to have someone they can talk to and who will be there for them when they don't feel comfortable talking to their parents because they don't want to have to choose between their mom and dad, or if their mom or dad tries to make it a competition between the parents with the kids stuck in the middle. Kids need someone who can fix things in court when they need to talk to the judge, so that one parent doesn't get to hurt them, or their other parent, and make the kids feel like it's their fault. I know Maria and I didn't do anything wrong to make our dad be a jerk, and neither did Mom, but I don't think anyone told the judge that when they went to court. I know Mom is trying to get her lawyer to fix it, but he's also trying to make sure everything is divided evenly between Mom and Dad. And that's not what I want. I don't want to be divided in half like a bank account. I want to live with Mom and not see the jerk again, and I should be able to tell the judge that. Then when Mom gets married again, I want to change my last name, so I don't have to even have that jerk's name associated with mine anymore. I really hope Mom gets married again before I grow up and have to get married myself to change my last name."

"Yeah, what Tia said," Maria added while Tia paused to take a breath.

Anthony was stunned speechless. He glanced over at Kay and saw that she seemed to be in the same state as he was. Luckily, he was turning into the parking lot of Mazzio's Pizza and didn't have to respond to Tia's speech because she changed the subject in an instant.

"What size pizza are we getting? Since Mom doesn't like spinach and pineapple, should we get two smaller pizzas and get different toppings on them instead of one large?"

"That sounds like a great idea." Kay finally seemed to be coming out of the trancelike state she'd been in on the drive. "I think I'd rather have chicken and tomatoes."

"Then you won't have any veggies, Mom," Tia pointed out as they started to unbuckle their seatbelts. "You know how important veggies are, so maybe add some onions. I know you like them."

Anthony had to rush to get out and open their doors, so he could help Kay and Maria down from the tall SUV before they opened their own doors. He was definitely going to have to up his treadmill training to get fast enough to perform his gentlemanly duties with these ladies.

Tia was too much of a tomboy to let him hold her hand while she jumped down, but he was cool with her not letting him be the gentleman his mom raised him to be when she took his hand to walk across the parking lot instead.

"Okay, I'll add some veggies if you add some meat to your pizza," Kay replied as they were walking in the door. "I know you get protein from the cheese and gluten, but you're still missing a food group if you don't add meat."

"We can add chicken to mine too," Tia shrugged. "I think it will go better with spinach and pineapple than pepperoni or ground beef."

"What about Canadian bacon?" Anthony looked down at Tia beside him. "I think ham goes better with pineapple than any other meat."

"Hmm," Tia tilted her head like she was thinking really hard about whether or not she was willing to try Canadian bacon. "I never thought about Canadian bacon being ham, but since I like the way Grandma Lee puts pineapple on her Easter ham, I bet I'd like Canadian bacon on my spinach and pineapple pizza. Let's try it."

"I'll eat your chicken and tomatoes, Mom." Maria rolled her eyes as Anthony opened the door for the ladies to all go in ahead of him. "But let's pick a different vegetable because I don't like onions."

The face she made as she said her last sentence was adorable in how she was trying to feign disgust.

"Okay, how about olives and mushrooms?" Kay asked her as they got to the hostess station to be seated.

"Technically, olives are still a fruit and mushrooms are fungi," Tia pointed out. "But I suppose we can pretend mushrooms are vegetables just like we sometimes do with savory fruits."

"Mushrooms taste like dirt." Maria scrunched up her nose, making another adorable face.

Anthony stopped himself from laughing but had to agree with her. *Yuck!* "Actually, my brothers and I decided they taste like dirty gym shoes." Maria looked up at him with a confused look on her face. "When I was about your age, the three of them held me down and made me do a taste test to verify it." Anthony shuddered to show his disgust.

"You have mean brothers." Maria tried to make a mean face, but she couldn't hold it without smiling. Anthony was unsure what that smile meant, but it looked a lot like the smile Kay gave him the previous weekend when she told him that he could ride with her and then laughed at him trying to get in her tiny car.

As they walked to their table, Anthony got the same feeling of everyone in the restaurant watching them that he'd gotten the other night when he and Kay went to the diner for breakfast. What he originally thought was because of their obvious size imbalance making him look like a sideshow freak, turned out to be more of a curiosity about him because he was a stranger to all the people who apparently knew Kay, Tia, and Maria quite well. They said "Hi" to at least a half a dozen people before they made it to the table, which was only halfway through the restaurant.

It was kind of strange to him that this small section of such a large city felt like how everyone knew everyone else in his small hometown. Heart's Destiny, Texas was doing good to maintain a population of about fifteen hundred people, so while he didn't personally know all of them, being a member of one of the founding families meant everyone knew him when he was there.

He'd been spoiled the last few years of being in the Navy, and then traveling so much with the GWA, that he was more used to being in big cities or more populated areas, where he blended into the background and didn't really feel like all eyes were on him when he entered a room like they were in Heart's Destiny. But it seemed that anywhere he went with Kay, they were the center of attention.

Anthony wasn't sure how comfortable he was with that. On the one hand, he didn't think Kay or her daughters were so outgoing that they were intentionally drawing attention to them. But on the other hand, he didn't think they were so fragile that the whole town had to act like they needed to protect them from him. Maybe after a few outings, her friends and family would get used to seeing him with them and he wouldn't feel so self-conscious every time they went anywhere together.

When they were finally seated, the conversation was fun. Kay decided on just adding olives to her chicken and tomato pizza, even though they were technically a fruit, since nobody wanted to eat sweaty gym shoes. Mostly the girls talked about all their friends from school and tried to decide what they wanted to dress up as for Halloween. Maria wanted to be a princess, but Tia couldn't decide if she wanted to dress up or not. She'd apparently decided that she was too old to go trick-or-treating anymore and would rather stay home to pass out candy instead.

Anthony was a little sad to think that he'd already missed all the years she was excited to dress up. Of course, he would be working on Halloween, so he wouldn't get to see them dress up or trick-or-treat this year, if Kay was back in Tulsa by then. *Please let her decide to take the job as a flight attendant*, Anthony thought, hoping that meant Kay and the girls would be traveling with him and they could all dress up for the company Halloween party.

Anthony wondered if he should mention it and see if Tia was more interested in dressing up for a party than she was for trick-or-treating, but he didn't want to make Kay feel like he was pushing her too fast in their relationship. In the end, he decided that he could safely plant the seed without making it too obvious that he wanted to have them with him by keeping the focus on what he was going to do for Halloween.

"You ladies all seem to have some great ideas for costumes, maybe you can help me out with mine for this year." Anthony looked directly at Tia but watched Kay with his peripheral vision. "I have to dress up for our company Halloween party and I have no idea what I want to wear."

"You have to dress up even though you're old?" Maria looked at him like that was the craziest thing she'd ever heard.

"Hey, I'm not that old!" Anthony scoffed playfully with her. "Yeah, everyone in the company dresses up in costumes for the party backstage at the show. Some of us go to another Halloween party after the show, too, so the guys who have to wrestle that night can dress up after their matches, but the whole company participates. Last year, my best friends and I dressed up as *The Three Stooges*."

Kay burst out laughing. "Which one were you?"

"The bald one, Curly," Anthony answered, smiling at her. *Damn, I love to hear her laugh.* "It wasn't long after I got out of the Navy, so I still had the buzz cut so I didn't have much to lose by shaving my head for the costume. I did have to stuff my shirt with pillows, though. James and Dean had to wear wigs for their costumes and complained about how hot they were all night. Not that either of the twins could pull off the body type of Moe or Larry, but we had fun with it."

Leah Mae Wright

Kay laughed some more, and Anthony knew it was because she knew what James and Dean looked like, so he knew she was able to imagine them in costume along with him to get the full picture in her head.

"What's so funny, Mom?" Tia looked back and forth between Kay and Anthony, like that would somehow make the joke clearer to her.

"Well, first of all, Anthony is like a foot taller than Curly and a lot thinner, so imagining Anthony fat and bald is comical before you add in the possibility of the slapstick comedy of *The Three Stooges*," Kay told Tia. "And his best friends are not much shorter than him, but with long hair and full beards. Please tell me they at least shaved for the costume?"

"Yeah, they shaved, but they didn't actually grow the beards as a more permanent feature until after that party," Anthony replied with a grin.

"So basically, ya'll looked like *The Three Stooges* if they became bodybuilders?" Kay giggled.

Anthony pulled out his phone to bring up the pictures, so they could all see how ridiculous he'd looked. "Yep, definitely bodybuilding stooges." Kay smiled widely as she passed his phone to the girls before handing it back to him.

"Do you need a group costume again?" Anthony could see the wheels turning in Tia's head by her thoughtful expression as she asked the question.

"Not necessarily. We just did it last year because it was the first time we were all together for Halloween since high school."

"It's too bad you won't be here in Tulsa." Maria tapped her fork against her lips. "If you were here, we could do a group costume with you."

"I don't have to be in Tulsa to do a group costume with you." Anthony winked at Kay over Maria's head. "How about I dress up as a king, Mom dresses up as a queen, and the two of you both dress up as princesses? Even if we're not in the same city, we can think of each other and know that we're dressed up to go together."

"That's a perfect idea!" Maria squealed. "See, Tia, you have to dress up, even if you just dress up to pass out candy, so you can be a part of our royal court."

"I'm not a princess." Tia crossed her arms over her chest defensively.

Anthony feared that there was a reason she seemed so defensive that had something to do with the way her father had been acting lately. It broke his heart to think that maybe her father used to call her princess but had stopped, or had recently made her feel like she wasn't worthy of the endearment. Anthony wanted to bolster Tia's self-image without triggering any self-doubt that her father had obviously been filling her head with, so he tried to do that with a little humor.

"Really?" He looked at her and tilted his head like he was examining her. Then he turned to look at Kay before speaking, hoping Kay would know what he was thinking to help set up the punch line. "Isn't there a test we can give her to see if she's a princess?"

"We can put a pea under her mattress to see if she can feel it." Maria's eyes lit up with mischief. "Or have her kiss a frog."

Okay, I guess Maria set up the punchline instead of Kay, Anthony chuckled in his head. He winked at Kay, who grinned back at him, before he replied to Maria. "Do I need to go find another frog for her to kiss? She's a bit young to be kissin' frogs, though." He scratched his head like he was thinking. "Maybe we just have to believe that since your mom proved to be a princess by kissing me last weekend and turning me into a prince, then we can just assume that as the daughter of a princess, she's automatically a princess, too?"

"You weren't a frog." Tia shook her head at Anthony's playfulness, but with the smallest of smiles.

"Ribbit," he croaked out to make a frog sound. They all three started laughing. He felt like he'd just achieved the greatest accomplishment of his life in making these three ladies laugh and smile. Anthony wanted nothing more than to spend the rest of his life making them happy.

When they were finished eating, Anthony followed Tia's excellent directions from the pizzeria to the fun park. He wondered if she'd ever tried to navigate from a map or if she just remembered the turns from the times she'd ridden to the places in the past. *Maybe I should get out some of my aviation maps and teach her to read the topography for flying?*

When they walked into the fun park, they decided to play mini-golf first. The girls fussed with each other a little wanting to pick teams, but Kay put a stop to that with an exclamation of "Every man or woman for themselves!" as she took off running toward the first hole.

Anthony was glad to see that Kay was more relaxed after dinner and seemed to be letting go of some of the stress of the night. He hoped it was at least partially because he was there to carry some of her load, but he knew a lot of it was that she was destressing by playing with her daughters like she was a kid again.

"How are we deciding who goes first?" Tia looked to her mother when they caught up with Kay at the first hole.

"Ladies first." Anthony nodded toward Kay. She smiled back at him, but it was that cute little ornery smile, so he was a little worried about what she was about to say.

"Oh, no!" Kay pointed at Anthony like she didn't want to go first. "Age before beauty."

Anthony chuckled at her reference to their conversation about him looking older than her the previous weekend.

"How about we go youngest to oldest?" Maria wore that same little smile Kay just had.

Yep, they both smile like that when they're being ornery.

"Sure, we can do that." Kay grinned at Anthony, and he just shook his head at her. He couldn't help but wonder if she was going to actually do that, or if she was going to let him go last so her daughters didn't know about their age difference.

"So, what do I do?" Maria looked up at Anthony for directions. "Will you teach me, Anthony?"

"Sure," he replied. "First, put your ball on one of the dots here at the beginning of the green. Now, stand sideways and hold your club like this." Anthony stepped up to the ball as if he was going to tee off and demonstrated how to hold a golf club. When he stepped away so she could get into position, she took the same stance and had excellent form for holding the club.

"You're standing on the wrong side of the ball." Tia pointed at her sister, when she looked up from where she'd been writing all their names on the scorecard.

"No, I'm not," Maria objected and hit the ball before anyone could give her any instruction on how to putt. "This is where Anthony showed me to stand, so I'm doing it just like he does. Now, what do I do next?"

Anthony was confused because she had a great shot and he wasn't sure why Tia thought it was wrong, so he just looked to Kay hoping she could see his confusion and clear things up for him.

She chuckled and shook her head, before looking up at Anthony. "Technically, she should stand on the other side because she's right-handed," Kay told Anthony before turning to Maria. "But since you got the ball only a few inches from the hole, I'd say you should go take your next shot and put it in the hole, even if you putt left-handed."

Maria easily made her next shot and started off under par, setting the stage for a fierce competition. Tia set up to putt next and walked around looking at the green and the various obstacles in the way before going back to actually hit the ball. The look on her face was fascinating and Anthony wondered what she was actually thinking as she took her first putt and got a hole in one.

"I'm going to lose this game." Anthony shook his head, but he smiled as the girls walked back over to where he and Kay were standing.

"Not necessarily," Tia reassured him, looking up at him. "Your height is actually an advantage because you can see over the taller obstacles to be able to calculate the angles to hit the ball without having to walk around the green first."

"That's what you were doing?" Anthony was completely dumbfounded, unable to fathom how she'd come up with the formulas, much less done the math in her head as quickly as she'd walked around the green and stepped up to tee off.

"Yeah, it's all just a mix of geometry and physics," Tia shrugged as if it was no big deal. "You just have to estimate the distance the ball has to travel, how hard to hit it to get it to go that far, and what angles to hit the obstacles at to get them to help you get to the hole."

Now I know why Kay thinks she's bad at math, Anthony thought. He had no idea how to reply to that and just stood there with his jaw hanging open in amazement at Tia's genius.

"You're next." Kay poked his side, bringing him out of his astonished stupor and surprising him that she'd admitted to their age difference in front of her daughters.

"What?" It was Tia's turn to look confused, a look he doubted she had often. "I thought it was youngest to oldest, so you should go next, Mom."

"Nope," Kay smirked. "Anthony is next."

"How old are you?" Tia tilted her head at Anthony.

Anthony wasn't sure if Kay wanted him to answer that honestly or not, so he just looked at her, still in shock.

"It's rude to ask someone how old they are," Maria told her sister, saving Anthony from having to say anything immediately.

He looked between Maria and Tia before looking at Kay. *Do you really want me to tell them?* He tried to ask her with his eyes. She must have understood his unspoken question because she nodded and smiled at him.

"I think it's only rude when you ask a lady her age." Anthony looked back at the girls. "I'm twenty-five." He finally answered and saw Tia's jaw drop like his had at her explanation of doing complex math to determine how to putt.

"So, you would have been thirteen when I was born and seventeen when Maria was born." Tia seemed to be thinking things over. Anthony didn't think it was a question, so he didn't answer her, not sure where her mind was going at the moment to know what to say. He was glad he hadn't said anything when she continued speaking. "I guess that's why you didn't meet Mom soon enough to be our dad, you had to grow up first. If you and Mom get married, would you actually be able to be our dad since you're not that much older than us?"

I like the way you think, Tia! Anthony thought and gave her the biggest smile he could before answering her. "There's not an age limit on being a stepdad that I know of, so I think we'll be okay."

The smile she gave him before throwing her arms around his waist to hug him was the biggest he'd seen from her yet. While he knew Kay was skeptical and didn't want him to push their relationship along too fast, he was thrilled to know that at least Tia seemed to want him and Kay to move on a faster timetable.

Anthony hugged her back, giving her a kiss on the top of her head, because he just couldn't help himself. When he looked at Kay over Tia's head, he hoped the small smile he saw on her face was because she was thinking about moving a little faster now, too.

~~~
~~~

Kay was unsure how to feel as they played mini-golf. She was enjoying being playful with her daughters and loving how well Anthony was getting along with them.

Anthony was right when he said he was going to lose the game. Tia beat them all, with Maria coming in second by only ten strokes. Kay didn't think she or Anthony were under par on a single hole, and they tied for third with scores twice as big as Tia's.

She felt a little bad that the girls were carrying most of the conversation with Anthony, but her emotions were all over the place and she had to get them straightened out in her head before she could have any kind of a real discussion with him.

Even if she wanted to talk to him about more serious subjects than they'd covered while at the pizza place or playing at the fun park, she didn't want to discuss them in front of her daughters, so she was being more reserved and quieter than she was with Anthony the previous weekend. She hoped he didn't think she was pulling back from him, but it couldn't be helped right then.

Kay took some of the time that Anthony had the girls distracted with video games to think about how the night was going. At first, she was completely mortified that Anthony arrived for the date to find Mark being belligerent. She was embarrassed that she'd been married to him for so long. She thought for sure that Anthony would think less of her for the bad decisions she'd made in her life, especially marrying Mark.

She'd been watching for signs all night that Anthony was looking for an escape from being around her and her problems, but she hadn't seen them like she'd expected. It had been just the opposite, actually. He'd truly acted too good to be true, playing the role of her knight in shining armor, not only rescuing her before Mark could really hurt her, but also finding a way to keep the girls from having to go with Mark at all until she could get the court to sever his visitation rights.

While he hadn't kissed her other than a soft brush of his lips on the top of her head while they were playing mini-golf, or given her any longing looks like he did the previous weekend, he'd shown his affection by holding her hand as they walked between activities, and given her comfort when she needed it with one-armed hugs and little touches that she doubted anyone else had noticed all night.

It was nice to feel like he wanted to be physically connected to her, and not just with the invisible strings they both felt. Every time their eyes connected, they both smiled. It wasn't just a sexual attraction between them. Kay was beginning to feel like he was the missing piece of her soul that had felt empty her whole life. Like the gap she felt in her heart was filled now that she'd met him.

He certainly seemed to know what she needed before she did to be able to help her when she didn't know how she was going to get through the stressful parts of the night. His brain seemed to be working three steps ahead of hers, like how he had the suggestion of a job interview, when she had no idea that she needed a reason to leave town with the girls so she wouldn't look like she was kidnapping them. It reminded Kay a lot of her dad.

Kay didn't know how her dad convinced Matt to change the petition to severing Mark's visitation rights and issuing an order of protection, instead of the petition to have only supervised visitation that Matt had been suggesting all week. It must have been because of their friendship for so many years that Matt changed his tune when her dad told him what happened that night.

Although, that was definitely not the reason that Matt altered his opinion about Kay taking off on a vacation with the girls when Anthony suggested it, since they'd never met. Kay hoped it wasn't that Matt just listened to them more because they were men. She hated feeling like she had to have a man to stand up for her or her daughters in order to get anything done to keep them safe.

At the same time, she was grateful that she had the men in her life if that was what it took. She knew her dad would always do anything to take care of his children and grandchildren. After the earlier events of the night, Kay was beginning to think Anthony wanted to always be there for them, too. He was certainly doing a good job of keeping her daughters laughing and distracted from how their father was acting.

Kay shuddered at the thought of how bad things could have gone if Anthony or her dad hadn't shown up when they did. She had to shake that off and not let herself think about the what if's or she would end up causing a panic attack and she really didn't want Anthony to see her in the throes of one of those.

Kay tried to sidetrack herself by thinking of the possibilities of what the jobs Anthony mentioned could be. She also wondered where they might be in Texas. She hated the idea of moving from Tulsa, where she'd lived her whole life and was close to her family.

But maybe it wouldn't be so bad if the job she got was near where Anthony lived when he wasn't flying all over the country. If it kept her daughters safe, she could handle not knowing anyone in a new city for a few years, especially if she could see Anthony more often than the once every six weeks that they'd planned on seeing each other with her living in Tulsa and him traveling all the time for work. *I'll have to ask him later after the girls go to bed.*

After another hour taking turns in the batting cages, where Tia and Maria both decided that they liked batting left-handed like Anthony, Kay saw her youngest daughter starting to fight to keep her eyes open. It was way past their normal bedtime, so she suggested heading home so they could get some rest before their early morning flight. Kay half expected the girls to grumble but was happily surprised when it wasn't a fight to get them to leave the fun park.

Apparently, their excitement about flying to Dallas with Anthony was enough to override their normal tendency to not want to leave when they were having a good time somewhere. They were both awfully quiet on the ride home and Kay wasn't surprised that Maria was sound asleep when they got there.

Anthony's gentlemanly behavior of opening their doors all night continued with him insisting on carrying Maria in instead of letting Kay. She wasn't sure how she felt about that. Kay was sort of used to her dad doing things like that for her, but he was the only one, so she was unsure how to take it from Anthony.

Part of her thought it was just proof that he was right when he told her the previous weekend that he would treat her daughters as if they were his own, so she should trust him to be there for all of them. But there was still another part of her that was afraid that it was too much, too soon, and not possible for him to really love them like a father within a few hours of meeting them.

Mark used to carry the girls to bed after a night out, too. What if Anthony starts acting like Mark in a couple of years?

"Which bedroom do I need to put her in?" Anthony inquired as they made their way through the living room.

"Last door on the left." Kay followed him down the hall. When he laid her on the bed, Kay moved over and took off Maria's shoes and socks.

"I'll be in the living room." Anthony kissed the top of Kay's head, walked back out of the bedroom, and closed the door behind him.

Kay quickly changed Maria into a nightgown and tucked her into bed. Kay then walked across the hall to her own bedroom, hung up her jacket, and left her purse on the desk in the corner. She looked at herself in the mirror over her dresser to make sure she still looked presentable to go talk to him.

Part of her wanted to invite him to her bedroom for the night, but she wasn't completely comfortable with that, since her daughters were right across the hall. *Don't overthink it!* Kay told herself in her head as she was leaving her room. *He's already said he's going to sleep on the couch and he's only staying to make sure the girls and I are safe from Mark. Be grateful for his help in keeping the girls safe and quit thinking about how bad I need him to hold me all night, so I feel safe, too.*

Before Kay could get through the hall to the living room, Tia almost ran her over as she shot across the hall from the bathroom toward her bedroom. She'd already changed into her pajamas and only stopped her sprint from the bathroom to hug her mother.

"Goodnight, Mom." Tia quickly let go of the hug. "I've already given Anthony a pillow and blanket for the couch. I told him the one in the den is bigger and more comfortable to sleep on, but he said he's going to stay in the living room because it's between us and the front door, in case he needs to stop anyone from getting through the house to us. He's really smart when it comes to protecting people, huh?"

"Yeah, he is." Kay wondered if that was all Tia had to say. Based on the ornery smile her daughter was giving her, she worried that Tia was going to pull a prank on Anthony, like she'd done with her girlfriends when they had slumber parties. Kay started to give her a warning not to do anything like that, but she didn't get another word out because Tia started talking again.

"Um, Mom, since my room is closest to the living room, do you think you could maybe take him to the den until I go to sleep?" Tia looked down sheepishly. Kay worried about Tia being afraid of Anthony being too close to her overnight. But before she could ask why, Tia looked back up at her mother with a big grin and said, "Because I want to be able to go to sleep fast, so I can get up early for our flight, and I'm afraid hearing you guys kissing will keep me awake!"

"Goodnight, Tia." Kay ruffled her daughter's hair. "And there won't be any loud kissing to keep you awake."

"Yeah, right, Mom." Tia shook her head at Kay. "Is there not going to be kissing because he's too tall for you to kiss? You know you can stand on the organ bench to be the same height as him, so you can kiss him goodnight easier, right? I don't mean that I don't want you to kiss him. Grownups are supposed to kiss after a date. I just don't want to hear it." With that, she darted into her bedroom and shut the door.

Kay giggled as she walked into the living room to see Anthony pulling a pair of sweatpants out of his suitcase. He'd already spread the blanket Tia gave him, a pink and white checkerboard quilt Kay's mom had made for her years ago, over the end of the couch and put a pillow in a matching pink pillowcase on the other end. Since the quilt wasn't even big enough to cover a twin bed, Kay knew it wouldn't be big enough to cover Anthony on the couch.

Her little giggle at Tia turned into a full-blown belly laugh at the thought of Anthony barely being able to cover his legs and torso with the pink quilt. *Maybe I'll have to sneak out here early in the morning to see if I can get a picture of that!*

Tia obviously had a similar idea. Realizing that her daughter was not only feeling the same sense of safety with Anthony that she was, but she was also already feeling comfortable with being her normal self around him, and happier than Kay had seen her in months, made Kay decide that she didn't care if anyone else thought they were taking things too fast. *My babies need him to make their lives better just as much as I do!*

"What's so funny?" Anthony closed his suitcase and dropped the sweats and a t-shirt on top of it.

"Tia." Kay pointed over her shoulder with her thumb as she moved over to sit on the couch between the pillow and blanket. "She's punking you by making you sleep under a girly quilt that's way too small to be useful."

Anthony chuckled and sat down beside her, picking up the quilt and pulling it over his lap. "Yeah, I don't think it's going to be so cold that I really need a blanket of any kind tonight, but I'm glad she brought me something I can at least camouflage things with tomorrow morning when I first wake up." He smiled and put his arm around Kay to pull her into his side.

"Camouflage?" Kay looked up into his deep brown eyes and batted her eyelashes at him. "What do you need to camouflage?"

He leaned over to whisper in her ear. "I told you I dream about you every night, remember? Because of those dreams, I wake up every morning with massive evidence of what I've been dreaming about doing to you, so I'm hoping I can wad this blanket up and hide that until I can wake up and get it under control."

Yeah, that quilt is going to be a one-pole tent in the morning!

Kay couldn't hold back the burst of laughter at the mental image of him waking up with a boner under a pink quilt.

She was relieved that he was still thinking of sex. After the night they'd had so far, she'd been afraid that he was going to have second thoughts about wanting to get mixed up in her crazy life, and would sneak out in the middle of the night, so he didn't have to deal with her problems. Kay feared she was too much trouble to have to deal with for most guys.

She brought more baggage to a potential relationship than most people would take on a yearlong trip around the world. Not that she thought of her daughters as baggage, but loving another man's children as if they were his own had to be difficult for most men. After meeting Kay's overprotective father and violent ex-husband, Anthony had probably been overwhelmed by all of her baggage. *Who am I kidding? They didn't just show him my baggage, they opened it up and spread it all over the front lawn tonight!*

Kay's laughter stopped at that sobering thought. She laid her head on the side of Anthony's chest and let out a sigh. She wished she could control the roller coaster her emotions seemed to be on that night. She'd gone from happy and excited at the prospect of her date and taking things to the next level with Anthony, to terrified when Mark was there. From worried about having to deal with Mark if he came back later and when they finally appeared in court, to laughing and having fun playing with her daughters and Anthony at the fun park. From feeling helpless, to feeling protected and empowered. She saw all the good that Anthony was bringing into her life and the lives of her girls, but she couldn't see what good she brought to his.

Kay didn't like feeling like she was dumping all her problems on him. She wished she knew what she could do for him to bring him more joy in his life. *I hope sex will be good enough for him to want to stick around. Not that I know when we'll actually have any time alone to be able to have sex.*

"Penny for your thoughts." Anthony softly kissed the top of her head.

"I'm sorry tonight didn't go as we'd planned," Kay answered with a long sigh.

"I'm not." Anthony's hand brushed up and down over Kay's shoulder and arm.

"You're not?" Kay sat up straight and turned her head to look up into his eyes. "I can't sleep with you tonight with my girls here, and I don't know how else I can possibly repay you for everything you've done for us tonight and the flight out of town tomorrow and possibly helping me find a new job. How can you not wish that we were able to stick to our original plan of going to dinner and then coming back here to spend the night alone together?"

He shook his head at her before turning sideways on the sofa, so they were face-to-face. He then brushed a lock of hair behind her ear and kissed her forehead before speaking in a low sultry voice. "Baby, it's not a quid pro quo. Do I want to have sex with you? Yes." He lowered his voice to a whisper of a shout to say, "Hell yes!"

He grinned and winked at her before continuing. "But sex isn't my ultimate goal with you. And I definitely don't want to have sex with you as long as you think it's how you can repay me for anything I do for you. I don't wanna take advantage of the stress of tonight to get in your pants either."

Kay was confused by what he was saying. It seemed like he was contradicting himself by saying he wanted to have sex, but he also didn't want to have sex. Being this close to him and smelling his natural musk mixed with mint was clouding her brain with pheromones and making her really wish he would push for sex right then. But after his explanation, she was wondering if it would have happened even if they were alone in the house.

"My goal for us is to be together long-term, like sixty or seventy years, way past when we're even capable of having sex." He took both her hands in his and stroked the backs of them with his thumbs. "That means we need to focus on building a foundation that doesn't rely on our sexual chemistry to connect us. I want to start us off right by doing things together now, like sharing laughs, playing mini-golf with the girls, me being a friend that you can lean on when you're going through a rough time like tonight, protecting you from anyone who wants to hurt you, and providing for your emotional needs, as well as your physical ones."

He paused to bring her hands up to his lips, so he could kiss her knuckles a few times before he said anything more. "And that goes both ways, not just me doing things for you, but you also being there for me to talk to and laugh with, too. It's not going to always be fifty-fifty. Honestly, most of the time I want to carry the majority of your burdens, so you can just relax and be happy. But I know there will be times, like when I get sick, and I'm a horrible patient when I'm sick, that you'll have to carry the majority of our burdens because I'm too busy being a big baby complaining about how bad I feel. I just hope that if I can keep you happy ninety-five percent of the time, then you won't want to leave me the five percent of the time I might be sick and need you to do everything for me."

"But I don't want to be a burden to you," Kay whispered, looking down at their joined hands resting on the couch between them. "I feel guilty for needing you to take care of me and my daughters."

"Sweetheart, there's no reason to feel guilty." Anthony reached up to stroke her face gently. "You're not a burden in any way. No matter what happens between us, I would never think of you that way. I think you're a precious gift to me; one I want to cherish. Please let me."

A precious gift? Looking into his chocolate brown eyes made Kay believe he really thought of her that way. *Lord, if you're listening, please don't let Anthony break my heart because I'm afraid it might kill me if he doesn't stick around.*

He was looking at her like he was waiting for her to say something. She wasn't quite sure what to say because she wasn't ready to admit how much she really wanted him to take all her burdens and cherish her.

What exactly does cherish entail? Is that a sexual innuendo? Gaw, I've been out of the dating game too long if I don't have a clue what is or isn't a sexual innuendo!

Kay slowly lowered her eyes and tried to hold back her smile as she tried to turn this from a heavy conversation to a more flirtatious one. *Please let me not have totally forgotten how to flirt!*

"I guess." She drew the words out slowly and nibbled her bottom lip. "But I'm not really sure what I'm agreeing to let you do." She slowly looked back up at him and was thrilled at the desire she saw in Anthony's eyes. "Is there a specific way you intend to cherish me?"

His lips turned up slightly before he spoke. "Oh, Baby, I have so many ideas of ways to cherish you. But since you told Tia there won't be any kissing tonight, I'll have to wait until tomorrow to show you the first of them."

"You heard that?" Kay felt her cheeks flush.

"I don't think you were as far away from the end of the hall as you thought you were," he chuckled.

Kay lightly laughed with him. She'd been told her whole life that she talked too loudly, so she wasn't surprised that he could hear her talking with Tia.

"Besides, I kind of liked Tia's suggestion about the organ bench. She's brilliant, solving a problem I didn't realize we might have in the future." Anthony gave her a big smile.

Kay looked at him quizzically because she didn't see how being able to stand on the organ bench to kiss him goodnight at the door would solve a problem in the future. *That'll only work when we're here.*

He obviously saw her confusion because he elaborated, "I practically had to fold in half to kiss you Saturday. Her idea sounds like it will save my knees and back, but I'm a little worried that everyone will wonder why we're carrying a bench with us through the airport tomorrow, so I can keep kissing you."

"We're not carrying a bench through the airport." Kay swatted at his shoulder in a playful manner. "You'll just have to pick me up next time instead of the awkward squat fold you did Saturday."

He wagged his eyebrows at her before saying, "I like the way you think." Then he put his hands on either side of her waist to pick her up to reposition her on his lap.

Kay was so shocked by the movement that she didn't even think about where she was putting her legs as he set her down and she ended up straddling him. Even through the quilt he still had on his lap, she could feel the bulge beneath his dress pants. *Damn. Why did I tell Tia that I wouldn't be kissing him tonight? Or did I? I think I said there'd be no "loud" kissing, not that there would be no kissing at all.*

"You know…" Kay ran her hands over Anthony's shoulders to put her arms around his neck. "…Tia is probably asleep by now. And I didn't say I wouldn't be kissing you tonight. I just said that there would be no *'loud'* kissing to keep her awake." Kay put extra emphasis on the word "loud" as she wiggled just a little in his lap.

"Then I'll be sure to keep this quiet." Anthony pressed his lips to hers.

It started off as a soft, sweet kiss, but as Anthony's arms wound around Kay's waist and his hands ran up and down her back pulling her closer, it became more passionate than she'd ever felt before.

One of his hands stopped to cup the nape of her neck and held her in place, so he could deepen the kiss. The other hand was on her low back, holding her in place with her core resting on his very large erection. *Mamma Mia! I hope those books are right about bigger being better!*

Even through their clothes and the quilt, Kay could tell that Anthony was much larger than she'd ever seen. Just the feel of him against her was more arousing than anything she'd ever experienced. She unconsciously wiggled her hips to rub against him. *Dry-humping certainly didn't feel this good when I was a teenager!*

Kay tried to meet his tongue lick for lick, but the feel of him rubbing against her was too much for her to be able to keep focusing on returning his kiss. Her nipples were so hard, and she loved the feel of them being pressed against his chest. Kay wished they were in her bedroom with the door locked, so they could be skin to skin instead of having the barriers of their clothing between them. Instead of taking things further like she expected, he slowly pulled his lips away from hers.

"You need to stop wiggling if you want me to be able to continue being a gentleman," he whispered as he looked into her eyes.

"Sorry," Kay whispered and pulled back, so she was still sitting on his lap, but wasn't rubbing intimately against him any longer. Kay knew they couldn't keep kissing, or they would go way farther than they should with her daughters just down the hall.

She had to think of something else to take her mind off of how good he felt rubbing against her, or she was afraid she would give in to her body's desires, instead of what she knew really needed to happen that night. Going back over the events of the evening in her head, Kay decided to skip the really scary stuff that was happening with Mark.

That was when she realized that they hadn't talked about the possible jobs he mentioned earlier. "How about you tell me about those jobs, so I know what I need to do to my résumé tonight before we leave to take it to them?"

"I'm not sure you'll even need a résumé to apply for them." Anthony rubbed his hands up and down Kay's arms. He looked nervous as he started to speak. "The one I hope you'll like the best and interview for on Tuesday is as a flight attendant for my crew."

"I'm not qualified for that." Kay shook her head at him as she felt her heart drop. As much as she loved the idea of working with Anthony and being on the same schedule as him to be able to see him all the time, there was no way her experience as a hostess in a restaurant, or her two years of college core credits, would be enough to qualify her for that job. "Unless they offer some kind of flight-attendant school as part of the benefits before I start."

"Naw, you won't have to go to flight-attendant school. It's with a private company, not an airline." Anthony's lips turned up slightly. "My boss actually asked me if I knew anyone with childcare experience to fill the position because so many of the guys are bringing their families with them that they need some extra hands on the flights to help with the kids more than doing the normal flight-attendant duties."

Does being a mom count as the right experience?

"Like I told you earlier, that one pays about fifty-thousand dollars a year, plus travel expenses and all the normal benefits like insurance and stuff. Plus, you can be on the same crew as me and we can all travel the world together, which I think is the best benefit."

"But what about the girls and school? How can I travel all the time with two kids?" Kay's hopes deflated at thinking of the one possible downside. *There's no way this will work. It's too good to be true!*

He took a deep breath and looked Kay in the eyes as if he was searching for what to say. She felt like he was looking into her soul and could see she worried that she was so caught up in the fairy-tale experience that she was going to get hurt really bad when it all fell through and didn't end in happily ever after like she was dreaming about.

"I know you want to keep the girls in school for socialization, but there are several kids that travel with the GWA year-round. They are classified as homeschooled, but Rick has a couple of tutors on staff, as well, to help them with anything the parents aren't comfortable teaching their children. That's probably going to be a big benefit to keep up with Tia's intellectual needs. The kids spend some time each day in an area backstage set up as a classroom to do schoolwork together and socialize, too. So, if you decide to take that job, then Tia and Maria will still get the socialization that you want them to get from school."

More stuff that sounds too good to be true, Kay thought. Instead of getting her hopes up that she would be able to get that job, she asked about the other one, thinking maybe it wouldn't sound as perfect so maybe it would be attainable.

Anthony spent the next hour telling her all about his family business. Apparently, the ranch he told her about growing up on was actually just one part of Burleson Incorporated. They didn't just own the ranch and a bunch of cows like Kay had pictured when he was describing it. They had oil wells on their land, refineries for the oil, a chain of gas stations, and an office in San Antonio to handle all the different ways his uncle and cousins were expanding and diversifying the corporation.

Anthony was on the board of directors and wanted to go back to school to take some business classes, so he could be more beneficial in the quarterly board meetings. *So much for thinking I'm dating a normal guy!* At least that meant there were lots of potential jobs that she could do when they got to San Antonio, if she couldn't get the job flying away with him.

Kay leaned over and put her head on Anthony's chest as he talked about the options he saw for their future. She drifted off to sleep listening to the soothing sound of his heartbeat and softly spoken words, dreaming about the possibilities he described.

Chapter Seven

Saturday, October 6, 2018

"Wake up! It's time to go to the airport," Anthony thought he heard Tia saying as he slowly drifted up out of a dream about holding Kay all night.

When he opened his eyes, he realized it wasn't all a dream. They were both still fully dressed, although Anthony wished they weren't. But since she was laying on top of him on her couch that was probably a good thing. Anthony couldn't believe they'd fallen asleep while cuddling on the couch talking.

He presumed they'd just both been too comfortable when he held her on his lap while they talked, and they both drifted off to sleep without realizing the compromising position they would wake up in. Apparently, once they were asleep, he just leaned back and pulled her on top of him as he laid them out on the couch without even realizing it.

Kay had leaned over and put her head on his chest while they were discussing the possible jobs she could get at Burleson Incorporated. Anthony couldn't resist rubbing her back while he told her about the family business, and how he wanted to take a few business classes to be able to be a bigger part of the company when he eventually tired of traveling all the time.

He didn't tell her that if she decided that she wanted to work there instead of with the GWA, he would be switching jobs much sooner than his current ten-year plan. Whichever job she decided on, he was going to be working with her, so they didn't have to be apart a single day from then on.

She looked so peaceful sleeping there with her face resting over his heart. He really wished he didn't have to wake her up. He was unsure how he was going to keep things camouflaged when she did get up, so he figured he would let her sleep until he could figure it out.

Anthony looked around and didn't see Tia, but he knew he heard her a moment ago. *Maybe it was just part of the dream?* Anthony thought and decided to go back to sleep since it was still mostly dark outside.

Anthony didn't know if he slept for another few minutes or another hour before he felt Kay being shaken on top of him and heard Tia again. "Mom, wake up, or we'll miss our plane." Tia put her other hand on Anthony's shoulder and shook him as well. "Anthony, didn't you say we have to be at the airport early? Wake up so we can go."

He opened his eyes and saw Kay slowly lifting her head and struggling to open her eyes as well. He smiled at her obvious confusion about how they ended up sleeping in their clothes on the sofa. "Good morning, Beautiful." Anthony pushed her hair out of her eyes and tucked it behind her ear.

"Since you're finally awake, I'm going to wake up Maria now." Tia ran back down the hall.

"Morning." Kay started to push up off of Anthony.

He pulled her back down so he could kiss the top of her head and whisper, "Don't move yet. I still need you to be my blanket for a few more minutes."

She giggled and wiggled a little, which didn't help his cock to deflate at all. Anthony groaned in frustration before moving to whisper in her ear. "Keep moving like that and we won't be able to get up without embarrassing ourselves."

"Embarrassing you, maybe," Kay giggled as she hopped up and backed away from the couch. Her cute little smile and the twinkle in her eyes, told him she was not embarrassed about the tent in his dress pants at all. "Bathroom is the first door on the right. You might want to get in the shower now before the girls come back in here." With that, she sauntered down the hallway.

Anthony quickly grabbed his suitcase and stuffed the t-shirt and sweats he'd gotten out to sleep in the night before back in it before taking it and his garment bag with him to the bathroom. He wasn't sure if he should lock the bathroom door or not.

While he wouldn't mind Kay coming in to join him in the shower, he doubted she would, and he didn't want to take a chance on one of her daughters not realizing he was in the bathroom and walking in while he was taking care of his morning wood situation.

Anthony felt a little guilty about doing his normal morning routine in Kay's shower, but since he didn't think he would be able to actually be with Kay any time soon, he had to do something to alleviate the intense need he felt to be with her.

Instead of using his bodywash as lubricant like normal, he used a little bit of her strawberry shampoo. Closing his eyes and smelling her, it didn't take but a few strokes to be done. Good thing, since someone was knocking on the bathroom door before he could even finish rinsing off.

"I'll be done in a few minutes," he announced loudly while quickly switching to his bodywash and taking the quickest shower of his life.

He quickly dried off with the fluffy white towel that was hanging on the shower door and got dressed, so he could open the door in case one of the girls needed the bathroom urgently. He left his shaving kit on the vanity, but carried the rest of his things back out with him.

"All yours," he broadcast as he stepped into the hall, since he had no idea who had been knocking earlier.

Maria ran past him from her bedroom and slammed the door to the bathroom before he could even get to the living room. *Maybe I should've waited until they'd all had a chance to use the bathroom before I showered?*

"I'm in the kitchen," Kay called out when he set his luggage down in the living room.

Anthony walked in there to see that she was still in her clothes from the previous night. Instead of changing clothes to get ready for the trip, she'd made a full breakfast of bacon, scrambled eggs, and toast, and was busy plating it all.

"Mmm, something smells delicious." Anthony smiled as he walked up and kissed the top of her head. "How can I help?"

"You can put the plates on the table and get the orange juice out of the fridge," she answered as she leaned her head into his ribs as if she were trying to hug him without stopping what she was doing or using her arms.

Anthony tried to hold back a chuckle because the way she rubbed her face over his ribs like a cat tickled, but he was not fully successful. She apparently noticed and he thought the little smile she gave him as she handed him two plates of food meant she was planning to use his ticklishness to her advantage at some point.

Please do, Baby! I can't wait to find out where you're ticklish, too!

Anthony turned to take the plates to the formal dining room, but he was quickly turned around by Tia coming into the kitchen.

"We normally eat in the den." Tia pointed to the built-in table on the other side of the kitchen island.

Within a few minutes, they were all seated at the table and quickly eating. The girls were excited, and kept asking questions about where they were going and what to expect while traveling with the GWA.

When he told them all to pack a mix of dress clothes, casual clothes, and stuff to workout in, so they could change depending on what they were doing, the girls started to pick on him for changing clothes multiple times a day. Maybe most people didn't change clothes as many times in a day as he did, but he couldn't change his ingrained tendency to dress in the proper uniform for each activity and look professional while he was at work or on a plane.

In addition to the dress code for while he was working, he preferred to wear a suit and tie while flying commercial, so he wouldn't stand out sitting in first class. But he couldn't work out with his friends or get in the ring for sparring or the self-defense lessons he wanted to give the girls in a suit and tie. And if they did any sightseeing or spent any time on the ranch, they needed to change into jeans and boots because that was the proper attire.

He just hoped the fact that he had his clothing laundered while traveling would prevent his excessive amount of laundry from being a negative about him in Kay's eyes.

He smiled when he thought about how Tia and Maria would make fun of him when he took them to the ranch and introduced them to not only his family, but the horses his dad had been training since he was a kid. Watching him tack his horse would give them plenty of material to poke fun at. He'd gladly enjoy hearing them laugh at his quirks.

Their questions reminded Anthony that he'd changed the flight but didn't do anything about the hotel reservations. As soon as they were finished eating, he called the hotel the company normally used in

Dallas and made the change, so instead of a king suite in the normal block of rooms reserved by the company for Tuesday night, he and Kay could check into adjoining king suites Saturday night through Wednesday morning.

After a crazy game similar to musical chairs to get all four of them through their remaining bathroom needs, when he squeezed in brushing his teeth and shaving while Kay curled her hair and put on her make-up, they were finally all ready to go with bags packed and got out the door.

The chaos of the morning reminded Anthony of growing up with five older siblings and made him grateful he'd grown up with more than one bathroom. It got him to thinking about how many bathrooms there should be in the home he wanted to buy with Kay. *Damn, I hope she's ready to buy a house with me soon!*

When Tia couldn't give him directions to the airport, Anthony learned that neither of the girls had ever been on a plane. He had a hard time holding in the emotion he was feeling at realizing he was about to take them on their first flight. *This is one of those firsts I thought I'd miss out on with my kids.*

He swallowed down the lump of emotion in his throat at feeling like he was exactly where he was supposed to be, taking his family to the airport for their first flight together. He gently clasped Kay's hand in his, bringing it to his lips to kiss the back of it as he pulled out of the driveway. He just reversed the directions he'd followed from his trip to their house the night before to take them across town to board the plane to their future.

They took up an entire first-class row when they boarded the plane. Since both girls wanted to sit by the window, Anthony and Kay took the two aisle seats. Anthony missed being able to hold Kay's hand during the flight, since they had to keep the aisle clear for the flight attendants.

He'd been constantly touching her in some way, either holding her hand or putting his hand on her back to guide her through the airport, since they left her house that morning. While he felt he needed to hold back sexually until Kay was ready, he struggled with controlling his need to feel connected to her by constantly having a hand on her.

Their conversation was light-hearted due to the excitement they were all feeling about flying. If Anthony hadn't already had an extreme affinity for flying, he knew he would have gained it from sharing in the joy Tia and Maria were showing as they peppered him with questions about the plane and how it flew.

He only hoped he was doing an adequate job of explaining aerodynamics. While he could explain in detail the procedures for a pilot, the parts of the plane, and the various gauges and functions of each switch and button in the cockpit, he wasn't as educated on the physics of flight to be able to explain it to Tia completely.

He glanced across the aisle at Kay and noticed her eyes were glazed over after listening to the flight training he'd given the girls. He winked at her and gave her a smile, hoping she wasn't too bored with all the technical jargon he was using while answering Tia's questions. Maria was being awfully quiet as she stared out the window on the other side of Kay.

About halfway through the flight, there was a bit of turbulence that was a bit too intense for Tia and Maria. Tia reached over and grabbed Anthony's hand, squeezing it like a vise. Maria squealed as she grabbed Kay's hand in a similar manner.

"Are we going to crash?" Tia questioned through gritted teeth.

"No, Tia." Anthony stroked the back of her hand with his thumb to comfort her. "That's just a little turbulence. Totally normal."

"I don't like turbulence," Maria choked out.

Anthony fought to keep from chuckling. "I don't know that anybody likes turbulence." He leaned forward to look around Kay at Maria. She smiled at him, though he could still see a little fear in her eyes.

Kay was gripping the armrest on her seat with her free hand, so Anthony reached over and took that hand in his to reassure her, too.

"Just think of it as a speed bump, like the ones in parking lots." Anthony hoped his explanation would reassure them all.

"Is that what it is?" Tia looked confused. "What did we hit in the air?"

"Kind of." Anthony contemplated how to explain it, so they wouldn't be scared. "It's usually a cross wind or an air pocket from a storm that pushes on the plane at a different angle than the rest of the air around us. They aren't very big and just make the ride a little bumpy for a few minutes. You have absolutely nothing to worry about."

"Unless one of us throws up," Kay added with a groan. Anthony looked over to notice that she looked a little green. Before he could move, both girls reached into the seat pockets and tried to hand Kay the little white bags they pulled out.

"Nope, don't even have to worry about that," Anthony chuckled out. "We're well prepared for that."

Kay gave him a weak smile, but took both of the emesis bags, just in case. He was grateful she didn't actually have to use them.

"Do you hit a lot of speed bumps when you're flying?" Tia queried him softly, still holding his hand.

"Not as many as we've hit on this flight." Anthony hoped to reassure her that the flights would be smoother if Kay accepted the flight-attendant job, and they were flying with him all the time. "I try to watch out for them, so I can fly smoothly over them."

"How can you see them if it's just wind?" Tia looked up at him with confusion written all over her face. "Wind is invisible."

"Yeah, but clouds aren't." Anthony pointed out the window at the cloud cover below them. "If I see an exceptionally fast-moving cloud or one that's moving in the opposite direction of the ones around it, I know there's a crosswind or strong winds near it and adjust to avoid it if I can."

Tia sat back and contemplated his statements and Anthony hoped she would accept them and feel safer flying with him in the pilot's seat. Hopefully, her genius IQ wouldn't clue her into the fact that most of the time he flew above the actual cloud cover and couldn't see potential turbulence any more than any other pilot. Parenting a kid smarter than him was going to be a challenge. One he welcomed with open arms.

After the turbulence passed, Anthony noticed that both girls were getting antsy and having a hard time sitting still for the rest of the flight. He decided that they needed to do something active when they landed to help the girls expend some pent-up energy. When he asked Kay if they brought bathing suits, she looked at him like he was crazy for thinking they needed swimwear for a trip in October. He had to explain that the hotel they were staying at in Dallas had an indoor, heated pool before she understood the reason for his question.

After a little disagreement over his insistence on paying for new swimsuits at the mall, they finally made it to the hotel prepared for an afternoon of swimming. With the girls all in the adjoining room, Anthony debated in his head whether he should change in the bathroom of his room or right there beside the king-sized bed, like he would have if they weren't in the room connected to his. In the end, he opened his side of the adjoining doors and went to change into his swim trunks in his bathroom, so they could feel free to come into his room without risking seeing him undressed.

He decided to leave his side always open, so they could come and go as they pleased. And if Kay opted to share his bathroom, so she didn't have to wait to get a shower after swimming while the girls got cleaned up, all the better.

He grabbed two of the four large towels in his bathroom and was holding them in front of him as he knocked on the adjoining room door. He was glad he had the coverage in front of his cock when Kay opened the door. She'd chosen a modest one-piece when they were shopping, but it didn't do much more than a bikini would have to conceal her curves.

Anthony was struggling to figure out how he was going to camouflage his erection while swimming when Maria came barreling around Kay and almost ran into him. He was glad his cock seemed to realize that he should go into hiding whenever kids were present. Maria's high-pitched squeals of excitement about swimming quickly solved his erection issues, so he could relax and enjoy swimming with them.

"I grabbed two towels from my bathroom." Anthony held up the towels as evidence. "I figured we could use these and two from your bathroom for swimming and still leave two in each bathroom for our showers afterward."

"Yeah, I was wondering what we were going to do with only one extra towel in the bathroom for swimming." Kay let out a self-deprecating chuckle. "I wasn't thinking about you having towels in your bathroom that we could use, too."

"I'm leaving my side of this door open, too, so you can come use my bathroom if you need it." Anthony felt exceptionally nervous about offering to share a shower with Kay. "I figured four showers divided between two bathrooms would be faster if we did two in each instead of three in one."

"Oh, uh, okay." Kay blushed beautifully and almost overrode Anthony's kid-induced erection control. "We can figure that out when we get back from the pool."

Kay went into their bathroom and got two more towels before they all made their way down to the pool.

As soon as they got to the pool area, both girls dove into the water like they were destined to be Olympic swimmers. "Wow!" Anthony exclaimed in amazement. "They're like a couple of blonde fish."

Kay giggled at his little joke. "Yeah, they both love to swim." She sat down on a lounge chair and laid the two towels she was holding on a table beside her. "My parents take them swimming daily in the summer, so they both swim better than I do."

Anthony put his two towels down beside hers and held out a hand to Kay. "You're not going to sit on the sidelines and let them show us up, are you?"

"It won't matter if I sit here or get in the pool, they'll show me up either way." Kay took his hand and let him lead her to the pool. "Tia has been able to beat me when we race for a few years now. And Maria finally started beating me this last summer."

Anthony thought back to his childhood years racing his brothers and cousins. Not just in swimming or running, but also on horses, ATVs, and even surfboards. When he was younger, he had a disadvantage being the youngest male Burleson. When he grew to be the tallest of them all as a teenager, though, he found out that his height and long limbs made it easy for him to win when it was a race based on using his body to propel him and not a piece of machinery or riding the fastest horse. He wondered if he could be competitive with the girls in a swimming competition with Kay riding piggyback. It would be fun to find out if his ability would help her get a win over the girls or if the extra load would slow him down enough to give the girls the victory.

"I have an idea." Anthony told Kay about his idea to race with the girls and even the playing field.

"Tia will love that idea." Kay smiled.

"Yeah, I figured it would give her a chance to mathematically predict a winner before we actually race to see if she's right." Anthony returned Kay's smile as they walked hand in hand down the stairs into the shallow end of the pool.

Kay called the girls over to where they were standing. She explained Anthony's proposed race and he could see the wheels turning in Tia's head as she contemplated the potential mathematical equations.

"This is a hard problem to figure out." Tia tapped her pointer finger on her lips. "Since Mom and I are the same height, the only reason I beat her is because she weighs twenty-five pounds more than me and her boobs make her less aquadynamic than me. Once I hit puberty and get boobs, we'll be more competitively matched."

Anthony was grateful he hadn't just taken a drink, or he would've had a spit take at Tia's casual mention of boobs. He tried to keep his face blank, but it was hard when Kay giggled at his obvious embarrassment. He luckily didn't have to say anything since he had no idea what to say as Tia continued her thoughts.

"Maria is almost as fast as me now that she's closer in height. I'm six inches taller but she's twenty pounds lighter and those numbers seem to negate any advantage for either of us. How tall are you? And how much do you weigh?"

"I'm six-foot-six and weigh two-hundred-and-twenty pounds," Anthony answered.

"So, you're eighteen inches taller than me and outweigh me by one-hundred-and-forty pounds. Taking only height and weight into consideration, then your height should increase your speed by a factor of four-point-five, but your weight should decrease your speed by a factor of seven, so I don't think we need to have Mom ride piggyback for me to be able to beat you swimming the length of the pool."

"Yes, but you can't just base it on height and weight," Anthony smirked. "My extra weight is more muscles that can produce more power than your smaller muscles, to propel me down the pool faster."

"And you don't have boobs to slow you down, so you want to borrow Mom's to make the race more fair," Maria piped up with a mischievous grin.

Kay covered her mouth as she busted out laughing. *Damn, I love that sound.*

"Something like that," Anthony chuckled at the precocious little girls.

"Okay, but I'm going to have to go look up the right formulas and the drag coefficient of water to be able to do the math." Tia started to exit the pool.

"How about we do that later when we get back to the room?" Kay gripped her daughter by the shoulders and turned her around to keep her in the pool. "And just have fun racing now."

"But the whole point was to predict a winner based on the math," Tia protested.

"Well, then we'll change it to you justifying the outcome with math after performing the experiment," Anthony offered as a compromise to keep them from having to exit the pool before he or Kay had even gotten fully submerged.

"Awesome!" Tia had a huge smile on her face as she splashed back through the water. "I like experiments."

They decided to do several races to make sure the results of the first one was accurate. Tia won the first race, but Anthony complained it was only because Kay was choking him by holding on around his neck. Kay adjusted to holding on around his chest with her arms and his hips with her legs and they won the next three races.

He thought three out of four was solid proof of a successful experiment, but Maria wanted another chance to win a race, so they kept going. Tia won rounds five and six, making them tied at three each.

Anthony wasn't sure if it was because he was getting tired, or if it was because Kay was distracting him by rubbing her feet across his cock while they swam. He wasn't going to mention that excuse with little ears present, though. He made sure to stay low in the water, even if it meant he had to be on his knees when they stopped in the shallow end, so nobody could tell the reaction his body was having to Kay's teasing. Even having the girls talking to them wasn't enough to negate his response when she was practically jacking him off with her feet.

Since they were tied, they decided to go until one of them won a fourth race. Turned out that Tia was also getting tired, and Maria had been conserving her energy during the first six races. Maria won races seven, eight, nine, and ten to be the ultimate victor in their challenge. Anthony couldn't wait to see how Tia wrote up the findings of their little experiment.

They opted to play a few rounds of Marco Polo when they were done racing. Anthony loved seeing Kay laughing and playing in the pool with her daughters, even if Kay wasn't plastered to him any longer like she'd been while they raced.

He reveled in the feeling that he was the reason she could relax as if she didn't have a care in the world while they splashed around. He wanted to carry all her burdens, relieve her of all her stressors, so she could always be as happy and carefree as she appeared as she splashed and played.

He hated the time they were apart when Kay and her daughters went to their own room to clean up after swimming and he was relegated to his own room alone. He got in the shower, leaving his side of the door between their adjoining rooms open, so Kay could come join him while the girls used their bathroom.

When she didn't come over to his room before he got out of the shower, he quickly dressed for dinner and knocked on the door on their side to let her know the shower was open. When Kay opened the door still in her swimsuit, he was glad he did. "I thought you might want to use my shower." He smiled and pointed over his shoulder with his thumb.

"Yeah, I think Maria is still *'swimming'* in our tub," Kay sighed, using air quotes when she said the word swimming. "Let me get her out and Tia started on her shower, and I'll bring my stuff over to your bathroom."

Kay turned and walked away from the door, leaving it open between their rooms. Anthony wanted to follow her and help her get the things she needed moved to his room, but he was afraid she would think he was overstepping and trying to get her to do more than shower there. Instead, he walked back to his bed for the next few days and sat down. He flipped on the television to see about the weather for the next couple of days, so he could plan some sightseeing activities for Sunday and Monday.

He looked up at Kay with a smile as she walked through the door, pulling her rolling suitcase behind her. She returned his smile before disappearing behind his bathroom door. *Damn, I wish she was ready for us to shower together! But at least I can sit here and picture her in my shower.*

A few moments later, Maria ran through the room and jumped on the bed beside him, effectively killing his fantasy thoughts. "What are you watching?" She eyed the television.

"Just trying to catch the weather, so I can figure out when we can go to the zoo without risking being rained out."

"We're going to the zoo?" Maria's eyes went wide with excitement.

"Yeah, I thought it might be a fun thing for us to do tomorrow." Anthony smiled at her before turning his eyes back to the television to see the weather report. *Awesome, no rain in the forecast the whole time we're in Dallas.*

"I wonder if they'll have a cool hybrid animal at the Dallas Zoo like we have in Tulsa," Maria mused.

"What kind of cool hybrid animal do you have at the Tulsa Zoo?" Anthony was curious about what Maria thought of as cool.

"Honker," Maria divulged as if that were all the answer he would need. "Since the weather is over, can I flip channels?"

"Sure." Anthony handed her the remote control. "What's a Honker?"

"Honker was our duck," she replied as she flipped the channels until she settled on cartoons. "Well, he's half mallard duck and half blue goose. Since he was a rare hybrid, he went to live at the zoo when he bit my tongue."

Anthony wasn't sure how to respond to her matter-of-fact statement. *Surely, she's pulling my leg?*

"What? How?" He stammered in confusion. "Why?"

"She stuck her tongue out at him when he tried to wiggle away when she wanted to give him a hug." Tia walked into the room and held out a hairbrush. "And he didn't go to the zoo because of biting Maria. He went to the zoo after the neighbor's dog bit him and our vet had to call in the vet from the zoo, since he hadn't ever operated on a hybrid animal before. Can you help me with my hair?"

Anthony really looked at her then, realizing that her hair was a wet, tangled mess. *I really should have paid more attention to what my sisters did with their hair as kids,* he thought as he turned to sit on the side of the bed and took the brush from Tia.

Leah Mae Wright

"I can try." Anthony felt nervous and unsure of how to detangle the little girl's long hair without hurting her. "Is there a special way I need to brush it?"

"Just start at the ends and work your way up." Tia turned her back to Anthony, so he could attempt to brush her hair that hung down to her mid-back. "I can't reach the ends in the back, but I can get it once you get the tangles out up to my shoulders. Mom usually helps me, like she did Maria before she got in the shower, but obviously, she can't help me from her shower."

"Obviously." Anthony tried to gently brush her hair an inch at a time. He picked up a chunk of her hair and brushed below where he grasped it so that if he had to pull it, he wouldn't pull it all the way up to her scalp and cause her discomfort. After a few minutes, he was mostly through the lower half of her hair, the task being easier than he originally feared.

"Wow, you're much better at this than Mom or Grandma," Tia praised as he moved up to the hair just above her shoulders. "They don't ever hold it like you do, so it feels like they're going to pull half my hair out."

Anthony looked up from his task to meet her eyes where she was watching him in the mirror on the wall across the room. He grinned at her and was rewarded with a beaming smile from Tia in return. *Thank fuck she can't tell I've never done this before and have no clue what I'm doing.*

He thought he was done since she could do the part above her shoulders, but when he went to hand her the brush, she didn't take it. "Can you do it all? I want to watch you in the mirror, so I can figure out how to hold my hair the way you do, so I don't pull out half my hair either."

"Sure," he choked out and continued brushing. He wanted to memorize every moment he got to feel like a daddy taking care of things he hadn't even realized would be needed by these precious little girls.

Kay walked out of the bathroom with her head wrapped up in a towel like a turban. She was dressed like her daughters in jeans and a t-shirt and cute little bare feet. Even without a drop of makeup on, she was the most beautiful woman he'd ever seen.

"I was trying to hurry, so I could do that." Kay pointed at Anthony brushing Tia's hair.

"You should let Anthony brush your hair, too, Mom." Tia gave her mom a bright smile. "It doesn't hurt or make me feel dizzy like when I try to lean over like you do to do it myself."

Anthony shrugged his shoulders and grinned when Kay looked at him quizzically. "Who knew I had a hidden talent?"

"You have a lot of experience as a hairdresser?" Kay smiled at him as she walked toward him and took the towel off her head.

"Nope, first time I've ever brushed anyone's hair but my own," he replied.

"Well, then I guess I have to test your natural talent." Kay turned to stand between his knees while Tia sat on the bed beside him to watch.

Anthony wasn't sure what alternate universe he landed in when they got to Dallas, but he loved feeling like he was right where he was supposed to be. With his family.

Later that night, after coming back to their rooms after having dinner in the hotel restaurant, Anthony laid in his bed contemplating life. After only being with Kay for twenty-four hours, he knew he couldn't be separated from her ever again. No matter what job she decided she wanted to do, he would work beside her. If that meant leaving the GWA and not flying again unless it were for fun with his family, he would happily plant both feet on the ground wherever Kay wanted to live.

He decided he needed to have a couple of options for her to do some interviews, so he sent a few quick texts.

Anthony: Kay is with me in Dallas. Feel like interviewing for that flight-attendant position on Tuesday?

Rick: I thought you weren't going to push her too fast?

Anthony: I wasn't. Then I got there for our date & had to step between her and her ex.

Rick: Fuck! Did you hurt him? Need an alibi?

Anthony: No, Kay's dad is the sheriff, so he took care of the heavy lifting. I just couldn't leave her or the girls there & risk him coming back & hurting them.

Rick: K. Tell her we'll do paperwork on Tuesday, & she can start work on Wednesday.

Anthony: Thanks. See you Tuesday.

After finishing up with texting his boss, he decided to be prepared in case Kay didn't want to take the job with the GWA.

Anthony: Can you get me a list of job openings at Burleson?

Dad: For you? You thinking about coming home?

Anthony: For Kay, & me if that's where she ends up. She's interviewing with the GWA on Tuesday, but if she doesn't want that job then I need to have other options for her.

Dad: I'll get with Jon tomorrow & email you a list of options.

Anthony: Thanks, Dad.

Dad: So, does this mean we'll get to meet your Kay soon?

Anthony: Yeah, she & the girls are with me, so you'll get to meet them when we fly into San Antonio later this week.

**Dad: I'll have your mom prepare bedrooms for while
you're here. Three?**

**Anthony: Don't know. She & the girls are sharing a room
at the hotel. I don't know if they will want to share
when we're there or not.**

**Dad: We have plenty of rooms, so I'll make sure there's
space prepared to spread out if that's what they want.**

Anthony: Thanks. Night Dad!

Dad: Night Son!

Anthony put his phone on the charger on his bedside table. He rolled over and tried again to fluff his pillow enough to help him sleep. It was hard to do when all he could think about was the fact that Kay was lying in bed on the other side of the door.

He'd left his side of the adjoining doors open in case one of them needed his bathroom. At least that's what he told them as the girls were closing their side to get ready for bed. Truth be told, he left it open so that if Kay wanted to sneak over to his bed in the middle of the night, she would have easy access.

Now that he was thinking about the possibility of her coming to his bed, his cock was responding as if she was already there. He'd been surprised at how well-behaved his cock had been all day. Normally, just thinking about Kay got him hard. He'd been afraid that spending the day with her would have led to him having an erection that lasted for so long, it became dangerous like in those erectile dysfunction commercials that said to go to the hospital if you have an erection for more than so many hours. But apparently spending time in dad mode kept him in better control than he expected. Other than during the races, when Kay was trying to make him lose control with her feet, he hadn't really had a full erection all day.

Oh, he still had a half-chub anytime he looked at Kay, especially when he put his hand on the small of her back as he walked with her. He thought about how different he felt holding Kay's hand when compared to holding Tia's or Maria's. With the girls, it was strictly a protective thing, a way to keep them safe as they were walking through a crowd or across a parking lot. With Kay, he still felt protective as he held her hand, but it was also arousing. Even a light brushing of her arm against his while they were standing in line made his dick twitch. Any arousal he felt disappeared, though, the instant he started interacting with the girls. *My girls,* he thought. *Fuck, I want them to be my wife and daughters!*

I really wish my almost wife would come to my bed right now!

After tossing and turning for hours, Anthony finally got up and went to the shower. If he was going to keep himself in check so he didn't overwhelm Kay, he was going to have to take a lot of showers. He should probably switch to cold ones.

<div align="center">~~~</div>

Sunday, October 7, 2018

Waking up Sunday morning in Dallas was much different than Kay's normal routine at home. Instead of waking up alone in her bed and going to church with her parents and daughters, or going in for an extra shift at work if the girls were with Mark, Kay woke in bed with her daughters and had plans to spend the morning with Anthony to explore downtown Dallas and then the afternoon at the Dallas Zoo.

Kay had enjoyed seeing Anthony interact with her girls. He was a natural when it came to parenting. Not only had he shared in their excitement about flying for the first time, but he also let Tia squeeze his hand in a vise grip and spoke soothingly to comfort her when she freaked out during a turbulent part of the flight that scared her.

After the stress of the flight, he was understanding in their need to expend some energy and insisted on stopping between the airport and the hotel to buy bathing suits, since nobody had thought to bring them. He didn't just give them an outlet for their pent-up energy in going swimming, either. He also found a way to engage Tia's brain in the physical activity in a way that Kay would have never thought of on her own.

Kay felt those ever more familiar butterflies as she thought back to their races with the girls. Seeing him in only a pair of board shorts was definitely a highlight of the trip for Kay. He had well-defined muscles, but was not bulky like a bodybuilder. He was long and lean with the body of a swimmer. The scar on his right side didn't detract at all from his physical perfection. He had just enough chest hair to be tempting, especially when it tapered down to a happy trail into his shorts. Kay wondered what it would feel like brushing against her naked breasts.

She could only guess that it would feel amazing, based on how her breasts pressed into his broad back felt through her bathing suit while she was riding piggyback for their races. She really enjoyed getting to wrap herself around him even if it was in a completely non-sexual way. She felt her nipples harden and her sex clench as she relived the feeling and recalled how quickly he'd responded when her feet slipped across the front of his swim trunks.

He didn't even acknowledge her attempts to show him that she still wanted more physically between them. He'd just nonchalantly reached down and pulled her feet back up around his waist, hooking them together over his chiseled six-pack abs, and carried on like she hadn't just given him a hard-on with her exploring feet.

They'd all laughed and splashed the afternoon away, leaving Kay feeling like he was the missing part of their family. He stepped into the daddy role effortlessly.

It looked like he intended to continue in the role as they headed out to explore the city Sunday morning. Anthony answered every question the girls had as they walked around Dealey Plaza and didn't even blink when Tia started asking questions about the JFK assassination that Kay would have had no idea how to answer.

He had a large base of knowledge, but he wasn't just lecturing her on the facts in a boring monotone like Kay's high school history teacher. Anthony had even given her some off-the-wall conspiracy theories to think about, and challenged her to play detective as they walked around to decide for herself what she thought was the truth.

It was a strange combination of how he could be so serious with Tia, but playful with Maria when they walked through the Dallas Cattle Drive Sculptures in Pioneer Plaza. It was like he already knew how he needed to interact with them differently because their personalities were so distinctive.

After hearing his stories of his family ranch, and actual cattle drives his dad and Pappaw Jerry went on, Maria wanted to go to his family ranch and play cowgirl. Kay never would have thought her little princess, who loved to play with dolls and dress up in frilly dresses, would ever be interested in doing something so tomboyish.

Tia was even interested in learning to ride the horses, and she'd never acted so relaxed before with anything other than something studious. It amazed Kay that Anthony was the one that brought out this never-before-seen side of her oldest daughter.

As they were leaving Pioneer Plaza to head for the zoo, Kay's cell phone rang in her pocket. She pulled it out and wished she'd remembered to text her dad the night before when they got settled for the night, since it was him calling.

"Hi, Dad," Kay answered the phone apologetically. "Sorry, I forgot to let you know we made it safely to Dallas last night."

"As long as you're there safe, that's all that matters." Her father's tone of voice was one Kay didn't know how to interpret over the phone. She couldn't tell if he was angry, or worried, or maybe both. "You are there safe and sound, right?"

"Yes, Dad," Kay answered in a more relaxed tone, hoping to alleviate some of his worry. "We had a mostly uneventful flight, other than a little unexpected turbulence. We spent the afternoon swimming at the hotel and when we checked in, they put us in the room right next door to Anthony, so he's close if Mark somehow finds out where we are and follows us. We're as safe as we can possibly be and are having a blast sightseeing. We're on our way to the zoo now."

"I'm glad, baby girl." Charles sounded a little more relaxed in his tone of voice, but he wasn't completely at ease. "I don't think Mark will be following you, unless you left anything at the house that said where you were going."

"No, I didn't," Kay answered thinking there was something troubling about how her dad worded that statement. "Not that it would matter if I did since Mark doesn't have a key to the house."

"Um, about that…" Her dad's voice trailed off, and she could definitely tell there was something he didn't want to tell her. "I think he broke in there last night."

"What?" Kay shouted, covering her mouth with her hand in shock. Kay knew Mark was acting strange lately, but breaking into her house was way over the line even for him. *Thank God we left with Anthony!*

"Calm down," Charles beseeched. "I've got it all covered here."

Kay took a few deep breaths and squeezed Anthony's hand that she hadn't even realized she'd reached over to grab. "Okay, Dad, I'm better now. Please tell me what happened."

"I noticed the front door standing wide open when we drove by on the way to church this morning. I stopped and called my best detectives to come and investigate. I sent your mom on to church and replaced the front door as soon as the pictures and evidence were taken. I'm going to be spending a few days on repairs, but I really don't think you should come home until the court date. I'm sending the crime scene photos to Matt for the hearing, too."

"Repairs? Crime scene photos?" Kay squeaked out.

"Yeah, baby girl," Charles sighed, and she could hear that he was choking up, too. "I'm really glad you and the girls aren't here to see this." He paused to clear his throat. "I didn't like the idea of you running off to Texas and possibly getting another job, so you could be with Anthony instead of here in Tulsa. But after seeing firsthand how far off the rails Mark is going, I've decided that it will be best if you stay in Texas for a while. When you come back for the hearing, get a hotel on the other side of town, and don't come near the house, or anywhere he might look for you. I've got an APB out for him, but I can't guarantee that I can keep him in jail. Even if I can convince a judge to not give him bail, I can't guarantee that his friends won't be watching for you."

"How bad is it, Dad?" Kay felt tears streaming down her face. She couldn't hold them back. Kay was so freaked out right then, not sure if she should be terrified of Mark, or grateful to Anthony for keeping her and the girls safe from him. *I really hate having to lean on him like this! But I'm so glad he's here for us right now.*

"Worse than anything I would have expected him to do," her dad answered. "Don't worry, I'll pack up whatever is left salvageable of your belongings and bring it to you in Texas when you decide where you'll be living there."

"Wha-whatever's sal-salvageable?" Kay croaked out with a little stutter. *What the heck has Mark done to our stuff?*

"Don't worry about the stuff here." Her father's tone made it obvious he was trying to calm Kay down while still staying angry himself. "You just focus on getting a good job in Texas and finding a place to live there where Mark can't find you. I'll focus on getting him locked up in Oklahoma, and taking care of the house and stuff here in Tulsa. Just make sure you have a spare bedroom for guests, so Mom and I have a place to stay when we come visit every month and to live after I retire in a couple years."

Kay had to laugh at her dad trying to get her to focus on something else. Only he would think threatening to move in with her was a good distraction from the chaos that was currently her life.

"Yeah, I'll get right on that, Dad," Kay told him as her chuckle died down. "Maybe one of these jobs Anthony knows about will pay well enough I can buy a house with a guesthouse for you and Mom."

Anthony's brow raised at hearing her conversation, but he didn't interrupt to ask the questions he was obviously thinking. He simply held her hand, giving her a reassuring squeeze and a small smile. Kay quickly got off the phone with her father and took a few cleansing breaths before turning in the seat, so she could look at him and her daughters in the back seat.

"What happened?" Tia enquired before anyone else could. She leaned up in her seat, gripping the back of Anthony's seat like she needed to hold on to something to feel safe. "Why was Grandpa talking about repairs and crime scene photos?"

Kay patted her daughter's hand on the seat. "Apparently, it's a good thing we weren't home last night. Someone broke into the house, so Grandpa has his best detectives investigating. But it's nothing we need to worry about. We're just supposed to have fun on our trip, and when I get a job and a new home for us, he and Grandma will bring us the stuff that wasn't damaged in the break-in."

"Dad did it, didn't he?" Tia looked close to tears.

"We don't know for sure." Kay wished she could protect her daughters from knowing the violent side of their father. "He is Grandpa's prime suspect, but it could have been someone else. You know how the justice system works. Innocent until proven guilty. Grandpa is going to make sure that the guilty party is arrested, but he has to investigate first to make sure he doesn't arrest someone who isn't actually guilty just because we think it was him."

Kay noticed the twitch of Anthony's mouth at her statement and felt guilty for defending the possibility of Mark's innocence. Her gut instinct said that Mark was definitely the one who had broken in and trashed her house, destroying not only her things but also their children's. She knew from the look on his face that Anthony believed Mark was the guilty party, too. But she hated the thought that her daughters would feel the shame of being sired by a violent man, so she really hoped that their initial belief that Mark was the culprit who trashed her home was incorrect. *Yeah, that's not real likely.*

"How about we follow Grandpa's instructions and go have some fun at the zoo?" Anthony gave them all a much-needed change of subject.

"Why did you call him Grandpa?" Tia sat back against her seat and looked at Anthony quizzically.

"Because that's what you call him," Anthony answered with a look back at Tia that said *"duh"* like Tia often did to everyone else.

"You did that Friday night, too," Tia pointed out, still looking confused. "You called my mom, Mom. Why didn't you use their first names like most adults do?"

"I guess I'm not like most adults." Anthony shrugged his shoulders as he parked the SUV they'd rented when they got to Dallas the day before. "I figured since I was talking to you, I should use the moniker you use to refer to them."

"But why?" Tia still looked confused as they all got out of the vehicle.

Anthony tilted his head and scratched his chin like he was deeply thinking about his answer. "I've never really thought about it before, but I guess somewhere along the way I was taught to use the same level of respect about others that whomever I'm speaking with uses as a way to show that I consider us to be on the same level." He gave Kay a wide smile over Tia's head before continuing. "It probably has something to do with dealing with the delicate egos of my fellow sailors who hadn't reached my same rank yet."

Kay giggled at his ego reference. He may have claimed to not be a cocky egomaniac, but Kay thought he just hid it well.

"So, it was your way of saying you're still a kid like us and respecting Mom and Grandpa?" Tia contemplated.

"But you're not a kid," Maria shouted, turning to look at Anthony and stopping them all in their tracks where they were walking toward the zoo entrance.

"No, I'm not a kid, but I can still respect my elders," Anthony smirked as he ruffled Maria's hair.

The girls both laughed. Anthony winked at Kay as he gave her a secret smile. *Is he teasing me about my age?* Kay thought as she shook her head and grinned back at him. *And why am I smiling about it?*

As they made their way through the zoo, Kay contemplated her life. Watching Anthony interact with her daughters was the best kind of distraction from the trouble back in Tulsa. She didn't want to think about Mark or his horrible behavior, so she let herself be swept away by her playful Prince Charming.

Anthony was a perfect gentleman, always opening doors or pulling out chairs for not just Kay, but also her daughters. He paid attention when any of them spoke, not just listening idly but not really hearing, like Mark used to do when they went somewhere as a family.

Anthony is nothing like Mark.

Anthony didn't just listen to let them talk, either. He focused on whoever was speaking and actually contemplated the things being said, so he could expand the conversation. Kay knew he was not just getting to know her but also her daughters.

I'm not the only one falling in love with him, Kay thought, realizing that her daughters were basking in the easy affection Anthony was giving them all.

Anthony was a very affectionate man. While they were walking around in the hotel, or a mall, or the various tourist exhibits, he was either holding Kay's hand or had an arm around her shoulders. If they were walking along a road or through a parking lot, he would put himself between them and any possible danger. He would hold one of the girl's hands while she held the other as they walked through areas where the girls needed to be kept close for their safety. He was constantly touching one of them, either holding a hand or running a hand over their hair.

Kay loved it when he ran his hand through her hair as he pulled her in for a hug. It made her feel safe and happy. But even with all his easy affection this weekend, Anthony hadn't touched her in a sexual manner, like she expected after their Skype call Thursday night. He hadn't even tried to kiss her again since they arrived in Dallas.

Probably because meeting my nightmare ex killed any sexual interest he had in me. He's probably just helping me find a job and get away from Mark because he feels sorry for me.

It made her worry that she would end up with a broken heart when the dust finally settled. And so would her daughters. She wasn't sure what to do to lessen the pain for all three of them when Anthony finally walked away.

While she frolicked and played with Anthony and her daughters, enjoying their playful competition of who could do the best monkey impression, she struggled to stay in the moment and enjoy her time with Anthony while it lasted. She knew her life was a mess. It just wasn't the right time to start a new relationship.

She had to deal with going to court and fighting with Mark first. Once the court case was settled, she had to focus on getting established in a new life with her daughters. She had to find a new job in a new town before she could really think about the possibility of having a relationship.

Maybe Anthony realizes that and that's why he's stepped back into more of a friend role? I can handle being friends, right?

Kay wasn't sure she could handle being only friends with Anthony. For some reason, meeting Anthony awakened her libido in a way she wasn't sure how to handle, especially if he only wanted to be in the friend zone. She wanted way more than that with Anthony.

Their Sunday night was similar to their Saturday evening, only taking showers after they got back to the rooms from dinner instead of before, like when they went swimming. As Kay settled into bed between her daughters, she wasn't sure how to feel.

As much as she longed to go to Anthony's room and take their relationship to the next level, she felt guilty for having that desire. He was so much younger and way more attractive than anyone else Kay had ever been involved with before. She knew he could have any woman he wanted with a lot less effort than he was having to put in to spend time with her. She didn't have a clue why someone as perfect as Anthony would ever even look twice at her.

He deserved to find the perfect woman. Someone tall and svelte and closer to his own age. As an older woman who was so vertically challenged that even a gain of a single pound looked like she'd packed on ten, Kay didn't feel like she was anywhere near the ideal woman for Anthony.

A single tear slid down her cheek as she resolved to appreciate Anthony's friendship and help in dealing with her messy life, but to make sure he knew she would never ask for anything more between them.

She drifted off to sleep, grateful that she could still live out her fantasies with Anthony in her dreams.

~ ~ ~

Monday, October 8, 2018

Monday morning, Kay was awakened by her phone ringing on the bedside table. Apparently, all the swimming and sightseeing over the weekend was exhausting enough for the girls that they were still sound asleep at almost ten in the morning.

Kay extracted herself from the bed without waking them to answer.

"Hello," she answered as she made her way to the bathroom.

"Good morning, Kay," Matt Monroe greeted her through the phone. "I just wanted to give you an update after my court filing this morning."

Kay was nervous about what he was going to say as she leaned against the vanity.

"I filed a petition for an order of protection and termination of Mark's visitation rights," Matt continued speaking. "I included the photos your dad gave me from your house, the evidence of Mark's fingerprints there implicating him in the break-in, and the preliminary statement of what happened Friday from your dad. I need you to get to a computer and send me an email with statements from you, the girls, and Anthony, in each of your own words about that as well, along with any other incidents you want to list in the past as previous altercations with Mark."

"Okay, we'll write those up today and email them as soon as they're finished." Kay wished she'd walked into Anthony's room instead of her bathroom, so he could have heard all this and helped her remember everything Matt asked for from them.

"The court date is set for Monday, November fifth," Matt stated curtly. "I need you, the girls, Anthony, and your dad there at eight a.m. and ready to testify. I'll email you a list of questions as soon as I go through your statements, so you can prepare for taking the stand. I don't want anyone to sound rehearsed while you're testifying, but I don't want any of you to feel lost or blindsided by what you might be asked. I can't say for certain that Mark's attorney won't still ask some off-the-wall questions, but hopefully at least having an idea of what you'll need to answer will be helpful. It should be pretty open and shut, though, especially with listing out Mark's violent outbursts, his vandalism of your home, and any other inappropriate interactions he's had with you or the girls. You'll have to justify moving to Texas on such short notice, but with a job that pays that much more than your last one, that should be easy. Any questions for me for now?"

"No, Matt," Kay sighed. "Thank you so much for taking care of all this. I'll get those statements sent to you and I'll call if I have any questions after we receive your emailed instructions."

They said their goodbyes and Kay quickly took care of her morning bathroom needs before dressing and knocking on the door between her room and Anthony's.

"No need to knock, Sweetheart," she heard Anthony chuckle from the other side. "It's your door that's closed."

Kay opened the door and saw Anthony sitting on his bed already dressed for the day. "Sorry, I didn't want to just walk in on you unannounced." Kay felt herself blush as she stepped through the open door.

"You can walk in on me unannounced anytime, Baby." Anthony stood and took the two steps needed to reach Kay where she'd stopped just inside his room. He clasped Kay by the shoulders before rubbing his hands down her arms and taking her hands in his. "What's wrong?" Anthony looked down into her eyes as if he could see through to her very soul.

"Nothing's wrong." Kay was unable to move once their gazes locked on each other. "Matt called. We have to write out our statements about what happened Friday and email them to him this afternoon. He has the court date set for Monday, November fifth. Do you know your work schedule to know if it will be a problem for you to be in Tulsa that day?"

"I can pull it up." Anthony released her hand to pull his phone out of his pocket. "But even if I'm scheduled to work that day, I'm sure Rick will be able to get another pilot that week if I need to be off."

He fiddled with his phone for a few minutes and then looked back to Kay with what she could only describe as a wicked grin. "The fates must be on our side," he grinned. "I'm off the fourth through the eighth, so we can do court the fifth, sixth, and seventh with no problems. Did Matt say how many days he thinks it will take?"

"No, he didn't say." Kay shook her head. "Maybe he'll have an idea when he sends us the question lists he's going to put together based on our statements. I don't imagine he can guess yet until he has an idea of how long each of us will need to be on the stand."

Anthony set his laptop on the table in the room and opened it up. "Do you want to use my laptop, or your new tablet, to send the email?" He pulled out the chair at the table for Kay to take a seat and then sat beside her.

"I thought that was an e-reader," Kay replied, feeling stupid for her lack of technological knowledge to know the difference.

"It's a tablet that has the Kindle app on it for reading e-books," Anthony answered with a slight upturn of his lips. "It also has a web browser, and we can set up your email on it, too, so you can use it like a computer."

"Don't tell Tia that or I'll never be able to use it myself." Kay's mood dropped when she realized she would have to figure out how to budget in a laptop to replace the desktop computer that Tia used at home for her online courses.

"I guess I should've ordered three of them," Anthony smiled as he logged into his computer.

"No, you shouldn't," Kay argued. "I owe you more than I can repay as it is. I'll be reimbursing you for our expenses on this trip as soon as I get my first check from whatever new job I can find this week, but I still have no idea how to repay you for helping me find a new job and place to live."

Anthony leaned over and kissed Kay on the forehead. "I won't take a dime from you for anything, Baby." Anthony ran his hand through

Kay's hair, tucking it behind her ear. "You don't owe me for anything, ever."

"Yes, I do," Kay retorted as she shot up out of the chair and started to pace through Anthony's room. "The flight and this hotel and the zoo, swimsuits, and everything else you've paid for this weekend are all my expenses because of my messed-up life. They aren't your expenses or your responsibility in any way. So, yes, I do owe you!"

Anthony leaned back in his chair and waited for Kay to get close enough he could reach her without getting up. As soon as she was close enough in her rapid walking circle, he pulled her onto his lap to stop her pacing.

"Baby," he drawled as he put both hands on either side of her face to make her look him in the eye. "It's not your mess or my mess, it's our mess. I'm trying to take things slow like you want, but Friday night forced us to speed up our relationship, whether you're ready or not. I'm doing my best to keep from pushing you to do anything you aren't ready for, but I still intend for us to end up married. Sooner rather than later. So, I'm going to go ahead and get started on taking care of my family's financial needs."

"But we're just friends," Kay protested. *He can't be real,* she thought. *He's the one who has been pulling back and putting us in the friend zone.* "We haven't even done…" She trailed off, feeling her face flush at her sexual thoughts. "…anything more than friend stuff."

"Friend stuff?" Anthony chuckled as he moved his hands down her body to grip her hips and grind his erection into her. "Baby, I'm sure you can feel how much I want to do with you that I would never do with a friend."

"Bu-but you haven't wanted to d-do any, anything in days," Kay stuttered, looking up at Anthony with wide eyes. She wasn't sure how to switch gears again after she'd just decided to be friends only the night before.

"Oh, Baby." Anthony leaned his forehead against Kay's, their mouths so close their breath mingled. "I've wanted to do a lot of things but couldn't because we haven't had any time alone so I could. Do you know how hard it was to hide this when we were swimming?" He ground his hips against her again, so Kay could feel his steel-hard erection.

The look in his eyes was smoldering, making Kay realize that whether she understood why he was attracted to her or not, he definitely wanted her. Just as their lips were about to touch in what Kay knew would be a panty-melting kiss, she heard her daughters stirring in the other room.

Kay jumped up off of Anthony's lap just as Maria came running into Anthony's room.

"Morning Mommy!" Maria barreled into Kay and hugged her tight. She released Kay and turned to Anthony, throwing herself into his lap and her arms around his neck. "Morning Anthony!" She released him and hopped back down. "What's for breakfast?"

"I'm not sure." Kay looked over her daughter's shoulder toward the door between rooms. "Is your sister up yet?"

"Yeah, she's in the bathroom." Maria bounced on her toes. "I figured I'd ask about breakfast while I'm waiting on her so I can get dressed." She was still wearing her favorite pink flannel nightgown and her blonde hair was a tangled mess from how she rolled around in her sleep.

"Baby, why don't you go help the girls get dressed and I'll order room service for breakfast?" Anthony gave her a panty melting smile. "After we eat, we can get started on those statements."

"Can I get French toast for breakfast?" Maria looked hopefully at Anthony.

"Sure, Princess," he replied. "Does Tia like French toast, too? Or do you think she'd rather have something else?"

"French toast is my favorite." Tia surprised them as she walked into the room already dressed, apparently already ready for the day.

"Perfect." Anthony smiled at Tia. Then he turned back to look at Kay who was still standing where she'd landed when she jumped off Anthony's lap, feeling overwhelmed by everything that had already happened that morning. "Kay, Baby," he cooed, reaching out to stroke her cheek. "French toast for four okay with you?"

Kay's gaze snapped back to Anthony's face. She looked into his eyes and realized that no matter how overwhelming her life seemed at the moment, Anthony wanted to be there to support her through it. *Can too good to be true really be true? Can I trust that the fairy tale is real?*

Kay decided in that moment to quit second guessing whether a relationship with Anthony was right or not, to not fight against it because she thought the timing was off, and to just live each day as it came, trusting fate to put her where she was supposed to be, with whom she was supposed to love.

Chapter Eight

Tuesday, October 9, 2018

Anthony was just as restless as the girls after spending all day Monday, and most of the morning Tuesday, in the hotel room while they each took a turn typing up their statements about the altercation Friday night with Kay's ex-husband.

Kay had let him set up her tablet with her email, but since it didn't have a traditional keyboard or word processing software, they opted to use his laptop for typing up their statements to send to her attorney. Everyone needing to use his laptop made him realize that he needed to find out what the girls would need to do schoolwork on, if Kay decided to take the job with the GWA, and homeschool the girls with the assistance of the tutors Rick already employed. There was no way they could both use his laptop and get everything done in a timely manner.

He hated that he couldn't get more time alone with Kay to fully settle their financial disagreement, almost as much as he hated not having alone time with her to get her naked. While he wanted Kay more than he'd ever wanted a woman before, he knew it was more than just a sexual attraction. He wanted to be not only her protector, but also her provider.

Regardless of how politically incorrect his caveman instincts were, he had no desire to try to tamp them down. He just hoped that his inner caveman wouldn't scare Kay off. *Maybe it won't if I can keep most of those caveman feelings hidden? Maybe I can be their provider without Kay noticing if I just order what they need for school without mentioning it to her first? Better to ask forgiveness than permission, right?*

While Kay was helping the girls on his computer, Anthony texted his boss to find out what they would need for school supplies. He covertly placed an order on his phone and had two iPads shipped to his parents' house in Heart's Destiny. He expedited the shipping, so the girls would be able to pick them up on Thursday, and be ready to start their new school on Friday. If Kay opted to take a job at Burleson Incorporated instead, the girls could use the iPads for whatever school they ended up in. Hopefully, Heart's Destiny Elementary and Middle Schools.

When Kay finally sent off the final email to her attorney with all four of their statements attached, Anthony was more than ready to get them all out of the hotel, and do something more active to help the girls expend some of their pent-up energy. Kay felt they should have lunch first, though, so instead of the additional sightseeing he wanted to do, they made their way down to the hotel restaurant to eat before going to the arena for Kay's interview with Rick.

To call it an interview was a gross overstatement, but Anthony knew better than to tell Kay that. She had the job already according to his texts with Rick, but Anthony knew that Kay wouldn't feel right about taking a job she didn't even interview for beforehand.

While they were seated in the restaurant, several of the wrestlers came in for lunch. They would be doing a workout at the hotel gym while the ring, cameras, lighting, and stage were being set up at the arena. Anthony introduced Kay, Tia, and Maria to as many of the guys as he could in the restaurant, but most of them were just people he knew in passing, not any of his closest friends.

"What time am I supposed to meet Rick for the interview?" Kay looked nervous as she pushed her food around on her plate more than she actually ate.

"He didn't give a set time," Anthony replied with a smile, reaching over to take her free hand in his, hoping to soothe her obvious nerves. "He's already at the arena to supervise the show set-up, so whenever we get there is fine."

"So, we should go there now?" Kay squeezed his hand. "Before he gets too busy with the actual show going on?"

"Yeah, we can go now, if you want," Anthony replied, masking his disappointment at not being able to spend another afternoon sightseeing with Kay and the girls. "I was thinking closer to two or three, so we could get in a trip to the aquarium first, but maybe now is better than later when he might be stuck in a meeting with the writers to make any final changes to tonight's show."

Anthony quickly paid for lunch and escorted his family out of the hotel and off to the arena. Once there, he found Rick sitting in his makeshift office. He introduced Kay, pointedly telling Rick that she was there to interview for the flight-attendant job, hoping his boss would get his point and not make Kay feel like she was being given a job for any reason other than her own merit.

While Kay was talking to Rick, Anthony showed the girls around the backstage area, making sure they saw the locker rooms while they were still empty, just so they would know where the women's locker room was if they needed a restroom during their time at the arena.

On a normal day, they would have all needed to change into workout clothes in the dressing rooms, but since Kay was going to do her interview while Anthony was showing the girls around and starting their self-defense training, they'd opted to dress for the workout at the hotel, so they didn't have to split up to change while Kay was in her interview still in her professional dress.

Anthony realized the mistake of wearing sweatpants when Kay had first walked into his room wearing her knee-length gray dress and black fuck-me pumps. It was sleeveless and form-fitting. She was a vision that caused his cock to come to attention and tent his sweats. She hadn't put on the matching long-sleeved jacket that was almost as long as the dress when he first saw her, so he was trying desperately to figure out how to quell his reaction. He was relieved when she put on the jacket that actually concealed her curves before they'd left their rooms to go meet his boss and coworkers.

Once Anthony and the girls made their way down to where the ring was already set up, he finally got to expend some of the pent-up energy they were all suffering with by teaching the girls how to run the ropes and flip to land safely before starting their self-defense training.

He may not be their stepdad yet, but he was definitely feeling like it already. And that meant he was going to make sure his girls knew how to defend themselves, even as he prayed they never, ever had to do it.

~ ~ ~

Kay was a nervous wreck as she took the seat in front of Rick Robertson's desk in the corner of the backstage area of the arena. She wasn't sure she was qualified to be a flight attendant based on the minimal information Anthony had given her about the job she was interviewing for, but she hoped she wasn't wasting the time of the owner of the company to even sit for an interview.

She'd at least dressed for the role in a dark gray sheath dress with a matching jacket and her tallest black heels, instead of one of the t-shirt and jeans combos she'd been wearing every day while they were in Dallas. She brought all three of her professional dress outfits with her for her interviews, but based on the fact that Anthony put dress pants and a suit jacket in a garment bag to go to the arena, so he could change out of his workout clothes after doing some self-defense training with the girls while she was doing the interview, she assumed she would need to buy a few more to be able to have more options to wear on the job. If she was somehow, miraculously, qualified and got it, anyway.

Considering how much she felt herself shaking when Anthony left with the girls, she feared that wouldn't be her biggest issue, since there was no way anyone would hire her for a flight-attendant position when she would obviously spill any drinks she tried to serve the passengers with her shaky hands. *Why did I feel so much more confident when he was standing beside me?*

"Anthony told me you have extensive childcare experience." Rick leaned back in his chair and looked at Kay across the desk.

"Yeah, yes," Kay stuttered, hating her own lack of self-confidence. "Mostly my own daughters, but I also did a lot of babysitting as a teenager." *But that's not what a flight attendant does, so why does that matter?*

"Perfect." Rick smiled. "The position title is technically flight attendant, but it's more of a mother's helper job while we're flying between cities and maybe some babysitting at the hotel if some of the parents need a night out. Mostly it's just making sure the kids all have whatever they need while we're flying, passing out snacks, keeping them entertained when they need to be distracted from their ears

213

popping or turbulence, and allowing those of us who have to work on the plane to not have to worry about our kids, so we can actually get some work done. That sort of thing."

Kay let out a sigh of relief. She could definitely handle a mother's helper job, and maybe not knowing anything about the plane, or the other duties of a flight attendant wouldn't be an issue. *And maybe I won't get any motion sickness that causes me to lose the job on the first flight.*

"The salary is fifty-two thousand a year, paid bi-monthly via direct deposit. The schedule is the same as Anthony's, five days on and five days off, where you just have to meet us wherever we are the day before you start your flight rotation. We take extra time off around the normal major holidays, taking off from the weekend before through the weekend after. It usually works out that whichever flight crew is working the Friday before our break comes back to work the Monday after, basically splitting their rotation into two or three days before and two or three days after. The other flight crew ends up with a longer holiday break that way, but it evens out when the opposite flight crew splits their shifts the next holiday. You'll be on the same flight crew as Anthony, so you'll get a longer break for Thanksgiving and split your shifts at Christmas."

Wow, Kay thought, feeling her nerves dissipate. *He's talking like I already have the job.*

"You have the standard insurance benefits, but time off is hard with our travel schedule. Our other flight crew members have to negotiate with their opposite crew counterparts to swap days if they need sick time or personal time, but since I haven't hired anyone for your position yet on the other crew, we'll have to figure out what to do if you need to take time off until we fill that position. To make up for the inconvenience of having to travel constantly, we provide tutors for your kids. There are three of them currently on staff, but if we need to add more to meet your daughters' needs, we will. After we do the paperwork to get you on the payroll, you'll meet with them to determine what needs to be done to set up the curriculum for your daughters based on the homeschool regulations in your state of residence and their individual intellectual levels."

Kay was astounded by the scope of how much Rick was telling her about the benefits of the job. *A free education for my girls? One that*

*is designed to work at their level, so maybe they won't be so bored
with what they're learning? How can I possibly turn that down, even
if I don't think I'm really qualified to do all the aspects of the job?
Fake it 'til you make it, I guess.*

"After you've worked a few flights, you'll get to know the other
moms and be able to trade out with them on babysitting at the hotel
some nights, if you want a night off with Anthony. The moms have all
been swapping out on that on their own, so there's not a set schedule
for if there is any extra babysitting. Technically, it's not part of your
job, so don't feel obligated to babysit every time they ask."

"Oh, I won't mind babysitting at all." Kay smiled brightly.

"I'm sure you won't," Rick replied with a little chuckle. "But after
years of traveling with the only alone time we get without our children
being when we can swap off babysitting with the other parents in the
company, I've learned that it's best to set some boundaries and only
swap babysitting nights when I get equal babysitting nights in return.
If you let them, these animals will have you babysitting every night,
not giving you and Anthony any alone time. I don't want you to get
burned out by not having any time to yourself, or lose both you and
Anthony when you both quit, so you can actually spend time alone
together."

"I would never do that." Kay shook her head, hoping he
understood she was more serious about the job than he seemed to think
she would be.

"I'm sure you don't intend to." Rick's lips turned up in a little
smile. "But I also know that you and Anthony are in a new
relationship, and need to spend your time building the foundation
you'll both lean on as your relationship grows. I'm just saying to
make sure you make time for yourselves, focus on each other for a
while, not my needy employees, who won't realize they're taking
advantage of your willingness to help out."

Is that relationship advice from my new boss? Kay saw a look of
sadness in his eyes that made her wonder if he was speaking from
experience. She didn't feel comfortable asking him about his personal
life during her interview, so she filed that away for the future in case
she ever got to know him or his significant other well enough to delve
deeper into his motivations for the advice he just gave her. Regardless

of his reasons, she would heed his warning to balance her time with Anthony with her time working.

Rick picked up a tablet that was laying on the desk. "I've got you signed in to fill out your HR paperwork." He handed the tablet to Kay. "Just put in your info on there and take a picture of your driver's license and social security card when the tablet tells you to. Once that's done, you can leave the tablet here on my desk and meet me in catering and I'll take you to where we have the classroom set up, so you can talk to the tutors and get started on the homeschooling process."

Kay fumbled through the procedures of filling out her electronic human resources forms, not quite sure when she was actually offered the job, or if she was accepting it by default by filling out the forms. The iPad was surprisingly easy to figure out how to use when it was already in the forms and gave her step-by-step instructions when she needed to photograph her identification.

Who'd have thought a wrestling company would be so high-tech? But I guess they can't travel with a bulky photocopier to be able to take copies of my identification like they did at my last job.

Once she was done, she wandered around the backstage area until she found Rick, since she wasn't familiar with their setup enough to know where catering was to actually meet him in the right part of the building. She was surprised that she didn't find Anthony or her daughters while she was exploring the expansive space.

Surely, they haven't left the arena to try to sneak in a trip to the aquarium? Kay thought as Rick walked her through a part of the cavernous building that she hadn't seen yet.

Rick opened a door and they walked into a room that Kay assumed was their temporary classroom. There were several tables and chairs, but only a couple of children were already there chatting with two women and one man. The man and one of the women looked to be in their mid-to-late forties and Kay wondered if they were a couple. The other woman looked to be closer to Kay's age.

"Daddy," screamed one of the children, a girl about Tia's age or maybe a year younger, with her brown hair up in a ponytail and wearing jeans and a t-shirt with a picture of a wrestler on it. She ran up and threw herself into Rick's arms.

"Hey, Pumpkin." Rick lifted his daughter off the ground and returned her hug. He shifted to hold her on his hip like Kay used to hold her daughters when they were toddlers and turned so they were both facing Kay. "This is Miss Kay. She's going to be helping out on our flights. And she has two daughters who are going to be traveling with us, too."

"Hi, I'm Britney!" The little girl held one hand out to Kay while her other was wrapped around her dad's neck.

"Nice to meet you." Kay shook the young girl's hand.

"Where are your daughters?" Britney looked around like she expected them to be right beside Kay.

"Um, I'm not sure," Kay replied with a smile. "Anthony was going to show them around the arena while I did my interview and I seem to have lost them."

Britney's smile fell from her face. Clearly, the child was disappointed to not be able to meet a couple of new friends. Before Kay could say anything to console her and let her know they would still be able to meet that day, the other people in the room walked over and started introducing themselves.

Kay decided she was going to have to come up with some way of remembering names better. Between the dozen people Anthony had introduced to her at the hotel and the half dozen she'd met so far at the arena, she was already swimming in a sea of strange names in her head, and knew she would only remember a few of them for at least the first couple of days on this new job.

She tried to prioritize which ones she needed to remember the most. Rick Robertson was her new boss and his daughter's name was Britney. They would be the easiest to remember for her because of how important they were in her getting the new job and her daughters developing a new friendship. Mr. and Mrs. Traverson, Dan and Ivy, were the tutors who specialized in math and science and would be her daughters' new teachers. Stacy Jones was the tutor who focused on reading, writing, and history with the younger children and would be able to work with Tia on her high school level literature requirements that Kay already knew she would test in at. Those would be the first names she definitely remembered. Hopefully, she would catch on to the names of all the wrestlers, their families, the other members of the flight crew, and the rest of the backstage staff quicker than she feared she would.

Apparently, the girls would need iPads to do their actual schoolwork, but the Traversons already had the software on theirs that the girls could use the first couple of days to test their knowledge base to start designing their personalized curriculum. Kay didn't know how much iPads cost, but she hoped she had enough in savings to cover it because she hated the idea of asking Anthony to cover more of her expenses. Then Kay remembered Anthony's words from the day before.

"Baby, it's not your mess or my mess, it's our mess. I'm trying to take things slow like you want, but Friday night forced us to speed up our relationship, whether you're ready or not. I'm doing my best to keep from pushing you to do anything you aren't ready for, but I still intend for us to end up married. Sooner rather than later. So, I'm going to go ahead and get started on taking care of my family's financial needs."

She hated that their conversation was interrupted, and she hadn't gotten a chance to finish it with Anthony since. She tried to analyze what he said and compare it to how he was acting toward her. Were the actions she felt were him stepping back into the friend zone, actually his way of not pushing her to take their relationship to the next level before she was ready? Was his insistence on paying for everything really because he thought he was taking care of his family? Kay wasn't sure which was the correct perception of how Anthony had been interacting with her and her daughters the last few days.

She kept second-guessing her own thoughts, so she decided to take advantage of being alone while she searched the arena for her children to call her best friend for a second opinion.

Deanna answered on the second ring. "Kay, thank God you called!" Dee screamed through the phone. "Mom said your house was broken into and you and the girls were missing, and you haven't answered your phone or returned my texts in four days!"

"Sorry, Dee," Kay sighed. "I've been too busy to even pull it out and look at my messages. And it's been on silent for my job interview today."

"Where are you? What the hell is going on?"

"Promise me you won't say a word about any of this to anyone, especially Mark." Kay pled with her friend while making her way down an empty hallway in the backstage area of the arena.

"Obviously," Dee replied with a huff. "I would never tell that asshole anything."

Kay spent a few minutes explaining to her best friend about the events of Friday night, how she ended up in Dallas with Anthony, hearing from her father about the break-in, her discussions with her attorney, how they were all going to have to testify in court, and that she would be starting a new job traveling with the GWA. After that, she told her best friend about how her discussions with Anthony before Friday were leading to them starting a sexual relationship, and maybe being more after she was comfortable introducing him to her daughters. Then Kay explained her feeling that after the mess that was Friday night, he hadn't acted like he wanted to follow their original planned path, so she thought they were actually living in the friend zone.

"But yesterday, in the only five minutes we've had alone since Friday, he mentioned still wanting to marry me." Kay confided in her friend as she stopped to sit down when she came to a secluded area where she felt like she could keep talking and not worry about running into anyone she didn't want to overhear her conversation. "And today when I was doing my interview with the owner of the company where he's worked for over a year, his boss, or I guess our boss now, was giving me advice as if he thinks we're already a couple. I'm so confused. I don't know if we're just friends, or if we're more. And with everything up in the air with court, I'm not sure now is the time to start a new relationship, so I have no idea what I should do."

"So, he's the one who mentioned ya'll getting married?" Dee sounded surprised as she asked the question. "It wasn't just your fairy-tale fantasies last week?"

"Oh, no," Kay replied, shaking her head, even though Dee couldn't see her. "I've really tried to take your advice and not let myself believe the fairy tale is real. He's the one who told my dad that he fell in love with me at first sight. But he hasn't even kissed me since Friday night. We've gone swimming and sightseeing with the girls, but the girls are with us twenty-four-seven, so it's more like I'm hanging out with a friend, like if you and I took a road trip with the kids, not something romantic."

"I have no idea what to say." Dee sounded astonished. "I mean, normally I'd tell you to believe his actions and not his words, and say you're in the friend zone. But since he's still talking marriage when the girls aren't there and he's telling others you're a couple, I have to wonder if his actions are just super friend zone because the girls are there."

"So, what should I do?" Kay fiddled her fingers nervously as she awaited Dee's answers to her inquiries. "Do I let myself start to believe a little in the fairy tale?"

"Maybe?" Dee drew the word out to multiple syllables like she wasn't quite convinced. "But maybe wait until after you go to court to make sure that doesn't blow it all up."

"Friend zone for the next month, got it." Kay was thankful her best friend could help her settle on a plan. "Thanks, Dee."

"Anytime, Kay," Dee replied cheerfully. "Now turn your phone back up and reply to my texts. I have at least two or three dates to tell you about."

"Don't wait to text, tell me now," Kay implored, wanting to hear something positive happening in her friend's life. "But hurry because I have to go find my girls and get them set up with their new tutors for testing in the next couple of days."

They continued chatting for another fifteen minutes where Dee described not two or three but four different dates with four different guys. None of which she would grant a second date, even the one she slept with, regardless of the fact that Dee claimed it was good sex. Kay finally had to get off the phone when Dee started to describe his dick in detail.

She got up from her seat and wandered back down the hall the way she'd come, hoping to not get too lost before she found Anthony and her daughters.

~~~

As the guys started arriving at the ring to do some run-throughs of their planned matches for the night and get in some extra sparring,
~~~

Anthony wondered what was taking so long for Kay to finish her interview and meet them at the ring.

"Want to sit ringside and watch the wrestlers practice?" Anthony entreated the girls.

"Can we?" Tia had a look of sheer excitement on her face.

"Yeah, Princess," he replied as he helped Maria over the ringside barricade. "We can stay and watch them spar for the next couple of hours if you want."

"I definitely want to watch." Tia put her hands on the top of the barricade and pushed up to be able to throw one leg over to sit straddling the three-and-a-half-foot tall, black-vinyl, padded barricade. "I like watching wrestling on TV and trying to figure out the physics of the moves, but it's hard to do with the size distortion of the television and the actual size of the wrestlers not being a known variable."

I have no idea what she's talking about, Anthony thought as he made his own way over the barricade and sat down in one of the ringside seats beside Maria. *Maybe I should talk to the tutors about helping me learn what I need to be able to understand what Tia is studying?*

"Yeah, I bet that does make it harder." Anthony scratched the back of his head. "What variables do you know when you're trying to figure out the physics of wrestling?"

"I use the height and weight announced for each wrestler and use that and my estimation of the angles of their bodies in relation to their opponent to estimate how much power they're producing to execute a specific wrestling move."

"Be sure to ask the guys their real stats, then," Anthony chuckled as his best friends walked down the ramp toward them.

"Their real stats?" Tia looked confused as she tilted her head inquisitively.

"Oh yeah!" Anthony smiled at her still sitting straddling the barricade. "The announcers don't always have their real stats, so your numbers may be off. Like with these guys." Anthony motioned to James and Dean as they walked up and stood on either side of Tia. "I know they're only six-foot-four, but the announcer always bills them at six-foot-five."

Tia turned to look back and forth between the twins.

"So, they lied to the announcer?" Maria's eyes widened in surprise as she looked up at Anthony. She turned to look at the twins. "Lying is a sin, so you need to tell the announcer your real heights."

Anthony fought not to laugh at the incredulous looks on his best friends' faces. The two large, long-haired, tattooed, badass, biker-looking men didn't appear to know how to take the reprimand of a precocious eight-year-old girl.

"Why you throwing us under the bus?" Dean turned his face toward Anthony and gave him a glare.

James chuckled, which only served to increase Dean's irritation. Dean punched his brother in the arm. "Don't laugh at me," Dean growled at his brother. "You're in trouble too."

"No, I'm not," James replied, holding his hands up in surrender. "I'm not the one who lied about our height. And no roughhousing around the girls." James turned to face Tia and stuck out his hand for her to shake. "I'm James, your Aunt Randi has told me all about you, Tia." After shaking her hand, he leaned across the barricade and reached out to Maria. "And Maria. It's a pleasure to meet you both."

"You know our Aunt Randi?" Tia looked at James like she wasn't sure she could believe him.

"Yeah, I met her the same night Anthony met your mom," James replied as he stood back up.

"Are you, her boyfriend?" Maria grinned mischievously.

"Um, uh," James started to stammer, clearly not expecting Maria's bold question. "We're just texting right now since I'm always traveling."

To save his friend from the girls starting a barrage of questions about him and their aunt, Anthony decided to change the subject by introducing Dean. "Girls, this is Dean." Anthony pointed to Dean. "He's James's twin brother. They've been my best friends since we were toddlers. They grew up on the next ranch over from me."

"You need to teach your friends not to lie." Maria wagged her finger at Anthony.

"I didn't lie," Dean protested, throwing up his hands in frustration. "It's professional wrestling. It's all acting. We're telling stories to entertain people. Saying we're bigger than we are is to enhance the gimmick, not lying. Just like it isn't lying to pretend to beat the crap out of our opponents and act like we really hate them when they're actually our friends. The character Dean Dangerous is six-foot-five and two-hundred seventy-five pounds. I can't help it that I'm not actually as big as the character I play in the ring."

Both girls started laughing at Dean's outrageous overacting with his arms flapping around like he was a bird trying to fly away during his rant. James gave Anthony a nod of thanks while the girls talked through whether or not acting was actually lying. After a brief back and forth with Dean, where it was determined that acting isn't really lying since it couldn't actually be a sin when the members of the church acted like a doll was really the baby Jesus in the Christmas pageant, they agreed to give Dean a pass even though Tia wasn't quite convinced that giving inaccurate height and weight information to build up the characters' mystique wasn't crossing the line to lying. Once she explained why she needed accurate data, Dean agreed to tell her his actual height and weight for her calculations, since she wasn't actually watching as a form of entertainment based on the suspended reality of the wrestling world.

Tia finally hopped down from the barricade and sat in the ringside chair beside Anthony as the Hunter brothers got in the ring to run through some moves with their opponents for the night. She watched their practice intently. Anthony was completely fascinated by the way her mind worked, even though he didn't understand it himself.

Maria, however, wasn't as enthralled by the action in the ring as Tia. Instead of watching the wrestlers in the ring, she started asking him a million questions.

"So, what's going to happen if Mom gets this job today?"

"Well, then you'll get to travel with us all the time and not just for this short vacation," Anthony replied.

"Does that mean we can do our group Halloween costume for the company party instead of trick-or-treating?"

"Definitely," Anthony answered.

"Awesome!" Maria shouted. "I've never been to a Halloween party that was for grownups."

Anthony wished she'd brought some of her toys on the trip to give him an idea of how to keep her entertained while they sat there, when her questions turned a little more personal about his relationship with Kay.

"So, are you my mom's boyfriend?"

Anthony wasn't sure how to answer that question. He liked to think he was, but he and Kay hadn't actually labeled their relationship for him to be able to honestly say yes. Before he could think of how to respond, she continued her string of questions.

"Are you going to marry Mom? If you do, can we change my last name to Burleson like you? Can Tia and I call you Daddy? Or do you prefer we just call you Anthony since you'd only be our stepdad?"

"Um," Anthony started to speak and floundered for a second while he wished Kay would come out from the backstage area to help him answer Maria's questions. He looked around the massive space, and not seeing Kay, he decided to just wing it and hope Kay wouldn't be pissed at him for his answers.

"Well, Princess," he drawled as he brushed a platinum ringlet of hair out of her eyes. "I haven't quite convinced your mom yet, but I do want to marry her."

"We'll help you convince her," Tia declared from his other side without taking her eyes off the action in the ring.

Anthony turned to look at her, but she was so focused she didn't look up at him. He turned back to look at Maria.

"As for your other questions…" Anthony trailed off as he ran a hand through his hair trying to be diplomatic and not insult their father, or reveal his caveman instinct to not only change their last name, but to also protect them from their asshole father, and anyone or anything else that could potentially be a danger to them. "It's going to all be dependent on how the judge rules when we go to court next month. We'll have to ask the judge if you can change your last name or not."

"What do kids normally call their stepdad?" Tia questioned softly.

Anthony turned back to her and was floored when he saw her looking up at him with her eyes filled with hope and trust. These two little girls might not have a drop of his blood, but they both had a huge part of his heart.

"I'm not sure," Anthony shrugged one shoulder and scratched his chin like he was thinking. "I imagine some kids call their stepdad by his name and others call him some version of dad. I think it just depends on what you want to call me. I'll answer to anything you want to call me, as long as you don't call me late for dinner."

"Late for dinner is a horrible name!" Maria exclaimed.

"It's an even worse thing to be," Anthony chuckled as he turned back to Maria, who he suddenly had an urge to tickle.

When he gave in and tickled both sides of her waist at the same time, Tia surprised him by coming to her sister's defense and tickling him the same way. They ended up rolling on the floor in an epic tickle fight that drew the attention of his friends in the ring. The next thing he knew he was face down on the floor with James and Dean holding him down, so the girls could both tickle him.

"Uncle!" Anthony shouted through his laughter as he tried to escape the torture. "Damn it, man! Let go of my hands, so I can tap out!"

"That's a bad word." Maria continued tickling his armpit.

"How should we punish him for saying a bad word?" Tia asked the guys watching them from in the ring.

"I'll start a swear jar as soon as you let me up," Anthony answered amid shouts from the ring of "swats" and "a time-out chair" from the wrestlers watching their antics.

"Naw, I think he needs a spanking," Dean laughed, letting go of Anthony's right leg to swat him on the ass.

"I think he needs five more minutes of tickle torture!" Tia exclaimed as she continued her onslaught to his ribs.

"I agree with Tia," James choked out through his laughter.

No amount of begging or pleading would convince them to let him up until the five minutes were up. Anthony vowed to return the torture to his best friends just as soon as he could get them all home at the same time as his older brothers were all there to help him retaliate.

When they finally stopped the tickle torture and released his arms and legs, Anthony laid there for a few more minutes to catch his breath. It took him a little longer than the average person to recover and felt way too much like his struggle to breathe with his collapsed lung right after the accident.

"Fuc, fudge," James quickly changed his normal frustrated curse. "You okay?" He checked on Anthony when he realized Anthony was still struggling for air.

Dean joined his brother in cursing under his breath, but the girls didn't hear him to reprimand him for saying bad words. "Dude, I'm sorry. We weren't thinking about your lung."

"It's okay," Anthony assured them as he finally pushed himself up off the floor to sit up. "I'll be fine, just takes a little longer to catch my breath than before."

"What's wrong with your lung?" Tia was sitting on the floor beside him and looking up at him with fear in her eyes. Maria was beside her with a similar look. Anthony never wanted to see that look on their faces, and hated that his decreased lung capacity was the cause of their fear at the moment.

"I'm okay, Princesses." Anthony took each of their hands and gave them a gentle squeeze to comfort them. "I had a collapsed lung eighteen months ago, but the doctor fixed me right up, so it won't collapse again. It just takes me a little extra time to catch my breath now, but it's nothing to worry about."

Tia looked at him like she wasn't quite buying his story, but at least she didn't look like she was afraid he was going to die anymore. "Can I use your computer tonight to look up the precautions you should be following based on your injury?"

"Sure," Anthony agreed, feeling humbled by Tia's need to take care of him. "In fact, I can probably get Doc Hayes to email me my last chest x-ray report, so you can see that my lungs are both fine now."

Her eyes went wide with excitement. "Do you think he can actually send the pictures? One of the classes I was looking at on Coursera for next semester was about how to read x-rays and diagnose things like bronchitis and pneumonia. It would be cool to see what your lungs look like compared to what they show us in the class."

What the fuck? She's twelve and taking online classes meant for doctors? A law degree might be a waste of her abilities. Anthony looked back and forth between the girls like Maria could read his mind and explain Tia to him. Maria just grinned and he read her expression to mean, *"Yeah, I don't get her either."*

"Um, yeah, I'll ask him," Anthony finally nodded. "Why are you taking medical classes when you want to go to law school?"

"Because these classes don't count for anything, so I just take anything that looks interesting," Tia replied matter-of-factly. "When I actually get to take college classes that count toward a degree, then I'll focus on the law classes. If I were to take them now, I'd just be bored having to take them again when I get to college."

"That makes sense." Anthony nodded once again. Tia rolled her eyes and gave him a look that said, *"duh"* before popping up and recruiting Maria to help her pull Anthony off the floor.

He feigned needing their help pulling on his hands to be able to stand just because he liked the look of confidence and achievement on their faces when they were able to lift him. He looked around the arena again to see if Kay had finally made it out to where she was supposed to meet them at the ring.

When he saw Rick standing on the stage talking to a couple of wrestlers and one of the writers, he knew she was done with her interview, so he started to worry about where she went after she was done meeting with Rick. So, he pulled his phone from his pocket and called her.

"Hey, Anthony," Kay answered after only one ring. "Where are you? I've been wandering all over the backstage area looking for you and the girls."

"We're sitting ringside watching the guy's practice," Anthony replied. "I'm sorry, Baby, I thought I told you I was taking the girls to the ring, so you could find us here when you were done."

"You did," Kay replied, her voice sounding breathy, like she was jogging from wherever she'd been backstage. "Between the interview and meeting the tutors, I just forgot you said that. Did you actually get to start the girls' self-defense training, or was the ring already occupied when you got there?"

"Yes, Baby." Anthony smiled. "But you missed your self-defense training since the ring is now full of wrestlers."

~~~

When Kay finally made it to the arena floor to meet up with her daughters and Anthony, they were walking up the ramp toward the entrance from backstage. Anthony's heather gray sweatpants and t-shirt with the word "Navy" printed across his chest were filthy. Kay wondered what on earth had happened during their self-defense training that had left him covered in dirt when neither of her daughters appeared to have a single spot on their t-shirts or leggings.
~~~

Leah Mae Wright

"What happened to you?" Kay reached out to dust off his chest and abs when they met on the stage at the top of the ramp.

"Tia the Terminator and Maria the Mauler," Anthony replied as he ruffled the tops of both girls' hair. "Teamed up with the Dangerous Twins to take me out in a tickle fight."

"Tia the Terminator and Maria the Mauler?" Kay looked back and forth between her girls and Anthony.

"Yeah, Mom, those are our new wrestling names." Maria struck a pose as if she were a wrestler about to take on an opponent.

"Dean Dangerous said he'd train us to be wrestlers since Anthony's self-defense skills weren't enough to defend himself from us. We've already learned to make a mean face to scare our opponents." Tia demonstrated as she scrunched up her face in what Kay presumed was supposed to look fierce.

Kay stifled a giggle at the ridiculousness of her daughters. Kay smirked up at Anthony. "My girls kicked your butt, huh?"

"I was holding my own at first," he replied, holding his hands up in surrender. "But the Dangerous Twins got up to their normal heel tactics and held me down for the girls' tickle torture."

Kay couldn't hold back the burst of laughter any longer. Her mental image of Anthony being held down by his two best friends while her daughters tickled him had her laughing so hard her eyes were watering.

Even covered in dirt from the arena floor, Anthony was the sexiest man she'd ever seen. Not because of what he was wearing or even because of his incredible body. What Kay found most attractive was how he interacted with her daughters, bringing out a fun playful side that brought new life and laughter to her girls. It was the most animated she'd seen her girls in years, maybe ever. And Anthony had been the one to ignite that spark of joy in them.

Maybe Dee was wrong about needing to stay in the friend zone until after court? Kay thought as she wiped the tears of laughter from her eyes.

"I wish I could have seen that," Kay finally admitted, when her laughter started to die down.

"I taped it on my phone," interjected one of the wrestlers who had been talking to Rick on the stage when Kay walked out from the back. "I can text it to you if you want."

"Oh, um, thanks," Kay replied, surprised by the stranger. "Can you email it to me, so I can watch it on my tablet? I think I need to see it on a bigger screen than my phone."

"Or he can send it to me, and I can project it to the jumbotron," Rick suggested, grinning at Kay.

I think this whole company is filled with pranksters.

"Naw, Anthony's head is already big enough, we don't need to inflate it to jumbotron proportions," Kay chuckled, actually feeling comfortable joking back with her new boss.

Anthony threw up his hands and muttered, "I don't have a big head," causing several of the guys standing nearby to chuckle.

Kay gave the wrestler, who introduced himself as Tank, her email address to send the video. He pulled it up and let her watch it once on his phone first before sending it. He hadn't actually got the beginning of the tickle fight for Kay to know who started it, but when the video started playing Anthony was on his knees with a large hand spanning the belly of each of her daughters. With his long arms holding each of the girls at arm's length, he could tickle their ribs with his fingertips, but they couldn't reach him to retaliate.

Less than a minute into the video, the twins stepped over the ringside barricade and made quick work of grabbing Anthony's hands and feet and stretching him out face down on the floor. That's when her daughters actually dove for his underarms and ribs to begin several minutes of tickle torture. It was every bit as hilarious as Kay had originally imagined it.

Anthony excused himself to go change into his suit while Kay took the girls back to the classroom area to meet with the tutors.

Kay loved seeing her daughters so comfortable with Anthony that they picked on him about having to go primp like a prima donna. No matter how much he playfully argued with them that he had to dress appropriately for the activity he was doing, they didn't see the point in changing clothes so many times a day.

He was in a suit when he was flying or anywhere he considered part of his job, even just going to the arena to check in for his flight rotation that wouldn't start until the next day. If he worked out at the arena, he changed into his workout clothes for that activity and then changed back into his suit as soon as he was done. For their sightseeing trips, he changed into jeans and more casual shirts.

Leah Mae Wright

Kay imagined there would be days while they were traveling that she would see him in three different outfits in a single day. With the way he filled them out, that was fine with her. It was acceptable to enjoy the eye candy, even if it made it hard for her to hold back from doing more than looking.

"Whoa!" Maria shouted as they got to the classroom area that was now full with a dozen kids and another dozen adults that Kay assumed were their parents. "This is going to be our new school?"

Ivy Traverson walked over to where Kay stood with her daughters. Britney Robertson was hot on her heels.

"Hi, I'm Britney." Britney waved excitedly as soon as she slid to a stop in front of the girls. "I thought you were really lost when your mom didn't bring you back before everyone else got here."

"We weren't lost." Tia looked back and forth between Britney and Kay. "We were just doing self-defense training with Anthony and watching the wrestlers practice while Mom did her interview."

"And beating Anthony in a tickle fight," Maria added, flashing Britney her ornery smile.

"Anthony got in a tickle fight?" Britney's eyes widened, a look of surprise on her face. "Are you talking about the same Anthony I know? The really tall guy who flies the plane and doesn't normally talk much to us kids?"

Kay had to smile at how Britney tried to jump to get her hand up as high as Anthony's height when she was describing him.

"Yeah, unless there's more than one Anthony who works here," Tia nodded before shrugging.

"You must be really fun to hang out with if you got him to do a tickle fight. The most I've ever gotten him to say to me was *Hey Shortcake* and that was only because I was wearing a Strawberry Shortcake t-shirt. What's your name? Oh, Ms. Ivy, can she be in my study group so I'm not the only girl anymore?"

Kay wasn't sure when Britney took a breath as she continued asking questions without allowing anyone time to answer them. Kay could tell by the looks on her daughters' faces that they weren't sure when to interrupt Britney's rant on why she needed a girl in her group. Kay didn't know either, so she just stood there until Ivy finally stepped up and took charge of the situation, like only a teacher could.

Once she introduced herself to the girls, Ivy informed them all that Tia and Maria would be assigned to study groups based on how they scored on the tests they would be taking over the next several days. Ivy got Britney to go back to her table and then walked Tia and Maria up to the front of the classroom.

"May I have everyone's attention for a minute," Ivy announced in a firm teacher voice that drew all eyes up from their tablets or papers in front of them. "We have two new students joining us, so I thought it would be nice for everyone to introduce themselves and make them feel welcome. We'll just go around the room and have each student say their first name, age, and favorite subject to study."

Ivy looked down at Tia and Maria as if she expected them to start the introductions, but before Kay's shy daughters could work up the courage to lead things off, Britney started for them.

"I'm Britney. I just turned twelve last month. And my favorite subject is reading."

"I'm Connor. I'm fourteen and my favorite subject is science," stated the blond boy seated beside Britney.

"I'm Cody. I'm thirteen and my favorite subject is P.E.," the dark-haired boy at their same table continued.

"I'm Sarah. I'm eight and my favorite subject is reading," one of the little girls at the next table shared.

"I'm Katie. I'm nine and my favorite subject is reading," the girl beside the last one imparted.

They continued through the room with a mix of boys and girls introducing themselves as a couple of ladies walked over to Kay.

"Hi, I'm Jana, I'm Sarah and Shawn's mom," the first one introduced.

"And I'm Emily, mother to Katie and Jason," the second one added.

"I'm Kay, and mine are Tia and Maria up in the front," Kay replied.

"Looks like one of yours is about the same age as our girls." Jana pointed to the two girls closest to Maria's age. "Since our girls are besties who are probably going to latch onto your youngest to plan world domination over the boys, we figured we'd do the same with you."

"Geez, Jana, you make us sound like the mean girls in high school." Emily swatted a hand at Jana. "We're really not cliquey like that. The GWA is a big family, and we all get along most of the time. Since we're the only moms with daughters about the same age as yours, we figured you'd be more comfortable getting to know us first instead of being overwhelmed by a couple dozen parents in your face the first day."

"Yeah, you're probably right about that," Kay replied with a shy smile. "I'm already struggling to remember everyone's names."

The GWA kids finished their introductions and Kay turned to look at her daughters, curious about what they would say their favorite subjects were.

"I'm Maria. I'm eight and my favorite subject is art," Kay's youngest announced.

Of course, it's art for Maria. That girl won't ever let anyone see her brain.

"I'm Tia. I'm twelve and I can't decide if my favorite subject is physics or calculus," Kay's brainiac oldest shrugged.

"You can't decide between physics and calculus?" Ivy exclaimed with a shocked expression on her face. "Um, Dan, do we have curricula for those?"

"I haven't explored the high school curricula yet since we've only needed the kindergarten through eighth grade so far, but I'm sure they're available," Dan replied from his seat. "What grade are you in currently, Tia?"

"In school, I'm only in eighth grade because the only time Mom let the school move me up a grade was when I skipped preschool and started kindergarten at four and a half," Tia explained matter-of-factly. "But I'm auditing Johns Hopkins University's Integral Calculus Through Data and Modeling, the University of Virginia's Introduction to Physics, and Rice University's Introduction to Mechanics this semester through Coursera online."

Kay noticed several jaws dropping around the room. She was torn between feeling proud of her daughter's brilliance and a need to shelter her from the spotlight shining on her in the quiet room. When Tia looked to her with confusion written all over her face, Kay decided to break the silence.

"Mr. Robertson, um," Kay started as she stepped up to the front of the room and took Tia's hand. "Rick assured me that ya'll would be able to help me customize her educational plan to match her intellectual level."

"Oh, we can definitely do that," Dan's voice boomed as a broad smile spread across his face. "Now that introductions are over, why don't we let the kids get back to work on their individual assignments? Ms. Stacy and Ms. Ivy can go back to what they were teaching and be available to anyone who has questions while I help Ms. Kay, Tia, and Maria get started on testing and customizing their lessons."

Once Dan had ushered them to a table on the side of the room, Kay felt a little more comfortable than discussing her daughters' special needs in front of all the other parents and students. Kay could see that her daughters felt the same when their posture was more relaxed, and their little faces didn't show as much anxiety.

They laughed and chatted for a few more minutes before Dan got the girls started on the first of their tests on his and Ivy's iPads. They each only got one test done before they took their dinner break and met back up with Anthony. Since neither Kay nor Anthony had to stay at the arena to perform in the show, Kay decided to just have the girls do their tests on the afternoons they would be at the arena between three and six. Not starting their actual classes until her next work rotation would give her time to figure out how to get each of the girls an iPad.

Not having to stay late at the shows meant she could also get them back on schedule with their normal bedtime at the hotel. The last four days of being off schedule and not getting them to bed at their normal time was really throwing Kay off balance and out of her comfort zone.

It would be better if they had their own room to go to bed on time and Kay could sit up for an extra hour or two to unwind and read. She supposed she could put them to bed in her room and sit up in Anthony's for a little while and they could actually have some time to talk, like they had the week before when he would call or Skype after the girls were in bed. The only thing that stopped her from suggesting it to him when they got to the hotel was her uncertainty about what she would be allowed to do after going to court.

If the judge didn't think she had a valid reason to sever Mark's visitation rights, he could order her to stay in Tulsa and stick to the current visitation schedule. She'd have to give up her new job and only see Anthony sporadically. They couldn't build a relationship if she was in Tulsa, and he was traveling all the time. She would never ask him to give up his dream job to move to Tulsa full time because he would just end up resenting her for it, and they would eventually break up over it.

She had to stay strong and maintain a little distance until after the judge's ruling. Once she was free of Mark and definitively able to move to Texas with the court's permission, then she would explore more with Anthony.

Until she knew for certain that the judge wouldn't rip her heart out by finding in Mark's favor, she had to maintain her friend zone with Anthony. She couldn't open her heart to him any more than she already had, or she might not survive the heartbreak if she had to let him go.

Chapter Nine

Wednesday, October 10, 2018

As soon as his early morning alarm awakened him, Anthony bounded out of bed to knock on the adjoining door to wake up his soon-to-be family. It was completely unlike his normal morning routine, where he put off getting up until he completely lost his mental image of the dreams of the night before and took his time in the shower to relive the fantasies while jacking off. He hadn't changed the routine since having Kay, Tia, and Maria with him. But since the girls had been sleeping later than the company's normal takeoff time, he hadn't slept as soundly as normal the night before because he was tossing and turning while worrying about them all being late for Kay's first day on the job. About midnight, he'd finally reset his alarm for an hour earlier than normal to give the girls time to get ready before they had to head to the airport.

"What time is it?" Kay yawned as she opened the door. She looked adorable in an oversized pink t-shirt that hung almost to her knees.

"Seven," Anthony answered, trying to keep the tent in his shorts hidden behind Kay and the partially opened door, so neither Tia nor Maria saw more than they should. Luckily, thinking about the girls quickly deflated his overeager cock. "We have to be at the airport at nine, so I figured I should wake ya'll up in plenty of time to get through showers. Thought you might need mine first, so you have time to do your hair and stuff while I'm in the shower."

"Yeah, sorry, I forgot to ask what time we needed to be ready this morning." Kay's voice was so soft it was hard to hear as she spoke through another yawn.

"It's okay, Baby." Anthony kissed the top of her head. "I usually get up at eight to leave the hotel by eight-thirty, but I reset my alarm for this morning when I realized that I hadn't told you the schedule before ya'll went to bed last night."

"Sugar," Kay squealed, turning on her heel to rush toward the bed to wake her daughters.

Did she just use sugar in place of the word shit? Anthony wondered as he watched her rushing around the room.

"Girls, get up, we've got to hurry and get ready for my first day of work," Kay shouted as she rifled through Maria's suitcase and pulled out a frilly pink dress. "Tia, help Maria get a quick shower and dressed as if we were going to church."

The girls were both sitting up in bed, yawning, and looking between Kay and Anthony in confusion. Kay tossed the dress, a pair of black patent-leather shoes, and a bundle of white cotton on the bed before grabbing the handle of her rolling suitcase and heading back toward Anthony where he still stood in the open doorway.

"What can I do to help?" He wasn't sure what to do as she started to rush past him.

"Brush and blow dry their hair and figure out breakfast since we don't have time for room service," Kay rambled without pausing for a breath as she disappeared through the door.

Anthony hoped Kay wouldn't mind him feeding the girls donuts from the continental breakfast the hotel put out in the lobby every morning.

He went back into his room and started packing up his electronics from where he'd left them out. The laptop on the table showed a new email in Kay's inbox from her attorney, so he left it there in case she needed to see it before they left.

Once his e-reader and all the various chargers were in his laptop case, he moved to the laundry bags that had been returned to them as they arrived back at the hotel the night before. Emotion welled in his chest as he sorted through the stacks of folded clothing. It was the mundane little things that he hadn't realized he was missing out on before that got to him the most.

Suck it up! He told himself. *Anybody sees you tearing up over getting to do something so domestic as putting away kids' clothes and they'll revoke your man card.*

He wiped the moisture from his eyes and put his socks, underwear, t-shirts, sweats, shorts, and jeans in his suitcase. Then he moved to the dry-cleaning bag hanging in the little hotel closet. He removed all the plastic and put his dress shirts, suit coats, and slacks on the sturdier hangers in his garment bag, only leaving one set out to put on after his shower. He put his dirty clothes from the day before in bags to give to the laundry service at the hotel in Austin, leaving the laundry bag out for the clothes he'd slept in and would take off to shower.

He'd just sat at the table and turned some music on from his laptop when Maria came in carrying a hairbrush and blow dryer.

"Morning, Princess," he greeted her, smiling at her cuteness in the light pink dress with a darker pink ribbon around her waist and darker pink lace trimming the hem just below her knees. "Why are you all dressed up this morning?"

"Morning, Sire." Maria grinned at him as she curtsied.

Freaking cute kid!

"Mommy said we have to dress professionally for work." Maria wrinkled her nose as she stood back up to her four-foot-six height. "I don't see why, when Tia and I aren't actually working, and we'll just have to change to get in the ring when we get to the arena. But I'm just a kid, so I don't get to have a say. I just get to do as I'm told."

Anthony chuckled at the adorable faces she was making at him as she lamented being a kid.

"Why aren't you dressed for work yet? You can't fly the plane in workout shorts and a t-shirt, or can you? As an adult, you can decide for yourself what to wear."

"Not unless I want to get fired," Anthony replied as he took the hairbrush and hair dryer from her and got set up to work on her tangled golden curls. "There's a dress code at work that I don't have any say in either. Professional dress on the plane, business casual at any company function, with the exception of workout clothes while exercising or costumes on Halloween."

"Since Mommy got this job, when are we going to start looking for our costumes?" Maria bounced on her toes excitedly.

"Well, our workdays are pretty booked up." Anthony thought about when they could work in a shopping trip as he started detangling her hair. "Today, we're flying to Austin. It's just a short flight, so we'll be there about eleven. We'll check in at the hotel and have lunch, maybe do some sightseeing before heading to the arena for the afternoon and evening."

"Are there costume stores in Austin? Can we look at them instead of sightseeing?"

"I'm sure there are costume stores there, but I don't know where they are. Besides, Austin is the state capital, so I thought you might like to see the capitol building and learn a little about Texas history."

"That's right, Mr. Dan said field trips like that would count as our history lessons for our new school," Maria grinned. Anthony could hear the enthusiasm in her voice even though she was facing away from him as he brushed out the back of her hair. "I love that our new school includes so many more field trips than Park did."

"Thursday, when we fly into San Antonio, I want to take you to our family ranch for the night instead of staying in a hotel or going to the arena. You think Mom will be okay with that for a field trip?" Anthony finished detangling her hair and turned on the blow dryer.

"YES!" Maria shouted over the sound of the hair dryer. "Can we ride horses while we're there?"

"Maybe not Thursday, but definitely at some point next week when we're off work." Anthony finger-combed her hair to make sure the heat of the hair dryer wasn't too high. "We'll only be there for half a day and then have to fly to Houston on Friday, Shreveport on Saturday, and New Orleans on Sunday. Then Monday we're off work and can fly back to San Antonio and stay at the ranch until we have to fly to Knoxville the following Friday to go back to work."

"We'll be able to stay on the ranch from Monday to Friday?" Maria whipped around and threw herself into Anthony's lap. She squeezed her arms around his neck so tight Anthony almost choked. "We're going to have so much fun with the horses and cows!" Maria squealed in his ear.

He turned off the hair dryer and returned her hug, though without the bone-crushing intensity.

"What's she so excited about?" Tia came into the room wearing a navy-blue skirt and light blue blouse. Combined with the low-heeled dress shoes, the outfit made her look more mature than her twelve years.

She needs to go back to little girl ruffles like Maria, Anthony thought, hating that he'd missed out on being her stepdad for so many years.

"We get to ride horses on the ranch!" Maria shrieked again as she grabbed Tia's upper arms and jumped up and down.

"I assumed as much when Mom instructed us to pack boots and jeans, and then Anthony extolled all the virtues of the ranch when we were in Pioneer Plaza." Tia shrugged her shoulders like she didn't understand how Maria didn't already know horseback riding was a given on their trip.

"Do we have a dirty clothes bag started for our clothes from yesterday?" Tia effectively changed the subject.

"I have one on the bed beside the stacks of ya'll's clean clothes, but I don't know if Mom has one started in ya'll's room or not." Anthony pointed to the stuff on the bed before restarting the hair dryer to finish up Maria's hair.

"Superlative." Tia picked up the stack of her clothing. "I'll pack these and pick up the dirty stuff from our room."

Tia carried the stack of clothes to the other room, returning after only a minute to stuff some things into the dirty laundry bag. She then carried the stack of Maria's clothes back to the other room. Anthony assumed she was packing their things in the other room while he finished drying Maria's hair.

When she hadn't returned by the time Maria's hair was dry, Anthony put his hand to his mouth and made a fake trumpet sound. "The royal hairdresser is summoning Princess Tia," he called out to her. The smile on her face as she reentered the room made him feel like he'd accomplished more with his goofball antics than he ever would in a career. *Being their dad is more rewarding than any job, even flying!*

~~~

Kay wasn't sure what she was expecting for her first day of work, but it definitely wasn't what she saw when she first stepped on the GWA plane. It was a lot larger than the commercial plane they'd taken from Tulsa to Dallas, so she assumed there would be twice as many seats
~~~

per row as the first-class section in the smaller commercial plane. *Nope, not even close!*

Instead of having two aisles like the commercial plane of equal size that Kay had seen before, it only had one down the middle, where the center section of seats had been taken out to combine the two aisles. Instead of eight seats per row like Kay remembered from walking past the first-class section on her only previous experience flying in a plane of equivalent size in the past, there were only two extra-large pods on each side of the wide center aisle per row. In addition to that, the odd-numbered rows were turned to face the back of the plane, effectively creating a feeling of separate seating areas where four passengers could congregate around a central table.

Kay wondered if each family had their own section to have a family breakfast on their morning flight or if they were configured that way, so the writers and performers could collaborate on planning the individual matches and overall events.

Anthony had introduced her to the other flight attendant, Janice, when they first arrived at the gate, but the lithe blonde stayed at the gate to make sure everyone got on the plane, so Kay couldn't ask her if there was someplace particular that she and her daughters should sit.

They'd dutifully followed Anthony down the ramp to board the plane, but he hadn't given her any instruction on what she should do once they were on board. He'd left them standing in the galley and carried his bags through a door that Kay presumed led to the cockpit.

"Where are we supposed to put our suitcases?" Tia looked around the plane, obviously trying to figure out where they were supposed to sit the same as Kay.

Kay shrugged her shoulders because she had no idea. She stepped into the main compartment of the plane hoping to be able to figure it out. *Shouldn't we have checked our bigger suitcases? Or is there a way to the cargo hold from up here?*

"Rick and the writers usually take up the first two rows." Anthony walked up from behind her. "They'll work the whole flight."

Kay turned to look up at him and had to stifle a giggle at the tilt of his head, as if he was trying to keep from brushing the top of his head against the ceiling, even though they were standing in the center of the aisle where there was more headroom than under the overhead bins on the sides of the plane.

"After that, it's just wherever anyone wants to sit," he continued. "But I'd avoid the second set of rows if I were you because that's where the guys who want a say in their storylines will fight over sitting."

"Where do the other kids usually sit?" Maria tugged on Anthony's sleeve.

"More towards the middle and back of the plane," Anthony replied. "There's another galley and more restrooms in the back of the plane. We use the back galley for extra storage, but since we only had one flight attendant before, the main galley is the only one she worked from. It's not like commercial planes where the flight attendant has to distribute drinks and snacks to every passenger on a set schedule. If anyone needs something they didn't bring with them, they'll push their call button to let you know what they need."

"So where do I need to sit to see when someone pushes a call button for me?" Without allowing time for Anthony to answer, Kay continued with another question while motioning to her oversized rolling suitcase. "And where are we supposed to put our suitcases that we can't lift into the overhead bins?"

"Janice usually sits in the jump seat in the galley where she can see the monitor that alerts her when a call light is pushed." Anthony turned and pointed to the seat in the galley. "But I think Rick wanted you to sit closer to the kids, so the parents can just ask you directly for whatever help they need. You're probably going to end up spending more time soothing fussy babies than getting snacks, but check with Rick to be sure 'cause he may want to have a snack service now that we have a second flight attendant."

"As for your monster suitcase," Anthony chuckled. "Strap it into an extra seat."

"It doesn't need to go down in the cargo hold?" Kay thought there was no way the lap belt would go around her suitcase even if she converted the pod seat into a bed, so she could strap it down on a flat surface.

"No, the cargo hold is full of catering tables and backstage furniture," Anthony replied and started walking toward the back of the plane. "We've got extra bungee cords stored in the back galley to safely strap down extra-large suitcases."

He disappeared behind a door in the back of the plane and quickly returned with a bundle of blue cords in his hand. Tia walked past Kay pulling her suitcase to meet Anthony about midway through the plane. Maria was hot on her heels, leaving Kay standing there at the front of the passenger section feeling lost and completely unprepared for her new job.

As Anthony put the girls' suitcases in the overhead bin above the window seats the girls had claimed, Kay pulled her suitcase behind her to claim the aisle seat beside Tia. Maria might be brave enough to sit in a backwards-facing seat, but Kay knew herself well enough to know that if she tried to ride backwards, she'd end up air sick.

Anthony lowered the handle on her suitcase and easily hefted it up to sit in the seat across from Kay. He had it strapped to the seat with three bungee cords wrapped around it faster than Kay could have separated the cords from the bundle.

"Preflight's done," Kay heard a deep voice say from the pocket of Anthony's suit jacket.

Anthony pulled a small walkie-talkie out of his pocket and pushed a button on the side to talk into it. "Roger that. Nate, come meet Kay before it gets too crowded with everyone boarding."

"Are you sure it's okay that my suitcase takes up a seat? Should we maybe store it in the back galley, so there's more room for passengers?" Kay felt guilty for taking up an extra seat that could be used by a person.

"Naw, Baby, it's fine." Anthony ran his hand over her head and through her hair. "There's at least a couple dozen extra seats and you won't be the only one with an oversized suitcase strapped to a seat."

Kay stood when she saw another man in a navy suit, which was almost an identical match to the one Anthony was wearing, walking toward them. He was a good six inches shorter than Anthony and his hair and eyes were both a lighter shade of brown than Anthony's, but the matching suits made Kay think of the newcomer as Anthony's miniature copy.

Who would have thought that I would ever think of a six-foot-tall man as a miniature, when two weeks ago his size would have intimidated me? If being around Anthony constantly for less than a week has changed my perspective that much, what all will have changed about me by the time we go to court next month?

"Ah, the infamous Kay." He reached out to shake her hand. "I'm Nate, the more dashing and debonair pilot on this crew."

Kay giggled as she shook his hand. "Funny, my first thought when I saw you was that you're Anthony's Mini-Me."

He released her hand to take his to his chest and mimed pulling a knife from his heart. "You wound me," he shook his head at Kay before looking up at Anthony. "No wonder you weren't afraid to introduce her to everyone, you've already got her brainwashed to defend your ugly mug."

Anthony chuckled and pulled her into his side. Before he could reply to Nate's jib, Tia jumped to his defense.

"Anthony didn't brainwash Mom." Tia crossed her arms over her chest to show her offense at Nate's statement. "They fell in love at first sight."

"Oh, my bad." Nate held his hands up in surrender. "I didn't know those were two different things."

"Are you sure he's smart enough to help you fly the plane?" Maria questioned Anthony. "Anyone who's dumb enough to think brainwashing and love are the same thing might need to go back to preschool, and surely isn't capable of flying a plane."

Kay held back her giggle at her daughters' antics. *Maybe I'm not the only one who feels more confident to show the sarcastic streak that runs in the family since spending time with Anthony.*

"Maria, we don't call people dumb," Tia chastised her sister. "It's insulting and demeaning. We refer to them as intellectually challenged and offer them help to learn, so they don't feel bad about themselves or worry that they won't be able to get any smarter."

"Dang, man, your family is mean." Nate pointed at Anthony. "I love it! I never thought anyone would beat out my mom for the queen of sarcasm title, but I think you have three solid contenders. You have to bring them to Mom's house for dinner when we're in Atlanta next month."

"Yeah, I don't think any of them were intentionally being sarcastic," Anthony chuckled.

"I was definitely not being sarcastic," Tia stated matter-of-factly.

Kay couldn't hold back her laugh then. Anthony joined her with a bark of laughter of his own. When they got themselves under control,

Anthony introduced Tia and Maria, then ordered Nate to get back to work.

"I'll meet you at the gate after we land, Baby." Anthony kissed the top of Kay's head. "If you can't get your suitcase down, just leave it there and I'll get it when I clear the plane in Austin."

He weaved his way through the passengers who were boarding, and Kay sat down to wait for the aisle to clear before going to check with Rick and then Janice about where she needed to be and what she needed to do on her first day of work.

On Tuesday when she'd interviewed with her new boss, Rick, she thought he was being extremely optimistic about her being qualified to perform as a flight attendant on his corporate jet. Earlier that morning as she got ready for the day, she'd expected to go through an intense training process to be able to learn all the proper procedures before she would actually be doing the job.

When both Rick and then Janice told her to just sit near the kids and assist the parents with getting kids snacks on the flight from Dallas to Austin, she really expected to spend the afternoon in Austin training with the other flight attendant on more of the features of the plane she would need to know in an emergency.

Instead, she was handed a safety manual to read, so she would know what to do in case of a crisis. There was no actual training on what to do in an unexpected situation because her job in an emergency would simply be to help keep the children calm. After almost thirteen years as a mom, she had more than enough life experience to do her new job—making the flights more comfortable for the children on board the corporate jet. *Easy Peasy!*

Once they were in the air and the fasten seatbelts sign was turned off, Kay got up and walked around to check in with the parents to see if they needed anything. She met several more moms than she had the day before, as well as a few babies and toddlers that hadn't been in the classroom area with the school-age children on Tuesday.

Her daughters ended up moving to sit with new friends while Kay helped with juice boxes and sippy cups and passed out bananas from the galley. Once all the kids' snack needs were met, she spent the rest of the flight sitting and chatting with new friends of her own. Anthony had been right when he'd told her the company was like a big extended family that would welcome her and the girls with open arms.

Kay may have only just met them, but their warm welcome made her feel like they'd known each other forever. Jana and Emily especially felt like they were her newest BFFs.

Kay just hoped she would be able to keep her dream job and get to live out the real-life fairy tale she felt like she was in after November fifth.

<div style="text-align:center">~~~</div>

Anthony loved how well Kay, Tia, and Maria seemed to blend seamlessly into his life. Other than a couple of small changes to his routine, like getting up an hour earlier to help them get ready to be at the airport on time and switching from going to the weight room and lunch with the guys to going to lunch, sightseeing, and self-defense training with Kay and the girls, he stuck to his normal schedule. While Kay and the girls went to the classroom, he sparred with his buddies and hung out with them until meeting back up with Kay and the girls in catering for dinner. The night before, they'd all hung out together watching the show on backstage monitors before going back to the hotel when the girls started getting tired.

All three of them seemed to be making friends with the other families. Anthony loved seeing them excited to go hang out with their new friends as they left the ring after their self-defense lesson while he stayed to spar with his friends.

He'd worried that they would miss their old friends and life in Tulsa too much to really want to change their lives so much by Kay taking this job and traveling with him all the time. But with as well as they were fitting into the GWA family, Anthony felt his worries had been misplaced. Not only was Kay his soulmate, but fate was also working in their favor to have them all traveling together, so they could become a family.

"Uh oh, he's got that goofy grin on his face again." Dean pointed at Anthony as he climbed into the ring to start their sparring session. "We'll have to go easy on him, so we don't hurt him while he's off in la-la land daydreaming about Kay."

Anthony just shook his head at his friend as he thought about how he would sneak in a takedown when Dean was least expecting it.

Leah Mae Wright

While his friends liked to trash talk during their sparring thinking it gave them a psychological advantage, Anthony preferred to let his actions speak louder than his words.

"What are we working on today?" Anthony asked when James joined them in the ring.

"Since you didn't seem to lose a step from high school while going back over all our old wrestling drills the last few times we've gotten you in the ring, we thought you might want to learn some pro moves." James smiled slightly.

"We want to practice a new finisher and thought you'd be perfect to practice on, so we don't hurt anyone who actually has to get in the ring for the show tonight," Dean smirked. "It's a combination of a suplex and a stunner. We'll get you up and hold the extension for the suplex and then as we're going down, we convert it to a stunner."

"Yeah, that's not happening." Anthony shook his head. "But I'll gladly sit ringside and watch you practice it on each other."

"What? You don't trust us, your best friends since we were babies, to keep you safe in the ring?" Dean simpered.

"It's precisely because I've known you since we were babies that I know better than to risk you breaking my neck in an untried move," Anthony deadpanned.

"I told you he wouldn't go for it," James chuckled. "We figured we'd just do takedown drills until the other guys get here to run through the choreography for our matches tonight."

They started working with just the three of them until a few other wrestlers arrived and they paired off to do three-minute rounds of grappling like Anthony remembered from his high school wrestling days. After Anthony pinned Dean in his mini-match, they stood ringside while James and Liam went through their round in the ring. James won his round and he and Liam joined Anthony and Dean on the floor while two other wrestlers took their place in the ring.

"Ya think it's the lasses in their lives that gave them the upper hand today?" Liam asked Dean.

"Yeah, the only reason they could beat us is because they're both powered by pussy," Dean replied. His voice went high-pitched at the end of his statement because he was surprised by Anthony's single-leg takedown on the ringside mats.

James and Liam both laughed at Dean sprawled on the mat while Anthony popped back to a standing position with ease.

"Serves you right, brother." James pointed at Dean as his laughter died down. "You know better than to say stuff like that about our ladies."

"I meant no disrespect." Dean held up both hands in surrender as he made his way back to his feet. "If anything, I'm envious."

"Definitely envious," Liam stated as he took a step back from the other guys as if he were afraid either Anthony or James would take him down next. "How's Kay settling into the gypsy lifestyle?"

"Really well," Anthony answered.

"It's like ya'll are an instant family," Dean added. "Your perma-grin shows how much you're enjoying living out those fantasies every night."

"Don't mention anything about those," Anthony warned, feeling his cheeks heat because he wasn't actually getting to live them out with two short chaperones sharing Kay's bed. In fact, he was beginning to fear he wouldn't ever get to live them out if Kay found out his friends knew her fantasies.

"You know we wouldn't say anything in front of your lass and her wee ones." Liam's expression went from jovial to serious.

"Yeah," Dean stated as he slapped Anthony on the shoulder. "We're just busting your balls 'cause ours are blue."

"Blue?" Liam looked quizzically at Dean. "I thought we were green with jealousy?"

"Dude, if your balls are green, we need to rush you to a hospital because that's abnormal," Dean chuckled.

Anthony turned to look at James who was struggling to hold back a laugh. "I swear these guys have been dropped on their heads too many times."

"Probably," James replied with a grin. "It's embarrassing to take them out in public."

"Definitely," Anthony agreed.

The conversation died down as the guys were called up to the ring to practice some of the choreography for their scheduled match that night, so Anthony hopped over the barricade to sit in a ringside seat to watch.

He wondered if he should make his way to the classroom to see if he could help Kay with whatever lessons the girls were doing. When he remembered that they didn't have their iPads, he realized that he couldn't be much help to them when they weren't even set up for lessons yet.

Still, he wondered what they were working on in the classroom without the technology to complete any real lessons. He wanted to go find them and suggest a longer tour of Austin but didn't want to push his way into their education. He feared the forced proximity of working together was already pushing Kay's limits. He didn't want to interfere with time she felt she needed away from him or make her feel like he was stepping over the line of her boundaries by trying to spend every waking minute with her.

Play it cool, he told himself as he watched his friends practice. *We've got the rest of our lives to be together. We don't have to have it all now. Being her man means taking care of her needs first. Right now, she needs a friend more than a lover. I can be patient and wait for her to be ready for more between us.*

<div align="center">~~~</div>

Kay enjoyed more time getting to know her new friends while her daughters took more tests on the tutors' tablets. Kay thought their instantaneous friendship was unusual, but the idea that it was too easy to be real never entered her mind. She just had two new friends that she felt as close to as her sister or her childhood best friend, even without the years of experience between them.

After hearing their meet-cutes with their spouses, she felt comfortable telling them how she and Anthony met, even telling Jana and Emily about how Anthony believed that he'd subconsciously recognized their connection on his first trip to Tulsa, and maintained it through his dreams for over a year, until they could actually meet and fall in love at first sight.

"So, you actually met him in the castle hotel?" Jana leaned back in her chair and smiled at Kay. "Sarah kept going on and on about meeting Prince Charming when we stayed there."

"So did Katie," Emily agreed, bouncing in her seat as she elaborated. "Matt wouldn't let me take the kids swimming there because he was afraid she'd meet a local boy at the pool and want to stay there with her prince. He was all freaked out about her being too young to be into boys already, and ranted about not letting her date until she's thirty."

"Jeff and I had a similar conversation where I had to explain to him that it had nothing to do with being interested in boys already." Jana playfully shook her head. "I had to explain that all little girls love believing in fairy tales, but he's the only Prince Charming in our family. That led to a fun night of playing *Sleeping Beauty* after the kids were asleep."

"Hopefully based on the adult book and not the Disney version," Emily leaned in and whispered while wagging her eyebrows.

"You know it," Jana whispered back conspiratorially as they all three giggled softly.

Kay made a mental note to look up the adult book version on her e-reader later, if she could figure out how to put a child lock on it, so her daughters wouldn't accidentally read it.

"It's so cool that you actually met your prince in the castle hotel." Emily had a dreamy expression on her face. "We'll have to tell the girls they were right about the castle hotel being the site of fairy tales coming true."

"You don't think I'm nuts for wanting to believe in the fairy tale of love at first sight?" Kay was still afraid they would think she was just carried away by the setting of her first meeting with Anthony, and fooling herself into believing they were meant to be together.

"Of course not," Jana reassured her. "I know you're still in the honeymoon phase where you're not sure if it's real or not. I felt the same way when I first met Jeff. But looking back now, I wish I could go back in time and kick myself for not believing at first. I regret the year I wasted with my doubts when I could have been with him."

"Yeah, don't listen to whatever voice in your head that's telling you it's not real." Emily nodded confidently.

"How'd you know I had a voice in my head telling me that?" Kay wondered how they could possibly have noticed the internal conversations she had in her head with imaginary versions of her family and friends.

"Because mine sounded an awful lot like my mother," Emily replied with a shrug. "You get the same look on your face when you think nobody's watching that I got when I was having a mental argument with my mother about Matt, so I figured you probably have someone in your head telling you not to follow your heart with Anthony."

"Yeah, more than one," Kay replied with a sigh. She explained how she'd gotten conflicting advice from her sister, Randi, and her childhood best friend, Deanna. She told them about her most recent conversations and texts with Randi telling her to loosen up and enjoy the sexy times with Anthony, but to guard her heart, so she wouldn't be crushed if it ended, and Deanna telling her to keep Anthony in the friend zone until he proved he wasn't really too good to be true. She didn't mention the legal issues in Oklahoma, but she did tell them how her parents were pushing her to maintain her independence to be a good role model for the girls, and not to be swept off her feet by a man she barely knew, and giving them the impression that she was weak and needed a man to take care of her.

"Well, don't listen to the negative Nellies," Jana implored. "They aren't here to see you with Anthony, so they can't see what we see between you two."

"And we've seen you both looking at each other when you don't think anyone is paying attention to see the love you share," Emily whispered softly. "It's real, so relax and enjoy living the fairy tale. The adult version, not the G-rated movie version."

Kay felt her cheeks flush from the thought of doing adult things with Anthony. She might feel like she'd been friends with Jana and Emily longer than she really had, but she still wasn't ready to open up to them about her current sleeping arrangements and how she might want to change them.

So, she changed the subject, asking them about the extra staff she saw backstage that hadn't been on the plane. She learned that the GWA also employed three separate ground crews that hauled the ring, stage, lighting, and audiovisual equipment around the country in eighteen-wheelers and RVs. One crew drove the East Coast to the Mississippi River. The second drove between the Mississippi River and the Rocky Mountains. And the third drove between the Rocky Mountains and the West Coast. Apparently, they booked the shows so the ground crews rotated every couple of weeks, and with enough people licensed to drive the big rigs to swap out drivers to stay within the legal limits of how many hours truckers were allowed to be behind the wheel when they were going to a different city each day.

The drivers were also the crew that set up the arena before the wrestlers arrived. As soon as they got the first truck unloaded, they met the plane to transport the catering and backstage furniture from the plane to the arena. The arenas provided the catering crew to feed them all, starting with the ground crew who slept during the late afternoon and evening while the wrestlers were performing. At ten o'clock each night, the ground crew came back to the arena to haul the backstage and catering furniture back to the plane. By eleven, they were breaking down the ring, stage, lighting, and audiovisual equipment to load it up and start their drive to the next city by one or two in the morning, so they could set up in the arena before the plane load of wrestlers arrived.

The logistics of it all boggled Kay's mind. She was just grateful that she seemed to have fit in easily in her small role in the company's grandiose show.

It felt too easy, too perfect a solution to all her problems, to fall in love with Anthony and spend the rest of her life traveling by his side with her girls and all their new friends. She hoped her new friends were right in telling her to enjoy living the fairy tale.

I want to believe that Anthony is my prince. My knight in shining armor, who has rescued me from my dragon of an ex, and is carrying me away to our happily ever after in his winged steed.

~~~

Thursday, October 11, 2018

On Thursday, when they flew from Austin to San Antonio, Kay breezed through her duties because it wasn't really work to pass out fruit and milk. She really didn't think it was work to cuddle a baby while his mother fed his twin and his father worked with the boss on planning storylines either.
~~~

Leah Mae Wright

What's that old saying about if you love what you do, you'll never work a day in your life? Kay thought with a smile. *Yeah, I love playing with kids and rocking babies, so this is definitely not work.*

Maria came over to sit beside her as she rocked the infant. "Hey, baby girl." Kay smiled at her daughter as she took a seat. "Are you having fun with your new friends?"

"Yeah." Maria nodded, looking at the baby in Kay's arms and not really paying attention to her mother.

"Are you sure?" Kay raised an eyebrow at Maria, wondering what was going through her youngest daughter's head.

Maria looked up at Kay then, finally meeting her eyes. Her expression was quizzical, so Kay waited for Maria to ask the question she clearly wanted to ask. Maria's lips turned up slightly in a cautious smile.

"Sarah and Katie are awesome," she finally confided. "I like your new job. It's like you get paid to hang out with us and we get to play with our new friends a lot more than we could with our friends at Park. I really like having our classes without having to go to school."

"Even though you're doing more than an hour of schoolwork a day?" Kay remembered back to a couple of weeks before when her daughter expressed her desire to shorten the school day.

"Yeah, but it's not like I'm actually in school." Maria's smile turned more mischievous. "We get to do things like field trips every day and our actual time with a teacher lecturing is a lot less than in my old school."

Kay wasn't sure she wanted to burst her daughter's bubble by telling her that she would have more lecture time when she completed all the testing they were doing to make sure they had the correct curriculum level for her needs. *Yeah, maybe she won't notice when it turns into more work if I don't tell her and just let her enjoy her new learning experience.*

Not that she got the chance to continue that line of conversation. Maria was much more interested in the baby Kay was holding than in continuing to talk about her school. She reached over and let him hold onto her finger, smiling and cooing at him. "What's his name?"

"Travis," the baby's mother, Tina, answered as she uncovered her other son, who was now full from his feeding, and lifted him to her shoulder to burp him. "And this is his twin, Trent."

"They're both cute." Maria looked up to see the other baby in his mother's arms across the aisle. "Can I hold one of them?"

Before Tina could answer, Anthony's voice came over the intercom. "Good morning, all. I'd like to be the first to welcome each of you to the best part of Texas. Welcome home to those of us who live in the San Antonio area. Please take a seat and buckle up for landing."

Kay helped Tina secure her sons in their infant seats before checking that all the other kids were back in their seats and securely buckled in. She then took a seat herself and buckled in. Once Anthony landed the plane, her responsibilities turned to making sure she and her daughters had all their belongings as they exited the aircraft.

She waited with the girls in the terminal while Anthony finished his end-of-flight procedures. When he finally exited the plane carrying his own bags, they walked together out of the airport. Instead of going to the rental car counter like they had in Dallas and Austin, Anthony directed them to the long-term parking lot in San Antonio, where he'd parked his extended cab pickup. Once he secured their luggage under the cover in the bed of the truck, he helped them all into the vehicle. *He's always such a gentleman!*

Instead of staying at the hotel with the rest of the GWA crew, they were going to stay at the Burleson Ranch. They would skip the girls' tutoring time and the evening show for one day because Anthony wanted to introduce them to his family, since they were as close to his hometown as the wrestling company ever went.

Kay was nervous to meet his family. He'd told her all about them, and her daughters were excited to get to see the ranch after hearing Anthony's stories about growing up there. Kay thought they probably wanted to meet the horses more than Anthony's actual family, but she hoped the humans would be as welcoming to the girls as the equine Anthony described. Her stomach was in knots the whole drive from the airport in San Antonio out to the ranch in the small town of Heart's Destiny.

She was so lost in her own world that she didn't realize they skipped the first Heart's Destiny exit off the highway and took the other exit closer to the Burleson Ranch. She was surprised when they turned off the paved road onto the gravel drive leading into the ranch.

Leah Mae Wright

Anthony had to key in a code to open the large wrought-iron gate with a stylized capital B in the middle. Once they drove through the gate, he stopped for it to close before continuing down the long drive.

They passed a fenced-in pasture and barn before the gravel road turned into what Kay would describe as the ranch version of a subdivision. There were several houses separated by wide expanses of yard. Anthony stopped the truck in the middle of the road instead of pulling into one of the driveways of the actual houses.

"That was my Pappaw Jerry's house." Anthony pointed to the first of the houses on their right. It was a large two-story home with dark blue siding, white trim, and a wraparound porch. "My sister Becky lives there now with my cousins, Julie and Jen. It was actually built by my fourth great-grandpa in the eighteen-seventies."

He then pointed to a smaller house set about fifty yards away from the first one. It was a single-story brick house about the same size as the one Kay lived in back in Tulsa. "That's where my sister Char lives now. It was originally built for my second-great-aunt who disappeared after World War I. Tia, if you want a mystery to solve, ask Char about the stuff she found in the attic and see if you can help her figure out what happened to our second-great-aunt Mary."

"She disappeared?" Tia looked at the house in awe. "Like here one day and, poof, gone the next?"

"There wasn't a poof in the story I was told," Anthony chuckled. "She went off to serve as a nurse in World War I. When the war was over, she didn't come home. The family looked for her, but was just told she was discharged and sent home by her commanding officers. Nobody knows where she actually went, but she didn't come home to Heart's Destiny. When Char moved in there, she found some boxes in the attic of her stuff. They contained a lot of things that were sent home for her while she was overseas, including a bunch of letters we think were from a boyfriend. I think she went to his home after the war instead of hers. I know the family would love to find her kids, or I guess it would be great-great-grandkids by now."

"Have you tried one of the ancestry tests?" Tia queried, clearly putting her thinking cap on to figure out the mystery. "That would probably be the easiest way to find them."

"I haven't, but I don't know if anyone else in the family has," Anthony replied. "You'll have to ask Char if she's tried that. She's the one who's been talking about trying to find them since she found those letters."

He pointed to the next house another fifty yards away from Char's. It was another brick house, but larger, a two-story almost as big as the first house. "That's where my cousin JJ lives. It was originally our great-great-grandparents' house. Grandpa Joshua was Great-Aunt Mary's brother. He built both houses in the early nineteen-hundreds."

"So, all three of those houses are over a hundred years old?" Maria asked.

"Actually, the first one is probably closer to a hundred-and-fifty years old, and the other two are like a hundred-and-ten," he replied. "If you follow this road to the south part of the ranch, there's another house that's almost a hundred-and-forty years old that was my third-great-grandparents' house. They were the first Burlesons on the ranch. Jonah Burleson came out here in eighteen-eighty-one and worked on the ranch for Bob Rogers. A year later, he bought the land due south of the original Rogers ranch and married Bob's daughter, Emma. When the Rogers passed, all the land was combined into the Burleson Ranch. My oldest brother, Bobby, lives in their house now."

Kay couldn't see the house his oldest brother lived in, but assumed it was similar to the ones she could see.

"Wow, you have quite a family legacy." Kay looked longingly at Anthony. She was envious of Anthony's deep family roots. She wished she knew as much about her own family history. "Do you have a family tree that I can see to figure out how you're related to all these people you keep talking about?"

"I'm sure someone has it drawn out," he replied with a wink. "The last house on the right and the house in the middle on the left were the next two built on the ranch. They were built in nineteen-thirty by my great-grandpa Robert and great-uncle Jonathan. My cousin Justin lives in the last one on the right. I think my brothers Josh and Jake still live in the house that was our great-grandparents', but since they're both still in the Navy, maybe it's just where their extra clothes are stored."

The last house on the right was another single-story house that really reminded Kay of her childhood home since it was also white with black trim. The house in the middle on the left was another two-story home, but also had white siding and black trim. It was approximately twice the size of her home back in Tulsa.

Anthony pointed to the house farthest from them on the left. "That's my Uncle Jon and Aunt Susan's house. It was built in the nineteen-eighties right after my mom and dad's house." He pointed to the closest house on the left, which looked like it belonged in a magazine about antebellum plantation mansions. It was all white, with huge columns holding up the gabled roof providing shelter from the weather for both the wide porch that ran across the entire front of the house and the two balconies on the second and third floors that were almost as big as the porch. The balconies were only set-in far enough to allow for the pillars to run in front of them from their bases on the porch to their capitals at the roof.

Kay was in awe of the two large homes that dwarfed the one between them. They were each at least three stories with huge porches and balconies on multiple levels. Based on the way the driveways wound around beside the houses, she assumed the garages were behind the buildings, so as not to take away from the impressive architectural lines of the homes.

"Are you sure your parents aren't Scarlett O'Hara and Rhett Butler?" Kay teased jokingly.

Anthony laughed. "Naw, our house is way bigger than Tara."

Kay giggled with Anthony until she realized her daughters were both looking at them like they'd lost their minds. "Sorry, girls," Kay apologized to her daughters as Anthony finally pulled the truck into the driveway beside his parents' home. "You haven't seen *Gone With The Wind*. It's a really old movie about life in the south during the Civil War. The main characters were Scarlett O'Hara and Rhett Butler. The plantation where Scarlett lived was named Tara."

"So, ya'll were laughing because it was an old people joke?" Maria asked with an impish grin.

"Yep," Anthony answered as he turned off the vehicle and unbuckled his seatbelt.

"Speak for yourself," Kay squealed. "I'm not old."

Anthony turned in his seat to look at Kay. "I didn't say you were old, Baby." Anthony wagged his eyebrows. "Just well-educated, so you can get my old man jokes." He gave her a wink and a grin before getting out of the vehicle to do his gentlemanly routine of opening their doors and helping them down from the super tall truck.

Before they could even take a step toward the house, a dark-haired woman who looked to be in her early fifties bounded down the steps in the center of the porch. She was dressed in jeans and a bright pink blouse that looked like it was a throwback to the nineteen-eighties. She was only a few inches taller than Kay, if you didn't count her big hair, which made her appear to be closer to six feet tall.

This must be Anthony's Mom, Kay thought just as she was engulfed in the woman's arms.

"I'm so glad you're here," she shouted as she squeezed Kay with way more enthusiasm than anyone should have at their first meeting.

Kay was barely able to get her arms up to halfheartedly return the hug when she was pushed back and held at arm's length by her shoulders. She looked up into Anthony's mother's vibrant green eyes and was about to introduce herself, but she didn't get the chance to speak.

"Kay you are absolutely as beautiful as Anthony described," she gushed before turning to the girls.

Kay caught a glimpse of trepidation on the faces of her children, and hoped they wouldn't say anything to offend Anthony's family.

"I'm your Memmaw Hazel." Hazel swooped in between the girls, so she could hug Tia with her right arm and Maria with her left. "I can't wait to get to know you both."

"Memmaw Hazel?" Tia mouthed to Kay, giving her a look that could only be read as confusion.

Memmaw Hazel? Kay agreed with her daughter's confusion in her head. *I guess he's told his family about wanting to marry me? But I don't get why he keeps saying that when he's not acting like anything more than a friend. Other than our make-out session Friday night and maybe some of the hand holding and extra affectionate touching the past few days, none of our time together this week has been anything I wouldn't do with my best friend, Deanna. Maybe he just hasn't told them everything that happened to make him pull back and put us in the friend zone?*

Or maybe he really means it when he says he intends to marry you, but you won't get your head out of your butt and finally agree, Kay's inner voice that sounded a lot like her little sister said in her head.

Maybe? Kay mentally replied to her inner sister-voice, while contemplating when her inner sister voice jumped on the fairy-tale bandwagon. *But can I really trust that the fairy tale is real?*

"Mom," Anthony shouted as he stepped in behind his mother. "Chill out. You're scaring them." He lowered his voice and put on a pout. "And I haven't gotten my hug yet. I always get the first hug."

"Oh, don't be silly, Anthony!" Hazel released the girls and turned to hug her son. "You gave up the first hug by bringing me a new daughter and grandbabies."

"We're not babies," Maria pouted.

"Sorry, sweetie." Hazel shook her head as she released Anthony from her embrace. "I just got so excited because you're my first grandkids that I said grandbabies when I meant granddaughters."

"But we're not related," Tia pointed out, looking perplexed.

"Maybe not legally, yet." Hazel gave Tia a beaming smile. "But legality and DNA don't matter, my heart adopted you as my granddaughter the instant Anthony told me about you."

Tia looked back and forth between Hazel, Anthony, and Kay. When her gaze finally landed on Kay, it seemed that Tia wanted to ask her mom if illegal heart adoptions were allowed. Kay shrugged and smiled at her daughter, hoping to convey her thought that while it might be a little weird to be welcomed into their family so soon, having more people to love is always allowed. Tia returned her smile before turning to Hazel and opening her arms for another hug.

"Cool." Tia embraced Anthony's mother. "I needed another grandma."

"Yeah, Grandma Lee needs help that can be with us outside of Tulsa until Grandpa Lee retires and they can move to where we live." Maria wiggled into the hug with Tia and Hazel.

"Can I get in on the granddaughter hugs?" a deep voice boomed from behind Kay, startling her.

Anthony pulled Kay to his side when he noticed her jump. She snuggled into Anthony's side as she turned to look at the older cowboy who had walked up. He was tall, only a couple of inches shorter than Anthony but just as broad. Kay would guess he was in his late fifties or early sixties with salt and pepper hair. *Anthony's Dad?* Kay wondered.

"Dad," Anthony confirmed her unspoken question with a smile as he reached out with his free arm to shake his father's hand. "I thought you'd be at the office today."

"Naw," he answered with a slow smile and shake of his head. "It's not every day a man gets to meet his granddaughters for the first time. That's an event worth playing hooky for don't you think?" He turned to look at Kay and extended his hand toward her. "Welcome to the family, Kay. I'm Bob."

"It's nice to meet you, Bob." Kay smiled as she shook Anthony's father's hand. She was grateful his greeting was much more sedate than his wife's because it was more like what she was used to in her normal life.

He turned to the girls and squatted down to be closer to their level. "Tia," he greeted looking at the correct child. "And Maria," he added as he turned to look at the other little girl. "Ya'll can call me Pappaw Bob."

"Why do you use Pappaw and Memmaw instead of Grandpa and Grandma?" Maria inched closer to him.

"No clue," Bob shrugged. "It's just what my family has always used. You can use Grandpa and Grandma if you prefer."

Tia tilted her head in thought as she and Maria looked at each other as if silently communicating their decision. Kay was always in awe of how easily Tia and Maria understood each other without saying a word because she thought that was only normal in twins, not kids born four years apart.

"No, we'll stick to Memmaw and Pappaw," Tia finally decided. "That way we won't get confused about which Grandma or Grandpa we're talking about if we don't use an actual name."

"Now that we've settled that, can your Pappaw have a hug from his granddaughters?" Bob opened his arms toward the girls. They almost knocked him over running into his arms.

"What rooms do you have ready for us?" Anthony moved to get their bags out of the back of his truck.

Kay was thankful he was finally getting them all moving toward the house because she felt awkward still standing in the driveway.

"I made up the beds in Char's old room for Tia, Becky's old room for Maria, and your old room for you and Kay," Hazel informed Anthony before turning and reaching for the girls' hands to lead them into the house. "I have lunch ready and then Pappaw wants to take you out for a horseback ride."

"Um," Kay stammered, not sure what to say about Hazel's plan for her to bunk with Anthony. All week, Kay had been sleeping in the same hotel room as her daughters both in Dallas and their night in Austin. Anthony hadn't pushed to take their relationship to the next level of sharing a bed with him, always retiring to his own room at the end of the day. He hadn't even pushed for a real kiss since their make-out session Friday night. *Surely, he doesn't think our first time together will be in his parents' house?*

She turned to look up at Anthony as everyone else walked into the house. His eyes dimmed as they met Kay's. His lips lifted into the smallest smile which Kay assumed was his way of covering his disappointment at her not being ready to share a bed with him.

"Don't worry, Baby." Anthony widened his smile as he started to turn toward the house. "It's a seven-bedroom house. I'll let you have my old room and I'll make up the bed in one of my brothers' old rooms for me."

Kay slowly followed him into the house, feeling completely overwhelmed by all the emotions flooding her system. Her emotional roller coaster was quickly replaced by a sense of awe as she stepped through the wide double doors and into a foyer that was as big as Kay's living room at home. There was a silver medallion in the middle of the marble tile floor that served as the landing for a double staircase that curved up each side wall to the second and third-floor landings. The foyer itself was open all the way to the ceiling of the third floor with a sparkling crystal chandelier that appeared to be centered over the medallion.

To the left, just before the stairs, was an archway that led into a room that looked like a library. To the right, the archway before the stairs led into a formal dining room that had the largest table Kay had ever seen. The double doors on the back wall of the foyer were closed and Kay wanted to go open them to see what was there. Since Anthony was leading her through the dining room, she made plans to explore the home and check out that door later.

Anthony led her through a doorway from the formal dining room into a gorgeous kitchen with stainless steel appliances, white cabinets, and solid stone countertops that were mostly white with silver marble veining. The walls were painted a blueish gray that offset the white cabinets and brought out the silver in the countertops. A huge island in the middle of the room separated it from a less formal dining area where her daughters were already sitting to eat lunch with their unofficially adopted grandparents.

Kay plastered on a happy smile hoping it would mask her whirlwind of feelings as she sat down at the dining table beside her youngest daughter. She was unsure how successful she actually was at hiding her emotional turmoil as she made small talk over lunch.

"I have four horses saddled and ready to ride," Bob informed them after finishing his lunch. "I figured I'd need three for the girls and I, but I wasn't sure if either of you would want to go with us. So, I just saddled one extra, thinking I can either saddle a fifth or unsaddle the fourth before we hit the trail."

"They've never really ridden before," Kay admitted sheepishly. "Don't they need a few lessons before going on a trail ride?"

"We've done the pony rides at the fair," Maria protested.

"But those horses were tethered to a wheel and could only walk in a circle," Tia reminded her sister. "I think Mom's worried that we won't know how to put on the brakes if the horse wants to go too fast or leave the trail."

Anthony and Bob both chuckled.

"The brakes are easy. You just say *Whoa* and pull back on the reins and the horse will stop." Hazel mimicked the motion with her hands as she emphasized the word "whoa."

"No need to worry, Kay." Bob reassured her. "Back when our kids were little and all wanted a horse of their own, I started working with the horses that we felt were old enough to retire from working, so they'd be gentle with my kids. The stable closest to the house currently houses a dozen retirees that we take to the schools and town festivals for kids to ride. They like to walk in line, nice and slow, and won't misbehave or get off the trail."

"Baby," Anthony drawled, as he took Kay's hand and stroked the back with his thumb. "A trail ride is actually the safest for beginners. The girls won't have to know how to do anything more than sitting in the saddle and holding the reins. The wooded trail keeps the horses in single file. They can only go as fast as the lead horse, and they have to stop if the lead horse stops. If we were to put them in an open pasture to give them lessons, the horses would have more freedom to be able to run. That's when the girls would need to know the commands and how to control the actions of the horses. We work up to that so both the riders and horses are comfortable and safe."

"Oh. Okay." Kay released a breath she hadn't realized she'd been holding, visibly relaxing at hearing they were planning the safest ride for her daughters. "In that case, let's go change clothes, so we can all ride."

~~~

Anthony had dropped their bags in the foyer on the way to the breakfast nook for lunch, so he backtracked through the kitchen and dining room to grab them, so they could all change for an afternoon trail ride. He was almost as excited about the girls' first trail ride as they were, but he tried to maintain a more stoic outer appearance than they were as they bounded up the stairs. He didn't want to give Kay any reason to think he was overstepping and trying to take their father's place because he knew that would be a surefire way to make her run for the hills, leaving him behind with only the bittersweet memories of his almost family.

He showed the girls to his sisters' old rooms on the second floor. The second and third floors of his childhood home were identically laid out. A hallway led off the central landing from the staircases. There were two bedrooms with a Jack and Jill bathroom in between on each side of the hall. The second floor had been dubbed the girls' floor until he was born. Instead of putting her infant son on the third floor with the rest of the boys, Hazel Burleson wanted him closer to her first-floor master suite.

Anthony hated it when he was a little kid and his brothers picked on him for being on the girls' floor. But as a teenager, when he realized that he didn't have to share his bathroom with one of his siblings since the bedroom on the other side of his bathroom was a game room, he didn't mind as much. His brother Bobby had the same setup on the third floor when they were growing up, so he decided to put his stuff in Bobby's old room after he got Kay settled in his old room.
~~~

He quickly changed into a t-shirt, jeans, and boots for riding and made his way down from the third floor to meet his girls in the foyer to take them over to the stables, where his dad had already gone to get the last horse tacked up. From the stairs he could see that they were already in the foyer and Kay had apparently found his old cowboy hat from when he was about Tia's age. The leather band around the old straw hat matched the boots and belt she wore. She looked sexy as sin with her baby blue vee-neck t-shirt showing off her ample cleavage and tucked into the waist of her skintight distressed denim skinny jeans. She wore the boots over the ankles of the jeans, and it was a look Anthony found hotter than hell. He couldn't believe she'd found his childhood stuff from before his growth spurt when he turned fourteen, and was actually small enough to wear his things.

His dick twitched at the thought of her wearing his old boots, belt, and hat. There was something primal stirred up inside him at her wearing his things, like they marked her as his. He had to get that under control before he made it all the way downstairs, or he'd embarrass himself by showing everyone how much he liked seeing Kay in his old things.

He quickly thought back to his twelve-year-old self when he was the runt of the litter, still even shorter than his sisters. He'd asked his parents what to do so he could grow up big and strong like his dad and brothers. They'd told him to eat all his vegetables and pray about it. So, he did. Nightly. For two solid years. At fourteen, he grew two inches in height and went up a shoe size every month. Nine months in and his momma told him to quit praying to get bigger because six-foot-six was taller than anyone else in the family, and it was really hard to find size fourteen shoes.

With his dick deflated after thinking about his mom, Anthony stepped off the bottom stair and flicked the brim of the hat on Kay's head with a single finger.

"Baby, where'd you find this old thing?" Anthony grinned down at her upturned face.

"It was the only one on the hat rack in your room that fit me." Kay shrugged as she smiled up at him with that special secret smile he loved seeing. "When I saw the matching belt coiled up under it and it was also my size, I had to look for the matching boots in the closet. I was shocked when they all fit, but figured they'd be better for riding than my boots with a four-inch heel."

"Definitely," Anthony chuckled. "I can't believe Ma hasn't gotten rid of these old things. I outgrew them over a decade ago."

"Those were yours?" Tia looked incredulously up at him. "How old were you when you were our size?"

"Those were the ones I wore most as a kid," Anthony replied. "Got 'em for my tenth birthday and didn't grow again until I turned fourteen." He explained how he'd been the runt and the advice his parents gave him that led to his epic growth spurt.

"Yeah, I don't think I'll pray to get taller." Maria shook her head, flashing her cute little half smile that Anthony was beginning to recognize as the one all three of them had before delivering the punch line of a joke. "I want to be taller than Mom and Tia, but I don't want to be as tall as the Jolly Green Giant."

"Hey, I'm not the Jolly Green Giant," Anthony playfully rebuked as he mussed the top of her hair.

The girls just giggled as they made their way out of the house and Anthony started walking them over to the stables.

Kay looked confused by the direction they were walking, and Anthony wondered what she was thinking. When their gazes met, he raised one eyebrow at her to silently ask.

"Are the horses not at the barn we passed coming in?" Kay pointed behind them at the first of several barns on the property.

"No, that barn is where we store a tractor, a few lawn mowers, and the four-wheelers we got in trouble for trying to use to herd the cows as teenagers," Anthony replied. "When we had livestock in the front pasture, we stocked the loft with hay, too. But Dad quit using that pasture and hayloft when Bobby got old enough to try to sneak girls up there. I'm not sure if he's started using it again since we all moved out."

"How many girls did you try to sneak up into the hayloft?" Kay teased him playfully.

"None," Anthony answered honestly. "Being the youngest, I had already seen all my brothers get in trouble for trying to get frisky on the ranch. So, I played it smart and snuck my alone time with a pretty girl on the other side of town."

"Can't do that anymore," Anthony's dad, Bob, said as they caught up with him. "Bobby made Luke put gates up on the north side of the Walker ranch when he caught your sister parking out there with some boy she'd brought home from college her senior year."

"Seriously?" Anthony shook his head in surprise. "Bobby's the one that told me about those trails back when I was too young to drive anything that far except a four-wheeler."

"Yeah, well, I guess when he made police chief, he figured it would look bad if he got caught out there where all the young'uns were makin' out, so he shut it down for everyone."

That made Anthony wonder where Bobby took his buckle bunnies because he knew Bobby wouldn't bring them back to his house on the ranch. His oldest brother only made that mistake once, back when he was eighteen and had just moved into his house on the south side of the ranch. Anthony was only thirteen at the time, but he still remembered the fuss Tammi Jo Willis had made about wanting to move in with Bobby for their senior year of high school. She wouldn't take no for an answer and showed up at his house every day for a week claiming to be his girlfriend, when Bobby swore he'd only taken her out on one date. Bobby finally got her to leave him alone but only after he was caught making out with another girl in the high school parking lot. And even then, he had to put up with her yelling at him about being a cheater in front of the whole school before she finally stomped away.

Anthony shook off his wandering thoughts when he realized that everyone else was moving toward the horses. His dad already had them lined up in the narrow space between the fences exiting out the back of the stable that led into the woods. He made his way over to the area outside the fence to the left of the horses where Bob was introducing the girls to the ones they'd each ride.

"Maria, I heard you like princesses, so I figured you'd want to ride Princess Buttercup." His dad stroked the side of the horse's neck over the fence.

"Is she named after *The Princess Bride*?" Maria grinned as she reached over to pet the horse's neck.

"I think that's the movie my daughters picked their names from," Bob replied. "Right behind her is her mate, Westley. Tia, you ready to climb the fence and hop on his back?"

"Climb the fence?" Tia scrunched up her nose at Anthony's dad.

"Yeah, Pop, uh, Pappaw put these split rail fences up to make it easier for us to get on the horses when I was a little kid too small to mount from the ground." Anthony stepped up behind her. "You just climb up and sit on the top rail of the fence, so you can reach the saddle horn to hold onto while you put your left foot in the stirrup. Then you stand up in the left stirrup and throw your right leg over the horse to sit in the saddle and put your right foot in the other stirrup."

"Yeah, I don't think that's actually going to be as easy as you're describing." Tia looked anxious about mounting the horse. "Can't you just pick me up and put me in the saddle like they did when we did the pony ride at the fair?"

"I can if you'd rather this first time." Anthony wondered where her fear was coming from, considering he hadn't seen her seem to be afraid of heights when she and Maria had climbed on the jungle gym they'd found on one of their sightseeing trips in Dallas. "But when we come back to the ranch next week, I figured we'd start teaching you the more advanced stuff, so you can do it all on your own. If you get as good with the horses as you are with swimming and math and everything else, my sisters are going to want to teach you to barrel race in the rodeo."

"No, I'd rather just have you put me on the horse anytime we go riding and stick to the trail where Pappaw has control of the horse I'm on." Tia's lips quivered with fear.

"Tia, sweetie," Kay cooed softly as she rubbed a hand up and down her daughter's back. "Are you afraid of the horse?"

Anthony went down on one knee beside them wanting to comfort and reassure Tia that there was nothing to be afraid of. "It's okay, Princess," he crooned tenderly as he reached out and took her hand in his, giving her a little squeeze. "These horses are all really well trained. There's nothing to be afraid of."

"Marmaduke was well trained too, but he still snapped and bit me for no reason!" Tia exclaimed, taking a step back from the horses. "And these horses are a lot bigger than he was. If I mess up the physics while trying to get on Westley, I could fall and get trampled to death."

"Oh, sweetie," Kay cooed as she wrapped her arms around Tia. "Marmaduke was a fluke caused by the irresponsible kennel owners inbreeding their dogs. I'm sure with their long history of ranching, the Burlesons don't have inbred animals here that are at risk for going crazy and forgetting their training."

"Your mom's right, Tia," Bob reached over to stroke Westley's neck. "We keep meticulous records on the lineage of all our animals, so we don't risk any genetic abnormalities tainting our stock. There's not a horse on this ranch that would ever step on a person on the ground. In fact, Westley here, actually saved my daughter Char's life once by standing perfectly still over her and neighing up a storm until someone heard him to come rescue her."

"Really?" Tia stepped out of Kay's embrace and looked back and forth between Bob and the horse. "What happened to her?"

"Well, she was misbehaving and had been running him through the woods when she knew better than to go that fast on the trail. It wasn't long after a bad thunderstorm and there was a tree that had been struck by lightning in the storm, and had a branch that was only partially broken and hanging down lower than normal. She wasn't paying attention and when they ran under that tree, the branch hit Char in the head and knocked her off the horse. Her right foot was still caught in the stirrup, and she was hanging off his side. Westley stopped on a dime and was still standing there under that low branch neighing his head off when our ranch manager, Carlos, heard the racket he was making and went to find them. As soon as Westley saw Carlos, he stopped neighing but continued standing perfectly still while Carlos got Charlotte free. If he would have moved at all after she got knocked off by that branch, she'd have had more than one knot on her head from it bouncing against the ground, but Westley didn't let that happen."

"So, he's like a hero horse." Tia stepped up to the fence, reaching through the slats to pet Westley just below where Bob was.

"Has Princess Buttercup ever done anything like that?" Maria inquired from where she was still leaning between the fence rails to stroke the other horse.

"No, none of the other kids were ever that reckless on the horses, so only Westley has had to be a hero," Bob replied. "Come to think of it, that's the only time Charlotte ever did anything reckless and that was fourteen or fifteen years ago now."

"Why don't I remember that?" Anthony figured he should have remembered the incident, if he'd been nine or ten at the time.

"Because Carlos called me at the office, and I told him to take her straight to Doc Hayes, instead of to your Ma back at the house. I met them at Doc Hayes's office. When we got home, we kept her downstairs with us, so we could wake her up every couple of hours. Your Ma arranged sleepovers for the rest of you with your friends or cousins for the weekend, so your rowdiness wouldn't impede her healing. Besides, we didn't want any of you to know what she'd done, so you wouldn't get any ideas of things to try for yourselves."

"Yeah, that was probably for the best," Anthony chuckled with his dad. He turned to look back at Tia. "Now, are we ready to mount up and ride?"

"Yep," she agreed with a nod of her head. "I'll even try climbing the fence and getting on myself if you'll stand right beside me, so you can catch me if I start to fall."

"I promise, I won't let you fall, Princess," Anthony vowed as he stood back up and put a hand on Tia's waist as she started to climb the fence rails. He didn't need to catch her because she mounted up with ease, but he was glad to provide the reassuring hand to make her feel safe in doing so.

"My turn!" Maria bounced with excitement. Anthony did have to use both hands on her waist to give her a little boost, but not much.

Bob walked past both girls to mount up on the lead horse named Tornado.

"You gonna be my safety net, too?" Kay quipped, once both girls were on their horses.

"Absolutely, Baby," Anthony replied with a wink at his woman. "I'll always catch you if you start to fall." He gripped Kay's hips as she climbed the fence, and it took all of his willpower to resist letting his thumbs trail over her ass cheeks as she mounted the horse.

"What's my horse's name?" Kay asked as she settled in the saddle.

"Leonardo," Anthony answered as he moved to mount his own horse. "And I'm on Donatello."

"I guess you boys didn't pick names from princess movies like your sisters, huh?" Kay giggled as she turned back to watch Anthony get on his horse.

"Naw, we preferred cartoon characters like the **Teenage Mutant Ninja Turtles**," Anthony replied as the horses started walking behind his dad's lead.

As the horses leisurely traversed the trail, Anthony enjoyed the view of Kay's perfectly heart-shaped ass bouncing in the saddle in front of him. Was it any wonder why he fell in love with her when all his favorite parts of her body were heart-shaped?

The conversation was mostly lighthearted as they rode for a couple of hours. Anthony and Bob told the girls about more of the family history, about the different parts of the ranch, and a little about the small town their ancestors had founded. Kay, Tia, and Maria talked about their lives in Tulsa, including elaborating on how Tia had been bitten by a family friend's dog when she was eight. Anthony decided her plastic surgeon must have been a miracle worker because he hadn't even noticed the scars under her jawline and hidden in her hair in the week they'd been together almost twenty-four-seven.

When they got back to the stable a couple of hours later, she tilted her head way back and pulled her hair out of the way, so she could show them to him properly. He was in awe of how strong that kid had to be to get through an ordeal such as that. He vowed to do everything in his power to protect all three of them from ever having to suffer through any kind of pain in the future.

He removed saddles and put them away in the tack room while his dad taught the girls how to brush the horses and get them cleaned up after their ride.

"That's why Anthony's so good at detangling our hair," Tia exclaimed. "Pappaw taught him how to be gentle brushing the horses."

Huh? Anthony thought. *I guess I did learn that dad skill from Dad.*

"Thanks, Pop!" Anthony gave his dad a pat on the back. "I didn't realize just how valuable that life skill was until this week with my girls."

"Did you teach him how to braid their mane?" Maria giggled. "He might need a refresher on that lesson since he couldn't braid our hair."

"No," Bob laughed. "We've never braided the horse's manes."

"You should." Maria started weaving the strands of hair in Princess Buttercup's mane together. "Princess Buttercup would look so pretty with pink bows at the end of a few braids in her mane."

Anthony hid his chuckle at the thought of his dad putting pink bows on his horses by ducking behind Donatello's neck where he was brushing out his own horse.

It had been an almost perfect afternoon. He loved having time as a family and seeing how quickly the girls were meshing with his parents. The only thing that would have made it better was some alone time with Kay. Maybe if he slowed down a little while taking care of the needs of Donatello and Leonardo, his dad would take the girls back to the house while he and Kay snuck a few minutes alone in the stables. There wasn't a loft in the stables, but there was an extra stall where they stored hay for the horses that he wouldn't mind rolling around in with her.

Unfortunately for him, nobody was slower in taking care of the horses than Maria, who had to brush out Princess Buttercup's mane a second time to remove the half-dozen braids she'd put in it even though she didn't have bows to tie them off.

When they finally left the barn, he took Kay's hand, so they could slowly stroll back to the house. If the girls ran far enough ahead, his dad would keep up with them to herd them where they needed to go to get cleaned up for dinner and Anthony might have a chance to sneak a kiss or two with Kay on the porch while everyone else was in the house.

~~~

Kay was excited at being able to go with her daughters on their first horseback ride. She spent the rest of the afternoon soaking up the joy and wonder of her daughters as they learned all about the horses and how to take care of them. The huge smile she wore on their trail ride was one-hundred percent real because she didn't need to mask her feelings while having so much fun laughing and getting to know another side of Anthony and his family history.

She forgot all about the stress of her life back in Tulsa, why she worried that things were moving too fast between her and Anthony, and even her fear that his slowing things down was really because he'd changed his mind about wanting to be with her. She embraced the joy of the here and now, and just let herself live in the moment.
~~~

By the time they finished taking care of the horses they'd ridden and were walking back to the house from the barn, Kay had completely forgotten about the current state of their sleeping arrangements and any anxiety she had about them. Instead, she reveled in the affection Anthony was giving her by keeping her close to him all day and holding her hand on their walk to the house.

He pulled her to a stop as they stepped up on the porch, allowing the girls to run ahead into the house to wash up for dinner.

"What's wrong?" Kay looked up at Anthony, trying to figure out why he stopped her from going inside.

"Nothing's wrong, Baby," Anthony murmured in his slow, Texas drawl.

Kay loved it when he called her "Baby" and drew the word out to twice its normal length. It made her feel special because he only said "Baby" that way when he was addressing her with it as a term of endearment.

"I just haven't had a moment alone with you in days and I'm going through withdrawal." Anthony picked her up and sat her on the porch railing. He stepped between her knees and wrapped his arms around her, so she couldn't fall backwards off the porch. "It was hard enough to go six days without kissing you when we weren't in the same state, but the last six days of not getting a moment alone to kiss you have been pure torture. So, I'm going to take advantage of having the girls distracted by my parents to hide on the porch and kiss you for a few minutes."

Anthony bent down to softly brush his lips across Kay's. She wrapped her arms around his neck and played with the longish hair at his nape as she returned his kiss. When his tongue came out to swipe across the seam of her lips, she eagerly opened for his exploration. Their tongues tangled together in the most erotic kiss Kay had ever experienced. Anthony's hands palmed her buttocks as he picked her up and pulled her into his body. Her legs instinctively wrapped around his waist as their bodies molded together.

Is this what my books described as "climbing him like a tree"? Kay wondered.

While she felt small and delicate compared to his large frame, she also felt like they fit perfectly together as his erection rubbed against her core. He speared her mouth with his tongue like she wished he would spear her with his extra-large erection.

What am I thinking? We're on his parents' front porch! I can't think about sex with Anthony on his parents' front porch!

Anthony's hands moved, one cupping her buttocks and the other moving up to the nape of her neck. Kay forgot all about where they were when he massaged her with both, moving her head to give him access to her neck, so he could trail open-mouthed kisses down it while he ground his erection against her in just the right way to stimulate her clitoris.

Just as Kay felt like she was about to explode in pleasure, she heard a soft female voice behind her. "Ooops, sorry, didn't mean to interrupt."

Anthony gently lowered Kay to her feet but made sure she stayed in front of him as she turned to see who was speaking. *Yeah, I'm not sure I'm tall enough to hide that erection,* Kay thought while trying not to show her embarrassment at being caught making out like a teenager.

"Mom said Aunt Hazel wanted us all to come for dinner tonight to meet the newest members of the family," announced a blonde woman as she walked up the stairs and onto the porch. "You must be Kay. I'm Anthony's cousin Jen." Jen extended her hand to Kay.

"It's nice to meet you." Kay reached out to shake her hand. Instead, she was pulled into another unexpected hug.

"Sorry, Cuz." Jen squeezed Kay. "We're a bunch of huggers in this family. You'll get used to it."

As soon as Kay was released from Jen's grasp, she was embraced by another woman. The second was a little taller than Jen, whom Kay guessed was about five-foot-four, but shared her blonde hair and blue eyes. "I'm Julie, Jen's sister, and Anthony's cousin." Julie released Kay from the hug.

Before she could catch her breath and introduce herself, she was embraced by a third woman. This one was about the same height as Jen, but she had light brown hair and green eyes. "I'm Anthony's sister, Becky," she introduced herself as she released Kay.

"It's nice to meet you all." Kay's head was spinning from the rapid-fire introductions. She turned to look up at Anthony as he took her hand and pulled her back to him and away from the growing crowd on the porch. She was sure he saw panic in her eyes, but thankfully he didn't acknowledge it in a negative way.

"How about we all go inside and see if Mom has some name tags laying around we can use to keep from confusing Kay." Anthony motioned behind him toward the door with a little grin. "And don't overwhelm the girls like you just did Kay." Anthony gave his sister and cousins a pointed look before leading them all into the house.

Instead of going to the kitchen where they'd eaten lunch earlier in the day, Anthony stopped just inside the formal dining room, where there were now two extra-long tables set with a third smaller table between them to create one large U-shaped table big enough to seat at least forty people. *Surely there aren't that many people coming to dinner tonight?*

"I should go wash up first." Kay lifted her hands up in surrender to Anthony, hoping he didn't see her trepidation at meeting so many of his relatives.

"Yeah, me, too." Anthony grinned, pulling her behind him through the double doors off the foyer, leaving Jen, Julie, Becky, and the other people who had arrived without introductions behind them. The double doors opened to a hallway that had two doors on the left, one on the right that Kay assumed was the other door she'd seen in the kitchen earlier, and another set of double doors at the opposite end. Anthony pulled her through the first door on the left and into a washroom with cabinets and counters that matched the ones in the kitchen.

Kay walked to the furthest of the double sinks in the room and turned on the water to wash her hands. She kept her gaze down not sure what to say to Anthony who had followed her into the bathroom.

"You okay, Baby?" Anthony inquired as he started to wash his own hands in the other sink. Their gazes met in the mirror and Kay could see he was worried about her.

"Yeah," she finally replied as she gave him a small smile. "Maybe a little embarrassed and overwhelmed."

Anthony opened a cabinet and pulled out two hand towels, handing one to Kay before drying his own hands with the other. "Nothing to be embarrassed about, Baby." He folded the towel and hung it on the towel bar beside the sink. "I'm sorry, I didn't think Mom would invite everyone tonight. I thought it would just be Mom and Dad and maybe

Char, Becky, and Bobby. I should've told her not to overwhelm you with the aunts, uncles, and cousins, too."

"How many of them are there?" Kay followed Anthony's lead and put the towel she was finished using on the towel bar as he had.

"Too many," Anthony chuckled as he pulled her into a hug. "You already know there are eight in my immediate family counting my mom and dad, but Jake and Josh aren't here right now. The other Burlesons are Dad's brother Jon, his wife, Susan, and their four children, JJ, Justin, Julie, and Jen. The Whitmans are Mom's sister, Maggie, her husband, Doug, and their two children, Dougie and Dani. The Harpers are Aunt Susan's sister, Sarah, her husband, Joe, and their three kids, Colt, Cam, and Colby." Anthony kissed the top of Kay's head. "So, twenty-one who might be here tonight."

Twenty-one? Kay thought, wondering how she was going to be able to remember all their names. "Where'd you say those name tags are?" They pulled apart and started to make their way out of the washroom and back to the dining room.

As they stepped back into the dining room, Kay stood as straight as she could trying to project confidence in herself, which she didn't really feel, so she could present a good example to her daughters. *They don't need to see how overwhelmed I am,* she thought as the introductions began anew.

"Why don't you have a nickname?" Tia looked up at Anthony as he pulled out a chair for her.

"Because he hated his nicknames as a kid," the woman who sat down across the table from where Kay was standing beside Anthony declared. Kay thought it was his sister Becky but wasn't certain. "He threw a fit and Mom made us quit using them."

"I didn't throw a fit." Anthony shook his head, moving to pull out chairs for Maria and Kay and taking his seat beside Kay once they were all seated.

"Oh, you definitely threw a fit with the first one," the other woman seated across from them chuckled. Kay couldn't remember if she was his other sister or a cousin. "But you were three at the time, so you probably don't remember."

"I don't remember that time, Char," the woman, whom Kay thought was Becky, shook her head at Charlotte. "I was talking about when he was twelve and we had been calling him Tony his whole life and he decided he hated it."

"Of course, I hated it," Anthony growled with an overacted grimace. "Ya'll said it with that fake accent that made me sound like a character on *The Sopranos*."

Kay couldn't contain her smile at the mental image of Anthony in the old television show.

"What's *The Sopranos*?" Tia looked around Kay at Anthony.

"It's an old TV show about mobsters in New Jersey," Kay answered her daughter. "Although, you do wear a lot of dark suits while you're flying, so you kinda look the part now." Kay giggled as she grinned at Anthony. "Maybe I'll call you Tony from now on."

Anthony leaned into Kay, speaking softly into her ear, so only she could hear. "You can call me anything you want, Baby, when we're alone and I'm making you want to scream it. But I reserve the right to spank you if you get my sisters started with calling me Tony again." He pulled back just enough for their eyes to lock on each other, almost close enough to kiss.

Oh my, Kay thought, noticing a twinkle of something in Anthony's eyes that she couldn't quite interpret. She wasn't sure why he was suddenly back to the sexual innuendo when he'd been avoiding it all week, but she liked it. Liked how he was looking at her and making her feel sexy and wanted. *Yeah, if you want to spank me, Tony, it won't have anything to do with your sisters. But maybe if we ever get out of the friend zone, I'll come up with another reason to try that out when we're alone.*

"Oh, no, you are definitely not Tony," Kay uttered a little too breathlessly as Anthony pulled back from her and leaned back in his seat. *I may want to scream it later, though,* Kay thought as she tuned back into the conversation around her.

"We could always go back to the first nickname we had for him." Char smirked.

"What was that, Aunt Char?" Maria looked at Anthony's sister inquisitively.

"Ant," Char replied and the girls all giggled. "He was the littlest one of us, was always the first in the food when we ate, and it was the first three letters of his name, so it was an easy nickname to come up with."

"He's not the smallest anymore." Tia giggled, smiling at Anthony. "And he always makes sure Mom, Maria, and I have a plate before he dishes up his own when we eat in catering, so I don't think he's an Ant anymore, either."

Kay could clearly see the wheels turning in Tia's head as she tried to figure out an appropriate nickname for Anthony. *What do kids normally call a stepdad?* After their make-out session on the front porch, Kay was back to thinking that Anthony wanted to keep moving forward with their relationship and would possibly be their stepdad one day. She decided to put off trying to figure that out until after the court date because the judge could still derail any plans she might try to make now.

"When will you be moving in next door?" Hazel asked, bringing Kay back to the present conversation around them.

"We'll be back here the fifteenth to move the stuff from my apartment to the ranch." Anthony looked decidedly uncomfortable at his mother's question. "But I just thought we'd store my furniture here, not move me into Jake and Josh's house."

"Don't be ridiculous." Hazel waved her hand around as if she was dismissing Anthony's suggestion. "Those boys aren't using the house. We can store their stuff here and redecorate the house with a more feminine touch for my new granddaughters."

"Mom, quit pushing," Anthony pleaded. "They still live in Tulsa, and we can't make any decisions about living somewhere else yet."

"And why not?" Hazel looked back and forth between Kay and Anthony. "You're clearly in love and going to end up married and living here, so why can't we get started planning the wedding and decorating your home? I know you asked her to marry you the night you met, so why aren't we planning it all now?"

"Technically, he didn't actually propose that night," Kay pointed out, looking at Hazel with an expression of incredulity.

"No, I knew better than to give her the chance to say no," Anthony smirked. "I told her we'll get married whenever she's ready as long as it's within a few months or a year."

"Okay, so why can't we go ahead and start planning the wedding and where ya'll will live?" Hazel pointed back to Anthony.

Kay threw her hands up in exasperation. As she turned her head, she saw Bob grinning from ear to ear as he leaned back in his seat and spoke to one of the other men. She couldn't hear what he said from across the room, but guessed he said "told you I raised him right" by reading his lips. She would have to remember to ask Anthony about that later. At that moment, she needed to clear things up with her want-to-be-mother-in-law.

"There are lots of reasons why I can't make any decisions about life right now," Kay explained, imploring Hazel to understand and back off. "First of all, we haven't known each other two full weeks. Second, we haven't even gone on a real date yet, much less gotten to know each other well enough to talk about marriage."

"I thought our first date was at the diner the night we met." Anthony reached over to clasp Kay's hand in his.

"And your second date was at Mazzio's and the fun park," Tia stated matter-of-factly. Anthony nodded in agreement.

"Those weren't real dates," Kay objected, looking back and forth between Anthony and her daughters.

"Our third date was a weekend away in Dallas." Anthony held up three fingers, ignoring Kay's disagreement.

"Really?" Maria gave Anthony her ornery smile. "I thought the plane ride to Dallas was the third date and swimming at the hotel was the fourth." She counted them off on her fingers as she spoke.

"Then dinner at the hotel was the fifth, sightseeing downtown was the sixth, and the zoo was the seventh." Tia continued the count, her smile matching that of her sister.

"Dinner after the zoo was the eighth," Maria added, continuing to count them with her fingers. "And room service breakfast was the ninth."

"Enough!" Kay reached over to stop her daughter from counting on her fingers. "You can't count every meal and place we went as a date. They weren't dates. We were just hanging out as friends, not dating."

"Baby…" Anthony slowly drawled out the word in his special way that made Kay's insides flutter. Kay wondered how she was supposed to maintain her argument when he made her feel butterflies. "I definitely thought of them as dates."

"No, the first night was you trying to talk me into going on a date with you, not actually a date. Then Friday, our date got canceled because of, well, you know." Kay didn't want to embarrass herself or her daughters by going into detail about the altercation with Mark on

Friday night. "The rest was just you being a good friend and helping me find a job. Dating is going out one-on-one, not hanging out with my whole family."

"A date also ends with a goodnight kiss." Tia's face lit up with her little half smile that Kay knew meant she was scheming. "So, you can figure out how many times it was really a date by how many times you've kissed. I know Friday night was a date because I had to cover my head with my pillow, so I couldn't hear you kissing."

"And today was a date," Anthony's cousin Jen interjected with a grin from her seat down the table.

"Does room service breakfast count if they were kissing before we woke up?" Maria turned in her seat to look at Jen.

"Definitely," Jen agreed.

Kay felt herself blushing and hated that she couldn't control it. "No, we didn't actually kiss then," she argued.

"Maybe I didn't actually get to kiss you then because Maria walked in, but we definitely did some other things that count as a date," Anthony smirked.

If he counts every time I was aroused by him or vice versa, he'll start adding days we weren't even in the same town to our date count, Kay thought, feeling her cheeks turning a deeper shade of red.

"And dating can definitely include hanging out with the whole family," Hazel argued. "When you're planning to become a family of more than just you and your spouse, you have to include everyone in the family while you're courting, so you know you're planning to marry the right person."

"Again, we just met," Kay protested, turning to Hazel. "It's impossible to know when you first meet someone that you want to marry them."

"Oh, that doesn't matter." Hazel waved off Kay's point before raising her voice, so Susan could hear her from the other end of the table. "Burlesons know the first time they see their mate. Isn't that right, Susan?"

"Yep," Susan replied, squeezing the hand of the man sitting beside her. "Jon told me we were getting married on our first date."

"And Bob told me he was going to marry Hazel the first day he saw her at church," said the man beside Susan that Kay realized was her husband, Jon. "She was only fifteen at the time, so he had to wait a while to tell her, but he knew the first time he saw her."

Kay turned to look at Bob, who agreed with a nod of his head and a secret smile to his wife.

"Love at first sight is the norm in Heart's Destiny," one of Anthony's other aunts added. Kay couldn't remember if she was Maggie or Sarah.

As Kay absentmindedly ate the meal, she didn't realize Anthony had placed in front of her, his family went on to describe not only the other two older couples in the room's romantic stories, but also talked about several neighbors and friends who also fell in love the first time they saw their spouse. Kay gave up trying to refute the possibility of a fairy-tale romance when it was clear that nobody in the room would believe her saying she couldn't be sure yet about wanting to marry Anthony. Not even her daughters, who were listening to all the stories of love with excitement and awe written on their cherubic faces.

That wasn't the real reason that Kay was holding back on moving forward with her relationship with Anthony, though. She felt uncomfortable with discussing her legal issues with her ex-husband in front of all of Anthony's extended family, but she saw no other option than airing her dirty laundry to get Hazel to stop pushing to plan a wedding and move them into the house next door.

"I have a court date next month that could prevent me from being able to move out of Tulsa or continue on this job!" Kay finally shouted over the roar of the various conversations going on around her. They all stopped talking at once at Kay's declaration. She looked around to see everyone looking at her with expressions of shock. Lots of wide eyes and several hands over mouths. *Well, sugar,* Kay thought. *I didn't mean to be that loud.*

She turned to look at Anthony, who leaned over and rubbed her back while giving her a sympathetic smile.

"The judge can't really tell us not to move, can he?" Maria's eyes filled with unshed tears.

"No!" Tia shouted as she jumped up from her chair, darted over to Anthony, and grabbed his arm. "You won't let the judge make us stay where he could…" She choked on her words making them unable to be understood as her tears started to fall.

Anthony pulled Tia into his arms, cradling Kay's sobbing daughter in his lap. "Don't worry, Princess," he cooed as he rocked her and rubbed his hand up and down her back. "I'm going to be there in court, and I won't let him near you. And no judge in his right mind will rule in his favor after we all testify."

Kay couldn't understand what Tia was saying as she clung to Anthony and cried into his chest. She was glad Anthony seemed to understand her as he continued to soothe her with his whispered replies to her statements.

Kay turned to look at her younger daughter, thinking she might need the same kind of soothing that Anthony was giving Tia. Maria wasn't in her seat any longer, which caused Kay's heart to race as she scanned the room looking for her baby. When she finally saw where Maria was, Kay wasn't sure whether to breathe a sigh of relief, or laugh at the sheer determination on her daughter's face as she sat on the police chief's lap.

She had a hand on either side of Anthony's oldest brother Bobby's face as she spoke to him. "You can coordinate with Grandpa Lee and arrest the judge for false imprisonment if he won't let us leave Tulsa," Maria instructed. "That's the right charge for making us stay somewhere we don't want to stay, right?"

"Uh, maybe," Bobby nodded with a confused look on his face. "But Tulsa is out of my jurisdiction, so I can't be sure what the law allows there."

"It's okay, Uncle Bobby," Maria shrugged as if that was no big deal. "My Grandpa Lee is the Sheriff in Tulsa, so he can do the actual arrest there, but you can come give us a police escort back here to your jurisdiction, so we can find a judge that will say we can live here where we want. It's a small town, do you even have a judge here?"

Several people laughed and Kay was relieved to realize that Tia was one of them.

"That would be me," announced one of Anthony's uncles. Kay tried to remember his name but failed. He made his way over and took the seat that Tia had vacated. "Maybe you can tell me what you're going to court for, and I can give you an idea of how a judge will see it. Obviously, I have no jurisdiction to intervene in an out-of-state case, but maybe a practice run can help you prepare for whatever you're about to have to face in Oklahoma."

"Thanks, Uncle Doug." Anthony smiled at his uncle before turning his head to look down at Tia, who was still sitting on his lap. "Tia, did you meet your great-uncle Doug?"

"Is this another of those heart adoption things that isn't really legal, like Memmaw and Pappaw?" Tia looked quizzically at Doug.

"For now." Doug smiled at Tia. "But I have a feeling it'll be legal eventually."

Tia smiled and got down from Anthony's lap. She walked over and took the seat next to Doug and started asking him all kinds of questions about what his courtroom was like and the types of court cases he normally saw. Once she was satisfied that he was qualified to give an accurate opinion of a judge, she started explaining the legalities of the situation with the detail and confidence of a seasoned lawyer.

Kay felt completely flummoxed by all the questions that were coming at her from every angle. She'd always felt like she had to hide the not-so-savory aspects of her previous marriage from everyone, including her own family, so opening up to Anthony's family about it was way outside her comfort zone.

The only way she could get through it was to disengage. As her daughters and Anthony, and even her father by phone, explained the disgusting details of her life, Kay closed off her emotions and observed as if she were hearing it all about someone else.

By the time dinner was over, she felt completely drained, even though Doug was reassuring in his belief that the judge would rule in her favor and allow her to move away and terminate Mark's visitation rights.

She was so numb by the end of the night that she fell into the bed Anthony showed her to and was asleep before she could even ask him where he was sleeping. She awoke the next morning without even remembering how she got to bed.

Chapter Ten

Sunday, October 14, 2018

Over the last couple of days, Anthony was pleased to see how well Kay and the girls were all fitting in with the rest of the company. Tia was quickly becoming best friends with Rick's daughter Britany, who was also twelve years old. Maria spent as much of her time as she could each day with two other little girls about her age that were the daughters of a couple of the wrestlers that Anthony didn't know well. He figured he would have to expand his circle of friends to be able to stay ahead of any mischief the girls would get into in the future.

Kay also seemed to have already made some new friends in the mothers of the two girls Maria was calling her two new best friends. Anthony could only refer to them as Sarah's Mom and Katie's Mom because in the evenings when they went back to their adjoining rooms, Maria couldn't stop talking about Sarah this and Katie that.

While he was glad they were all making friends and settling into life traveling with the company, he was frustrated at not being able to get any time alone with Kay. Their mornings were a rush of getting everyone ready, which was only slightly less chaotic than the day they had to all use one bathroom before leaving Tulsa, even with the addition of a second bathroom being available for four people to shower and dress. As soon as they got to the airport, Anthony had to focus on his preflight duties while Kay and the girls got settled in the passenger section.

Once they landed, they had a little time together while they checked in at the hotel and turned their dirty laundry over to the hotel staff for cleaning while they grabbed lunch. They'd explore the sights of whatever city they were in and then head to the arena for about an hour of self-defense training before the wrestlers started showing up to use the ring.

They only stayed to watch the wrestlers practice the first day, when Kay did her interview, but since then the girls went to the backstage area set up as a classroom as soon as the rest of the kids and tutors showed up. Kay always went with them, either working with the tutors to get the girls homeschooling set up properly or socializing with the other mothers.

While they were occupied by their new friends and the girls' education, Anthony went back to his previous schedule of hanging out with his friends, first doing a little extra sparring in the ring, and then sitting in the locker room watching the show on monitors. He'd tried to meet up with Kay and the girls in catering, so they could watch the show together. But as soon as they were all finished eating, the girls all rushed off back to the classroom with shouts of "See you later, Anthony!" and not even so much as a hug or kiss on the cheek from Kay.

They would find him again a little before nine to go back to the hotel. Kay had reinstated a bedtime for the girls, moving it to nine each night from their previous eight-thirty. They all three disappeared behind the closed door adjoining their rooms, leaving Anthony alone in his to sit up for a couple of hours missing them.

He felt like a total jackass for being jealous of the time that Kay and her daughters spent with their new friends and tutors. He wanted to push to be involved in that part of their lives as well, but he was afraid he'd already pushed Kay too far by orchestrating the easy transition into her new job that forced her to travel with him constantly. He knew that if he tried to push his way into the few hours of the day that they weren't already with him, he would push way past the boundaries Kay was trying to keep up between them.

He was already all in and wanted to be her husband and the girls' dad, but Kay wasn't there yet. Anthony thought the girls were ready for them to be a family, especially after the family dinner on the Burleson Ranch. Maria especially had asked a few times over the two days since they'd left the ranch when they were going back to see Memmaw and Pappaw and the horses. She'd even started giving Anthony daily drawings of the house ideas she had for building on the ranch. Of course, they all looked like castles because she was a firm believer that she was a princess and needed to live in a castle. Anthony wanted nothing more than to convince her mother and sister of the same thing.

Unfortunately, he had no idea how to do it when he couldn't get more than a few minutes alone with Kay each day to steal a kiss or two before the girls woke up and wandered through the open door of their adjoining rooms. He still hadn't convinced Kay to allow him a good night kiss as she shut the door each night at bedtime.

Anthony decided he needed to figure out how some of the families on the tour managed to squeeze in couple time to keep expanding their families while traveling with their children. Since his closest friends weren't parents, he was back to trying to figure out how to make friends with the wrestlers he only knew as passing acquaintances. *I don't think asking them how they manage alone time with their wives while traveling with their kids is the best thing to ask to get to know them.*

Anthony hung his head as he stepped out of the cockpit and started his post-flight walkthrough of the plane after landing in New Orleans. As he checked the emergency exits, he noticed that Rick was still on the plane. Figuring he was just finishing up something before departing for the arena, Anthony continued on his post-flight checklist, so he could hurry to meet Kay in the airport.

"Hey, hold up!" Rick raised a hand to stop Anthony as he walked past him on his way back to the front of the plane.

"Hey, Boss." Anthony turned to see what his boss had stayed on the plane to talk to him about alone. "What's up?"

"I just wanted to check on you." Rick crossed his arms over his chest and leaned back in his seat. "How are things going with you and Kay?"

"It's good," Anthony replied, not sure what his boss was really asking. "She seems to be settling into the routine and happy with the job."

"I know that already." Rick looked up at Anthony like he was trying to read his body language for more of an answer than Anthony had given. "How is your relationship with her going?"

Anthony wished at that moment that his standard professional attire didn't include a tie because he felt like it was choking him under his boss's scrutiny. He shrugged as he sat down in the seat across from

Rick. If he was going to have this talk with his boss, then he was going to at least do it while sitting comfortably instead of hunching over because he was too tall to stand at his full height under the overhead storage compartment without scraping the bottom of it.

"It's fine, I guess," Anthony finally sighed. "Hard to be anything more when we can't get any time alone."

"I was afraid of that." Rick tilted his head as he looked at Anthony. "I told Kay to make sure she gets equal babysitting time with the other parents, so you guys can have a date night, but I don't think she knows anyone well enough to be comfortable leaving her daughters with any of us yet."

"How does that work?" Anthony realized then that his boss might be able to give him some insight into how the other parents managed alone time while traveling. "The swapping babysitting and getting adults-only time, that is. I thought having adjoining rooms would give Kay and I some time together at night after the girls go to bed, but she closes the door between our rooms and goes to bed with them."

"The girls are cockblocking you?" Rick chuckled.

Anthony stifled his own chuckle. "Yeah, but that's not really the problem." He ran his hand through his hair, trying to figure out how to word his feelings. "Last week, when we were in California and she was in Tulsa, I got to talk to her more than I have this week, even though we're traveling together now. We would text off and on throughout the afternoon and either call or Skype at night after the girls went to bed."

"And now you're together more but not getting to have those deep conversations because you have little ears always listening." Rick nodded, showing his understanding.

"Yeah," Anthony huffed. "I wish there was a way I could have some time alone with her, but I don't know how to get it. How do the other families do it?"

"Do it?" Rick smirked.

"Not necessarily *it*, it." Anthony hoped he didn't appear too embarrassed to talk about sex with his boss. "But traveling with kids and still getting alone time with their wives?"

"Well, they don't sleep in separate rooms than their wives." Rick was still smirking. "We put the families in suites, so the kids have rooms with multiple twin or bunk beds and the parents have a separate bedroom with a lock on the door."

"That would be great," Anthony replied with a sigh. "But I don't think Kay is ready for sharing my bed with the girls in a separate bedroom on the other side of the suite."

"They also have a sofa bed in the living room area in most of them, so you wouldn't necessarily have to share a bed, and could still get your talking time on the sofa after the girls' bedtime," Rick explained. "I spend half my nights sitting on the sofa working while Brit's asleep, so I know they can be comfortable enough to talk more than you and Kay are now."

"Any chance you can get us switched into a suite for tonight?" Anthony would probably still have to sleep on the couch and give Kay the king-sized bed in the private bedroom, but he was okay with that if he could get an hour or so of sharing the sofa with Kay before bed.

Rick pulled his phone out of the pocket of his suit coat. After a few taps on the screen, he looked back up at Anthony. "Done." Rick slipped his phone back into his pocket. "Let me know tomorrow if it helps your situation and I'll change all your future rooms, too."

"Thanks, Boss." Anthony smiled as they got up from their seats and made their way off the plane.

When they checked into the hotel, Anthony felt guilty for having Rick change their room assignment. He didn't know how to explain it to Kay without seeming like he was trying to manipulate the situation to get her in bed. He was nervous as they exited the elevator and he carried all of their larger bags and followed Kay to the room door, so she could use the keycard he'd handed her to open the door to the room she didn't know they would be sharing yet.

Kay opened the door and looked around the suite with an expression of awe at the lavish surroundings. "Are we in the right room?" She turned and looked up at Anthony.

"This is a room like our friends usually get," Tia answered as she walked over to one of the doors off the living room and opened it. "This is our room, Maria."

She went into the room and Maria followed her, leaving Anthony and Kay alone in the open floor plan living and kitchenette area of the suite. After apparently putting down their backpacks, both girls came back out of the room and walked over toward Anthony.

"I'm confused." Kay looked at her daughters and then back to the room that appeared to have two twin beds.

"It's a family suite." Tia waved an arm around the room. "Since the company pays for our hotel rooms while you're working, they put families in suites, so the kids have a room, and the parents have a room, and the company only pays for one room instead of two separate hotel rooms with an adjoining door. It's more cost-efficient for the company."

"But it's not really more cost-efficient for the company to put us in a suite and still have to pay for a second room for Anthony." Kay still looked confused. Anthony hated that he was probably about to cause Kay to lose that adorable, confused look.

"Yeah, Baby, about that," Anthony stated sheepishly. "I'm booked into this suite, too."

"Bu-but, we're not a family," Kay stuttered out as she motioned between herself and Anthony.

Anthony smiled at Kay, glad that she still looked adorably confused. "Yet." He winked at her, closing the distance between himself and Kay. He took both of her hands in his and went down on one knee so he could look Kay eye to eye. "I'll keep asking every day until you finally agree to marry me."

"And I'll keep telling you no." Kay stomped her little foot like an insolent child. "I can't make any decisions about the future until I know what the judge will allow me to do."

"Baby," Anthony crooned in his slow Texas drawl. "The judge can't order you not to marry me. And I want to be there with you to deal with anything else he does order."

"You're already going to be there." Kay shook her head. "We don't need to be married for you to go to court with us."

Anthony hung his head, trying to pull back and quit pushing Kay to move their relationship faster than she was ready for. *She'll get there eventually,* he thought. *I just have to control myself and quit pushing until she's ready.*

Anthony stood back up, giving Kay a kiss on the forehead as he did, before going back to the large bags he'd left sitting just inside the door. He picked up the two for the girls and put them in their bedroom.

When he went back into the living room area of the suite, he looked back and forth between his and Kay's suitcases for a moment while the girls were distracted checking out the contents of the fridge in the kitchenette area. As much as he wanted to carry both of their bags to the other bedroom, he didn't want to make Kay feel like he was solely focused on progressing their sexual relationship.

He wanted Kay more than he'd ever wanted any other woman in his life, but he didn't just want her for sex. He wanted so much more. The best friend. The constant companion. The co-parent. The partner in life. She wasn't just his sexual mate. She was his soulmate. His everything.

He put his own bags down at the far end of the sofa, resigned to the fact that he would be sleeping on the pull-out bed that night, before carrying Kay's large bag to the other bedroom.

~~~

Kay was confused and overwhelmed as she went through the motions of her normal day. Anthony's abrupt change from getting on one knee and proposing to giving her a chaste kiss on the forehead and putting their bags in separate rooms had given her emotional whiplash. After the craziness of his family dinner Thursday, he hadn't limited his talk of marriage to only when they were alone, but he also hadn't shown any sign of wanting to move the sexual side of their relationship to the next level.

Friday night in Houston while they were all sitting in catering having dinner, he asked Rick's opinion on picking a wedding date, so everyone in the company could attend. That got the girls started on asking about where they would live after the wedding, and if they could build another house on the ranch, so his brothers could have theirs back when they got out of the military. Maria had even started drawing him pictures of houses she liked to give him ideas of what to build for her.

Saturday afternoon in Shreveport while they were in the ring for a self-defense lesson, Anthony pinned Kay to the mat and enlisted the
~~~

help of the girls to tickle her while he held her down, claiming they wouldn't stop until Kay agreed to marry him. The only reason Kay got out of actually agreeing was because of the position Anthony was in where he straddled Kay, holding her hands down with his and her legs down with his ankles, left him vulnerable to Maria's elbow where she was tickling her mother. Needless to say, the girls learned that an elbow to the nuts would stop even a man as big as Anthony from continuing to attack, and Kay was able to get up without saying yes.

But as much as he was bringing up marriage and planning to be a family, he wasn't actually acting like he wanted Kay the way she longed to feel desired. He was still openly affectionate, holding her hand or putting his hand on her back or his arm around her shoulders as they walked together, but his kisses were mostly chaste and to the top of her head or her forehead, like right before they left their suite in New Orleans on Sunday afternoon.

Even the few times they were alone in the mornings while the girls were in the other room, either still sleeping or starting to get ready for the day, he'd barely given her a peck of a kiss on the lips. Certainly, nothing as hot as their make-out session the previous Friday on her couch in Tulsa or as passionate as on his parents' porch Thursday after horseback riding.

Even if she didn't have the worry of the upcoming court date preventing her from making any future plans, Kay couldn't possibly plan a future with Anthony when he was sending her such mixed signals. Now that her libido had been awakened, she wanted to know if she could actually experience the intense, erotic lovemaking described in the books she read, not get stuck in a marriage where she only got chaste kisses. If she wanted a sexless marriage, she could have stayed married to Mark. Kay shuddered at the thought of that.

"You okay?" Emily reached out to put a hand on Kay's shoulder.

While Tia had also started to bond with a new best friend on the first day they met Britney, Kay learned that Britney's mother had left her and Rick when Britney was five. Kay had hoped to make friends with all the mothers of the children who traveled with the company, especially the mothers of her daughters' closest friends. But after a couple of days being around Britney, she knew meeting her mother would never happen. But at least she was able to become fast friends with the moms of Maria's new besties.

"Yeah, I'm fine," Kay replied to Emily, trying to make herself focus on her new friend instead of letting her mind wander any longer.

"You sure?" Emily gave Kay a quizzical look. "The way you were shaking a moment ago, and went really pale, didn't look fine to me."

"Sorry." Kay shook her head. "My mind wandered off to a bad place for a second there. Nothing that will actually ever happen again, so no need to worry about me."

"Your ex?" Jana also looked at her with a concerned expression.

"Yeah," Kay replied. She hadn't talked to either of her new friends about the situation in Tulsa, so she was shocked they picked up on her thoughts so easily. But since the girls referred to Anthony by his given name, it was probably obvious to everyone in the company that he wasn't their father, so they could easily figure out that Kay had issues with her ex-husband regardless of whether or not she actually mentioned anything.

"You don't have to talk about it if you don't want to." Emily gave Jana a strange look.

"But we overheard the girls talking last night in catering when they went back for their late snack." Jana shrugged.

"Ha," Emily snorted. "She calls it a late snack like they ate an apple or something healthy. When we all know they just wanted to get a second dessert and act all grown up by sitting alone at their own table."

Kay laughed with her friends at the shenanigans their daughters were up to, grateful they were only innocently trying to sneak an extra piece of cake.

"Anyway," Jana shared when their laughter died down. "While they thought their table was secluded enough to talk without anyone hearing, they were talking about Maria's father and having to go to court next month."

Kay gasped and covered her mouth with her hand, completely astonished that her daughter was talking about that with her newest friends. She felt like the world's worst parent for watching her daughter with her friends from the opposite side of the room and not realizing how heavy their conversation had been.

"It's not a big deal," Emily reassured Kay. "They weren't talking about the reasons you're going to court. Maria was more focused on how Anthony's going to fix it and if he can't do it alone, then her grandpa the sheriff, or her new uncle the police chief will help him convince the judge to rule in your favor. It was all positive about how she wants it to go, so Anthony can be her new dad."

"What Emily means is that what the girls were talking about was how Anthony is Maria's hero," Jana added. "And all little girls need a father figure that they can consider a hero."

"Not just little girls," Emily smirked. "Us big girls need heroes to lean on once in a while too, but they are our partners or spouses instead of our father figures."

"So, even if you don't want to talk to us about why you have to go to court or what you were thinking that made you look like you were about to faint, we hope you'll eventually get comfortable enough to tell us when Anthony is being your hero," Jana added with a knowing grin.

Kay giggled at their obvious fishing for information about her relationship with Anthony. She felt a little strange about talking about her love life with women she'd only known a few days. But traveling with them the way she was made her feel closer to them than she would have normally felt about people she'd just met. Kind of like she felt closer to Anthony than she had to any other man in her life.

She embraced the quick connection of new friendship and gave them a brief overview of her short-lived relationship with Anthony, glossing over their texts, calls, and Skype conversations as merely communicating while she was in Tulsa, and he was flying them around California. She explained that they were going to go on their first date that Friday and how her ex-husband's inebriation and belligerence derailed their original plans. She pointed out that when she expected a romantic dinner for two, she got a night at the fun park with her kids and her new friend, Anthony.

"I'm so confused about my feelings for Anthony," Kay finally admitted. "I thought we were starting a romantic relationship, but it's more like I'm on a road trip with a friend."

"Damn, that's got to be frustrating." Jana lowered her voice to a whisper, so the girls couldn't hear from across the room. "Like seriously, no bow-chicka-wow-wow at all?"

"No, not really," Kay whispered back, realizing that while they'd already been speaking softly, she wanted to make sure there was no chance at all for her daughters to hear her talking about anything sexual. "We talked about it while he was in California, but then after Anthony saw the baggage I have with my ex, he hasn't pushed to go there. We made out a little that night after the fun park, but it was only kissing on my couch and we both fell asleep there still fully clothed. Then when we went to see his family last Thursday, we were interrupted by his sister and cousins arriving when we were making out on his parents' front porch. But since then, even when we're alone in the morning and could do more, he's only given me a peck of a kiss, nothing like those or the night we met. It feels like he's changed his mind and just wants to be my friend now."

"Then what was all that about picking your wedding date the other night?" Emily softly inquired.

"The night we met, he said he wanted to marry me." Kay rolled her eyes. "I thought it was a joke, but he finally said that we didn't have to fly off to Vegas and get married immediately since I wasn't comfortable introducing him to my girls yet. He said he'd wait six months or a year to plan our wedding when I was finally comfortable with him meeting the girls. Then when he met the girls a week later and we went to his parents' house less than a week after that, his mom started in about how we should start planning our wedding now. He's brought it up daily since then, but surely it's just him continuing the joke, right?"

"I didn't get the impression that it was a joke," Jana disagreed, shaking her head.

"Me either," Emily agreed with Jana. They both reached out to take one of Kay's hands, making her feel like she could depend on these women and should pay attention to their opinions and advice.

"How long have you actually had alone in the mornings with Anthony?" Jana squeezed Kay's hand.

"Usually only five or ten minutes," Kay responded. "Then the girls are up and running into the room."

"You've been in adjoining rooms all this time, right?" Emily asked but didn't give Kay a chance to answer. "So, you slept in the room with the girls and when you got up to go to Anthony's room, you left the adjoining door open, right?"

"Yeah," Kay answered sheepishly, feeling her cheeks heating up.

"Then you need to switch to a suite like the rest of us, so you can put the girls in their own room and actually get some alone time with

Anthony overnight," Emily declared with a conspiratory glint in her eyes.

"We're in a suite tonight," Kay sheepishly admitted, wondering if her new friends might be able to help her plan to get Anthony's bags moved into her room after the girls went to sleep. There was no way she wanted him to sleep on that couch when her room had a king-sized bed that he would fit in better. Even if him wanting to only be friends meant she slept on the sofa. "But when he was putting our bags in the room, he put his beside the sofa in the living area and mine in the master bedroom. Like he's planning to sleep on the sofa instead of with me because he just wants to be friends."

"Or he thinks you need more time to be ready to sleep with him." Jana gave Kay a knowing smile.

"I bet that's it," Emily whisper-shouted excitedly, a little louder than they'd been speaking. She turned to look at their daughters and when they didn't seem to acknowledge their mothers' conversation, she turned back to Kay and lowered her voice again. "Between you already being forced to introduce him to the girls before you were ready and being overwhelmed with the shitstorm that is your ex and having to go back to court, I bet he thinks you need more time to be ready for s-e-x."

"You think?" Kay tilted her head quizzically.

"Definitely," Jana agreed. "He's always been quiet, only speaking to most of us in passing or a greeting when we board or exit the plane, but I've always gotten a vibe from him that he'd be one of those guys who would sacrifice his own wants to meet the needs of someone he loves. I bet he's holding back on the passion because he thinks you need a solid friend to lean on more."

Huh? Kay thought. *Could he really think I need him to be a friend more than a lover? If so, how do I convince him that what I really need is a passionate lover and multiple orgasms?*

Emily spit out the drink she'd just taken from her water bottle and pointed at Kay. She opened her mouth as if to speak, but just closed it a second later because she was speechless.

"Did I say that out loud?" Kay was confident that the blush in her cheeks had spread across her whole body.

"Yep," Jana choked out through her raucous laughter. "I recommend putting on your sexiest nighty and going to get a drink of water after the girls are asleep."

"I don't have a sexy nighty." Kay wished she'd thought to go lingerie shopping to prepare for her first date with Anthony. "It was a spur-of-the-moment trip, and I didn't even think about packing anything like that."

"No problem." Emily waved away Kay's worries. "We're in New Orleans and the girls are currently being supervised by their tutors, so we have a couple hours to do a little shopping." She hopped out of her chair and walked over to Stacy who had just stepped away from the table where she'd been working with a group of younger kids. Kay couldn't hear what Emily said to Stacy, but she thought Stacy's nod meant they were fine leaving all of their kids with the tutors for a little while.

"Let's go," Emily directed them as she got back over to where Kay and Jana were sitting. "We just need to be back by six when they'll break for dinner."

It was only a little after three o'clock in the afternoon, so that left them plenty of time for a quick shopping trip. Kay was excited to spend some time with her new friends and enjoyed the afternoon getting to know them both better.

She was shy at first when they got to the first store and were browsing through racks of nighties so sheer, they were see-through. Her new friends wouldn't let her feel embarrassed like she normally would, though, and settled her nerves by picking out a few things for themselves, as well as insisting on them all going into the large dressing room to try on their selections. It was hard to be embarrassed when they were comparing C-section scars and helping her pick items that accentuated her best features while disguising the fact that her belly wasn't as flat and toned as Kay thought it should be.

While they were at the mall, Kay enlisted her new friends' assistance in picking out a couple more professional dress outfits to supplement the few she'd brought with her. She spent a little more from her savings than she really wanted to spend but decided that it would be okay since it wasn't more than the difference between what she would have earned in a week in her old job and how much she'd already earned in the first week with the GWA. She would just have to remember to transfer the money back into savings from her first paycheck.

Even if she no longer had to have the savings to buy iPads for the girls after Anthony had surprised them with the new tablets at his parents' breakfast table on Friday morning, she still wanted to save as much as possible. Until she got through the looming court date, she had to save as much as she could in case she had to give up her new job and move back to Tulsa without a job there anymore. She wanted to be as optimistic as Anthony about how that day would go, but she couldn't quite achieve it.

When they stopped for a quick detour to the hotel to drop off their purchases, they were cutting it close to the kids' six o'clock dinner break. It couldn't be helped though, because there was no way Kay wanted to have to explain where the bags of lingerie came from, or give Anthony or her daughters an opportunity to peek at what was in the bags.

By the time they got back to the arena, a half-hour past the kids' dinner break, she knew all about how her new friends met their husbands, the birth stories for not just the two girls her daughter was friends with, but also the crazy ones when Jana and Emily each had their younger sons, and both family's best tips for traveling all the time with kids. She'd shared her own stories with them, as well as asked their advice on how to move forward with Anthony.

Although she still wasn't quite sure she could agree to marry him before finding out what the judge would say about her new job and traveling all the time being a valid reason for terminating Mark's visitation with the girls, she agreed with her new friends that she didn't need to be married to enjoy a physical relationship with Anthony.

Even if the judge ordered her to move back to Tulsa, she could still enjoy a fling with him for the next three-and-a-half weeks. And thanks to her new friends, she had a plan to seduce him into it. And more than one naughty nightie to pick from to start on that when they got back to the hotel later.

~~~
~~~

Anthony left the group sparring in the ring just before five o'clock to go check in with Rick to make sure the pilot for the other flight team had arrived. Once he verified that both he and Kay were cleared to leave for their time off, he went to the area designated as the classroom with a plan to take them all on an evening walk through the French Quarter and maybe go on a ghost tour. He loved being able to take what Maria was calling "mini field trips" with them in the different cities they visited to a variety of historical and cultural sites.

When he got to the classroom area, he was surprised to find that while Tia and Maria were there with their tutors and new friends, Kay was nowhere to be seen. *Maybe she went to the bathroom,* he thought as he took a seat at a table at the edge of the area. The girls were actively engaged in working on their tablets, so he figured he would just sit there and wait for Kay to come back from wherever she'd gotten off to. He pulled out his phone and spent some time surfing the net and texting with family while he waited.

"Mom's not back yet?" Tia looked around as she walked up to him and put her backpack on the table beside him.

Anthony checked the time and realized he'd been sitting there for about an hour. The fact that Kay hadn't come back in that time worried him. *Where did she go?*

"No, Princess," Anthony replied as Maria walked over with her two friends. "Do you know where she went, so we can go find her?"

"Miss Kay went with our moms to run some errands," one of Maria's friends told them.

One of the tutors walked over with two little boys. Anthony wasn't sure of their ages, but they were at least two or three years younger than Maria and her friends.

"Hi, I'm Stacy," the tutor introduced herself. "Are you taking all of the kids to catering for dinner? Or would you like me to help you with them?"

"Uh, I don't know," Anthony sputtered in confusion. "I'm not sure."

"He's here for Maria and me," Tia explained, and Anthony was grateful for her help.

"Right, but since Kay left with Jana and Emily, I thought he might be escorting Sarah and Shawn to their dad, Jeff, and Katie and Jason to their dad, Matt, too." Stacy smiled at Tia. "I'm assuming the ladies just got stuck in traffic on their shopping trip and will meet us all in catering since they know we break for dinner at six. No biggie, we can all walk over there together."

"Yeah, I know Matt and Jeff, so I can help you find them." Anthony stood to walk with the crowd of kids. *And maybe they can tell me where our wives went.*

When they got to catering, it only took a minute for the four extra children to find their dads. Once they all had full plates, the kids all ended up sitting at one table with their dads, the tutors, and Anthony at the one beside them. Since neither Kay or either of the wrestlers' wives had arrived yet, Anthony decided to ask Matt and Jeff if either of them knew where the ladies had gone.

"What errands did the ladies go on?" Anthony inquired before starting to eat.

"They just said shopping," Stacy replied, leaning in a little too close to Anthony. "It's no big deal, we had plenty for the kids to do to stay occupied, so they could go get whatever supplies they needed."

"I think he's more concerned because it's the first time Kay's left in the middle of the day, and they're late coming back," advised the male tutor that Anthony thought he remembered was named Dan.

Hearing they were late alarmed Anthony even more, so he pulled out his phone and tried to call Kay. After not getting an answer, he sent her a text hoping she'd at least reply to it.

Anthony: Hey, Baby, where are you? We're waiting in catering. I thought the girls might like to do a ghost tour this evening since we're clear to leave early.

He laid his phone on the table while he continued eating. He heard a phone buzz, but it wasn't his. Jeff pulled his phone out of his pocket and gave the screen a longing look. He appeared to be scrolling through photos and moved his fingers as if to zoom in on one.

"They had to stop at the hotel to drop off their bags, so the kids didn't see them." Jeff turned his phone toward Anthony. The photo on the phone was a close-up view of a gift bag with a *Trashy Diva* logo. "I think we're all going to have a good night tonight," Jeff smirked as he turned his phone back to flip through his photos again.

Trashy Diva? Is that an adult toy store or a lingerie shop? Holy Fuck! They went lingerie shopping! Damn, I hope Kay actually bought something, too!

Looking over at Tia and Maria sitting with their friends eating dinner made Anthony doubt that Kay would have actually bought anything to wear for him yet. There was no way he would be seeing Kay in something sexy and skimpy when her daughters would be sleeping in the same suite.

He resigned himself to slowing down his pursuit of Kay. He could continue taking care of his needs in the shower each morning, so he could be the helpful friend she could lean on without feeling pressured for sex. He would continue making sure she knew he still wanted to get married but would follow her lead on the physical aspect of their relationship. She had enough on her plate and didn't need him piling on more.

Just as they were finishing eating and Anthony had gotten up to help the girls clean up their table, Kay walked in with her two friends.

"Sorry, we're late," the blonde who walked over to hug Jeff apologized. *Jana.*

"It's okay." Stacy greeted the ladies with a smile before turning to place a hand on Anthony's arm. "Anthony helped me get the kids all down here to catering to find their dads."

While Anthony wasn't comfortable with Stacy touching him without permission, the brief flare of jealousy that he saw in Kay's eyes was worth the few seconds of discomfort before he pulled away to pick up the trash on the kids' table.

Kay didn't say anything, just turned and walked over to fix herself a plate. When she returned to the table to sit by the girls and eat, she finally spoke. "Sorry, girls, I didn't think we'd be gone that long."

Anthony wasn't sure if Kay was only apologizing to the girls and not him because she was trying to pull back from him, or if she was just acting out in a fit of jealousy because of Stacy still being there trying to flirt with him. He hoped it was the latter. Not that he wanted her to be jealous, or that there was anything going on that warranted her jealousy, but if she was jealous that meant she had romantic feelings for him more than just the need for a friend. And he definitely wanted her to have romantic feelings for him.

He hoped he could reassure her that they were both still feeling their soul-deep connection by making sure she knew he was still only focused on her.

"Baby, where's your phone?" Anthony reached over to run a hand down her arm. "I tried to call and text, but you didn't respond to either, so I was starting to get worried."

"It's here in my purse." Kay dug through her bag for her phone. When she pulled it out, she looked up at Anthony. The expression on her face made her appear quite chastened, so Anthony smiled at her to let her know he wasn't mad, just wanted to know she was okay. "Sorry, I guess I forgot to turn it back on when we got off the plane this morning."

"You seriously have issues with your phone," Anthony chuckled. He then bent over, stroked a hand over her hair, and kissed the top of her head. "I'm just glad you're back safe and sound."

After a little more small talk with Jeff, Jana, Matt, Emily, and all of their kids while the ladies ate dinner, Anthony finally got Kay, Tia, and Maria out of the arena to do a walk through the French Quarter even though he couldn't convince them to do a ghost tour.

When they finally got back to the suite at the hotel, Tia and Maria said an early goodnight and retired to their room. They had their own bathroom and a television in their bedroom on the wall between the two twin beds, so even if they didn't go to sleep immediately, they would be comfortably ensconced in the room for the night. Kay said she was going to go and enjoy the jacuzzi tub in her bathroom and disappeared into the master bedroom, leaving Anthony in the living room alone.

He grabbed a pair of sweats and a t-shirt and walked into the guest bathroom off the living area to change for bed, wondering how he got stuck with the smallest bathroom with only a shower stall that he was too big to fit in.

After changing clothes and brushing his teeth, he grabbed a bottle of water from the mini-fridge and flopped on the sofa. He didn't bother pulling out the bed, assuming it wouldn't be any more comfortable to sleep on than leaving the couch as it was. He turned on the television and flipped channels for a bit, finally settling on a music station to listen to while he surfed the internet on his laptop.

~~~

When they first arrived back at the hotel, Kay picked up their clean laundry from the front desk and took it to her bedroom to sort through and put away. Her hands were shaking as she sorted through their things and hid her new purchases in with the clean clothes she was putting in her suitcase. She decided that she'd just have to figure out a way to handwash her new lingerie and dry it with her hair dryer, so the girls wouldn't catch a glimpse of it.

She left Anthony's dry-cleaned garments hanging in her closet but carried his stack of folded clothing out to put it on the coffee table for him when she delivered her daughters' clothing to their room. The girls had already changed into their pajamas and were laying in the twin beds in their room watching television when she left them to go to sleep.

Anthony was putting his things in his suitcase when Kay walked back through the living room. She excused herself to go take a bath as Anthony pulled out his sweats and t-shirt to change for bed.

As Kay filled the jacuzzi tub with water, she hoped the jets would relax her enough to lessen the anxiety she was feeling about her plans for the night. She mentally walked through her list of tasks as she slipped into the tub and checked them off as she did them.

Enjoy the jets massaging the tension from my tight shoulders. Check.

As she laid there soaking away the tension, she tried to analyze how she felt about the events of the afternoon and evening. She felt so guilty for making Anthony worry about her by not telling him she was leaving the arena. It wasn't that she'd actually done anything wrong by going with her friends that she felt guilty for. If she felt anything for her actions that afternoon, she should be excited about the surprises she bought to wear for him while they were shopping.

But she felt remorseful because he'd worried about her, and she hated being the cause of his unease. It wasn't because she'd been unsafe in leaving the arena, because she felt perfectly safe having left with two other women instead of going alone.

It was more a case of her feeling shameful for not thinking about his feelings, or how he would react to her leaving without telling him
~~~

in advance. As much as she wanted her insensitivity to his feelings to be because their relationship was so new and she wasn't used to needing to check in with anyone prior to meeting him, she knew that wasn't the real reason.

She'd checked in with her parents when living with them, even after her divorce, so not being accustomed to checking in with someone wouldn't just be a poor excuse, but an out-and-out lie, even if she only tried to use it to convince herself.

She'd also checked in with Mark most of the time they were married, so she couldn't say she had experience with not needing to keep a significant other apprised of her whereabouts either. She mentally added *"Apologize to Anthony before trying to seduce him"* to her mental checklist when she realized that she didn't tell him she was leaving because she didn't want to have to explain where she was going. It was just like the last couple of years she was married to Mark, when she quit checking in with him because she didn't want to give him a reason to lash out at her. She kicked herself for punishing Anthony for her wrongly assumed prediction of how he would respond the same way her idiot ex would have.

Kay knew Anthony better than to ever really believe he would act like Mark. If she'd told him she was leaving and whispered where she was going in his ear, maybe she wouldn't be so anxious while soaking in the tub. If she'd been open and honest with him, maybe he would have already moved his bags into her room and joined her in the bath.

When she looked down at her body as the jets stopped stirring up the water, she decided that it was probably best that she was alone for her grooming before he joined her for more. She went back to her mental checklist to prepare for the rest of the night.

Shave everywhere I don't want Anthony to see hairy. Check.

Scrub every inch of my body, especially focusing on exfoliating the important parts. Check.

Shampoo and condition my hair. Check.

Once she got out of the tub, she continued her mental checklist as she slathered on her lotion, brushed and blow dried her hair, and put on the barest minimum of makeup, so she felt her most attractive.

Put on the royal blue nightie and thong because it's Anthony's favorite color. Check.

Leah Mae Wright

Cover it with the fluffy white hotel robe, so I can make sure the girls are asleep before trying to seduce Anthony into my bed. Check.

Sit on the end of the bed for what seems like forever trying to work up the courage to actually go out there and try to seduce Anthony into my bed. Check.

Get sidetracked by imagining what I want him to do to me like I'm writing one of the love scenes from the romance novels I love to read. Check.

UGH! Quit thinking about how you want him to kiss and touch you. Just get up and go out there! She told herself. She flopped back onto the bed with a groan.

She was not a sexually aggressive person. She didn't know how to push past her fear of rejection to actually go through with her plan to seduce Anthony. She feared she would never be brave enough, confident enough, or feel worthy enough to actually go ask Anthony for the passion she wanted.

Even if she couldn't work up the courage to attempt seducing Anthony, she still had to go check on her daughters before going to bed. Maybe if she spent a few minutes talking to Anthony while covered in the fluffy robe that literally covered her from her neck to her toes, where it dragged the floor since it was obviously for a taller woman, she might be able to work up enough daring to open the robe. Maybe a peek at her skimpy lingerie would entice Anthony to be more sexually aggressive when Kay couldn't be.

~~~

Anthony was typing up lyrics to a song about Kay when she came out of her room wrapped in a white fluffy robe. He wished he would have been home with his guitar where he could actually play the tune he was hearing in his head, but he'd settled for typing the song his heart was writing for his Kay. Maybe one day he would be able to play it for her without scaring her off with his overpowering feelings for her.

Anthony tried to adjust his position and use his laptop to conceal his reaction to seeing Kay and imagining her wearing nothing under the robe. Kay opened the door to the girls' room, but she only poked
~~~

her head in for a moment before stepping back and pulling it shut with a soft click.

"They actually sleeping or still watching TV?" Anthony smiled up at Kay as she walked over toward him.

"The TV is still on but they're both out cold," Kay replied as she stopped walking and stood a couple of feet away from Anthony, between the other end of the sofa and the coffee table he had his feet propped up on. "Between the self-defense and the sightseeing, I think you finally drained their never-ending batteries."

"Naw, Baby." Anthony grinned at Kay and patted the sofa to invite her to sit with him. "Any energy we drained from them today will be recharged by morning."

Kay returned his smile, but she didn't sit down. She looked a little nervous and Anthony was concerned about what she was about to say. *Please don't break up with me,* he thought to himself. *I'll get us back in adjoining rooms on our next working day, so you won't feel like I'm pressuring you into more than you're ready for, just please don't say you don't want me even that close to you.*

"Baby, what's wrong?" Anthony moved his laptop to the coffee table, since his fear of losing Kay had killed his boner so he didn't have to keep trying to hide it. "Sit down here and talk to me, please."

"Nothing's wrong." Kay shifted her weight from side to side but still made no move to sit down or even get close enough that Anthony could reach out and touch her. She bit her bottom lip and wrapped her arms around her midsection like she was trying to protect herself, but Anthony had no idea from what. "I'm sorry I didn't tell you I was leaving the arena today."

"It's okay, Baby." Anthony spoke softly, hoping to soothe her. "You know I'm not mad about that, right?"

Kay nodded her head and a single tear slipped down her cheek. Anthony wanted to pull her onto his lap and kiss away her tears, but he didn't know if she would accept the comfort from him.

"Is there a reason you didn't want to tell me you were leaving?"

"I honestly didn't think about it at the time." Kay wiped the tear off her face. "We're so new that I didn't think about needing to tell you I was leaving when it happened." Kay motioned between the two of them. "And I went with two other people, so I felt safe to go with people who knew their way around to get us back on time. I honestly didn't think you'd even know I'd left, much less have time to start to worry about me being gone."

She paused and took a deep breath. Anthony's eyes were naturally drawn to the movement in her chest as she inhaled and exhaled. The robe was securely wrapped around her and kept the swell of her breasts completely covered, but Anthony's cock responded to the movement regardless. He hoped she wouldn't notice as he stayed quiet to allow her to gather her thoughts, so she could finish explaining what was still bothering her.

"But while I was soaking in the bath, I realized that I was sneaking out like I would have back when I was married to Mark, and I feel so guilty for that." Kay sniffled, and more tears started to fall.

Anthony opened his arms, imploring Kay to step into them, so he could comfort her with a hug. "Come here, Baby," he softly commanded. She flew into his arms, and he had to adjust her position to cradle her on his lap as she cried into his chest. He held her close and stroked one hand up and down her back and the other hand over her hair. "You have nothing to feel guilty about, Baby."

Anthony couldn't quite understand everything Kay was sobbing into his chest, but he got the gist of it as her feeling bad because she didn't tell him she was leaving because she didn't want him to tell her she couldn't go shopping with her friends like her ex-husband would have.

I hate that controlling bastard!

"Baby, you know I only wanted to know you were safe, right?" Anthony whispered softly into her ear. "I wouldn't ever try to stop you from going shopping with your friends. I might have tried to give you my card to pay for anything you wanted, but I wouldn't try to stop you from going."

Kay pushed up from his chest to look into his eyes. "I know," she whined. "That's why I feel guilty, because I treated you like I had to deal with him, and you don't deserve that."

"Baby, it's okay." Anthony brought both hands up to cup her face. "Like you said, we're still new. I don't think you consciously tried to sneak away from me. You're just not used to having someone worry about you as much as I do, but we'll get there."

"You're really not mad at me?" Kay moved her hands up to either side of his face, holding him the same way he was holding her.

"No, Baby," he replied as he swiped his thumbs under her eyes to clear the streaks of her tears from her face. "I love you way too much to ever be mad over a little misunderstanding."

Kay looked deeply into Anthony's eyes as if she were trying to see into his soul to determine if she could believe him. "Do you really?" Kay whispered softly. "I'm so confused and don't know how I really feel or what to believe."

"Yes, Baby," Anthony replied. "I really love you. You can believe in that."

"This is the first time you've actually said it and you've only really kissed me a couple of times. All that time in between, when you're more like a platonic friend, makes me doubt that you really mean it when you say it."

"I'm sorry, Baby." Anthony tucked her hair behind her ear. "I have definitely not been thinking like a platonic friend. I certainly don't mean to act like one, but I don't want to embarrass you or the girls by kissing you like I want all the time in public." He took her hands in his, holding them between them.

"Yeah, I was mortified when your cousins walked up on us the other day," Kay grimaced.

"How about we have our own secret way of saying I love you that won't draw attention to us in public, so you can be reassured when you think I'm being too platonic?" Anthony squeezed her hands in his.

"Like how you're squeezing my hands now?" Kay's expression lightened, the sparkle coming back into her eyes that he'd missed all evening.

"Exactly," he replied with a smile. "We hold hands a lot, so nobody will notice it's any different. And anytime one of us squeezes, we'll know we're saying I love you."

Kay quickly squeezed his hands three times. "One for each word." She smiled as she looked up at him. She might not be ready to actually say the words to him, but he was grateful that she was willing to tell him in her own way. He returned the three soft squeezes.

"It's been so fast, though," Kay cautioned imploringly. "How do you know we can trust these feelings to last?"

He brought their foreheads together, praying she could see in his eyes what he didn't have the words to explain. "I don't know how..." His words trailed off as their breath mingled. "...I just know."

Leah Mae Wright

They sat there silently connecting through their eyes for a few moments, basking in the emotional bonds they were building.

"It's like, when I first saw you," Anthony started, hoping to explain without sounding like a woo-woo nut job. "I didn't just see you with my eyes. My heart and my soul saw you too, and they recognized their other halves. I don't just love you because you're beautiful. I also love how strong you are to have gone through hell with your ex and are not only still standing, but you're coming out swinging in the fight against him. I love how you aren't afraid to show your softer side as you compassionately care for not just your kids, but every child you meet. You're a great mom, and seeing you with the girls makes me want to be your partner in parenting them, and maybe a couple more if you're willing to adopt. I feel like you're what's been missing in my life, and I don't want to live without you anymore. I trust that my love for you is never-ending because I love you more each day and can't fathom there will ever come a day that I don't love you more than the day before. I know you're scared, Baby. But love is nothing to fear. Lean on me and let my bottomless well of love and trust be enough for both of us."

"How am I supposed to say no to all that?" Kay giggled.

"Does that mean you'll finally agree to marry me?" Anthony gave her a peck of a kiss on the lips before she had the chance to answer.

"Oh, Anthony," Kay sighed. "I do believe I'm falling in love with you, and I really want to say yes, but I can't yet."

"Because you're worried about going to court?" Kay nodded and with their foreheads touching it made him nod his head with her. "Baby, you know the judge can't order us to not get married. He may insist we live in Oklahoma if he doesn't want to terminate visitation, but he wouldn't have a legal leg to stand on if he tried to order you to quit your job to stick to the current visitation schedule. The worst-case scenario would be adjusting the visitation schedule to match our work schedule, but I don't think that's even a possibility with all the evidence your dad has against Mark. The judge definitely won't order you to take the girls to visit him in jail and based on what your dad was saying he's charging him with, he will definitely be going to jail soon."

"We don't know that for sure, though," Kay groaned, shaking her head. "Dad can only do so much with gathering evidence and presenting it to the D.A. to file charges. The D.A. can still say he doesn't want to pursue it as hard as Dad wants him to and drop the case against him altogether."

"Regardless of what the D.A. decides, that's all out of our hands. So, we shouldn't worry about any of that when we're talking about our future. I'm going to love you no matter what happens with the courts and your ex. The only part of our future that will be impacted by that is whether we live in Tulsa or Heart's Destiny most of the time."

Kay huffed out a breath. "Fine, maybe you're right. But I'm still not going to say yes to marrying you until after we go to court next month."

Anthony grinned, already planning to try to change her mind. "We'll see about that. I'm gonna keep tryin' to wear you down by proposing every day until then."

"You haven't properly proposed to me yet," Kay complained, her lips turning down in an adorable little pout. "And what happened to asking my dad for my hand like you told him you'd do when you met him?"

"Yeah, Baby, I talked to him on the phone Thursday night when my Uncle Doug had you call him, so he could hear the case against Mark." Anthony smiled. "He not only gave me his blessing, but he also told me to give him as much notice as possible for the wedding date, so he can bring your whole family to Heart's Destiny for the ceremony."

"Seriously?" Kay had an expression of shock on her face. "We've barely known each other for two weeks and my dad even agrees we should get married?"

"Yeah, Baby," Anthony replied. "And if I have my way, we'll be married before we've known each other two months. So even if you won't say yes yet, tell my mom what you want for a wedding the weekend after Thanksgiving."

"You are so not right in the head," Kay giggled. "There's no way we can plan a wedding by Thanksgiving. Besides, my momma taught me to always take a test drive, so I don't get stuck with a lemon, and I haven't taken you for a test drive yet to make sure you're not a lemon."

"Test drive away, Baby," Anthony replied, wiggling his hips, so she could feel his erection. "I'll gladly prove I'm not a lemon." He hoped her declaration of needing a test drive meant Kay was ready to move their conversation to the bedroom. He was tempted to push her in that direction by kissing her right then, but he still wanted to let her feel in control of how fast and how far they went, so he sat there waiting for her to kiss him.

When she didn't move or say anything for a few minutes, he felt his self-control slipping and thought he should warn Kay. "Baby," he growled in a low, gravelly tone. "It's taking every ounce of self-control I possess not to pick you up and carry you into that bedroom to give you the ride of your life. I'm trying to be the man you need and let you set the pace, but if you don't kiss me soon and tell me you're ready to really be with me, it might be safer for both of us for you to get off my lap, go to your room, and lock your bedroom door between us."

Anthony stifled a groan as Kay got off his lap. As much as he wanted her, he didn't want to coerce Kay into anything she wasn't ready to do. Instead of running to the bedroom like Anthony expected, though, Kay slowly took only a few steps back from Anthony and put her hands on the tie of her robe.

"I *am* ready," Kay whispered shyly, slowly starting to untie the knot in the belt of the robe as she continued her slow walk backwards. "I'm so ready that I snuck out of the arena today to go shopping for something special to wear for you tonight."

Fuck Yes!

Kay took another step backwards as one end of the belt came out of the knot. "Why don't you come to the bedroom with me, so I can show it to you and that locked door will keep the girls from walking in on us?"

She didn't have to ask him twice. Anthony jumped up from the sofa and stalked toward Kay. He caught up to her in three of his long strides. Instead of letting her continue the slow walk, he scooped her up into his arms and carried her bridal style over the threshold of the bedroom. He sat her down at the foot of the bed and turned to shut and lock the bedroom door. When he turned back to Kay, her hands were back on the knot in the belt that she was struggling to undo.

"Baby, stop," he ordered, his voice deeper than normal from arousal. "I want to unwrap the present you're giving me tonight."

He dropped to his knees in front of her, making them approximately the same height. Kay lowered her hands to her sides as Anthony's replaced hers working on the tie of the robe. It only took him a moment to untie the knot, slip the belt off the robe, and let it drop to the floor. The robe fell open a few inches, revealing a swath of royal blue silk. He gently stroked his hands up the lapels to push the fluffy white robe off of Kay's shoulders. When the robe fell to a puddle on the floor around Kay's feet, Anthony feared he would explode in his pants like an overexcited teenager from just the sight of Kay in the short sexy nightie.

She'd obviously chosen it because it was both of their favorite color. There were thin straps over her shoulders that led down to a bra-like bodice that barely contained her sumptuous breasts. Her nipples were hard and trying to poke through the thin material. Just under her breasts, there was a band of ribbon where the lower portion of the gown was gathered and flared out to just over her hips. Kay's legs weren't long, but every inch of them was on display for him. He noticed an old scar on her left knee and had an extreme urge to trail his tongue across it.

Not this time, he thought. *But one day I'm going to tie her to the bed, so I can leisurely examine every inch of her and kiss away any residual pain from every scar on her sexy little body.*

"You're sure, Baby?" Anthony itched to reach out and touch her. "If you're not sure, please tell me now because once I touch you, I can't guarantee I'll be able to stop."

"I'm sure." Kay's voice was breathy as she reached out to brush his hair back out of his eyes. "I want you to show me how real our love is, Anthony."

He pulled her into his arms then and kissed her passionately. Her palms ran over his chest as she eased her arms up and around his neck. One of his hands slid down from the small of her back to cup her ass while he threaded his other through her long, lustrous hair. Gently tugging on the soft strands, he guided her to tilt her head, so he could deepen the kiss. Anthony reveled in the feeling of her running her fingers through the short hair at the base of his skull as their tongues slid against each other.

It was the best kiss of his life and he hated that it had to end, so he could get them off the floor and up into the bed. He tried to pull back from the kiss, but he couldn't keep his lips off her for more than a millisecond before he was right back to kissing her. He finally started to trail his lips down her throat, licking and sucking his way down to her collarbone before moving back up to just under her ear.

"Baby, you taste amazing," he whispered in a low, gravelly tone. "I want to taste every inch of your delectable body."

"Yes, Anthony," Kay moaned, the soft sound resonating against his lips on her throat.

As he moved his kisses down and across her shoulder, he slowly slipped the thin strap of the gown down onto her arm with his tongue. He moved to repeat the action on the other side before pulling Kay's arms down, so the nightie could slip down enough to reveal her breasts.

Fuck, her tits are perfect.

He trailed his tongue across the top of her cleavage as he slipped the straps down and off her arms, the gown sliding to a sapphire puddle on the floor at her feet.

She was standing in front of him in only a little matching blue thong and Anthony sat back on his heels for a moment to gaze at her. He let his eyes travel over every curve and crevice he could see, wanting to memorize all he could about their first time together. Her belly was soft, mostly flat with just a little rounding below the evidence of her having given birth to at least one of the girls via a C-section.

I really need to spend some time worshiping her there.

He reached out to cup her breasts, stroking over her nipples with his thumbs. Her tan tips seemed to harden even more than they already were at his touch. He leaned in and replaced one thumb with his tongue, lavishing her taut nipple with open-mouthed kisses.

Fuck, she tastes sweet, like honey.

He moved to give her other breast equal treatment as Kay's hands went to the back of his head as if she wanted to hold him there to keep suckling forever. He loved the feel of her nails against his scalp and followed her direction to keep going back and forth between her perfect peaks.

He ran his hands up and down her body, needing to touch her everywhere at once. When his palms ran across the sides of her thong, he slipped a finger under the satiny fabric over each of her hip bones and slowly slid them down her legs. Once she stepped out of them, he pushed back up onto his knees, gripped her hips to pick her up, and sat her on the end of the bed.

He ran his hands down her legs from her hips, over her thighs, down the backs of her calves, to her tiny little feet. He continued to softly stroke his hands up and down her legs as he looked up into her lust-filled gaze.

"Baby, I have to know if you taste like honey everywhere." Anthony ran his hands up the insides of her lower legs. When he reached her knees, he gently pushed her legs open and leaned in to kiss his way up her inner thigh. "You're so sweet, Baby." He moved back down to kiss his way up the other thigh.

"You don't have to do this," Kay protested, her hands in his hair as she tried to pull his head away from the place he most wanted to be. "I know guys don't like it."

Anthony smiled up at her before licking his lips. "I'm not just going to like it. I'm going to love tasting you." Anthony hoped his words reassured her.

She still sat there stiffly, which made Anthony fear that she'd previously had a bad experience with oral sex. Not wanting to bring up bad memories, but needing to know how best to move on with their night, he asked, "Baby, is there a reason you don't want me to eat your pussy? A bad experience? Or you just don't like it?"

"Na, No," Kay stammered. "Nobody's ever wanted to before."

"Nobody's ever tasted this pretty pink pussy?" Anthony ran a finger over her freshly shaved folds. Her smooth cunt glistening with her arousal was the most perfect thing he'd ever seen. He ached to taste it, teasing her clit with little licks and sucks alternated with longer licks of her folds and actually fucking her with his tongue.

"I'll stop if you tell me you don't like it, but we can't know if you like it or not until you let me eat your pussy." Anthony looked into her eyes and saw her trepidation. "I'm betting you'll like it so much that you'll come in my mouth at least three times before you finally beg me to stop and fuck you." He wagged his eyebrows at her suggestively.

"Anthony," Kay groaned in a pleading tone. "You know I don't normally, um, you know, once."

"Baby..." Anthony cut her off. "What you've done in the past is irrelevant. If it wasn't good for you before, it's because you weren't with the right guy. Trust me to make this good for you, better than you've ever experienced before, because I'm the right man for you."

Kay nodded at him, but he wanted her verbal assent and not just a nod of agreement. He teased his fingers through her damp lower lips, spreading the moisture up and over her clit. He kept his touch light, not yet giving her the pressure he knew she needed.

"Tell me what you want me to do, Baby." He leaned closer to the junction of her thighs, so his breath could tease across her sensitive nub as he maintained eye contact. "I need to hear your words, Baby."

"I want you to, uh, li, lick me," Kay stuttered out, her fingers loosely running through his hair.

Anthony leaned down and licked the line where her right thigh met her groin. He leaned back far enough her hands fell from his head and removed his hand from her perfect pussy. Kay put her hands down on the bed beside her and her lips turned down into an adorable pout.

"What's the matter, Baby?" Anthony arched an eyebrow at her. "I did exactly what you said you wanted."

"You know that's not what I meant," Kay sulked, her hands fisting the comforter.

"Then tell me exactly what you mean." Anthony's lips lifted in the barest hint of a smile. "I want to hear all your dirty words, Baby."

He loved watching her blush spread from her cheeks down to those delectable double D's as she sat there silently contemplating what to say. He could tell she was struggling, her innocence holding back her inner bad girl from saying the naughty things she was thinking. *Come on, Baby, let me see that inner bad girl.*

"Tell me to eat your pussy," he ordered, his voice sounding deep and commanding even to his own ears. "Tell me to suck your clit. Beg me to fuck you with my tongue."

"Eat my pussy," Kay whispered, her voice so soft he could barely hear her.

"What was that?" Anthony cupped his hand to his ear to taunt her into speaking louder.

"Eat my pussy," Kay stated in a more normal tone of voice. "Suck my clit," she whisper-shouted a little louder. "Fu, fuck me with your tongue," she stuttered out breathlessly.

"Oh, Baby, I love hearing your pretty little mouth talk dirty." Anthony dove between her thighs and devoured the most delectable dessert he'd ever had. *She's even more delicious than I dreamed. A luscious mix of tangy and sweet.*

~ ~ ~

Oh, Fuck! Kay thought. If he really loved hearing her talk dirty, she figured she'd better start thinking more vulgar words, so she could make herself comfortable actually saying them to him. *He was so right in thinking I would like this! That I would like him eating my pussy.*

She fell backwards onto the bed, unable to maintain a seated position when Anthony moved her thighs up onto his shoulders. She couldn't tell exactly what he was doing because he didn't start slow with a long lick through her slit like he had on her thigh. No, he was kissing her cunt as passionately as he'd kissed her mouth a few minutes earlier.

He swirled his tongue around through her folds, then flicked her clit with the tip a few times before sticking his tongue farther into her than she ever dreamed he could reach. He pulled out and sucked on her clit like he had her nipples earlier before starting back with the swirly patterns through her folds.

It was pure heaven. Kay couldn't control her body's response to how wonderful he made her feel. She rocked her hips involuntarily, grinding her pussy on his face. It only took a few minutes before her whole body tensed and her climax exploded through her. As her inner walls squeezed his tongue tight, he rubbed her clit with his finger, applying just the right amount of pressure to extend her orgasm.

"Oh, yes, oh, Anthony," she panted over and over, not even caring how loud she was chanting his name.

He didn't stop. Didn't pull back to allow her to come down from the high. He stayed focused on her, continuing to engulf her in pleasure until her first orgasm rolled into a second. How it was even more intense than the first, she didn't know. It felt as if she was shattering from the inside out. She was so overcome with the intensity of her release that she couldn't stop breathing out his name repeatedly.

Again, he didn't pull back, didn't stop kissing and sucking on her sensitive flesh. He moved his hand from fingering her clit to insert a finger. He gently stroked it in and out as he refocused his oral onslaught on her clit.

His other hand moved up to fondle her breasts, going back and forth between them to lightly pinch and pluck her nipples. While she was focused on how tight and tingly he was making her breasts feel, he inserted a second finger, scissoring them apart to stretch her opening. *What is he doing down there? Surely, I don't need to be stretched that much for him to be able to fit.*

When he inserted a third finger, it seemed to target in on a secret spot inside her that no one else had ever found, bringing her to the brink of yet another climax in only seconds.

"Anthony, oh, God, Anthony," she breathlessly panted. "Please, Anthony."

"Please what, Baby?" he asked in the brief moment he lifted his mouth from her.

"Please make me come," Kay begged. "Please, please, make me come with your cock."

"I will, Baby," he replied between licks on her clit. "But first come one more time from this. Now. Come now on my tongue and fingers."

He slurped as he increased the suction on her clit and rubbed on that perfect spot inside her. Her whole body contracted as her third climax consumed her. It was the most intense orgasm Kay had ever experienced, her cum flooding from her and into Anthony's mouth.

As she floated on a cloud of ecstasy, Anthony softened the strokes of his fingers before gently pulling them out. He kissed her mound one last time before standing up and stripping off his own clothes.

Kay could barely open her eyes to watch as he did the one-handed t-shirt removal she'd only read about before. Seeing the expanse of his chest with the sprinkling of dark hair that led down to chiseled six-pack abs and the V-cut of his torso aiming at the tent in his pants revived her from her orgasm-induced lethargy. She pushed up onto her elbows and opened her eyes wide, so she could savor the view of his body as he finally revealed it to her.

"Fuck," Anthony groaned as his hands went to the waistband of his sweats. "Be right back, Baby. I gotta go get a condom from my bag."

"Don't go," Kay implored, reaching out to invite him into the bed. "I'm clean, and if you are too, then I don't want anything between us."

She already knew he was sterile, so it didn't matter that she wasn't on birth control.

"Yeah, I'm clean." A sexy grin spread across his face. "And I don't want anything between us either."

He pushed his sweats down quickly, his triple extra-large erection aimed directly at Kay. *Yep, I definitely needed to be stretched if he's going to try to put that monster in me! Guess I'll finally find out if my books are right about bigger being better.*

Kay scrambled up onto the bed, so she could lay her head on the pillow as Anthony crawled onto the bed over her.

"Where are you going, Baby?" Anthony hovered above her with his forearms supporting his weight on either side of her head.

"Just moving up, so there's room for you on the bed too," she replied, reaching up to wrap her arms around his neck and pull him down for a kiss.

Anthony took advantage of her being focused on the feel of his tongue engaging with hers to roll them both across the bed, so she ended up on top of him, her legs straddling his abdomen. She felt the wet tip of his cock lightly brushing against her buttocks, causing her core to flood with her own arousal.

Anthony's hands ran from her hips up to cup her breasts, where he stroked and lightly pinched her diamond-hard nipples. When the kiss ended, so they could both take a breath, Kay sat up and looked down into Anthony's chocolate brown eyes. Her whole body flushed when she realized that she was leaving a wet spot on his abs where she'd been grinding into him.

Anthony continued his exploration of her body, softly trailing his fingertips over her breasts, up to her neck and shoulders, then back down between her breasts. A single fingertip trailed across the scar on her lower abdomen from the births of her daughters.

Kay stiffened at his touch there, feeling self-conscious about the extra weight she couldn't lose directly under it.

"You are the most beautiful woman in the world," Anthony growled huskily.

"I'm already in bed with you, Anthony." Kay softly slapped at his shoulder. "You don't have to lie to me to keep me here."

"I'm not lying, Baby." Anthony grabbed Kay's hips, lifted her up so his cock could spring back towards his abs, and moved her back a few inches to straddle his erection. "You are the most beautiful woman in the world to me. Only you turn me on." His fingers dug into her buttocks as his thumbs pressed into the soft skin on the front of her hip bones. He used his tight grip on her hips to rub her wet slit up and down the underside of his cock. "Only you make me this hard."

"But I have scars and belly fat I can't lose," Kay protested. "That's not beautiful."

"It is to me," he replied, his thumbs stroking the ends of her C-section scar. "This scar," he choked out. "It's proof of how strong you are, of how big your heart is. Having babies wasn't easy on you, but you love so much that you not only suffered through a rough delivery and recovery once, but twice. Even knowing what pain was coming, you willingly went through it again because of how much you love the girls. The way you love them is the most beautiful thing about you. Now let me show you how much I love you."

"Yes, Anthony," Kay choked out over the lump in her throat from the overwhelming emotion Anthony's words filled her with.

Anthony gripped her hips and lifted her up, so his cock could stand up from its previous position of being pressed into his abdomen by her weight on him. "Touch me, Baby," Anthony ordered, his voice deep and dark. "Line me up, so I can take us both to heaven."

Kay reached down and softly stroked him, feeling playful and wanting to tease him a bit first. Anthony groaned and his cock twitched at her gentle touch. "You're killing me, Baby," he moaned. "No teasing, please, Baby. I need you too bad."

When her fingers wouldn't meet around his girth as she tried to grip him, she reached down with both hands to squeeze him tight as she lined him up with her opening. She rubbed his tip through her folds, his precum mixing with her juices to coat them both.

Slowly, Anthony pulled her hips to lower her onto him one agonizing inch at a time. He paused only partially inside her to allow her to adjust to his size while he reached up with one hand to fondle her breasts again.

"Baby," Anthony moaned, his voice sounding strained. "You feel amazing."

"So do you," Kay sighed breathlessly as she pushed herself down farther onto his shaft.

Once she was fully seated, feeling fuller than she ever had before, Anthony held her still. Kay took a deep breath and focused her gaze on Anthony's expressive face while her body relaxed and adjusted to accommodate his impressive length.

The way he looked up at her from the bed made her feel like the beautiful woman he described. She could see in his eyes the soul-deep love he felt. At that moment, their connection, the unseen bond between her and Anthony was all that existed in the world.

Anthony slowly started to move, thrusting up into Kay's body and filling her more completely than she ever dreamed possible. *Bigger is definitely better,* Kay thought as Anthony stroked against that spot deep inside that she hadn't even known existed before being with him. She tried to match him thrust for thrust as she felt herself coming closer and closer to the edge.

"Yes, Baby," Anthony moaned out. "Ride me, Kay."

She braced herself with her palms on Anthony's pectorals as their rhythm synced up, the speed and intensity of their thrusts increasing, causing Kay's breasts to bounce uncomfortably. Not that she really noticed or cared in the moment, but she would feel it the next morning. Anthony reached up to cup her breasts, holding them still, so he could lift his head and run his tongue over the tips.

"Feels so good, Baby," he breathed out over her nipple. "Can't hold back much longer. You feel too fucking perfect." He latched onto her other nipple and sucked hard.

Kay couldn't hold back her own moans of pleasure as her arousal engulfed her. "Don't hold back," she shouted breathlessly. "I want all of you, Anthony."

"Yes, Kay, Baby," he grunted. "Come now, Baby!" Kay felt him swelling inside her. "Come. With. Me." He punctuated each word with a powerful thrust up into Kay.

"Yes, Anthony, yes," Kay shouted as she shattered, her inner walls squeezing around Anthony's cock like a vise.

"Fuck, Kay," Anthony shouted, dragging the words out to multiple syllables, as Kay felt him release inside her. He repeated her name over and over with each spurt from his shaft.

Kay collapsed on top of him, her head resting over his heart. She felt as if she was floating on a cloud from the intensity of her orgasm. Anthony wrapped her in his arms, stroking one hand up and down her back and the other through her hair, his softening cock still inside her as they both recovered from their explosive joining.

A few moments later, he rolled her over onto her back, resting her head on a pillow. He pulled out slowly and gently kissed her lips before disappearing into the bathroom. When he returned, he gently ran a warm wet washcloth between Kay's legs.

"What are you doing?" Kay looked at him through half-closed eyes.

"Just taking care of you, Baby," he replied as he dried her off with a hand towel. He took them both back to the bathroom before crawling back into bed with Kay.

He pulled back the comforter and rolled them both underneath it. He laid on his back diagonally across the bed, so his feet wouldn't hang off the end, and pulled Kay into his side closest to the headboard. She rested her head on his shoulder, her arm across his chest, and her leg bent up over his abdomen. He wrapped both arms around her, cradling her to him, making her feel cherished and loved. She drifted off to sleep without a care in the world because she knew in her heart that Anthony would be there to take care of her through anything that came their way.

Chapter Eleven

Monday, October 15, 2018

Anthony woke the next morning laying on his side, one arm under a pillow beside him that was covered in Kay's long dark hair, his other arm draped over her, his hand cupping her breast. He couldn't quite tell what part of her body was pressed against his morning wood, so he opened his eyes to figure out exactly how they were laying. They were both on their sides, her back to his front, but their height difference didn't allow them to line up with both their heads on the pillows while their hips were also aligned.

The pillow that was covered with Kay's lustrous locks was angled down so that her head was cradled on one end and actually lined up with his chest. If she were turned the other way, she could have woken him up by licking his nipples. His cock twitched at the thought, pressing between her thighs like he had a mind of his own and knew exactly where he wanted to be and was working on getting there immediately.

Anthony closed his eyes and breathed in the soft strawberry scent of Kay's shampoo. He wanted to memorize everything about the first time he woke up naked with her. The feel of her hair as it tickled his nose. The softness of her skin pressed against his. Every point of contact between them, every sensation where their bodies were touching. The weight of her breast in his hand. The wet heat between her thighs clasping his cock. Even the ice-cold chill of her feet tucked up between his knees and her ass rubbing against his lower abdominals.

How can her ass feel like an ice pack when it's so close to the heat of her pussy?

She wiggled against him, and it took every ounce of self-control he had not to thrust up into her. He could feel the wetness of her opening on the head of his cock tempting him to wake her with round two, but he didn't want to take a chance that she was too sore from the night before to be ready for more.

"Good morning, Baby." Anthony's voice was gravelly from sleep.

"Mmm, morning," Kay purred, rubbing her frozen parts into him.

He squealed and pulled away when she hit a particularly ticklish spot with her icy ass. "Why is your ass that cold?" Anthony sputtered through his laughter. "Did you bring an ice pack to bed while I was sleeping?"

She rolled onto her back, smirked up at him, and shrugged one shoulder. "I read this really great scene in a book once where a couple used an ice cube to heighten the sensation in bed, so I figured I'd see if my butt was cold enough to do the same." Kay graced him with a cheeky smile.

"Yeah, I think I'm supposed to be the one using the ice cube on you." Anthony leaned over her, his mind filled with fantasies of tying her up and teasing her with the different sensations of running a multitude of items over her beautiful body. With their faces only inches apart and their eyes locked on each other's, he stroked one fingertip down her throat, over her collarbone, and down to circle the swell of her breasts. "Would you like me to lick up the trail of water left behind, Baby?"

"Yes, please," Kay whispered in a breathy tone that went straight to his cock.

He couldn't resist her pouty pink lips a moment longer and dove in for a passionate good morning kiss. Unfortunately, it was interrupted by the sound of his phone alarm ringing from out in the living room.

He jumped up from the bed and quickly donned his sweatpants, so he could rush out to turn it off, hoping he could silence it before it woke the girls.

Just as he swiped to dismiss the alarm, the door to the girls' room opened. Maria walked out, yawning, and rubbing her eyes. She looked adorable in My Little Pony pajamas and her blonde hair a mass of curls in all directions.

"Good morning, Princess." Anthony watched her walk to the mini-fridge and get a bottle of water without even really opening her eyes.

When Maria didn't reply or even seem to hear him, he looked over her head at Kay, who was standing in the master bedroom doorway wearing only the fluffy robe from the night before. "Is she still asleep?"

"Probably." Kay bobbed her head. "Both girls have been known to sleepwalk, but normally they talk in their sleep too and make it hard to tell that they're still asleep."

Maria carried her water bottle to the couch where she curled up on one end and hugged it to her like it was her favorite stuffed animal.

"She's okay, though, right?" Anthony wasn't sure what to do for a sleepwalking child.

"She's fine," Kay replied as she walked over to sit beside Maria. "We just have to wake her up now that she's settled back down. I'll get them both started on baths if you want to go ahead and get the shower going in the master bath."

"You know there's a small shower in the guest bath." Anthony pointed at the door to the small bathroom between the two bedrooms. "They can each have their own bathroom, while you and I share a shower."

Anthony wagged his eyebrows at Kay suggestively. She flashed him that secret naughty smile he'd missed the last week, which he took as her agreement to meeting him in the shower. He grabbed his suitcase and garment bag to take to the master bedroom, leaving his laptop bag on the floor beside the coffee table where his laptop still sat.

Kay gently stroked back Maria's hair and cooed softly to her, "Wake up, Sleeping Beauty."

He couldn't hear any more of what Kay said to the girls as he put his bags on the bed and got out his toiletries to take into the bathroom. He brushed his teeth first, kicking himself for not thinking of morning breath before kissing Kay earlier. He pulled out his electric razor, thinking that shaving before his shower would give Kay plenty of time to get the girls started on their morning routine, so she could join him in the shower.

Even if she was too sore to fuck, they could still live out some of his fantasies about getting each other off in the shower. The boner that had gone away when Maria walked into the living room was back at full force at the thought of fucking Kay's tits in the shower.

Kay walked in as he finished shaving. *Perfect timing,* he thought as he cleaned his razor and put it away. Kay brushed her teeth as he put his shampoo and bodywash in the shower and turned the water on to warm up. He plucked her bottles off the side of the bathtub and put them in the shower while he waited for her to finish.

Anthony stripped off his sweatpants before unwrapping the gift of his gorgeous girlfriend from her fluffy bathrobe. He picked her up and kissed her as he carried her into the shower. He loved how her petite frame made it easy for him to carry her around or put her in places most people wouldn't fit, like seated on the high ledge around the shower at the perfect level for him to eat her pussy for breakfast.

Thank fuck for eight-foot ceilings and six-foot-high ledges meant for shampoo bottles.

"What are you doing?" Kay squealed as her ass cheeks touched down on the cold tile. She rounded her back and leaned forward, so she didn't hit her head on the ceiling. She put both hands on the top of his head, presumably to hold herself up, though Anthony knew he would never let her fall.

"Having breakfast." Anthony lowered his mouth between her open thighs. He kept both hands gripped on her hips to make sure there was no risk of her falling or getting hurt. "Remember to be quiet since the girls are awake," he cautioned before swiping the flat of his tongue from her slit to her clit.

"Oh, my, Anthony," Kay moaned quietly as she dug her hands into his hair.

He enjoyed the slight nips of her fingernails against his scalp as he devoured his favorite treat. Since he couldn't look into her eyes in this position, he closed his eyes and allowed his other senses to sharpen, savoring her taste and smell. Tangy and sweet with a musky aroma that could only be described as essence of Kay.

He settled into a rhythm, cycling through his favorite ways to arouse her orally. Suckling her clit, long licks through her slit with his tongue flattened out, swirling designs through her folds and around her most sensitive nub with just the tip of his tongue, and fucking her with his tongue while applying gentle pressure to her clitoris with his nose. It only took a few moments before her inner walls were clamping down on his tongue as she came, repeating his name in a breathy moan.

Anthony was not a believer in one-and-done when it came to Kay's orgasms, so he continued his oral onslaught until she went over the edge a second and third time, whimpering his name repeatedly. He savored her taste on his lips as he slowly slid her down from the ledge, her soft, satiated flesh rubbing against his still hard and aroused manhood long before her feet reached the floor of the shower.

He stopped her descent when they were eye to eye, holding her skin to skin while she recovered from her orgasm enough to be able to stand. She wrapped her arms around his neck, pulling his head to hers for a passionate kiss. He loved the way she returned his kisses with just as much passion and desire as he felt. It was like their tongues were dancing, sliding against each other as they twirled around the dancefloor that was both their mouths.

As much as he didn't want their kiss to end, he wanted to live out one of his dreams more. So, he released her lips and let her slide the rest of the way down his body until her feet hit the floor. Once he was sure she was stable on her feet, he pushed her backwards under the rain shower head and grabbed her bottle of shampoo.

"Wait," Kay protested as he poured some of the strawberry scented shampoo into his hand to wash her hair. "I want breakfast too."

She reached out and grabbed his cock with both of her petite little hands, one at the base and the other just below the head. When her little thumb stroked over the sensitive ridge, where the head flared out, and up to spread the precum that was already leaking out over the whole head of his cock, Anthony groaned in pleasure. He loved the feel of her touching him but had to stop her, so he didn't come before he could live out his favorite shower fantasy.

"Baby," he moaned as he started to scrub her luscious locks. "As good as that feels, I need you to stop."

"But we haven't taken care of you yet," Kay purred, her little pink tongue coming out to lick his head.

His cock twitched from the hot, wet contact and Anthony couldn't contain the low growl that escaped his throat. He had a primal urge to push her mouth down on his cock and fuck her face like a wild animal, but he wouldn't let himself do anything that might be too rough with his precious Kay. Instead, he took advantage of the fact that his hands were tangled in her hair where he'd worked up a lather with her shampoo and had been massaging her scalp. He lightly tugged on her soapy hair to pull her head back away from his cock.

"We're gonna take care of me, Baby," he growled out as he angled her head under the spray of water to rinse the shampoo from her hair. He used one hand to block the shampoo suds and water from dripping into her eyes, while he stroked the fingers of his other hand through her long locks to make sure he got all the bubbles rinsed away. "But I've dreamt of fucking your tits in the shower so many times that I absolutely have to live out that fantasy now that I actually have you in the shower with me. Please, Baby, just be patient and stand there. Let me live out this dream and make us both feel good."

"I'll try." Kay smiled up at him. "But patience is a virtue, and I lost my virtue a long time ago, so I may not be able to be patient for long."

"Hopefully, you'll enjoy this enough to be patient." Anthony picked up a washcloth and Kay's bottle of bodywash. It smelled of more berries mixed with a light floral scent that was intoxicating as he squirted some onto the cloth.

"But if your inner brat can't be patient, I can always switch to another fantasy I've had, and spank you in the shower," Anthony warned in a low, deep voice as he knelt in the shower and started washing Kay with the soapy washcloth. He started with her shoulders and arms, meticulously washing between her fingers and over the palms of her hands.

He hugged her to him, so he could enjoy the feel of her pillow-soft breasts pressed into his chest as he scrubbed her back. He released his hold on her when he came around from her low back to wash the soft curve of her belly. He avoided the parts of her body that they both wanted him to touch the most, teasing her with anticipation as he washed both of her legs and feet.

Kay groaned when he rinsed out the washcloth before washing her most intimate areas. Her soft mewling sounds went straight to his cock. His dick twitched in solidarity with Kay's frustration at how Anthony was moving slowly to draw out their anticipation.

He hung the cloth on a hook in the tile wall and picked up the bottle again. He drizzled her bodywash over the tops of her breasts and replaced the bottle on the shelf before using his hands to spread the soap over her tantalizing titties. When they were both adequately covered in suds, he moved his hands down to spread the fluffy pink bubbles over her pussy and ass. He didn't want even a thin washcloth between them as he washed her intimately.

"Oh, Anthony, don't stop," Kay protested when he pulled his hands away from her body and stood. "I was so close."

"But, Baby, I need my hands for this." Anthony cupped her breasts, squeezing them together to tighten the area where he would soon have his cock. "Squat down just a little bit and touch yourself, so we can both come from me fucking your tits."

His low, gravelly voice sounded commanding, even to his own ears, and he hoped Kay was aroused and not put off by his domineering tone.

"Yes, Sir." Her words came out in a breathy tone as she followed his orders.

He squeezed her boobs around his cock and started to thrust through her soap slickened cleavage. He couldn't decide where he wanted to look most, at his cock between her tits, at her fingers in her pussy, or at her beautiful face where he could see her pleasure in her expression and her love in her eyes.

"Oh, Baby, it's even better than I imagined," Anthony groaned out as his thrusts became more rapid. "I'm not going to last much longer."

"Oh, Anthony, oh, yes, Anthony," Kay moaned as her hand started to move faster between her legs. The sight of her thumb pressing on her clit while she had two fingers knuckle deep in her pussy caused a tingle in his spine and his balls to tighten in preparation of his release.

"Yes, Kay, now," he growled. "Fuck, Kay, come with me now!"

They were both chanting each other's names as they came together. Ropes of his hot, sticky cum shot over Kay's breasts and his abs. She closed her eyes when one shot to her face but only stopped chanting his name long enough to lick it off her lips. That visual was enough to trigger another wave from Anthony.

They both stood there, perfectly still for a moment, while they caught their breath.

"I guess you'll have to spank my inner brat next time." Kay gave him a cheeky smile as she stood up from her mini squat and pulled back from Anthony.

He returned her mischievous smile with a wag of his eyebrows. "I look forward to it, Brat."

He grabbed the washcloth and bodywash and cleaned her up where he'd gotten her dirty again after his first time washing her body. They each washed their own hair, hers needing a second cleaning to get his cum out of it. She followed her shampoo with conditioner while he put his own bodywash on the rinsed-out rag. Before he could wash more than his shoulder and right upper arm, she was pushing him to sit on the bench built into the shower and taking the washcloth from his hand.

She was much more efficient at washing him than he'd been with her, but he was grateful for her speed when they got out and he realized the time. They had to hustle through drying off, dressing, and packing their things, so they could get to the airport on time for their flight.

As soon as he could throw on his slacks and a button down, he dried off and packed his toiletries and carried his bags out to the living room. He put his socks and shoes on the floor by the sofa and draped his suit coat over the back of the chair, so he could put them on after getting everything else packed. Since he wasn't actually flying the plane on their trip home, he opted to skip his normal tie.

"Don't forget these." Kay carried out the dry-cleaning bag. "I left it in the closet last night when I brought you the rest of your clean clothes."

"Thanks, Baby." Anthony took his plastic covered suits from her and kissed the top of her head. Her hair was still wet, even though she'd already gotten dressed.

Kay practically skipped back to the master bedroom to finish getting ready. Anthony took a moment to appreciate the extra bounce in her backside that he hoped was brought on by their sexual shower escapades. He quickly repacked his things that hadn't already been put away.

Soon, all the girls were in the living room with their things and ready to leave the hotel. They stopped in the lobby for beignets for breakfast. Neither Kay nor her daughters had ever heard of the deep-fried doughy goodness and Anthony basked in his fatherly feelings at another first with them.

~~~
~~~

After their commercial flight into San Antonio, Anthony drove Kay, Tia, and Maria out to his family ranch once more. Instead of pulling into the drive of his parents' home as Kay expected, he pulled around to the two-car garage on the back of the smaller house next door. She knew the plan was for him to move into this house while they were in town this week, but she didn't think it would be ready for them to stay in it until after a couple of days of packing and moving not just his stuff from his apartment but also his brothers' stuff from this house.

"Why are we here?" Kay turned to look at him as he turned off the truck. "I thought we would be staying with your parents until you actually get moved in here."

"I don't have that much to move from my apartment." Anthony grinned at her. "After last night, I figured it would be best if I got my dad to help me get it all this afternoon, so we can sleep here tonight."

He wagged his eyebrows suggestively at her, making her think he was planning on them sharing a room in his new home. She gave him a small shake of her head and pointedly looked into the backseat at her daughters, hoping he understood she meant for him to quell the discussion about their sleeping arrangements until after the girls were out of earshot.

"Memmaw said she'd have our rooms ready when we got home today." Maria bounced with excitement in her seat. "I can't wait to see my princess room."

"When we got home?" "Princess room?" When did my daughters start thinking of this as home and plan bedroom themes with Anthony's mother?

"Memmaw confirmed on Skype last night that the smelly boy stuff has been moved out and Maria and I's rooms have been painted and set up already," Tia explained as they all started getting out of the vehicle. "She said she painted ya'll's room blue but didn't set up anything else in the house since she didn't know what you would want, Mom."

Kay noted that her daughter had referred to her and Anthony as a plural but only mentioned one room, making her wonder if her belief that her daughters hadn't noticed that she and Anthony had shared a room the night before was merely her delusion. She floundered for a moment trying to figure out what to say to her daughters.

I can't exactly say, "Yeah, I'm sleeping with this guy I just met two weeks ago but only until the judge orders me to give him up and move back to Tulsa" to my eight- and twelve-year-old daughters, Kay thought to herself.

Before she could figure out how to explain her current sleeping arrangements, the subject was dropped because the girls were both focused on the excited squeals of Hazel coming around the corner of the house. Kay was grateful for Hazel's distraction because she did not want to explain to her girls that she was taking advantage of the short window of time she thought she'd have with Anthony to enjoy a fling.

She didn't want her daughters to know what a fling was, much less enjoy one in the future. She wanted them to stay little girls who believed in fairy tales and happily ever after for as long as possible. Just because marriage to their father had tarnished Kay's gilded view of love, didn't mean she wanted them to share her doubts and insecurities.

Kay wanted her daughters to grow up to be strong, confident women who weren't afraid to follow their hearts into lifelong loving relationships. She didn't want them to be as weak as she felt; she didn't want them to settle for the ill-treatment she'd endured in her marriage. She wanted them to make their own decisions about who they loved, regardless of anyone else's opinions, not to feel like they could only sneak a few weeks of happiness with their soulmates until a higher power tore them apart.

That's what she felt like she was doing with Anthony, sneaking a few weeks of happiness with the love of her life, but expecting him to be ripped away from her by the judge in less than a month. She might not be strong enough to overrule the directive of a Tulsa County Judge, but she desperately wanted to enjoy what little time she got to have Anthony in her life until fate came between them.

Kay found herself being swept through the garage and a laundry room and into a huge country kitchen. The cabinets were painted a pale aqua to match the aqua tiles that were alternated with light pink tiles on the countertops and backsplash. The walls were painted pale pink to match the rest of the tiles. The floor was covered with black and white checkerboard linoleum. Kay wasn't sure if any of it was original to the nineteen-thirties home or if it had been updated over the years, but it was definitely not what she imagined was Anthony's style. She had to admit to loving the butcher block top on the island in the center of the room, but that was more for its usefulness than as a design choice.

"We got rid of the old chrome table and chairs years ago." Hazel waved her arms around as if pointing out where the old table had been in the kitchen in decades past. "I think your brothers just ate at the island instead of buying a new dining table."

"That's fine." Anthony leaned his elbows on the island in question. "I have a table and chairs in my apartment."

When did he have time to sneak off and change clothes? Kay wondered when she noticed he was dressed in a t-shirt, jeans, and sneakers instead of the suit he'd worn on the trip from New Orleans to the ranch.

"We left the library furniture, because that's all antiques from your great-grandparents, but got rid of the bachelor pad garbage Josh and Jake had left in the other rooms," Hazel continued. "We repainted all four bedrooms. Maria's is now princess pink and Tia's is a lovely lavender. Their beds, dressers, and desks have all been set up, as well as the Jack and Jill bathroom between them, so they're set for the night. I assumed you'd want your bedroom furniture from the apartment in the master, so I painted it royal blue since Tia said it was also Kay's favorite color. I figured we'd wait and see what you had and what you didn't before buying curtains and towels and such for your ensuite."

"Thanks, Mom." Anthony looked frustrated. "Now Dad and I need to get going if we're gonna get everything from the apartment this afternoon." He pushed off the island and stalked over to where Kay was standing. He took her hand in his and Kay felt tingles shoot from their joined hands throughout her whole body.

Kay wished he would pull her with him out the door to go to his apartment in the city to pack his things instead of leaving her on the ranch with his mother. Her hopes were dashed as he took his wallet out of his pocket with his free hand and pulled a credit card out to leave with her.

"Mom can show you where to shop in town to get the curtains and stuff for our bedroom and bathroom." Anthony practically forced the card into her hand. "I've already added you to my accounts at the bank, so you can use this for now. But if you have time after shopping, stop by there to get your own cards."

"Anthony," Kay started to protest using his cards or being the one to decorate his bedroom. Before she could say more than his name, he was squeezing her hand in their secret three-squeeze code for "I love you" and giving her a chaste kiss to stop her speech.

She returned Anthony's secret "I love you" and then he was rushing out the door, leaving her standing there, speechless. And still holding his credit card.

"Mom, come see our rooms!" Maria squealed from somewhere else in the house and brought Kay back to her senses.

Not knowing exactly where her daughters were in the house she hadn't had a full tour of yet, she reverted to their tried-and-true method of playing hide and seek that they'd used since her daughters were old enough to learn the classic pool game and decided to bring it on land. "Marco!" Kay yelled.

"Polo!" Tia and Maria both yelled back. Kay followed the sound of their voices out of the kitchen and into an empty room that she thought was previously a formal dining room. After a few more rounds of calling out for each other, she'd made her way through another empty room with a huge brick fireplace that caused Kay to imagine nights cuddling with Anthony in front of a roaring fire, the library Hazel had mentioned that was wall to wall bookshelves, still half full of books that looked as old as the house and was fully furnished with dark wood tables and antique leather wingback chairs, and found the front foyer and staircase up to where she could hear her girls. The woodwork in the house was impressive, from the dark hardwood floors to the matching door frames, moldings, and stair rails. It made Kay wonder why they would have covered the gorgeous hardwoods in the kitchen with linoleum.

As she got to the top of the stairs, she was happy to see the hallway had been recently painted in a creamy neutral tone that wasn't as garish as the gold flowery wallpaper in the downstairs rooms. While Kay didn't think it was her place to make any of the decorating decisions in Anthony's home, at least until she was sure she wouldn't have to leave him and move back to Tulsa, she couldn't help but want to take down that hideous wallpaper.

She walked down the hall and found Tia in the first room on the right. It was indeed a lovely lavender and fully furnished. Besides the previously mentioned full-sized bed, dresser, and desk, there was a bookshelf already stocked with young adult paperbacks, dark purple bedding to complement the lavender walls, and an entire new wardrobe that Tia was going through.

"Mom, come see my room," Maria called out in a sing-song voice as she emerged from a door into Tia's room from the Jack and Jill bathroom.

"I'm coming," Kay replied as Maria grabbed her hand and pulled her through the bathroom that was very femininely decorated in a mix of lavender and light pink to match each of the attached bedrooms.

Where Tia's room was feminine but subdued, the room appearing more mature like its occupant, Maria's room was an explosion of pink princesses that could only be enjoyed by a little girl. From the gauzy pink canopy over the full-sized bed to the castle-themed bedding. The bookshelf already held a copy of every Disney Princess book Kay could recall and a few she didn't recognize. In one corner there was a three-foot-tall dollhouse—a princess castle dollhouse—with several princess dolls on the shelf beside it.

Both girls were babbling on about how much they loved their new rooms, but Kay was too overwhelmed by it all to comprehend everything they were saying. She loved seeing her girls laughing and happy but wished it wasn't brought on by Anthony and his family's over-the-top spoiling. She hated knowing that she would have to be the bad guy in their fairy-tale story if the judge ordered her to move them back home to Tulsa and leave Anthony behind with all these new things. She was torn as to whether or not she should burst their happy bubble right then or wait and let the judge do it in a few weeks.

Looking between her daughters' happy faces as they fluttered about showing her their favorite new things, she couldn't bring herself to crush their dreams by telling them that they should reject the gifts because they probably wouldn't get to live in these bedrooms after they went to court. Instead, she joined them in the excitement of living in the moment and enjoying their time with Anthony while they could, and prayed that they wouldn't all end up with broken hearts after the legal issues in Oklahoma were settled.

Maybe they won't see me as the bad guy if it's the judge that orders us back to Tulsa without Anthony, Kay thought hopefully.

"We don't have time for a fashion show right now." Hazel ruffled Maria's hair. "We have to show your mom her room, so she can pick out what she wants when we go shopping and we can get back with enough time to wash the new bedding and towels for them to use tonight."

Kay followed Hazel out of Maria's room since she didn't know which of the two doors on the other side of the hall led to the master bedroom. Since she still wasn't sure how to handle discussing her sleeping arrangements with her daughters and felt really uncomfortable about talking to Hazel about sharing a bed with her son, she opted to go with the plan of picking out stuff for Anthony in the master suite and asking about the fourth bedroom for herself.

"You said there are four bedrooms?" Kay queried as they stepped into the hall. "I should probably get bedding for that room as well."

"It's not really a fourth bedroom." Hazel shook her head as she directed Kay to the door closest to the stairs across the hall. As they stepped into the small room, Hazel continued explaining. "It's really more of a sitting room since it opens up into the master, but it was used as a nursery and then a home office in the past. We just painted it to match the master, so you could decide how to use it now."

"Oh," Kay sighed, all hope of keeping her sleeping arrangements a secret lost.

Hazel showed her through the door to the huge master bedroom and pointed out the doors to the ensuite bathroom and walk-in closet. When Kay opened the closet door to take a peek, she found where Anthony had already dropped their suitcases and hung his garment bag. His bags were on the left side of the closet and hers on the right like he already had a plan for how they would share the space. His suitcase was still open from where he'd gotten out clothes to change and his suit from earlier was hanging beside the garment bag.

"We should probably add hangers to your shopping list." Hazel poked her head into the closet where Kay was standing. "He'll probably bring some from the apartment, but I'm sure it won't be enough for both of you."

"I'm going to have to make a list." Kay pulled a small notepad and pen from her purse to start jotting things down.

Hangers

King-sized bedding

Bathroom towels

She walked into the bathroom and was pleasantly surprised to see that the tile work wasn't as garish as the kitchen. The walls had been painted a lighter blue than the bedroom, but Kay was glad of that because the darker color would have been overwhelming if it was everywhere.

The large tiles on the floor almost looked like natural stone. On the right as soon as she got in the door was a long vanity with double sinks. The vanity and double sinks were solid-surface, similar to the ones in Anthony's parents' home next door but in a soft gray instead of white.

The subway tile backsplash on the vanity matched the walls of the huge shower that started at the end of the vanity and was just as long and twice as wide as the vanity. The built-in ledges for storing shampoo, glass shower doors, and bench on one end of the shower reminded Kay of the shower at the hotel in New Orleans. She blushed as she remembered her morning shower with Anthony.

She turned to examine the rest of the room and prayed Hazel wouldn't notice her pink cheeks when she turned away from the mirror over the vanity. There were two doors in the wall across from the vanity. She opened the first one to find shelves for storing towels and other bathroom necessities. When she opened the second, she almost laughed at the toilet hidden in a small closet.

She quickly closed that door and made her way around the corner to see the large claw-foot tub that had to be original to the home. It wasn't the jacuzzi she'd enjoyed the night before, but Kay could easily imagine soaking up to her neck in bubbles in the glorious white antique tub. But only after putting some privacy curtains over the window behind it that looked out at Anthony's parents' house next door.

Bathroom curtains and curtain rod

"Do you know the window sizes?" Kay walked back into the master bedroom.

"No, but I can run next door and grab a tape measure, so we can make sure we have the right sizes."

While Hazel was gone to find a tape measure, Kay quickly ducked into the walk-in closet to change into something more comfortable for working on setting up the house. She had a feeling she would appreciate her own jeans and sneakers for her afternoon of work on Anthony's house.

<div align="center">~~~</div>

Anthony had a pensive smile on his face as he and his father Bob loaded his truck with his belongings at his apartment on Monday afternoon. He hated having to leave Kay and the girls with his mom, especially after seeing the apprehensive look on Kay's face when he gave her his debit card to pay for the things he wanted her to pick out for their bedroom. While he wanted to spend every moment with Kay, he needed the time alone with his dad to help sort through his feelings about her.

Anthony was conflicted because his possessiveness for Kay, Tia, and Maria was the exact opposite of how he was raised to treat his wife and children. He hoped his dad could help him understand why he was feeling the way he was, and help him figure out how to control his primal urges, so he could love them the way they deserved.

"So, Son, what's on your mind?" They walked side by side up the stairs to get the next piece of furniture.

Anthony looked at his father incredulously, wondering how his dad always knew when he needed to talk.

Bob just grinned at Anthony before answering Anthony's unasked question. It was as if he could read his son's mind. "I know my kids. We may not talk as much as your momma and sisters, but all the Burleson boys need to talk things out once in a while. So, is it about Kay?"

"Yeah, Dad," Anthony chuckled. "I know she's *The One*, but I'm not sure how to make it happen."

"Seems like it's happening all on its own," Bob replied. "Maybe you need to quit stressing and just let fate take its course."

"Yeah, that's hard to do when I'm so worried about fate letting her get hurt again," Anthony grumbled.

"Hurt by who?"

Anthony took a deep breath and blew it out slowly before answering. "Her ex, her family." He took in another shaky breath. "Me."

Bob looked at his youngest son like he had three heads. "You would never hurt her," he emphatically declared.

"Not intentionally." Anthony dropped his head, his chin coming to his chest. "But some of my thoughts are scaring me that I might without meaning to."

"What kind of thoughts?" His dad looked concerned.

"Like I want to take the three of them to a deserted island and keep them away from anyone or anything that might hurt them." Anthony's voice was filled with anguish. "Like I don't want Kay to be my partner in life, because I want to take care of everything for her and the girls, so all they have to do is relax and enjoy life. Like extreme jealousy, where I want to be everything for them and not share them with anyone else. It's driving me crazy, Dad. It's not how you taught me to treat my wife and children."

Bob laughed; a deep belly laugh like Anthony hadn't heard from his dad in a long time, if ever. Anthony stopped before picking up one end of his sofa and just stared at his father disbelievingly. *What the fuck? Did I just cause Dad to have a mental break by sharing my inner demon?*

"It's not funny, Dad," Anthony grumbled as Bob bent to pick up the other end of the sofa. "I'm even having violent thoughts of how to kill her ex-husband. Like extremely graphic, bloody visions of tearing him limb from limb. It took all I had not to act on them when I stepped between him and Kay last week. What if I can't control those urges when we go to court next month?"

Bob straightened up lifting his end of the sofa, his face taking on a serious expression. "First of all, your feelings about Kay and your desire to beat her ex are two different things. You did the right thing protecting Kay, but not throwing punches when they weren't needed. Keep that up. Find someplace else to get your aggression at him out. Chopping wood and pounding in fence posts always helped me when I felt the need to hit someone."

"You felt the need to hit someone?" Anthony took long strides to keep up with his father as they carried the sofa down to the truck. He was seeing a side of his dad that he hadn't known before, and it surprised him.

"Oh, yeah," Bob chuckled. "When your mom was sixteen and still too young for me to date, I came home from college on spring break to see her walking through town holding hands with a punk teenager. I wanted to knock him upside the head and stake my claim on her like you wouldn't believe. We ended up with all new fencing on the ranch between then and her twentieth birthday. Your Pappaw Jerry tried to convince me that I needed to wait 'til she was twenty-one, but I just couldn't hold out any longer before asking her out."

"Yeah, I think I'll stick to sparring with James and Dean to get out my aggression," Anthony mumbled, hating the thought of working in the Texas heat to put in all new fence posts on over ten-thousand acres of land.

Bob laughed again before saying, "Yeah, you never did like working on the ranch."

"I like some of it, Pop." Anthony smiled at his dad as they put the sofa down on the bed of the pickup. "Like riding the trails around the ranch. I just don't like the hard work. I don't think God made me to sweat that much."

Bob shook his head as he returned Anthony's smile. "Now, back to how you're feeling about Kay. You know we all have those thoughts and feelings about our families, right?"

Anthony reached up and scratched the back of his neck. He felt confused by hearing his dad's words. It was like he was seeing a different version of his father than the man he grew up with. "But that's not what you taught me growing up."

"Of course not." Bob gave him a knowing smile. "Your momma would have tanned my hide if I'd have taught you boys about our natural caveman tendencies. Women changed a lot in our generation and they're even more independent now. So, while we still want to drag them back to our caves where we can provide and protect and hide them away from the world as our most prized possessions, we have to evolve, too. Or at least pretend to be more evolved than we are."

Anthony wanted to laugh with his dad, but he was still too scared of not being able to control his inner caveman. "But you and Mom always made it plain that she was your partner and worked just as hard as you did. I don't want Kay to have to work as hard as Mom does."

Bob chuckled. "Your Mom doesn't work as hard as she's made you think she does."

"Yeah, she does," Anthony protested. "It takes her, Aunt Susan, and Rosa working all day in the kitchen to feed all the hands. And I remember several times when she'd ride out with you to help mend a fence on the ranch over the years. Mom works a lot harder than I do."

Bob threw back his head as his laugh roared out of him. When he finally caught his breath, he slapped his son on the back. "Anthony, do you really think your petite momma helped me mend a fence?"

Anthony just nodded his head.

"No, Son." Bob kept chuckling. "Now that you're stepping into a dad role and having to find some alone time with Kay, I'm sure you can see that your momma and I just needed some adult time without six kids interrupting."

Gross Dad, I don't need to hear about you and Mom getting freaky in a cow field, Anthony thought, his face contorting in a grimace.

"As for the work she does feeding the hands," Bob continued. "Yeah, maybe some of that is harder work than you do flying around all the time. But that's just their way of hanging out and having girl talk. Most of that time is spent plotting how they're going to fix up their kids 'cause they all want grandbabies. Just be glad you found Kay when you did since I suspect you were going to be their next target for a bad blind date."

Anthony visibly shuddered at the thought of his mother, aunt, and their closest friend planning to fix him up with a blind date. He knew he needed to get this conversation back on track. Back to him and Kay.

"I'm scared I'm going to take over her life and she'll end up resenting me for it," he finally admitted awkwardly.

"Are you taking over her life?"

Am I? Yeah, I basically strong-armed her into leaving Tulsa to get away from her ex. Anthony's heart sank at the thought.

"Yeah, I pretty much demanded she leave town with me to keep her ex from being able to take the girls for his court-ordered visits," Anthony admitted with a sigh. "When her dad and lawyer both gave her other options and reasons why she shouldn't leave with me, I argued the points until I got my way."

"Did you? Really?" Bob gave Anthony a skeptical look. "Or did you point out the ways their options weren't safe for Kay or the girls and gave them the only option that would keep them from possible harm? What would have happened if they hadn't left with you when you did? What would have happened if you were all still there when her ex broke into her house? Do you think whatever knife he used on her furniture and clothing might have been used on you, or Kay, or one of those innocent little girls? Don't feel guilty for keeping them safe." Bob's tirade came to an abrupt halt, so he could lower his voice from the thunderous roar it became during his rant.

"And you also helped her get a job, one that pays well, so she can still feel independent like a woman needs. That's compromise. That's being a partner. You didn't unilaterally make the decision for her. You didn't just tell her what to do. You not only talked it out with her, but also with her dad and her lawyer. That's not taking over her life, that's giving her the best option and allowing her to make the final decision. That's being the man your momma and I raised you to be. One who can hide his inner caveman and truly love the right woman."

Anthony felt a little of the weight being lifted from his shoulders. *Maybe I'm doing this right after all.* "Thanks, Dad," he finally said as they walked back up the stairs to his old apartment. "Did you tell Josh and Jake that they've been evicted from their house?"

"Naw, we just moved their stuff into their old rooms at our house. They'll figure it out, if and when they actually come home on leave."

"Josh and Jake aren't going to be happy with that," Anthony pointed out, thinking his brothers would feel like they were being pushed out of their home.

"They'll be fine with it." Bob grinned. "They never furnished half the house because they really only slept there for their senior year of high school. They knew when they left that with so many siblings and cousins, they'd probably lose the house when they weren't home all the time."

"Yeah, I suppose it's just a place to store their stuff now."

"We really only moved their clothes and personal belongings. We left the bedroom furniture for Tia and Maria to use when ya'll are home." Bob started taking apart Anthony's bed to load it into the truck next. "Besides, they know that as soon as you get married and get your trust fund, you'll be building a house for your family, and they can have it back then if they're even home by then."

"Why do I need to wait to get my trust fund to build?" Anthony started helping his dad with dismantling the king-sized bed. "I haven't really spent much of my income the past couple of years. I have over a million just in my checking account, so I could start building something now."

Bob chuckled as he moved to pick up one end of the headboard to move it down to the truck. "I suppose you don't if you just want to build a normal house. But if you wanna build Maria her castle, you might need a little more than a million that's liquid and not tied up in your investments."

Anthony's smile widened as he thought about Maria's description of her dream house, a fairy-tale castle with her bedroom in one of the turrets.

"I can't get that money for five years though," Anthony pointed out.

Bob looked at his son like he was confused.

"Don't I have to be thirty and married first?" Anthony arched an eyebrow.

"No, you get it as soon as you get married," Bob replied. "Or when you turn thirty, whichever comes first."

Visions of Maria's dream castle on a ridge overlooking one of the ponds or creeks on the Burleson Ranch appeared in Anthony's head.

"Dad, do you think we could build a castle on the ridge just south of Bobby's house overlooking the creek and pond?" They finished loading the headboard and started back up the stairs to get the rest of the pieces of the bed.

"That sounds like a great place for a castle," Bob chuckled. "So, when can we start planning the wedding and building?"

"Just as soon as I can convince Kay," Anthony replied with a chuckle of his own. "I told her yesterday that I want to get married the weekend after Thanksgiving, but I haven't gotten her to say yes yet."

"Maybe you need to plan a better proposal." Bob picked up one end of the footboard as Anthony picked up the other to carry it down and load it on the truck. "Have you bought her a ring yet?"

"Naw, I haven't had a chance to go ring shopping with our crazy schedule," Anthony answered as they made it down the stairs. "I need that before I can do a fancy proposal. And with the way she keeps saying she won't say yes until after she goes to court next month, I haven't wanted to do it up big yet for her to just keep saying no."

"You know I have your Memmaw and Pappaw's wedding rings if you'd rather use them." They strapped the posts together on his headboard and footboard, so they wouldn't wobble on the drive back to Heart's Destiny.

"Really, Pop?" Anthony had a lump of emotion in his throat as he spoke. "They belonged to your parents. Are you sure you don't want to keep them for a while?"

"Why would I want to keep them?" Bob looked at Anthony like he'd lost his mind.

"They're pretty sentimental," Anthony pointed out as they made their way up the stairs to get the mattress.

"Yeah, that's why I thought you'd want them, seein' as how you're my most sentimental son," Bob replied. "Your Ma and I don't need them because we already have our rings. They've just been sitting in your Ma's jewelry box collecting dust since Dad died. They're still on the chain he wore them on around his neck after she passed. Maybe if you put that chain around Kay's neck it'll give her an incentive to say yes sooner."

"Maybe," Anthony choked out feeling unsure if he should chuckle at his dad's idea to manipulate Kay into saying yes, or let the tears fall that were threatening to escape his eyes at the sappy emotions he was feeling at using his grandparents' wedding rings to marry Kay.

Once he got his feelings in check and schooled his features, he choked out, "Thanks, Dad. I'd be honored to use their wedding rings."

"I'll go clean them as soon as we get all this stuff unloaded, so you can have them tonight." Bob pulled a handkerchief from his pocket and blew his nose. Anthony wondered if his dad was having to cover some of his own emotions when it looked like he might have also wiped a tear from his eye.

They finished loading the furniture in Bob's truck bed, then moved on to pack a few boxes of books, kitchen supplies, and various pictures and mementoes and several garbage bags of clothes, bedding, and towels under the tonneau cover of Anthony's pickup. Anthony's guitars, amps, and electronics went in the back seats and floorboards where they were the safest for the drive.

All in all, it only took them about three hours to get everything in his apartment loaded up for the move. They did a cursory cleaning of the kitchen and bathroom, dusted the windowsills, and vacuumed the whole apartment before Anthony turned in his keys to the office and left the apartment for the final time. After adding the driving time between Heart's Destiny and San Antonio twice, it had been about five hours since Anthony had seen Kay and he was desperate to get back to her.

~~~

After spending thirty minutes measuring the windows in the master bedroom, ensuite bathroom, and sitting room and jotting down all the sizes she needed for curtains and curtain rods, Kay was more than ready to go to town and get the things Anthony would need whether she got to stay there with him or not. Hazel tried to convince her to do the same for the rooms downstairs and start to plan color schemes for the formal living and dining rooms, as well as a less formal den that Hazel described as a rumpus room for the kids. But Kay didn't feel comfortable decorating a home she wasn't sure she would actually get to live in.

She couldn't exactly tell her potential future mother-in-law that, though. Kay was trying to figure out how to be diplomatic while still urging Hazel to quit fussing with the house, so she could drive Kay into town to buy the things they already knew Anthony needed.

"I'd rather have him here before I start planning out the rest of the house." Kay hoped she didn't come off as too weak-willed, like she needed Anthony's opinion on everything. That was definitely not the image of a strong independent woman her parents wanted her to
~~~

project or that Hazel appeared to be. "Until he gets back with the stuff from his apartment, I won't know what he already has to be able to match his things with any accessories in my decorating ideas. I'd hate to buy anything now and just have to return it because our styles clashed, or I duplicated some of the things he already has."

"I didn't think about that," Hazel sighed. "Okay, let's go to town, then. Tia! Maria! Load up, so Memmaw can show you around town."

Both girls barreled down the stairs. Kay wasn't surprised that they'd both changed into new clothes. She added laundry supplies to her shopping list as they walked over to get in Hazel's SUV.

"Why does everyone drive big trucks here?" Maria buckled her seatbelt as soon as she was seated in the back of Hazel's sports utility vehicle.

"There are a few places on the ranch that can be tricky to get to if you don't have four-wheel drive," Hazel answered.

"Mom, we'll need to trade in your slug-a-bug for an SUV when we move our stuff down here," Tia declared as if that was a foregone conclusion.

Considering the damage to her cute little Volkswagen that her dad had described, Kay didn't think it would be worth enough to trade in for an ATV, much less an SUV. Another vehicle was just one of the items on a long list of unnecessary expenses Kay was facing after Mark's vandalism of her home. She wasn't optimistic about being able to collect the cost of the damages from her ex-husband, regardless of whether he was convicted or not.

Kay felt her anxiety rising as she thought about all the money she would need to replace everything in her home in Tulsa. It wasn't just furniture and clothing he destroyed. Her dad had already replaced the front door and had been spending every night there for the past week going through the debris to see if there was anything salvageable before throwing everything away, so he could replace the drywall where Mark had punched holes in the walls and spray painted them with hateful messages to Kay.

Mark had even gone so far as to take a sledgehammer to the toilet and sinks and left water running from the faucets when he couldn't get to the pipes to break them. He'd unplugged the refrigerator and then shot the cooling unit on the back of it, so any food would be ruined even if someone got there in time to plug it in again before it went bad. He was, at least, smart enough not to shoot the gas range, but the sledgehammer through the glass front of the oven would still make it an expensive fix for Kay.

Kay was appalled at the damage described in the email she'd gotten from Matt when he sent her a list of questions to be prepared to answer on the stand, including her gut reaction to the destruction of her home. Kay had a hard time conceiving it all to be able to answer that question. Not that her dad or her lawyer would let her see the crime scene photos for Kay to know exactly how bad all the damage was. She hoped the fact that they were sheltering her from the atrocity of it all wouldn't backfire on them when she saw those photos for the first time in front of the judge.

"It's like an Old West town," Tia exclaimed, pulling Kay out of her head to realize that she'd zoned out in ex-husband hell, instead of paying attention to the drive to know how to get back to the ranch from town.

She wanted to kick herself for yet another time that she'd disconnected from her surroundings and gotten lost in her head. It was like she couldn't focus on real life because of being so overwhelmed by the negative aspects of her recent past. Kay hated the feeling of closing herself off in her own mental torment, and wished she knew a way to make herself stay present in the moment instead.

As she looked around at the buildings they were passing, she had to agree with Tia's assessment. The buildings were all rustic with wood façades and even wooden walkways instead of sidewalks. She could easily picture horses tied to the wooden railings while their riders were inside the businesses.

"Oh, yeah!" Hazel smiled into the rearview mirror at the girls. "We're proud of our cowboy charm in Heart's Destiny."

Kay was enchanted by the City Hall building that sat in the dead center of town. The large brick building sat in the middle of a well-manicured lawn; each side of the lot was a full city block. The traffic on the surrounding streets had the option of parking in marked spaces either facing City Hall or facing the businesses that surrounded it on the opposite side of the streets. The downtown streets were all named after breeds of cattle and horses.

"I figured we'd get some lunch first." Hazel pulled over on Longhorn Lane in front of Millie's Diner. "Heart of the Home is just over there on Appaloosa, so we can head there after we eat."

Kay turned to look in the direction Hazel had pointed, which was at the cross street they'd just passed when she parked. *At least it's close,* Kay thought as she unbuckled her seat belt and got out of the vehicle.

They made their way into the diner, where they were greeted by a loud "Howdy" from the woman behind the counter. Kay estimated her to be in her early forties, with flawless caramel skin and her jet-black hair covered in a hairnet. She wore jeans and a dark blue t-shirt with the diner's logo on the chest instead of a traditional waitress's uniform.

"Afternoon, Jane." Hazel led them to the counter. "This is my future daughter-in-law, Kay, and my new granddaughters, Tia and Maria. We're on a shopping trip to set up their house with Anthony, but I figured we needed to fuel up before we shop 'til we drop."

"Oh, how exciting," Jane gushed as she passed out menus when they took seats at the counter instead of picking a table. "When's the wedding?"

"We're not actually engaged yet," Kay answered at the same time that Hazel talked over her, saying, "The weekend after Thanksgiving."

"Oh, are you going to do it before we decorate the church for Christmas or after? I love all the poinsettias and holly we put out then, but I don't think I'd want it as the décor for my wedding."

"Before," Hazel answered, not giving Kay a chance to say that she hadn't agreed to a wedding yet, much less dates or décor choices. "Anthony wants a blue and white color scheme because royal blue is both his and Kay's favorite color."

"Oh, that will be beautiful." Jane pressed her hand over her heart. "We can still put up the white Christmas lights and make the church look like a winter wonderland for the wedding."

Kay wasn't sure how to feel as her daughters joined in the wedding planning discussion, giving Hazel all their ideas of how to make it perfect, and not giving Kay a chance to object. She didn't even get the chance to place her own order for lunch as Hazel announced that they would all have the daily special and sweet tea. Instead of fighting with her possible future mother-in-law, she sat there and ate her meatloaf, mashed potatoes, and broccoli and let her mind wander.

She imagined the wedding everyone else was discussing since it was a much happier vision in her head than where she'd gone earlier. *If I'm going to get lost in my head, I'd much rather it be daydreams of being married to Anthony than the nightmares of my real life*, she thought.

She remembered the church they'd passed on both trips to the ranch and assumed that would be where Hazel was planning the wedding. Kay pictured it with royal blue tulle wrapped around the white pillars at the church entrance and railings on the walkway and stairs leading into the old-fashioned white building. While she hadn't seen the inside of the church before, she thought it probably looked a lot like the church she attended at home in Tulsa and pictured it with similar wooden pews and pulpit, only stringed with white twinkle lights and more blue tulle.

She imagined her sister Randi and her best friend Deanna in royal blue bridesmaid dresses and carrying bouquets of blue and white wildflowers. She envisioned her daughters in matching dresses as they tossed flower petals down the aisle. Waiting at the end of the aisle, she pictured Anthony waiting for her in his Navy dress whites. His best friends standing beside him in white tuxedos with royal blue bow ties and vests.

Instead of the knee-length casual dress that she'd worn for her courthouse wedding to Mark, she envisioned herself in a long flowing white satin gown with iridescent lace accents at the bust and across the train.

Since she was imagining a dream wedding with Anthony, she pictured the full bridal experience that she'd dreamed of as a child. Her dad walking her down the aisle in a tux that matched the groomsmen. The cascading bridal bouquet of blue and white flowers accented with more of the iridescent lace, like her dream dress.

Instead of a traditional veil that covered her face, she imagined more of that iridescent lace coming down the back of her head from a silver crystal-encrusted tiara. She would wear her hair down, so it would show through the layers of lace. Her makeup would be flawless, a little more than she normally wore, so she would look glamorous instead of her normal natural look.

She was hearing the music in her head as she envisioned a family unity candle before saying their vows. She'd just gotten to saying "I

Do" in her head when everyone else standing to leave brought her back to the moment.

Kay hoped she covered her daydream daze as she told Jane how delicious the meal was and how nice it was to meet her before following Hazel and the girls out of the restaurant. They walked across Longhorn Lane toward City Hall before crossing Appaloosa Avenue to get to Heart of the Home to begin their shopping.

Hazel made a similar introduction to how she'd announced them at the diner as another woman that Kay estimated to be in her forties greeted them. Her long black hair that she wore in a braid down her back, high cheekbones under dark brown eyes, and olive complexion reminded Kay of her Native American neighbors in Oklahoma. With the name Honeysuckle Deere, Kay was certain the woman was Native American. She wanted to ask her what tribe she was descended from but figured it would be rude to ask as a first question to someone.

Kay remembered conversations with her grandmother when she was a child when she was told one of her great-grandparents was Cherokee, but she couldn't remember which one. After hearing about all of Anthony's ancestors and being reminded of her possible Native American ancestry, she made a mental note to ask her parents about her family tree, so she could pass on their family history to the girls.

Hating that her mind was wandering again, Kay shook herself out of her random mental rabbit holes to focus on the task of shopping for Anthony's household needs. Honey was extremely helpful in guiding her to the various parts of the store to pick out the towels, bedding, curtains, and rods she had on her list. She picked items in a mix of royal blue, light blue, and white, so she could accent the light blue bathroom with the darker shades and the darker blue bedroom with the lighter ones. She opted for solids and stripes because they were more masculine for Anthony than the floral or paisley patterns Hazel kept pointing out.

Hazel also kept trying to steer Kay into the section of the store that showcased the custom furniture Honey's husband, Brent built. While it was all of excellent quality and Kay could easily picture several pieces in Anthony's home, she still refused to buy anything other than what Anthony had specifically asked her to purchase or she thought they would definitely need immediately. Not even an extra bed for Kay to use in the sitting room attached to the master bedroom.

Since everyone already assumed she would be sharing Anthony's bed, she decided to just go with it, so as not to draw her daughters' attention to whether or not it was appropriate for them to be sleeping together so soon after meeting.

Kay cringed at the total she spent on Anthony's card. Since it was all things that he would need whether she was there or not, though, she tried not to feel too guilty for not using her own debit card to cover the costs.

Once she'd checked out at Heart of the Home, Hazel tried to convince her to go next door to Destiny Dresses to look at options for the wedding.

"We don't have time to do that now," Kay objected. "I still need to go to the grocery store and get back in time to wash all these towels and the bedding we need to sleep on tonight."

"You have to go to the bank and get your new cards, too," Tia reminded her.

No, I don't, Kay thought but didn't say out loud because she didn't know how to explain to her daughters how uncomfortable she was with being added to Anthony's accounts.

"Oh, the bank is just on the other side of City Hall." Hazel pointed in the direction of the bank as she pulled the keys to her SUV out of her purse and held them out to Kay. "You can go put this stuff in the car and go take care of the bank stuff while the girls and I go look at dresses."

"I don't really have to go to the bank today," Kay argued as she tried to juggle all the bags and not drop the keys that Hazel was pressing into her hand.

"Of course, you do." Hazel pointed the way and started ushering the girls in the opposite direction. "Anthony has plans for ya'll the rest of the week, so you need to go ahead and get that done while we're right here. If we're not in Destiny Dresses when you get done, we'll be over in Flora's Flowers. It's right over there, across Angus Avenue."

Unable to convince Hazel to skip the dress shop and florist, or that she didn't really need to go to the bank, Kay struggled under her heavy load as she walked back to the SUV and put her purchases in the back. She looked down the block as she shut the back hatch and could see that the Bank of Heart's Destiny was only a block away. She walked down the sidewalk in front of Millie's Diner, making note of the ice cream shop, The Creamarie, next door, and the bakery, Kara's Kakes, at the end of the block. She begrudgingly walked toward Mustang Lane in her walk toward the bank as she weighed her options once she got there.

Option one, she could walk around City Hall and not actually go to the bank. That would give Hazel the time she wanted to look at dresses and flowers for a wedding Kay wasn't sure would ever actually take place and keep Kay from feeling uncomfortable getting cards on Anthony's account.

Option two, she could actually go get the cards for the accounts Anthony had already added her to and wonder how many people in the bank would see her as a gold digger. Either option would give Hazel the time she wanted. The question for Kay was what would feel worse for her, the humiliation of strangers thinking she was after Anthony's money or Anthony being disappointed in her for not doing as he'd asked.

"It's not like I actually have to ever use the cards," Kay told herself as she crossed Mustang Lane to get to the bank. "What a bunch of strangers think doesn't matter nearly as much as Anthony's opinion."

She squared her shoulders and stood up straight as she walked into the bank. She stopped just inside the door and looked around, unsure if she should go to a teller station or ask for an officer of the bank.

"How can I help you?" asked a twenty-something blonde who walked up to Kay.

"Um, I'm not sure who I need to see," Kay stammered. "My, uh, boyfriend told me to stop by here to get cards in my name."

"You must be Kay," the woman stated as she reached out to Kay. "I'm Sierra. Follow me and we can get you all set up."

"Oh, okay," Kay stuttered as she shook Sierra's hand and followed her down a hall to an office on the right side of the building. "I guess you're the person Anthony talked to when he added me to the account."

"Oh, no," Sierra replied as she ushered Kay into her office and closed the door behind them. She took her seat behind her desk as Kay sat down in one of the chairs across from her. "I'm just an account rep. Anthony actually spoke to the bank president last week. Mr. Hunter informed all the employees to watch out for you."

Sierra turned to her computer and her hands flew over the keys. She asked for Kay's identification and had her sign a couple of signature cards. After just a few minutes, she opened a door on the side of her desk and fed card blanks into a machine that Kay assumed would print her information on them. As she was working on printing the cards, she gave Kay instructions to enter a pin number into a keypad. Kay was confused when she was asked to do it a second time, but just used the same pin thinking it was just a verification of the correct pin number. A few minutes later, Sierra handed Kay two cards and a printed page with a list of accounts that she'd been added to.

"This is your debit card that accesses both the checking and savings accounts." Sierra pointed to the first card. She pointed to the second card as she continued. "This is your credit card for purchases that exceed the debit card limits. You've been added to all of Anthony's accounts and investments. This list explains what each is and any limits or restrictions on usage. I didn't print any balances or complete account numbers, so you don't have to worry about keeping this page in a secure location, but I can tell you any balances you're curious about now."

"Oh, that's not necessary." Kay shook her head, feeling uncomfortable with discussing account balances with anyone, especially a woman she'd just met. "Anthony will be the one to keep up with those things."

As soon as she had the cards and paperwork put away in her purse, she thanked Sierra for her help and left the bank. Since she'd seen the businesses on three sides of the blocks surrounding City Hall, she opted to walk the other side to see what else was in the area on her way to find her daughters and Anthony's mother.

Across Angus Avenue from City Hall, she first saw The Caffeinated Cowpoke, which looked like the Old West version of a coffee shop. Next door to it she found a store she actually wished she had time to explore, The Book Nook. Through the large front window, she could see that the bookstore housed a mix of new and used books that she could spend hours perusing.

As she contemplated whether she could give in to the temptation of the bookstore or not, her daughters barreled out of the flower shop next door, followed closely by Hazel. All three of them had armfuls of catalogs and bridal magazines and were animatedly talking about their favorite dresses and flowers for the wedding. *Crap! How do I avoid planning a wedding I'm not sure will actually happen without crushing their dreams?*

She quietly contemplated that as they made their way back to Hazel's SUV, through their grocery shopping at H.E.B., and on the drive back to the ranch. As soon as they were unloaded at Anthony's house, Kay started washing the first of many loads of sheets, towels, and a comforter for them to use that night. The whole time feeling numb, like she was closing in on herself because she didn't know how to communicate her whirlwind of emotions to anyone else, even her daughters.

<p style="text-align:center">~~~</p>

As soon as Anthony got back to the ranch, he had to find Kay. He knew he shouldn't feel so out of sorts after only a few hours away from her, but he didn't yet know how to control his need to be with her constantly. Just being in the same room with Kay brought him peace.

He found her on a ladder in the master bedroom hanging heavy white draperies. "Beautiful," he sighed at the sight of her.

Unable to resist her being at eye level with him, he grasped each side of the ladder, effectively caging her in, so he could kiss her senseless. She wrapped her arms around his neck and returned his impassioned kiss.

"I take it you like the curtains," Kay giggled as they pulled back from the kiss.

Her arms were still draped over his shoulders. He moved his hands from the ladder to embrace her, lifting her off the ladder to hold her against him. She hooked her legs around his waist, making him wish that neither of them were wearing jeans, so he could push her up against the wall and slip inside her.

"What curtains?" Anthony brought his lips back to hers. Their mouths opened, their tongues tangled, as they thrust their hips together against the royal blue wall of their new bedroom.

Anthony was contemplating how to quickly shuck their jeans without stopping kissing Kay when he heard his name being called in a little girl voice. He broke their kiss and took a giant step back from the wall as Maria ran into the room.

"Pappaw wants you to come help him unload his truck," Maria said as Anthony lowered Kay to the floor.

"On my way, Princess," Anthony answered as he turned to Maria. "I just had to make sure your mom was ready to direct us for where to put the bedroom furniture first." *And sneak in some sweet Kay kisses while we had a minute of alone time.*

"Oh, uh, yeah," Kay stammered as she looked around the room. She pointed to the wall with a window in each corner and plenty of wall space between them for a king-sized headboard. "I'm thinking that wall for the head of the bed. What other bedroom furniture do you have?"

"Bedside tables, a dresser, and a chest of drawers." Anthony listed out the pieces of furniture as he bent down and kissed the top of Kay's head. He took a deep whiff of her strawberry scent before walking toward the door. "We'll get started with the bed while you figure out where you want the others."

They'd parked in the front of the house, so it would be easier to carry the large pieces of furniture in through the front door and straight up the stairs to the bedroom. While he was out there with his dad unloading the truck, his cousins, JJ and Justin, got home from their day at work in the Burleson Incorporated corporate office. Seeing that Anthony was moving furniture, they quickly changed clothes and offered their assistance in unloading the trucks.

With so much help, it didn't take nearly as long to get everything unloaded and in place in the house as it had taken to get it out of his apartment. Anthony ordered pizza from Pistol Pete's to feed everyone in appreciation of all their help.

"Dude, where's the beer?" Justin joked as they all gathered in the kitchen to eat. "Don't you know you're supposed to pay movers with pizza *and beer*?" He added extra emphasis on the words "and beer" as he slugged Anthony in the bicep.

"Sorry." Anthony shrugged one of his shoulders. "I didn't think to plan ahead to grab any on the way home. Just be glad Pistol Pete's delivers or you wouldn't even have gotten the pizza."

"I stocked the fridge with bottled water, milk, and juice today." Kay waved a hand in the direction of the refrigerator as she started putting slices of pizza on paper towels to pass out to everyone in the kitchen, since they hadn't unpacked his plates yet. "I didn't know what else you might want, or I would have gotten it earlier."

"Thanks, Baby." Anthony wrapped his arms around her from behind and kissed the top of her head.

Since they also hadn't unpacked glasses, Anthony started passing out bottles of water from the fridge for everyone to wash down their pizza with while they all chatted and ate. Although, when he thought about the fact that his set of dishes and glasses was only a service for four, he realized it wouldn't have mattered if they'd been unpacked because they wouldn't have had enough for everyone anyway. He hadn't needed more than four plates, bowls, glasses, or coffee cups when he was living alone in the apartment, so he hadn't thought about needing more now that he was back on the ranch and would need enough for any family that might show up around mealtime.

He figured what he had would be enough for them to use for the next morning's breakfast, but made a mental note to take Kay back to town to fully stock their kitchen the next day. That probably wouldn't be the only thing they would need to get while they were in town, since Kay had only gotten what they needed for their bedroom and bathroom. Having to spend another day working on setting up their new home meant he would have to delay his plan to leave the girls with his mom, so he could get some alone time with Kay to show her his favorite place on the ranch.

As much as he was looking forward to a naked picnic with Kay in his private oasis by the stream that fed into the southernmost pond on the property, he was glad that wouldn't be the only alone time he got with Kay during their time off. He was looking forward to having her in his bed every night while they were home.

It had only been twelve hours since he'd been naked with Kay in the shower and less than twenty-four hours since they'd been intimate for the first time, but Anthony was suffering from withdrawal-like symptoms from not being naked with her again soon enough. He felt like an addict. He was addicted to loving Kay. But if he had to have an addiction, he couldn't think of a better one than making love to Kay.

Once everyone was finished with their pizza, the crowd cleared from the kitchen. His parents and cousins went to their homes, leaving

Anthony alone with Kay, Tia, and Maria. They worked on unpacking the boxes and bags from his apartment and cleaning anything that needed it before putting everything away. When it got close to the girls' bedtime, Anthony opted to leave the unpacking and washing of the clothes, towels, and bedding he'd packed in bags for the next day.

As soon as the girls had gone to bed, Anthony left Kay in the kitchen where she was washing and putting away the last of the dishes. He went up to the master bedroom closet and unpacked both his and Kay's suitcases. He'd only planned to get their bathroom stuff, so he could run her a bubble bath, but when he dug through her suitcase to find her toiletries, he found more of her lingerie purchases from her shopping trip in New Orleans.

He loathed the fact that she'd felt guilty for sneaking away from the arena to go shopping for a sexy surprise for him. He despised the fact that his irrational worry about her, whenever she wasn't glued to his side, was the cause for her guilt-ridden feelings. He didn't know how to fix the situation either. He didn't want to be one of those over-the-top controlling guys who always had to know his woman's whereabouts, but he didn't know any other way of stopping the illogical anxiety for her safety that he felt whenever he couldn't see her, either. He just hoped he could cover the worst of his fears, so she would see him as just a little overprotective and not as an overbearing asshole.

He wanted to do something special for her to show his appreciation and love. Without any other ideas, he quickly unpacked her suitcase and filled the right side of the dresser and closet with her things. *Maybe she'll realize that I'm glad she went shopping when she sees that I put her sexy lingerie front and center in the top drawer, so it's the easiest to access.*

Since he still needed to get into his suitcase for his bathroom supplies, he figured he should unpack himself as well, filling the left side of the dresser and closet. When he didn't find any bubble bath, as he was putting their things away in the bathroom, he used her strawberry shampoo to fill the tub with bubbles before going back downstairs to find Kay.

She was drying her hands on a paper towel when he swooped her up into his arms, bridal style.

"Oh," Kay squealed in surprise. She tossed the paper towel over her shoulder in the direction of the trash bag they'd been using since he didn't move a trash can with him and smiled up at him before putting her arms around his neck. "Anthony, what are you doing?"

"Taking care of my Baby." Anthony smiled down at her and started walking toward the front of the house and the stairs up to their bedroom. "Work time is over for the day. Now it's time for you to let me cherish you."

"I've been wondering what all cherishing entails." Kay laid her head against his shoulder.

He took the stairs two at a time to rush them up to their room. As soon as he crossed the threshold, he kicked the door shut with his foot and turned around, so Kay was between him and the door. "Hit that lock, Baby," he commanded. "I don't think the girls will come looking for us, but just in case…"

"Good thinking," Kay agreed as his voice trailed off. She took one hand down from around his neck to lock the bedroom door before quickly returning it to his nape.

In a few of his long strides, they were in the bathroom, where he lowered her to stand on the rug beside the steaming, bubbly tub. He'd already found the towels that Kay had bought and washed earlier in the day and had two of the royal blue bath sheets hanging on the towel rack beside the tub and a washcloth draped over the side of the tub.

"Wow!" Kay was breathless as she looked around and saw his preparations. "Where'd you find bubble bath? I didn't think to buy any today at the store."

"I, um, didn't," Anthony sputtered sheepishly, hoping he hadn't made a mistake in using her shampoo. "I used your shampoo. But I'll put more shampoo and bubble bath on our list of stuff to get when we go shopping together tomorrow."

He pulled his phone out of his pocket and added them to his list of things he thought they still needed. Then he switched screens to a music app and picked a country channel because he knew Kay liked more songs in that genre than any other, and figured it would be more likely to play romantic music than his normal go-to classic rock channel. He sat his phone on the windowsill to provide a soundtrack for worshiping his queen.

He took his time undressing her, lightly trailing his fingers over her newly exposed skin after removing each garment. Once she was standing before him completely nude, he picked her up and gently lowered her into the tub of bubbles.

She made a soft moaning sound as she sank into the warm water that went straight to his already overly engorged cock. He quickly stripped off his own clothing and had her sit up, so he could slide into the tub behind her. He pulled her back between his legs, so her back was resting on his abdomen and chest, and her head was laying on his shoulder.

"I didn't realize just how big this tub was," Kay cooed as she relaxed back against him. "But I guess if your great-grandfather was as tall as you and all the other men in your family, then he would have installed the biggest tub he could find when he built the house, huh?"

"Yeah, I guess," Anthony grimaced, not really wanting to think about his great-grandparents, and what they might have done in the tub a few generations back. "I just thought we could both use a long hot soak after the hard work of the day."

"Mmm," Kay purred as her eyelids fluttered closed.

Anthony took that as her agreement and relished laying back and holding her in his arms as they soaked away the stress of the day. They laid there for a while, not talking, just appreciating being close to each other.

As the bubbles started disappearing and the water started to cool, Anthony reached for Kay's bodywash and the washcloth he'd draped over the side of the tub. He gently washed her front, starting at her neck and moving across her arms and torso as far as he could reach without asking her to move.

"You remember when you wanted me to tell you about my naughty thoughts over text when we first met?" Kay asked as he was running his soapy hands over her breasts.

"Yeah," Anthony replied softly, eager to hear all her dirty daydreams.

"This was actually one of the things I dreamt about," she revealed. "Not just the bath together, but the carrying me around like I'm precious to you. I never thought I'd get to live out my silly fantasies about feeling special."

"Oh, Baby," Anthony whispered softly into Kay's ear as he hugged her to him. "This is just the first of many times I plan to fulfill this fantasy. I want to make all your dreams come true. Not just the sexual fantasies, but anything else you've ever dreamed of, too. Your dream vacation, your dream job, your dream house. All you have to do is tell me what you want, and I'll make it happen."

Kay pulled out of his arms to turn around and look him eye to eye. For a long moment they stared into each other's eyes and Anthony felt like they were seeing deep into each other's souls.

"You really mean that," Kay whispered in awe. "It's not just sex, and it's not because you don't think I can achieve my dreams on my own."

Anthony wasn't sure how to reply, so he sat there for a bit collecting his thoughts and trying to figure out how to convey them to her without showing too much of his inner caveman.

"Baby, you're the strongest woman I know," he stated as he reached out to stroke his hand down her face and neck. "As much as I want you to need me, I know you don't need me to make your dreams come true. Once you set your mind to something, I know you can achieve it on your own."

"You're the only person who's ever thought that." Kay spoke so softly he could barely hear her as her eyes filled with unshed tears. She went on to tell him about how her parents had been pushing her to be independent but still trying to steer her toward a career of their choosing instead of pursuing her dream of becoming an author.

"Fuck," Anthony exclaimed. "Please tell me that you don't think I was doing the same thing by pushing you to take the GWA job. You know you can still travel with me for as long as you want and spend your time writing instead if that's what you want, right? I just suggested the job because I thought it would play best with the judge, and show how independent you are while allowing me to be with you all the time to keep you safe."

"I know." Kay moved to straddle his hips and wrapped her arms around his neck. "I don't know how I'll ever thank you enough for thinking it all through and coming up with the best solution when my dad and Matt weren't able to figure it out."

"No thanks necessary, Baby." Anthony pulled her to his chest and placed his lips on hers. He kept the kiss chaste and brief as the water was starting to dip below lukewarm, and he wanted them out of the tub and dry, so he could make love to her in their bed for the first time.

"How exactly do you want me to need you?" They pulled apart and he resumed washing her body.

"The same way I need you, Baby." Anthony grinned. "It's not a monetary thing, or a materialistic, *what-can-we-get-from-each-other* thing. And while I do feel a strong sexual need for you that I hope you reciprocate, that's not it either."

He dropped the washcloth and scratched the back of his head as he tried to fathom how to explain. "I just," he started, paused to take a deep breath, and then continued. "I need to be with you. To be in your life. To see you smile every day. To be the one who makes you laugh. To be the one who holds you when you cry. To be there for you to lean on when you're stressed. To be the wind beneath your wings when you fly. And I need you to need to be with me just as bad as I need to be with you."

"Oh, Anthony!" A single tear slipped down her cheek. She threw herself into his chest, splashing water out of the tub as they wrapped their arms around each other. As much as he wanted to hear her verbally profess her need for him, he took her passionate kisses to be her physical expression of her feelings.

Their tongues tangled; their hands roamed as their bodies joined in the frigid water. Their height difference meant that he could only get the tip in while they were kissing and Anthony didn't want to risk any deflation from the water temperature separating them, so he picked up Kay as he stood in the tub. Once he'd stepped out onto the bathmat, he grabbed the first of the bath sheets to wrap over her back. He reached for the second one but didn't really use it as he carried Kay to their bed.

Instead of drying their bodies with the towels, he spread the second one out as best he could while still joined with Kay. He crawled up onto the bed and hoped the two towels would be enough to keep them from soaking their bed as he laid her out beneath him.

It took every ounce of self-control he possessed to keep himself from pounding into her like an animal. He'd only breached her opening with his crown in the tub. The walk to the bed had only bounced her enough to take another inch of him. She was tiny all over—*Except her tits*, he thought—making her a tight fit for his cock.

He didn't want to hurt her, so he took his time working his way into her inch by agonizing inch to allow her inner muscles to adjust to his sizable invasion. When he was finally fully seated in her tight, wet heat, he held still to savor the experience of being balls-deep in the woman of his dreams.

Impatient Kay started to rock her hips, trying to get him to move. Instead, he pulled back, not quite almost out, to reposition them, so he could sit back and watch her while he fucked her. He unwound her legs from around his hips, holding them straight up in the air, and shoved a pillow under her lower back, so her pussy was elevated enough for him to fuck her while on his knees looking down at her laying across the bed.

Once in position with her feet resting on his shoulders, he gripped her hips and slowly started pushing back into her tight channel. The new angle allowed him to go all the way in without as much resistance, so he could be a little rougher without risking hurting her. He still held himself in check though, so he didn't risk crossing any lines of how hard she could handle.

"Oh, yes, oh, Anthony," Kay chanted repeatedly as he settled into a rhythm of stroking all the way in and then almost out of her dripping, wet pussy. She was so wet, and he didn't think it had anything to do with the water from their bath.

With his fingers digging into her hips, Anthony reached over with his left thumb to stroke her clit. After just a few strokes with just the right amount of pressure on her little bundle of nerves, he felt her inner walls spasm around his cock as she reached her first peak. Her repeated chants of his name got a little louder and mixed with her rapid, panting breaths as she came. Between her breathy moans of his name and the sight of her breasts bouncing in time with his rhythmic thrusting, Anthony had to slow his pace and pull back to only going halfway in to keep from coming with her.

Anthony watched her expression change from her O-face with her mouth open and her eyes closed to a satiated smile and her ocean blue eyes fluttering open. As the waves of her inner walls contracting slowed, so did her breathing as she came down from her first release.

"Play with your tits, Baby," Anthony commanded as their gazes met. "I want to watch you touch yourself while I fuck you."

He could tell by the uncertainty in her eyes that she was stepping outside of her comfort zone, but she didn't hesitate to cup her breasts. She squeezed them together as if she was presenting them to him and he wished he was flexible enough to bend down and take her perky peaks into his mouth, while still thrusting his cock deep inside her.

"Fuck, Kay, you're so hot," Anthony almost shouted as he increased the speed of his thrusting hips. "Play with your nipples, Baby. Lightly, with just one finger first."

She complied with his request, and he felt her inner walls start to quiver. She was on the edge with her second release, and he wondered how much of it was from liking being told what to do.

"Now get a little rougher, Baby," he ordered, wanting to find out how much he could get her to do before she went over again. "Flick them and pinch them, just enough to have a hint of pain turning to pleasure. Oh, yeah, Baby, just like that. Can you bend your head down far enough to lick your nipples?"

Kay's cunt started to clamp down on his cock like a vise as she complied with his instructions and Anthony was afraid she would milk him of his own orgasm as she flew over the edge a second time. She gripped him so tight, he couldn't move in or out as she screamed, "Oh, God, Anthony!"

His inability to move in her vise-like grip prevented him from getting the friction he needed to reach his own release. "Fuck, yes, come, Kay," Anthony moaned as he fondled her clit to prolong her intense orgasm while he held perfectly still inside her to enjoy the way she was clutching his cock.

When her inner walls relaxed and her panting slowed to only a mildly elevated respiration rate, Anthony started to move inside her again. He watched as she went back to playing with her rosy, tan nipples. She cupped both breasts, pushing them up high enough that she could just touch the tip of her tongue against her skin to swirl around the hardened nipples. She alternated pinching one between her thumb and first finger while licking the other, going back and forth so they both got equal treatment.

The sight was the sexiest thing Anthony had ever seen. The fact that she was doing it just because he wanted her to made him feel ten feet tall and bulletproof. He wondered if she would ever trust him enough to let him explore some of their darker fantasies, like tying her up and teasing her until she begged him to fuck her or letting him play with her tight little ass.

Just the thought of the possibility of doing those things one day was enough to push his limit of control. His fingers dug into her hips hard enough to bruise as his pace increased and his thrusts became more powerful.

"Fuck, fuck, fuck," he chanted as he lost control and rutted into her like a wild, beastly animal. He hated thinking he might be hurting her, but he couldn't make himself stop as he pounded into her. "You feel so fucking good, Kay. I can't stop. I need you too much."

"Yes, please, more, harder," Kay breathlessly begged, releasing Anthony from his self-imposed guilt at the possibility of being too rough with her already. "Fuck, Anthony, I need you just like this. Now!"

At her shout, they both exploded in ecstasy. Anthony released jet after jet of cum into her as they repetitively spoke each other's names. It was the most powerful orgasm of his life. When he felt completely drained and unable to come anymore, the waves of her muscular vaginal walls contracting around his cock milked yet another torrent from him.

Anthony collapsed onto his side on the bed, rolling Kay with him, so he could stay inside her without smothering her while they caught their breath. He held her to him, enjoying the feeling of her breasts pressed into the lowest part of his chest. She turned her head and pressed her ear against his heart. As hard as it was beating out of his chest, he hoped she wouldn't end up with a bruised ear.

"Wow," Kay breathed out the word as she caught her breath. "That's just, wow."

Anthony chuckled, agreeing with her performance assessment, but unable to put it into words.

"I mean, after last night and this morning…" Kay tilted her head to look up at him. "…I didn't think it could get better, more intense, but you just keep proving me wrong about all I ever thought I knew about my sexuality. That was like a thousand times bigger and better than I ever dreamed I could orgasm. Is it always like that for you, or is that just the tip of the iceberg and you're going to keep working me up to even bigger orgasms?"

"Oh, Baby." Anthony rolled onto his back and pulled Kay on top of him. His softening cock slid out of her as he pulled her up, so he could kiss her perfect pink lips. "It's only like this for me with you. That's the most intense I've ever come in my whole life."

She shut him up by kissing him again. As much as he loved laying there under her, stroking his hands up and down her back and ass while they kissed like they couldn't live without their tongues touching, he had to make sure he hadn't gone too far and hurt her by being so rough at the end. He gently pushed her up to a sitting position on his abs to break the kiss.

"Baby, are you sure it was all good?" Anthony tucked a lock of Kay's hair behind her ear. "I didn't, uh, hurt you? It wasn't too much when I lost control there at the end?"

"It was way better than good." Kay smiled as she weaved her fingers through his chest hair. She looked down at her hands on his chest as if she was too shy to look him in the eye as she told him how she felt. "That was actually another of my fantasies. Not so rough that it really hurt, and you definitely couldn't be that rough at first. I love how you're so gentle at first to allow me the time I need to adjust to your size. But I've also always wanted to feel like I'm so desirable that you can't control your inner beast and lose control and get a little bit rough because you want me so bad."

Anthony tipped her chin up with his finger, so she had to look into his eyes. "That was exactly what happened just then." He smiled up at her as their gazes met. "You're sure I didn't scare you even a little bit?"

"No, Anthony, you didn't hurt me, and you didn't scare me," Kay replied. "Not even a little bit."

"It's not just that I don't wanna hurt you, I don't even wanna scare you a little bit. I've seen how you get when you're scared and go off in your own world in your head to deal with the fear, and I don't ever wanna be the cause of that."

"You noticed that, huh?" Kay's breasts heaved as she took in a deep breath and sighed it out. "I was definitely not lost in my head at any point tonight. I might have been floating on an orgasm high, but I was still focused on what we were doing. When I get lost in my head, it's different. It's not only when I'm scared. I kind of get lost in my head whenever I'm thinking about anything. I'm not always trying to figure out what to do about a problem or a scary situation. Sometimes I'm just daydreaming about, um, happy things."

Her sexy secret smile told him that her "happy things" were really her dirty sexual fantasies. "Oh, yeah, I recognize those times too, Baby." Anthony returned her sexy smile. "Your facial expression changes depending on what you're thinking about, and I want to make sure that I'm only causing your sexy smile when you're lost in thought about me."

"Anthony," Kay purred his name, bringing his cock back to life. "You have to know that if I have a sexy smile on my face then I'm only thinking about you."

"Good." Anthony picked Kay up to take her back to the bathroom and clean up the mess of cum that was now all over his abs where it leaked out of her.

"What other faces do I make?" Kay inquired as he sat her down in the shower and started moving supplies from the tub surround to the shower shelves.

"You get a cute little scowl sometimes." Anthony grabbed two more towels. "But I think that's when you're trying to figure out a problem. I wish you'd talk to me about whatever is bothering you and let me help you with it, but your scowl is so cute that I'm okay with waiting for you to trust me enough to talk those things out."

After putting the towels on the bar on the outside of the shower door, he stepped into the shower and turned on the water, standing between Kay and the spray until the temperature was just right.

"It's when you look frightened that I can't stand seeing." Anthony moved, so Kay could step under the showerhead. He picked up her shampoo bottle and started washing her hair. "I wish I knew what to do to alleviate your fears."

Kay reached up and clasped his forearm since both of his hands were working up a strawberry lather in her hair. She squeezed three times, their secret code for "I love you." "Just do that if I zone out and look scared. If I'm focusing on you, I can't stay in my head with my fear."

Anthony squeezed her hair three times with both hands as a smile spread across his face. "I can definitely do that."

He rinsed the shampoo from her hair before applying her conditioner. He took his time washing her from top to bottom and enjoyed every moment of her returning the favor. He actually used the towels to dry them both off once they were both clean again. He even blow-dried her hair as he brushed out the tangles, so it wouldn't be a mess the next morning from going to bed with it wet.

When he carried her to bed, he was pleasantly surprised that the first two towels had prevented most of the water from their bath from soaking the new bedding. There was a small spot on the top of the blue and white striped comforter, but none on the powder blue sheets.

When he went back to the bathroom to put the towels in the pile of dirty clothes in the corner, he grabbed his phone from the windowsill. He turned off the music app and added *"clothes hampers"* to his shopping list. He plugged his phone into the charger on his bedside table and was about to ask Kay for her phone to plug in with his when he noticed she was already asleep. He found her purse where she'd left it in the closet by her suitcase. He hoped she wouldn't be offended by his invasion of her privacy as he searched through it for her phone.

When he pulled it and the charger out, he realized it was off again. He turned it on as he plugged it in to charge and was shocked at the number of notifications that popped up on the screen. He tried to find the smart settings to program it to go to airplane mode every morning from nine to noon, but apparently, the generic phone wasn't that smart. He added *"new phone for Kay"* to his shopping list as he settled into bed.

He rolled onto his side, so he could spoon her to drift off to sleep. Pulling her into his arms, he was hit with a sense of peace. Holding her while they slept didn't just feel right, it felt like more. Now he knew what his great-great-great-grandfather, Jonah Burleson, meant about finding his heart's destiny that was the inspiration for the town's name.

Kay is my heart's destiny, he thought as he drifted off to sleep with a smile as big as Texas on his face.

Chapter Twelve

Kay awoke the next morning with her body deliciously sore from the activities of the two previous nights. She would have stretched, but she couldn't move with Anthony wrapped around her from behind. Her head was on one of his biceps as a pillow with his forearm over her shoulder, so he could cover her breasts with his big hand. His other arm was banded around her midsection with his hand covering her mound. He also had a leg thrown over her thighs, effectively pinning her to the bed.

Kay didn't mind being pinned down though, especially when she wiggled back against him and felt his erection pressing between her butt cheeks. *I think I've discovered the benefit of being with a younger man,* she thought as her lips turned up in a grin. *He still has the sex drive and stamina of youth at the same time I'm starting to come into my sexual prime.*

Her wiggling was apparently enough to entice Anthony to thrust his hips, really rubbing his glorious erection between her cheeks. She felt naughty for enjoying the feeling as much as she was, and hoped he wasn't awake to see her head-to-toe blush from the forbidden images running through her mind.

She quit wiggling, thinking that if she laid perfectly still, he'd drift back to sleep if he'd slightly woken. After a moment, his thrusting stopped. But instead of loosening his hold in sleep as she'd hoped, so she could get up to go to the restroom, Anthony squeezed her tighter and growled, "Mine," in a sleepy, gravelly, tone.

"All yours," she replied, not sure if he was actually awake to hear her. Laying in his arms like she was, she couldn't deny her feelings for him. Somehow in the short time they'd known each other, she'd fallen completely, head over heels, in love with Anthony.

She still didn't know how her pending court appearance in Tulsa would affect their relationship, but she couldn't worry about it while he was holding her. It was like his touch was enough to calm her mind and put all the possible negative outcomes in a box labeled "Not Gonna Happen" and left her with only room in her head to envision the wonderful, romantic possibilities for their future together.

Since she didn't hear any noises in the house to indicate the girls might be up and needing breakfast, she settled back into her cozy cuddling partner, closed her eyes, and reviewed the daydreams from the day before. The wonderful visions she'd had of her dream wedding with Anthony replayed in her mind. When she got to their vows, she imagined herself pledging to "love, honor, and obey" Anthony, and Anthony pledging to "love, honor, and cherish" her.

Is that a throwback to last night? She wondered with a giggle. *Because he cherished me, and I obeyed his directions in bed? Maybe I won't complain about those vows and demand they be changed this time like I did the last time I got married. Anthony will only give me sexy commands that I won't mind obeying.*

While she wasn't completely comfortable with making any official plans until after going to court, so she would know how the ruling would affect their lives, she knew in her heart that she and Anthony would eventually get married.

Before she could drift back into her daydream wedding, Kay heard the bedroom door rattle. Apparently, the girls were up and trying to get into the room where she was laying in Anthony's arms. The room where they were both naked and intertwined. Still unable to extricate herself from Anthony's embrace, Kay laid there and listened to her daughters' conversation through the door.

"Why is their door locked?" Maria questioned.

"Because grown-ups need privacy," Tia answered.

"But we have to go wake them up, so we can go with Pappaw to learn how to be ranch hands," Maria whined.

"Yeah, but we have to have breakfast before we go with Pappaw, so we can go fix some cereal first and give them time to finish their grown-up stuff while we're eating," Tia replied.

"What grown-up stuff are they doing?" Maria inquired.

"Nothing we need to see," Tia explained. "Come on, we'll knock on their door if they aren't up yet when we get done eating."

"I hope they're making us some little brothers like Travis and Trent," Maria wished as their voices started fading like they were walking away from the bedroom door.

Their quiet walking down the hall didn't last long and then it sounded like a stampede as the girls ran down the stairs. Kay let out the breath she hadn't realized she'd been holding, feeling relieved that she had a few minutes to get up and dressed before seeing her daughters.

Anthony chuckled behind her, and she found herself giggling with him even though she didn't have a clue what they were laughing about.

"I guess it's a good thing we remembered to lock the door last night," he mumbled in a sleep-roughened voice that made her nipples hard and her core tingle.

"Yep, and even better that they didn't realize they could get into this room from the sitting room because I don't think we locked it last night," Kay giggled as she rolled to face him.

"Nope, completely forgot that one," Anthony admitted as they both started laughing again.

"I'll be sure to lock the door from the hall to the sitting room from now on," he declared as their laughter died down. "Speaking of the sitting room, what do you think we should put in there?"

"No clue," Kay replied. "Your mom said it was a nursery and a home office before, but I don't think we'll need either of those. With already having the library downstairs, we don't need it for that either."

"What do you think about a music room? I put my guitars and amps in the den yesterday, but if I set up the television in there, I won't be able to play when the girls want to watch TV."

"That sounds like a great idea for it, then." Kay thought she would want a comfy couch or something in there, too, so she could sit and listen to him play his guitars.

"Any chance you'll be moving your organ down here?" Anthony sat up, his face lighting up with the possibilities he was thinking of for the music room. "We can put it in there, too, and maybe write some music together."

Kay sat up, pulling the sheet around her, as if it would shield her from the vulnerability she was feeling at the reminder of the damage her ex-husband had done. "No, Dad said it was damaged beyond repair." Kay shook her head as she tried to hold back the tears filling her eyes.

Anthony pulled her into his arms and dropped a kiss on the top of her head. "I'm sorry, Baby," he whispered as he rocked her against his chest. "I got all excited about our shared love of music and didn't even think before I said that. I know it won't be the same or have the same sentimentality as your old one, but we can go into San Antonio this week to let you pick out a new one if you want."

Kay shook her head into his chest and almost laughed through her tears as his chest hair tickled her nose. "No." She pulled back and looked up into his eyes. "I don't want another organ. I only had that one because my mom upgraded hers when she moved last month. She's the church organist and wanted to groom either me or one of the girls to take over for her one day. I actually preferred playing classical music on the piano when I was a kid and rocking an electronic keyboard as a teenager, but never really liked playing hymns on the organ."

"Well, then, we'll look at pianos and electronic keyboards instead." Anthony gave her a quick kiss before jumping out of bed. He walked over to the dresser where he opened a drawer and pulled out a pair of navy-blue boxer briefs. As he slipped them on, he pointed to the right side of the dresser. "I unpacked your suitcases last night and put all your clothes in the drawers on the right. I hung your dresses that were on hangers in the closet, but we need more hangers if you want to hang up any of the shirts or jeans that you had folded in your bag."

Kay was shocked that he'd done that for her, and she hadn't noticed. As he bent to get into a lower drawer on his side and pulled out a t-shirt, Kay realized she was being ridiculous feeling self-conscious about being naked in front of him. She dropped the sheet and went to explore the dresser drawers to find her own clothing.

"Damn, I wish we didn't have to rush to get dressed this morning," Anthony groaned as he looked her over from head to toe and back again. "It should be a crime to cover up all your sexiness."

"Whatever!" Kay rolled her eyes at him as she pulled open the top drawer on her side of the dresser. Instead of the sensible white cotton bras and panties she expected to find, it was filled with the more colorful and less practical thongs and lacy lingerie she'd bought in New Orleans. The blue satin nightie she'd worn Sunday night and hand-washed and blow-dried Monday morning was folded right on top.

Why would he have put this stuff where the girls could easily find it?

"I wanted it front and center, so you'd know how much I appreciate you going shopping for special things to wear for me." Anthony pointed at the contents of her drawer as he pulled a pair of jeans out of his bottom drawer.

Kay wasn't sure if he'd read her mind to answer her unspoken question, or if she'd slipped and actually vocalized the question she believed she'd only thought in her head. Regardless of whether she'd actually spoken the question or not, his answer relieved her of any residual guilt she felt about not telling him when she left the arena.

"I like your reasoning." She grinned up at him. "But with girls who snoop, this kind of stuff has to be hidden in the back of drawers and under hideous clothing they won't want to borrow."

"Okay," Anthony chuckled as he finished getting dressed. "I'll add *hideous clothes to hide the good stuff under* to my shopping list." He grabbed his phone from the bedside table and was typing with his thumbs as he went into the ensuite restroom.

Kay continued going through her drawers to find her normal daily underwear and a navy t-shirt and jeans to match Anthony's attire for the day. She wasn't sure what the plan was for the day to know if she should put on sneakers or boots, so she just left her socks on the top of the dresser until she found out from Anthony which she should put on over them.

He was stepping out of the toilet closet as she walked into the bathroom, and she was grateful for the door when she took her turn in there. Even though she knew she wanted to marry him, they were still too new for her to be able to pee without the privacy of that door between them.

When she was done with her business in the toilet closet, she washed her hands and brushed her teeth in the sink beside Anthony. He finished brushing his teeth and started shaving while she brushed her hair and pulled it up into a ponytail.

"What's the plan for today?" Kay shifted on her bare feet. "I wasn't sure if I should put on sneakers or boots."

"Whatever you're most comfortable wearing, Baby." Anthony smiled as he ran his electric razor over his sexy stubble. "I figured we'd spend the morning going through the house and figuring out what else we need and then head to town to shop. I figured I'd show you around town, if Mom didn't already show you everywhere yesterday. And then we could come home and work on setting up the house, maybe get started stripping off the downstairs wallpaper. That's probably going to take more time than we have this week, especially since I want to take you on a long ride around the ranch before we have to go back to work. But we can at least get started on getting the walls ready to paint next time we're home."

"Home, huh?" Kay mused as she put her brush back in the top drawer between the sinks. Well, her dad had told her to find a place to live in Texas with room for her parents to visit. While there wasn't room in this house for them to sleep, Kay's future in-laws had plenty of spare bedrooms, so she figured making Anthony's house into her new home would meet her parents' criteria while making her happy because she would be with Anthony. *Hopefully, that judge in Tulsa will agree.*

"Baby," Anthony drawled out as he put his razor down on the counter and took Kay's hand. He squeezed three times and she realized that she must have let her apprehension about the court interfering with their making his house their home show in her expression. "This is just one of the places we'll call home. We'll work on fixing it up the way we want now, so we'll be free to do the same with your home in Tulsa next month. After the judge issues the order of protection, so it's safe for us to take the girls to visit your family, we'll want our own home there, too, so we can alternate where we go on our days off."

"Is that really what you want to do?" Kay returned his three squeezes. "You don't want to just move here full time?"

"Baby," he moaned as he picked her up with both hands on her butt and brought their foreheads together. Instinctively, Kay's arms went around his neck and her legs went around his waist, so she could cling to him like a monkey in a tree. "I just want to be with you, wherever you want to live. If you just want one house in Tulsa, we'll scrap all the plans for this one and figure out how to add another bathroom to your house in Tulsa. Or if it's too hard for you to go back there because of the break-in, we'll buy another house in Tulsa that has all the bathrooms we need. Or if you want ten houses in ten different cities, we'll house hunt as we travel for work. Home to me isn't a specific house. You're my home. So, as long as I'm with you, I'm home."

"How can you say that with a family legacy like the Burleson Ranch?" Kay was incredulous at his definition of home.

"The same way my great-great-great-grandpa Jonah could decide to settle down here where he had no family or friends because he knew the first time he saw my great-great-great-grandma Emma that she was his heart's destiny," he replied as he slid one hand up her back to cup her neck and his other hand covered her whole rear end. "You're my heart's destiny, Kay. You're my home, even if you don't want to live in the town my family named after their love."

Kay was speechless at his declaration. Not that it would have mattered if she'd tried to speak, because he would have silenced her when he crushed his lips to hers. All of Kay's worries—about court, where she would be allowed to live after the judge's ruling, the issues with her ex, the destruction of her home in Tulsa, the guilt for feeling like a burden to Anthony with all her baggage and unnecessary expenses, and even her torn feelings about the expectations of others—disappeared from her mind as their tongues tangled.

It was more than just a passionate kiss. It wasn't just about their explosive sexual chemistry. It was a physical representation of their hearts' promise to one another—to always be home together. No matter what the future held, or what anyone else wanted them to do, they would get through it together. She knew in that kiss that she was ready to tell him "yes" the next time he proposed. *But only if he actually does it right and gets down on one knee with a ring!*

She didn't get a chance to tell him that, though, because their kiss was interrupted by the girls banging on the bedroom door.

"Wake up!" Maria shouted through the door.

<p style="text-align:center">~~~</p>

Anthony reluctantly pulled back from kissing Kay and slowly slid her down his body until her feet were on the floor. He made sure she wasn't as wobbly on her feet as he felt from the intensity of their kiss before releasing her from his grasp, so they could exit the bathroom.

"I guess it's a good thing I didn't put on makeup this morning," Kay giggled as they stepped back into their bedroom. "We'd have both needed to wash it off before the girls saw the mess we'd have just made of it."

Anthony chuckled at her silliness, but he wasn't sure he would have actually felt embarrassed enough to wash off her smeared lipstick from his mouth had she been wearing any.

He strode to the door and unlocked it as Kay grabbed her sneakers out of the closet. He barely got the lock turned before the door opened, and Maria bounded in past him to jump on the bed. He saw Kay grab a pair of socks from the top of the dresser before sitting down on the bed beside Maria, presumably to put on her shoes and socks.

Realizing he hadn't put on his own yet, he grabbed his own socks from the dresser drawer and his sneakers from the closet to join them on the bed.

"Pappaw said we get to meet the ranch foreman today and they would teach us all about how to run the ranch." Maria was already dressed for ranch work in her boots and jeans. Her pink t-shirt even had a picture of a horse on the front. Anthony wondered if that was why she'd chosen it for the day.

"That sounds like fun," Kay grinned at her daughter as she tied her first shoe.

Not really, Anthony thought but didn't say because he didn't want to burst Maria's excited bubble.

"Did he tell you what he was going to show you first?" Anthony asked instead.

"We have to learn more about riding the horses first," Tia stated as she walked into the room, also already dressed for ranch work in boots, jeans, and a red western shirt like his sisters would have worn for riding in the rodeo. "He said we can't herd the cattle until we learn how to communicate with the horses where to herd them to."

"I think I'd rather milk a cow than herd a whole bunch of them to a different pasture," Maria grumbled.

Oh shit, I hope she doesn't think this is a dairy farm!

"We don't milk our cows." Anthony hoped he wasn't about to traumatize the girls. "You do know the difference between a cattle ranch and a dairy farm, right?"

"Yeah, a ranch is bigger than a farm," Maria stated matter-of-factly. "But we still get milk from cows, so I want Pappaw to teach me to milk them first."

"I don't think I want Pappaw to show me the cows anymore," Tia whispered, sounding nervous. He looked up from tying his shoes to see that she looked a little paler than normal. "I think I might have to give up hamburgers if I meet the cows they come from."

"Are vegetarians allowed to live on a cattle ranch?" Kay tried to hide her ornery smile behind her hand.

"I'm not sure," Anthony chuckled. "Maybe we can have Pop teach Tia how to do a cost breakdown and feasibility study for converting the ranch over from beef production to a dairy? If she can do the math to make it look more profitable, maybe we won't have to move again today."

"We don't have to become vegetarians as long as I don't meet the beef before it's on my plate," Tia announced. "But I'd still like to learn the math for ranching, just maybe not the herding cattle so much."

"Don't worry, Princess." Anthony tried to offer Tia a reassuring smile. "You're not the first girl on the ranch with similar objections. My sisters didn't want to herd the cattle either for the same reason you don't. Now that I think back, maybe I should have used that same argument, since they got out of it, and I didn't."

"He made you herd the cattle when you didn't want to?" Maria looked irritated for his younger self.

"It wasn't a regular chore for me, but I had to go on one cattle drive," Anthony replied with a grin at her. "He wanted all of us to know as much as we could learn about the family business, so we'd appreciate all the work that our employees do and know how to run everything when it's time for us to take over the company."

"How are you going to take over the company if you don't already work there?" Tia looked confused. "Is that why he wants to teach us, so we can take over when he retires since you don't work there now?"

"Actually, I do work for Burleson Incorporated now." Anthony made a mental note to check out the corporate charter to find out about the possibility of leaving shares in the company to stepchildren. "But since my only responsibility to the company is to attend the quarterly board meetings, I haven't had to do much for them since we met."

Anthony reached over and took Kay's hand as he referenced the night they met, so he could give her their silent "I love you" squeezes while talking to the girls. She smiled up at him and returned the gesture.

"So, you're a member of the board of directors?" Tia's expression turned inquisitive. "Don't you have to research the options you're given to vote on at those meetings to decide the direction of the company?"

Yeah, that's why I'm thinking I need to go to school for a few business classes, he thought while feeling less qualified to do his job as a board member than the intellectually gifted Tia.

"Actually, that's something you might be able to help me with," Anthony stated. "I've just been on the board since my Pappaw Jerry passed away a couple years ago. Since I was in the Navy then, my cousins who work at Burleson full time started putting together packets of information on what was going on, so those of us who aren't there all the time could understand what we were voting on. I've been thinking that since I have a lot more free time in my job now, I'd like to take some online business classes, so I can learn how to be a better board member. Think you can help me find the right ones to take?"

"Oh, I can definitely help you do that!" Tia's excitement lit up her face. "Maybe we can take some of the same classes, so my tutors don't have to try to learn material they've never studied before to help me if something is confusing. Mrs. Ivy said she has a degree in math, but she was confused by my integral calculus assignment the other day, so I'm not sure her degree covers more than teaching the normal high school math classes."

While Anthony didn't feel qualified to help Tia with integral calculus any more than it sounded like the tutors could, he did like the idea of doing some business classes online that they could learn together. Apparently, Kay did, too, since she squeezed his hand again at the suggestion. *"I love you,"* he silently clutched back.

Wanting to not only help her with classes they could take together, but also to find a way to help her in the classes she was already taking, he tried to think of who in his family might be best to help Tia with her complex math classes. His brother Jake was undoubtedly the smartest of them and would be her best option, but since he was in the Navy and stationed in Washington, D.C., he couldn't be much help at the moment. So, he cycled through the degrees the rest of his siblings and cousins had earned to see if any of them might have taken a comparable class. A lightbulb went on in his head when he realized who would be best to tutor Tia.

"I would love to take some business classes with you." Anthony's lips curved up into a wide grin. "And I know just the person to help you with your calculus assignments. You remember my cousin Justin?"

"Yeah, he helped move furniture yesterday," Tia nodded.

"His degree is in chemical engineering and that requires a lot of complex math," Anthony nodded along with her. "We just have to make sure that he doesn't try to recruit you to go to work for him in R & D instead of finishing school."

"Research and development? What's he working on that you think he would want me to help with now with no degree?" He just thought she looked excited a moment ago. Apparently, research and development sounded like more fun than online business classes.

"Alternative energy sources," Anthony replied. "JJ and Justin have been working to convert Burleson Oil into Burleson Energy. Instead of looking at new drilling sites for oil, JJ's already turned some of our dried up well sites into wind farms. And Justin has R & D working on improving the battery life for electric cars and finding ways to use things like used cooking oil and cow manure instead of crude oil to make a form of fuel that will work in a normal car, so individuals don't have to spend a fortune to convert their vehicle engines over to run on alternative fuels."

"Won't cow manure make the car stink?" Maria wrinkled up her nose in disgust.

Kay burst out laughing and tried to cover it with her free hand. Anthony wasn't sure what Kay thought was so funny, but he couldn't stop himself from chuckling with her. Laughter was contagious, apparently, because the girls were both giggling, too.

"Saw-sorry," Kay stuttered, waving her hand around like she could shoo the laughter away. "I just got the craziest image of gas stations being replaced by manure trucks and …" She trailed off as she burst out laughing again. "…and, and…" She sucked in a breath before continuing. "…wo-wondered how small the shovel had to be to put the manure in the gas tank. Or if it would just lead to a lot of manure accidents like in *Back to the Future*."

Anthony couldn't contain his own laughter, not from her mental imagery but from the delight he felt at seeing Kay so giddy. He loved seeing her happy and laughing and vowed to do anything in his power to keep her bubbling with bliss for the rest of their lives.

~~~

After their crazy conversation with the girls, Kay found herself being dragged next door to Anthony's parents' house before she even had a chance to put on a pot of coffee or eat a bite of breakfast. Lucky for her, Hazel's kitchen was a hive of activity with Hazel, Susan, and Rosa—who Kay learned was the wife of the ranch manager and one of Hazel's best friends—all working diligently to prepare the days meals for all the ranch hands and anyone else who happened to be there and in need of breakfast. Anthony made their plates as she poured them each a cup of coffee, so they could sit at the table and talk to Bob about what he wanted to teach the girls.

Apparently, Bob's schedule was a mix of days on the ranch coordinating with the ranch foreman about cattle movements and horse training, and days in the office dealing with the actual business of beef production and whatever else he did with the other divisions of Burleson Incorporated. He'd taken off on Monday to help Anthony move, but he was back to work on the ranch Tuesday and wanted to spend at least part of his time working with the girls on their riding skills.
~~~

"What are you going to do while we're with Pappaw all day?" Maria inquired between bites of her second breakfast of the day.

Kay couldn't tell if Maria was asking her or Anthony, so she looked to him before answering. He just shrugged at her like he didn't know what the plan was after their earlier discussion in the bathroom had been derailed. He was willing to give up his home and family to move to Tulsa with her full time, if that was what she wanted. But looking into his soulful brown eyes right then, she knew that wasn't the path she desired for their lives.

"Well, Anthony and I have to go through the house and figure out what all we need to do to make it our home," Kay replied as she smiled at him. "You said we'd be planning and making lists this morning and going to town to start buying supplies this afternoon, right, Anthony?"

"Yeah, Baby!" Anthony placed his hand on her thigh since she had her coffee cup in one hand and her fork in the other, so he couldn't hold her hand. He squeezed it three times and she smiled at him since she couldn't return his silent "I love you" right then. "But I wasn't sure if that was the plan you wanted to go with, since it was only the first option for the day, and we didn't get a chance to discuss any others."

"Well, when you give me the best ideas first, there's not much need to waste time discussing the other options." Kay smiled, hoping he understood her meaning.

She wasn't talking about the actual plans for what they would do that day. She was talking about planning for their future, where they would have homes near both their families. She wanted to be optimistic and plan their future without thinking about the obstacles stuffed in the "Not Gonna Happen" box in her mind. She metaphorically duct taped that box shut, so those issues couldn't come out and get in the way of her happily ever after with Anthony.

As they looked into each other's eyes, Kay tried to project her message clearly to him without words. She wasn't one-hundred percent certain that he comprehended everything she was trying to impart, but she thought the glint in his eye shined with recognition of her hidden meaning when his lips turned up in a wide smile.

Anthony lifted his hand from her thigh and reached up to cup her nape, pulling her to him as he leaned toward her. He brushed his lips across hers in a very chaste kiss compared to their fervent kisses when they were alone, but it was still the first time he'd kissed her lips in front of her daughters and enough to make them both comment.

"Mommy and Anthony, sitting in a tree, K. I. S. S. I. N. G.," Maria merrily sang.

"I know the saying is supposed to be, *'get a room,'* when people are kissing in public, but since ya'll already have a room next door, I'm changing it to, *'go to your room,'* while we're here," Tia snickered.

"We have a whole house full of rooms." Anthony wagged his eyebrows suggestively as they pulled back from the kiss. "What do you say we leave the rugrats with their grandparents while we go kiss in every single one while planning how we want to decorate them?"

"That sounds like an excellent idea," Kay agreed.

"Anthony, I need a word with you before you head out." Bob stood up and motioned for Anthony to follow him.

"Sure, Pop," Anthony replied as he too stood up from the table. He bent to kiss Kay on the top of her head and said, "be right back, Baby," before following his father out of the room.

Kay cleared their dishes from the table, rinsing them off and putting them in the dishwasher, while waiting for Anthony to return.

"You don't have to do that," Hazel admonished when Kay went back for Bob's dishes and the girls milk cups.

"It's no trouble," Kay replied, suddenly feeling guilty for not offering to help with the meal prep the other ladies were all focused on. "I'd stay and help you with the rest of the meals you're making, but…"

"Nonsense," Hazel cut Kay off. Hazel waved her hands around like she was shooing flies, or at least Kay, out of her kitchen. "You're gonna be way too busy redecorating the house this week to have time to visit with us while we're cooking."

"I think she'll be doing a little more than redecorating," Rosa giggled and winked at Kay. "Unless redecorating is the new word you kids have started using for canoodling."

"What's canoodling?" Tia looked quizzically at Rosa. "I don't think that word is in the dictionary Grandpa Lee gave me."

"Oops, sorry." Rosa made a face as the older ladies all chuckled. "We're gonna have to get used to having little ears around again."

Leah Mae Wright

"What's so funny?" Anthony queried as he and Bob walked back into the room.

"Is it a bad word that we're not old enough to say yet?" Tia inquired at the same time.

Kay couldn't control her own giggles then at the look of horror on Tia's face from thinking she'd said a bad word.

"No, sweetie." Susan was apparently the only one of the ladies who could control her laughter for a few seconds to get a couple of words out.

"What word?" Bob's deadpan delivery of the question renewed the round of giggles in the kitchen.

"Canoodling," Tia answered when none of the adult ladies in the room could talk over their uncontrollable hilarity. "Mrs. Rosa asked if *redecorating* was the word now being used to replace the word *canoodling,* and I didn't know the definition since *canoodling* isn't in my dictionary."

Kay noticed Bob starting to blush and that just made the situation funnier to her.

"No, Princess," Anthony chuckled. "Canoodling isn't a bad word. It just means kissing. It's the word old people use to describe young people making out."

"Is it kissing or making out? Because making out is more than just kissing like ya'll were just doing at the table," Tia pointed out, obviously confused by Anthony's attempt at an explanation. "Making out means kissing with tongues and over the clothes touching."

Anthony's mouth opened and closed like he didn't know how to reply for a moment before he declared, "Just kissing, with no tongues. You don't need to know about making out or anything more until you're at least thirty."

I guess he was right in saying he'd treat them like his own, Kay thought. *That's definitely a Dad response.*

The room erupted in another round of laughter.

"Does that mean you can't do more than kiss Mommy until you turn thirty?" Maria put her hands on her hips like she was about to argue with him.

Kay sat back down at the table, enjoying the show, and wondering how Anthony was going to dig himself out of the hole he found himself in with the girls.

"I'm never going to get a little brother if I have to wait five more years for you to be old enough to make out with Mommy and make me one," Maria huffed.

Anthony gaped back and forth between Maria, Tia, and Kay. Kay almost felt sorry for him because the poor guy looked lost. She wondered if he understood what he was getting into when he'd said he would love them as if they were his own. This was just one of the many ways her girls would test his mettle as a parent as their relationship progressed. Kay couldn't wait to see how he passed their tests.

After floundering a moment longer, Anthony finally replied. "We don't have to wait five years to adopt you a little brother." Anthony smirked as he ruffled Maria's hair.

"Awesome!" Maria squealed as she threw her arms around Anthony's waist to show her gratitude with a hug.

"Welcome to parenthood," Kay chortled as Anthony's dark chocolate eyes met hers. Time seemed to pause for them to recognize the fact that they were really becoming a family with broad smiles and mouthed words of love from across the room. They didn't have to be touching for Kay to feel their connection. She saw it in his eyes from ten feet away.

When Anthony looked down at Maria as she released him from her bear hug, Kay realized that the world hadn't really stopped while she was lost in Anthony's gaze. The giggles had died down and conversations resumed. She looked around the room and appreciated the love and acceptance of everyone around her. She took a moment to say a silent prayer of thanks for being blessed with her expanding circle of friends and family.

There was a knock at the back door just before an older, Hispanic cowboy let himself in and greeted Rosa with a kiss on the cheek. Kay and the girls were introduced to Carlos Diaz, Rosa's husband, and the Burlesons' ranch manager.

Carlos and Bob would be holding the lead ropes on the horses while the girls got comfortable in their saddles and learned how to command the horses to walk in the direction the girls wanted them to go in the corral closest to the stables.

After being reassured that her daughters would be well supervised for the day, Kay and Anthony walked back to their new home.

Our house, Kay thought, feeling a sense of peace as they walked in the front door. No matter what uncertainty lay ahead of them, she knew she was exactly where she was supposed to be. With Anthony. No matter what the future challenged them with, they would get through it together.

"What room do you want to start with?" Anthony questioned as they stood in the entryway.

She turned to the right and looked at the black leather sofa with built-in recliners on both ends that Anthony had moved from his apartment. It, along with the two side tables and entertainment center that were also in the room, were entirely too modern for Kay's taste. The glossy black surfaces clashed with the classic dark wood on the lower half of the walls and the floor.

"Is this supposed to be a formal living room?" Kay wandered across the room, thinking his furniture looked more like it belonged in a man cave or game room instead of the formal living room of a home.

"Yeah, my stuff's not really formal living room furniture, is it?" Anthony scratched the back of his head as he looked around the room. "Maybe we can move all this to the den? Turn it into a game room for the girls?"

It wasn't going to clash any less with the woodwork in the den, but Kay agreed that it would be better suited to turning into a game room than the formal front room of the house. "Excellent idea. Now what do you think you want to put in here?"

"First we have to take down this tacky gold wallpaper," Anthony cringed as he ran his hand over the wall. "I like all the wainscoting, but the walls above it need to be painted. I don't know what color, but I think it needs to be a color that will brighten up the room."

"Agreed. I'm thinking of a seating area over here. Sofa, end tables, coffee table, and a couple of chairs, but leaving the area in front of this window open for putting up a Christmas tree. We can decide on the wall color after we pick out the furniture, so we can coordinate it with the upholstery. Same with curtains."

"Sounds good." Anthony nodded in agreement, pulled out his phone, and started typing in his list. "Sofa, end tables, coffee table, chairs. What about lamps or artwork? And do we want a TV in here or just in the game room? Might be nice if we had a couple more televisions, maybe in the bedrooms, so we're able to watch TV while they play video games or whatever."

"Yeah, maybe a TV in each bedroom, so they don't fight over the one in the game room when they want to watch different shows," Kay conceded, trying not to let herself feel guilty for Anthony spending more money on her daughters when they didn't necessarily need their own televisions. "But I don't think we need a TV in here. This room is more for socializing with company, not lounging around watching television. Maybe some extra chairs in the corners in case more than a couple of people come to visit."

"Perfect." Anthony tucked his phone in his pocket and bent down to kiss Kay. He still kept it chaste since there were no curtains covering the windows yet and anyone walking by could see them.

They spent the next hour going from room to room discussing what they wanted for the formal dining room, game room, and music room. They opted to leave the library as it was for the time being, and let the girls pick the paint color and accessories for the game room. They also went over the things they hadn't thought about yet for the kitchen and their bedroom, continuously adding to Anthony's list on his phone and kissing when they completed their planning in each room.

By the time they finished their planning in their bedroom, Kay was more than ready for their kissing to go beyond the chaste pecks in the other rooms. When Anthony started to bend down to kiss her, she held up a finger to tell him to hold that thought for a moment. She locked the doors, both the main one leading into the master bedroom and the one leading into the sitting room from the hall, before returning to his side.

"Ms. Lee, why would you lock the bedroom doors in the middle of the day?" Anthony swung her up into his arms and carried her to the bed.

"I figured we should practice canoodling." Kay grinned before putting her arms around his neck and pressing her lips to his.

Anthony instantly took over and deepened the kiss as he tenderly laid her out diagonally across the bed. Their tongues twined and their hands roamed as he pinned her to the bed with his body.

Kay loved the feel of Anthony's hair between her fingers as she massaged his scalp with her right hand. Her left hand trailed across the hard planes of muscle in his shoulder and upper back as she tried to pull him even closer to her, as if their bodies could merge into one.

Anthony rolled to lay on his side beside Kay as they pulled back from the kiss to take a breath. "Are you trying to corrupt me, Ms. Lee? Tempting me into canoodling before I'm old enough?" He trailed a single fingertip down Kay's neck, across her collarbone, and down to swirl patterns on her breasts.

"Oh, no, Mr. Burleson." Kay shook her head as she let her fingers play across his perfect pecs. "You are definitely old enough to canoodle. In fact, I think it's you who's corrupting me into doing more than just a little canoodling."

"More than canoodling?" Anthony raised one eyebrow with the question. "Does that mean I get to touch you under your clothes too?"

"I don't know, Sir," Kay murmured in a breathy tone, hoping he picked up on her role-play idea without her having to actually tell him the fantasy. "You're the one in charge of teaching me how to do more than canoodling."

"Remember your lessons, Ms. Lee." Anthony looked down at her with a stern expression. "You're to address me as Professor Burleson when I'm instructing you in kinky sex ed."

"Yes, Professor Burleson," Kay cooed in breathless anticipation.

Anthony lifted Kay's arms above her head, then pushed her up the bed until she could reach the corner post of the headboard.

"Lace your fingers around the bedpost, Ms. Lee," he instructed. She complied immediately. "You're to lie completely still while I teach you to be patient and enjoy the anticipation of what's to come. If you let go of the bed or move in a manner meant to entice me into going faster or touching you differently, I will stop and the lesson will be over for today, leaving you aching with the need to come. But if you're a very good girl and follow my every instruction, I'll reward you with the orgasm you so desperately want now. Do you understand, Ms. Lee?"

"Yes, Professor Burleson." Kay was hardly able to contain her exhilaration as she eagerly awaited his touch.

Anthony pushed her t-shirt up around her shoulders, exposing her white cotton sports bra. Instead of a traditional sports bra that went on as one piece over the head, Kay had to wear specialized sports bras that had almost a dozen hooks up the center front to get them on over her abundant breasts. She almost regretted the practical undergarment, but the look on Anthony's face as he methodically unfastened the upper clasps to expose her breasts gave her reason to think he liked it. He left the last two clasps hooked, pushing the material down under her breasts to effectively turn her supportive sports bra into a push-up bustier.

"Beautiful," he whispered as he started lightly trailing his fingertips over her breasts, across the upper curve of her cleavage, down the sides, and along the bottom, where the material of her bra lifted them up, back up the center where she longed to feel his cock again. He avoided the areola and nipples, but that didn't stop her nipples from turning painfully hard in response to his touch.

"It's so tempting to fuck your perfect tits," he growled as he slowly trailed his hands down her abdomen. "But if I let my cock have his way, we won't get anything else done today, so that will have to wait for later."

He pulled back and unfastened her jeans, sliding them and her panties down to her mid-thigh. She wanted him to pull them completely off, so she could open her legs for him. But she had to obey the rules of his dirty lesson and stay perfectly still while he played with her.

"I should have shaved you in the shower last night," he groaned as he stroked a single finger through her folds. "Would you like me to do that for you, Baby?"

"Yes, Professor Burleson." Kay felt herself gush with wetness at the wicked image in her head of him running a razor over her mound. Him seated on the floor of the shower while she sat spread eagle on the bench in front of him.

"You're so wet, Ms. Lee," he whispered as he dipped a finger into her slit, stroking slowly in and out, but not coming close to the sensitive spots she really wanted him to touch. "I love how wet you get for me."

"It's only for you," Kay moaned breathily as she struggled not to wiggle her hips. Being a good girl and laying still while he touched her was the sweetest form of erotic torture. She both loved the feeling of anticipation and hated being forced to patiently wait for him to do more.

Her hips involuntarily twitched as he pulled his finger out of her. He brought his hand up to his face, sniffing her arousal on his finger.

"I love the way you smell, the way you taste," he uttered, and Kay assumed he was about to lick her juices off his finger. "Have you ever tasted yourself?"

"No, Professor Burleson." Kay shook her head slightly, unable to take her eyes off his finger still in front of his mouth.

"Mmm, then you're in for a treat, Ms. Lee." Anthony brushed his finger over her lips. "Open your mouth and suck your sweetness from my finger."

Kay obeyed his command and was shocked at the tangy sweet taste as she swirled her tongue around his digit before sucking him in until her lips met his knuckles. He sucked in a breath, and she thought she felt his cock twitch against her thigh, but wasn't sure because of the layers of denim between them.

"Such a naughty girl, trying to tempt me with your mouth." Anthony pulled his finger from her.

"No, Professor Burleson," Kay pleaded. "I wasn't being naughty. I was trying to follow your instructions."

He raised a brow at her as if questioning her honest intentions.

"Please don't stop our lessons, Professor Burleson," Kay begged. "I'm trying really hard to be a good girl for you."

"You are a very good girl, Kay," he agreed with a slight smile. "Let's see if you can get your reward from just my mouth on your tantalizing titties."

He slid down the bed and rolled back on top of her, burying his face between her breasts. He licked and sucked all around her breasts, still avoiding her rock-hard nipples. Kay fought the urge to release her hold on the bedpost, so she could grip his hair and guide his mouth to her needy nipples. It was a sensual struggle that may have lasted only minutes, but felt like years to Kay.

When he finally trailed his tongue across first one nipple then the other, Kay felt her pussy tingle and start to clamp down on nothing but air. When he suckled them in turn, she felt the first waves of an impending orgasm. She chanted his name as she felt herself getting closer and closer to the edge.

"Yes, Kay, always say my name when you come," Anthony commanded as he switched breasts.

The slight pinch of pain as he bit down lightly on her nipple sent Kay careening over the edge. She shattered from the inside out, coming harder than she could have ever imagined possible from breast stimulation alone. He laved her with his tongue to ease the slight sting from his bite as she started to float down from her orgasmic high.

Just when she thought the orgasm was almost over, he repeated the gentle bite on her other nipple, sending her soaring again. He prolonged her floaty feeling with soft nips and licks all over her breasts, up her chest and neck, until he joined their mouths in an ardent kiss.

She heard a phone ringing that broke the spell of lust they were under. Anthony rolled off of her to lay beside her as he pulled his phone out of his pocket. She saw "Dad" on the display and immediately sat up and started righting her clothing in case she needed to rush out to her daughters.

"Hey, Pop, everything okay with the girls?" Anthony quavered as soon as he'd answered the call and put it on speaker.

"Oh, yeah, everything's fine here," Bob drawled through the phone. "We just wanted to ask you to pick up some ice cream on your way back from town."

"We haven't even left to go to town yet." Anthony watched Kay stand up to pull her pants back up.

"Oh, um, okay," Bob stuttered.

"We had to go through the whole house to decide how we want to decorate and make a list of what to buy in town first," Anthony explained with a wink to Kay. "We just finished that and were about to head out, but it's gonna take a while for us to get everything. Do we need to bring the ice cream back first? Or can you wait for it until this evening when we're done in town?"

"Yeah, this evening's fine," Bob drawled. "Just need some vanilla bean from the Creamarie to go with the apple pies your Ma's making for dessert tonight."

"Sure, Pop, we'll pick it up on the way home, no problem." They said their goodbyes and Anthony disconnected the call.

"Don't forget your phone." Anthony pointed to Kay's phone on the bedside table as he got up from the bed. "You might want to check your messages, too. You had a lot of notifications last night when I turned it on and put it on the charger for you." He turned and started walking toward the bathroom.

"Oh, yeah, thanks." That's when Kay realized that she hadn't even turned it on after their flight from New Orleans the day before. She scrolled through her messages and sent a short reply to each of her parents, her sister, and her friend Dee to let them all know she was fine, just too busy to talk. She then stuffed it in her purse before going to the bathroom to pull her sex hair back into a respectable ponytail for their trip into town.

"Um, do you think we have time to take care of that before going to town?" Kay pointed at the bulge in Anthony's jeans that hadn't gone down after their playtime. She felt guilty that he'd given her so much pleasure and hadn't taken any for himself.

"Naw, Baby," Anthony drawled as he finished combing his hair. "I told you, if Mr. Happy comes out to play, we won't get anything else done today."

"But I was the only one who got anything a few minutes ago. You took the edge off for me, I want to do the same for you." Kay started brushing her hair up into position to replace the hairband that she'd lost in the bed. "And I haven't tasted you yet, not really, and I really want to."

"Baby, there is definitely not time for that," Anthony groaned as he pressed a hand to his crotch like he needed the pressure against his cock even through the layers of clothing. "As bad as I want your mouth on me, I want to make sure I have plenty of time to savor every minute your lips are around my cock. Not squeeze in a quickie before rushing through our shopping list."

Kay finished fixing her hair as he continued talking.

"And you weren't the only one to get anything from what we did earlier. The gift of trust you just gave me was the most sensual thing I've ever experienced. And now I get to enjoy the memory of you—laid out on the bed, exposed for only me, letting me do whatever I wanted—all afternoon while I enjoy the anticipation of what I'm going to do to you when we go to bed tonight."

Kay opened her mouth to reply but closed it again when she couldn't make herself form words. She had too many images in her mind of Anthony doing dirty things to her while she was tied to their bed to do more than follow him quietly out to the truck, so they could go into town.

Maybe I should write these down, so I can actually share them with him later?

~~~

Anthony loved seeing the dreamy look on Kay's face as they got in his truck to head into town. He knew she was daydreaming about what he'd planned for her in their bed later. But as much as he liked being the reason she was zoning out, he also wanted her to come back to him in the moment, so she could actually learn her way around town and wouldn't get lost the first time she tried to go on her own.

He reached over and took her hand, giving her their silent "I love you" signal to bring her out of her head as he pulled out of the driveway and onto the gravel road through the ranch. He waited for her to look over at him before speaking. He only met her gaze for a moment before he had to turn back to focus on driving, but was sure she was actually listening to him as he told her how the town was divided up.

"Way back before there was even a Burleson on this land, three ranchers worked together to buy the land that would eventually become the town. It started as four quadrants. The southwest quadrant, where we are now, was owned by my fourth-great-grandfather, Bob Rogers."

"Until your third-great-grandpa married his daughter, and they combined it with the land south of here to expand the Burleson Ranch," Kay replied, showing that she remembered the family history he'd previously told her.

"Yeah." Anthony smiled over at her. "The northwest quadrant was owned by Lucas Walker and the southeast quadrant was owned by William Hunter. The three of them each put up the money to buy the northeast quadrant, so they'd have a say in how a town was started. At first, they just had two roads, Rogers Road runs north and south and Walker Road runs east and west. The first thing they built on the northeast quadrant was the train depot. Supposedly, they named it Hunter's Depot, but since nobody put up a sign saying as such, it
~~~

became the Heart's Destiny Depot when the town was incorporated. We're turning on Rogers Road to get out of the ranch and head into town."

Anthony made the left turn and stole glances at Kay as she looked around at their surroundings.

"So, across Rogers Road is the Hunters' ranch, where James and Dean grew up?" Kay pointed out the window at the park-like setting of the Hunters' property.

"Yeah," Anthony nodded. "Now their parents have turned the place into a bed and breakfast instead of a working cattle ranch. They still have horses in case any of their guests want to do trail rides or whatever."

"Wow, I would never be able to do that." Kay turned to look at the Hunters' property. "I'd be too worried about not having enough guests to pay the bills."

"Naw, they don't have to worry about that," Anthony shook his head. "David Hunter, James and Dean's dad, is actually an investment banker and our bank president. His parents taught him young how to pick winners in the stock market because they had no desire to continue running a cattle ranch. Mandi, James and Dean's mom, is actually the one running the B and B. And I think she only did it because my Ma talked her into it since there wasn't a hotel in town and she wanted Pop to stay in town when she was pregnant, and he needed to have a place to stay locally for anyone he needed to meet with for Burleson Incorporated to be able to come to him instead."

Kay giggled and shook her head but didn't comment.

"This is Walker Road, so this intersection is dead center of the original land purchased to create our town." Anthony pulled to a stop at the junction of Rogers and Walker roads. "If we were to turn right here, the Hunters' ranch would be on the right and the official town of Heart's Destiny would be on our left. We can only go about six miles east on Walker before we hit the edge of town at the railroad tracks and interstate thirty-five. There's a main road every mile, all named after cows."

"The roads that run north and south in town? I noticed the roads running east and west were named after horses, too."

"Yeah." Anthony was surprised she'd already noticed the way the roads were named. "If we were to turn left, the Burleson Ranch would be on the left and the Walker Ranch would be on the right. About three-quarters of the way across the original land is where the oil wells start, between four and five miles from here. This side of Walker Road actually goes about eight miles before it dead ends at the refinery. Back when the Burlesons first hit oil, they bought more land to the west to build the refinery. And the Walkers bought more land west of their ranch to build housing for the refinery workers. Eventually, they turned the western half of their ranch into subdivisions, too. They still live in the southern part of their original land and set up all kinds of trails for dirt bikes and four-wheelers on the northern part."

"Where ya'll went parking as teenagers?" Kay smirked.

Anthony rolled his eyes and nodded, not really wanting to think back to his teenage activity with Nancy on the trails. Instead, he shifted Kay's focus by pointing out the Heart's Destiny Community Church as he drove across Walker Road and turned right into the church parking lot so as not to block traffic.

"If we'd have gone straight on Rogers, we'd pass all the schools and athletic fields on the right, with what's left of the Walker ranch on the left. It only goes another eight miles and ends at Clydesdale Street, which is the only other street with access to interstate thirty-five. There are a few businesses on Clydesdale, but most of the places we need to go today are either in the center of town, or the business area on Walker. Maybe if we have time, we can check out the business areas on Clydesdale and Charolais after our shopping."

Anthony pointed to the church in front of them. "This is the only church in town, originally built in the eighteen-seventies by our three founding families. They donated four square miles of land for the church, the cemetery, and the pastor's house. I don't know if they had a specific religion in mind when they built it, but it's pretty much non-denominational now."

"I guess if it's the only church in town, this is where your mom is planning our wedding." Kay looked up at the white building.

"Probably," Anthony grinned. The rings his dad had given him that morning were burning a hole in his pocket, ready to jump out and latch on to Kay's hand. "You ready to say yes, yet?"

"I don't know…" Kay trailed off her words, her lips only half lifting in a smile. "…maybe, if I get a really enticing proposal."

Anthony imagined proposing to Kay at sunset in his favorite spot on the ranch, the bluff overlooking the creek and pond. Now he just had to plan it all out and figure out how to get her there alone while still getting as much done on the house as possible in the two-and-a-half days they still had on the ranch before flying out Friday to go back to work.

"Oh, I'll make it enticing," he cooed as he leaned over and gave her a quick kiss before pulling out of the parking lot onto Quarter Horse Drive, the road that ran between the church and the cemetery. He crossed over Brahman Blvd. and made the right on Angus Avenue to pull into the Burger Barn on the corner of Angus and Walker.

"Please tell me you don't think the Burger Barn is the right place to make a proposal enticing." Kay rolled her eyes at him as he parked.

"No, Baby," Anthony chuckled as he got out and went around to open her door for her. "I just figured we needed to fuel up with lunch before our epic shopping spree. And I thought you might like a taste of some Burleson Beef."

"I wanted a taste of your Burleson beef before we left the house, but I guess I'll settle for a burger instead," Kay sassed as they walked to the door of the restaurant.

Anthony enjoyed seeing her come out of her shell and show him her saucy side. As they stepped through the door, he bent down to whisper in her ear. "You'll get as much of me as you can swallow tonight, Baby."

He took advantage of her shocked expression to steal a not-so-chaste kiss before standing back up and pulling her toward the counter. She was full-on blushing as he introduced her to Tom and Tiffany, the proprietors of the Burger Barn, but it started to fade when he gently squeezed her hand three times. She returned his silent "I love you" and showed no more signs of embarrassment as she placed her burger order.

As they sat eating lunch, he started to explain how City Hall was situated in the very center of town with the blocks bordering it being the main business district. She'd apparently figured that out on her own the day before when she walked all around the center of town while his mom had taken the girls to look at bridal wear and flowers for the wedding.

"I told you to tell her what you want," Anthony pointed out. "If you don't, she'll just go with whatever the girls tell her they think you'll like and you'll end up dressed as a princess on our wedding day."

"I can't do that," Kay protested. "What if we make all these plans and then the judge orders us to move back to Tulsa immediately, and we can't follow through with what we plan?"

"Baby, that's not going to happen," Anthony groaned. "And even if we're ordered to move to Tulsa, we can still follow through with most of the plans, just in your church in Tulsa instead of the church here. Or maybe we can convince the judge to officiate right there in his courtroom, so we can get married, and I can adopt the girls all at one time."

Kay dropped her burger to her plate and gaped at Anthony.

Fuck, I probably shouldn't have said that last part out loud.

"You want to adopt the girls?" Kay finally asked after a moment of floundering with her mouth opening and closing like a fish out of water.

Fuck, I told her the night we met that I wouldn't try to take their father's place and now, not even three weeks later, I'm telling her that's exactly what I want to do. She's got to be thinking I'm either indecisive, or I originally lied to her. How do I convince her that I meant what I said originally but changed my mind after seeing what a scumbag their father is?

"Yes, I want to adopt your daughters." Anthony put his own burger down and took both of Kay's hands in his, across the table, needing to feel their connection as he explained. "I know I said I wouldn't try to replace their father the night we met, and at the time I really meant that. But after meeting him and seeing how he's treated you and the girls, I don't think he deserves the honor of being their dad. I'm not sure I deserve that honor either, but damn it, I'm just selfish enough to want it."

"That's not selfish," Kay corrected softly as she squeezed his hands. "I love you" he pressed back. "That's selfless because you want to be the dad they need and protect them from the monster they don't deserve to have in their lives."

Thank fuck, she gets it!

Kay pulled out her phone and dialed a number. As it started to ring, she put it on speaker and sat it on the table between them. The name Matt Monroe was on the display. Anthony felt his heart skip a beat when he realized she was calling her attorney.

When the receptionist answered, Kay introduced herself and asked to be transferred to Mr. Monroe. Within seconds, the line clicked, and the attorney was speaking through the phone's speaker. "Kay, what can I do for you? How's Texas?"

"Texas is great, better than great, it's perfect," Kay answered with a tentative smile. "I have you on speaker and Anthony with me, so we can both ask you some questions."

"Okay, I take it you've gone over the potential questions I sent you to be prepared to answer on the stand and have questions about how to word your answers," he assumed incorrectly.

"No, not exactly," Kay drawled out. "We'd rather know what we need to do, so Anthony can adopt the girls."

"He can't unless Mark's parental rights are terminated," Matt explained. "The petition we've filed is to terminate visitation, not parental rights."

"How hard would it be to change that?" Kay looked over at him with hope in her eyes. "With as much as Mark has complained about having to pay child support, I'm thinking you might be able to work a deal with his lawyer to terminate his parental rights. A deal that Mark will want, so he doesn't have to keep paying and we don't have to go through the mess of dragging each other through the mud in court."

"It's possible," Matt stated over the sound of rustling papers. "I'll call his attorney and try to work it out. But even if he takes the deal, you'll have to appear in court to get the judge to sign off on it."

"Will we be able to do the adoption the same day?" Anthony barely kept himself from crossing his fingers as he waited for the attorney to answer.

"I doubt it," Matt replied. "You'll have to get an attorney to draw up the adoption papers and submit the petition for adoption to the court. They won't even put you on the docket until after Mark's rights are terminated."

"Can you go ahead and draw up the papers and submit them as soon as the judge terminates Mark's rights?"

"Technically, I'm Kay's attorney and it could be a conflict of interest," Matt started but Kay cut him off.

"And as my attorney, it's not a conflict of interest for you to represent my future husband as he adopts our daughters."

"No, I guess not," Matt chuckled. "Congratulations. When's the wedding?"

Kay looked at Anthony across the table and shrugged. He'd already told her he wanted to get married the weekend after Thanksgiving, so he took her shrug as her yes to the wedding date.

"Saturday, November twenty-fourth, unless the judge needs to marry us in Tulsa while we're in court, so he can do the adoption," Anthony answered as he smiled across the table at his blushing bride-to-be.

"He couldn't marry you in his courtroom that day either," Matt replied, his tone of voice full of mirth. "There's a three-day waiting period after your blood tests before you can get married in Oklahoma."

"I thought they did away with that requirement?" Kay sounded like she was asking a question even though her words could also be construed as a statement.

"Well, it has been a few years since I got married," Matt chuckled. "Maybe it has changed, but I still don't think the judge will require you to get married immediately in his courtroom before starting the adoption process. I'll get started on all these paperwork changes and call Mark's attorney now. I'll let you know what he says. Hopefully, he'll agree and make your court date an easy appearance to sign some paperwork and set another date to come back and sign some more paperwork to finalize the adoption."

"Thanks Matt," Kay smiled.

"Thank you," Anthony added as they disconnected the call.

"You'd better not dawdle on that enticing proposal." Kay gave him a pointed look as she picked up her burger to finish eating her lunch. "I can't officially start planning the wedding until you put a ring on my finger."

Anthony almost got the rings out of his pocket right then, eager to see the diamond sparkling on Kay's hand. But he decided to tease Kay a bit instead and stick to his plan for the perfect proposal.

"I'd put a ring on your finger right now if you hadn't already said the Burger Barn wasn't the right place for me to propose." Anthony smirked before popping the last bite of his burger into his mouth.

"Haha," Kay feigned laughing, sticking her tongue out at him before finishing off her food. "I know you haven't had a chance to go ring shopping, so I know better than that. And I don't want to pick out my own ring, so don't even think of suggesting we stop at a jewelry store today."

Anthony was glad she had no idea what was in his pocket. *Maybe she won't suspect a thing if I can get her out on the bluff before we have any time apart when I could shop without her?*

"Nope, no jewelry store today," Anthony agreed as they bused their table before leaving. "But we do need to get on with the shopping, so we can get back to the ranch in time for dinner."

When they left the Burger Barn, they went straight to Heart of the Home to pick out the furniture and other household items on their list. Kay picked out coordinating curtains, but didn't buy them since they hadn't measured the windows to know what size to get for each room. She wanted the formal living and dining rooms to have sunny yellow walls to offset the teal blue upholstery and draperies.

The tables in the formal living room were all a dark wood to match the wainscoting. The design was the same style as the furniture she picked out for the formal dining room. The table only sat twelve instead of the sixteen of the smallest table at his parents' house, but their dining room was smaller than his parents' so that seemed appropriate. They found the same style of dishes and silverware that he already had and bought enough to serve twelve.

She picked out a tablecloth, napkins, and napkin rings with yellow and teal patterns, so the color scheme would flow from the formal living room to the formal dining room. The teal was darker than the aqua in the kitchen, but she said if they found some artwork with both shades and maybe some pink accents, it would help the kitchen coordinate with the rest of the house, so they wouldn't have to renovate the kitchen any time soon.

Anthony wasn't sure he could really picture it—and wasn't really fond of the pink in the kitchen—but he was on board with whatever Kay wanted, so he looked for artwork with all the shades of blue-green, yellow, and pink he could find to help her pick a couple of pieces.

They found a super comfy dark brown sofa that Kay wanted to put in their music room off their bedroom that Anthony was looking forward to spending some time on while writing her song. She'd already hung the curtains in that room since they matched the ones in their bedroom.

They decided not to pick out anything for the game room, opting to have the girls design it with them. Thinking of the girls brought a smile to Anthony's face at thinking about their conversation with Matt about the adoption.

"When do you think we should talk to the girls about the adoption?" Anthony questioned Kay as he was carrying their smaller purchases to the truck. The furniture was scheduled to be delivered Thursday, giving him Wednesday to take down wallpaper, and hopefully paint the two rooms while they were still empty.

"Not until we get confirmation from Matt that Mark is willing to sign away his rights," Kay answered as he helped her into the truck. "I don't wanna get their hopes up that it's a done deal and then have Mark screw everything up at the last minute."

"Yeah, that makes sense." Anthony nodded his head as he closed her door. He walked slowly around the back of the truck to take the time to school his features, so Kay didn't see his disappointment at not being able to tell them immediately as he slid behind the wheel.

They left the town square to head over to the Hometown Hardware on Walker Road between Longhorn Lane and Brangus Street. Kay picked out several small sample cans of various shades of yellow paint, while Anthony picked up the supplies to strip the wallpaper. He supposed it would be easiest if she painted swatches of a few different colors on the walls to see which one she really liked best while he was working on the wallpaper removal. They'd come back to the hardware store once she decided which shade they needed to buy in full size cans of paint.

Once that was done, he headed back up Longhorn Lane to Eldon's Electronics for three televisions for the bedrooms and Kay a new cell phone that was actually smart enough to set up, so she didn't have to remember to switch it to and from airplane mode every day.

Leah Mae Wright

She balked at him buying her a new phone, claiming hers was just fine for how little she used it. When he explained why he wanted to get her a new one, so he wouldn't worry about her if she went somewhere with her friends because it would remember to turn airplane mode off for her, so he could call her, she finally relented.

Since Eldon's wasn't affiliated with her provider in Tulsa, Anthony just added her new phone to his plan and made sure she had all the bells and whistles of a top-of-the-line phone. They copied her contacts and other info from her old phone, so she could send everyone a text with her new number and cancel her old one whenever they went back to Tulsa.

When she said something about possibly passing it down to Tia for her birthday, Anthony just shook his head and made a mental note to buy Tia a new phone for her birthday. He could argue with Kay about it later if she still had her old phone line active by then.

Finally, they made it back to the center of town to pick up his dad's ice cream at the Creamarie. Apparently, Marie Milton, the owner of the Creamarie was offended that Kay had walked by the day before without coming in to introduce herself and started putting up a fuss as soon as they walked in.

"I'm sorry, Nana Marie," Anthony apologized, hoping to appease his honorary grandmother. "I didn't come to town with her yesterday, and I wanted to introduce her to you myself."

"Your Momma coulda introduced her to me when they had lunch next door," Marie huffed, swatting his arm as soon as he got close enough to the counter for her to reach across with the paper in her hand.

"Yeah, well, from what I heard, Ma was too busy trying to pick out wedding stuff to think about making introductions," Anthony grinned. "Besides, I only get to introduce my handpicked grandma to my future wife once, so I didn't want Ma doin' it for me."

"Well, get on with it then," Marie ordered, waving her paper around in front of him.

"I will as soon as you quit fussin' at me." Anthony smiled at her before turning to look at Kay. "Kay, I'd like you to meet my Nana Marie. She was best friends with my Memmaw Judy before she passed and stepped up to help us all remember her love."

Anthony turned back to look at Marie and finished the introduction. "Nana Marie, this is the other half of my heart, Kay. She reminds me a lot of you and Memmaw Judy with how she tries to take care of everyone around her, so I hope you'll welcome her to the family with the same love that you've had for me since I was born."

Anthony thought he saw Marie's ebony cheeks turn a little pink as she came out from behind the counter to embrace a shell-shocked Kay.

"It's so nice to meet you, Nana Marie." Kay returned the older Black woman's hug.

"It's nice meeting you, too, Kay," Marie blubbered as they released each other. "We may not be blood, but the Burlesons are closer to me than some of my other family."

"Hey, now, don't be spreading those rumors about not being blood," Anthony objected with a wink at Kay. "Pop said we got our brown eyes from you, and I know you don't want to make him out to be a liar."

"Oh, yeah." Kay played along. "I definitely see the family resemblance."

"Oh, stop," Marie protested. "Ya'll are gonna get people wondering about my wild youth and questioning your Memmaw and Pappaw's marriage with neither of them here to refute the rumors."

After a little more small talk, they got the ice cream and headed back to the ranch. Of course, they couldn't just drop the ice cream off at his parents' house and go for a sunset trail ride like Anthony wanted. They had to stay for dinner and dessert.

Between discussions about all the work he had to do on the house and wedding plans that Kay wouldn't sign off on yet, Anthony sent a text to his cousin Justin to find out when he'd be available to help Tia with calculus. *Maybe he can help me make excuses to get out of here before sunset?*

> **Anthony: You had to take complex calculus classes for your degree, right?**

> **Justin: Yeah, why?**

> **Anthony: Don't know if you noticed in the couple of times you've met her, but Tia is a genius & has some**

> **homework I'm not quite sure how to help her with.**
> **Wondered if you'd mind helping her while we're here.**

Justin: Sure. Now?

Anthony: Give me a few to get finished @ Mom & Dad's
> **and herd everyone home.**

Justin: K, see ya in 15.

"Thanks for a delicious dinner, Ma." Anthony pushed his chair back and rubbed his overly full belly. "But we need to get home and get started on my long list of chores."

"I wasn't planning to start on any of that until tomorrow, so the girls and I can stay awhile and relieve Hazel of dish duty," Kay argued as she smiled over at Anthony.

"Oh, um, okay," Anthony sputtered, unsure what to do to get Kay to quit derailing his plans. "But, um, Justin is gonna be at our place in a few minutes to help Tia with her calculus homework."

"Really?" Kay glared at him, looking confused. "I didn't realize you'd had a chance to call and ask him since we discussed that this morning."

"Yeah, I just texted him." Anthony held up his phone as if he needed to show her proof. "He's only available in the evening after work, so I wanted to give him as many evenings as possible to help her before we fly out. And I need his help to move that sofa to the girls' game room, so I can clear out the front room to start stripping wallpaper and painting tomorrow."

"Then I guess you and Tia should head on over there while Maria and I take over dish duty," Kay asserted, standing and kissing Anthony's cheek before starting to clear the table. She stacked up about half of the empty plates to carry to the kitchen. Maria popped up from her seat and kissed his other cheek before following her mother from the dining room with a plate in her hands.

"Let's get the bridal books for you to take with you, Tia," his mom suggested as she got up and left the dining room with Tia following closely on her heels.

"What just happened?" Anthony looked to his dad for guidance since they were the only two people left in the dining room.

"You're learning what it means to be a husband and father," Bob replied, his lips turned up in the slightest smirk. "You make plans only to change them to accommodate the wife and kids."

"Yeah, well, I can't make her my wife if she keeps derailing my plan to propose," Anthony grumbled, running a hand through his hair in frustration. "I was gonna get Justin to watch the girls while he helped Tia with her homework, so I could get Kay to the bluff to propose at sunset. I guess I should have thought it through better. There's no way I could get everything set up this late in the day."

"Might be better off if you enlist your sisters to help you tomorrow," his dad suggested. "They'll be a lot better at helping you plan a proposal."

"Thanks, Pop," Anthony replied as Tia came back into the room with an armful of bridal magazines.

"I'm ready to go," she announced.

Anthony stood and stacked up the rest of the dishes to carry them to the kitchen for Kay before he and Tia went to meet Justin. She and Maria were emptying the dishwasher of the load his mother had already run—from breakfast or lunch or maybe the ranch hands' meal prep she did daily—when Anthony walked into the kitchen. He placed the stack of dirty dishes beside the sink with the ones Kay had already piled there.

"See you at home in a bit, Beautiful." He kissed the top of her head. He and Tia walked out the back door and around to the front of their house to meet Justin on their front porch.

As soon as they stepped in the front door, Tia bolted up the stairs to get her tablet.

"Help me move this sofa while she's getting her homework?" Anthony indicated with his hand toward the other end of the heavy black leather, double-recliner sofa that was still in the front room.

"Kay didn't like it in the front room, huh?" Justin chuckled as he bent to pick up the end opposite Anthony.

"Nope, this stuff is all going to go in the den," Anthony replied as they each hefted an end of the heavy piece of furniture. "We're going to turn it into a game room for the girls."

"Sweet," Justin whistled as they walked through the hall back to the den at the back of the house across from the kitchen. "If you have the Xbox set up by the time we're done with Tia's homework, maybe we can get in a game or two tonight."

While Anthony hated missing out on the opportunity to propose at sunset, he couldn't complain about how he ended up spending the evening. While Justin and Tia worked on calculus, Anthony moved his guitars and amps up to the music room and his former living room furniture and electronics to the new game room. He unloaded the things he and Kay had purchased earlier in the day and stored everything in the garage, so it wouldn't get messed up while they stripped wallpaper and painted.

He mounted televisions in the bedrooms and was pleasantly surprised by having satellite cables already in the rooms to hook up to. He made a note in his phone to check that the utilities were transferred into his name from his brothers' the next day, along with ordering any equipment he would need for the televisions to pick up the appropriate channels. He also made a note to set up internet service since he thought Tia was still using his parents Wi-Fi from next door to do her homework.

When Kay and Maria got home, he made sure the game room was laid out the way the girls wanted before hooking up the television, stereo, Xbox, and surround sound. He then spent a couple of hours of quality family time teaching the girls how to play the GWA's video game and laughing with them at the crazy characters they made up for their avatars.

Justin only stayed for the first couple of rounds as they took turns playing, leaving as soon as each of the girls had beaten him in their virtual matches.

"This was more fun than I thought it would be." Kay leaned into his side. Anthony was reclined on one end of the sofa watching Tia and Maria battle it out on screen while both sitting in the recliner on the other end of the couch.

He pulled Kay off the center cushion and tighter into his side as he scooted over to make room for her to extend her legs on the recliner with him. Anthony thought it was a perfect time to count his blessings. He had the love of his life, whom he'd be marrying in a little over a month, cuddled up to his side, and two laughing little girls that he couldn't wait to legally claim as his daughters playing just a few feet away on the other side of the sofa.

I hope I can be the man they all deserve. A loving husband and devoted dad. I hope I can protect them from the evil in the world without being too controlling. I want to keep them safe and make their dreams come true. That's possible without taking over their lives and stifling their independence, right?

Chapter Thirteen

Kay glanced at her new phone on the bedside table to see the time as she slipped out of Anthony's arms to take care of her morning bathroom needs. She figured she'd only woken up before six a.m. because of the nap she'd taken the evening before when she fell asleep cuddling with Anthony while they watched the girls playing video games. Since the girls had stayed awake much later than Kay the night before, she assumed they would sleep later than normal, giving her time to repay Anthony for the way he worshiped her body the previous day.

She quickly brushed her teeth and hair, then stripped out of the t-shirt and panties Anthony had left on her when he carried her to bed last night. She vaguely remembered him helping her undress for bed while she was half asleep.

He'd helped her out of her shoes, socks, and jeans and was going to tuck her in still wearing her bra, panties, and t-shirt. She'd protested and took the t-shirt off, so she could remove her bra. Once she had the bra off, Anthony had put her t-shirt back on and growled, "You have to wear this, or I won't be able to let you go back to sleep."

Smiling at the memory, she tip-toed to the dresser to slip on another slinky negligée without waking Anthony. After checking that both doors to the hallway were locked, so the girls couldn't walk in, Kay slid under the covers from the foot of the bed.

Kay ran her hands over Anthony's hairy legs as she crawled up the bed, trying to coax him to roll onto his back, so she could wake him with a special morning kiss. She wasn't super confident in her blow job skills, and was pretty certain she wouldn't be able to take near enough of him in her mouth to be more than a tease, but she wanted to taste him way more than she feared being bad at giving head.

As he rolled onto his back, she crawled over the leg closest to her, so she could start kissing her way up his inner thighs. She wasn't sure if he was awake or not, when he spread his legs wider, so she could kneel between his thighs. She was shocked when her hands found the bottom of his boxer briefs, thinking he would have gone to bed naked like he had the previous two nights they'd shared a bed.

Should I go in from the bottom to play with my hands? Or pull them down from the top with my teeth?

She decided to run her hands over his erection on the outside of his boxer briefs at first, wondering how far she would get before he woke up and took over. While she wanted to have a little playtime with her in charge, she couldn't wait for him to take control and direct her on how to please him the most.

After dealing with her domineering ex-husband, Kay thought she'd never want to give up control of her body to another person. But it was different with Anthony. Mark was brutal and tried to force Kay to do what he wanted by using his fists. Anthony would never do anything to hurt her like that. Kay found his commanding, deep voice arousing when he took control. Probably because she knew that if she had even the slightest objection to whatever he wanted her to do, he would back off and discuss it with her instead of reacting with violence.

Unlike Mark, who wanted to control her every move because he was an insecure little man and could only feel good about himself when he was intimidating others, Kay knew Anthony's need for control was from his fear of loss. He wanted to know where she was and be able to call her when they were apart, not because he wanted to be the big man in charge of her life, but because he was afraid of something happening to her like had happened to his high school girlfriend and unborn child. If she'd been with him in Florida where he was stationed, neither she nor the baby would have died that horrible day. At least that's what Kay thought Anthony believed.

Understanding that his need for control was because he wanted to keep her safe was why Kay felt comfortable giving it to him in all aspects of her life. She knew he might eventually push her to the limit of what she could handle sexually, but it would only be exciting and pleasurable, not frightening, or painful. She trusted him completely, heart, body, and soul.

After rubbing his full length with her hands several times and cupping his balls through the thin cotton, she hooked her fingers into the waistband of his boxer briefs to slowly pull them down and free his cock. She tucked the front waistband under his balls instead of trying to pull them out from under him, where he was trapping the back between his butt and the bed. As she tentatively stuck her tongue out to take her first lick from his base to his tip, Anthony threw the sheet and comforter off of them and pushed up on his elbows to look her in the eyes.

"I have to see you, Baby," he growled, his voice hoarse from sleep.

Kay stopped mid-lick, like a deer in the headlights, unsure what to do next.

"Don't stop," Anthony moaned. "Please, Baby, I just want to watch while you take what you want."

Buoyed by his words and the pleading look in his eyes, Kay continued her oral exploration of his erection. She trailed the tip of her tongue up the full length of his manhood, swirled little circles in the especially sensitive spot just below the head. She lapped up the drop of precum that was already leaking from the slit before closing her lips over the head and sucking him to the back of her throat.

"Oh, fuck, yes, Kay," Anthony groaned as his left hand weaved through her hair. He didn't pull her hair or try to control her movements. It was more of a caress, like he just had to touch her in some way and that was the only way he could reach to touch her. "Just like that, Baby."

Kay's head bobbed as she moved her mouth up and down on him, taking him as deep into her mouth as she could and then backing off while sucking hard. She couldn't take him all in her mouth, so she stroked the root with her hand to lavish attention on his whole length. She cupped his balls with her other hand and gently squeezed, just enough to give him a little pressure without causing any pain.

His breathing was ragged as he panted out her name repeatedly. His grip on her hair tightened slightly, as he tried to pull her mouth off of him. "Fuck, Kay, you have to stop, Baby."

Kay shook her head no, since she couldn't verbally respond, as she continued sucking and stroking him. She could feel his balls tighten in her hand and knew he was close to coming. She wanted him to deliver on his promise the day before, to give her as much of him as she could swallow.

"Kay, Baby, if you don't stop now, I'm gonna come in your hot, wet mouth."

Good, that's exactly what I want, Kay thought as she squeezed his base tighter, sped up her stroking, and sucked him as deep as she could without triggering her gag reflex.

"Fuck, Kay, Baby," Anthony grunted as he started to spurt down her throat. Kay struggled to swallow it all as the thick ropes of cum exploded out of Anthony's cock into her mouth while he recited her name again with each burst.

When she couldn't swallow another drop, she sat up, her mouth coming off the end of his cock with a little pop. She continued stroking his dick with both hands as the final few shots of viscous white ejaculate painted Anthony's abs.

Anthony broke their visual connection when he collapsed back onto the bed.

"Good morning," Kay chirped as she smiled at her man while he recovered from his orgasm.

"Best, fucking, morning," Anthony replied as he opened his eyes and lifted his head just enough to make eye contact with Kay again. The broad smile he gave her matched the one she was giving him. "Give me a minute to catch my breath and go clean up. Then I want to examine every detail of that sexy little surprise you're wearing."

Anthony got up and went to the bathroom. Kay stretched out on the middle of the bed, arranging herself in a sexy pose and adjusting the nightie to keep everything covered, if only slightly, by the thin purple silk.

The look of lust in Anthony's eyes as he appreciated the view when he walked back into the bedroom made her nipples tighten and her pussy flood with arousal. He trailed one hand up her top leg as he crawled on the bed. When he reached her hip, he pushed the hem of the negligée up to her waist, exposing her bare sex. He gently pushed her hip to roll her to her back, using his other hand behind her other knee to spread her legs for him.

Once he was positioned on his belly between her legs, he trailed his hands and mouth up and down her thighs, over her hips, and across her pelvis. He took his time teasing and taunting her before he finally lowered his mouth to her core. The anticipation was almost too much, causing Kay to nearly explode with the first swipe of his tongue across her sensitive clit.

Kay felt like she was floating in another plane of existence as he ate her pussy. She wasn't sure what was different between this time and the other times he'd lavished her with oral affection, but it seemed like more. He didn't just take a little taste, titillating her to an orgasm. He devoured her, consumed her, and made her shoot off like a rocket into another dimension.

She panted out his name as fireworks exploded behind her closed eyelids. Her climax was so extreme she felt like she shattered into a million, sparkling pieces, as if her body was one of the mortars shot into the sky on the Fourth of July.

Anthony wouldn't let her stay shattered, though. He kissed and stroked her back together as he worked his way over her body. He cradled her to his chest as he sat up in bed, leaning his back against the headboard and setting her on his lap. Her head rested over his heart, and she loved hearing its steady thumping as he wrapped her in his arms.

"Wow," she whispered when she finally felt like she'd floated back down to earth with him. The feel of his erection pressing into her hip let her know he was ready for round two, as soon as she recovered.

When she asked about round two, he positioned her on her hands and knees, with her feet hanging off the side of the bed, so she was at the right height for him to stand beside the bed and fuck her from behind. This was another position where he could go deeper and really stroke that secret spot inside her that only he could find.

Kay thought it might be her favorite position, especially when he got past the first few slow, gentle thrusts to allow her to adjust to his size, and started pounding her harder. It was primal, raw, and animalistic. He fucked her like a man possessed. She felt claimed, marked as his by the impression of his fingers on her hips.

She wasn't surprised when her orgasm was more intense than the last one, as he fingered her needy nub while he fucked her from behind. Kay felt so intoxicated by his hedonistic ravishing that she wasn't sure her slurred incantation could be coherently understood as his name. He decelerated his pace to let her come down from the high, telling her he wanted her to come again before he reached his own release.

He pulled his hand back to her hip, then slid them both back farther to rub across her butt cheeks. "Tell me you're mine," Anthony demanded as he gently stroked her.

"I'm yours, Anthony," Kay moaned breathlessly.

"I want you in every way possible for a man to have a woman," he growled as his pace accelerated.

"I'm yours, any way you want me," Kay replied, feeling her next climax building.

"Do you really mean that?" Anthony plunged more powerfully into her.

"Yes, Anthony, yes," Kay chanted on the brink of her next O.

"Even if I wanna fuck you here?" Anthony spread her cheeks and circled her anus with his finger coated in her cream.

Kay couldn't answer because the feeling of him pushing the tip of his finger past the ring of muscle sent her over the edge to ecstasy. Her vaginal walls spasmed around his cock, milking him of his own orgasm.

"Fuck, yes, Kay," he groaned as he held himself as deep inside her as possible to ride out his release.

Finally, he bent forward, running his hands over the silk on her sides as he leaned down to kiss the back of her neck. He stroked her hair over her shoulder, moving it out of his way, so he could kiss up her neck. Kay turned her head, so their lips could meet in a passionate kiss before they collapsed to the bed, spooning on their sides.

"Um, about your last question," Kay started when she was finally able to speak again. "I, um, I don't know if I'll ever be able to handle all of you there. But I liked, um, what you did with your finger."

"Really? I couldn't tell," Anthony chuckled sarcastically as he hugged Kay closer. "I wasn't sure if it made you come harder than ever, or if you hated it and were trying to tell me by crushing my dick inside you."

"Oh, are you okay?" Kay rolled in his arms to face him. She wanted to see his expression to know if she'd actually hurt him with her massive orgasm. She'd heard about some gruesome injuries being possible to male genitalia, but she thought it was just the testicles that were susceptible, not an erect penis. "It was definitely the most intense orgasm ever. But maybe we should back off some if I hurt you when I come that hard."

"You didn't hurt me, Baby," Anthony chuckled. "I was just teasing you a little bit. I actually love the way you clamp down on me when you come. You get so tight I can't even move, like you're not gonna let me pull out until we're both spent. You feel fucking amazing."

"You make me feel amazing." Kay smiled at him as they looked longingly into each other's eyes.

"How 'bout we continue to feel amazing together in the shower?" Anthony wagged his eyebrows suggestively.

"Sounds like a plan, Professor Burleson." Kay batted her eyelashes, flirting cheekily. "I seem to recall some lessons you planned to teach me in the shower."

"I've been looking forward to those lessons all week, Baby." Anthony grinned as he bounded out of bed.

Kay laid there for a second looking at him in all his naked glory. The sex-tousled hair, the smoldering look in his dark brown eyes, his smooth tan skin stretched tightly over his broad shoulders, chiseled pectorals with a smattering of dark hair. Even the scar over his ribs couldn't mar the perfection of his torso, as it tapered down to six-pack abs and that flawless V of muscle that pointed to the end of the happy trail of hair, down to the most picture-perfect penis Kay could imagine. Long and thick, absolutely proportionate to his height, glistening with their combined juices from their earlier activities, and standing at attention, aimed directly at Kay.

"Like what you see, Ms. Lee?" Anthony's question caused Kay's eyes to snap to his from where she'd been staring at his cock and licking her lips.

"Yes, Professor Burleson." Kay slowly started to sit up and move to the edge of the bed.

Anthony gripped her hips to pick her up. She instinctively wrapped her arms around his neck and her legs around his waist. He moved his hands, so one supported her butt and the other covered her upper back, hugging her to his chest. His cock poked at her core, but only the tip entered her as his long strides carried them to the shower.

He didn't even turn on the water as he pressed her back against the wall of the shower and slowly started pushing into her wet heat. The cold tile against her back was a sharp contrast to the heat of their bodies becoming one. When his hands moved to each cup a butt cheek, Kay expected him to increase the speed and intensity of his thrusts. She figured it was a good grip to be able to bounce her on his cock as hard and as fast as he could.

Instead, he pressed his body into hers with a leisurely, sensual intention that made Kay feel more than she expected. The feel of his chest hair tickling her sensitive nipples was tantalizing in a way she never imagined possible. The way he applied pressure to her clit with his pelvic bone as he filled her to the hilt teased her to the edge. The way he flexed as he lifted her up to deliberately drag his head across that secret spot inside her, as he pulled back but never completely out, was the best kind of erotic torture. Instead of their normal raging inferno of passionate lovemaking, Anthony was building a slow-burning blaze in the fireplace for them to have romantic nights in front of for years to come.

Even with every part of her wrapped around him, touching skin to skin, she felt their connection the strongest in their eye contact. He whispered words of love, how he wanted to show her how much he loves her, but he didn't want to risk making her too sore for more. Even if she couldn't hear the sentiments coming from his lips, she would have read them in his soulful chocolate eyes.

"I love you, too," she replied, hoping he could read the sincerity of her words in her eyes. "So much, it's scary sometimes, but also the safest I've ever felt."

"Oh, Baby, love is nothing to be scared of," Anthony crooned. "I'll always keep you safe."

Kay couldn't tell if they were there for minutes or hours, making love deliberately, cementing their sensual connection with their bodies, their hearts, and their souls. Truly becoming one, as they experienced another explosive mutual climax.

<div align="center">~~~</div>

Anthony was walking on cloud nine as he and Kay made their way downstairs after they finished their shower. With eight orgasms between them that morning, he was kind of surprised they were able to walk down the stairs. That was why he'd slowed things down in the shower, hoping to keep her from being too sore from the times he'd lost control of his inner beast and been rougher than he wanted with Kay.

Damn, if slowing things down didn't make our connection feel even stronger in the shower, he thought. *I'll have to remember that the next time my inner beast tries to make an appearance, so I don't accidentally hurt her by losing control.*

He bent to give Kay a quick peck of a kiss when they got to the bottom of the stairs. He watched Kay's heart-shaped ass sway as she walked down the hall to the kitchen to start breakfast. He knew he couldn't act on the desire he had to carry her back up to their bed for the rest of the day, but he could certainly enjoy the view while he didn't have an audience around to prevent the instant erection he got whenever he looked at Kay.

While she was starting breakfast, Anthony started going through the bags from the hardware store to find the steamer he was going to use to remove the wallpaper from the walls in the formal living and dining rooms. After he got it set up, and while he was waiting for the water to heat up in it for him to be able to actually use it, he started a group chat with his sisters.

Anthony: Hey, I need ya'll's help so I can propose to Kay tonight.

Becky: Do you have a plan you need us to help set up? Or do we need to help you with a plan for how to propose?

Charlotte: Congrats! Have you already picked out a ring?

Anthony: I want to take her to the bluff south of Bobby's house & propose with the sun setting behind the creek.

Anthony: Yes, Pop gave me Memmaw & Pappaw's rings yesterday.

Becky: Okay, so what do you need our help with?

Charlotte: I always loved Memmaw's rings. I'm sure Kay will too! <3

Anthony: I need ideas for how to get her out there. Yesterday's attempt failed.

Becky: Take her for a horseback ride?

Charlotte: What did you try yesterday?

Anthony: Figured if I suggested a horseback ride, it wouldn't be just the 2 of us.

Anthony: I had Justin helping Tia with homework & thought I'd take her on an ATV while he was able to watch the girls. But Kay insisted on staying & doing dishes for Ma & we missed the sunset.

Becky: You're right about the horses. Sorry, didn't think of that.

Charlotte: What are your plans for the day?

Anthony: Just working on the house. Maybe going back to the hardware store for paint if Kay picks a color.

"What's that thing?" Tia pointed at the wallpaper steamer as she walked into the front room, where Anthony was sitting on the floor beside the steamer that was apparently warmed up and ready for use.

411

"It's a wallpaper steamer," Anthony answered, setting his phone down in the windowsill and standing to start using the steamer. "It's supposed to make it easier to remove the wallpaper, so we can paint these rooms."

"Can I help?"

"If you want." Anthony started trying to steam the first section of wallpaper. "But I figured you and Maria would be working on your plans for how you want to decorate the game room this morning, so we can go buy the paint and stuff this afternoon."

"Oh, we already know how we want to decorate in there." Tia waved her arm in the direction of the room they were planning to use for the game room. "We want to turn the wainscoting panels into chalkboards and paint the tops of the walls pink to match the kitchen."

"Maybe I should have gotten more than one of these." Anthony indicated what he meant by lifting the steamer in his hands. "So we could work on more than one room at a time."

"We can get another one when we go get the paint." Tia had a huge smile on her face as she started looking through the hardware store bags. "Why didn't Mom get bigger cans of paint yesterday?"

"She's not sure which one she wants to go with." Anthony looked over his shoulder to see Tia lining up the small sample cans on the floor in front of her. "Why don't you go put on some painting clothes, so you can paint her swatches on this wall as soon as I get the first section of wallpaper down?"

"I was waiting for Maria to get done with her bath, so I could shower and get dressed." Tia shrugged one shoulder as she stood and tugged at the bottom of her purple pajama shirt. "But I should probably shower after painting and not before, huh?"

"Maybe," Anthony grinned. "Depends on how messy you get when you paint."

"I'm not nearly as messy as Maria, but I have ended up with paint in my hair before, so I should probably wait." Tia bounced out of the room to go change.

Anthony finished getting the wallpaper down on the first section of wall before checking his phone to see what ideas his sisters had for him.

Charlotte: How about we plan on coming to your house
     about 5 & taking the girls on an ATV ride? While Becky
     & I take them west from Bobby's, you can take Kay
     south for the proposal.

Becky: Great idea, Sis! We can ride over on ours, so he
     has to walk Kay over to the barn to get his to cover for
     us getting separated.

Charlotte: Agreed. Do we need to put a blanket & picnic
     basket on your ATV, or would you rather have the
     champagne ready to pop at home to celebrate with
     everyone when you get back?

     Anthony: Considering I don't have champagne or fancy
          champagne glasses here, maybe you can pick those up
               & have them ready & waiting when we get back?

Becky: We have plenty of glasses at our house. I'll add
     Jen & Julie to this chat, so whichever one of us gets
     home first can make sure they're all clean & ready to
     take to your house as soon as you & Kay leave.

Charlotte: I'll pick up a bottle of champagne on my way
     home from school & chill it at my house.

Jen: Congrats, Cuz! I'll get with the fam here & make sure
     we all leave the office early enough to converge on
     your place @ 5:30.

Julie: Awesome, I'm so excited! Char, I'll pop over to your
     place to grab the bottle while you're on ATV duty.

     Anthony: Thank you! Thank you! Thank you! Ya'll are
                         the best!

"Do you think Mom will mind if we get paint on these clothes?" Tia surprised him as she walked back into the room wearing jeans and a navy-blue t-shirt. Maria was right behind her in a similar pair of jeans and a pink t-shirt, with her hair still wet from her bath. Anthony assumed Tia had brushed out the tangles for her while she was upstairs changing. "We didn't pack any of our older stuff that already has paint stains when we left Tulsa."

"But these are the oldest clothes we brought with us." Maria gave him an impish smile. "We knew better than to try and paint in any of our new clothes Memmaw bought us."

"Um, I'm not sure." Anthony placed his phone back on the windowsill. "Let's go ask her before we open the paint. If not, I'm sure I have some old t-shirts we can turn into painting smocks in those bags in the laundry room."

They made their way to the kitchen just as Kay was heading toward them to let them know breakfast was ready. They discussed the smock possibilities while scarfing down scrambled eggs, bacon, and toast. The girls drank chocolate milk while Anthony and Kay had coffee.

Anthony reveled in the feeling of family surrounding him at the breakfast table. He hadn't really felt like he belonged on the ranch after leaving the Navy. Too many bittersweet memories haunting him when he thought he'd lost his only chance to be a father. Kay, Tia, and Maria were not only proving to him that he could still be a dad, but also that they all fit in perfectly on the Burleson Ranch.

After breakfast, he found a couple of old white t-shirts for the girls to wear over their clothes while painting. Tia opted to change into shorts under hers since it only covered down to a few inches below her knees, and she didn't want to get paint on the bottom part of her jeans. Anthony's old t-shirt almost reached Maria's ankles, so she was fine just rolling up the cuffs of her jeans. But they did have to tie some knots in the back, so the neck opening didn't fall off her shoulders and risk getting paint on her pink t-shirt under the improvised smock.

Kay started sorting through the laundry in the bags to wash it and put it all away, while Anthony and the girls went back to the living room to remove wallpaper and paint a dozen spots with different shades of yellow. Tia noticed his phone screen flashing a notification and asked him who he was texting earlier.

"I was in a group chat with my sisters and cousins," he replied while he worked on the wallpaper on the other side of the window from where the girls were painting yellow squares. "We've finished making our plans for tonight, so they can wait for me to reply after I finish this."

"I can reply for you if you want." Tia waved her hand toward his phone. "Unless you're ready to teach me how to do the steamer, so you can reply yourself while I work on the wallpaper."

Anthony contemplated which option would be best, risking her getting paint on his phone or risking her getting burned with the steamer, and opted to let her reply to his family group chat.

"It looks like they expanded the group to include your brothers, the rest of your cousins, and Memmaw and Pappaw," Tia told him after she read through the messages. "They want to know if you want to surprise Mom with an engagement party tonight after you propose."

Of course, they do, Anthony thought. *Only my family would turn a chat asking for help getting Kay alone into a planning meeting for a party for fifty of our closest friends and relatives.*

"Um, I don't know," Anthony replied. "Do you think your mom would like a surprise engagement party when we haven't had time to change out of our work clothes?"

"No, I told them to plan the surprise party for her birthday tomorrow instead." Tia shook her head. "The furniture won't be here until tomorrow either, so I figured it would be better to have everyone over after we've finished painting and actually have places for everyone to sit for the party."

"Good idea." Anthony scraped the next section of wallpaper down off the wall. "Maybe we can get most of it done today, so we just have the finishing touches in the morning when the furniture arrives and have time to get dressed up and go into San Antonio for birthday shopping and dinner."

"I thought you already gave Mom her birthday present?" Maria looked questioningly at him as she painted another square of yellow on the wall between the window and foyer where Anthony had removed the first section of wallpaper.

"Yeah, but I sent her the e-reader when I thought I wouldn't be able to see her on her actual birthday," Anthony shrugged as he moved around the corner to the next wall. "And I want to give her something else since I get to be with her on her special day."

"Do you think you can take us shopping for her tomorrow, too?" Tia requested.

"Definitely," Anthony replied. "I was thinking we'd all go to the music store in San Antonio before dinner. I want her to pick out the instruments she wants for the music room, and I thought that would be a good gift from all of us."

With his back turned to the girls while he was steaming the wallpaper off of the wall at the other end of the room from where they were painting and texting, Anthony didn't see the faces they made at his suggestion of Kay picking out her own present.

"Maybe we can get Memmaw to take us to town in the morning when she goes to pick up the cake for the party, so we can have time to wrap her presents and they can be a surprise instead of something she has to pick out herself." Tia was still tapping away on Anthony's phone while Maria went on to paint the next color on the wall.

Anthony heard the disapproval in her tone and realized the faux pas of his plan to shop with the birthday girl present to pick out her own gift. Not knowing what she would pick out for herself, though, he didn't want to order her an electronic keyboard and risk it not being exactly the one she wanted the most. He racked his brain for other ideas of things he could get for Kay.

More sexy lingerie? No, because she wouldn't want to open that in front of the girls. A laptop, so she can type the books she wants to write? No, I can't do that without knowing what software she needs to format it the way a publisher will want it. Jewelry? Maybe, but she never wears any, so I don't know what style she'd like. Hell, I'm not even sure she'll like the style of the rings in my pocket.

At a loss for ideas, he finally decided to ask the girls for better recommendations than his lame ones. "Since letting her pick out her own birthday present was obviously my worst idea, what do you suggest we get her?"

"Music boxes," Tia and Maria chimed in unison.

"Huh," Anthony pondered whether or not he could find a single music box in Heart's Destiny within the next twenty-four hours, much less three of them.

"Mom used to collect them." Tia finally put his phone back in the window and moved to paint her swatches of yellow paint on the other side of the window from where Maria was painting. "She had a whole bunch of them when we were little, but only three or four survived the move to Grandma and Grandpa's house. And now they're probably broken, too. If we get her music boxes that she can keep here, she can restart her collection, and you'll keep them safe for her if we have to go back to Tulsa."

Hearing the trepidation in her voice at the possibility of having to go back to Tulsa felt like a knife to Anthony's heart. He wanted to reassure her that she wouldn't have to live there ever again, if she didn't want to, but knew he couldn't yet. He hated being stuck in limbo, waiting on word from Kay's attorney, and their day in court, to tell the girls he wanted to adopt them. He'd promised Kay the day before that he wouldn't say anything until she got the "all clear" from Matt, and he wouldn't go back on his word to Kay, but that didn't mean he couldn't offer them some reassurance that he was doing everything he could to make sure they never had to see their sperm donor again.

"Don't worry, Princess." Anthony smiled at Tia. "I'm going to Tulsa with you when we have to go to court. I won't let him near you girls, or your mom, while we're there. And I'm working on making sure the last time you ever have to be in the same room with him is that day in court. That way we can all go visit your family in Tulsa and not have to worry about it being unsafe anymore."

"You really think we're going to be able to stay here and only visit Tulsa?" Maria's lower lip trembled.

"Yes, Princess, I absolutely do," Anthony replied reassuringly.

"Awesome," Maria squealed. "But we need to move your music stuff back down to the game room, so you can make that other bedroom our brother's room when you adopt him."

"Naw, we'll just put his crib in your room," Anthony joked while struggling to maintain a deadpan expression. "Since you're the one who wants a baby brother, I figured you'd want to be the one to get up in the middle of the night to feed him and change his diapers."

Maria's jaw dropped, and so did her hand, while holding the open can of paint. Anthony quickly flipped off the steamer, so he could drop it to the ground and rush to clean up the yellow spill on the hardwood floor. Even as he rushed to quell the mess, he couldn't help but chuckle at Maria's shocked response to his kidding with her.

"I was only kidding, Princess." Anthony knelt down beside her, capped the paint can, and wiped up the spill with one of the old towels he'd also brought in from the laundry bags for just that purpose when he found the t-shirts the girls were wearing as smocks. "We won't adopt until after we build a bigger house, so we have room for a couple of little brothers, and nobody has to share a room but Mom and I."

"Not a bigger house, a castle," Maria insisted, waving around the paintbrush in her hand and painting a yellow stripe on Anthony's forearm.

"We're supposed to paint the walls, not each other," Anthony heard Kay say through a giggle from behind him. He turned to look at her, needing to see her smiling face. "Although, now that I see them all up on the wall, I think I like the shade on Anthony's arm the best."

"That would be this can." Anthony handed Kay the can he'd just closed up from Maria's spill.

"Are you close to being ready to go to town to get the paint?" Kay looked around the room at what all they'd gotten done so far.

"I can be if you want me to be." Anthony wiped the paint off his arm with another old towel. "Or you can take the truck and the girls to pick out the paint for the game room while I finish taking down the wallpaper in here to give you a room ready to paint when you get back."

"Um, maybe," Kay sputtered, looking nervous.

"It's only about four miles to the hardware store." Anthony hoped to reassure her that she could find it and not get lost. "Make a left out of the ranch on Rogers, then a right on Walker. It's at the corner of Walker and Longhorn. You can't miss it."

"It's not that I'm worried about getting lost…" Kay trailed off, looking down sheepishly. "I'm not sure about driving your truck."

"Why not?" Anthony wondered aloud. "I actually prefer thinking of you driving my truck instead of your little car, so you're less likely to get hurt if you have an accident."

"Bigger doesn't mean safer," Kay retorted. "In fact, for me, bigger vehicles are less safe because I can't reach the pedals and see over the steering wheel at the same time, so I'm a lot more likely to have an accident."

Anthony laughed at the mental image she conjured with her description of trying to drive his truck. "Come on, Shorty," Anthony chuckled as he stood. "Let's go see if we can adjust the seat to where you can drive my truck. If not, I'll clean up and drive ya'll to town."

The girls took off their t-shirt smocks and followed them out to the truck. Anthony adjusted the driver's seat as far forward as it would go, which was quite a bit different than his normal setting of all the way back. The girls climbed into the back seat, while Anthony helped Kay into the driver's seat.

"Wow, there's a lot more room back here when Mom's driving," Maria shouted. "I can't reach the back of the seat with my feet anymore."

Kay adjusted the seat back, so it was also as far forward as it would go, putting her sitting up straight, as if she was going for perfect posture. Anthony showed her how to adjust the steering wheel down, so it would be more comfortable for her to drive. Once it was adjusted along with the mirrors, she had to concede that she could indeed see over the steering wheel to drive while engaging the gas and brakes as needed.

He made sure she had her purse and phone before handing over his keys, so she could go to town for her first trip on her own. He felt a tingle of fear as she pulled out of the driveway. He knew it was ridiculous to be afraid of her getting in an accident and dying anytime he wasn't the one driving her around. That's why he was pushing to conquer his fear by sending her on this short little errand in his hometown, where he felt reasonably assured she would be safe.

He watched until she made the turn on Rogers Road before he went back inside and went back to work on taking down wallpaper. He checked his phone after every section of wallpaper that came down, catching up on the family group chat when he had no messages from Kay.

He had to smile at how Tia had orchestrated his family into planning Kay's surprise birthday party, even getting recommendations for where to shop for music boxes and the suggestion to leave Kay to supervise the furniture delivery while Anthony, Tia, and Maria went shopping.

Leah Mae Wright

Tia's elaborate plans started first thing in the morning with breakfast in bed for Kay—cinnamon rolls with a birthday candle in Kay's that were being delivered to Tia by one of his cousins from the bakery downtown. Followed by their speedy shopping trip, giving Kay a gift basket of bubble bath and other girly stuff to spend the afternoon having a spa day in their master bathroom, and dressing up for a late afternoon birthday lunch. While the four of them were off at lunch and a little sightseeing, Anthony's family would be decorating the house with balloons and a birthday banner, and sneaking in the cake and drinks to surprise Kay upon their arrival at home with her birthday dinner.

As he called to make their late-lunch reservations for the next day, Anthony wished he could have come up with some of the ideas on his own because he wanted to be the one to pamper Kay on her special day, but he was grateful for his family's help in planning and executing more than he could have done on his own with so little time. He hoped Kay felt as loved and accepted by them as he did.

When he finished getting the wallpaper down in the living room, he cleaned up the mess where he'd been piling the old wallpaper on the floor. He wiped down the walls with the specialty cleaner that was supposed to make sure no glue residue remained on the walls. He spackled any areas where the old plaster walls were showing their age with cracks or chips where it had come off with the wallpaper.

He pulled the electric sander out of the shopping bag from the day before and set it up, so he could smooth out the spackle once it was dry, wanting to give Kay a perfect surface for painting.

He checked his phone again for messages from Kay before moving the steamer and supplies to the dining room. He almost texted her to check in, but he stopped himself when he imagined her getting in an accident while trying to read his text as she was driving home.

He pushed the horrid images from his mind, replacing them with visions of her painting the wall he was tackling with the steamer. It was a trick his Navy shrink had taught him, using positive mental imagery to fight off the nightmares that he had immediately after the aircraft carrier bombing that caused his Navy career-ending injuries. He used his fantasies of Kay to fight off his fears until she and the girls finally got back from the hardware store.

~~~

Kay couldn't contain her broad smile as she floated through her day. She was so happy with Anthony that she couldn't hold all the joy inside. She felt like she'd laughed more in the twelve days she'd spent with Anthony than she had in the twelve years before she met him.

While her family and friends weren't around to see her every day to witness firsthand how her spirits were lifted in comparison, they'd backed off on their initial assertions that Anthony was too good to be true. Even with the limitations of only brief communication with Kay and her daughters through phone calls, emails, and text messages, those closest to her had seen enough of an improvement in her mood to change their tune. Even her dad, who had been pushing her to be strong and independent and avoid men at all costs after her disastrous divorce, was now singing Anthony's praises and looking forward to walking her down the aisle at their wedding. Though now that she started trying to figure out who could walk her daughters down the aisle since none of the boys in either of their families were age appropriate, she'd started thinking about having Tia and Maria walk her down the aisle instead.

Kay'd called her parents that morning while making breakfast and filled them in on the change of plans for their day in court, the hopefully impending adoption of the girls by Anthony, and the tentative wedding date that Anthony had set for them the day before. After her mother's squeals of delight died down, her father had given her a hearty "congratulations" and said he would go ahead and schedule their travel arrangements for a family Thanksgiving and wedding in Texas.

Kay'd also texted her sister and childhood best friend, asking them each to be her bridesmaids. She may have told Anthony that she couldn't officially plan the wedding until he properly proposed, but she didn't think informing her family of the potential date counted as officially planning anything. Even if it did, she'd already said yes to his proposal in her heart, so she wouldn't worry about planning too soon.

Randi and Deanna were both excited and congratulated her with text messages full of heart emojis and gifs of wedding cakes. They
~~~

were each going to coordinate with Kay's father, Charles, about their travel arrangements. Kay let them know to be expecting calls from her future mother-in-law, Hazel, to get their measurements for their dresses, but it might be a week or two before she actually picked out a style from the catalogs Hazel had the girls going through already.

After breakfast, she started working through the laundry that Anthony had haphazardly shoved into garbage bags when he packed up his apartment. She wanted to wash everything, since some of his clean clothes had been stuffed in the same bag with the sheets he'd removed from the bed the day of the move.

She emptied all the bags and sorted everything into loads to run through the washer and dryer, starting with the dirty bedding. One bag was all his old Navy uniforms, and she wasn't sure they could be laundered at home. She hung them on the rod in the laundry room and pulled out her new phone to look for a dry cleaner in Heart's Destiny. Once she called and verified that they could handle his uniforms, she carried them out to Anthony's truck, so they could drop them off the next time they went to town and put a note in her new phone to pick them up on their first day home the next week.

She surprised herself with how much she was using her new phone. Anthony had been so enthusiastic when he showed her how to use it like a virtual assistant that she actually wanted to use it more than she had her old one. She'd never been big on using the latest technology or social media like most of her peers. With her ex in the Army, there had been restrictions on what she could say on social media, so she just avoided it altogether to keep from accidentally breaking the rules. Now that she had a phone capable of more than calls, texts, and Skype, she wondered if she should explore more of the sphere of social media, even if it was way outside her comfort zone.

After cleaning and putting away everything they'd bought for the kitchen the day before, Kay found Anthony cleaning up where Maria spilled paint on the floor. She didn't hear all of their conversation, but she got the general gist of their kidding around leading to her mess and the stripe of yellow paint she'd apparently painted across Anthony's forearm.

It was such an adorable father-daughter moment that Kay wanted that shade of yellow for their walls even if it wasn't the best match, just so she could remember the moment every time she walked into their living room.

When she informed them of her choice of colors, Anthony sent her and the girls to the hardware store in his truck. While she was slightly nervous driving such a large vehicle, he gently coaxed her into conquering her fear by making her comfortable behind the wheel before sending her off.

The look in his eyes was all confidence and love, showing her that he trusted her to not wreck his truck. His belief in her was all it took to shore up her own self-confidence that she could navigate the town while easily maneuvering the massive vehicle.

Just pick the biggest parking spaces and don't try to back up where you can't see how close you are to what's behind you, she told herself as she drove into town. First, she dropped Anthony's Navy uniforms off at Destiny Dry Cleaning, making a mental note that it was next door to the electronics store they'd gone to the day before on Longhorn Lane.

Instead of risking hitting something by trying to back out of the northeast-angled parking spot across both lanes to drive south on Longhorn Lane, Kay only backed into the northbound lane and drove north to Appaloosa Avenue, where she turned right. When she got to Brangus Street, she made another right turn to head back to Walker Road to go to Hometown Hardware. That put her parking at the hardware store facing the correct direction to head back to Rogers Road and the Burleson Ranch without having to struggle to maneuver Anthony's big truck in a complex turn to go the direction she wanted.

She purchased four gallons of yellow paint for the living room and dining room, two gallons of pink paint and two gallons of chalkboard paint for the girls' game room, and several drop cloths, paint rollers, trays for using the paint rollers, and trim brushes, so they wouldn't have to come back to the hardware store to finish the painting.

When she checked out at the register, she used her own debit card since her first week's pay had been direct deposited two days earlier. She may have gotten cards for Anthony's accounts, but the only time she actually used his card was when she bought the bedding, curtains, and towels and hadn't checked her own bank balance first. She didn't know what it would take to make her comfortable using his accounts.

As long as her job kept putting her deposits in her account, she didn't think she'd feel right spending money from any other accounts.

When they got back to the ranch, Anthony had finished removing the wallpaper in both the living and dining rooms. He'd cleaned up the old wallpaper mess and spackled a few spots in each room. Anthony was sanding the dry spackle in the living room when Kay, Tia, and Maria walked in the door, each carrying a can of paint or a bag of supplies. He put the sander down and kissed Kay quickly before going out to unload the rest of the paint and supplies from the back of the truck.

Kay went to the laundry room to swap out the loads she was washing and drying. She folded the first load of dry sheets and put them away in the upstairs hall closet before going to the living room to help with the painting.

As soon as Anthony finished sanding the rough spots on the living room walls, they spread out a drop cloth and taped off the dark wood wainscoting and trim, so the girls wouldn't get yellow paint on any of the woodwork. Kay and the girls worked on painting what they could reach of the walls, while Anthony worked on moving the game room furniture and electronics to the center of the room and covered it all with a drop cloth.

He started steaming off the wallpaper in the game room, but he had to stop when Kay called him into the living room to paint the top of the walls where none of the girls could reach without a ladder, since they'd returned his parents' ladder the day before. As soon as they were finished painting the living room, Anthony went back to removing the wallpaper in the game room, while Kay sanded the dry spackle in the dining room and the girls took a break from painting to have a snack.

The girls surprised Kay and Anthony by bringing them each a sandwich where they were working. At some point, Anthony turned on some music from his phone and put it in the hallway, so they could all hear it no matter what room they were working in downstairs. As they worked through the afternoon, he turned their workday into an impromptu classic rock concert, schooling the girls on a genre of music they wouldn't normally listen to on their own.

They worked together like a well-oiled machine with Anthony removing wallpaper and preparing the walls for Kay and the girls to paint. He would come help with the painting where they couldn't reach as a break from preparing the walls in the next space. They'd finished the living room, dining room, and the pink part of the game room walls, when Anthony moved to prep the walls in the hallway, while Kay and the girls were painting the wainscoting panels and dark wood trim in the game room with chalkboard paint.

When Anthony started steaming the wallpaper off the hallway walls, Kay realized they hadn't thought about what color to paint the downstairs hallway that ran the length of the center of the house. With every room on the lower level opening up into the hallway, she couldn't figure out how to make it flow from the dark wood in the library, to the yellow of the living and dining rooms, to the pink and black of the game room, to the pink and aqua of the kitchen, to the not quite white in the laundry room, mud room, and downstairs powder room. Maybe they should have planned to repaint the laundry room, mud room, and downstairs powder room in a neutral color that didn't just look like dirty white walls and carry that neutral color down the hallway.

When Kay suggested they pick another color to paint those rooms the next day, Anthony objected. "Naw, Baby, we have other plans for tomorrow, so we'll have to finish the painting next time we're here."

"What plans?" Kay didn't think the furniture delivery should keep them from spending the day painting.

Before he could answer, there was a knock on the front door and Anthony's sisters, Charlotte and Becky, and cousins, Jen and Julie, walked in the house.

"Hey, all," Becky shouted as they all came down the hallway toward Kay and Anthony.

"We're here to take the girls for a ride on the four wheelers." Charlotte smiled brightly when they reached them.

"Oh, um," Kay stammered, not sure how to politely decline Anthony's overwhelming family. "I don't think they'll have time today. We're going to be painting for a couple more hours and it'll be dark before we finish the game room."

The four women looked back and forth between Kay and Anthony like they were confused by Kay's response. Anthony shrugged like he didn't know how to answer their unasked questions.

"What are you working on?" Jen poked her head into the game room to look. "If we all pitch in, it won't take nearly as long, so we can still get everyone out on the four wheelers."

"I'm finishing removing the wallpaper in the hall and the girls are finishing painting in the game room." Anthony held up the steamer in his hands.

Charlotte, Becky, and Jen walked into the game room and started helping the girls with the chalkboard paint. Julie asked Anthony to teach her how to use the steamer and he promptly started showing her. With all the paint rollers and brushes in use, Kay found herself unsure of what she could work on. She'd already finished all the laundry, as she'd taken several breaks from painting to swap loads between the washer and dryer and put away everything when it was finished.

"I guess I'll go start dinner." Kay mentally started planning to double her normal amount of spaghetti, so there would be enough to feed all their extra helping hands.

Before she could turn toward the kitchen and take a step, Anthony stopped her by saying, "Naw, Baby, it's too early for dinner."

"It's going to take at least an hour to fix," Kay argued, turning back to see Anthony handing Julie the steamer.

"Then we still have time for a ride on the four wheelers, while my sisters and cousins help the girls finish our chores for the day." Anthony reached out to take Kay's hand.

"I'm not going to go play and leave our guests to work on the house," Kay objected, not moving when Anthony tried to tug her hand to get her to follow him outside.

"Now I see why you needed our help," Becky giggled as she poked her head out of the game room where she was painting by the door. "I think you only have two options to get her to go with you. Ruin the surprise by telling her where you're taking her and why, or take advantage of your superior size and strength by carrying her out of the house while she continues to object."

"You planned for them to come over, so you can take me somewhere?" Kay wondered what he could possibly be up to.

"Yeah, I wanted to show you something last night, but you insisted on doing Ma's dishes instead, so I had to enlist their help to try again today," Anthony explained as he bent down and picked Kay up, tossing her over his shoulder like a sack of potatoes. "And since you're stubbornly refusing to come with me, I'm choosing Becky's second option, so I don't ruin the surprise."

"The keys are still in the four wheelers out front," Charlotte shouted as Anthony started walking down the hall toward the front door. "So, you don't have to carry her all the way to the barn to get yours."

"Thanks, ladies," Anthony called back loudly as he opened the front door. "We'll be back in a little while."

He walked over to the closest ATV and put Kay on before getting on behind her. It felt weird riding in front of him when he reached around her to turn it on and grip the handlebars to steer.

"Aren't I supposed to ride behind you?" Kay wiggled her butt against his crotch as he started down the gravel road, grinning as his cock hardened against her.

"I'm not taking any chances on you jumping off," Anthony replied as he increased his speed once they were past the houses that Kay thought of as the ranch subdivision. "This way I can keep my arms around you, so you can't escape until we get where we're going."

A couple miles later they passed another house that Kay assumed was his brother Bobby's. They kept going south, past a few more buildings that Kay thought were a second stable, barn, and bunkhouse. They eased southwest, around a fenced in pasture, and took off on a trail going uphill through a wooded area. Kay estimated they'd gone about five miles from the house in the fifteen minutes they were on the four-wheeler, when the woods opened up to a field of wildflowers and they stopped at the top of a bluff.

Anthony turned off the ATV before they both got off the machine. Anthony took Kay's hand as they walked toward the edge, where the bluff sloped down toward a wide-open field with a creek running through it and into a pond. The sun was setting into the horizon, painting the sky in a glorious mix of blue, purple, yellow, and orange. It was a stunning view that took Kay's breath away.

"Wow!" Kay was breathless with awe at the gorgeous sunset.

"This is my favorite spot on the ranch." Anthony waved his arm to indicate the field around them, as they stood there enjoying the view. "I want to build our house on this bluff, so we have this view every night. Maybe put in some pavers to make a natural-looking stairway down to the creek for swimming in the summer."

Kay turned to look at the field of flowers, trying to picture a home there that would blend in with the natural beauty of the area. "I can see why." Kay turned back toward the sunset. "It's a beautiful place to live."

As the orange light of the sun started to sink below the horizon, Anthony pulled something out of his pocket and dropped to one knee. Kay turned to look at him when he clasped her left hand in his right, realizing that he was about to propose. She'd known it was coming but she was still stunned that it was actually happening.

"I love you so much, Baby," Anthony shared as they stared into each other's eyes. "I want to spend the rest of our lives together, living our dreams, raising our kids, and loving each other more each day."

Kay was nodding her head in agreement before Anthony could even ask the question.

"Kay Lynn Lee, will you marry me?" Anthony held up a sparkling, square-cut, diamond solitaire. Kay couldn't tell if the ring was silver, white gold, or platinum, not that it really mattered. It was what Anthony had chosen for her and she would have loved whatever he picked for her even if it was made of plastic.

"Yes, yes, yes!" Kay shouted as Anthony slid the ring on her finger before standing and scooping her up into his arms. Their lips locked together as her arms and legs clamped around him. The kiss was impassioned, a sensual expression of their love.

When they pulled back to take a breath, Anthony carried Kay over to the ATV, putting her down on it. He reached into his pocket again, pulling out a silver rope style chain with two silver bands on the necklace like charms.

"These were my grandparents' wedding rings," Anthony explained before Kay could ask him when he'd been able to sneak off to a jewelry store. "Memmaw passed away when I was thirteen and Pappaw wore her rings on this chain around his neck until he passed away ten years later. My dad put Pappaw's ring on the chain when we lost him, but they've just been being stored in Ma's jewelry box for the last two years. When I talked to Dad while we were moving Monday, he suggested we use them. But if you don't like the style, or if you want gold instead of platinum, we can pick something else."

"No, I don't want anything else." Kay shook her head slightly, reaching out to touch the chain and pull the bands hanging on it closer to her face, so she could see them better. She put her left hand up next to the bands, so she could see all three together. "These are perfect. I not only love the style, but I also love the sentimentality of passing them down through the generations of your family."

As it was getting too dark for Anthony to feel comfortable trying to put the necklace around Kay's neck without losing one of the rings, he put them back in his pocket to drive them back to their house first. As soon as they walked in the door to their home, they were swarmed by family members wishing them well.

Kay somehow managed to get them all into the kitchen, so she could start fixing dinner while they offered their congratulations. Eventually, Anthony went back to work on the hallway wallpaper, while his sisters and cousins helped the girls finish painting in the game room.

When Kay was finished fixing a huge pot of spaghetti and meatballs with corn on the cob, green beans, and garlic toast, and everyone else was finished cleaning up the painting supplies, and all the wallpaper was removed, they settled into the kitchen for a family dinner.

Since their dining room furniture wouldn't arrive until the next day, Tia and Maria ate dinner at the table for six in the kitchen with Charlotte, Becky, Jen, and Julie. Anthony and Kay sat on the stools at the island, so they could visit with everyone while eating.

After another evening of extended family time that Kay enjoyed immensely due to all the stories about Anthony in his younger years, their guests left and the girls went up to get baths and go to bed, back to their normal bedtime routine. Anthony and Kay worked together to clear the table. Once the dishes were all stacked by the sink, Kay rinsed them off and handed them to Anthony, so he could load the dishwasher.

"Now that we're alone," Anthony stated, pulling the necklace and wedding bands back out of his pocket. "I think this will look better around your neck than mine."

"Really? I figured since I have this ring to show I'm taken…" Kay gave him an ornery little half grin, holding her left hand up and pointing to the ring with her right. "…you'd wear those until the wedding to warn off other women."

"If that's what you want, I'll wear them." Anthony looked down at the necklace in his hand to see how the clasp worked before putting it on his own neck. He tucked the rings under his t-shirt before continuing. "But since you're the only woman who will ever see me without a shirt to see them, I don't know how effective they'll be at warning off all these invisible women you seem to be concerned with."

Instead of continuing to rinse the plates under the running water in the sink, Kay grabbed the sprayer attachment under the guise of using it to rinse the large stockpot she'd boiled the pasta in, but instead she turned it to spray Anthony. It was her playful way of getting back at him for calling her out on her jealousy.

"They aren't invisible," Kay insisted as she soaked Anthony's shirt. "Stacy was blatantly flirting with you the other night."

"Oh, Baby, they're all invisible to me since I met you," Anthony disagreed as he easily disarmed Kay of the sink sprayer nozzle. He captured both of her wrists in one hand and held them over her head, so he could saturate her shirt with the spray. "And if we're having a wet t-shirt contest, you have to get yours wet, too."

"Stop, stop, it tickles," Kay squealed, squirming but unable to escape from Anthony's firm grasp on her wrists.

"I'll stop when you admit that neither one of us has a reason to be jealous because everyone else is invisible to us," Anthony demanded as he made sure her nipples were visible through her white bra and pink t-shirt by focusing the spray of water directly on her breasts. "If anyone else tries to flirt, we're oblivious because we're too focused on each other to take notice."

"Yes, fine, they're all invisible," Kay squealed when the stream hit an especially ticklish spot on her side.

Anthony put the sprayer back in the slot on the back of the sink and turned the water off. Then he scooped Kay up with one arm behind her back and the other under her knees. He carried her toward the front of the house to the stairs.

"Anthony, wait," Kay objected even as her arms wrapped around his neck. "We haven't finished the dishes."

"I'll do them in the morning," he replied as he carried her up the stairs toward their bedroom. "I need to dry off my fiancée now."

He carried her through the bedroom and into the bathroom before he sat her down in front of the vanity. He dropped to his knees beside her, evening out their height difference. He took his time as he removed her clothing. Slowly stripping her of each piece, reverently stroking her newly exposed skin with his hands, as if he couldn't move on to the next item until he'd touched every inch that he'd just revealed.

He started with her t-shirt, then went to her shoes and socks before removing her jeans. He ran his hands over her entire body with the exception of where she was still covered by her bra and panties. She loved how he touched her everywhere, but she really wished he would hurry up and get to the good parts.

She wanted to speed him up by removing her bra but when she went to undo the dozen hooks down the front, he stopped her by saying, "No. Keep your hands down by your sides. I want to unwrap you like the precious gift you are."

Yes, please! Kay thought before asking, "When do I get to unwrap you?"

"Later, Baby." Anthony started unhooking her bra. "After I spend at least an hour or two worshiping you, my queen."

He dropped her bra to the floor with her other clothing. His gentle touch as he stroked his fingertips over her breasts was such a tease. She longed for him to apply more pressure, to squeeze and knead her bountiful flesh, to pinch and bite her nipples, and to push her to find her limits where pain became pleasurable.

"More, please," Kay whimpered.

"More what, Baby?" Anthony's thumbs flicked across her nipples.

"Harder, rougher." Kay ached for him to quit torturing her. "Quit teasing me with light, tickly touching. I'm not made of glass; you don't have to be gentle."

"Baby," Anthony groaned. "I don't want to risk hurting you."

"You're not going to hurt me, Anthony," Kay insisted, wrapping her arms around his neck, and pressing her lips to his for a long sensual kiss.

Anthony's arms wrapped around her, pressing her bare breasts to his wet t-shirt covered chest. The denim of his jeans was rough against her thighs, as he thrust his still covered erection against her.

He deepened the kiss, fucking her mouth with his tongue in sync with the prodding of his hips.

"Fuck," Anthony groaned when he finally pulled back to take a breath. He sat back on his heels and ran a hand through his hair like he was frustrated with himself.

Kay felt guilty, thinking her request might have ruined the mood. "I'm sorry," she sighed.

"No, Baby." Anthony came back up on his knees and gripped Kay's shoulders. "You have no reason to apologize. I'm sorry. I'm the one who's letting my fear stop me from giving us both what we want."

He hugged her to him, burying his face in her hair as he rested his head on her shoulder and nuzzled her neck. "I want you more than I've ever wanted anyone in my life," he whispered in her ear. "I wanna do things to you that I've never wanted before. Dark, dirty things that scare the hell out of me."

"Oh, Anthony," Kay cooed soothingly as she rubbed her hands up and down his back.

"I love you, Baby," he crooned. "So much that I don't wanna ever risk hurting you."

"I love you, too," Kay replied. "And I trust you to push our limits without actually hurting me."

"Really? How?" Anthony lifted his head to look her in the eye. "I don't trust myself not to lose control and accidentally go too far, so how can you?"

Before Kay could answer him, he stood and started pacing the bathroom while ranting. "It's been less than twelve hours since I was inside you last, and I'm frantic to fuck you. We've fucked more in the last four days than either one of us has in the last four years. I know I need to back off and give you a break, or you won't be able to walk by the end of the week, much less enjoy being fucked. That's why I'm trying to control my inner beast that wants to be rough and fuck you like a wild animal. I'm trying desperately to be gentle, so I don't leave you too sore to do more tomorrow. But as soon as I touch you, it's like the beast takes over my body, and I completely lose control. And it's killing me to think I might accidentally go too far."

"Stop," Kay commanded, stepping into his path, so he had to quit stomping around the bathroom or run her over. When he stopped just a few inches in front of her, she arched her back and dropped her head back to look up into his eyes. "You haven't been too rough so far, so if your inner beast took over during the rougher moments, you can let him out anytime because it's not too much for me. And if the dark, dirty things you want to do are more intense than what we've already done, then we'll talk about them first, and use a safe word if needed, so we can both test our limits. I think we'll find that our limits are evenly matched, and we can both live out all our dark, dirty desires."

She smiled up at him and started to slide her arms around his waist. He grabbed her hands before she could fully embrace him and dropped back to his knees. He placed her hands on his shoulders before embracing her, their mouths meeting in a passionate kiss.

"You're so fucking perfect," Anthony growled as he pulled back just slightly, their lips not quite touching. "I don't know how I got so lucky to find you. I don't know if I'm good enough to deserve you, but I can't ever let you go. You're the missing piece of my heart, my soulmate, my everything."

He kissed her again, a deep, possessive kiss that made Kay feel like he was claiming her. He slid his hands down to her hips and slid her panties down her legs. Once they were on the floor, he picked her up by the hips and sat her on the vanity as their lips parted.

"Right now, I want to test your upper limit for orgasms while being worshiped with my mouth," Anthony implored as he stroked his hands down her thighs and spread her legs.

Kay gripped the edge of the vanity, her outer thighs pressing into her wrists, and resisted the urge to lean back against the mirror and close her eyes. Her ocean blue eyes looked longingly into Anthony's dark chocolate depths. Their soul-deep connection was expressed in their eye contact even more than where their bodies touched.

Anthony maintained their eye contact even as he lowered his head between her legs. He lightly blew out a long breath over her sensitive bundle of nerves before flicking it with the tip of his tongue.

Kay had never felt as aroused as she did with Anthony. Just that one little flick of his tongue across her clit and she was on the edge. She knew that if he applied even a little more pressure on his next lick, she'd explode in pleasure. He wasn't going to make the first orgasm that easy for her, though. Instead of focusing on her sex, he trailed his tongue up from her mound, making patterns on her belly with just the tip, as he worked his way up her body to her breasts.

She weaved her fingers through his hair, trying desperately to get him to move back down to her needy core. "Yeah, Baby, pull my hair," Anthony demanded between swipes of his tongue over her diamond hard nipples. "I want to feel your sex kitten claws in my back while I make you purr."

"You're going to have to do more than tease me if you want me to purr," Kay taunted as she moved her hands down to rub across the wide expanse of his upper back and shoulders.

He latched on and sucked hard in response to her goading. He scraped the edge of his teeth over her tight bud, as he pulled back and moved to repeat the actions on her other breast. That slight hint of pain was like a lightning bolt shooting straight to her sex, pushing her even closer to the edge.

His big hands clamped onto her pelvis, covering the crease where her thighs met her torso, and holding her still when she started to writhe with need. He teased her with his thumbs, spreading her folds but not touching her needy nub, as he continued to nibble her nipples.

As he moved his mouth from one side to the other, he bit down a little harder on the swell of her cleavage. The thought of having a mark from his teeth, lasting a few days on her breast, was enough to send Kay soaring over the edge. She cried out his name, as her pussy clamped down on nothing but air, immersed in her first climax of the evening.

"Fuck, I love watching you come," Anthony whispered reverently against her skin. He soothed any remaining sting from his teeth with open-mouthed kisses across her breasts, laving each bite mark with his tongue. He sat back on his heels as he trailed more open-mouthed kisses down her torso.

Just as she felt like she was floating back down to earth, he devoured her pussy with his mouth, sending her soaring for a second time almost instantly. She floated on wave after wave of pleasure, unsure when one orgasm ended, and another began.

Or maybe it was just one? Can a single orgasm last an hour?

She didn't realize she'd dug her nails into his back as she floated in an ocean of ecstasy. It was a truly mindless, out-of-body experience.

She wafted through the heavens as he cleaned her up and carried her to bed.

"We need to put some clothes on to sleep, so the girls can surprise you in the morning without finding us naked in bed," she only vaguely registered Anthony saying as he slipped one of his t-shirts over her head.

The last thing she remembered was him pulling her into his arms and kissing her forehead as she drifted off to sleep.

Chapter Fourteen

Anthony awoke to the sound of a soft knock on the bedroom door, glad he'd planned ahead and put Kay in one of his t-shirts and slipped on a pair of athletic shorts before they fell asleep wrapped around each other.

"Come in," he called out to the giggling girls on the other side of the door. His voice was hoarse from sleep, making him especially grateful for the tray of mostly full juice glasses Tia carried in for Kay's birthday breakfast in bed.

He sat up in bed and gently nudged Kay to wake her, as Tia carefully placed the tray of juice on the bedside table. Maria wasn't as careful with the two bakery boxes she was carrying. She bounced up on the foot of the bed and dropped them both on the comforter beside Anthony's knees.

When Kay finally stirred and started to sit up, the girls simultaneously sang and shouted, "Happy Birthday, Mom!"

"Oh, goodness," Kay yawned, trying to cover her mouth with her hand. "What's all this?"

"Breakfast in bed for your birthday," Maria shouted and started to open the boxes. The first contained one giant cinnamon roll with a single candle stuck in the middle, which she handed to Kay. The second was a bigger box with another half-dozen large cinnamon rolls.

"Aunt Jen said you'd light the candle for us." Tia handed Anthony a candle lighter that was lying between the juice glasses and a stack of plates on the tray she'd carried in, along with one of the plates to put it on.

"Why's mine so much bigger than the others?" Kay helped Anthony put her giant cinnamon roll on the plate.

"Because it's your birthday, so yours is special," Maria answered as she took out one of the other cinnamon rolls and put it on one of the other plates that Tia had put beside the other breakfast box.

Anthony lit the candle on Kay's cinnamon roll while the girls plated the smaller rolls, two each for the three of them. They sang a slightly off-key version of **Happy Birthday** to Kay before she blew out the candle and they all dug into their breakfast.

"Thank you." Kay looked lovingly into each of the smiling faces surrounding her. "This is a wonderful birthday surprise."

"Oh, we're just getting started," Tia snickered, giving Anthony a conspiratorial grin. "We've got to run to town to finish getting the next surprise ready, but Memmaw said that if we go early enough, we can get back before the furniture delivery, so you can spend a leisurely morning lying in bed reading while we take care of the housework today."

"Are you going to give me any hints about the surprises?" Kay queried between bites of her cinnamon roll and sips of her orange juice.

"Nope," the girls chirped in unison before popping pieces of cinnamon roll into their mouths.

"That takes all the fun out of the surprises," Anthony added as he finished off his breakfast and drained the last of his juice. He reached over to the bedside table where all of his and Kay's phones and tablets were charging, picked up Kay's e-reader, and handed it to her. He gave her a chaste kiss before getting out of bed. "Happy Birthday, Baby. Now you relax and read, while we get dressed and head to town."

Anthony grabbed a pair of boxer briefs from the dresser, a pair of jeans and a t-shirt from the closet, and went into the master bathroom to get ready for the first part of the day. While he was brushing his teeth, shaving, and changing his clothes, the girls carried the dirty dishes down to the kitchen and finished getting ready to go.

"We shouldn't be gone more than an hour," Anthony told Kay as he snuck another kiss when he was done in the bathroom. He sat down on the side of the bed and put on his socks and sneakers. "And the furniture isn't supposed to be here until ten, so we should be back with plenty of time to meet the delivery. So, you don't have to worry about a thing other than relaxing today."

One more quick kiss and he was out of the bedroom and headed downstairs to take the girls to town. They were already waiting for him at the truck, excitement lighting up their cherubic faces.

They headed downtown to the three stores where they were most likely to find everything they needed. The first stop was the Knick Knack Shack on Mustang Lane, where they had three different music boxes gift-wrapped for Kay. They then walked to the craft store next door, A Stitch In Time, where they were able to get most of the stuff to make their own gift basket—a basket, some filler for under the gifts, and some spa-scented candles for the bathroom. After putting those purchases in the truck, they walked around the corner to the Book Nook to find birthday cards.

In the bookstore, Anthony was inspired with gift ideas that might entice Kay into starting to write her first novel. He found a book of writing prompts, a dark blue hardbound book filled with lined pages for her to handwrite her first book, and a royal blue bejeweled pen. He asked the clerk if they could gift wrap the items together as they approached the counter, and was happy to have one less item he might need to wrap himself.

"Why are you buying a blank book?" Tia gave him a quizzical look when he put the items on the counter to check out.

"I thought your mom might want to handwrite her first book," Anthony replied.

"I didn't know Mom wanted to write a book." Tia looked deep in thought about the possibility.

"What's Mom want to write about?" Maria bounced by her sister's side as Anthony paid for their purchases.

"She hasn't told me any specific storylines." Anthony wondered if he should really be the one to explain the romance genre to the girls. "But I know she wanted to be an author when she was a teenager, and I thought these things might inspire her to follow her dreams."

"That's a much better gift idea than having her pick out an instrument." Tia nodded her approval as they made their way back to the truck after paying for their purchases and waiting for the gift wrapping. "I always got the feeling that she only played the organ because Grandma Lee wanted her to for church. She didn't ever really look like she enjoyed it much."

"Yeah, when she and I talked about it, she said she liked the piano when she was a kid and the electronic keyboard in high school, so I was thinking she'd pick one of those instead of an organ," Anthony explained as they got in the truck.

Anthony pulled out on Mustang Lane heading east, then turned south on Angus Avenue to go down to the grocery store, H.E.B., for wrapping paper, bubble bath, and whatever else the girls wanted to put in Kay's spa day gift basket.

"Is there a beauty supply store here?" Tia inquired as she was looking at the limited selection of makeup and nail polish.

"Um, maybe?" Anthony was unsure where else to go to get the things the girls wanted to get. "Let's ask the cashier when we pay for this stuff."

They walked to the front of the store and put the wrapping paper, tape, scissors, and large bottle of strawberry bubble bath on the conveyor belt, and waited their turn in line. When Anthony recognized the cashier as Tammi Jo Willis, he wasn't as confident in his plan to ask about a beauty supply store. His oldest brother's ex was known to be catty and might send him on a wild goose chase just because he was related to Bobby. He didn't get the chance to change lanes to find a different cashier to help them, though, because the girls were already introducing themselves to Tammi Jo.

"Hi, I'm Tia and this is my sister Maria. We're new in town and wondered if you could tell us where the closest beauty supply store is." Tia reached across the conveyor belt and offered her hand to shake with Tammi Jo.

Tammi Jo ignored Tia's outstretched hand and turned to Anthony before speaking. "Hey, Anthony, are these girls with you?"

"Hey, Tammi Jo," Anthony replied, hoping to keep things civil and escape the grocery store ASAP. "Yes, these are my soon-to-be stepdaughters, Tia and Maria."

"You're marrying their mother?" Tammi Jo gasped, holding a hand to her chest in disbelief.

"Yeah, they're getting married the weekend after Thanksgiving," Maria answered for him. "But we're trying to find the stuff for a spa gift basket for Mom's birthday today."

"And we're kinda in a hurry." Tia tapped her foot impatiently as she pulled her hand back and motioned at the things on the conveyor belt that Tammi Jo hadn't even started to scan. "So, if you could scan these things while telling us where the nearest beauty supply store is, that'd be great."

Anthony wasn't sure if he should reprimand Tia for being rude, or pat her on the back for getting Tammi Jo to refocus on her job, instead of starting the shitstorm he'd expected from her. In the end, he just kept his mouth shut, so he didn't misstep.

"Um, yeah, Beautiful Destiny is over at the corner of Arabian and Brangus," Tammi Jo sputtered as she scanned their items.

Anthony quickly swiped his card and said a quick "Thanks" as she handed him the receipt. He picked up the bags and ushered the girls toward the door.

"Tell Bobby I said hi," Tammi Jo shouted to their quickly retreating backs.

"I don't like that lady." Maria shook her head as they got into the truck.

"Me either," Anthony replied as he started the truck to head to the beauty supply store.

"Why did she want you to tell Uncle Bobby hi?" Tia looked perplexed. "He wouldn't want to date someone that rude, would he?"

"No, he wouldn't," Anthony chuckled. "In fact, if you want to see Uncle Bobby scared, you tell him about meeting Tammi Jo and that you want to fix him up on a date with her."

"Uncle Bobby doesn't like her either?" Maria questioned.

"No, Uncle Bobby doesn't like her either," Anthony replied as he parked on Arabian across the street from Beautiful Destiny. He was thankful for the walk across to the store being enough to distract them while he changed the subject. "So, what're we getting here for the gift basket?"

"A manicure kit, nail polish, and maybe the stuff for a facial if it's not too expensive." Tia listed out the things she thought her mother would like best, releasing his hand where she'd been holding it as they walked through the crosswalk, so he could open the door to the store for them to enter.

"When we do spa days at home, it's usually just the stuff from the dollar store," Maria told him as they got a basket and followed Tia down the first aisle of beauty supplies.

Damn, how does she look so fucking beautiful with only discount beauty supplies?

"Well, we don't have to worry about the cost today," Anthony insisted. "So, why don't we get her all-new makeup too?"

"Maybe we should text our aunts to make sure we get the right stuff?" Tia looked flustered at the huge variety of face creams on the first aisle.

Anthony pulled out his phone and started a group chat with his sisters and female cousins.

> **Anthony: At the beauty supply store to fill a spa day gift basket for Kay's birthday. What do we need to get for facials and makeup?**

The chat started filling up with beauty brand recommendations that completely confused Anthony. Just when he thought the chat wasn't such a great idea, his sister Charlotte threw him a lifeline.

> **Charlotte: I'm assuming you're at Beautiful Destiny & didn't go into SA for this shopping trip. If so, ask for Cassidy at the front counter. She'll help you pick out what you need to buy.**

> **Anthony: Thanks!**

"Char said to ask for Cassidy at the front counter and she can help us find everything we need," Anthony explained, ushering the girls back toward the front counter.

Anthony easily recognized Charlotte's friend, Cassidy, remembering her from when his sisters had friends over for slumber parties when they were kids. She was already at the front counter, so Anthony quickly explained that Charlotte had recommended she help them fill the spa day gift basket.

"Okay, so what all are you trying to fill this gift basket with?" Cassidy requested as they started walking back through the aisles of the store. "Are you talking about recreating a full spa experience with massage oils and mud wraps? Or more of a day of beauty with mani-pedis, facials, hair, and makeup?"

"A day of beauty," Tia replied just as Anthony answered, "All of that."

"And we have to make sure there's no aloe in anything," Maria added. "Mom's allergic to aloe."

"I didn't check the bubble bath," Anthony exclaimed, kicking himself for not knowing about Kay's allergies.

"That's okay," Tia reassured him with a pat on his forearm. "Mom's bought that brand before, so I don't think it has aloe in it."

"Okay, we'll start here with facial supplies." Cassidy directed them to the correct aisle, picking up a tub of cream and reading the ingredients. She put it back on the shelf and moved on to a different product, eventually starting to fill the basket with a pump bottle of yellow cream that she said could be used as a daily face wash and makeup remover that wouldn't need to be followed with a toner, whatever that was, because it was included in the product. She added a clay masque, a peel, and several different face creams, a heavy-duty one for the morning, another heavy-duty one for at night, and a couple of lighter options, in case Kay preferred lighter over heavy-duty.

They moved on to makeup, adding foundation, powder, a couple of eye palettes that Cassidy said would be perfect to accentuate Kay's blue eyes, another palette for her cheeks, and a couple of different colors of mascara, eyeliner, lipstick, and lip liner. Anthony just hoped Cassidy was correct in assuming the colors would work for Kay based on the girls' skin tones.

While the girls were focusing on picking a few different colors of nail polish to go with the manicure kit they picked out, Anthony stepped around to the next aisle and picked out some sensual massage oils. Instead of putting them in the gift basket from the girls, he opted to surprise Kay with them after the girls went to bed, even if massaging every inch of Kay was more of a gift to him than her.

Since Kay had just stocked up on shampoo, conditioner, and detangler when she bought their bathroom supplies, they didn't bother with any hair supplies. Which was probably good since the hour they spent in the beauty supply store put them way over the estimated time he'd told Kay he would be shopping with the girls. He pulled out his phone and texted her as they made their way to the register.

> **Anthony: Sorry, Baby, I completely underestimated how long it would take for the girls to shop. We're almost done & should be home in 15 minutes or so, but you may need to get up & dressed to meet the furniture delivery if they get there before we do.**

> **Kay: I figured when you weren't back by 9 that the girls were showing you their shopaholic sides. I'm already dressed & downstairs.**

> **Anthony: Relaxing & reading, I hope. I'm gonna clean up the mess we left in the kitchen as soon as we get home.**

> **Kay: Um, maybe? {blushing smiley face emoji} Are you going to spank me if I already cleaned up the kitchen?**

> **Anthony: Yes, you Naughty Girl. Instead of an erotic birthday spanking like I had planned for tonight, now I have to punish you for disobeying my instructions to relax & read this morning.**

> **Kay: Best Birthday Ever! I'm looking forward to my spanking, Tony.**

Anthony couldn't help but laugh at her response. While he'd teased her about spanking her, he hadn't ever really intended to follow through with the act. When they first met, he'd fantasized about giving her a few playful love taps to her bare ass before fucking her from behind. After she opened up to him about the abuse her ex had inflicted on her, he'd dropped the idea completely because he didn't want to risk triggering a bad memory.

With her bringing it up again, though, he wondered if he could control his inner beast to make it playful and safe to explore their boundaries a little more. Their dirty fantasies certainly seemed to be similar in nature. And she'd proven multiple times over the last few days that she trusted him to push her boundaries. The problem was that he wasn't sure he could trust himself not to lose control and accidentally go too far. With their massive size difference, he could easily hurt her without meaning to, if he didn't keep his inner beast on a tight leash.

"Whoa!" Tia exclaimed, bringing him back to the present from where he'd gotten lost in dark thoughts. "Are you sure this stuff isn't too expensive? We can put some of it back if we need to."

Anthony looked at the total on the card reader screen—it read $215.74 —and swiped his card.

"Nope, we're good, Princess," Anthony smiled as he keyed in his pin to complete the transaction.

The girls held his forearms, so he had his hands free to carry the bags as they walked through the crosswalk back to the truck. He opened both passenger side doors, so he could put the bags in the front seat and hand the items to the girls in the back seat to put them in the gift basket. Then he spread the roll of wrapping paper out on the hood of the truck and wrapped the things that weren't already gift-wrapped and wouldn't fit in the gift basket before driving them home.

Once they got to the ranch, he saw the delivery truck backing up through the lawn to the front porch, so he took the driveway around to the back of the house. He parked beside the garage, since it was still full of the lamps and accessories that they didn't want to move into the rooms until they were finished painting and had the furniture in place to put the various items on. As they were getting out of the truck, he put the gifts for later in one of the bags to keep hidden in the garage until they got home from their afternoon outing. Then he helped the girls carry in the gift basket and other wrapped spa day supplies. They left it all sitting on the island in the kitchen and went in search of Kay and the furniture delivery.

~~~

After Anthony and the girls left, Kay laid in bed and read for a little while, only stopping because her phone was blowing up with birthday
~~~

well-wishes from family and friends. After a brief conversation with her parents, she replied to the messages from her sister and friends. It was a little before nine in the morning when she signed off on the conversations, so she could take a quick shower before Anthony got home with the girls, since she was expecting them home any minute.

After she was dressed for the day, she put her phone in her pocket and carried her tablet with her downstairs. When she found the downstairs as empty as the upstairs, she started to worry about the fact that they were gone more than the hour Anthony'd thought they'd be. But then she remembered that while Anthony had seamlessly stepped into the fatherly role in their family, it had only been a couple of weeks that he'd been a part of their lives. That was obviously too little experience shopping with her girls to be able to estimate the time it would take for them to pick out whatever they were planning to get for her birthday. She resigned herself to having to meet the delivery truck and hoped they sent more than one delivery person, so she didn't have to try to assist in carrying in the heavier pieces of furniture.

She went to sit in the kitchen, since that was the only room with seating downstairs at the time that also had a window where she could see the gate to watch for the delivery truck, and found the mess that they'd left in the kitchen the night before, along with their cinnamon roll plates and juice glasses from their birthday breakfast in bed. Instead of sitting down to read some more the way she'd planned, she quickly finished rinsing everything off and loading the dishwasher. She wiped down the counters and table, then decided to start a load of laundry to make sure they all had clean clothes to pack for going back to work the next day.

She carried the hampers down from both upstairs bathrooms and sorted the loads in the laundry room. Once she started the first load of clothes in the washer, she carried the hampers back upstairs to the bathrooms before returning to the kitchen to try again to read on her e-reader. Just as she sat down, her phone buzzed in her pocket with a new text notification.

**Anthony: Sorry, Baby, I completely underestimated how
    long it would take for the girls to shop. We're almost
    done & should be home in 15 minutes or so, but you**

Leah Mae Wright

> **may need to get up & dressed to meet the furniture
> delivery if they get there before we do.**

>> **Kay: I figured when you weren't back by 9 that the girls
>> were showing you their shopaholic sides. I'm already
>> dressed & downstairs.**

> **Anthony: Relaxing & reading, I hope. I'm gonna clean up
> the mess we left in the kitchen as soon as we get
> home.**

Oops! Kay thought for a minute about how to break it to him that she'd already cleaned up the mess. She thought back to some of their previous conversations, about how he'd hinted at having a dominant side early on in their relationship and how just the night before he'd tried to hold that part of himself back from her. She knew he would never hurt her. And hated that his fear of accidentally going too far was preventing him from being his true self with her. She had a feeling that some of her kinkier fantasies would dovetail nicely with his darker, forceful desires. *Maybe I can use my morning disobedience to show him just how much I want to submit to his dominance?*

>> **Kay: Um, maybe? {blushing smiley face emoji} Are you
>> going to spank me if I already cleaned up the kitchen?**

> **Anthony: Yes, you Naughty Girl. Instead of an erotic
> birthday spanking like I had planned for tonight, now I
> have to punish you for disobeying my instructions to
> relax & read this morning.**

Yes! It worked! Kay thought before replying one more time.

>> **Kay: Best Birthday Ever! I'm looking forward to my
>> spanking, Tony.**

She heard the sound of a heavy truck and looked out the window to the back of the house to see the delivery truck coming through the gate at the entrance of the ranch. She put her phone in her pocket and walked to the front door, assuming it would be best to move the furniture through there instead of trying to come through the mud room and laundry room to get to the hallway.

She stepped out on the front porch just as the truck turned the corner around Bob and Hazel's house next door. She waved for them to see where they were delivering the furniture. They stopped the truck on the gravel road in front of the house, so Kay walked out there to discuss with them the best way to park the truck to be able to unload the furniture.

Instead of blocking the driveway that led around to the back of the house that she knew Anthony would need to use to park the truck by the garage where he'd been parking it all week, she had them back up in the front lawn, so they could lower the ramp straight onto the front porch.

As she stood on the porch trying to help direct the truck, she saw Anthony drive by going to the back of the house. Just as the driver exited the delivery truck when it was finally parked, Anthony came out the front door and scooped her up into his arms, their lips meeting in a greedy kiss that left Kay feeling breathless. It was a little more passionate than he'd ever kissed her with an audience and pushed her to her limit for appropriate PDA in front of her daughters.

She was so lost in the kiss that she didn't realize he'd carried her back in the house until he released her lips as he lowered her feet down to the second step from the bottom of the staircase in the foyer.

"Baby, go upstairs and read while we get the house set up," Anthony instructed and started to turn away from her.

"But my e-reader is in the kitchen." Kay stepped down to the first step, thinking she needed to go to the kitchen and get it in order to take it upstairs and read.

"Tia," Anthony shouted as he blocked Kay from stepping down off the stairs.

"On it," Tia hollered and took off down the hall toward the kitchen.

"Your next surprise is in the kitchen, so Tia's going to bring your e-reader to you, so you can go upstairs and read and not ruin the surprise while I'm moving furniture," Anthony explained.

"Yes, Sir!" Kay cheekily gave Anthony a mock salute before turning to slowly walk up the stairs. She shook her butt at him when she got to the third step.

"Behave yourself, Brat," Anthony chuckled and lightly slapped her left butt cheek.

She felt like she was floating up the stairs after successfully goading him into that one little swat. She sat at the top of the stairs, wanting to watch him. Seeing his muscles work as he did the heavy lifting was a definite turn on for Kay. A few minutes later, Tia delivered her e-reader, but Kay didn't even bother turning it on to read. She preferred watching the show below as Anthony set up their home.

She had to get up and move out of the way when they carried in the sofa she'd picked out for their music room. It was a dark brown microfiber with overstuffed cushions and pillow top armrests. It was going to be a dream to lay on while listening to Anthony play his guitar. She flopped down on it as soon as Anthony and the delivery driver put it in place. She stayed there waiting until he'd brought up the tables they'd picked out for that room before going back to the top of the stairs, leaving her tablet sitting on the end table.

It looked like the china cabinet for the dining room was the last thing they carried in before the delivery driver left. She was confused when the delivery driver left and neither Anthony nor her daughters appeared to tell her she could come back downstairs.

Maybe they need a few minutes to set up their surprise in the kitchen? Kay sat there at the top of the stairs waiting patiently for the first five minutes. After ten minutes, her patience started to wane, but she remained where she was, even if her knees were bouncing in excited anticipation.

It only took thirty minutes to unload all the furniture, so why is it taking so long for them to come get me for the next surprise? Kay wondered as she checked the time on her phone to note that it had been a full fifteen minutes since the delivery driver left. At the twenty-minute mark, her patience had worn so thin, it was almost nonexistent. She slid off the top step, dropping her butt to the next step down, like she would have when she was a child.

I'm thirty-three years old and acting like a three-year-old trying to sneak down the stairs to catch Santa on Christmas Eve. She smiled at the thought and slid down another step. She slowly continued slipping down the stairs for the next ten minutes and was about halfway down the staircase when Anthony and the girls emerged from the hallway carrying the lamps and accessories for the living room through the foyer to put them in place.

"Can I come down now?" Kay barely got the words out before Anthony stepped through the archway to the living room.

"Just a couple more minutes, Baby." Anthony smiled up at Kay and lifted the lamps in his hands a few inches higher. "This is the last room we have to finish and then we'll get back to your birthday celebration."

"You already decorated the other rooms?" Kay frowned, sliding down three more steps as Anthony disappeared into the living room.

"Just putting things in the right rooms and moving the furniture in the game room back to where we originally had it before we had to move it to paint." Maria came back out of the living room and ran up the stairs to Kay. "Anthony said he didn't want to hang anything up until you could supervise to make sure it's exactly the way you want it."

"Well, I can come down and help with that now." Kay slid down the next step.

Seeing the way Kay was sliding down the steps on her butt, Maria ran to the top of the staircase to do the same all the way down. She went a lot faster than Kay had, however, and quickly passed Kay on the fifth step from the bottom. When she landed on her butt on the floor of the foyer, she jumped up and raised her hands in victory, shouting, "I beat you to the bottom, Mommy!"

"Only because you cheated by not telling me we were racing," Kay playfully chided, poking her tongue out at her youngest daughter. "Let's race again and see who wins when we both know it's a race."

Kay put her phone down on the table just inside the living room, so she didn't risk breaking it while racing her youngest daughter. They both ran up the stairs to the top, plopping down on the top step. "Ready, set, go!" Maria shouted and they both slipped off the top stair, trying to be as fast as possible to the bottom, while making sure their backsides made contact with every step. They stayed neck and neck the whole way down to the bottom, laughing the entire way, until Kay barely hit the floor a split second before her youngest daughter.

"I win!" Kay exclaimed as she pulled her daughter onto her lap and tickled her ribs. Maria tried to retaliate, and they ended up rolling around on the foyer floor, laughing through their tickle fight.

"Do we still need to sweep the foyer, or do you think they got up all the dirt we tracked in with their clothes?" Tia inquired, drawing Kay's attention to where she was standing beside Anthony in the archway between the foyer and front room.

"I'm gonna call it done for now, but only because we don't have time for more chores if we're gonna give her the next surprise and make our two o'clock reservations." Anthony reached down to help Kay stand up from the floor.

Tia helped Maria up and then started dusting off her sister's back. Anthony helped Kay dust herself off before ushering them all toward the kitchen.

When they got to the end of the hallway, Anthony covered her eyes with his hands and walked behind her, as the girls each grabbed one of her hands to guide her into the kitchen.

"Happy Birthday!" They all yelled in unison as Anthony dropped his hands from her eyes.

On the butcher-block top of the island was a basket full of beauty products and three unusually wrapped packages. It looked like they hastily tried to wrap the two large bottles and a shorter round jar, maybe, when they wouldn't fit in the basket. The paper was wrapped up from the bottom and twisted at the top with tape wrapped around the twisted part to hold it all together.

"Thank you!" Kay exclaimed, unsure where to start with unwrapping.

"Open this one first, Mommy," Maria insisted, handing her the biggest of the wrapped bottles.

She opened it to find a pump bottle of facial cleanser. Tia handed her the second one, which she opened to find a bottle of the bubble bath she usually bought for the girls at home. The third one was a light blue jar candle, the scent labeled as "Waterfall" smelled relaxing.

"We tried to get everything you'd need for a spa day at home, so we can do our nails and facials, and you'd have all new makeup to get dressed up for the next surprise," Tia explained the gifts, pushing the basket toward Kay.

Kay looked through the items in the basket, finding a variety of full-size products that were too big to carry with her when they flew off to work. She made a mental note to buy some airline-approved small containers to transfer some of the new products into, so she could use them in the hotels where they'd be staying while working. She noted the brand name makeup and nail polish and couldn't wait to find out how much better they looked than her dollar store knock-off brands.

Kay was overwhelmed by the feelings their thoughtful gift elicited. She tried to stave off the tears that were threatening to leak out of her eyes by imagining the scene they must have made when Anthony followed Tia and Maria up and down the aisles of a beauty supply store. Her tears turned to giggles at the mental image.

If he was comfortable shopping for this stuff, I wonder if I can get him to use some of it and actually participate in this spa day they planned for my birthday?

"You'll be joining us for our spa day, right Anthony?" Kay batted her lashes up at him.

"Um, I figured I'd measure the windows for curtains while you and the girls were doing all that girly stuff," Anthony sputtered, looking slightly flustered by her suggestion.

"Men get manicures and facials, too." Kay smiled up at him. "Just without the colorful polish and makeup."

"And I want you to paint my toenails." Maria pulled on Anthony's hand to try to coax him to come upstairs for their spa day.

"Please, Anthony," Tia implored, getting into the act of coercing Anthony into participating in their spa day. "It's a spa day for the whole family."

Anthony closed his eyes and took a deep breath. He opened his eyes as he exhaled and looked back and forth between the three of them. "I can't say no to the three of you," he finally capitulated. "Just don't tell the guys or they'll revoke my man card."

"We won't tell anyone." Maria had a gleam in her eye that made Kay dubious of her actual intentions of telling Anthony's friends.

"Just let me swap the laundry before we get started." Kay motioned to the laundry room across the hall from the kitchen.

"Already done." Anthony shook his head, redirecting her toward the stairs. Kay was flabbergasted by his doing laundry as she'd never known a man capable of operating a washing machine before. "And I'll swap the rest out while you're doing your makeup after my part of this facial stuff is over."

They made their way upstairs, where Kay started organizing the various products on the vanity between the sinks in the master bathroom. Anthony pulled out his electric razor and shaved while Kay was arranging everything. They started with the facial cleanser, then put on the mud masque before piling onto the bed to teach Anthony about how to properly cut, shape, and buff fingernails. There were two laser etched glass files in the manicure kit, so Kay worked on Maria's nails while Tia demonstrated on Anthony's left hand and then let him practice on her nails. Once the girls' hands and feet were both done, Kay focused on her own nails while the girls took turns working on Anthony's.

Once all of their nails were shaped and buffed, they went back to the bathroom to wash off the green crackled masques. As there were a variety of face creams in the basket, each of the girls picked a different one to use.

"Aren't you going to pick a face cream?" Kay arched an eyebrow at him when Anthony just stood there looking confused.

"As I have no idea what I need in a face cream, I'll leave that selection to you, Baby." Anthony dropped a kiss on the top of her head.

Kay looked over the selections and opted to go easy on him picking the pump bottle of argan milk. It had a thinner consistency than the others and would feel lighter on his face than the thicker, gooier creams.

"Do we have time to paint our nails?" Maria looked back and forth between Kay and Anthony.

Kay went to check the time on her phone and remembered it was still downstairs in the living room when it wasn't in her back pocket.

"Um, I don't know." Anthony looked at his phone for the time. "How long does it take for nail polish to dry?"

"Depends on the polish and how many coats we have to apply," Kay answered vaguely.

"We should probably save that for tonight when we get home then. We only have about forty minutes before we have to leave, and we still have to change clothes and ya'll need to do your hair and makeup still."

That sent them all into a frenzy as the girls' plans for fancy updos turned into simple French braids. Kay's playtime with all the new makeup had to be cut down to the bare minimum she could put on in about ten minutes. When she finally left the bathroom, she found Anthony sitting on the bed, already dressed in a navy-blue pinstriped suit with a white shirt and a royal blue tie.

Laying across the bed was a navy blue floral jacquard wrap dress with a shoe box beside it.

"I, um, ordered these last week." Anthony looked a little embarrassed as he motioned at the items. "I figured you'd need a few more dresses and matching shoes for work, but I only ordered the one set to make sure the size was right. When the dress and shoes arrived in the mail the other day, I didn't know how to give them to you without it seeming creepy. I don't want to be the overbearing boyfriend who picks out all your clothes or anything. I just saw this dress in a magazine and thought it would look good on you, so I went to the website on my phone and ordered it with the matching shoes."

He rambled on about wanting to respect her boundaries and how he would try to quell his tendency to accidentally overstep them, but he needed her to be patient with him as he was learning how to mesh their lives together without taking over her life.

"Anthony," Kay interrupted him, cupping his face with a hand on each cheek. "Stop, take a breath, and quit worrying so much about scaring me off." She gave him a peck of a kiss before pulling back and starting to remove her t-shirt and jeans, so she could change into the new dress. "If I'm not allowed to feel guilty for burdening you with my issues, then you're not allowed to feel guilty for taking care of them for me."

"I don't feel guilty for taking care of you, Baby." Anthony leaned forward to rest his elbows on his knees, while Kay changed into some of her nicer new undergarments. "It's more that I don't know where these caveman tendencies are coming from, and I feel like an asshole for doing things without even asking your opinion. I was raised to treat my future wife like a partner in life, but instead, I feel like I've been taking control of your life and not allowing you any choice in the matter. I don't want to do that, so please point it out when I overstep and demand I be a better partner for you."

"You really don't know why you need to take control?" Kay tied the inner tie on the new dress.

"No." Anthony shook his head before covering his eyes with the palms of his hands, his long fingers extending up into his hairline. "And it's unsettling to not feel like my normal self."

Kay finished tying the outer belt of the dress before walking back to him and hugging his face into her chest. His arms went around her waist in a loose embrace.

"I'll admit, I was a little overwhelmed by your need to know where I was at all times when we first met," she confessed as she stroked her fingers through the hair on the back of his head. "But after I realized why you need to know, why you need to take control, I understood that it's because you're not an overbearing asshole. It's because you're a natural protector and provider. You don't take charge to be cruel. You do it to keep us safe. You don't buy things for the girls and I to take away our choices of what we want. You're providing for your family with thoughtful gifts that we need, or you think we'll like. I think it all goes back to when you were a teenager. Back then you weren't in control, and you lost the people you loved. Now that you're in love again, you're subconsciously taking control, so you don't risk losing us, too. And I'm perfectly fine with you taking any and all control you need to feel as safe as you make me feel. The only time I'll complain is when you're holding back and not acting on your natural instincts to dominate me."

Anthony's head came up and his dark brown eyes bored into her baby blues. "Seriously?" His arms tightened around her, pulling her closer between his knees. "You, you want me to dominate you?"

"Yes!" Kay nodded once before wagging her eyebrows suggestively. "I have some really hot D/s fantasies that I hope we get to explore in the near future. I was thinking I might need to write them down for you if you didn't figure them out on your own soon."

"Fuck," Anthony groaned. "I wish we had time to explore them now."

He pressed his lips to hers in a hungry kiss, just starting to nibble her bottom lip when the girls walked into the room and announced that they were ready to go. Anthony released her so she could slip on the navy pumps in the shoe box. Her black purse didn't match her outfit, but she grabbed it anyway as they left the bedroom.

"If you want, I can put your phone and driver's license in my pocket, so you don't have to carry a bag," Anthony offered. "I don't think you'll need anything else this afternoon."

"Oh, okay," Kay agreed as she dug out her wallet and handed her driver's license to Anthony. "My phone is still downstairs where I put it down to keep from breaking it while Maria and I were butt slide racing on the stairs."

He put her driver's license with his in his wallet as they walked down the stairs. She grabbed her phone from the living room and tucked it into the pocket of his suit coat as they made their way out to the truck.

"You don't need to check your messages while we're driving to San Antonio?" Anthony looked at her like he was surprised that she'd just put it in his pocket without looking at it.

"Nope!" Kay made an extra loud popping sound as she said the word. "I've already talked to my parents and texted with everyone else I know this morning, so nobody's expecting me to check my messages again for a couple of days."

Anthony just shook his head as he helped them into the truck. Kay knew he didn't understand her nonchalance when it came to her phone usage. She chalked it up to a combination of their age and financial status differences. It probably wouldn't be the only quirk they discovered about each other over the years to come.

"So, where are we going?" Kay turned in her seat to look back at the girls in the back seat as they drove through the gate to leave the ranch.

"It's a surprise," Maria declared at the same time Tia announced, "A fancy late lunch."

"I kinda figured that much when we had to dress up and have a two o'clock reservation," Kay giggled. "But where are we eating?"

Maria shrugged as Tia replied, "We don't know. Anthony didn't tell us the name of the restaurant."

Kay turned back toward Anthony, who just smiled at her instead of answering.

"You're seriously not going to tell us where we're going?" Kay pouted up at him.

"Nope." Anthony took her hand and brought it to his lips, kissing her left ring finger, just beside her engagement ring.

"But what if it's someplace we don't want to eat," Kay faux-whined, trying to think of something that would be fancy that she wouldn't want to eat. "Like a fancy French restaurant that serves snails."

"They don't serve snails," Anthony deadpanned.

"Is it Tex-Mex?" Kay wondered how many things she could guess before figuring out where they were going. "I've heard the Mexican food gets better and better the further south you go in Texas."

"No, it's not Tex-Mex." Anthony's lips turned up slightly.

"Is it a seafood restaurant?" Kay shuddered at the memory of the one time she went to a seafood restaurant in Tulsa and her fish was served whole. "I can't eat fish if it's looking at me when it's served."

"They do have some fish dishes on the menu," Anthony chuckled. "But I'm pretty sure it's filleted before being served. And it's not just seafood on the menu. I'm sure there are plenty of other options to choose from to not risk looking into the eyes of your lunch."

"Do they serve Burleson Beef?" Kay's cheeks felt warm when she thought about the beef in Anthony's pants.

"I'm not sure." Anthony shrugged, either not acknowledging Kay's innuendo, or not catching it since he was focused on the road ahead of them and didn't see her blush to know what she was thinking about. "We'll have to ask Pop if they're one of the restaurants we supply in the area."

Kay deduced from his answers that it could be any of the major chain restaurants she knew of that served standard American foods. And not knowing anything about local restaurants that were exclusive to the San Antonio area that served similar cuisine, she had no chance of actually guessing the name of the restaurant where they were going. So, she changed the subject, asking Anthony to tell them some of the history of the area.

He talked about the Alamo and how it fit into the history of Texas fighting for independence. He talked about how one of his ancestors went from being a commander in the Texan Army to the Vice President of the Republic of Texas. It was fascinating how much he knew of not only his family history, but also how his ancestors impacted the history of the world.

The hour-long drive into San Antonio flew by as Anthony schooled them all in Texas history. They parked in a parking garage and had a less than ten-minute walk before they got to their destination, the Tower of the Americas. Anthony purchased their tickets for the Observation Deck, Flags Over Texas, and the 4D Theater Ride, but took them up to the revolving restaurant first.

They spent a glorious afternoon eating gourmet burgers for lunch, before exploring the tower to learn more about the state of Texas. Kay got more knowledge about Texas out of their afternoon excursion than she learned about her home state of Oklahoma in the entire semester of Oklahoma History she'd taken in high school. The girls were even excited to go home and write up reports about what they'd learned to submit to their tutors for their homeschool history credit. They were chatting away about what they would write while riding in the backseat as they headed home in the early evening.

It was a new experience for Kay to have a partner in Anthony, who really saw her and catered her birthday experience to focus on what was most important to her—spending quality time with her daughters. Her parents had always done a party and given her gifts, including the girls in their plans, but it wasn't the same as being seen by her future husband.

When she was first married to Mark, he would get her a card or a small gift, but they were always so impersonal that Kay couldn't even remember any of them specifically. Kay knew she would remember this birthday for the rest of her life, because Anthony knew her well enough to know that she treasured that quality family time more than anything, so that's what he gave her for her birthday. The actual gift items were simply a means to get them all together for the experiences.

She was so lost in her thoughts, rejoicing in how well Anthony had seamlessly meshed himself into her family, how quickly he became an integral piece of their life-puzzle, that she almost missed the fact that the front porch was lit up with twinkle lights and covered in balloons as they pulled into their driveway. Instead of pulling around back to park like he'd done all week, Anthony parked on the driveway in front of the house.

"What on earth?" Kay covered her mouth with her hand as Anthony's family all started pouring out of their front door.

Leah Mae Wright

"Surprise!" Tia and Maria shouted in unison. "It's your birthday party!"

"Happy Birthday, Baby." Anthony gave her a peck of a kiss and helped her down from the truck. They walked hand in hand up to the porch where Kay was greeted with hugs and birthday well wishes from Anthony's extended family.

"Thank you, everyone!" Kay exclaimed, feeling overwhelmed, but very much loved and accepted into their family.

"Be right back, Baby." Anthony kissed her on the top of her head as they made their way into the house. "I have to go get the rest of the presents from the garage."

He took off down the hall as soon as they stepped into the foyer. Her daughters flanked her, walking her from room to room, where she found more streamers and balloons decorating pretty much everywhere. When they got to the dining room, she couldn't even see the new dining table because it was covered with presents and party supplies. At one end of the table was a giant sheet cake. The base frosting was white, and it was trimmed with royal blue frosting flowers. In the middle it read, "Happy Birthday, Kay!" Directly behind the cake, stacks of paper plates and plastic utensils were waiting to be filled when the cake was cut. The other end of the table was almost overflowing with gifts.

"I figured you'd wanna see the cake before we cover it with candles." Hazel stepped up to where Kay was looking at the cake. "But since our bigger tables wouldn't fit in here, we figured we'd start in the kitchen with chili for supper first. And after everyone's finished mingling while we eat, we'd try to get as many people in here as we can fit, and put the candles on the cake then to sing *Happy Birthday* and have you open your presents."

"Don't let her fool you, Kay." Susan rolled her eyes and shook her head at Hazel. "While we did plan to do dinner before the cake, seeing the cake first isn't the reason she hasn't put the candles on it yet."

"It's because my sister didn't know how many candles to put on it," Maggie giggled and smiled. "And she's too embarrassed to admit that she doesn't know how old you are."

"She's thirty-three today." Tia shrugged her shoulders. "Sorry, Mom, I thought Anthony already told them how old you are, so I didn't think about it to tell them when I was helping plan the party."

"I'd already told you that." Anthony pointed at Hazel as he walked in and put a few more gifts on the table.

"Well, yes, you did," Hazel admitted, looking sheepish. "But I guess I just didn't believe you because she looks ten years younger than she is."

"I say we go with Hazel's age estimate and just use twenty-three candles," Kay giggled. "I like the idea of staying twenty-three forever, so I won't ever get old."

"I think you just want to say you're younger than me," Anthony joked as he kissed the top of her head and started guiding her out of the dining room. "But I'll love you at any age, Baby."

As they walked into the kitchen, she heard music start playing behind her. She turned to look and saw Anthony's oldest brother, Bobby, holding up his cell phone. "I found you the perfect theme song, little brother." Bobby grinned as **Older Women** by Ronnie McDowell filled the air. "Maybe you should learn to play it for her on your guitar."

"Robert Adam Burleson, turn that off," Hazel grumbled as she swatted at his phone. "It's not appropriate with little girls in the room."

"Sorry, Ma." Bobby turned the music off and tucked his chin to his chest, looking utterly chastened.

"That's actually one of Grandma Lee's favorite songs," Maria informed her new family with a little shrug, like she didn't understand what the issue was since she'd heard the song several times before.

"And it has a positive body image message for women who might otherwise feel like they are old and frumpy and can't see their own beauty because they're comparing themselves to younger, thinner women," Tia pointed out. "It's one of the songs Grandma Lee used to explain that our beauty comes from the inside, like how we treat the people around us, no matter what we look like on the outside."

"Oh, well, um, okay then," Hazel stuttered, looking flustered. "I guess I never thought of it from that perspective."

"Thanks, nieces," Bobby grinned again, holding his hands up to high-five each of the girls. Kay couldn't help the giggle that escaped her when they slapped hands. He put a hand on each of the girls' upper backs and steered them toward the island where there were stacks of plastic cups and multiple bottles of soda. "Now, what do you want to drink? Uncle Bobby is pouring."

"I'm not sure if my girls are being a bad influence on your son, or if your son is being a bad influence on my girls," Kay teased as she wrapped an arm over Hazel's shoulders.

"I'm afraid it goes both ways," Hazel smiled, finally laughing with Kay.

"I'm a good influence, though, right, Baby?" Anthony handed Kay a disposable bowl of chili with a plastic spoon already in it.

"Yes, Dear," Kay replied at the same time Hazel muttered, "Hopefully."

The women both giggled as they made their way over to the table, where there were bowls of optional add-ins for the chili.

"I didn't know exactly what Tia was talking about when she said your favorite food was Frito Chili Pie," Hazel explained, pointing to the bags of Fritos on the table. "So, I just made sure I had everything she said went in it thinking we could mix it individually. If it's actually a specific recipe that has to be baked like a pie, then I'll need to get it from you for next year."

"This is perfect." Kay started to add Fritos and cheese to her bowl. "My Mom usually layers everything in a casserole dish and heats it up in the oven to melt the cheese on top, but it's just as good either way."

Anthony walked over with the girls, each carrying a bowl of chili, Anthony carrying two. He handed one of the bowls he was carrying to his mother before they all started adding things to their bowls. Kay noticed that her girls followed Anthony's lead and skipped the onions.

After stirring up their concoctions, Tia took a bite and then looked around the kitchen before asking, "Mom, where's the sugar?"

"The big canister beside the coffee pot," Kay replied. "Put a scoop in one of the extra bowls and bring it over to the table for everyone else, please."

"Will do." Tia put her bowl down on the table beside Kay, then walked over to the other side of the kitchen to get some sugar to add to their chili.

"Sugar?" Hazel arched an eyebrow questioningly. "In chili?"

"Oh, I have to try this." Bobby smiled so big his dimples popped.

"You would." Charlotte wrinkled her nose in disgust.

The cousins all started debating the idea of adding sugar to chili, leaving no chance for Kay to try to explain why they ate it that way.

Tia came back with a disposable bowl filled halfway with sugar with a plastic spoon resting in the middle. She sprinkled a spoonful of sugar into her bowl before passing the sugar to Kay.

"Thanks, baby girl." Kay sprinkled her own spoonful of sugar over her Frito chili pie.

"Since you're putting sugar in yours too, I'm assuming this is one of the ways Tia tried grossing you out and it was actually good instead." Anthony waved a hand at Maria as she put sugar in her bowl next.

"Nope, this is a trick Mom taught me when she was helping me with a food science class a few years ago," Tia replied without giving Maria the chance to answer Anthony. "It balances out the flavors. Some people use salt to do the same thing, but since too much sodium is bad for heart health, we use sugar instead. And a teaspoon of sugar only adds sixteen calories and four grams of carbohydrates. With the protein and fat in the beans, meat, and cheese lowering the glycemic index of the meal as a whole, even a diabetic can have a little sugar in their chili."

"That was another class like the integral calculus one I helped you work on the other day?" Justin inquired as he added sugar to his chili.

"Yeah, but Mom knew about using sugar instead of salt in chili before I took that class," Tia explained between bites of her food. "Where did you learn about it, Mom?"

"High school home economics," Kay replied with a shrug before scooping her next bite onto her spoon. "But we didn't learn about the glycemic index or any of the detailed nutritional science stuff from Tia's online class back when I was in high school. I think my home ec teacher just liked sweet chili because she used a lot more than a teaspoon in hers."

A few more people tried it when the first few said they liked the taste. The reviews were mixed overall, some loved it, some hated it, and some refused to even try it. Kay was pleasantly surprised by the fact that no matter what any individual person stated as their opinion, everyone was supportive of their belief. Had she had this same discussion with her ex's family, it would have ended up in a yelling match because everyone in that family was of a similar belief as Mark, that anyone who disagreed with them was wrong, stupid, and unworthy of being treated with respect.

She shoved those negative thoughts back in the "Never Gonna Happen Again" box in her mind before she started hearing Mark degrade her in her head like he'd done when they were married, and she disagreed with him.

She looked around the room, crammed wall to wall with Anthony's supportive, loving family. She'd only met them a week before (except for Anthony), but they were all there—standing to eat because there wasn't enough seating for everyone—welcoming her and her daughters into their family to celebrate her birthday. A tear threatened to escape because she was so overwhelmed with emotions. Wonderful feelings of love and acceptance. Like she finally found her place in the world, a true sense of belonging with this wonderful family that she never thought she'd feel with anyone but her parents, siblings, and children.

Anthony noticed when she went to wipe her eyes, trying to prevent the tears from falling. "Baby?" He put his bowl down and gripped her shoulders to turn her toward him, so he could see her whole face. "What's wrong?"

"Nothing's wrong," Kay insisted as her eyes started overflowing. "Just happy tears from being so grateful to have all of you in my life."

"Oh, Baby," Anthony drawled as he hugged her tightly.

She couldn't make out exactly what else he was saying because one of her ears was pressed into his chest and the other was covered with his big hand. But she got the gist of it as not liking to see her cry, even if they were happy tears. His other hand pressed into her upper back, while his thumb stroked up and down just below her neck. He finally stopped talking and kissed the top of her head before releasing her. She stopped crying and snickered lightly at the surrealness of the moment.

"I finished all of my dinner." Maria showed Kay and Anthony her empty bowl. "Can we have cake now?"

"Absolutely," Anthony exclaimed, taking her empty bowl, and stacking it with his and Kay's before throwing them all in the garbage.

The rest of the family followed his lead, tossing their empty bowls in the trash can as they walked into the dining room, where they found Hazel arranging candles on the cake.

"I made the executive decision that we're all just going to have to stop aging at twenty-four, since that's how many candles are in a box," Hazel declared as she lit the last one.

They all laughed at Hazel's declaration before singing **Happy Birthday** to Kay. Once she blew out the twenty-four candles, Hazel started cutting and plating the cake. The first piece went to Kay, who was instructed to sit and open presents between bites.

"Open mine first," Maria insisted, handing Kay a beautifully wrapped box, one of the four that Anthony had brought in that looked to have been professionally wrapped, unlike the ones from earlier in the day.

"Oh, what could it be?" Kay took the box and shook it lightly by her ear, as if she could hear it make noise and know what was inside.

"Don't shake it, you might break it!" Maria squealed.

"Oops!" Kay brought it down to her lap and carefully untied the ribbon from around the box. She slid a fingernail along the seam where the paper was taped down to cut the tape, so she could unwrap it without tearing the paper. Once it was unwrapped, she found a beautiful mahogany music box. She opened it to hear **Beauty and the Beast**, as their figurines twirled like they were dancing.

"Oh, it's beautiful!" Kay exclaimed. "Thank you, sweetie. I love it."

"Mine next." Tia handed her the next gift.

Kay took her time and opened the next package with the same deliberate motions. Inside, she found a round pink soapstone music box with a beach scene carved into the top. She couldn't place the song when she opened it, but the box said it was **Imagine** by John Lennon.

"Another beautiful music box." Kay smiled at her daughters. "Thank you."

When the third package she was handed turned out to be a pewter heart shaped music box that played **I Just Called To Say I Love You** from Anthony, she started to sense a theme for the gifts she was opening. Instead of handing her the last of the four gifts he'd brought in for the party, he handed her one of the boxes from his family. Yet another music box, this one played **Ave Maria**.

The more presents she opened the more music boxes ended up spread across the dining room table. **Amazing Grace**, **Blue Danube**

Waltz, a couple of different pieces by Beethoven that she recognized from her childhood piano lessons, and several songs she didn't recognize even with the packaging stating their names.

"How on earth did ya'll coordinate this, so you didn't get two of the same one?" Kay probed after thanking yet another person for a music box.

"When Tia told us that you used to collect music boxes, but they were damaged when your house was broken into, we wanted to rebuild your collection." Hazel waved toward the first three music boxes she'd opened. "Since there were only three in Heart's Destiny, and we wanted Anthony to be able to take the girls to get those for you this morning, the rest of us had to go into San Antonio, or have someone who was already in San Antonio pick one up for us. We had a whole group chat going, texting pictures of each of them, so we didn't duplicate."

"And some of us were stuck on duty in Heart's Destiny and didn't think to call a cousin who was working in San Antonio," Bobby shrugged as he handed Kay another gift. "So, I stuck with the musical theme, even though it's not a traditional music box."

Kay opened his gift to find Big Mouth Billy Bass, the singing fish mounted to a plaque. She laughed with glee at the nonsensical gift.

"Where on earth did you find this?" Anthony reached down and pushed the button to make it sing *Take Me To The River*. "I didn't know they still made these."

"The Tackle Box," Bobby replied, shrugging one shoulder. "I noticed them the last time I was in there buying bait, and for some reason I remembered them when I was trying to figure out where to find a musical gift since I didn't have any other ideas for a music box."

"Well, I'm glad you did." Kay smiled at her future brother-in-law. "I'm going to have to figure out how to rearrange my decorating plans to be able to display most of these, but I know exactly where to put this one. Billy is going to be mounted on the wall in the music room upstairs."

"Perfect." Anthony kissed the top of her head and placed the last gift in her lap.

She opened it to find a bedazzled pen, a hardbound journal, and a book of prompts for writers. "Oh, Anthony," Kay breathed out the words, moved by his thoughtful gift. He was following through with his declaration a few days prior, when he said he wanted to help her achieve her dreams. He was the only person she'd ever told of her aspiration to write romance novels, and he was giving her the tools to start writing down the stories that previously only lived in her head.

She gently placed the items on the table beside the music boxes before jumping out of the chair and launching herself into his chest. He instinctively bent down to wrap his arms around her, and she took advantage of being able to get her arms around his neck. She climbed him like a tree and wrapped her legs around his waist as she kissed him like nobody else was in the room.

"I think that's our cue to leave," Kay vaguely heard one of Anthony's male relatives say, but she was too focused on kissing the love of her life to care.

"Nope, now it's time for us to go play video games," Maria decided, her daughter's voice finally starting to penetrate Kay's brain.

"Mom, Anthony, go to your room," Tia teased and the whole room erupted in laughter. Even Kay and Anthony chuckled, as their lips parted, and Anthony sat her back down on her feet.

"Thank you," she mouthed, unable to choke out the words around the lump in her throat from the overpowering emotions brought on by truly being seen and understood by the man of her dreams.

"Alright, I have to know. What's so great about a blank book to get that kind of a thank you?" Bobby circled his hand in Anthony and Kay's direction. "And will it work with just any woman, or is this a unique Kay trait?"

"Bob, you need to have another talk with your oldest son," Hazel huffed. "He needs to quit trying to kiss every girl he meets, and find one to settle down with like his youngest brother."

"I didn't say I wanted to kiss every girl I meet," Bobby backtracked, throwing up his hands. "I know part of it is 'cause they're gonna get married. I just wondered if I found a woman I want to think about settling down with, would giving her a blank book make her want to commit and kiss me like that."

"It wouldn't work for me." Charlotte shook her head. "I mean if I got a blank book as a gift from a guy I was actually interested in. Not you, because we're related and all."

"Me either," Jen agreed with a little shrug.

Leah Mae Wright

"You know you're the only person I've ever told about that dream." Kay looked up at Anthony. "So, even my parents wouldn't understand the significance of that gift."

"Um, no, I didn't realize it was a secret." Anthony looked sheepishly down at Kay and then over to the girls, who were giggling. "If I had, I wouldn't have told the girls about it when we were shopping this morning."

"Oh!" Kay was surprised, wondering how long before her daughters told everyone, so she didn't have to overcome her fear of being denigrated for her dreams. "Then I guess we can share it with everyone else."

Kay took a deep breath and blew it out before turning to face Anthony's family. He rested his hands on her shoulders from behind her, showing her his support, and making her feel stronger than her fear.

"When I was a teenager, I wanted to grow up to be an author," Kay confessed. "My college major was English Literature, but my family thought it was because I wanted to be a teacher or college professor. If I'd finished school, I probably would have actually been a teacher, since it's a much more stable job than an author."

Kay paused to collect her thoughts and pointed at the books on the table. "This is Anthony's way of encouraging me to write," she choked out. "To follow my dreams even while working in a different field. That's why it means so much to me."

"Because he sees the real you and believes in your ability to achieve the dream." A single tear slipped down Jen's cheek.

Kay could only nod, too emotional to vocalize her agreement with Jen's observation.

"So, I've gotta find a wannabe author to give a blank book to for it to work." Bobby grinned, bobbing his head. "Yeah, I like that idea. A smart, creative woman. Kay, would your bridesmaids be smart, creative women like you?"

"Um, yeah, maybe," Kay replied, only slightly worried about where Bobby was steering the conversation.

"Have you already picked out your bridesmaids?" Hazel asked expectantly.

"Yes," Kay admitted, turning to look at Hazel. "My sister, Randi, and my best friend since sixth grade, Deanna Wolfe. I told them both that I'd give you their phone numbers to get their measurements when I decide on dresses from the catalogs you picked up the other day."

"Did you say Deanna Wolfe?" Anthony's cousin JJ choked out the question, a strange expression on his face.

"Yes," Kay replied. "Oh, do you know her? She works for an oil company in Tulsa, but I don't remember the name."

"Maybe," JJ replied as he ran a hand through his dark brown hair. "I can't imagine there's more than one Deanna Wolfe who works for an oil company in Tulsa, but anything's possible. Such a small world if it's the same woman, though."

"Well, since my cousin seems to already have an interest in your friend, tell me about your sister." Bobby arched an eyebrow and gave Kay another dimple-popping smile. Kay looked over at JJ, who opened his mouth as if to object to Bobby's statement, but just closed his mouth without actually saying anything.

Interesting, Kay thought, wondering if she would see sparks fly for her BFF at her wedding.

"Sorry, Bro." Anthony slapped a hand on his brother's shoulder. "James has already claimed Randi."

"James Hunter?" Becky's eyes darted to Anthony, looking at him in what Kay could only read as shock and maybe a little disappointment.

"Yeah." Anthony ran a hand through his own hair like he couldn't figure out how to break the news to his sister that James was off the market. "He met Randi the same night I met Kay and they've been talking and texting every day since."

"I suppose the Hunters will be your groomsmen?" Hazel hypothesized to Anthony. He just nodded his agreement, looking like he wanted to get off the subject of his best friends as soon as possible.

"Well, when you see them this week, have them text me their measurements for their tuxes as well," Hazel changed the subject back to the wedding before turning to Kay. "Have you started looking through the catalogs to pick tuxedo and dress styles yet?"

"No, but I was thinking white tuxedos for the groomsmen." Kay looked up at Anthony. "That way they would sort of match with Anthony's dress uniform from the Navy."

"Perfect." Anthony bent and kissed Kay on the forehead. "I just have to find it, since it hasn't made it to the closet yet in the move."

"It's at the dry cleaners." Kay smiled up at him. "I dropped it off when the girls and I went to get paint, and we're scheduled to pick it up next week when we get back in town."

With the party turning into a wedding planning discussion, most of Anthony's family said their goodbyes, leaving Kay to peruse the wedding catalogs with her daughters, Anthony, and Hazel. When they couldn't decide on their favorite styles from the pictures in the catalogs before it was time for the girls to go upstairs for baths and bedtime, they all agreed to go to Destiny Dresses and Benny's Formalwear the following Friday morning to see the actual items to make the final decision.

<div align="center">~~~</div>

Anthony was glad when his mother finally left, and the girls went upstairs to get baths before bed. He had a couple more surprises for Kay for her birthday. He got the last present for her out of the garage while Kay was putting away the last of the laundry in the girls' rooms. He left the wrapped gift on her bedside table and went into the music room, where he called out to her to join him as she stepped out of Tia's room.

He put his laptop on the coffee table, opened up the document he'd started with his notes on the song he was writing for Kay, picked up his acoustic guitar, and sat on the sofa. He made sure it was in tune before he started playing the song for the first time.

Kay came in and sat down on the other end of the sofa, watching him as he played. He fiddled with the notes and played it through a couple of times, singing the words in his head to make sure they matched up with the notes he was playing. When he opened his mouth to start to sing, he turned to look at Kay as he sang her song directly to her, enjoying seeing the emotions crossing her face as she listened.

♫ *I'll love you for a long time.*
You're always on my mind.
I need you more every day.
Every time I look at you,

I'm amazed by the things you do.
And by the words that you say.
Even when I'm all alone,
I hear your voice, with that tone,
that makes me glad that you're mine.
When I see your smiling face,
it lets me know that I have a place.
In my heart, your love will shine.
Yes, I love you.
Yes, I love you.
More than you'll ever know.
Yes, I love you.
Yes, I love you.
More than you'll ever know.
You're my heart.
Yes, I want you.

More than you'll ever know. ♪♫

"Happy Birthday, Baby," Anthony crooned as the final note faded.

"Did you just write me a song for my birthday?" Kay questioned breathlessly, as she looked at him adoringly.

"Technically, I've been working on it in my head for a couple of weeks, but this is the first chance I've had to pick up my guitar and actually play it," Anthony admitted, reaching over, and turning the laptop, so she could read the lyrics and note ideas on his screen. "I type up my song ideas on my laptop when I'm sitting in hotel rooms, and then usually spend a little time playing when I'm home to polish them up into actual songs."

"That's amazing." Kay tilted her head as if a question popped in it. She bit her lip before asking, "Is that why you wanted me to get a keyboard? So, we can write music and play it together?"

"Yeah." Anthony nodded, looking down sheepishly and hoping he wasn't pushing her into doing something he loved, but she didn't really want to do. "But if you don't want..."

"No!" Kay exclaimed, cutting him off. "I do want to get a keyboard, so we can play together. I just didn't see when we'd have time to go to a music store with everything else we were trying to get done on our time off."

Anthony leaned the guitar against the end of the sofa and picked up his laptop. He opened an internet browser and typed in the web address for his favorite music store. He opened the page for electronic keyboards before passing it to Kay.

"How about you pick one of those and we order it online to be delivered next week?" Anthony requested when she put the laptop on her lap.

"Okay." Kay started scrolling through the listings of various electronic keyboards. "Some of these are pretty expensive."

"Don't look at the prices." Anthony scooted closer to Kay on the sofa to be able to look at the screen with her. "Just look at the features and pick the one that has the ones you want."

"Anthony." Kay drew out his name to make it sound like an objection to his idea.

"Kay," Anthony groaned, drawing out her name in a similar manner. "Don't argue, just get what you want. If I think you're picking something because it's the cheapest, I'll just order the most expensive one, too."

"You wouldn't," Kay gasped.

"I would," Anthony replied as he leaned over and kissed her forehead. "I want you to have the best of everything, Baby, even if I have to fight tooth and nail with you to accept it."

"How about we compromise with this one?" Kay pointed to an electronic keyboard on the laptop screen. "It's not the cheapest, but it's not the most expensive, either. It has all the features I need, and a few that just look like fun."

"Then it sounds perfect." Anthony reached over to click the button to add it to the online shopping cart. Since he was already logged into his account, it was just a few clicks to check out and have it scheduled to be delivered the following week, when they were back in town.

"Now you have one more surprise." Anthony stood up and scooped Kay up into his arms.

He shut the door to the hallway from the music room with his foot and Kay reached down to flip the lock on the door handle before he carried her into their bedroom. They repeated the close and lock procedures on the bedroom door to the hallway before he laid her down on the bed. He handed her the last gift, the box containing four different flavors of sensual massage oil.

"I'm assuming there's a reason you didn't give me this one at the party." Kay smiled her secret, sexy smile, as she slid her nails along the tape to unwrap the present.

She took her time opening it, just like she had all the gifts downstairs. He didn't understand why she didn't just tear the paper since it ended up being wadded up to be thrown away.

"I didn't think you'd want anyone else to see it and know what I have planned for you tonight." Anthony sat down on the bed beside her.

"Oh, is it a paddle for my spanking?" Kay stopped unwrapping the present and looked up at him hopefully.

"No," Anthony shook his head, feeling nervous about the turn of their discussion. "I would never use a paddle on you, Kay. The only spanking I want to give you is a light one with the palm of my hand, just enough to be erotic, and never painful."

"Well," Kay huffed, sticking her bottom lip out in a pout. "That's not much of a punishment for misbehaving today."

"I would never really punish you, Baby." Anthony smiled down at her. "At least not with anything that could cause you pain. Now finish opening your present, so I can explain how I am going to punish you for being naughty this morning."

Kay finished removing the paper from around the box and ran her finger over the bottles to turn them all facing forward in the opening on the front of the box, so she could read the different flavors.

"I'm not sure how giving me a massage is going to be a punishment," Kay sighed.

"The massage itself isn't the punishment." Anthony loosened his tie, ready to wrap it around her wrists to tie her to the headboard. "Not being allowed to come while I massage every inch of your delectable skin is the punishment. I plan on taking you right to the edge and keeping you there for a long time tonight, Baby. When I finally command you to come, it will be the most explosive yet from the hours of anticipation and teetering on the edge. And just to make sure you can't reach down and touch your pretty little pussy while I'm teasing you everywhere else, I'm going to tie your hands to the headboard. You said you want me to dominate you. Is that still true, Kay?"

"Yes, Sir, please," Kay begged, her eyes dilated, and her breathing rate increased. Anthony could see her nipples were hard, even through her dress and bra. He loved knowing that he could turn her on with just his words, especially since his cock had been hard as steel since the moment they were finally alone in the music room earlier.

"I don't want to be some random Sir," Anthony admonished as he trailed a hand up her thigh, pushing her skirt up. "You're my Baby, my Kay. I want to hear you saying my name whenever we're playing these kinky games."

"Yes, Anthony." Kay's voice came out breathy from her arousal. "Or is this when I'm allowed to call you Tony?"

He actually liked the way she said "Tony" in that breathy voice. His cock twitched in response to the way she said it, so he nodded in agreement. "Yes, you may address me as Tony when we're playing. We can use a safe word if you want, but know that all you have to say is *no* and I'll stop. I don't want to do anything to make you uncomfortable or cause you pain. This is only for our mutual pleasure."

"I don't need a safe word tonight, Tony," Kay purred, and Anthony's cock twitched again in response. "But, um, maybe in the future, we can use one, so we can, um, do a little role-play where I say *no* but mean *yes*."

"Fuck, yeah, Baby," Anthony growled, excited at the dark desires she was hinting at them exploring in the future. "But tonight, I only want to torture you in the best way. Get you so worked up that you beg me to fuck you, beg me to let you come on my cock."

"Yes, please, Tony," Kay moaned, her hips starting to wiggle as his hands moved closer to them on her thighs.

"Don't move," Anthony commanded as he stood and removed their phones from his pockets, putting them on the chargers on his bedside table. He swiped his phone screen to open the app to play the country love songs playlist he'd set up when he realized they were Kay's favorites. He removed his suit coat and hung it up in the closet. He toed off his dress shoes and socks, leaving them in the closet to walk out to the bed.

Kay was still laying in place, holding the box of warming massage oil. He sat beside her on the bed and took the box from her hand, opening it to remove the first bottle of oil. He sat the box with the other three oils on her bedside table before commanding her to stand and strip for him.

Kay sat up and awkwardly crawled around him to get off the bed. She stepped out of her heels and started to untie the wrap dress with shaky hands.

"Baby," Anthony drawled out, placing his empty hand over her shaking ones on the dress's outer tie. "Relax. Why are you so nervous?"

"I, um," Kay stammered, looking down at their hands on her waist, instead of up at his face. "I, I don't know how to do a sexy striptease, so I figured I should just hurry and take everything off, so we could get on with the massage stuff, but I worried I'd screw up and make this a knot instead of actually untying it, and you'd realize that I'm too much of a dork to be sexy."

"Baby," Anthony drawled out the endearment once again, making it three syllables. "You're not a dork and you don't have to do anything to be sexy to me. It doesn't matter if you do the most sensual dance, and touch yourself while you slowly tease me with removing your clothes, or if you get this tie so knotted up that I have to cut you out of the dress, I'm still going to think you're the sexiest woman on the planet. Instead of stressing about what you think you're supposed to do, or worrying about whether or not I'll think it's sexy, focus on looking into my eyes. I'm sure you'll see how turned on I am as you do whatever feels best for you."

Her eyes popped up to meet his at his command to look into his eyes. "Good girl," he praised her, letting his hand drop from hers. "I've never tried this before, so understand that my knowledge of dominance and submission is limited to the little bit I found online earlier this year when my dreams started including a bit more kink than I was prepared for. After thinking back to what I researched then, I think what you said about me needing to take control of some aspects of your life, so I feel safe to love you is pretty spot on with what I read about being a Dom. From what I read, I think my job as your Dom is to provide for your physical and emotional needs, so you feel safe and secure enough with me to be able to let go of all your worries and just feel pleasure from me. It's supposed to strengthen our connection as a couple by focusing on each other, bonding us in our true intimacy by building our trust in one another. Is that what you want out of trying D/s?"

"Yes, Tony," Kay cooed, keeping their gazes locked together.

"Good, that's what I want, too." Anthony smiled at her. "Now, clear your mind of any extraneous thoughts or worries. Stay focused on me. Just do what I tell you, however it feels most natural to you. There is no right or wrong. Your only choice is to obey or tell me *no* if what I ask you to do is painful. And I promise I won't ask you to do anything that will cause either of us pain."

"You're not supposed to ask me to do anything, Tony," Kay whined, practically purring the words. "You're supposed to command me to do what you want."

"Are you back talking me, Brat?" Anthony growled, lowering his voice to sound deep and commanding.

"No, Tony," Kay denied, her eyes widening at his imposing tone.

"Good girl." Anthony praised her again, maintaining the dark dominance in his voice. "Now strip."

Kay started to sway her hips as she nimbly unfastened the outer tie on her dress. She sensually ran her fingers over her midsection as she moved toward the inside tie at her other hip. Instead of untying it as she'd done the first one, she stroked her fingers over it before moving them up her body and playing with her bountiful breasts as she danced to **Strip It Down** by Luke Bryan.

Seemed like an appropriate song for her sensual striptease in Anthony's opinion. He still held the bottle of massage oil in his left hand, so he pressed his right hand over his erection that was desperately trying to escape the confines of his clothing at the sight of Kay touching herself for him. When she finally undid the other tie and let the dress slip from her shoulders, Anthony squeezed his cock through the fabric trying to relieve a little of the pressure from the sight of her in her sapphire blue lace bra and matching thong.

How the fuck did I miss her changing into them when she got dressed earlier? He thought she'd left on the white cotton bra and panties she had on under her jeans and t-shirt that morning when she changed to go to lunch.

"Fuck, Baby, you're so fucking sexy," Anthony moaned, barely maintaining control of himself at the sight of her teasing her nipples through the thin lace.

He was leaking so much precum that it was soaking through his boxer briefs and a small wet spot appeared on his slacks. While he normally would have cringed at the thought of having to explain the stain to the dry cleaners, he couldn't even think about that possibility as he kept his focus on Kay.

She teased like she was reaching back to unhook the bra, but then ran her hand back around to the front of her body. She trailed her fingertips over the swell of her breasts before slipping the straps off her shoulders. Her expression changed, giving Anthony the impression that she was thinking too hard about how to unhook the back clasp in a sexy manner, and he wondered if she hadn't unhooked it when she reached behind her the first time because she couldn't quite reach the clasp.

"Come here, Baby," he ordered, wanting to save her the awkwardness of pushing it down and spinning it around her body to be able to unclasp it herself. When she stepped between his knees, he wrapped his free arm around her and deftly unhooked her bra. As it slipped down her body and eventually off her arms to the floor, Anthony lowered his mouth to her deliciously delectable double D's.

He suckled and stroked, alternating between the two gorgeous globes, so they each got equal treatment from his mouth and hand. He savored the taste of her, salty and sweet, the essence of Kay, as she ran her fingers through his hair. As much as he loved the feel of her hands on him, he couldn't wait a second longer to tie her to the bed.

"Give me your hands," he directed as he pulled back from her bodacious breasts and pulled the tie from under the collar of his shirt.

As she held her hands out between them, he made quick work of tying one end of his tie around her right wrist. He tested the knot by slipping two fingers between the silky material and her wrist and tugging. He didn't just want to make sure the knot wouldn't come loose if she pulled, he wanted to make sure the binding wouldn't become too tight around her delicate wrists if she lightly struggled against the bonds once he had her bound to the bed.

Anthony thought of tying Kay up as symbolic of him taking over control of not just her body, but also anything occupying her mind.

While in bondage, she didn't have to worry about anything else going on in her life because he was there to take care of her needs. He often fantasized about combining bondage with a blindfold to free her from all distractions, so her only task was to feel the pleasure he gave her. He was aroused by the trust in him she showed by submitting to being bound and vulnerable, knowing that he would never take advantage and cause her harm.

He explained those thoughts as he scooped her up and laid her in the center of the bed. "I'm not going to blindfold you tonight, though, Baby," he elaborated as he looped the tie around the bedpost and secured her other wrist with the other end. "Tonight, I want to see your beautiful blue eyes, so I can see in them how much you're enjoying being bound and at my mercy, unable to do anything but endure the erotic torture, as I have my way with you."

Once she was safely secured to the bed, Anthony opened the bottle of massage oil and slowly drizzled it over her shoulders and arms. He straddled her body, so he could massage the oil into her skin, hating that he had to remain dressed, so he didn't lose control and go straight to fucking her.

Kay wrapped her fingers around the tie where it extended up to the bedpost, gripping it tightly when he moved down her body, starting to drizzle the oil on her chest. He thoroughly enjoyed massaging the oil into her breasts, avoiding the taut tan nipples and areolas. She whimpered when he continued down her body without touching her needy nubs.

He lightly caressed the oil into the soft swell of her stomach, especially focusing on her C-section scar. He slipped her sexy thong down her thighs and eventually off her petite feet, bringing it to his nose to smell her musky, sweet scent before tossing it off the bed in the direction of where her dress and bra were already resting on the floor.

Sitting back on his heels between her spread legs, he pulled her right foot up to rest on his thigh. She giggled as he started massaging the oil into the top of her foot. Her giggles turned to explosive laughter when he moved to the bottom.

"Oh, my Baby has ticklish feet," Anthony crooned at her as he tried to keep ahold of her foot to keep massaging the oil in as she writhed and kicked.

"Stop, stop, stop," Kay squealed, and Anthony released her foot and slid up to massage her calf and shin instead.

"Sorry, Baby, I'll try not to be so tickly when I get to the other foot." Anthony worked his way up her right leg, drizzling on more oil and massaging it into her thigh. She started to giggle again when he got to the inside of her thigh, so he applied a little more pressure, thinking that maybe the light pressure was why it was tickling her.

When he got to the junction of her thighs, he intentionally skipped over her sex. He lightly massaged the oil into her hips and pubis, but avoided her lower lips. He went down her left leg, massaging her in the opposite order as he had her right. When he got to her left foot, he applied more pressure and was relieved when she didn't have the ticklish reaction that she had to the lighter pressure on the right.

When he was done with the front of her body except for her most sensitive erogenous zones, he flipped her over, the tie twisting around itself as he settled her face down on the bed. He used one hand on each leg, massaging his way up her body, starting with the thin strip down the middle of the backs of her thighs that he missed when she was laying on her back.

"I believe it's time for your birthday spanking," Anthony growled as he reached her heart-shaped ass. "Count it out for me, Baby."

Kneeling between her spread thighs, he lightly swatted her right ass cheek.

"One," Kay announced in that sexy breathy tone of voice that Anthony loved hearing.

He repeated the light swat on the left cheek and decided he didn't like the angle. He wanted to see her sweet cunt to know if she was being aroused by the swats.

"Two," Kay counted as Anthony pushed her knees up, not quite under her hips but spread a little wider, so he could see her pretty pussy while he spanked her. He shoved a pillow under her belly for support.

He proceeded to play her perky ass like a pair of bongos as Kay counted out each of her birthday spanks. After each swat, he ran a finger through her slit, loving that she was wetter every time.

"Such a naughty girl, getting wet from being spanked," Anthony playfully admonished as he trailed his cream-covered finger up between her cheeks, spreading her own arousal on her anus. He watched as even more of her juices flowed down her thighs, when he pushed his finger in her asshole up to the first knuckle.

She moaned in pleasure as he finger-fucked her asshole between slaps on her ass cheeks. He wasn't sure how much longer he could hold out before he had to be inside her. He had to get her to the point where she begged for his cock soon, or he was afraid he would be coming like a teenager in his pants.

"I think my dirty girl likes being finger-fucked in the ass even more than she likes being spanked," he growled as he continued alternating the tasks of his hands.

"Yes, Tony," Kay cried out as she pushed back on his finger like she wanted him deeper in her ass.

"That's it, Baby." Anthony pumped his finger in her ass like he wanted his cock in her pussy. "Fuck your ass on my finger. Fuck, that's so fucking hot."

When she started panting like she was close to coming, he pulled his finger out of her tight little hole and finished off the last few swats of her birthday spanking as quickly as possible.

"Oh, I was so close," Kay groaned in frustration at the removal of his finger from her snug anal opening.

"Remember, Baby, you don't get to come until I tell you to," Anthony admonished as his palm landed on her ass for the final time.

"Thirty-three," Kay's final count came out breathlessly.

Although he tried to keep each strike light so as not to hurt her, her cheeks were a pretty pink when he was finished. He picked up the bottle of oil again and massaged it in thoroughly to ease any residual sting. He worked a little around her tight ring of muscle, teasing her a little more even though he knew he couldn't open her up enough to take his cock there that night.

"Maybe I should've gotten a plug for this pretty little ass," he mused as he finally moved his hands off her sexy derriere. He drizzled the oil on her back and massaged it in as he continued with his dirty thoughts. "Maybe even a whole set of plugs, so we can get you opened up enough to take my cock there."

"Yes, Tony, please," Kay pleaded.

"Please, what, Baby?" Anthony continued stroking her back.

"Please plug me, fuck me, fuck my ass, however you want just make me come, Tony, please."

"How can I possibly deny you when you beg so prettily?" Anthony hastily unfastened his pants and freed his overly engorged cock. He stroked himself a couple of times to spread his precum down his shaft. His precum and her cream mixed to provide more than enough lubricant for him to slide balls-deep inside her in one smooth stroke. He gripped her hips, holding her still for him to pump into her from behind.

"Fuck, yes, come, Kay," he shouted as he pounded into her slick wet channel. "Fuck, yes, I love how tight you squeeze me when you come on my cock."

He reached around and fingered her clit, trying to draw out her pleasure as long as possible. He wanted her to still be coming when he unloaded inside her. He felt the tingle start in his spine as her inner walls milked him. It only took a few more strokes before he held himself still, as deep inside her as he could get, releasing rope after rope of his semen into her womb.

He rounded his body over hers, kissing the back of her neck between whispers of how fucking perfect she was and how much he loved her. He reached up and untied her wrists before pulling her with him as he rolled onto his side. He spooned her there for several moments, allowing them both to catch their breath.

"Are you sure the bathroom, closet, and hall are enough separation between us and the girls' rooms that they couldn't hear us?" Kay wiggled her ass against his softening cock.

"Shit, I hope so," Anthony groaned, feeling a little guilty for losing control and shouting his command for Kay to come. "Even if they heard us, I'm sure it was muffled enough that they couldn't understand exactly what we were saying."

"If they ask about it tomorrow, I'll let you explain it to them," Kay giggled.

Anthony wasn't sure if he should be nervous about the possibility of having to discuss the birds and the bees with the girls, or proud that Kay trusted him to truly be the girls' dad and handle the hard discussions with their daughters. He opted to let his chest fill with pride, electing to push off the nerves until the time came that he was actually called upon to discuss sex with his kids.

He scooped Kay up into his arms and carried her to the bathroom to clean them both up from their earlier activities.

"Do you think we can wash these pants here at home?" Anthony beseeched Kay as he stripped off the clothes that he hadn't taken the time to remove earlier. "Or will they be ruined if they aren't dry-cleaned?"

Kay looked at the pants in question as Anthony stepped out of them and laughed. "I don't know that dry cleaning can get those stains out." She pointed at the crotch that was covered in a mix of their bodily fluids. "I can try throwing them in the washer tonight and if they come clean, we can hang them to dry in the morning before we leave. I think it's really the hot dryer that would cause them to shrink, which is why they are labeled as dry clean only."

"Okay, but first let's get you clean." Anthony started the shower and took care of his Baby one more time in the final hours of her birthday.

Chapter Fifteen

Their work week seemed to fly by for Kay as she found herself reminiscing over what all they'd done while on their flight from Indianapolis back to San Antonio. They'd settled back into the traveling routine easily.

Their mornings started with a steamy shower, in more ways than one, before working together to get everyone packed up and ready to go for the day. Then they grabbed a quick continental breakfast as they checked out of the hotel each morning before going to work.

Kay enjoyed her job, feeling more like she was hanging out with friends the whole time instead of actually working. She'd made several new friends, in addition to the two new besties she'd gotten to know on her first week of work. They would all socialize during the morning flights, while their children were having classroom time, and during dinner each evening in catering. Kay had even added a few of them to the group chat, with all of her and Anthony's female family members and friends, where she was making wedding plans.

Her bestie, Deanna, had been a little worried when she first realized that Kay was marrying into the Burleson family that owned Burleson Oil, thinking they wouldn't want her involved in the wedding because of her employer. Kay's future in-laws quickly dispelled her friend of her fear of rejection, even going so far as to offer her a job if her boss decided to fire her for attending the wedding of a business rival. Kay thought back to how JJ had acted after hearing that Deanna was going to be in the wedding. She couldn't contain the smile she had at the thought of how Hazel and Susan would probably be playing matchmaker for them when they were all in Heart's Destiny for the wedding.

Getting back to her own whirlwind romance, her mind wandered back to their daily routine while working. When they arrived in whatever city they were going to for the day, they would check in at their hotel before exploring the city for their daughters' field trips. Except when they had days when the outings didn't fit into the middle of the day, like the Saturday night trip to the Grand Ole Opry in Nashville. That night they skipped dinner in catering to leave the arena for an evening of music appreciation, which the girls decided to classify as a humanities field trip for school.

There were a couple of other days, when they didn't go exploring historical areas, instead going shopping for their Halloween costumes, or dragging the Hunters to a bridal shop to get measured for their tuxedos. Kay loved the fairy-tale royal costumes that they found in Columbus, Ohio.

Regardless of what their midday outing looked like, though, they would go to the arena by two o'clock to have self-defense training time in the ring until the wrestlers arrived to do their daily training and rehearsals. Anthony had cut back on his previous sparring time with his friends to accompany Kay and the girls to the classroom, where he took an active role in working with the girls on their education.

His previous experience, with taking CLEP tests to get through his college core credits faster than taking the actual classes, was proving invaluable as he worked with Dan Traverson to accelerate Tia through the rest of her high school classes, and get her set up to start working toward a college degree in the new year. Since she was getting the socialization aspect of school with the other kids that traveled with the GWA, Kay couldn't object to Tia actually going to college online once she realized that she wouldn't physically attend any classes on campus. Anthony even had Tia reviewing his corporate reports in preparation for when they would be taking some business classes together the next semester.

Kay hadn't found time to start writing yet, even though she brought her birthday gift with her to try and pen her first novel. Any free time when she wasn't working was spent helping the girls with their lessons, or going through the multitude of catalogs Hazel had sent with Tia to pick out possible wedding options. She even had Anthony and her friends going through them, when they weren't working on something else while backstage at the shows.

They had a round table discussion one night in catering, so all their friends could chime in with their opinions about the wedding. Anthony pointed out that the traditional white tuxedos Kay had picked out in the catalog wouldn't match his Navy dress white uniform because of the collar style. Then Jana had pointed out that it might look better to only have Anthony and Kay in white and have the rest of the wedding party in royal blue, so it didn't look like there were three grooms.

In the end, they did an online search for royal blue tuxedos with a mandarin collar, in order to send Hazel some pictures that she could hopefully get Benny's Formalwear to special order. Kay wasn't super hopeful that they would be able to find all the dresses and tuxedos to match before the wedding, but when Anthony reached across the table to squeeze her hand in their secret code for "I love you," she let go of any doubt.

It would all work out in the end. No matter what the wedding attire looked like, or where they had their wedding, they would end up married and that was all that really mattered. Regardless of whether they got married in Texas or Tulsa, no matter the outcome of their future day in court, she was marrying the man of her dreams. The man who fulfilled all her fantasies, multiple times a day.

The best part of her new job with the crazy schedule was that she got to spend every night with Anthony. Once they were through with all their obligations for the day, they went to their family suite at the hotel. After the girls were tucked into bed each night, she and Anthony would either sit on the sofa in their suite and talk for a while, or retire to their bedroom to make love before cuddling and talking late into the night.

Anthony was usually quieter when there were others around, but when they were alone at night or early in the morning, he engaged Kay in long deep conversations about anything and everything. They may have only known each other almost four weeks, but spending three of those four weeks practically glued together made it feel like they'd known each other forever.

Kay was brought out of her ruminations by Tia grabbing her hand when the plane shuddered as it encountered turbulence.

Leah Mae Wright

"I don't like speed bumps in the air," Maria complained from the other side of Anthony. The two of them had been drawing house plans for most of the flight while Kay and Tia were reading.

"Anthony, can you go give the pilot a break and fly us the rest of the way to San Antonio, so we don't hit anymore?" Maria requested, making Kay cover her mouth to hide her giggle.

"Sorry, Princess," Anthony replied with a barely hidden chuckle. "I don't work for the airline, so they won't let me fly their plane."

"They should," Maria argued. "You're a much better pilot than…"

Kay was grateful her daughter's words were cut off by the flight attendant asking to collect their empty cups, napkins, and peanut packages. The look on Anthony's face told her that he was also grateful for the conversational change. He was definitely not as cocky as she'd originally thought him to be, based on the slight flush on his cheeks from the possibility of the commercial flight crew hearing Maria say he was a better pilot than the one flying the plane.

Soon, they were descending into San Antonio and on their way to enjoy a few days off. Well, a few days when they weren't working for the GWA. Their days were still scheduled out and crammed full of work, even though work now meant working on fixing up their home and planning their wedding instead of flying and taking care of the kids on their flights for the GWA.

Maybe I can sneak in some writing too?

~~~

Friday, October 26, 2018

Anthony was in heaven, waking up with Kay's lips wrapped around his cock. It was hard to believe the shy woman, who thought she was asexual less than a month before, had blossomed into his almost insatiable sexual match in their short time together. He'd been so worried that her petite size would prevent her from being able to physically handle his more intense sexual desires, and had tried futilely to hold back with her at first. He was pleasantly surprised to learn that not only could she handle them, but she also craved him in ways that were even darker than he'd previously imagined.
~~~

Since she didn't normally like to initiate their sexual encounters, preferring for him to take charge of her body, commanding her to bring them both the ultimate pleasure, he wasn't quite sure what she was up to by waking him up with such a spectacular blow job. He decided to just lay there and enjoy the exquisite wet heat of her mouth. It wouldn't take long before she clued him into what she really wanted.

It took every ounce of self-control he had to not grab her by the hair and fuck up into her hot little mouth. *Maybe that's what she wants?* He thought back to the other morning when she'd asked him to fuck her face while they were in the shower. It was the hottest thing he'd ever experienced, making him explode in pleasure as she deep throated him. Just the memory was making his balls draw up, ready to shoot another load down her throat any second. He couldn't let that happen, though, because Kay always came first. Usually multiple times, before he let himself go.

"Fuck, Baby, you have to stop," Anthony groaned as he laced his fingers through her long umber tresses, and gently pulled her off his cock. "You know the rules, Baby. I don't come until you do."

"Sorry, Tony." Kay didn't look the least bit apologetic as she sat back on her heels beside him on the bed, a coy expression on her face. "Are you going to spank me for trying to break the rules?"

Ah, so that's what she's after this morning. I haven't spanked her since her birthday, and she wants it again.

"Yes, Baby." Anthony sat up in the bed and leaned back against the headboard. "Lay over my lap. I think you've earned twenty this morning. Ten for trying to break the rules and make me come first, and ten for trying to be too full of cum to eat a healthy breakfast."

She pushed up onto her knees and crawled over to drape herself across his thighs. The underside of her breasts barely brushed against the outside of his right thigh where they hung down toward the mattress. He spread his legs a little, just to make sure her hips were supported on his left thigh. He stroked his big hand over the globes of her ass. She was so small that his palm covered one cheek while his fingers covered the other.

"Spread your legs a little more, Baby." Anthony stroked his hand over her. "And put your hands behind your back."

When she crossed her wrists in the small of her back, he clamped his right hand around them both, loving the feeling of holding her at his mercy. When she widened her knees on the mattress, he stroked a single finger down through the slick, wet folds of her sex.

"Fuck, you're so wet already, Baby," Anthony moaned. His cock pressed into her side as he slowly fingered her pussy. "My naughty little brat likes being spanked."

"Yes, Tony," Kay answered, even though he'd spoken it as a statement and not a question.

"If you count all twenty and don't come until I tell you to, I'll give you a special treat at the end of your spanking." Anthony raised his hand and gave her the first soft slap across her ass.

"One," she counted breathlessly.

He kept the first few swats light, warming her up before starting to push her limits a little with harder smacks.

She kept counting, "two, three, four, five." When he went a little harder on the sixth slap of his palm on her perky heart-shaped ass, she sucked in a sharp breath before saying, "six."

He massaged out the sting in her cheek before dipping his hand between her thighs to find her dripping wet from the harder blow. "Yeah, my naughty baby likes it," he growled before giving her another harder spank on the other ass cheek.

"Oh, seven," Kay gasped as her hips started to wiggle. Anthony couldn't be sure, but he thought she was trying to rub her clit into his thigh to alleviate the intense need she felt to come.

He squeezed her ass as he commanded her, "Be still, Baby, or you won't get to come today."

She stilled instantly, not knowing that he wouldn't actually follow through with that threat, since it would be just as much of a punishment for him as it was for her.

"Good girl," he praised her before continuing with her spanking. He continued alternating sides as he increased the power behind the slaps until he finished the fifteenth swat. She moaned in pleasure as she counted every single one.

Her ass was a rosy shade of pink, that he enjoyed seeing more than he thought he would. He wondered how long her skin would retain his mark. Precum dripped from the end of his cock onto her side as he thought about all the ways he wanted to mark her as his.

Even wanting to leave his mark on her, he decreased the intensity of the last five swats as he didn't want to leave a lasting bruise, or have her too sore to sit comfortably as they went through their day of picking out stuff for the wedding. He would have to make sure her cotton panties covered any residual redness from their play time, in case anyone went in a dressing room with her to help her into the wedding dresses she would be trying on later.

Once she'd finished counting the last of the swats, he rewarded her by fucking her with his fingers while she was still draped over his lap.

"Oh, Tony, please," Kay moaned out in that sexy, breathy tone Anthony loved to hear.

"Please, what, Baby?" Anthony cooed as he stretched her tight channel by inserting a third finger.

"Please, may I come?" Kay begged.

"Such a naughty girl, wanting to come from being held down, spanked, and finger-fucked," Anthony chuckled. "Good thing I like it when you're naughty. Huh, Baby?"

"Yes, please, Tony," Kay breathed out. "I don't think I can stop it."

"Don't stop it, Baby," Anthony ordered as he sped up the thrusts of his fingers into her creamy cunt. "Come now, Kay. Come on my fingers."

"Yes, fuck yes, Anthony," Kay cried out in the throes of climax.

Anthony held his hand mostly still, lightly stroking her G-spot with the tip of one finger as her inner walls clamped down on his digits. Her whole body quivered as she came, and it was one of the sexiest sights he'd ever witnessed.

As soon as she released the vise-like grip her pussy had on his fingers, he moved his hands to grip her hips. He picked her up and spun her to face him, bringing her down to straddle him, impaling her on his cock. Her arms came up around his neck and she pressed her lips to his.

He quickly took control of the kiss, fucking her mouth with his tongue in a similar manner to how he was fucking her tight, wet pussy with his hard-as-steel dick. He kept a firm grip on her hips, bouncing her on his cock as he thrust up into her.

Within seconds, she was crying out from her second orgasm. He swallowed her cries of pleasure as he continued to kiss her through the climax. He wasn't sure how he found the will to resist coming with her, but he somehow held on to his control as she drifted back down to earth.

His goal was to maintain a ratio of three-to-one. Kay coming three times for every one of his own orgasms. So far, he'd only slipped a couple of times to a one-to-one or two-to-one ratio, even though they made love almost every night and again each morning. He wished he had more opportunities to get Kay alone in the middle of the day, so he could make love to her a third time each day, too, but he just hadn't figured out how to sneak that in yet.

"Fuck, you feel so good, Baby," he crooned into her ear before kissing down the column of her neck. "You're so fucking tight, so fucking wet."

"You're so fucking deep," Kay whispered softly in his ear, where she'd buried her face in his neck, her head resting on his shoulder. "I was so scared it would hurt the first time with you."

"Never, Baby," Anthony whispered back. "I would never hurt you, Baby."

"Oh, Anthony, I know that." Kay's breath tickled across his neck. "I meant that I was afraid you were too big to fit inside me." Her little tongue licked across the pulse point at the base of his throat. "You not only fit, but you also reach places inside me that I never knew existed. Really, really good places that only you can reach inside me."

"Damn straight, I'm the only man who will ever be inside you," Anthony growled as he increased his pace. "You're mine, Kay, and I'm never letting you go."

"I'm yours," Kay panted against his jaw after kissing her way up his neck. "And you're mine. I'm never letting you go either."

"Fuck, Baby, I need you to come again," Anthony requested in a deep, demanding tone before suckling Kay in the hollow above her collarbone where her neck and torso met.

"Yes, Tony, yes," Kay chanted as she pressed her beautiful breasts into his chest.

"Now!" Anthony exclaimed when he couldn't hold back a moment longer. His orgasm barreled through him like a freight train, his spine tingling as his balls drew up. He felt rope after rope of white hot cum as it shot out of his cock and into her tight wet channel. "Fuck, yes, Kay."

They continued repeating each other's names as they rode out their mutual release. Her inner walls squeezed him in waves as she came, milking his dick of every drop of ejaculate until he felt completely drained.

They sat there in bed, wrapped in each other's arms as they came down from the heights of ecstasy. Anthony didn't want to lose their physical connection, even as he felt himself softening inside her. He stroked her back soothingly as he whispered words of love and affection to the woman of his dreams. He knew he was fully recovered when he felt himself hardening inside her again.

Time to take care of my Baby in the shower, he thought as he tucked her legs around his waist and slid over to the edge of the bed. He stood up, still inside her, and carried her to their shower, so they could get ready for their day. He loved giving her aftercare in the shower, almost as much as he loved watching her blast off in the heights of pleasure.

He kept one arm clamped around her, cradling her ass in his hand, so she didn't slide off him as he used his other hand to adjust the water temperature. Once it was raining down over them with just the right amount of warmth to be hot, but not scalding, he started thrusting his hips to gently bounce her on his cock while he washed her hair and most of her body.

They whispered sweet nothings as they came together one more time. She was a wet noodle in his arms, languid and sated. He didn't trust her legs to hold her up when they were done, assuming she was as weak-kneed as he felt from their morning machinations. He sat her down on the bench built into the end of the shower and knelt between her knees to shave her pretty pink pussy.

By the time he was done, she'd recovered enough to insist on shaving her legs and underarms herself, while he washed his own hair and body and watched her with hungry eyes.

Who knew watching a woman shave her legs would be sexy as fuck? No, not any woman, just my woman, Kay. Kay makes everything look sexy as fuck because she's sexy as fuck. Because she's Kay. Because she's mine. I can't believe I'm the lucky bastard that gets to be with her for the rest of our lives.

They finished their morning rituals in the bathroom and went downstairs to make breakfast together. While they were in the middle of eating with the girls, his mother walked in the back door, announcing that she was ready to go shopping for the wedding.

They quickly finished eating and loaded the dishwasher before walking out the door to head into town. Anthony opened the passenger doors for Kay, the girls, and his mother to get in his truck, but was surprised when his mom walked back toward her house, instead of getting in the truck.

"Did you forget something, Ma?" he asked her quickly retreating back as the girls got into the truck.

"Nope," Hazel shouted over her shoulder. "I'm taking my own car, so if Kay finds her perfect wedding dress, I can bring it home without you seeing it."

"Okay," Anthony chuckled as he helped Kay into the truck and shut her door. He walked around to the driver's side and got in, continuing speaking to Kay as they buckled up. "Are we really doing the whole not seeing your dress before the wedding thing?"

"Yes," Kay drawled, her eyes sparkling with mischief. "I'm not taking any chances with bad luck before the wedding, so while I want you to be there to help me decide on the bridesmaid's dresses and the groomsmen's tuxes, I want you to go get your uniforms from the dry cleaners while I look at wedding dresses."

"You know it'll take me less than ten minutes to pick up the dry cleaning," Anthony pointed out as he turned left out of the ranch on Rogers Road toward town. "How much time do you think I need to kill while you try on wedding dresses?"

"It shouldn't take more than an hour," Kay declared, her voice sounding chipper. "Maybe you can figure out our options for music at the reception, and then we'll meet you at the florist."

"Yeah, okay," Anthony sighed, taking Kay's hand, and bringing it to his lips to kiss the back. "I'll go bug Bobby at the PD and see if he knows of any bands in town, so we don't have to hunt down wedding musicians in San Antonio."

"Perfect," Kay grinned as she squeezed his hand in their silent way of saying, "I love you." He returned their secret declaration of love as he parked on Appaloosa Avenue right in front of Destiny Dresses and Benny's Formalwear.

He walked around to open Kay's door and the back passenger door for the girls just as his mother parked beside him. As soon as he had his girls out of his truck, he spun on his heels and opened his mother's car door for her as well, knowing she expected him to be on his best gentlemanly behavior.

"Do you have the measurements for the Hunters' tuxes?" Hazel probed as they made their way towards the interconnected stores.

"Yes, I made a note in my phone when we took them to be measured in Indianapolis on Wednesday," Anthony replied, pulling his phone out of his pocket with his right hand while holding the dress store door open for the ladies with his left.

"Are we sure they aren't identical twins?" Maria hypothesized as they walked into Destiny Dresses. "Their measurements were all the same and other than their tattoos I think they look identical, but they keep saying they aren't."

"No, James has darker hair than Dean, and Dean's nose is bigger than James's," Tia replied. "And I think Dean's eyes are wider apart than James's, too, so they're not quite identical."

"James was a half inch longer when they were born, too," Hazel told her granddaughters. "And slightly heavier, but I can't remember if it was two or three ounces. That was why the doctor listed them as fraternal twins instead of identical, but for a while there when they were kids, it was really hard to tell them apart. It made me really grateful that my twins were so obviously different."

"When will we get to meet Uncle Josh and Uncle Jake?" Tia inquired.

"They're both coming home for Thanksgiving and the wedding," Hazel told her as Louella Benson walked over to them to get them started looking at bridesmaids' dresses.

Kay was thrilled when Louella led them over to a rack of royal blue dresses that she'd pulled to show them based on the pictures Kay had flagged in the group chat as her favorites. Hazel had apparently already shown Louella all the pictures, so she could have samples of each ready.

"Hang on a second before we start going through all of them." Kay pulled both of her phones out of her purse. "I have to Skype my mom and sister, so they can see them, too."

She opened Skype on her new phone and connected with her family. She also turned on her old phone for the first time since she got the new one, thinking she would need to use it to text pictures to Deanna, since she was at work and couldn't connect to the video chat. She didn't want to try to juggle two apps on the one phone to communicate with both of her bridesmaids because she knew she would inevitably disconnect the video call if she tried to switch back and forth between it and texting.

Her old phone started pinging with notifications, which was weird since she'd given her new number to almost everyone she knew. When she saw they were all texts from her ex, she bit her lip unsure what she should do about them.

"What's wrong, Baby?" Anthony inquired at the same time her sister squealed from her phone as the Skype call connected.

"Um, hang on a second, Randi." Kay passed her old phone to Anthony. "I need to text pictures to Dee on this phone, while we're Skyping with Mom and Randi on my new one. Can you, um, maybe do that for me?"

"Sure, Baby, no problem." Anthony smiled, taking her old phone, and kissing the top of her head.

Kay turned back to the phone in her hand to see her mother and sister squeezing together to both be seen on the video call. She said "hello" to them before turning her phone around to introduce them to Hazel, Louella, and Benny. Then, she focused the phone on the dresses Louella was showing her from the rack, only turning the phone back, so she could see them to discuss each option.

Anthony took pictures with her old phone and texted them to Deanna. He read Dee's reactions to the texts out loud, so everyone could hear her thoughts about each dress as well. They all seemed to agree with her pick for her favorite, but understood her reluctance to pick it because of not seeing a similar dress in the children's sizes her daughters would need.

"That's because that particular line doesn't publish a catalog for their flower girl dresses," Louella told them. "But we can get that exact same dress in children's sizes."

"Aren't the lace sections a little too revealing for children's dresses?" Hazel wrinkled her nose.

"Oh, no, the lace sections in the skirt don't go above the knee on most people." Louella pulled out the adult version of the dress again. "The only reason you're thinking this is even slightly risqué is because this dress is meant for a woman at least five-foot-seven, so the lace inserts seem to go higher in the skirt to hit at knee level on a taller woman. With you and Kay both being petite, you have to imagine losing the bottom six or eight inches of this skirt to convert it to fit a petite person."

Louella held the dress up to Hazel and folded one of the lace panels up about six inches from the bottom and it did indeed look like the lace panel would still hit about knee high on Hazel with the bottom of the shortest section of the asymmetrical hem still being about mid-calf. Unaltered the longest part of the dress would drag the ground on someone as short as Hazel's five-foot-three.

"Well, I'm five-foot-six, so we'll still need to hem that one for me." Randi pointed in the direction of the dress from the screen of Kay's phone.

"We'll actually order them specifically for your measurements," Louella replied to Randi.

"That's why I had you and Dee go get measured at the bridal boutique this week," Kay explained to her sister.

Louella took down the measurements Randi rattled off to her for her dress before getting the measurements Dee had texted from Anthony.

"I also have the Hunters' measurements for their tuxes." Anthony swapped phones with Louella, so she could get the guys' measurements from his phone.

"And I have sample tuxedos for you to look at." Benny carried over three different blue tuxedos. "I figured you'd probably want to compare them to the dress you picked to find the closest color match."

"Oh my goodness!" Kay's mother, Mary Lee exclaimed when she saw the blue tuxes. "I'm not sure your father will want to look like a blueberry walking you down the aisle."

Kay burst out laughing at her mother's imagery. When she got her giggles under control and caught her breath, she finally explained to her mom, "Dad tried to give me away the first time and I came back like a bad penny. This time I'm having the girls walk me down the aisle, only instead of them giving me away, we're going to claim Anthony as ours."

"I'm happy to be claimed," Anthony chuckled as he kissed the top of Kay's head. "And the groomsmen are fine with looking like blueberries as long as they don't turn into blueberries like that kid in the candy factory movie."

"Her name was Violet and she turned violet, not royal blue," Tia said matter-of-factly while pointing at the blue tuxedos. "So, I think they'll be safe in royal blue suits."

"So, those tuxes are only for the groomsmen?" Mary asked.

"Yes," Anthony and Kay answered in unison.

"Do you have anything picked out for the parents?" Louella queried. "We have a nice selection of mother's dresses."

"I don't have any preference for what our parents wear." Kay shook her head, looking to Anthony for confirmation from him that he didn't have a preference.

He shook his head and concurred, "Me either."

"Well, since the two of you will be in white and the rest of the wedding party will be in royal blue, maybe we should wear navy blue?" Hazel took Kay's phone from her, so she could talk directly to Mary. "I'm sure your husband is much like mine and has a classic navy-blue suit in the closet. And you and I can have fun shopping for new navy-blue dresses to match our spouses without being too matchy-matchy with the royal blue and white wedding."

"Excellent idea, Hazel," Mary beamed from the phone.

They picked the tuxedos that best matched the bridesmaid's dresses. Kay was glad they took the time to look at them in person and side by side with the other options, since the three tuxedos that were all listed as being royal blue varied dramatically based on the material they were made out of and how much the material shimmered. They picked a linen blend that didn't sparkle, since it was closest to the chiffon of the women's dresses.

As Anthony was getting ready to leave, he pulled Kay aside to hand her old phone back to her. He bent down to whisper in her ear, "I moved the message thread from Mark to a folder, so the girls won't see it if you want them to text pictures of the wedding dresses to Dee while you're trying them on. I also blocked him, so he can't call or text you on that phone anymore. I sent the folder to Matt and your dad, so they have the messages in case they need them for court, then password-protected it on your phone. I would have deleted it entirely, so there was no possibility that the girls could guess the password and open it, but you have to have the originals if they're needed in court."

"Oh, thank you." Kay breathed a sigh of relief that she didn't have to open the messages and send them on. "I'm assuming, since you sent them to Dad and Matt, that they were pretty bad."

"Yeah." Anthony hugged her to his chest. "Bad enough that I wish I could get him alone for about fifteen minutes with guaranteed immunity from prosecution for what I'd do to him in that time. But since that's not possible, I'm letting your dad and Matt take care of him. I know you didn't give him your new number, but when you're done on Skype, block his number on that one too, please."

"I will." Kay hoped she could figure out how to block someone on her new phone. *Or I'll have you do it while we're at the florist,* she thought. "And thank you again for taking care of that, so I don't have to see the messages."

"Anytime, Baby." Anthony gave her a quick peck of a kiss. "I'll always protect you, Kay. I love you."

"I love you, too," Kay replied, hugging him tight around the neck one last time before he had to leave to get his uniforms from the dry cleaners while she tried on wedding dresses.

As Anthony walked out the door, Kay handed her old phone to Tia. "You're in charge of texting pictures of the wedding dresses to Aunt Dee," Kay told her oldest daughter before turning to Hazel, who still held her new phone. "And you can keep Mom and Randi up to date, so I don't accidentally flash anyone by trying to take my phone into the dressing room to try on wedding dresses."

Kay spent the next hour trying on the sample dresses that Louella had pulled based on the pictures Hazel had shown her of Kay's favorites from their group chat. She was glad her future mother-in-law had already informed her to only pull the petite samples for Kay to try on, even though several of them were still too long.

Everyone's comments about how much they loved each one she tried were making it hard for Kay to make a final decision. Until Louella presented her with the final dress, the one with the iridescent lace overlay that Kay had imagined in her first daydreams about her wedding with Anthony.

It's perfect! Kay thought as she changed into her dream wedding gown. The solid white satin bodice had a sweetheart neckline that cinched in at the waist like a corset due to the buttons up the back. The sleeves were part of the iridescent lace overlay, so even though they were long sleeves, they weren't hot due to only being made of lace and not having the layer of satin that made up the rest of the dress. The trumpet style of the gown meant it started to flare out at the hips, making it easier to walk in than the mermaid styles that only started to flare out at the knees.

Even though it was a petite dress, it would need to be hemmed, so the front wasn't dragging the ground like the short train. But Kay had already known any dress she would find would need to be hemmed due to her extremely short stature. *Although, with a gown this long, I could get mega-high heels and actually look like I'm taller. Anthony will still tower over me, even if I put on eight-inch platforms.*

Kay giggled at her own thoughts as she poked her head out of the dressing room and asked for someone to help her finish buttoning the back of the dress. Louella stepped up and finished the buttons that Kay couldn't reach, then handed her a pair of five-inch heels to slip on to see what she thought of the dress with shoes tall enough to lift the front just off the floor.

Kay was surprised at how comfortable the shoes were to walk in as she made her way out of the dressing room and back out to the stage that was set up with mirrors all around, so she could see the dress from all angles and so could her family.

"Oh, Kay," her mother, Mary, gasped from her phone that Hazel was aiming at her as she stepped onto the platform. "That's definitely my favorite."

"It's exquisite," Hazel agreed.

"I think this is the one." Kay beamed at her mom and future mother-in-law. "And with these shoes, I don't think it will even need to be hemmed."

"Let me see," Randi demanded from the phone. Apparently, she had to crowd her mom to be able to see the screen on their end to see the dress. "Oh, Sis, it's perfect! Lift it up and let me see the shoes."

Kay lifted the front of the dress and poked out a foot to show off the satin-covered stilettos.

"They'd be sexier if they weren't bridal white," Randi joked when she saw the shoe.

Mary swatted Randi away from the phone and Kay knew it was so her sister wouldn't make any comments about "hooker heels" or "stripper shoes" that would embarrass everyone else who could hear the conversation.

"You look like a fairy princess, Mommy." Maria smiled up at Kay.

"It's beautiful, Mom." Tia grinned as she snapped pictures of Kay from every angle to send to Deanna.

After they all agreed that it was definitely the wedding dress she should wear, Louella helped her try on the matching veil for more pictures before she went back to the dressing room to change.

When she carried the dress, shoes, and veil out of the dressing room to Louella to package them for transport back to the ranch, she found Mary, Hazel, and Louella discussing the payment for everything related to the wedding. Mary was trying to get Louella to take her credit card information over the phone because she thought it was her place as Kay's mother to pay for the wedding. Louella was explaining to the two mothers that Anthony had already left his card information to pay for everything, with instructions not to let Kay switch it to her card, unless it was her card on his accounts. Hazel was trying to mediate, but she wasn't having much luck.

Kay took a deep breath before stepping into the fray. She handed the items to Louella, who stepped away to put the shoes in their box and the veil on a hanger, so it could go in the garment bag with the dress.

"Mom!" Kay shouted, holding her hand out for Hazel to hand her phone back to her. Once she could see her mother on the screen, she continued in a more normal conversational tone. "Thank you for wanting to pay for my wedding. I love you and appreciate how you've always taken care of me. But I've learned in the last few weeks that I'm not nearly hardheaded enough to win an argument with Anthony, when he insists on paying for something that I think is my responsibility. So, I'm going to let him have his way anywhere he's already set up payment for wedding stuff, and let Daddy argue with him when ya'll come down for the wedding, if there's something you really want to pay for the wedding. They are much more evenly matched in the stubbornness department, so maybe Daddy can convince him to let ya'll reimburse him for some of this stuff."

"Don't hold your breath on that one." Hazel smiled as she looked at Mary on the phone over Kay's shoulder. "Burleson men are known to be very determined when it comes to providing for their families. Bob wouldn't even let my parents continue paying for my college classes once we started dating. The only reason my mother was able to buy my wedding dress is because we went shopping in Austin when Bob didn't know."

"Gracious, they sound a lot like my Charles," Mary grinned. "Alright, I guess I can't fuss over a good man wanting to take care of my baby girl."

With that, they made sure that Louella and Benny had all the measurements for the bridesmaids, the groomsmen, and both of Kay's daughters to order their wedding attire to fit. Kay found a royal blue garter that she added to the purchases she was taking with her that day. Or rather that she was sending home with Hazel that day, so Anthony wouldn't see them before the wedding.

They said their goodbyes and put their purchases in the back of Hazel's SUV before walking over to the florist to pick out the bouquets and any other flowers they would need to decorate the church and reception venue. Kay didn't see Anthony's truck but knew he would be meeting them there soon.

~~~

After leaving the dress shop, Anthony quickly picked up the uniforms Kay had put in to be dry-cleaned the week before. Then, he made his way over to the police station at the corner of Mustang Lane and Brangus Street to see if his oldest brother was there. While he didn't have high hopes that his brother would know about band options for the wedding reception, he did want to show him the texts he'd just taken from Kay's old phone and sent to her dad and attorney.

The Tulsa County Sheriff was most likely to be the one to arrest Kay's ex-husband, Mark, but Anthony still thought it was wise to inform his brother to keep a look out for him, since his latest threats
~~~

indicated he knew that Kay had taken the girls to Texas, and he was coming after them.

"Good afternoon, Mabel," Anthony greeted the receptionist as he walked into the station.

"Anthony!" Mabel shouted, jumping up from her desk to give him a hug, as only a southern motherly figure could get away with while wearing a police uniform. "Congratulations! I heard you're gettin' married."

"Yes, ma'am," Anthony replied, returning her hug. "Any chance you know any local bands that play at wedding receptions? I thought about asking Bobby, but figured he'd only know the bands that play at Tully's."

"You know your brother." She shook her head, swatting him in the shoulder as she pulled back from the hug. "And I doubt you want a honky-tonk band to play at your wedding, so I'll save you from his awful recommendations, and give you the numbers for a couple of youngsters I know that would be better suited to the performance."

"Thanks, Mabel." Anthony grinned. "Any chance he's in, so I can ask him about some actual police business, while you're writing down those numbers for me?"

"Yeah, yeah, go on back." Mabel waved him off with one hand, as she sat back down at her desk and started scrolling through her phone to look up the numbers with the other.

Anthony made his way back to his brother's office, only waving at the detective in the outer office as he walked through, so he didn't get stopped for another conversation before talking to Bobby. He knocked once on the door before opening it and walking on in to find his brother eating lunch at his desk.

"Hey, Bro," Bobby choked out after swallowing a bite of his burger. "What's up?"

"I think I might actually have some official police business for you." Anthony sat down in the chair in front of his brother's desk and pulled his phone out of his pocket. When he had the folder open that contained the text message threats from Mark to Kay, he slid it across the desk to his brother. "I copied those off Kay's old phone this morning. Since her ex seems to have an idea of where she is, I figured you might need a heads up to keep an eye out for the asshole."

Bobby picked up Anthony's phone and scrolled through the messages. "Shit, man," he cursed as he read. "Have you sent these to her dad or her lawyer?"

"Yeah," Anthony replied. "From her phone, at the same time I sent them to myself. Her dad has an APB out to pick him up for the vandalism of her house in Tulsa, but I'm a bit worried that he's not going to be able to lock the jackass up. Especially if he's already in Texas looking for them, like those messages say."

"You think he knows exactly where in Texas?" Bobby handed Anthony's phone back.

"Not sure," Anthony shrugged as he put his phone back in his pocket. "I'm hoping that he was just able to track them to Dallas because of the girls flying there from Tulsa. But with no record of them flying commercially out of Dallas, maybe he lost the trail, and won't see any of our commercial flights into and out of San Antonio."

"What does Sheriff Lee think?" Bobby inquired.

"Not sure," Anthony replied. "He thanked me for the info via text, but I haven't actually talked to him about the threats."

"Well, then, let's call him. See if we can't get a few departments to coordinate our efforts to bring the dirtbag in and protect your girls. You have his cell number, or do I need to call the office and see if he's in?"

"I have his cell." Anthony pulled his phone out of his pocket again to dial the number. He put it on speaker and sat it on the desk between them as it rang.

"Anthony," Sheriff Lee's voice came out in a clipped tone as he answered the phone. "I trust my girls are still safe and sound with you."

"Technically, they're safe and sound with my mother and Skyping with your wife while Kay tries on wedding dresses. And I've been barred from the building, so I don't see her dress before the wedding." Anthony's words caused Charles to chuckle through the phone. "I figured while they're all occupied, I'd meet up with my brother and make sure his department is keeping an eye out for Mark, in case he somehow figured out where we are. I have you on speaker in Bobby's office now. I'm not sure if ya'll formally met when we were passing the phone around at our family dinner a couple weeks ago, but Sheriff Lee, this is my brother, Police Chief Bobby Burleson."

"Nice to officially meet you, Chief Burleson," Sheriff Lee said through the phone.

"You too, Sheriff," Bobby chuckled. "But we're a pretty laid-back small town here, and we're about to be family, so please call me Bobby."

"I suppose you're right, family shouldn't be so formal," Charles chuckled along with Bobby. "You can call me Charles, as well. I assume you're calling about the messages Anthony forwarded to me earlier?"

"Partially," Bobby replied. "I just read through them and wanted your opinion on the likelihood that Mark was able to track them past Dallas, since they didn't fly commercial out of there."

"Honestly, I'm not sure how he was able to track them to Dallas," Charles groaned, sounding frustrated through the phone. "Mark's not exactly tech-savvy enough to be able to track Kay's phone."

"I assumed he checked with the airlines for the girls' names on flights out of Tulsa when he couldn't find them that first weekend," Anthony explained his theory. "While they're not really supposed to give that information out to just anyone, he could have easily manipulated an airline employee to give him information about his daughters. I just wasn't sure if he would be smart enough to have that employee search for their names on flights that don't go through Dallas to be able to find them from the other commercial flights we've taken into and out of San Antonio."

"How many flights into and out of San Antonio are we talking about?" Charles questioned, sounding concerned.

"Three, so far," Anthony replied, trying to remember the dates, so he could list them for Charles. "From New Orleans on the fifteenth, to Knoxville on the nineteenth, and from Indianapolis yesterday. We're scheduled to fly out to Fargo, North Dakota on Monday. Then on the fourth of November, we'll be flying from Seattle to Tulsa. Those are all commercial flights that he might be able to track with the girls' names. With four of the five being into or out of San Antonio, it'll make it pretty obvious where we are most of the time. If he has my name from the witness list and does any digging into me in the San Antonio area, it will lead him directly to the ranch. That's why I wanted to loop Bobby in, to make sure he doesn't get near the girls."

"And why I wanted to find out how likely you think it is that he was able to figure out exactly where they are," Bobby added. "If you think he's still in Dallas, then I'll just keep watch from a distance, but if you think he could be here in Heart's Destiny, then I'll head over to the bridal shop now, so I can provide close cover while the ladies are out of Anthony's sight. And I'll have my officers double up on shifts, so we can search the whole town for him."

"I honestly don't know what to expect from Mark anymore," Charles huffed. "When I read the texts that said he was going to Dallas to…" His voice trailed off, like he couldn't repeat the threat to Kay out loud. He cleared his throat before speaking again. "I notified DPD of his possible presence in their city, but I don't have high expectations of them actually tracking him down and extraditing him to Tulsa County."

"I have some contacts in DPD, as well as the Rangers." Bobby turned toward his computer. "I'll make a few calls and see if I can get their assistance in locating him. Also, what's the likelihood of you getting a warrant to track his phone, since he's wanted in your jurisdiction?"

"Between slim and none," Charles sighed. "While it would be really nice to track down criminals using their cell phone signal, the courts here have declined to let us do that, claiming it's an invasion of their privacy."

"You think Uncle Doug would let you do it?" Anthony grilled his brother.

"Probably," Bobby smirked as he tapped out a text on his phone. "But I don't have the capability with computers to actually do it from here, so I usually rely on confidential informants to call me with locations that I can't get myself."

"You have confidential informants that can track cell phones?" Charles sounded intrigued.

"I have one." Bobby's grin widened. "Who I happen to have just texted to see if he can locate someone for us."

Anthony didn't know how legal it was for Bobby to ask someone to locate a cell phone signal without a court order, but if it helped him keep Mark from getting near Kay or the girls, he was okay with it not being perfectly legal. He looked at his brother quizzically as he watched Bobby texting back and forth with his informant. *I wonder who it is?* Anthony knew their brother Jake was capable of doing anything with a computer, but he wasn't sure he would risk his job in naval intelligence to illegally track a cell phone. *Maybe someone Bobby knew when he was in the Navy?*

Anthony shook his head at his random thoughts. Regardless of whom Bobby was communicating with to help Charles find the jackass, Anthony wasn't in law enforcement, so he didn't need to know anything more about how they went about doing their jobs. He made sure Bobby and Charles exchanged cell numbers, so he could excuse himself from the conversation.

Once he'd disconnected the call with his future father-in-law, he said goodbye to his brother before leaving the station to head over to Flora's Flowers to meet his bride-to-be and their daughters. He walked in there only a few minutes after Kay. When he saw her sitting with Tia, Maria, and Hazel looking at pictures of bouquets, while Florence was gathering sample flowers to show them, he opted to leave the last chair for Florence, and scooped Kay into his arms, so he could sit where she'd been with her on his lap to make their final decisions on flowers for the wedding.

They quickly picked the bouquet flowers and were looking at table centerpieces for the reception when they hit a snag. He pulled his phone from his pocket and called his best friends' mother to find out how many tables would fit in the ballroom. She informed him that it depended on the layout they picked for the room and how much space they needed to leave open for the dance floor. Since they were already scheduled to meet with her the next day to look at the ballroom, they let Florence know they'd call her back to place the final order once they had the information from Mandi about how many tables they needed floral centerpieces for after that meeting.

Once they were done at the florist, they went to Millie's Diner for lunch, then popped over to Kara's Kakes to confirm their cake-tasting appointment for Saturday afternoon. They finished their afternoon by going back to the craft store to get all the stuff to start putting together wedding favors and printing their own wedding invitations.

Considering the long guest list, they were lucky to get the invitations printed that weekend and would be working on the favors every free moment they had at home in the next four weeks.

~~~

Sunday, October 28, 2018

As they walked into the Heart's Destiny Community Church on Sunday morning, Kay realized that her mental picture of the inside of the church from her daydreams about the wedding was pretty close to accurate. The pulpit and pews were all solid maple with exquisite woodwork. The carpeting was all a dark gray, probably so it wouldn't show dirt as much as some other colors. Kay was glad that it was so neutral that it wouldn't clash with whatever color scheme was used for various events, specifically her upcoming wedding. There had been a time at her home church in Tulsa when the carpet was a hideous orange shag that Kay dreaded seeing in her friend's wedding pictures because of how badly it had clashed with their chosen wedding colors.

The Burlesons all sat together, taking up two pews on the right side of the church. Kay met more Harpers and Whitmans that Anthony claimed as cousins by marriage, but Kay wasn't sure how they were all related. She also met more Hunters, Deeres, Miltons, and Bensons, but she was pretty sure they weren't related to Anthony or his family.

Once they all got settled in their seats, Pastor Harrison delivered a sermon that was very similar to what she was used to in the Baptist church back home, so she didn't think her parents would object too much to the non-denominational church for her wedding. Kay was glad that she was able to stay present in the moment and actually listen to the preacher, instead of daydreaming the way she had the last time she'd gone to church with her parents, even with Anthony's arm resting on the back of the pew behind her, so he could rub his thumb over her shoulder throughout the sermon.

Maybe it's because he's here with me that I'm able to enjoy the moment and not daydream about when I'll get to see him next?

After the service was over, they made their way to the fellowship hall for the potluck lunch that was apparently a weekly occurrence in Heart's Destiny. Kay walked over to the food table where Anthony had placed their cooler before the service, glad the potato salad she made the night before was still chilled as she removed it from the cooler to put it out to serve with the other dishes. She tucked the
~~~

cooler under the table before going to get in line with Anthony and the girls to make their plates.

There were lively conversations all around them, including Tia and Maria making new friends with girls their ages from their Sunday school class that morning. Pastor Harrison came to sit with them while they ate, giving Anthony and Kay the opportunity to not only confirm the wedding date, but also to do a mini marriage counseling session with him since they weren't scheduled to be back in Heart's Destiny until the fourteenth of November, only ten days before their wedding. He still wanted to meet with them at least once in the week before the wedding to confirm all the plans.

Kay almost couldn't believe just how welcome she felt in this small town. It was feeling more and more like home every day she was there. While she would always want to go visit her family and friends in Tulsa, she wasn't sure it was her home anymore, like it had been all her life. When she really thought about it, even the arenas and hotels they were in while working for the GWA felt more like home than Tulsa now. All because Anthony was with her in those environments. She was starting to understand what he meant when he said she was his home. It was a sentiment she could definitely agree with him on because he was now her home, as well.

After they finished eating and helping clean up from the potluck dinner, Kay and Anthony left their daughters to spend the afternoon making cookies with Hazel while they went for a romantic horseback ride to their special spot on the ranch. They let the horses drink from the creek before tying them up in the shade.

~~~

Anthony laid out a blanket a few feet away from the horses for he and Kay to lay among the wildflowers and enjoy what he'd packed in the saddlebags, a bottle of sparkling wine, cheese and crackers, and a mix of berries they could feed each other with their fingers. This had been his original plan to propose to Kay, so he wanted to make sure she got the whole romantic experience, even if it was a little later than the actual proposal.
~~~

Leah Mae Wright

"What's all this?" Kay looked over the spread that he'd laid out on the blanket.

"This is me, trying to properly court you, the way you deserve." Anthony took her hand and lightly tugged to get her to sit and relax beside him. "I wanted to do all this the night I proposed, but since I didn't have time to grab everything before we left the house that night, I figured we'd enjoy a redo. Maybe make our proposal story for our grandkids a little more romantic than me throwing you over my shoulder and driving you out here on a four-wheeler."

"I already thought your proposal was romantic." Kay snuggled into his side. "Telling me about the history of our rings and proposing where you want to build a home for our family was extremely enchanting."

"Yeah, maybe." Anthony didn't sound convinced, even to his own ears, as he uncorked the small bottle of wine. "But you deserve more, and I wanna do more to show you how much I love you."

He poured the wine into the two plastic wine glasses and handed one to Kay. "A toast to my beautiful bride." They clinked their glasses together before taking a sip.

He then opened the containers of crackers, cheese, and fruit. He put a slice of cheese on a cracker and held it to her lips.

"I can feed myself, you know," Kay giggled, but she took a bite of the cheese and cracker.

"I know, Baby." Anthony popped the rest of the cheese and cracker into his own mouth. "But it's more fun to share." He wagged his eyebrows at her after he finished chewing and swallowing the morsel. He reached for the berries next, but Kay stopped his hand, apparently wanting to feed him as well.

They alternated feeding each other their late afternoon snack while discussing what they each envisioned for the house that they would eventually build at the top of the bluff a few yards away from where they were laying on the bank of the creek. They talked about how they wanted to clear away some of the brush at the edge of the creek, so they could actually play in the water in the summer. While they didn't get the really frigid temperatures in South Texas that Kay was accustomed to in Oklahoma, they agreed that the spring-fed creek was too cold to get in except in the hottest part of the year.

Soon their lighthearted talk about their future plans, while feeding each other, turned to more carnal teasing when Kay sucked the berry juice off of Anthony's fingers. She swirled her velvet soft tongue around his thumb, and Anthony would have sworn he felt it in his cock. He was as hard as the rocks beneath them in an instant.

"Maybe it's a good thing we haven't started clearing the trail to make a road and run power out here yet," Anthony growled, his voice sounding deeper than normal, even to his own ears. As soon as she released his thumb from her mouth, he sat their mostly empty wine glasses aside and pulled Kay onto his lap. "I think we need to christen this spot before we have anyone out here to start construction."

"Yes, Tony," Kay cooed just before their lips met.

With one hand in her hair, holding her lips to his, and the other on her ass, pressing her core into his overly engorged erection, Anthony took control of the kiss. He didn't just leisurely tangle their tongues. He fucked her mouth with his, like he wanted his cock to fuck her tight cunt.

Kay had one hand in his hair and the other digging into his back with her nails, like she couldn't pull him close enough to her. She wrapped her legs around his waist and was using them to increase her leverage, as she writhed against his manhood.

"Too many fucking clothes," he groaned as he pulled back and moved to pull her t-shirt up. She lifted her arms, so he could get it off, then went to work on the dozen front hooks on her bra, while he quickly removed his own t-shirt.

"Way too many," Kay breathlessly agreed, as she stood and unfastened her jeans. She kicked off her boots and shucked her jeans and panties faster than Anthony could get his jeans unbuttoned and down to his mid-thighs. His cock sprang free as he took his boxer briefs down with his jeans, the tip already glistening with precum from just a few minutes of dry-humping.

"That's far enough." Kay moved to straddle him again without letting him completely remove his jeans and underwear. She gripped his cock to line him up with her opening and started to sink down on him before he could protest that he hadn't had enough time to prepare her yet.

"Fuck, you're so wet, Baby," Anthony groaned as Kay impaled herself on his cock. "And way too tight to take all of me that fast."

He gripped her hips and held her still, making sure her body relaxed to accommodate his size before allowing her to move. Once he was sure she was feeling no pain, he let her set the pace and enjoyed how she rocked her hips as she rode him. He fondled her bountiful breasts, ducking his head to lick her pebbled peaks, as she bounced up and down on his length.

They were louder than normal, almost screaming as they cried out their passion, instead of the way they normally whispered words of love and affection. Anthony loved hearing her shout, "Oh, fuck, yes, Tony," as she came almost as much as he loved hearing her shout, "I love you, Anthony." He liked knowing that the only time she cursed was in the throes of passion with him; that he was the only person who ever heard her say a dirty word.

He returned her ardent cries of love, even as he held back his own release. She may have been too impatient to let him get her off with foreplay first, but he was still going to make sure that she came at least twice before he let go.

She cuddled into his chest, wrapping her arms under his to rest her palms on his shoulder blades, as she came down from the high of her orgasm. He took advantage of her limp-noodle, satiated state to slow down his hip thrusts, and switched to more of a slow grind of their bodies where they were joined. The constant pressure of his pubic bone grinding on her clit sent her over the edge once more.

"Oh, Anthony," Kay cooed as her tight channel clamped down on his cock in wave after wave of pleasure.

"Fuck, yes, Kay," Anthony shouted, as he gave one final thrust to be as deep inside her as possible when he came. With every wave of her vaginal walls squeezing his cock, he released another stream of cum deep into her womb.

They rested there wrapped in each other's arms for several long moments, as they floated back down from the heights of ecstasy.

"Fuck, I didn't think to bring anything with us to clean up with," Anthony groaned as they disentangled their bodies, and he watched his cum start to drip down Kay's legs.

Kay looked around at the blanket and the plastic containers that the food had been in before glancing over at the creek.

"No, Baby, it's too cold to rinse off in," Anthony protested, afraid she was about to go get in the freezing cold water of the spring-fed creek. With the air temperature only being in the low seventies, he didn't think it was warm enough to air dry after a dunk in the forty-something-degree water.

"It's either that, or we wipe off with this blanket and throw it straight in the washer when we get home. And we'd still need to shower before going to get the girls from your parents," Kay insisted, still looking back and forth between the blanket and the creek.

"We'll go straight to the house, and I'll go back to the stable to take care of the horses after we get cleaned up." Anthony tried to stand with his pants around his knees, so he could shake out the blanket to find the cleanest part to wipe off the majority of the sticky mess off their most delicate places.

Once they wiped off what they could, they quickly dressed and put the empty wine bottle, glasses, and plastic food containers in one saddlebag, and the blanket with the evidence of their copulation rolled to the inside of the ball in the other.

"My panties might still be glued to my body by the time we get home," Kay giggled as Anthony helped her onto her horse.

"Then I'll be extra careful removing them for our shower," he replied with a grin as he mounted his horse for their ride home.

Chapter Sixteen

As they boarded the plane in Seattle to fly to Tulsa for their court appearance the next day, Anthony reflected on the last week of life with his soon-to-be family. They may have technically been at work, but every minute felt like quality family time. From dressing up for the Halloween party as a royal family living out their own fairy tale, to swapping nights babysitting with the girls' friends' parents, and having his socks frozen in a bowl of water because he fell asleep too early when he was supervising the girls' slumber party. He loved every second.

Even having to thaw his socks out of the block of ice with the hotel hair dryer was a fun new experience that he would've missed out on if he hadn't met Kay. He was looking forward to scheming with the girls to pull a few of those slumber party pranks on his siblings, cousins, and friends for years to come.

Not as much as he was looking forward to more alone time with Kay, but he couldn't imagine ever looking forward to anything as much as he wanted more naked nights with Kay. Their time alone in their hotel room when the girls were spending the night with their friends was one he would never forget. Kay had found a dirty fairy tale on her e-reader, and they'd donned their king and queen costumes to role-play the sexy scenes.

Anthony had to stop himself from mentally reliving how he awakened his sleeping princess by kissing her lower lips because it wasn't appropriate to have a boner while sitting on a plane beside his future daughter. He tried to look across the aisle at Kay, but that just made the bulge in his pants grow another inch. He had to think of something else quickly, or he'd be pushing his tray table up without using his hands.

Luckily, Maria asked him to quiz her on her most recent list of spelling words, so she'd be ready for a test that Kay would be giving her in a few days. She pulled up the list on her tablet and handed it to Anthony. His cock deflated quickly as he randomly picked words from the list and said them for her to verbally spell for him. When she got them all mostly right, they went back through all of the third-grade spelling lists that had opened up so far in that school year, to make sure she knew the words the other kids had learned in the modules before she began the program, just in case they were different than the spelling lists she'd done at her school in Tulsa.

While there weren't very many that she didn't already know, it kept them occupied the rest of the flight into Tulsa, so both Kay and Tia could write without being disturbed. Once they landed in Tulsa, they checked into a hotel near the airport, not wanting to take a chance on Mark looking for them at the Camelot, since Kay had worked there for so many years.

Kay called her parents as soon as they got to the room. The Lees opted to skip the evening service at church to come across town to meet at the hotel restaurant for dinner. Anthony easily recognized Charles Lee as he walked into the lobby, even though he was in a suit instead of the sheriff's uniform he'd been wearing the first time they met. Seeing the petite woman walking in beside him made Anthony wonder if he was getting a glimpse of he and Kay in the future.

During one of their many late-night talks, Kay had told him about how her parents met when she was two years old, and that Charles had adopted her as soon as they were married. That was probably why Charles was so understanding and accepting of Anthony's feelings for Kay and the girls. He'd been in the same situation a little over thirty years before. Anthony hoped to follow in his footsteps and be just as good a dad to Tia and Maria as Charles had been to Kay.

"Grandma! Grandpa!" Tia and Maria squealed in unison as they ran across the lobby to launch themselves into the arms of their grandparents.

Introductions were made, since Anthony hadn't previously met Mary Lee. He was slightly surprised at how similar she was to his own mother. Mary was only an inch or two taller than Kay, so probably an inch or two shorter than Hazel, but they would be very close in height. They had similar hairstyles, but Mary's hair was jet black to Hazel's dark brown. It was Mary's eyes that struck him as being almost the exact same shade of green as his mother's.

I wonder where Kay and the girls got their blue eyes, since it wasn't from Charles?

Once they were seated, it was mostly small talk over dinner. Since Charles had informed them the week before that he'd arrested Mark, they already knew that he was out on bail while awaiting trial for felony vandalism, so they avoided any mention of him in front of the girls.

The girls told their grandparents about all the cities they'd visited and how much more they were learning through tourism than they would've studied in the previous month at their former schools. When the conversation turned to focus on the wedding, Anthony tried to talk Charles into coming down to Heart's Destiny on Saturday the seventeenth to spend the entire week getting to know not just Anthony's biological family, but also their GWA family that would be there for their holiday break.

"While I would love to do that, Anthony," Charles argued between bites of his dinner. "It will depend on hotel availability. When I called the bed and breakfast you mentioned, I was informed that they're booked up that entire week. We could get a room the Thursday before, or the Monday after, but apparently there aren't any rooms available Thanksgiving week."

"Oh, sorry, Dad." Kay covered her mouth, and quickly swallowed the bite of food she was chewing. "I forgot to tell you that Rick booked all the rooms for the GWA crew, so our family will all be staying on the Burleson Ranch."

"There are enough rooms on the ranch for all of us?" Mary queried, looking at Kay. "I thought you said there's not a spare bedroom in your house."

"There are actually eight family houses on the ranch." Anthony hoped to clear up the confusion. "Even if my brothers are able to come home on leave and need their old rooms in my parents' house, there's still four empty bedrooms there. Another four empty bedrooms at my Uncle Jon and Aunt Susan's house. And at least one extra bedroom in each of the five houses my siblings and cousins live in on the ranch. If you need more than the fifteen or so bedrooms we have available, we also have a secondary bunkhouse that we haven't used since we discontinued the bull breeding program a few years ago."

"Oh, alright." Charles looked a little more relaxed. "We won't need nearly that many rooms, only six or seven, depending on whether or not David can get the time off from work to come down with his wife and kids. If you're sure your family is okay with us staying with them that long, we should be able to come down early. I'm not sure about Randi or your girlfriends and their work schedules, but I'll see if I can't convince them all to come down with us and spend the whole week."

With that mini-crisis averted, the conversation turned to whether or not the girls could have a sleepover with their grandparents while they were in Tulsa. Erring on the side of caution, they opted to have the girls stay with Kay and Anthony at the hotel the first night, and would play it by ear after court the next day to see if they could have their sleepover that night.

Overall, they had a nice evening visiting with Kay's parents until it was time for the girls to get their baths, so they could get to bed by their nine o'clock bedtime. Anthony loved their nightly ritual of coming to him for help detangling their hair before goodnight hugs and kisses, even though he missed the years when they were young enough to want to be tucked in and read a bedtime story.

"What's that wistful look for?" Kay questioned him as they sat together on the sofa in their suite after the girls had left the common area to go to their bedroom for the night.

"Just wishing I hadn't missed so much of their younger years, when I could have tucked them in and read them bedtime stories." Anthony wrapped his arm around Kay's shoulders and pulled her into his side.

She cuddled in closer, resting her head on his chest. "Maybe, if all goes well tomorrow, we can start looking into what we need to do to adopt the little brother Maria wants and you won't miss bedtime stories anymore."

"Mmm, maybe." Anthony sat there, wistfully enjoying the cuddle time on the couch with Kay. "How many kids do you want to adopt?"

"I've never really thought about it." Kay snuggled in closer and slipped her legs across his lap. "When I was a kid, I wanted to grow up to have a big family, but I didn't have a specific number of kids I wanted. As I got older, and especially after having the girls, I pretty much decided that I'll be just as happy if I only have them, as I would be if I had a dozen more. So, I'll let you decide how many more we adopt."

He wrapped his arms around her and adjusted her, so she was fully seated on his lap, and he could hold her close.

"You remember I told you about my dreams," he murmured as he brought his lips to the top of her head.

"Yeah," she practically purred.

"They weren't just about you," he confessed. "They were about our family. I dreamed of us raising two daughters and two sons. The faces of my dream family were always fuzzy until the day we met, but I knew our girls would be blonde and our boys would have darker hair like yours and mine."

"Are the faces clearer now?" Kay rubbed her arms where she had goosebumps.

"Yeah, clear as can be." Anthony took over rubbing Kay's arms.

"Tell me about them," Kay whispered, softly.

"In my dream last night, we were celebrating Tia's sixteenth birthday by giving her a car. I parked it in the circle drive, in front of our castle that we're gonna build on the bluff where I proposed to you, the night before. When the kids all woke up, we sent Tia on a scavenger hunt through the house to find her birthday presents. You wrote out a story for the clues that sent her through all the rooms in the back of the house, so she couldn't see it through one of the front windows."

"That sounds like a fun way to surprise her," Kay giggled. "But tell me about the other kids."

"The other kids were all helping her figure out the clues to know where to search next. Maria looked a lot like Tia does now, probably because she would be about Tia's age now in the dream. The oldest boy looked to be about seven or eight years old. His name's Antonio and he kept trying to confuse Tia to make it harder to figure out the clues. It wasn't malicious, just a boy being a boy and trying to make the game last longer."

"Antonio? Sounds like you're describing yourself as a child," Kay giggled again.

"Maybe a little," Anthony chuckled with her. "His hair was darker than mine, though, almost black, complexion too. I'm guessing his biological family is Hispanic, and we'll keep the first name he was given at birth, since we'll adopt him as an older child."

"Yeah, sure, we'll go with that," Kay teased with another chuckle. "What about the other little boy?"

"He looked to be two or three, with medium brown hair and blue eyes, and he kept trying to get everyone to stop reading the clues to wrestle with him. After each of the other kids took a turn tickling him, I ended up carrying him as we followed Tia around the house and eventually out front to her new Jeep."

"You think Tia's gonna want a Jeep for her first car?" Kay laughed. "Tia isn't into jacked-up four-wheeling vehicles. She'll want something cute, like my Bug, or a sports car. You might wanna clue your dream self in for the reality of the future."

"Haha," Anthony deadpanned, tickling Kay to make her keep laughing. "My dream self is already clued in. And just like my real self, he's not gonna buy a cute little death trap for his family. And it wasn't a jacked-up Jeep Wrangler. It was a Jeep Patriot like my mom drives now. Safe while still being capable of going anywhere on the ranch."

"Oh." Kay sat up straighter and looked into his eyes. "I like your mom's SUV. I just didn't realize it was a Jeep."

"Good, then we'll look for one for you when we know for sure where we'll be living most of the time," Anthony declared, instantly wanting to kick himself for how he ended the statement. He should have said they would look for one for her when they got back to Heart's Destiny, so Kay wouldn't have stiffened up at the reminder of their court appearance the next day. "Baby," he groaned, not quite sure what to say to get them back to laughing and imagining their future with their kids.

"Don't," Kay barked, clearly trying to hold back tears. "Thank you for distracting me with your fantastic dreams for our future, but don't treat me with kid gloves, like I'm not capable of dealing with the possibility that tomorrow will be a nightmare, instead of our dream future."

"I know you're capable of dealing with whatever happens in court tomorrow, Baby." Anthony hugged her to him, to comfort himself as much as her. "I just hate seeing you worried about all the *what ifs* that might never really happen. I prefer you being your normal, happy, carefree self, only having to tap into your inner strength when a situation actually arises. We'll deal with whatever happens tomorrow. Together, tomorrow. Tonight, we'll just enjoy living in the moment, focused on each other, not what may, or may not, happen in the future."

Kay moved her arms from where she'd been hugging herself, wrapping them around Anthony's neck. She ran her fingers through the hair at his nape and pulled him down to brush their lips together. Anthony understood her nonverbal cues as her shy way of asking him to carry her to bed, so they could focus on each other and their mutual pleasure the rest of the night.

He took over the kiss, applying a little more pressure with his lips to show her that she could let go and just feel while he took care of her. He moved his arms, taking the one that had been over her legs to under her knees and the one that had been around her waist higher up her back, so he could stand with her cradled in his arms to walk them to their bedroom.

He laid her out on the bed before going back to the door to shut and lock it. He quickly stripped off his clothes, but he took his time as he slowly undressed Kay. As each new section of skin was exposed, he gently stroked his fingers over her delicate flesh. He followed his fingers with open-mouthed kisses, worshiping every inch of her. Paying special attention to her perfect, plump peaks and petal soft pussy. Whispering words of affection and love the whole time.

He loved the feel of her hands, whether she was running her fingers through his hair or rubbing her hands over his shoulders and back. Where she touched him didn't matter, only the intense sensuality he experienced from her delicate exploration of his body.

Knowing they wouldn't line up for the missionary position because of their height difference, Anthony reversed their positions as soon as she came down from her first climax, so she could explore the front of his body as he had hers. He ran his fingers through her long dark hair to pull her in for a deep, sensual kiss.

He kept his hands in her luscious locks as she moved to trail kisses down his neck. The feel of her hands rubbing across his chest was exquisite. When she followed them with her hot little mouth and lightly sucked his nipples, he felt a tingle in his spine and his balls drew up, as if he was about to come like an inexperienced teenager. And the only part of her touching his cock was her belly where she was laying on top of him.

"Fuck, Baby, I need you now," he moaned. "Please ride me, so I can feel your tight little pussy all around my cock."

He released her hair, running his hands down her body as she sat up. He stroked his cock a couple of times as she moved into position, rubbing his precum down the length even though he wouldn't need the extra lubrication based on how her sex was glistening from being so wet. He gripped the stalk, holding himself up for her to slowly slide down around him.

He moved his hand out of the way, lightly gripping her hips, so he could help her take him all the way to the root. The velvet glove feel of her channel on his dick was pure heaven. They synced up their movements, him tenderly thrusting up into her, while she smoothly rocked her hips down onto him. She traced her fingers over his abs, while he cupped her breasts and circled his thumbs over her nipples.

They reverently whispered their feelings for one another as they made love long into the night. Anthony held on as much as he could, trying to prolong their pleasure to the maximum extent. Each time she came it was getting harder and harder to stop himself from going over the edge with her. After her fifth orgasm, she collapsed onto him, her breasts pressing into his upper abs, and her head resting over his heart.

"Just relax, Baby," he commanded as he wrapped his arms around her. "I've got you."

He laid there letting her float in her satiated state of euphoria until her little pink tongue darted out to lick his nipple. Then he gripped her hips, so he could move her with him as he resumed his rhythmic thrusting up into her pliant pussy.

"Oh, Anthony, that feels so good," Kay cooed while still teasing his nipples with her fingers and tongue. "It's like I'm a blow-up doll that you're using to jack off with."

"No, Baby," Anthony chuckled. "I've never tried one to be sure, but I don't think a blow-up doll could ever feel as good as you do."

"You won't ever have to try one either, because I'm happy to be your real, live fuck toy," Kay moaned as her inner walls clamped down on his cock.

Leah Mae Wright

"Mmm, yeah, Baby." Anthony sped up his thrusts as he moved her up and down his length. "Be my good fuck toy and come from being used to jack me off. I want to feel your tight little cunt milking my cock."

"Oh, Anthony, yes," Kay chanted as her cunt started contracting around him in wave after wave of pleasure.

He couldn't hold back any longer, repeatedly saying her name with each burst of cum he released inside her. They clung to each other as they basked in the glow of their mutual climax. He knew he needed to get up and get a washcloth from the bathroom to clean her up afterward, but he couldn't make himself move in his satiated state.

Maybe I can stay inside her all night, and we won't need to clean up until morning, he thought as they drifted off to sleep, with her still draped over him, and their bodies still connected.

~~~

Monday, November 5, 2018

Kay was a nervous wreck as she walked into the courthouse with Anthony. She, Anthony, and her daughters met her parents and attorney in the hall outside the courtroom about ten minutes before they were to appear before the judge.

Kay's mother, Mary Lee, greeted them with hugs. First a warm motherly squeeze for Kay before she threw her arms around Anthony in an unexpected embrace. "Thank you, again, for protecting my babies."

Anthony gently patted Mary on the back to return her hug, but he didn't get a chance to speak before she continued.

"I don't know how we would've gotten through the last month if you hadn't taken them with you." Mary wiped at her eyes as she stepped back beside her husband, Charles.

"I couldn't have made it through the month either without them with me." Anthony gave Mary a small smile before extending his hand to Charles. "Good to see you again, sir."
~~~

"Yeah, you too," Charles replied as he shook Anthony's hand. "This is Kay's attorney, Matt Monroe." Charles gestured to his long-time friend as he released his handshake with Anthony.

"Anthony Burleson." Anthony extended his hand to the attorney. The two shook hands quickly before Matt turned to Kay to speak.

"Okay, you'll be sitting at the table with me. Anthony and the girls can sit right behind us with your parents. I'm going to introduce the new petition first. Since I haven't been able to get Mark or his attorney to respond to our suggested out of court settlement, I'm not sure if the judge will be willing to sign off immediately, or if he'll still want us to present our case. As the petitioner, we get to call witnesses first, so I'm going to put you on the stand first, then Anthony, then Charles, and end with Tia. I fully expect his attorney to balk at the girls testifying because of their ages, so I doubt we could get both of them on the stand."

"But I wanna testify, too," Maria pouted, gripping Kay's hand.

Matt squatted down to be on Maria's eye level before speaking again. "I know, sweetie, but I'm not sure the judge will even think Tia's old enough to testify. If we can't get permission for either of you to testify in court, I'll see what I can do about having the judge meet with the two of you in his chambers, so you can speak with him off the record. Once he talks to you, I'm sure he'll realize that you're wise beyond your years and well capable of testifying in court."

He winked at her as he stood. "Okay, time to go in. Remember, just sit quietly during the proceedings and remain calm while you're on the stand."

They all filed into the courtroom and took their seats. Tia and Maria sat on either side of Anthony, who sat directly behind Kay. Charles and Mary sat beside Maria filling up the first bench on their side of the courtroom.

Mark Fox sat next to his attorney on the other side of the courtroom. Kay could see his parents and brothers on the bench behind him. She worried about what they would say on his behalf, but hoped the fact that he'd been arrested for the vandalism of her home, and was only able to appear in court because he was out on bond before his trial, would override any testimony his family would give later in the hearing.

After Judge Anderson came in and called the court to order, their case was announced, and Matt began by requesting the change in proceedings to reflect the new wording of the petition to sever the parental rights of Mark Fox, instead of the previous petition to terminate visitation.

The judge ordered the change and had Matt bring him the paperwork he'd written up for the new petition. Judge Anderson took a moment to read over the new paperwork before calling for the attorneys to give their opening statements.

Matt delivered a precise opening statement, stating that due to Kay's new job and move out of state, as well as Mark's violent behavior, Kay was requesting full custody of her minor children with all parental rights and responsibilities of Mark Fox being permanently severed. Due to her fear for her safety and the safety of her minor children, she was also requesting an order of protection to prevent Mark Fox from having any further contact with the three of them.

When Matt was finished and took his seat, Mark's attorney stood and stated that he wished to defer his opening statement until after the plaintiff's case presentation was completed. Essentially, he wanted to present his opening statement when he presented the defense's case to the court.

The judge allowed the postponement of the defense's opening statement, and Matt called Kay to the stand. She was so nervous she was afraid she would trip as she stepped up to be sworn in. Placing her hand on the Bible was the only reason it stopped tremoring.

"Ms. Lee," Matt began, "you're here today petitioning the court to sever the parental rights of Mr. Fox with your daughters. Why is that?"

Kay opened her mouth to speak, but she struggled to get the words out. She closed her mouth and eyes and took a deep breath, trying to calm down, so she could get through her testimony. "I fear for my daughters' safety if they're alone with their father." Kay's voice was barely above a whisper.

"Bullshit," Mark cursed, but he tried to cover it with a cough.

Kay looked over at him when she heard his outburst, but she had to turn away from his angry glare. She looked at her daughters sitting beside Anthony. They were each holding one of his hands. Anthony smiled at her before mouthing, *It's okay, Baby, just keep going.*

Kay nodded and tried to return his smile to thank him for being there, lending her his strength, but she was afraid her lips fell flat.

"Why do you fear for their safety?" Matt prodded.

Kay turned her attention back to her attorney, then looked up at the judge. "Because he's starting to be verbally and emotionally abusive to the girls, like he was toward me at the end of our marriage. Right before I left him, his abuse turned physical. Now that I'm not there to abuse, he's started it with them, and I won't let it escalate to him doing more than yelling at my daughters."

"That's a lie," Mark shouted as he stood waving his fist in Kay's direction.

"Control your client," the judge directed Mark's attorney. The attorney pulled Mark back down to his seat by his forearm. They whispered quietly to each other for a moment before Matt went back to questioning Kay about the end of her marriage to Mark.

Kay described the last couple of years of her marriage, explaining how Mark started by insulting her in private, then escalated to demeaning her in front of his friends. She talked about how he spent more time at the bar than at home, but then he blamed her for their financial problems because she was too stupid to work at anything more than a minimum-wage job. Finally, she described how their arguments turned physical, prompting her to leave him, and how he hit her again when she and the girls were moving out of the family home.

It was hard to hold back the tears as she relived that time while on the stand. When she looked at her family, she took comfort in the love and support that showed in her parents and Anthony's faces. Maria's face was buried in Anthony's side. He had an arm around her to comfort her as she heard the bad parts of her parent's marriage. His other hand holding Tia's seemed to be the only thing holding her oldest daughter back from an angry outburst. Tia's face was red, and she was obviously gritting her teeth. The hand she wasn't using to hold Anthony's was tightly gripped around the wooden railing in front of her. If looks could kill, Mark would be dead from the angry glare Tia was giving him.

"Why do you believe that your ex-husband has now transferred his verbal abuse from you to your daughters?" Matt asked, bringing Kay's attention back to her testimony.

Leah Mae Wright

"After their last visit with Mark, my daughters told me about how he yelled at them," Kay replied.

"Objection," Mark's attorney shouted. "That's hearsay, Your Honor."

"Sustained," the judge announced. "Strike that last question and answer," he directed the court reporter.

"No problem." Matt smiled as he turned back to Kay. "We'll review their last visit when the girls testify. Describe the events of Friday evening October fifth."

"After not returning any of my calls the week before, so we could discuss changing the visitation schedule, Mark showed up to pick up the girls for his visit an hour and a half late. When I opened the door, I almost gagged from the overwhelming stench of beer. He was obviously drunk. When I refused to let him drive drunk with my daughters in the car, he shoved his way in the house. He didn't just force the door open, he shoved me out of the way, so he could walk in. I told the girls to go to the bedroom and call my dad, Sheriff Charles Lee."

Kay paused to take a breath before continuing. "I tried to talk to him, but he was belligerent. I tried to hold him back, so he couldn't go down the hall after the girls, but he shoved me away again and turned to yell at me some more. Then my, um, friend, Anthony, showed up and stepped between us, so Mark couldn't hit me. Dad showed up a couple moments later. Dad then sent Mark home in a cab and had his car towed from my driveway."

"And the next day?" Matt probed.

Kay wasn't sure how to answer that because she knew if she mentioned the break-in that Mark's attorney would object, since she hadn't actually seen any of the damage or been there when it happened.

"My daughters and I flew with my friend Anthony to Dallas, so I could go on the job interview that Anthony set up for me." Kay shifted in her seat to face the judge. "I actually started the job the following Wednesday. My daughters will be traveling with me while I'm working and have already started working with private tutors for their education. It's a wonderful opportunity for them to learn based on their intellectual level, instead of being bored in public school, while I'm earning triple my previous income."

"Please explain your previous income compared to the income from your new job." Matt smiled at Kay because he knew this was a point to make the judge understand her need to be able to travel for her job with her daughters.

"At my previous job, I worked for minimum wage. Even with a full forty-hour week, that was only two-hundred-and-ninety dollars a week. If I could work an extra shift, it only added eighty-seven dollars, giving me a gross of three-hundred-seventy-seven dollars a week before taxes and insurance. After those deductions, I was lucky if my take-home pay was over two-hundred per week, and that only happened when I worked an extra shift."

Kay paused to take a breath and do some mental math. "My new job is a salaried position, paying fifty-two-thousand dollars a year, or one-thousand dollars a week before taxes and insurance. My weekly take-home pay is now about seven-hundred dollars a week. Looking at the gross income, I now make three-point-four times the amount I made at my previous job. Looking at the take-home pay, I now bring home three-point-five times the amount I brought home in my last job. I rounded down when I said I now earn triple my previous income."

Kay saw Anthony chuckle and slightly shake his head. She knew from the tiny grin on his face that he would point out her quick mental math later. *Maybe he's right and I don't really suck at math.*

Matt asked her a few more questions, which she easily answered, being bolstered by the feelings of confidence in herself that she gained from Anthony being there to silently support her. Mark's attorney declined to question her, so she stepped down and walked confidently back to her seat.

Matt called Anthony to the stand next. While he was being sworn in, she felt each of her daughters reach over the railing between them to put a hand on each of her shoulders. Kay reached up and patted each of their hands, leaving her hands on top of theirs while Anthony gave his testimony.

"Mr. Burleson, can you explain what you witnessed at the home of Kay Lee on the evening of October fifth?" Matt began his questioning.

"When I arrived, the front door was standing wide open. I heard shouting from inside, so I ran in, so I could protect Kay and her daughters from whoever was threatening them." Anthony visibly took a deep breath to calm down. "Mark had his fist raised and was about to punch Kay, so I stepped in between them to keep her from getting hurt. I told him that he needed to leave, just as Kay had already asked him to do. Instead of vacating the premises, he continued shouting insults and being belligerent. Before I could take further action to physically remove him from Kay's living room, her father showed up and took control of the situation."

"Was there any physical contact between you and Mr. Fox?"

"No," Anthony responded. "I did physically move Kay behind me, so I could protect her, but I never touched Mark Fox."

"Could you describe Mr. Fox's appearance that evening?"

"Obviously inebriated." Anthony looked in Mark's direction, disgust written all over his handsome face. "Disheveled, as if he hadn't paid attention to his grooming for a while. Like he just threw on whatever clothing was laying around regardless of wrinkles or cleanliness."

"You said he was belligerent. What exactly was he shouting?"

"First he asked who the *'fuck'* I was." Anthony used air quotes when he said the F-word. "Then he demanded that the girls were going with him for their visit. When it was pointed out that he was too drunk to drive, he called Kay a *'slut'* and referred to me as her *'john of the week.'* He then threatened to tell the judge that I assaulted him, so he could get full custody of the girls. He then turned whiney when Charles said he was going to arrest him for trespassing."

Kay struggled to hide her smirk at Anthony's description of Mark as whiney.

"Is there a reason that you insisted on Kay bringing her daughters with her to go to the interview you set up for her with your employer, instead of leaving them in Tulsa with their father or grandparents?"

"Based on Mark's behavior, I feared for their safety if they were to stay with him. A real dad would never drink and drive, much less do so with his daughters in the vehicle. But that really had no bearing on the need for the girls to be with Kay during the interview with Rick."

Anthony turned to look at the judge before continuing. "You have to understand the nature of our jobs. We fly to a different city daily, rotating with a second flight crew every five days. So, we work five days and then have five days off. As part of the flight crew, we actually have time to go home for a few days between shifts, but the wrestlers and writers are on the plane daily, even if they aren't wrestling every day. Because they are constantly traveling, their families travel with them. The GWA employs multiple tutors to provide for the educational needs of all of our children because of the constant travel. Technically, the kids are classified as homeschooled, but they actually have customized curricula for each child based on not only the standards required by their state of residence, but also on the intellectual level of each individual student. Since Tia and Maria are both intellectually gifted, having the tutors available as part of the benefits of Kay's employment means they won't be bored while in school because the material is beneath their levels. But they still needed to be there when Kay interviewed for the job to make sure they were comfortable with the educational system from day one. Not only did Rick interview Kay to see if she would be a good fit with working for the GWA, but Kay, Tia, and Maria were able to interview the tutors before deciding on the best course for the girls' education."

"It sounds like a complex system. Are you sure it's not too much for young children like Tia and Maria?" Kay thought she heard a growl from her daughters at Matt questioning their intellect.

Anthony chuckled. "Since Tia does mental calculations of physics and geometry equations, which she figures out in her head in the middle of a game, as she plays mini golf, I'm sure she can handle the complexity of the educational system."

The judge cracked a smile. Matt ended his questions for Anthony, but Mark's attorney stood to ask some of his own.

"Why were you at Ms. Lee's home on October fifth? Was it just to pick her up to take her to an out-of-town interview?" Mr. Johnson snarled.

Kay shifted in her seat, hating how nervous she felt about how Mark's attorney would twist her relationship with Anthony against her. If Anthony felt any anxiety about the question, it didn't show when he turned to look at her with a smile before answering.

"Actually, I was there to pick Kay up for a date." Anthony turned back to look at the attorney. "I had just heard about the job opening the night before and wanted to surprise her with the interview over dinner."

"So, the phone calls about changing the visitation all week weren't because Kay was planning to move to Texas?"

"As I was not a party to those phone calls, I can't say what they were," Anthony shrugged. "But as I had actually asked Kay to marry me the weekend before and I live in Texas, I'm assuming she was trying to prepare for the possible move while she considered my proposal."

"So, you're now engaged to Ms. Lee?" Mr. Johnson looked incredulously between Anthony and Kay.

"Yes," Anthony smirked. "Our wedding is scheduled for Saturday, November twenty-fourth."

"No more questions," the attorney huffed in frustration as he stomped back to his seat.

Anthony stepped down and Charles Lee was called to the stand. Anthony kissed the top of Kay's head as he took his seat behind her. Tia and Maria both went back to holding his hands while they listened to their grandfather testify about walking in to see Mark pinning Kay to the wall and rabbit punching her in the kidney on the day she left him. Kay hated that her daughters had to hear about that.

Charles also testified about the recent altercation before detailing the criminal charges that Mark was now facing for the vandalism of Kay's home while she was out of town. He also mentioned the threatening texts that Mark had sent to Kay, but explained that the current laws in Oklahoma didn't have a provision for charging him with anything related to the texts until he followed through with the threat of violence.

Once he was finished testifying, he stepped down and Matt called Tia to the stand. Kay was proud of the strength her daughter showed as she squared her shoulders and marched proudly up to take the stand. Tia kept her gaze focused on whichever officer of the court was speaking, as she was sworn in and took her seat. She never even looked in Mark's direction as she testified, focusing instead on Matt when he asked her questions, or the judge when she answered, and occasionally looking at Kay or her family seated behind Kay, as if she needed their support to testify.

"Please tell the court about your last visit with your father, Mark Fox," Matt directed instead of asking a specific question.

"I assume you mean the weekend beginning Friday, September twenty-first and ending Sunday, September twenty-third, since that was the last time we actually went with him for our weekend visitation. And not Friday, October fifth, when he assaulted my mother and should have been arrested by my grandfather," Tia stated matter-of-factly.

"I would like you to tell us about both of those actually." Kay could hear the amusement in Matt's tone of voice, even though she couldn't see his facial expression to know if he was smiling at Tia. "You may begin with whichever one you wish."

"The most recent time I saw Mark Fox was on Friday, October fifth," Tia stated, confidently looking up at the judge. "He was supposed to pick us up at five o'clock that evening, but he didn't arrive until six-thirty. Mom barely had the door open about three inches when he shoved it into her. She told him we weren't going with him because he'd been drinking, and he shoved her again, so he could stomp past her. Mom yelled at Maria and I to lock ourselves in the bedroom and call Grandpa Lee, while she tried to keep him from chasing us down the hall. Maria and I ran down the hall then, so I don't know if he shoved Mom any more times before Anthony got there to protect her. I stopped in my room to grab my baseball bat in case he got past Mom and I needed to keep him from hurting Maria or I. As soon as I got into Maria's room, I locked the door and called Grandpa Lee. He was just around the corner and stayed on the phone with me until he got to the house. I couldn't hear what was going on in the living room to tell him what he was walking into, but he wanted to make sure we were safe in the bedroom. Once he said he was there, we hung up and I waited in the bedroom trying to calm Maria down, until Mom came in and told us it was safe to come out. That's when we met Anthony, and he took us all on their date for pizza and to play mini golf at the fun park."

"What about the other weekend you mentioned?" Matt inquired, drawing Tia's attention back to him.

"On Friday, September twenty-first, he was only an hour late picking us up." Tia again looked up at the judge as she testified. "He wasn't drunk when he picked us up, so we went with him to his apartment. As soon as we got there, he started drinking beer. When we asked what was for dinner, he started yelling about not having the money to buy extra food, and complained about how we should have eaten before coming to his house."

"The little bitch is lying," Mark shouted as he jumped up out of his chair. "I fed them dinner! Not that I should have to! Neither one of the little brats look like me, so I don't think either one of them are mine. I shouldn't have to take them every other weekend, or pay their bitch mother another dime in child support, just because I was the idiot she roped into marrying her fat pregnant ass! If you want me to pay more, you're gonna have to order a DNA test to prove I'm their father, 'cause I don't believe it for a second!"

"Order in the court," Judge Anderson bellowed as he slammed his gavel down repeatedly. "Mr. Johnson, control your client or I'll find him in contempt of court."

~~~

Anthony couldn't sit there and let Tia suffer through being alone on the witness stand a moment longer. *That jackass doesn't want to be her father? Fine by me! I'll be her dad! Starting right, fucking, now!*

While the judge was banging his gavel and trying to get Mark to calm down and stop screaming at Tia, Anthony leaned forward and lightly touched Kay's shoulder, whispering just loud enough that Kay could hear, "Baby."

Kay turned in her seat to look at him, catching her attorney's attention, who also turned. They ended up in an impromptu huddle of Anthony, Kay, Matt, Charles, and Maria who had moved to sit on her grandfather's lap when he'd come back to his seat from the witness stand.

"I love you, Baby. And I love your daughters too much to let Tia suffer through more time on the stand. So, I'm taking over now and fixing this." He kissed the top of her head before turning to look at the attorney. "Get Tia off the stand, give me a couple of minutes to talk to the girls, and then recall me," he told Matt. "Ask me about the parts of the statements I sent you that you didn't include before."

Matt turned back around and stood. "Your Honor," he interjected as he stepped out from behind the plaintiff's table. "I know it's a bit unorthodox, but I'd like to have Tia step down, so her family can comfort her and help her through the latest round of her father's verbal abuse."
~~~

"Agreed," the judge nodded. He then turned to look at Tia before speaking directly to her. "You may step down, young lady."

"No!" Tia defiantly crossed her arms over her chest and looked at the judge with what Anthony could only describe as sheer determination. "Not until you tell me that I don't ever have to be around that jerk again." She threw her arm out and pointed directly at Mark when she said, "that jerk" and Anthony couldn't help but smile at her. *Damn, she's going to be a handful as a teenager, and I can't wait to see it all.*

The judge's lips slightly lifted, like he was fighting to hold back his own smile at Tia. "I can't do that yet, because I can't give a verdict with anyone on the witness stand." Anthony couldn't be sure, but he thought the judge might have just winked at Tia with the eye turned away from the courtroom, so only she could clearly see it.

"Oh, okay then." Tia bobbed her head once and stepped down, standing tall and walking confidently back to her seat. She hugged Kay and then Anthony before sitting down between him and her grandfather.

Anthony turned to face the girls and dropped to one knee in front of them. If the proper position was to be on one knee to propose marriage to their mother, he thought it was an appropriate position to propose adoption to the girls. He took each of their hands in one of his before speaking. "Tia, Maria, I already feel like the luckiest man on earth to get to marry your mom and be your stepdad. But now I have to ask you if you'll do me the honor of allowing me to adopt you and be your real Dad."

"Yes," they squealed in unison before launching themselves at him. He caught a girl in each arm and returned their exuberant hugs.

"Your Honor." Matt turned away from Anthony and the girls and back toward the proceedings, again addressing the judge. "I'd like to recall Anthony Burleson to the stand."

"Objection," Mark's attorney shouted. "We've already heard from that witness. There's nothing more we need to hear from him. I'd like to have a chance to call my client to the stand and present the evidence we have against the former Mrs. Fox."

"Yes, well, circumstances have changed since his earlier testimony," Matt explained confidently. "I think what he has to say now might negate the need for further proceedings today."

Leah Mae Wright

The judge looked from Matt to Anthony. Anthony felt the weight of the judge's appraisal. He stood to his full height, still holding a daughter in each arm, letting the judge analyze him and hoping that he would see the need to let him speak.

"Objection overruled," the judge decided with a nod of his head. "Mr. Burleson may retake the stand and is still under oath from his earlier testimony."

Anthony put the girls down to sit on the bench beside their grandfather before he walked confidently to the stand and took his seat.

"During the defendant's outburst a few minutes ago, you not only conferred with my client, but you also asked me to recall you to the stand and ask you about the parts of the written statements you sent me back in October that we haven't addressed thus far," Matt stated.

Anthony wasn't sure if it was actually a question or not, but he answered anyway. "That is correct."

"Please tell the court what was included in those written statements that we haven't previously addressed."

"In the first statement, I explained to you that while I hadn't actually witnessed Mr. Fox interact with Tia or Maria, I believed from my interactions with them that he'd been verbally and emotionally abusive toward them. I told you in the first statement, the one dated October eighth, that I feel it would be in the best interest of the children that Mark's parental rights are terminated, and I am allowed to adopt them when Kay and I get married. I explicitly stated that the girls need a dad who loves them and protects them from abusive assholes, and I want to be that dad."

Anthony saw the girls giggle when he called their sperm donor an asshole. Kay's father just shook his head at the term, but his lips turned up slightly. Anthony worried that he might have shocked Kay's mother, though, based on the hand covering her mouth. She was so quiet and reserved that he almost forgot she was there. He would have to work on remembering to act like he would in front of his own mother when Mary Lee was around. Southern women of their generation hated profanity, and deserved the respect of their beliefs that Anthony normally gave his mom by not cursing in her presence. He wanted to kick himself for not giving Kay's mom the same respect, but he wasn't sure how to have actually done that when he was quoting his words from his written statement.

"Please tell the court about the second written statement that you emailed to me on Friday, October twelfth."

"In that statement, I told you about how scared Tia was the night before when this court appearance was mentioned at dinner with my family. I explained that the way she was shaking, and crying was more than just the normal nerves about having to testify in court, or anxiety about what the outcome might be of these proceedings. Her exact words as I tried to soothe her were 'please don't let him hurt me again' and I told you in that statement that I believe that Mark Fox has physically abused her."

"Objection, hearsay," Mark's attorney stood and shouted, interrupting Anthony's testimony.

"Overruled," the judge bellowed. "As Tia is present in the courtroom, we can recall her to clarify her actual statements and detail any physical abuse once Mr. Burleson has finished his testimony, if needed."

"Thank you, Your Honor." Matt nodded to the judge. "I don't think we need to speculate what might have happened and will let Sheriff Charles Lee investigate any possible abuse in case charges need to be filed in the future." He turned back to Anthony. "Now, as to the change of circumstances that occurred during the defendant's earlier outburst. Please tell the court what transpired between you and the plaintiff, Ms. Kay Lee, and her daughters, at that time."

Anthony turned to look directly at the judge. "I'm not sure if you noticed, Your Honor." Anthony smiled at the judge. "While you were having to reprimand Mr. Fox, I got down on one knee and asked Tia and Maria if they would do me the honor of allowing me to adopt them. They said yes. So, now I'm asking you to not put my family through any more abuse at the hands of Mr. Fox or his attorney. His outburst clearly showed that he doesn't want to be their father. I don't care whose DNA they have and don't think we should waste the court's time or resources to do the DNA testing Mr. Fox is requesting. I want to be their dad. Please terminate Mr. Fox's parental rights and let me adopt my daughters."

Judge Anderson gave Anthony the longest stare before finally nodding his head and turning to observe the rest of the courtroom.

Leah Mae Wright
When his gaze landed on the defendant's table, he pointedly asked, "No objections, Mr. Johnson?"

"No, Your Honor," Mark's attorney replied.

Judge Anderson turned back to Anthony. "You may step down now, Mr. Burleson."

Anthony made his way back to his seat where both girls moved to sit on his knees, Tia on his left and Maria on his right. He put an arm around each of their backs to help them balance, but they didn't say anything as the judge started speaking again.

"Mr. Monroe, do you have any other witnesses to call to the stand?" the judge queried.

"No, Your Honor," Matt said. "We rest our case."

"Mr. Johnson, I'm required to allow you to present your defense of Mr. Fox, but I feel the need to warn you that if you use these proceedings to denigrate his ex-wife or extend his verbal abuse of the children, I will hold you in contempt of this court."

Anthony had felt scrutinized under the gaze of Judge Anderson while on the stand, but he was grateful to not have been subjected to the glare of utter contempt that the judge gave Mark and his attorney. Apparently, it was more than Mark could handle based on how he slumped in his seat. His attorney seemed to fare better as he stood to begin his portion of the proceedings.

"At this time, Your Honor," the attorney started, "Mr. Fox would like to request that the court terminate his child support and parental rights. As Ms. Lee had previously filed for only the termination of his visitation and an unnecessary order of protection, we had planned to offer testimony as to why Mr. Fox should not be required to pay support for children he would no longer have any part of raising. In light of Ms. Lee's fiancé testifying that he wants to step into their paternal role, we're willing to forgo the testimony of our witnesses, so long as all of Mr. Fox's parental rights and obligations are permanently severed as of this date." The lawyer sat back down next to his client.

"You forgot to mention dropping the charges against me," Mark grumbled to his attorney, clearly too agitated to remember to keep his voice down, so only his attorney could hear. "Your Honor," Mark started trying to address the judge, but stopped suddenly when Judge Anderson slammed his gavel down.

"Mr. Fox, you were not called to address this court and any further statement from you will put you in jail for contempt of court." Judge Anderson looked directly at Mark. "As to the criminal charges pending against you, they are not a part of this legal proceeding, as you are currently sitting in family court, which is a civil court and has no jurisdiction to affect criminal charges. Any issues you have with the criminal justice system will have to be addressed by a criminal court judge, which I am not."

Judge Anderson scanned the courtroom until his eyes landed on Kay, who was turned slightly in her seat, so she could hold Anthony's right hand at Maria's side and still stay mostly turned forward toward the judge. Judge Anderson looked from Kay, to her hand holding Anthony's, to Anthony holding both girls on his lap, before returning his gaze to Kay to address her.

"Ms. Lee, normally I would take a recess to go to my chambers and deliberate how to rule in a case such as this, but I don't think I need to do that today. Instead, I'm going to ask you a couple of questions, considering you as still under oath, even though I'm allowing you to answer from your seat, so you have the support of your fiancé and family when you answer. I'll issue my ruling as soon as I have your answers to these questions."

Kay nodded to the judge in agreement before he continued. Anthony squeezed her hand in their silent "I love you" to show her he was there for her to lean on if she needed him.

"Did you only request termination of visitation initially because you wanted Mr. Fox to continue financially supporting your daughters?" the judge questioned.

"No, Your Honor," Kay gasped. "I didn't even think about the child support. Now that I have my new job, I don't really need Mark's help in providing for my girls. I just wanted to keep Mark from being around my girls, so he couldn't abuse them, and the termination of visitation is what my attorney recommended at the time we originally filed."

"Why did you change your petition from terminating visitation to completely severing Mr. Fox's parental rights and obligations?"

"Because today wasn't the first time Anthony mentioned adopting the girls to me," Kay admitted. "We actually talked to Mr. Monroe on Tuesday, October sixteenth about what would need to happen in court today for him to be able to adopt them when we get married. He's been trying to get a response from Mark, or his attorney, ever since then because we were hoping Mark would just sign away his rights, and we wouldn't have to waste the court's time with an ugly fight. But since they wouldn't return a phone call, Mr. Monroe had no other option but to change the petition this morning."

"You've been trying to settle out of court to sever his rights and responsibilities for the last three weeks?" The judge smiled.

"Yes, Your Honor," Kay and her attorney answered at the same time.

"Mr. Fox, you should have had your attorney return your ex-wife's attorney's call." Judge Anderson shook his head at Mark. "Let the record show that the court finds in favor of the plaintiff, Ms. Kay Lee, and hereby grants the petition of the plaintiff, Ms. Kay Lee, to sever the parental rights and obligations of Mr. Mark Fox in relation to the minor children currently known as Tia Lee Fox and Maria Mae Fox. The court also issues an order of protection for Ms. Kay Lee and her daughters currently known as Tia Lee Fox and Maria Mae Fox, preventing Mr. Mark Fox from any contact with them from this day forward, whether in person, via telephone, or other electronic communication." He hit his gavel on the bench again.

Before adjourning the court, he turned to Kay's attorney and told him, "Mr. Monroe, please bring Mr. Burleson's adoption papers to me as soon as you can get them written and schedule with my clerk for them to appear in my chambers to finalize them on the next weekday when they are available to be in Tulsa. We'll change the girls' names on today's orders then as well."

"I actually have them already, Your Honor." Matt pulled out the adoption petition from his briefcase.

"Very well." The judge smiled once more. "File them with my clerk as soon as we're adjourned and schedule a time for them to meet me in my chambers tomorrow morning, either before or after my scheduled court time."

The judge hit the bench with his gavel one last time to adjourn the court session and they all stood to leave.

Tia turned to look at Anthony. "Does this mean you're our new Dad now?"

"It won't be all legal and official until the judge signs the adoption papers tomorrow," Anthony replied. "But yeah, Princess, I'm your dad from now on."

"So, Mom was wrong when she said we couldn't replace our old lying one with a new dad," Tia stated matter-of-factly. "I knew I had seen it online where we could divorce him, too, but I just wasn't sure if we could do the sever petition the judge ordered today, or if we had to do the emancipation petition that I was reading about online."

"I wasn't wrong," Kay objected with a playful pout. "I just said it wasn't normal and told you how stepfamilies normally work."

"Normal is boring," Anthony smirked. "Who wants to be just like everyone else and do what others expect you to do? It's a lot more fun to be unique and forge our own path in life."

"I agree with Daddy." Maria smiled up at Anthony and made his heart swell by calling him Daddy. "I never want to be normal. I'm special and unique."

"All my girls are special and unique." Anthony grinned down at Maria, then he turned to smile at Tia, "My Princesses." Finally, he reached down and clasped Kay's hands in his, "And my Queen."

~~~

After they left the courthouse, Kay convinced her family to have a celebratory lunch at the restaurant in the Camelot Hotel, so they could share their good news with Randi while she was at work. Kay hoped that her sister could take her own lunch break to eat with them but since she'd already taken her break, they settled for talking to her while she took their lunch order.

Kay was a little uncomfortable when she noticed her former boss glaring at her from across the restaurant. *Guess he's still bitter about me quitting last month when he denied my last-minute vacation request,* she thought as she smiled and waved at him to show she didn't have any hard feelings toward him or the hotel.

"Stop, you're gonna get me fired too," Randi whispered through a giggle as she grabbed Kay's hand and stopped her from waving at Mr. Brooks.
~~~

Leah Mae Wright

"I wasn't fired from here," Kay told her sister. "I quit when he said I couldn't use my vacation time for a family emergency."

"That's not what he's telling everyone here." Randi leaned in, so only Kay could hear her. "He's telling everyone that you were fired when you didn't show up to work your normal shift without notifying him in advance, so he didn't have anyone in to replace you."

"Well, he's full of bull," Kay huffed, not caring if the whole restaurant could hear her. "I called him on Friday night and told him that I needed to use my vacation time starting the following Monday for a family emergency. He told me that I couldn't use my vacation time, so I quit. He had the whole weekend to find someone to work when he knew I wouldn't be there."

"Baby," Anthony spoke in his slow sexy drawl, redirecting her attention to him from her anger at her former boss. "What do you recommend we order?"

"Anything you want, it's all good," Kay replied before turning back to her sister.

"I think he was trying to get you to focus on something else and quit making a scene, so I can keep my job," Randi whispered softly.

"Sorry, Sis, I wasn't thinking." Kay lowered her voice and felt like an idiot for not thinking before speaking. "I just wanted to come here for lunch, so we could update you on court this morning. I didn't mean to make work difficult for you."

"Oh, yes, I need the scoop." Randi completely waved off Kay's apology.

I have to remember to ask Rick if he's still looking for someone for my job on the other flight crew, Kay thought, planning to recommend her sister for the position, if it was still available.

"We won in court." Tia gave her aunt a beaming smile. "Anthony's now our dad and we don't have to see the old one ever again."

"Awesome," Randi exclaimed as she raised her hand for Tia to give her a high five.

They quickly ordered their meals, so Randi wouldn't get in trouble for spending too much time at their table.

"So, how long are you going to be in town?" Mary inquired as soon as Randi walked away from the table.

"I didn't know how many days we'd need to be in court, so I booked our flight out of Tulsa to Kansas City for Thursday on the off chance we'd be done and could go back to our normal work schedule," Anthony replied.

"Can we have sleepovers at Grandma and Grandpa's house until then?" Maria asked, bouncing in her seat.

"Yes," Mary answered her granddaughter but then turned to Kay and Anthony. "But only if your mom and dad say it's okay."

"I think that can be arranged," Kay replied, looking at Anthony and thinking about the ways they could spend their time alone for the next three nights.

He reached over and clasped her left hand in his right hand under the table and gave her their "I love you" squeezes and a smile, which she promptly returned. "We do need to have them with us tomorrow when we meet with the judge." Anthony turned his smile to the girls and then Kay's parents. "Would you like to meet us at the courthouse again in the morning? Or would you prefer us to pick them up from your home and bring them back after?"

"I guess that will depend on where you're staying the night tonight," Charles asserted, just as Randi delivered their drinks. "I've repaired most of the damage on the house, but haven't replaced any of the furniture, since I figured you'd want to do that yourself. Now that you have a restraining order in place, I think it would be safe for you to go furniture shopping this afternoon, and stay at the house, instead of a hotel tonight, if you want."

"There really wasn't anything salvageable?" Kay squeezed Anthony's hand, since they still had their fingers intertwined and resting on Kay's thigh. Charles shook his head.

Kay turned to look up at Anthony before shaking her head. "I thought we might go by there and see what was left, but I don't think I want to stay there."

"Then we can go take a look this afternoon and go back to the hotel tonight." Anthony had nothing but love and compassion shining through his eyes as he smiled down at Kay.

Kay turned back to look at her parents, wanting to look them in the eyes as she told them about her decision to move to Heart's Destiny with Anthony. "Actually, I don't think I even want to go take a look. I'd rather remember my childhood home as it was when we were all living there and happy. Since we're moving to Heart's Destiny, I don't need to taint my memories with a final trip to see the destruction or repairs."

Kay dug into her purse and got out her keys that she hadn't used in a month. She handed the whole ring to her father since it only contained keys to the house and her car. "Let me know if you need me to do anything, so you can junk the car and transfer the utilities out of my name."

"You're sure, baby girl?" Charles hesitated as he took the keyring.

"Yes, Dad, I'm sure." Kay felt more confident in her decision than she expected, since she hadn't ever lived outside of Tulsa before. "I'd rather you and Mom use it for rental income than it sit empty most of the time. We can stay in a hotel anytime we come to town to visit."

Their meals were delivered, and the conversation turned to all the sights Kay wanted to show Anthony while they were in Tulsa. When they left the restaurant, Anthony and Kay went to their hotel to get the girls' things to take to the Lee residence on their way to Chandler Park that afternoon. Charles and Mary would meet them at the courthouse the next morning with the girls, since the hotel was on the other side of town and the courthouse was halfway in between there and the Lees' home.

When they heard that Kay and Anthony were going to the park, the girls insisted it should be a family trip. Kay was only slightly disappointed to not be alone with Anthony to sneak in some outdoor sexy times, like they had on their picnic on the ranch the week before. But even on a school day afternoon, the park was too crowded for them to do more than a chaste kiss or two. Besides, Kay's mother, Mary, enjoyed spending the afternoon telling her granddaughters and Anthony the same stories about her father, Kay's grandfather, doing the rock work in the park that she'd told Kay and her siblings when they were kids.

When they left the park, Anthony insisted on taking Kay for the romantic dinner date that they'd missed the month before. He'd somehow wrangled last-minute reservations at a steakhouse downtown that they barely made it to after their stop back at their hotel to change for dinner.

Had they actually followed through on their hotel room teasing, they would have missed it altogether. As it was, they continued their whispered innuendo and hidden caresses under the tablecloth all through the meal, which they rushed through to get back to the hotel.

As soon as the door to their room closed behind them, Kay was lifted into Anthony's arms and pressed back against the door. They kissed passionately as he hiked her skirt up to her waist and ripped off her panties. Within seconds, he unfastened his dress pants and impaled her on his massive erection.

It was hard, fast, and primal as they came together the first time that night. Round two in the shower was only a little less intense, but round three, when they finally made it to the bed, was the slow, sensual seduction that made Kay feel the most loved and cherished. After three weeks of daily lovemaking, Kay realized that while he wanted to be intense and let his inner caveman out about a third of the time, Anthony preferred spending as much time kissing, licking, and softly stroking every inch of her body, and making her come with his fingers and tongue, as he actually wanted to spend with his cock inside her. And at least half of the time that he was inside her, it was slow and gentle, and meant to strengthen their connection through lots of eye contact.

No matter how they came together, though, Kay loved the experience. Rough and raw, kinky and commanding, or soft and sensual, it didn't matter. Anthony had awakened a sexual part of her that she hadn't known she possessed before. Considering how wet she got, and how her nipples puckered, anytime Anthony even looked at her, no matter where they were or who was around, she didn't think she'd be going back to the asexual person she'd been before meeting him anytime soon, if ever at all.

The fact that he liked to cuddle afterwards, as much as she did, was just icing on the cake. She couldn't say that cuddling afterward was her favorite part of sex anymore either, though she did still enjoy it. She couldn't decide on a favorite position or specific carnal act that she liked best. Every time she thought she might have a favorite, Anthony would show her something new and different that she enjoyed just as much.

If hard pressed to say what she loved most about their sex life, Kay would have to say that it was that no matter what they did or how they did it, it was an expression of their love for one another. That's why they always said, "I love you" instead of "goodnight" as they drifted off to sleep in each other's arms.

<div align="center">~~~</div>

Tuesday, November 6, 2018

Anthony's phone had been blowing up with texts from his family and friends since the day before, everyone wanting to know how things went in court. While Kay's family was there and already knew what had transpired, Anthony didn't want to tell his family and friends over text messages or phone calls until after their second appearance in the Tulsa County Courthouse. He wanted to have the paperwork in hand to physically show them before doing a video call with his parents. Maybe he could text everyone else later, but he wanted to make sure it was all legal and officially done before he told his parents first. So, he'd left his phone on silent since entering the courthouse on Monday morning, and he had no plans to reply to anyone until after they left the courthouse Tuesday afternoon.

Their appointment with the judge in his chambers was set for noon, which was when he would normally take a recess in court for lunch. Anthony was glad that the girls had spent the night with Kay's parents, so they could spend the morning making love. Distracting himself from his nerves about meeting with the judge was only one sliver of a thought at the bottom of a long list of reasons for wanting to spend his morning focused on loving Kay.

She'd been more worried about the day before with having to face her ex in the courtroom. But Anthony was more anxious about the judge changing his mind and not signing off on the adoption. Just as he'd soothed her nerves Sunday night by worshiping her body, he sought comfort in her silky wet sex Tuesday morning.

Since they missed breakfast while they were tangled in the sheets, they stopped at Daylight Donuts on the way to the courthouse for chocolate long johns and coffee. Kay seemed surprised that he added just the right amount of sugar and cream to her coffee, while she was talking to the cashier, like she hadn't realized he'd been watching her every morning to know exactly how she liked it. He just smiled and thought of all the other little things he knew she liked that he couldn't wait to surprise her with in the future.

They were about fifteen minutes early for their appointment with the judge when they met up with the girls and Kay's parents at the courthouse. Charles and Mary Lee waited in the hall outside the courtrooms while Anthony, Kay, Tia, and Maria walked around the corner to the hallway leading to the offices of the court officials.

They walked into the outer office where Judge Anderson's staff was working at a couple of desks. A gentleman that looked to be somewhere between Anthony and Kay's ages was at the desk on the left, and a woman who looked to be in her forties was at the desk on the right.

"How may I help you?" the woman asked as she looked up from her computer at them.

"We're supposed to have a meeting with Judge Anderson at noon." Anthony hoped she was the clerk, who could direct them to exactly where they were supposed to be.

"Our attorney, Matt Monroe, should be here soon as well," Kay added with a smile.

"Yes, if you'll just have a seat." The woman pointed to a row of chairs by the door. "They should both be coming straight from court this morning, so it depends on where they are in testimony in the current case. They may be a few minutes late, but it shouldn't be too long of a wait."

They all sat in the chairs the clerk had directed them to, and Anthony could tell by how the girls were fidgeting in their seats that he wasn't the only one nervous about the meeting. He decided to try to distract them by whispering questions about what they had for dinner with their grandparents, and what they were planning to do with them for the next couple of days.

The girls quit fidgeting as they told them about the roast beef they had for dinner, and the pancakes they had for breakfast, in soft voices that didn't seem to disturb the people working in the office. They didn't have time to discuss any other plans before Matt Monroe walked in the same door that they'd entered a few minutes before.

Anthony stood and shook Matt's hand in greeting before the clerk told them they could all go back to the judge's office. Anthony hoped nobody else could hear his heart beating out of his chest as they walked between the two desks and through the door into the judge's chambers.

"It's good to see you all again." The judge pointed at the chairs in front of his desk before they all shook hands and took the seats he directed them toward. "We're a lot less formal in chambers than in the courtroom. I've already read the petition for adoption that Mr. Monroe filed with my clerk yesterday and believe everything seems to be in order, so we can sign everything today to get these young ladies' last names changed. I just need to verify with each of the girls that they do indeed wish for Mr. Burleson to adopt them."

He turned his attention to the girls before asking specifically, "Tia, Maria, are you here of your own free will to have Anthony Burleson become your dad?"

"Yes, sir." Tia smiled at the judge.

"Um, I think so." Maria looked at the judge like she was confused by the question. "I want Anthony to be my Daddy, but I don't know what *Free Willy* has to do with him adopting us."

"Not *Free Willy*, the movie." Tia rolled her eyes at her sister as the adults in the room chuckled. "He asked if we're here because we want to be and not because someone forced us to be here to be adopted."

"Oh, okay." Maria grinned. "Then yes, I'm here because I want Anthony to adopt us and be our Daddy."

"Then let's sign these papers and make it official." Judge Anderson was still grinning at the precocious girls.

They signed a few papers and made sure the girls' new birth certificates would be mailed to their address in Heart's Destiny. Technically, they were officially Tia Lee Burleson and Maria Mae Burleson as soon as the judge signed the adoption papers, but they needed the new birth certificates, along with the adoption papers that Anthony had tucked into his inside coat pocket, to change their last names on their social security records. The judge believed they would have them in the mail around the date of their wedding, so they could all three change their last names with the social security department the week after the wedding.

When they got back out to the main hallway, where the Lees were waiting for them, Anthony pulled out his phone and swiped the screen to set up a Skype video conference with his parents, since his mother would be at the ranch and his father would be in San Antonio at the Burleson Incorporated headquarters.

"Oh, Anthony, we've been so worried since you haven't answered your phone since court yesterday," his mother, Hazel, wailed as soon as the conference connected.

"Everything okay, Son?" Bob inquired before Anthony could reply to his mother.

"Everything is fabulous!" Anthony exclaimed, squatting down to try to squeeze Kay, Tia, and Maria into the frame with him to talk to his folks. "I didn't want to risk jinxing things by telling ya'll too soon. That's why I didn't answer my phone or texts."

He paused to pull the official adoption papers out of his pocket. Once he unfolded them and turned them around facing the phone, he continued speaking. "We had to come back to court today, so the judge could sign these." He lifted the papers, so they were in front of the camera on his phone where his parents could read them, or at least read the top line that specifically said what they were. "Figured I'd better officially introduce you to Tia Lee Burleson and Maria Mae Burleson, your one-hundred percent, legally adopted granddaughters."

"Oh my, goodness, gracious," Hazel shrieked, fumbling her phone in her excitement. "I didn't think that was even a possibility this soon! But it's so awesome!"

"Congratulations, Son." Bob looked a little choked up. "When will you be back in town, so we can celebrate with the newest Burlesons?"

"We're staying here in Tulsa to celebrate with our other grandparents until Thursday," Tia replied, when Anthony didn't recall their schedule quickly enough.

"Yeah, then we're working and won't be back home until the fourteenth," Kay added with a smile at him.

Anthony loved hearing her referring to Heart's Destiny as home. He reached over and squeezed her hand with their silent "I love you." She rapidly returned the gesture.

"And you said the GWA crew will be here the sixteenth and Kay's family on the seventeenth?" Hazel inquired.

"Yes, as far as I know that's the arrival dates for everyone coming from out of town for the wedding," Anthony verified, looking over the phone at the Lees to confirm. When Charles nodded at him, Anthony turned the phone to point the camera at the Lees. "Mr. and Mrs. Lee, these are my parents, Bob and Hazel Burleson. I know it's an unusual way to meet, but Mom, Dad, these are Kay's parents, Charles and Mary Lee."

"Actually, Hazel and I met on the video call while Kay was trying on wedding dresses," Mary reminded Anthony before turning to direct her comments to the phone. "It's good to see you again, Hazel."

"You too, Mary," Hazel replied through the phone.

Their parents chatted for a few minutes, making sure they all had each other's phone numbers and confirming the accommodations for the week the Lees would be in Heart's Destiny. They disconnected the Skype session and exited the Tulsa County Courthouse. The girls went with their grandparents to the zoo, leaving Anthony and Kay to go exploring the various sights of the city alone.

"Where to, Baby?" Anthony queried as they buckled up in their rental car.

"I know you were planning for me to show you around Tulsa…" Kay trailed off, looking up at him with mischief written all over her face. "But I think I'd rather take advantage of being child-free for the next couple of days, and go back to the hotel to practice for the honeymoon."

"Mmm, I like the way you think, Baby." Anthony wagged his eyebrows at Kay, deciding to have his parents watch the girls for a couple of days after their wedding, so he could surprise his wife with a beach bungalow on Padre Island for their honeymoon, as he rushed them to their hotel for their practice honeymoon.

He knew in his heart that he would spend the rest of his life feeling like he was still in the honeymoon phase of his relationship with Kay. He couldn't wait to experience the next fifty or sixty years with her.

Epilogue

Thursday, November 15, 2018

Hazel Burleson appeared to be working diligently to prepare the day's meals for the ranch hands alongside her best friends. In addition to her sister-in-law, Susan Burleson, and Rosa Diaz, the wife of the ranch manager that usually assisted her in the daily cooking duties, Mandi Hunter was there under the guise of finalizing the details for Anthony and Kay's wedding reception. In reality, while they were completing those tasks, they were really meeting to plan who they were going to try to match with their mate next.

"Do you really think we'll be able to match at least two of the guys with bridesmaids at the wedding?" Mandi looked skeptically at Hazel.

"Absolutely," Hazel affirmed, going back to chopping the vegetables she was working on for the stew they were making.

"Mandi wasn't at Kay's birthday party to see the look on JJ's face when Kay mentioned Deanna," Susan pointed out, as she rolled the dough that she was working with into balls to make rolls to go with the stew. "I recognized that look in my oldest son's eyes, so I'm sure we can push the two of them together."

"I'm sure that's true for your boy, Susan," Mandi replied, as she peeled the apples to go into the pies. "But I'm not so sure about my boy. James hasn't mentioned anything about Kay's sister to me, so even if they did text each other after meeting in Tulsa back in September, I'm not so sure it will really go anywhere."

"Maybe you should call Kay over, so we can find out what she knows about her sister and James?" Rosa fluted the pie crust she'd just put into the next to last pie tin.

"Good idea," Hazel nodded, setting down her knife and washing her hands to call Kay. She put the phone on speaker as she dialed, so everyone could hear her future daughter-in-law when she answered.

"Good morning," Kay giggled through the phone.

"Kay, is there any chance you can leave the girls with Anthony for a bit and come help us with a project?" Hazel set the phone down to dump the cut vegetables into the stockpot.

"Sure," Kay agreed in her cheerful tone. Hazel was so glad her youngest son had found himself such a happy bride. "I'll be right there."

They said a quick "goodbye" and "see you soon" before going back to working on the meal prep. A few minutes later, Kay breezed in through the back door and into the kitchen.

"What project do you need me to help with?" Kay moved to the sink to wash her hands, obviously thinking it was something meal prep related.

"We need to know all about your sister." Hazel smiled conspiratorially at her future daughter-in-law. "And any other single people who will be here for the wedding."

"Oh!" Kay looked a little befuddled before her face broke out in a wide smile. "Are you planning to do a little matchmaking at my wedding?"

"Maybe a little." Hazel held her hand up to pinch her thumb and first finger close together to show how little she intended to interfere with the young folks meeting their mates.

"More like a lot," Rosa laughed, spreading her arms wide, just like her smile, to contradict Hazel.

"We're all ready for grandbabies," Susan grinned. "And now that Hazel has a couple, she's helping us try for our own."

"Speak for yourself!" Rosa pointed at Susan, laughing. "My babies are still teenagers, so I'm not ready for grandbabies yet. But I'm happy to help the rest of you pair off your kids."

"Oh, this is going to be a fun week." Kay giggled with glee. "I take it you noticed JJ's expression when I mentioned that Dee is going to be a bridesmaid?" Kay nodded toward Susan, who nodded in return. "And you want to know more about my sister because she's been texting with James for the last month and a half?" Kay prodded as she turned to Mandi.

"Yes, but he hasn't mentioned her to me in all that time, so I'm not so sure our matchmaking will be productive."

"I have a feeling Randi and James won't need much help from anyone else to get together." Kay's smile widened. "I think the only thing keeping them apart is that Randi is in Tulsa and James is traveling all the time. To be honest, I'd already planned to introduce our boss to my sister, and see if he could find a job for her like he did for me, so they can actually spend some time together."

"You really think that's all it will take for them?" Mandi looked less skeptical than she had earlier.

"Definitely," Kay nodded. "Anthony could probably tell you more about how James feels about Randi, but my conversations with my sister have been enough to convince me that she's a smitten kitten over James."

Hazel smiled, thinking about how shy, quiet James Hunter deserved to have a woman fawning over him.

"What about Deanna?" Susan finished prepping the rolls for their final rising time. "Do you think she shares JJ's interest?"

"I'm not really sure about Dee." Kay hemmed and hawed, biting her lower lip like she was concerned about something to do with her friend. "I love her like a sister because we've been best friends since sixth grade. But we have differing opinions about love and relationships."

Kay went on to explain that her closest childhood friend changed a lot in college and no longer seemed to believe in true love. Apparently, she dated a lot, but didn't have many second dates with the same man.

"It sounds like she's guarding her heart because she hasn't been able to trust the men she's dated in the past," Rosa pointed out.

"Exactly," Kay replied as they all made their way to sit at the table now that the last of the food was cooking and didn't need their constant supervision. "I think that's true for her professional life as well. The text conversation we all had last month with her, when Jen and Julie offered her a job at Burleson if her boss fires her for coming to the wedding, might have been the first of a whole lot of baby steps to getting her to trust people again."

"Then, we'll definitely make sure Bob and Jon follow up with that job offer while she's here," Hazel decided aloud, taking a sip of her coffee. "If she's been hurt before, we'll have to play a long game with her and JJ. But if we can get them on the same team at work, maybe it won't take too many years before he proves to her that he's trustworthy enough that she'll let down her guard and fall in love."

"I agree," Susan sighed. "It sounds like if we try to push them too much, they'd both run in the opposite direction. But proximity should be enough to let nature take its course with them eventually."

"Are there any other singles coming to mingle at your wedding?" Rosa smirked.

"Randi's bringing her housemate, Amy, as her plus one. She was Randi's college roommate and when they moved out of the dorms, they just rented a house together to stay roommates. I'm not exactly sure what she does for a living, but it has something to do with chemistry. There aren't many single women who work for the GWA, except the tutor Stacy who isn't coming to the wedding. And a couple of the single, female wrestlers, but I don't know them that well, so I don't think they're coming either."

"Stacy's the one the girls mentioned the other night when they were trying to talk Charlotte into taking her job, right?" Hazel was curious about that situation and whether or not it could lead to her oldest daughter pairing up with one of the single wrestlers.

"Yeah, and I really wish Charlotte was interested in the job." Kay huffed out a breath of frustration. "Stacy's flirting with every man in the company has gotten so bad that several of the mothers have complained and most of the fathers avoid the classroom area to try to avoid the conflict."

"So, the fathers aren't taking an active role in educating their children?" Mandi gasped.

"If they're involved, it's not during the set hours when the kids have classroom time with the tutors," Kay replied, looking irritated.

"I hope Anthony hasn't let her run him off from helping you with the girls' education during that classroom time." Hazel could understand why Kay looked annoyed if the woman was being so unprofessional.

"Oh, no," Kay chuckled. "I put my foot down the first day Anthony was in the classroom with us, and I saw her start to try to flirt with him."

"Oh, I have to hear this story." Rosa leaned in toward Kay conspiratorially.

"Stacy has a tendency to touch people when she talks to them, whether they want her to or not." Kay's expression changed to a little half grin. "She bent down between Anthony and Tia and put a hand on each of their shoulders. Anthony turned in his chair, pulling away from her, but Tia froze and just stared at her hand. I think Tia was actually mad about what Stacy was saying about how to format the paper she was writing and not the hand on her shoulder, but I just saw her touching my family without permission. I came halfway across the table at her and demanded she keep her hands to herself, like we were all taught back in preschool. I then made it clear that I'm perfectly capable of taking care of any language arts instruction my daughters need, so she has no reason to ever interact with our family."

Hazel was surprised to hear that Anthony had just smiled at Kay in agreement instead of unleashing the overprotective Burleson male instinct that would have had his father or brothers taking charge of the situation had they been there. She smiled at Kay, glad to have a daughter-in-law who was strong enough to stand up for herself and her family, and a son that would have his wife's back without making her feel incapable of handling things without his help.

"What about single men coming to the wedding?" Susan changed the subject. "We do still have some daughters to match up, too."

"Yeah, there are a few of the wrestlers who are coming that are single," Kay smiled. "And our boss, Rick, is a single dad. He's the other reason I thought it might be nice if Charlotte took the job."

"Tell me about this single dad you think my Char should meet." Hazel imagined her oldest daughter walking down the aisle and giving her another grandchild.

Next in the Heart's Destiny Series

Anthony and Kay return for their wedding in <u>Courting Kay Bonus Scenes</u>, which contains deleted segments from this book, new scenes, and some spoilers for the second book in the series…

Wrestling with Randi

Randi Mae Lee felt like she was stuck in a rut and had no idea how to crawl her way out of it. She'd tried to portray herself as outgoing and confident all her life, but she felt awkward in the good girl role everyone expected her to play as the sheriff's daughter. After a traumatic lecture from her parents as a teenager, she mostly repressed her sexuality and any part of her personality that she thought might cause a repeat. She struggled with feelings of guilt anytime she acted on her baser instincts, never letting a boyfriend turn the relationship sexual until after at least a month of dating, and always breaking up with them within a few days of their first time together. Randi secretly longed to find a way to start standing up for herself and living life on her own terms. She wanted to find her dream job and break her bad relationship cycle, but fear kept holding her back.

James Hunter lived a pretty great life. After an idyllic childhood on the family homestead in the small town of Heart's Destiny, Texas, James had completed his college degree before going on to act as a bad boy of professional wrestling. He teamed with his brother as the Dangerous Twins, an outlaw biker tag team, for the Galactic Wrestling Association. He was living the dream, traveling the world while working at a job he loved. The only drawback was the feeling of jealousy he had at seeing the married wrestlers who traveled with their families. At twenty-five, he was starting to feel like it was time to cut back on the nights out at bars and start settling down to build a family. Random one-night stands weren't fulfilling anymore, but it was hard to find "*The One*" when he was traveling three-hundred-and-twenty days a year and not in one place long enough to really start a relationship.

When good girl meets bad boy, sparks fly. Fate seemed to be pushing him in the right direction the night James met Randi. It was instalove for the pro wrestler and the sheriff's daughter. They fell hard and fast for each other, but could they maintain their love when his travel schedule reduced them to a mostly texting romance? Or could they find a way to be together more than the nine days they got together for his Thanksgiving vacation and her sister's wedding to his other best friend?

He was the dirty-talking alpha man of her dreams, and she was the sexy, sweet woman of his. When a pregnancy mix-up pitted the lovebirds against her overprotective father, things looked bleak for their future together. Would James's love be enough to help Randi find and accept who she really was deep inside? Would he be able to pull back on his alpha tendency to take over her life and protect her from the world long enough for the wonderful woman inside her to shine when she's ready to show her true self to the world? When all is said and done, will James and Randi finally get their happily ever after?

DISCLAIMER This sheriff's daughter, good girl meets a dirty-talking, alpha, pro wrestler bad boy, instalove, pro sports romance book contains profanity, graphic sex scenes, therapy to deal with childhood emotional trauma, and a surprise pregnancy for secondary characters that is temporarily believed to be the main characters' baby by several of their family members and the surrounding small town residents. It is intended for adult readers (18+) who are not easily offended.

Books by Leah Mae Wright

Heart's Destiny Series

Galactic Wrestling Association Series

About The Author

Leah Mae Wright lives in Florida with her husband and fur babies. Her head has been filled with romantic stories for as long as she can remember, beginning with fairy tales as a small child growing up in Oklahoma and carrying through to countless ideas of her own throughout the years, as she's moved around to live in several different states. Now that her children are grown and life has slowed down, she's letting them out of her head, so they can join the libraries of her fellow fans of romance. Leah's literary world is a wonderful place that has no Covid, no real politicians, and a few unreal towns. Her favorite part about her characters living in her literary world is knowing that they are guaranteed a happily ever after.

You can keep up to date with Leah's future book plans at:
www.leahmaewright.com – Be sure to sign up for the Newsletter to receive emails about new releases, sales, and freebies.
www.facebook.com/LeahWrightAuthor
www.amazon.com/author/leah_wright
https://www.instagram.com/leahmaewrightauthor/
https://www.pinterest.com/LeahMaeWrightAuthor/

Provide your feedback to the author at:
Leah's Literary World Facebook Group
LeahWrightAuthor@gmail.com
Leah@LeahMaeWright.com

You can also review Leah's books on Amazon, Apple Books, Barnes and Noble, Bookbub, Fictiondb, Goodreads, Google Play Books, and Kobo.